Harmony Trilogy

Harmony Trilogy

Nancy Mehl

BARBOUR
PUBLISHING

ISBN 978-1-61626-697-4

Scripture taken from the HOLY BIBLE, NEW INTERNATIONAL VERSION®. NIV®.
Copyright © 1973, 1978, 1984, 2011 by Biblica, Inc.™ Used by permission.
All rights reserved worldwide.

Some scripture quotations are taken from the King James Version of the Bible.

This book is a work of fiction. Names, characters, places, and incidents are either
products of the author's imagination or used fictitiously. Any similarity to actual
people, organizations, and/or events is purely coincidental.

For more information about Nancy Mehl, please access the author's website at the
following Internet address: www.nancymehl.com

Cover design: Lookout Design, Inc.

Published by Barbour Publishing, Inc., P.O. Box 719, Uhrichsville, Ohio 44683,
www.barbourbooks.com

*Our mission is to publish and distribute inspirational products offering exceptional value
and biblical encouragement to the masses.*

 Member of the
Evangelical Christian
Publishers Association

Printed in the United States of America.

Simple Secrets

DEDICATION

A parent always hopes that in some way, they will be their child's hero. But I am blessed because I have a son who is my hero. I love you, Danny, and I will always be thankful to God that He has allowed me to be your mother.

ACKNOWLEDGMENTS

No writer writes alone. There are always others who help to make a story ring true. I want to thank the wonderful people who helped me to create Harmony, Kansas and its citizens—past and present.

First of all, my thanks to Judith Unruh, Alexanderwohl Church Historian in Goessel, Kansas. I don't know what I would have done without you.

A big thank you to the woman I now call my "fruity friend," Sarah Beck, owner of Beck's Farm in Wichita. You are a joy to work with!

Thank you to Marjorie Shoemaker from the Mennonite Heritage Museum in Goessel who took the time to answer all my questions and give me a "guided tour."

Thanks to Penny and Gus Dorado for helping me with my Mennonite research. You guys are real blessings in my life.

To my wonderful and unique friend Elly "Singer" Kraai: thanks for the Sunrise!

I also want to acknowledge my wonderful agent and friend, Janet Benrey and my first editor, Susan Downs, both of whom have opened doors of blessing for me.

My deep and abiding appreciation to Becky Germany and all the incredible folks at Barbour for giving me a chance.

To my wonderful husband, Norman: I love you so much. This "writing thing" would be impossible without you.

To my critique partners Faye Speiker, Kim Woodhouse and Alenc Ward: thanks for your invaluable help.

To my readers who have been so encouraging and supportive: you'll probably never know in this life how much you mean to me. YOU are the reason God gave me this opportunity. I will never take you for granted.

To the Mennonite people who have given our country such a rich heritage of faith and taught us to respect the things in life that are really important: I hope I've represented you well. I've certainly grown to love and admire the principles you stand for.

Lastly, and most importantly: to my Very Best Friend. You are the air I breathe. . .

Chapter One

"She wants a talking pizza on the cover."

Grant slid my proposal across the desk until it rested in front of me. His dark eyes narrowed, warning me not to argue. We both knew it was useless, but I couldn't stop myself. I'd worked hard on a menu cover for Pizzazz Pizza. The lines were clean and bold, the graphics eye-catching.

"You know pizzas don't actually speak, right?" An attempt to keep a note of sarcasm out of my voice failed miserably.

He sighed and ran his hand through his short salt-and-pepper hair. Managing an advertising agency isn't easy, and Grant works with more problem clients than most. Grantham Design is a mid-range firm. Not the worst but not the best. Grant's dream is to make it to the top like Sawyer, Higgins, and Smith, the number one advertising firm in Wichita. I'm pretty sure I knew what those guys would tell Olivia Pennington to do with her chatty Italian pie if this was their account. But unfortunately for Grant and me, we couldn't afford to lose her as a client.

I sighed and picked up my beautiful proposal. Maybe I could make it work for someone else—a client who was savvy enough to leave designing to the designers.

"A talking pizza," he said once again. "And don't get too creative, Gracie."

"Exactly what every designer strives for, a complete lack of imagination."

"Just make it work." With that, he turned and strolled out of my office, leaving me with a rejected design and a verbal food product in my future. I stared out the window at the deli across the street. Feeling hunger pangs, I glanced at my watch. Maybe I could consider the new menu design over lunch. Uptown Bistro serves the best hummus in town. Just thinking about it made my mouth water. My jaw dropped when I saw the time. Nine thirty? How could it only be nine thirty?

I flashed back to the excitement I'd experienced two years earlier when I graduated from college with a degree in graphic design. I was determined to set the design world on fire. But since then I'd discovered that the real world is a lot different than what I'd imagined. Most clients aren't interested in seeing *my* ideas. Instead, they boldly declare that they "know exactly what they want." Unfortunately, their brilliant suggestions are simply remakes of overused, hackneyed concepts, completely inappropriate for their needs. Like a talking pizza. I rubbed my forehead, trying to rid myself of the beginnings of a tension headache. Sometimes I felt like a kid who'd been handed a box of crayons and admonished to "color in the lines" without any chance for creativity or fresh ideas.

I put the Pizzazz Pizza packet in my drawer and stared at my computer screen. Well, if she wanted chatty food, I'd give her chatty food. At that moment, several ideas popped into my head that would make for interesting dialogue. Of course, none of them were appropriate for a family night out at the local pizza parlor. Then I began to wonder just what a pepperoni-covered pastry would say if it could talk. I was pretty sure it would scream "Help!" as loudly as possible since it was about to be sliced into pieces and devoured. However, I doubted seriously that Olivia Pennington would appreciate the humor behind such an idea. A few other entertaining concepts were drifting through my mind when the phone rang.

"Hello, Snicklefritz!"

I sighed into the phone. "Dad, I thought you were going to stop calling me that."

"Grace Marie, I've been calling you Snicklefritz ever since you were a little girl. You used to like it."

I leaned back in my chair and stared at the framed photograph of my parents that sat on the edge of my desk. "But I'm not five anymore. What if you accidentally use it in public again—like you did at graduation?"

My dad laughed. "Your friend Stacy said I was 'darling.'"

"Stacy was not and never will be my friend, Dad. She told everyone about that silly nickname. There are still people from school who call me Snicklefritz."

My dad's hearty laughter made me grab a strand of hair and twirl it around my finger—a nervous habit I couldn't seem to shake.

"So what's up?" My stomach tightened a notch. He usually never contacts me at work unless something's wrong. Like two weeks ago when he told me he'd broken his leg and would be out of commission for a while. And the call last year after Mom was diagnosed with cancer. Thank God, she's fine now.

"Honey, we got word today that your uncle Benjamin passed away."

My stomach relaxed, and I let go of my hair. I'd never even met my father's only brother. He lived in a little Mennonite town somewhere in northeast Kansas.

"What happened, Dad?"

There was a prolonged silence. When he spoke, my father's voice trembled slightly. "It was his heart, Gracie."

"Are you okay?"

"I'm fine, honey. I just wish. . ."

"You tried everything you could to mend your fences with him, Dad. You have nothing to feel guilty about."

A shaky sigh came through the receiver. "I know that, but it doesn't make it any easier right now."

"Do you need me to come home? When's the funeral?"

"The community has already held the service."

"You mean no one told you about your own brother's funeral?" I didn't even try to keep the indignation out of my voice. "What kind of people are these? Is it because you're banned or something?"

"Now don't jump to conclusions. Turns out Benjamin left strict instructions that this was the way he wanted it. The pastor who called me felt badly but didn't know what else to do except to honor my brother's wishes. He—he also wanted me to know about Benjamin's will."

"So what did he leave you?" It couldn't be much due to Benjamin's lifestyle.

"He didn't leave me anything, honey. My brother left his house in Harmony, along with all of his belongings to you, Gracie."

Goofy talking pizzas had obviously warped my brain. My father's words made no sense.

"What? He left what to who?"

"Left what to *whom*, Gracie."

"Dad, this is *not* the time to correct my English. Why in the world would Uncle Benjamin leave me his estate? He didn't even know me."

"I don't know, honey. The congregation we belonged to when I was young believed in The Ban. Benjamin embraced the practice the rest of his life, even though the church as a whole doesn't do it anymore. You were born after your mom and I left Harmony. Since you were never part of the church, I guess in Benjamin's mind you're the only relative left who isn't off-limits." He sighed.

"You know, my brother wasn't always so judgmental. Originally, Benjamin fully supported my decision to leave Harmony. But after your mom and I settled in Fairbury, something happened. He changed—and not for the better." My father paused. "I wish I'd taken him with me when I left. Maybe things would have turned out differently."

"I'm sorry, Dad. I really am. But this still doesn't make any sense." It would take some time before I could grasp the idea that I was now a property owner in a little Mennonite town.

"I wish I could help you more, Gracie. But with this leg, I can't travel. And Mom needs to stay here to take care of me. I'm overnighting the papers so you can look at them yourself. You'll have to decide what to do from there."

"Seems to me that Uncle Benjamin took a big chance leaving everything to someone he didn't know. I might decide to sell the land and plant a Motel 6 in the middle of Harmony."

My dad chuckled. "Well, that would definitely shake things up a bit." He hesitated for a moment. "Your mother and I left Harmony because the bishop of our church opposed our marriage even though our parents supported us. He ruled that town, Gracie. His judgmental attitudes made life unbearable. But your mother reminds me that he's been gone a long time. Pastor Mueller, the man who called today, seemed nice. Very understanding. Not at all like Bishop Angstadt. I'm not crazy about the idea of your going to Harmony alone, but your mother tells me I'm overreacting. Pastor Mueller said he would do everything he could to help you. He sounded very sincere."

"Send me the papers, Dad. I honestly don't know what I'm going to do about this."

"I don't want to make your mind up for you, Snickle. . .er, Gracie. But maybe you could go for at least a week or two. See if you can find someone to buy the place. The money would certainly create a nice nest egg for your future. And while you're there, you could rescue some of the possessions that belonged to Mama and Papa so they can stay in the family. When my folks left Harmony, they deeded the house to Benjamin and left almost all their belongings behind. My guess is that Benjamin kept most of our family heirlooms. It would mean a lot to me if we could get them back." He paused and took a deep breath. "But once you get them, if you feel uncomfortable in Harmony, I want you to turn around and come home. Forget the stuff. You're more important than any heirlooms. Promise me, Gracie."

"Okay, I promise." My dad tends to be overdramatic when it comes to me. His emotional response to their old hometown didn't alarm me. I suddenly thought of my grandfather. "Dad, are you going to tell Papa that Benjamin died?

"No. Mom and I have talked about it. I don't know if he even remembers Benjamin anymore. It would just confuse him, I'm afraid."

Papa Joe lived in a nursing home and was in the last stages of Alzheimer's. Mama Essie had passed away almost five years ago. They'd never been able to understand why Benjamin had turned his back on the family and stayed in Harmony. Now it was too late for them to reconcile. At least in this world.

Harmony. Strange name for a place that had brought so much destruction to the Temple family. Would this gift from my uncle help to heal the past, or would it bring even more pain? It was impossible to know the answer to that question by just sitting in my office.

I smiled down at the sketches of Pizzazz Pizza's new logo. Let Grant figure out what conversational cuisine says.

I was going to Harmony.

Chapter Two

With a promise from my best friend, Allison, to look after my cat and a warning from Grant that I had to be back in two weeks for an important client meeting, I took off Friday morning for Harmony, Kansas. After leaving Wichita, the only towns I saw along the way were small, rural places where life looked much slower and more relaxed than it did in the city. I was reminded of life in tiny Fairbury, Nebraska, where I'd been raised. As a teenager, I felt as if I lived behind a big picture window, destined to watch the world go by without actually being a part of it. Getting a job and moving to the big city had been a dream come true. Surprisingly, as I watched the countryside rush by, I felt a twinge of nostalgia for the way things used to be. My reaction surprised me. I had everything I wanted in Wichita—a job with an ad agency, an apartment downtown, and more friends than my entire high school class in Fairbury. I dismissed my errant feelings as a case of homesickness. It had been almost two months since I'd seen my mother and father. After I returned from Harmony, I'd schedule a weekend trip to Nebraska.

I stopped for lunch in a place called Walalusa. As with many small towns, the local diner had two distinct qualities you could count on—curious stares from the regulars and a burger loaded with grease, fried onions, and dripping cheese. Thirty minutes later I left with a full tummy, a bag of homemade peanut butter cookies, a pat on the back from a waitress named Floreen, and a vow to stop by again on the way home.

After about an hour and several wrong turns, I finally found an old, crooked, weathered sign that pointed the way to Harmony. I kept the notes I'd written from my father's verbal directions on the seat next to me and drove slowly, watching street signs so I wouldn't get lost. Homes with modern farm machinery were interspersed with older farmsteads that had horses, ancient tractors, and plows.

I rolled my car window down and breathed in the aroma of wet earth and burgeoning fields planted with wheat, alfalfa, and corn. I'd almost forgotten what the country smelled like.

Eventually I found a signpost that announced my entrance into Harmony. Instead of heading straight to Benjamin's, I decided to drive around a little. I turned onto what seemed to be the main road, a wide dirt street dotted with buildings. On the corner sat a large white building with a bell tower and a sign that read BETHEL MENNONITE CHURCH. A group of people stood in the front of the church, laughing and talking together. Most of them wore the kind of clothing I'd expected to see. The men had on dark pants, solid-colored shirts, and black or dark blue jackets along with the large brimmed hats that made them recognizable as Mennonites. The women wore dresses that reached almost to their ankles. A couple of them had added another covering—almost like a jumper or apron. A few sported the traditional head covering. But to my surprise, there were also women and men in more contemporary outfits. Jeans, sweatshirts, flannel shirts—even one young woman who wore shorts and a T-shirt.

Several of them looked my way. At first I wondered if it was because of my car, a bright yellow Volkswagen Beetle. But a quick look around revealed I was mistaken. Along with the black buggies and horses I'd expected, quite a few cars were parked on the streets. Some plain and dark with painted bumpers and others quite modern—even new.

On the other side of the huge church was a park with a massive stone water fountain, a small lake, various types of colorful flowers that reached up from well-tended garden plots, freshly painted shelters, and wooden picnic tables large enough to hold an entire family. The landscaping and careful maintenance showed extreme care and concern. I promised myself a visit some afternoon during my trip, accompanied by one of the novels I'd packed away in my suitcase.

As I drove farther down what was obviously the main drag, I couldn't help but notice the street signs. Although I was currently on the obligatory Main Street, the other interconnecting roads had interesting names like Bethel, Resurrection, and Charity Lane. I wondered if Hope Road was ahead somewhere since Uncle Benjamin had lived north of Main Street and Faith Road.

Harmony certainly had a small town atmosphere, but unlike so many of the abandoned and dying rural communities throughout Kansas, this place was vibrant and alive. I checked out some of the various businesses. Among the rows of neat, colorful buildings with hand-painted signs, I discovered a meat market, a bakery, a candle shop, a clothing store, and a secondhand emporium. Ruth's Crafts and Creations caught my eye, and Mary's Kitchen looked to be doing a brisk business, even though it was three in the afternoon. Lights sparkled from inside several buildings, and a bearded man in dark clothes and a wide-brimmed straw hat was using a phone attached to the wall outside. Old-fashioned streetlamps lined both sides of Main Street, and benches sat along the boardwalk, each one filled with men deep in conversation or women doing needlework while they talked and laughed together.

Harmony bustled with activity, and the residents certainly

weren't the dour, grim people I thought I'd encounter. This wasn't the town my father had described at all, but a charming place full of happy people. Spring flowers blossomed in window boxes. Honeysuckle bloomed over handrails and climbed up the sides of buildings. Children ran up and down the covered, wooden sidewalks, giggling and playing just like children anywhere else. I had the strangest feeling I'd stepped back in time and landed inside a Norman Rockwell painting. The real world seemed far away from this place—as if Harmony had found a way to banish it outside its borders.

I drove all the way through town, continuing to draw stares from people I passed. Just like every other small town, everyone knows when a stranger is among them. Feeling a little uneasy with the attention, I headed for Uncle Benjamin's. At the place where the businesses ended and houses began, I found the hand-painted street sign that read FAITH ROAD. At the corner of Faith Road and Main Street stood another church, this one much more modern. The square redbrick building sported a sloping roof and a large metal cross attached to its front face. A sign sat a few feet from the road that read HARMONY CHURCH. Two churches in a town this size just added to my list of surprises. Dad had only mentioned Bethel—the Mennonite church my family had once attended.

Following my father's instructions, I turned north and drove for about a mile, leaving the town behind. This area was much more rural with only a few simple houses nestled in the middle of fields planted with newly budding crops. Before reaching my final destination, I came upon a huge, red Victorian-style house with white trim. It sat back from the road and was surrounded by a large orchard. I slowed my car and stared. It had a wraparound porch with a creamy white railing. Two gleaming ivory rockers sat on the porch, and baskets of flowering green plants hung from the roof. The effect was striking—almost breathtaking. I noticed a very modern tractor parked next to a large red barn and an old beat-up truck in the driveway. I'd anticipated stark houses without beauty or style. Either my preconceived notions were wrong, or the people who owned this house weren't Mennonite.

I continued down the dirt road until I found Uncle Benjamin's. His house had the plain white paint I'd expected, but the two-story structure was actually quite charming. A nice-sized porch was attached to the front of the home. Large yellow tulips bloomed next to the steps, and beautiful purple irises, surrounded by a circle of stones, graced the middle of the yard. Purple irises. Mama Essie's favorite flowers. Had she originally planted the garden? Since it was late April, the flowers were anointed with the joie de vivre of spring, and as I stepped out of the car, their aroma greeted me. An old oak tree sheltered the porch, and a lone, cream-colored rocking chair sat waiting for an owner who would never return. I'd seen quite a few wooden rockers on Main Street. It was a safe bet they'd been crafted in Harmony.

As I approached the steps, I noticed two sparrows sitting on the railing. I thought they'd take flight when they saw me, but instead they stared at me with interest until I put my foot on the first wooden stair. As I watched them fly away and land on a branch in the oak tree, I discovered the reason for their lack of fear. Dangling from the branches was a brightly painted bird feeder. There were also several birdhouses hanging nearby, along with a large, multiholed house attached to the trunk of the tree. I'd never seen birdhouses like these. Each was solidly built out of wood and adorned with pictures of birds and flowers. Beautiful and colorful cardinals, blue jays, and sparrows decorated each structure. Tiny heads poked out of the houses while the birds from the porch sat on branches near the large feeder. They were obviously used to being cared for.

I fumbled around, trying to find the key that had been sent with Benjamin's papers. I'd just grasped it when the sound of a loud, gravelly voice split the silence. I almost dropped my key.

"Hey, just whatcha think you're doin' there, lady?"

I turned around to find a woman staring at me suspiciously. A round orb of a human being, she wore faded denim overalls over a dingy, torn T-shirt. Her feet were encased in old ratty sneakers caked with dirt. A lack of makeup and graying hair pulled into a messy bun made it hard to determine her age, but I guessed her to be somewhere near sixty.

She took a few steps closer. "I asked you just what you was doin' at that door, lady," she said, her face screwed up like a prune. "I knowed the man who lived there, and you ain't him. You ain't even his ghost."

After my initial shock, I recovered my voice. "I–I'm Benjamin Temple's niece. He—he left this house to me." I cleared my throat and forced myself to calm down. "I'm Gracie Temple," I said more forcefully. "And you are?"

Unfortunately, she took this as some kind of invitation and clomped her way up to the porch. She squinted as she looked me up and down. I met her gaze without flinching.

"Well, I guess you might actually be lil' Gracie," she said finally, her face cracking a smile that showed some gaps in her teeth. "You sure look a lot like old Benny. He was a nice-lookin' man, your uncle. Even more important, he was a good man. We was close friends. I been watchin' for you ever since he passed away. Promised Benny I'd keep an eye on this place."

"My uncle told you I was coming?"

The old woman leaned over the porch railing and spat on the ground. "Yeah, he did. It sure was important to him. In fact, it was all he talked about toward the end."

"Well, thank you for watching the house." I flashed her a smile and put my hand on the doorknob, hoping she would take it as a dismissal. I wanted to get inside, unpack, and settle in.

Instead of taking my hint, she extended her grimy hand. "I'm

Myrtle Goodrich, but folks call me Sweetie. Pleased to know ya. I live just down the road a piece. I'm sure we'll be good friends."

I couldn't help but stare at the hand she held out. She noticed and pulled it back, wiping it on her overalls. "Sorry. Been workin' in my orchard." After transferring most of the dirt on her hand to her clothes, she reached out again. This time I took it, forcing myself not to check it for cleanliness. Her grip was firm and her hands rough and calloused.

"Nice to meet you, Myrtle." I looked my new neighbor over carefully. Besides the fact that I didn't like cutesy names, if I was ever knocked senseless and a name like Sweetie fell out of my mouth due to severe brain damage, I still wouldn't apply it to this odd woman. I couldn't even call my cat "sweetie." Of course, with a name like Snicklefritz, he'd already suffered as much indignity as any one cat should have to. He'd acquired his name as a defensive maneuver on my part. Hopefully, the next time my father called me by that loathsome nickname, I could claim he had dementia and had confused me with my feline friend.

She flashed me another strange grin. It reminded me of a baby with gas. "Yep, when I was born, my mama took a gander at me and said, 'Will you look at that little sweetie?' And that was my name from then on."

"Well, that's interesting." I tightened my grip on the doorknob. "It was nice to meet you. But I really need to get unpacked. Maybe we'll see each other again before I go." Feeling as though I'd handled my escape the best way possible, I began to fiddle with the key, attempting to fit it into the keyhole. Instead of taking the hint, Myrtle advanced again.

"It's a good thing you finally got here," she said, looking around as if someone was hiding around the corner, listening. Of course her loud, rather rough voice pretty much made any attempt at secrecy useless. "Your uncle had a troubled mind, Gracie girl. I 'spect I never seen a man so full of worry. He sure was countin' on you comin' here. Toward the end it was all he talked about."

I took my hand off the doorknob, disturbed that my uncle was afraid and focused on me before he died. "I thought Uncle Benjamin died of a heart attack. Are you saying he knew he was going to die?"

Myrtle shrugged her rounded shoulders. "His heart was bad for years. He got worse and worse this last year. Then a couple of months ago, he started gettin' real weak and sickly. Couldn't stay on his feet for long. He figgered his time was finally up. Guess he was right."

"I—I didn't realize he had a heart condition. He didn't keep in contact with his family."

She nodded vigorously. "It's a cryin' shame, too." She swiped at her eyes with her muddy hand, leaving a trail of grime on her face. "He was a good man, Gracie girl. A good man."

"Thank you." I put my hand back on the doorknob. "Now if you'll excuse me. . ."

"Sure, sure." She frowned and took a step back. "Well, if you need anything, alls you gotta do is set this pot of petunias on the porch rail." She bent down to pick up a large pot of flowers sitting near the steps and handed it to me.

"Wouldn't it be easier if I called you?"

She exploded with coarse laughter, and her face turned beet red. "You're gonna have to get used to livin' like the old Mennies," she sputtered after regaining her voice. "There ain't no phone here."

No phone? I hadn't counted on that. "I have a cell phone. . ."

"I wouldn't count on it workin' out here," she said, interrupting me. "But you can go down to one of them shops in town. There's phones there. Not all these Mennies live by the old rules like your uncle. Only a handful of those kind left now." She grinned at me like a deranged Cheshire cat. "You got lucky and inherited one of the few houses around without no electricity or a working phone. For a city girl like you, it'll be quite an adventure, I reckon."

I stared at the woman as I set the flowers on the porch. Even though I found her irritating, it occurred to me that she might be one of the only people who really knew my uncle. Although I abhorred the choices he'd made, seeing the house where my father had grown up sparked a desire to learn what I could about Benjamin. "You know, I am rather curious about my uncle. Maybe while I'm here you could answer some questions I have about him."

"Well," she said, staring up at the sky, "it's gettin' pretty late. I got a roast in the oven that'll be burnt to a crisp if I don't get a-goin'." Myrtle waved once and jumped off the porch. Then she headed down the road like her overalls were on fire.

I shook my head as I watched her scurry away. Had I scared her off? Maybe it was best not to question my good fortune. I had to consider that maybe old Sweetie was a few bricks shy of a full load. Besides, I was determined to stay focused on my goals. I fully intended to sell the house, grab a few things for my mom and dad, and leave well within my two-week deadline. Trying to learn more about my uncle would probably only sidetrack me.

Before opening the front door, I glanced up and down the road. Besides the big, red home in the distance, I spotted a couple of other houses on Faith Road. They sat like silent sentries in the middle of crop fields. It didn't make any sense, but I suddenly had the strange feeling they were watching me—wondering what I was going to do next. A curious sense of uneasiness filled me, and I couldn't stop my fingers from trembling as I slid Benjamin's key into the lock.

Chapter Three

I had to jiggle the ancient key several times before the front door creaked open. Anticipating the worst from a lifelong bachelor, I was pleased to find a clean, orderly, and rather attractive living room. A bright rag rug lay on the polished hardwood floor, adding a splash of color to the surroundings. To the right of the entryway, a carved wood staircase led to the upstairs. The massive cherry secretary next to the window was beautifully carved and intricate, with a drop-down lid that doubled as a desk. The makeshift desktop held paper, pens, and a large leather Bible. Another wall was lined with bookcases. A rocking chair, a close cousin to the one on the porch, sat in the corner, and against the farthest wall, I was surprised to find a lovely couch upholstered in a rich gold brocade fabric. The material had been well cared for but appeared somewhat faded by time. Someone had carefully folded a colorful handcrafted quilt and laid it across its back. In another corner of the room, next to a cast-iron stove, was a brown leather upholstered chair, and next to it stood a tall grandfather's clock made from some kind of dark wood. Perhaps mahogany. The pendulum sat unmoving. I fumbled around on top of the clock and found the key that unlocked the front piece. Same place we kept our key at home. After checking my watch, I set the time, pulled up the weights, and started the pendulum moving. The slow ticking filled the silent room, making it feel as if life were coming back into the abandoned house.

The furniture surprised me. Rather than being plain and without character or design, I found well-crafted pieces that had obviously been created with excellence.

I checked out the old potbellied stove that was probably used to supply heat to the main room during the winter. Good thing it was spring. I didn't relish the idea of having to gather wood and start a fire on a frigid Kansas morning.

Two paintings hung in the living room. One was of horses standing near a fence. The other, a landscape depicting a field of golden wheat under gathered storm clouds. Both displayed a high level of talent, and I wondered about the artist. Against the far wall a large cross-stitch sampler declared "Fear not for I am with thee." The scripture touched my heart, as if God were speaking directly to me, reassuring me that even in this rather strange situation, I wasn't alone.

As I began my search through the rest of the house, I felt happy beyond words to find a fairly modern bathroom. The large claw-foot tub was different than what I was used to. I found the lack of a shower rather annoying, but I could make do. I'd been expecting an outhouse. I still remembered the summers my family went camping and fishing at a lake not far from our home. The only available facilities left much to be desired. Not much more than holes in the ground, I visited them only when absolutely necessary. My cousin, Jonathon, used to tell me stories about big, hairy spiders that lived at the bottom of the toilets. Needless to say, any outing to the bathroom was made in great haste and with severe trepidation. Thankfully, I wouldn't be having nightmares about spiders while I was here.

I liked the kitchen with its lemon yellow paint and handmade oak cabinets. A small oak table with two chairs sat near a window that looked out on the property behind the house. The table was covered with a green-and-white-checked tablecloth, and matching valances hung over the windows. A large tublike sink with a water pump sat directly under one of the windows. Two colorful rag rugs lay on the floor. A white hobnail hurricane lamp hung from one of the wooden beams that stretched across the ceiling. The stove and refrigerator bordered on antique, but at least they appeared to be clean. A stainless-steel teapot waited on the stove. As Myrtle warned, I couldn't find any electrical outlets. I peeked out the window and discovered that a propane tank had been set up next to the house. That explained how the appliances worked.

A sudden knock on the front door startled me, and I sighed with frustration. So far, my visit to what I'd pictured as a peaceful Mennonite community had turned out to be something quite different. Hoping Sweetie hadn't made an unwelcome return, I cautiously opened the front door. A nice-looking man stood on the porch, dressed in jeans and a blue-checkered shirt. I guessed him to be not much older than me. He flashed me a crooked grin.

"Sorry to bother you," he said, "but I wonder if you're Benjamin's niece, Grace?"

For crying out loud, did everyone in this town know me? "Yes, I'm Gracie Temple. And you are?"

He brushed a lock of sun-bleached hair out of his face. "I'm Sam. Sam Goodrich."

"Goodrich? Any relation to. . . ?"

"Yeah," he answered a little too quickly, his face flushing. "I'm her nephew. Don't tell me she's been here already."

"Yes. In fact, she introduced herself before I even got inside the house."

He shook his head. "Sorry about that. My aunt was pretty close to your uncle. She took his death hard. I think she's still trying to look out for him."

I couldn't leave this man standing on the front porch much longer. It was becoming evident he wasn't going anywhere. Reluctantly, I pushed the screen door open. "Would you like to come in?"

"Thank you, I would. But first let me get something from my truck. I brought you a housewarming gift."

I watched as he bounded off the porch and hurried over to a battered, weather-beaten truck that must have been blue at one time before rust took over. With a start, I realized it was the truck I'd seen parked in front of the beautiful red house down the road. Did this guy live there? I found him handsome in a roughshod, country kind of way. Not anything like the guys back home. Most of my dates came through hooking up with other people in advertising. I was used to the slicked-down, suited-up type who sported black-framed glasses and had their hair carefully styled to look messy. Never could quite understand the popularity of that look. I achieved it every morning when I rolled out of bed, and it didn't cost me a cent.

Frankly, Sam reminded me more of the boys in Fairbury—the ones I'd wanted to get away from. Funny how they'd never made my heart beat faster—the way it did now. Sam grabbed a large wicker basket from the back of his truck and trudged back to where I stood waiting.

"I thought you might like some fresh fruit," he said, smiling. "I have a farm about half a mile down the road. I brought you some fresh blackberries and strawberries. I also grow peaches and apples, but they're not ready to harvest yet. I stuck in some jars of peaches from last season, along with some apple preserves and a jar of apple butter." He carried the basket straight to the kitchen. He'd obviously been here before.

"Thanks. I appreciate it. It will be nice to have something to eat. I haven't had time to look around to see if there's anything else in the house."

He set the basket on the table in the corner of the kitchen. "You don't need to worry about that." He stepped over to the refrigerator and swung the door open. To my amazement it was stocked with food. "After your father called Pastor Mueller to say you were coming, we made sure you'd have what you needed." He stepped over to a door next to the kitchen cabinets. "There's also quite a bit of food in the pantry."

Inside a small room lined with shelves, I found almost every kind of canned food imaginable. Lots of collard greens, spinach, hominy, and bags of white beans sat waiting for someone who might appreciate them. That sure wasn't me. I was relieved to see a jar of peanut butter, a loaf of bread, and on the floor, a few bottles of pop.

"There are two wooden boxes on the floor near the door," Sam said. "They contain bird food and squirrel food for Ben's friends."

"I saw the bird feeder, but where did he feed the squirrels?" I closed the pantry door and almost ran into Sam. He colored slightly and took a step back. "There's a feeder on the south side of the roof. Ben has a ladder leaning up against the house. Just carry the food up there and dump it in. You'll have all kinds of squirrelly visitors. I mean besides my aunt and me." He grinned when I laughed. "Why don't you let me feed them the first time? It will only take a few minutes."

"Thanks. That would be great. I. . .I can't thank you enough for everything. If you'll tell me how much you spent on supplies, I'd be happy to write you a check."

His friendly smile ratcheted down a notch. "You don't owe us anything. That's just the way things are done around here. Besides, Ben was our friend."

Although my first reaction was to insist once again that he allow me to compensate him, I could tell it was best to back off. I didn't want to offend him. "Why don't I get us something to drink while you feed my uncle's pets? Then maybe we could visit for a while?"

His answering smile indicated that our rather awkward moment had passed. Sam showed me where the glasses were kept. Then he shoveled some bird and squirrel food into two metal pitchers and carried them outside. I checked out the fridge and found a pitcher of fresh lemonade. As I poured some into our glasses, I heard the ladder hit the side of the house. I carried the ice-cold lemonade into the living room and waited for him to finish. As promised, it took him less than five minutes. He came in, put the pitchers back in the pantry, and joined me in the living room. I sat on the couch while he took the rocking chair.

"I have to admit that the furniture in this house surprises me," I said after he'd made himself comfortable.

He smiled. "You thought it would be plain? A lot of straight lines and lack of decoration?"

I nodded.

"You're thinking of Shaker furniture. For the most part, even Old Order Mennonites were allowed to have nice furniture." He pointed at the secretary. "I believe that's been in your family for many years. If I remember right, Ben told me it was built by your great-great-grandfather."

"Really? My dad sent me down here to rescue our family heirlooms. I'm certain he'll want it." I shook my head. "There's more furniture here than I anticipated. We'll have to rent a pretty big trailer to get all this stuff to Nebraska."

Sam nodded and took a drink from his glass. After a few seconds of awkward silence, he smiled. "One of the reasons I came by was to show you how to use the propane tank and explain how the plumbing works.

"We do have plumbing in the big city."

He laughed. "I know that, but in this house, water is collected in a cistern that flows into a tank in the basement. If you want to take a bath or wash clothes, you have to turn on a small gas-powered generator that runs water through your pipes."

"Well, how does the...um...the..."

Sam grinned and put me out of my misery. "I won't explain all the intricacies to you, but an air compressor allows everything else in the bathroom to work the way you're used to. And let me put one other rumor to rest. Old Order Mennonites do use toilet paper. You'll find it in the bathroom cabinet."

The relief I felt must have shown in my face, because he chuckled again. I liked the way he laughed. It was deep and real. His irises were an unusual shade of bluish gray. I'd never seen eyes that color before. His blond hair almost reached his shoulders, and he kept pushing it off his sunburned face. It gave him the kind of romantic look many movie stars would probably sell their souls to possess.

"One other thing," he said. "There's an old wringer washer downstairs. Not very modern, but you'd be surprised how clean it will get your clothes."

"Thankfully, my grandmother used a wringer washer when I was young. She taught me how to operate it. When it broke down, she finally got a modern washer, but she always swore that her old machine got her clothes cleaner."

"My aunt used to say the same thing. However, she was willing to trade cleanliness for convenience. She'd never go back to the old way."

Feeling that we'd exhausted the clothes washer topic, I tried another tack. "Sam, do you mind if I ask you a few questions?"

He shook his head. "Of course not. That's why I'm here."

"It's about my uncle. You see, I never got the chance to know him. I must say I'm shocked he left his property to me. I have to wonder about it. You and your aunt were close to him. Do you have any idea why he'd pass along his inheritance to a niece he'd never met?"

Sam cleared his throat and frowned. "I'm sorry, I don't. He made it very clear that his personal life was off-limits. I guess he was friendlier with me than most, but there was always a side of Ben that he kept to himself. As you know, he was raised in the Old Order. Never really left it. Most of the other folks in town have adopted more modern ways, although they hold true to the Mennonite principles, plain living, and everything. But not Ben. He and a few others clung to the old ways. Funny thing was, he didn't hang around them much either. It was like he was protecting himself against something and he couldn't allow people to get too close." He stared down at the floor, looking uncomfortable. "Toward the end, he said some things I didn't quite understand. I got the feeling he hadn't meant to let them slip out." He lifted his head and looked at me. "Honestly, I'm not sure I'm comfortable telling you something said in private. If I really thought it was important, I would be willing to chance it. But at this point, I don't see how it would help anything."

A good-looking man with principles. Quite a rare find. Without realizing it, my eyes drifted to his left hand. No ring. For a few seconds, I felt a sense of relief. Then I realized I was having some rather serious thoughts about a hick farmer in a town so small it wasn't on most maps. This wasn't what I was looking for. I'm definitely a big city girl. I forced my mind back to the situation at hand.

"You said my uncle didn't spend much time with people who believed the way he did? Didn't he go to church?"

Sam shrugged his broad shoulders. "Well, the Old Order folks don't have a formal meeting house anymore. They hold services in each other's homes. Ben went to all the meetings and did everything he was supposed to do, but he rarely just sat down and carried on a conversation with anyone, even those who believed the same way he did. There were a few people he trusted, including my aunt and me. But I can't say he was ever completely forthcoming with us." He gulped down some lemonade then set down the glass. "I believe there was something going on with your uncle—something he never talked directly about. As far as I know, he died without ever sharing it."

"But he did tell you about me."

Sam frowned and leaned forward. "Ben asked me to come by and talk to him about something 'private' a couple of months ago. I thought he was finally ready to share whatever it was that bothered him so deeply. But he only talked a little about your family—who you were and how he hadn't seen you for so long. Didn't really explain why except to say there were some differences that separated you. Then he told me that I should watch for you to come. He even told me that he'd had all his property put in your name." He sighed and leaned back in his chair. "That was as personal as he got. I only wish he would have trusted me more. I think he went to his reward with a heavy burden. That shouldn't have happened. Benjamin Temple deserved better."

"Maybe he would have told you if he'd had more time," I offered.

Sam stared at his empty glass. "Possibly, but I don't think so. Ben knew he didn't have long. His heart was giving out. In the last year, he got worse and worse."

I felt a rush of indignation. "Why in the world wouldn't he call my father to let him know how ill he was? Except for my grandfather who is in a nursing home, my dad was his only close relative."

"He had his own way, Grace. It might not make sense to you, but over the years I came to respect your uncle for many of his beliefs. He didn't choose an easy life."

"But turning your back on people who don't believe the same way you do isn't right."

Sam shrugged. "I don't agree with it either, but I think in Ben's mind it was the only choice open to him. I guess he thought somehow your dad and your grandparents would repent and come back into the fold."

"That's ridiculous. My parents and grandparents are the best people I've ever known. They have nothing to 'repent' from."

Sam pushed back his chair and stood up. "Well, Pastor Mueller agrees with you. He talked to Ben several times and encouraged him to contact your family. Your uncle wouldn't budge. I tried to reason with him, too, but he shut me down. I finally let it go because I didn't want to lose his friendship."

I smiled at Sam, but I was thinking that although his words sounded right, I wished someone had been more forceful with my uncle. He'd left a lot of hurt behind him, and that certainly didn't seem very Christlike to me.

"I've got to get going," Sam said, "but first I want to make certain you know how to fire up all your appliances."

I obediently followed him around while he demonstrated each piece of equipment. I wanted to grumble that in Wichita, all I had to do was turn a knob, but I kept my mouth shut. I appreciated his help. After our informative tour, I walked him to the front door.

He put his hand on the doorknob to leave but suddenly hesitated. "Why don't I stop by tomorrow and take you to breakfast in town? You'll get a chance to visit a few of our shops and meet some of Harmony's residents. There are still a few folks who remember your family. I'm sure they'd love to meet you."

I started to turn him down. I wanted a few days to myself before taking on the town of Harmony. But as I looked into his incredible smoky gray eyes, I forgot what I'd wanted to say. Instead, I found myself nodding and asking him what time he'd be by. After agreeing to nine o'clock, I said good-bye and closed the door after him. As it clicked shut, I breathed a sigh of relief. Finally, some time alone. Hopefully, there wouldn't be any more interruptions from friendly neighbors.

It was still early, so I decided to carry my bags in from the car, poke around some, and then have a little supper. I'd already noticed several oil lamps scattered throughout the house. I searched until I found some matches in my uncle's desk. At least I would have some light after the sun went down.

As I closed the drawer, my eyes were drawn to the black leather Bible that lay on the desktop. I'd picked it up, intending to see if Benjamin had written family information in the front, when something slipped out from between the pages and fell to the floor. It was an envelope. I gasped involuntarily when I bent down to look at it.

My name was scrawled in large block letters on the front.

Chapter Four

I left the letter sitting on Benjamin's desk while I carried in my bags and had supper. I assumed my uncle had written it, but I couldn't decide if his message from beyond the grave was something I really wanted to read. Was this some last-ditch attempt to seek forgiveness? I didn't have to scratch very deep to uncover the resentment I felt toward him. The hurt he'd caused my family made it difficult for me to forgive him no matter what he had to say. Of course, my uncle may have left a very different kind of letter—a scathing missive full of judgment and retribution. Except that Sam and Myrtle had painted him in different colors. Unfortunately, most people have two faces—the one they show in public and the one they keep hidden behind a carefully constructed mask. Not knowing my uncle made it impossible for me to guess his motives.

A look through the refrigerator presented me with several options for supper. I finally settled on a bowl of beef stew that smelled absolutely wonderful. I found myself searching for the microwave before I remembered where I was. I discovered a small metal pan that I filled with stew and set on the stove. After locating a box of matches, I turned the knob under the pan, struck the match, and watched as the flame whooshed beneath the raised burner. A few minutes later, the aroma of homemade stew filled the homey kitchen. I added a slice of bread and butter, and before long my meal was ready. I sat down at the kitchen table and gazed out the window. A row of trees lined the back of the property. I wondered what was on the other side and decided to scout it out when I had time.

I finished my supper, put the dishes in the sink, and lit the oil lamp on the table. My mother had kept a couple of oil lamps in Fairbury even though we had electricity. A holdover from her childhood, I guess. The smell of burning oil took me back to leisurely nights on our old porch swing, listening to the cacophony of cicadas while my mother's old lamp burned in the window. I'd been in such a hurry to leave Nebraska I guess I'd forgotten a few of the things I'd actually enjoyed.

I grabbed my largest suitcase and headed for the stairs. Since the main floor consisted of the large living room, a bathroom, the kitchen, and the pantry, the bedrooms had to be on the second floor. The stairs were much steeper than I was used to, and each step creaked as I climbed. They twisted at the top and ended at a dark hallway. It occurred to me that perhaps it would have been better if I'd checked out this part of the house before the sun had gone down. The light from my lamp cast a rather ominous glow that made my surroundings look a little spooky. I left my heavy suitcase on the landing and proceeded down the hall.

There were three rooms upstairs. The first bedroom had probably been Benjamin's. The bed was covered with a rather plain blue bedspread. There was a mahogany dresser with a mirror. The top of the dresser held a comb, some kind of hair tonic, a small bowl of change, and two bottles of prescription medicine. An old wooden chair sat next to the wall, and a small battered trunk rested at the foot of the bed. Across the room I found a closet door. I slowly opened the door, which protested loudly in the silence.

An array of men's slacks and shirts hung on wooden hangers. All the pants were either black, dark brown, or dark blue. The shirts varied from light to dark. It was almost impossible to distinguish exact shades in the yellowish glow of the lamp. A wide-brimmed black hat hung on a hook on the side of the closet, and another hat just like it, but made out of straw, sat on a shelf.

I closed the door and stood in the middle of the room. "Hello, Uncle Benjamin," I said softly into the still, quiet space. "You wanted me here, and I'm here. Too bad you didn't make a move to see me while you were alive."

Feeling a little silly for talking to myself, I left that room and stepped out into the hallway. I held the lamp out in front of me and followed its flickering light to the next door. I turned the knob and swung it open. This room was larger than Benjamin's. A beautifully carved bed was pushed up against the back wall, next to the windows. A colorful patchwork quilt covered it. I walked over to the bed and ran my fingers across the hand stitching. I recognized the design. Mama Essie. She'd made one just like it for me. I'd tucked it away in my closet at home, afraid to use it because it was so precious I didn't want to damage it.

Of course, Mama hadn't seen her creations as something to be protected. "Why, honey," she'd said when I confessed to storing the precious gift away, "I made that quilt to be used. When you wrap yourself in it, I want you to imagine you're getting a big hug from your grandma."

I swung the lamp around and found a dresser like Benjamin's—but bigger and more ornate. A large homemade rag rug lay on the floor, and a cast-iron stove in the corner waited for the next chilly night. This had obviously been Papa Joe and Mama Essie's room. This was where I'd sleep. I could almost feel my grandparents, and the sensation gave me a sense of peace. I wondered how long it had been since the room had been thoroughly cleaned. I ran my fingers across the dresser and found it relatively free of dust. The quilt and the bedsheets looked freshly laundered. Had Benjamin tidied up in anticipation of my visit? The thought made me feel a little funny—as if he'd reached out to touch me from the great beyond. A shiver ran up my spine. Of course, as sick as he'd been, it was more likely Myrtle or Sam who had spruced the house up. I doubt my uncle thought much about housework during the last days of his life.

I lit the lamp that sat on the dresser but kept the one I had with me so I could use it to navigate my way back up the narrow stairs in the dark when I was ready for bed. I swung it around and had turned toward the door when I noticed an old photograph on the wall. I held the light close to it. It was a family portrait. A young Mama Essie and Papa Joe looked stoically at the camera. Mama was lovely, her dark hair pulled back into a bun with a few loose curls caressing her cheeks. Her dark eyes were framed by thick eyelashes that didn't need any help from mascara, and although the picture was in black and white, her cheeks were shaded with what might have been a rosy hue had the photograph been taken in color. Papa Joe stared at the camera with a rather humorless expression. But the hint of amusement in his eyes was unmistakable. I knew that look. He'd had it every time he'd told me one of his awful jokes. I didn't figure out how bad they were until I was an adult. To a child who worshipped her grandfather, Papa Joe put the professional comedians on TV to shame.

"Did you ever wonder why bread is square and lunchmeat is round?" he'd ask. Or "If you're eating cured ham, Gracie girl, don't you ever wonder just what was wrong with it before it got well?"

I also recalled the times he'd swing me around in circles with his strong arms, singing "I've Been Working on the Railroad." After leaving Harmony, he'd worked for the railroad until he retired. I guess that's why he loved the song so much. But even more than that silly song, Papa Joe had loved me—and I loved him and Mama. Seeing them so young made me realize how much I missed them. Even though Papa was still alive, he seemed only a shadow of the robust man he had once been. I'd give almost anything just to hear another one of his terrible jokes. I moved the lamp a little closer. I'd never seen any pictures of my father as a child—but there he was, probably all of ten years old. And next to him a smaller boy with deep, piercing eyes. Eyes that spoke of intelligence and reason. Uncle Benjamin. Although hair color is difficult to define in a black and white photo, it was easy to see that while the rest of the family had dark hair, Uncle Benjamin's was lighter. I would have bet all the money in my checking account, which wasn't much, that he'd had red hair like me. And that the spots across his nose were freckles just like mine. Although my mother told me my dimples came from an angel's kiss, I found that, in fact, they'd come from my uncle. I wondered if his eyes were green, too. They looked lighter than my dad's, which were brown.

It took a little while for me to recover from the shock I felt. Why hadn't anyone told me I looked so much like Benjamin? Had it been too painful for my parents and grandparents to talk about? When my father looked at me, did he see his brother?

I turned on my heels and left the room, slightly disturbed. Looking at that picture, I'd experienced a feeling of connection with an uncle I'd never met and never would on this side of life. Benjamin's actions toward my family had left me a solid sense of disdain for him. Finding out that I looked like him left me feeling confused.

One room remained at the end of the hall. I tried to turn the door handle, but it was either locked or jammed. I pushed against it a couple of times but couldn't get the door to budge. For tonight this last room would have to remain a mystery. At one time, it must have been my father's bedroom, but he'd been gone for thirty years. Probably relegated for storage, lack of use had caused the door to stick.

I put my suitcase in Mama and Papa's room, unpacked some of my clothes, and put them in the dresser drawers. When I opened the closet door, I discovered several women's dresses. According to my folks, Benjamin had never married. They must have belonged to Mama Essie. I'd look more closely tomorrow, when I had enough light to see them better.

I pushed my empty suitcase under the bed, picked up the lamp, and walked across the squeaky floor to the stairs, being careful to grasp the wooden railing with one hand while I held the lamp out in front of me with the other. Once downstairs, I realized I was going to have to get better at figuring out this lighting thing. If I'd lit a couple of lamps down here before I'd gone upstairs, the house wouldn't be so dark. I quickly fired up a lamp in the living room and put the one in my hand back in the kitchen. It sure wasn't like having electricity, but at least I could see well enough to get around.

I moved the bag with my makeup and toiletries into the bathroom, and grabbed the remaining overnight bag, carrying it into the living room to unpack. Although with my mother's prompting I'd purchased a windup alarm clock, I quickly realized that my cell phone charger was useless. Maybe I could buy an adapter for my car. That way I could at least charge my phone once in a while. Since I hadn't seen any kind of auto parts store in Harmony, I would probably have to drive to Council Grove.

The silence around me seemed almost deafening. In Wichita, I'd grown used to the sounds of cars honking, people talking as they walked past my windows, and long train whistles that woke me up in the middle of the night. It had been a long time since I'd been in the country—and so far Harmony was turning out to be even quieter than Fairbury, where the neighbors lived much closer. At least in Fairbury, you could hear dogs barking at night.

Suddenly remembering something else I couldn't get in Wichita, I went out on the front porch and down the steps. After walking a few feet away from the house, I stopped and looked up. Across the dark expanse of the night sky, the vista of stars sparkling like scattered jewels almost took my breath away. This was a sight only visible in the country. The lights of Wichita muted the stunning portrait of God's heavens, but in Harmony, they glittered with fire, anointing the night with His majestic, creative touch. It was beyond beautiful. I stood there, staring up until my neck began to ache. Reluctantly, I made my way back into the house, reminding myself that I had two weeks here—several more chances to behold this awesome sight.

Once inside, I checked my watch. A little after eight. I crossed my arms and gazed around the room. This was the time of night I'd usually pop popcorn, turn on the TV, and veg out until I got tired enough to go to bed.

"Not much to do here, Uncle Benjamin. What did you do for entertainment?" My voice sounded strange in the quiet. Like it didn't belong. Maybe it didn't. Maybe I didn't. I glanced over at the bookshelf and considered checking out the books lined up there, but I knew I was only trying to put off the inevitable.

My eyes rested on the letter lying on Benjamin's desk. Might as well get it over with. Funny how I dreaded reading it even more now that I knew about the similarities I shared with my uncle. Would my opinion of him be altered? And if so, which way would it go? I scolded myself for trying to anticipate something I couldn't possibly know anything about unless I actually got enough gumption to open the envelope. I moved the lamp to a small table next to the rocking chair, picked up the letter, and sat down. With trembling fingers, I pulled out the sheets of paper, unfolded them, and began to read:

Dearest Niece Grace,
    It is difficult to write this letter for many reasons. First of all, I am unsure that you have even honored my bequest.

I am aware that this letter might fall into different hands than yours. I placed it within our family Bible, believing that only a family member would discover it. I pray my assumption proves correct. However, since I cannot be sure of the outcome, it is with great trepidation that I pen these words.

First of all, I must tell you that although my family believes I have rejected them, I assure you I have not. I love them deeply and miss them. It is true that they have chosen to leave the old ways, but I cannot judge them right or wrong for this. God's love transcends our habits and choices. The reason for my separation from them is for motives they have never been made aware of. However, as I am dying and will not be able to protect them much longer from a terrible secret that has held me captive all these years, I have no choice but to pass it to someone else. And unfortunately, that person, my dear niece, must be you.

I cannot see into the future, and I don't know you, so I have no idea if you will be able to discover and navigate a path never found by me. However, my conscience will not allow me to die with this secret buried beneath years of deceit and lies. I have asked God's forgiveness for keeping it to myself—and for my part in it. But even with that forgiveness, justice has still not been served. Perhaps it never will. Unfortunately, you will now have to decide the matter. I pray your choices will be better than mine have been.

Reading by the light of the old lamp proved difficult, and my uncle's cramped script wasn't easy to read. His words filled me with a sense of dread. Either I was about to find out something I was pretty certain I didn't want to know—or I would discover that my poor deranged uncle had fallen way off his wooden rocker. With a sense of misgiving I turned the letter over and once again held it near the flickering lamplight.

Many years ago, an evil man lived in Harmony. Maybe you think I am being dramatic by using the word evil, *but I assure you that this man epitomizes the term. On the night my brother, Daniel, your father, planned to leave town with Beverly Fischer, the young woman who would become your mother, Jacob Glick was killed. No one in Harmony knows this. They believe he left town because he was so disliked. All these years I have been the only person who knew the truth. Now I must pass it on to you. Sadly, it is yours to bear alone.*

You see, I found Jacob's body that night. He'd been struck on the head with a large rock that still lay near his feet. The force of the blow took his life. I buried his body, the bloody rock, and a suitcase filled with his belongings amid the grove of trees on our property. His body lies there still.

I had to read the last paragraph several times to be certain I understood its meaning. My uncle had buried a body—here? A feeling of cold fear moved through me. I tried to tell myself that he was sick and that this letter was the result of his illness. But the thoughts seemed so well constructed and clear of confusion. With dismay, I continued to read.

You are probably asking yourself why I would do something like this. Why would I bury the body of a man who obviously lost his life by the hand of another and spend the rest of my days separated from my family, afraid to leave this property because the truth might be revealed? The answer will shock you, my dear niece, but I cannot keep the matter hidden any longer. It is because the man who killed Jacob Glick was my brother—your father, Daniel.

I put the letter in my lap. "This isn't true," I whispered into the dark corners of the room. "My father would never do something like that."

Of course, there was no response. What kind of a man would leave a poisonous letter like this behind him? What was he trying to accomplish? I knew my father. He was a man of peace—of forgiveness. The idea that he would take a human life was ludicrous. I had no desire to read another word of the hateful letter, but something compelled me to pick it up again. My hands shook, causing the paper to quiver beneath the amber-tinted glow of the lamp. I pulled the second page to the front and continued to read.

Please understand that I love my brother. I know this sin of murder was not planned. Jacob must have done something to provoke Daniel. Jacob was reprimanded many times for conducting himself inappropriately with several of the town's young women. Perhaps his conduct toward your mother was the impetus for my brother's reaction. I will never know the answer to this question in my lifetime. And please understand this: I am confident my brother did not know of Jacob's death. I came upon them when they were having words, arguing about something. I have no idea as to the nature of their disagreement. I left them to their contentious confrontation and went home. I found Jacob a couple of hours later. I am certain Daniel had no idea his blow had taken the man's miserable life. If my brother had been aware of the result of his anger, he would have stayed and paid for his crime. But I, in my desire to protect him and the girl he loved, took matters into my own young hands. I wanted Daniel and Beverly to get away from Harmony and have the life I knew could be theirs. So I took care of the problem and spent the rest of my days protecting our secret.

There are days when I regret my actions, even though

*I still love my brother. There are days when I hate him for
what his careless actions have cost me. But there are many
more days when I love him as much or more than I did when
we were children.*

With apprehension I turned the second page over and read
further.

*Now, dear niece, I am forced to turn my secret over to
you. You must decide what to do with it. Should you call
the police, my brother will probably be arrested for murder.
Should you keep this horrible secret, you may suffer the same
fate I have—life in Harmony, protecting the land that holds
the proof of my brother's dreadful deed.*

*Forgive me for passing this terrible legacy along to you.
I realize it is unfair, but I did not know what else to do.
I could not die with this unconfessed sin on my conscience.
Perhaps I forfeited my life on earth to protect my family,
but I am too weak to forfeit eternity.*

Please know that I have prayed earnestly for you.

Your loving uncle, Benjamin Temple

My fingers trembled so much as I attempted to refold the
horrible letter, I dropped it on the floor. All I could do was stare
at it. It couldn't be true. It had to be the rantings of a man sick not
only in his body but also in his soul.

I tried to figure out what to do next. Should I call my father
and read the letter to him? But what if Benjamin was telling the
truth? I knew my dad. If he thought he'd really caused the death
of another human being, he would contact the authorities. And
then what? Would he go to prison? And what about my mom?
The cancer that had tried to take her life was in remission. Would
the stress cause it to return? And what if I decided to keep this

secret to myself? Burn the letter and leave town without revealing Benjamin's secret? Someday, someone would probably find Jacob Glick's body. Would they tie it to us? Even though confusion jumbled my thoughts, I attempted to think the situation through. This property had been in my father's family for several generations. Glick's death would certainly be blamed on a Temple. Would it be Benjamin? For a moment, the idea of pointing the finger at him seemed to be a way out. But if the body was identified, my father would realize the truth and take responsibility for it. Of that I was certain.

My legs felt like lead. I couldn't move. Suddenly, an odd noise from outside caught my attention. What was it? Again, a scratching sound near the window drew my eyes there. I got up slowly, actually stepping on the letter, and crossed the room. I moved the curtain aside and looked out. I couldn't see anything, but another sound—a bumping noise—came from the other side of the house. I quickly realized how incredibly vulnerable I was.

I ran to my purse and pulled out my cell phone. Although it was almost out of power, there was still a little juice left in it. I quickly punched in 911, not knowing if emergency services even existed out here. All I got was a series of beeps telling me I didn't have enough power to make this call—or any call. I could run out to my car and drive to Sam's, but I had no intention of exposing myself to the darkness—and whatever waited outside.

It was entirely possible that the noises I heard belonged to an animal—but what kind of animal? I knew that in Kansas I wouldn't have to contend with a bear or a lion, but there were other things to consider. Like packs of wild dogs that banded together after their owners dumped them in the country. And rabid smaller animals that would attack humans if they felt threatened.

And of course, there was the possibility that whatever waited outside was altogether too human. Someone who knew there was a woman alone in this house without any way to get help.

Simple Secrets

I checked the front and back doors, making certain they were locked. Then I sat down on the couch and wrapped myself up in the quilt that lay over the back. Probably another one of Mama Essie's. "I need a hug, Mama," I whispered. As I sat there shaking, I put my trust in the only One who could really help me now. I repeated the comforting verses in Psalm 91 until the noises outside ceased, and I fell asleep.

Chapter Five

A loud knock on the door roused me. Was I late for work? Would Grant be mad? I opened my eyes and looked around. Where was I? This wasn't my apartment. I was in Harmony, and there was a body buried on my property.

The knock came again. I got up and shuffled to the front door. When my hand touched the knob, I remembered that someone or some*thing* had been outside last night. Daylight streamed in through the windows, so I felt safer, but still. . .I yearned for my door in Wichita. There was a peephole where I could see who stood outside, waiting to come in. I'd just stepped over to the front window, hoping I could get a look at my visitor, when a face popped up right in front of me. I shrieked involuntarily before I realized it was Sam, looking as surprised as I felt. Trying to pat my hair into place, I cracked open the door.

"Do you scream at everyone who stops by?" His eyes were still wide with alarm.

"No, just you." I swung the door open so he could come in.

"Is that what you're wearing to breakfast?" He stared at my rumpled clothes.

"Oh. Breakfast. I forgot." I pointed toward the living room.

"I'm sorry. Come in. It will only take me a few minutes to get ready."

Sam entered the living room and walked straight to Benjamin's letter, still lying on the floor. "Did you drop something?"

I reached over and grabbed it out of his hand before he had a chance to look at it. "Yes, sorry. Please have a seat. I don't have any coffee. I—I just. . ."

"Woke up?" He offered me an uneven smile. "I couldn't tell."

"Funny."

He glanced at the letter in my hand and then looked at me strangely. I'd planned to put it back inside the Bible, but that was out now. I'd have to take it upstairs with me.

"I had a rough night. Something outside. Guess I'm not used to living this way—so far from other people."

He chuckled and plopped down in the rocking chair. "I understand. It definitely takes some adjustment."

"Actually, it was rather frightening. And I had no way to contact anyone."

"I'm sorry," he said, the smile slipping from his face. "It's important to have a way to get help if you need it. We'll work out something." He pointed toward the roof. "Most of the time, squirrels only feed during the day, but Ben mentioned that he heard something at night sometimes. Could even be raccoons or possums. That's probably the noise that frightened you."

I frowned at him. Great. Nocturnal squirrels or something even bigger. His explanation might explain the scratching noises, but it certainly didn't cover the odd thumping. Unless these were the biggest critters in the world.

"Excuse me while I get ready."

"Sure. Is it okay if I wait inside? It's a little nippy out there this morning."

I nodded, clutched the letter to my chest, and hurried away, somewhat charmed by the idea that he'd actually asked if he could stay inside the house while I changed my clothes.

First I stopped by the bathroom to brush my hair and fix my makeup. Then I ran up the stairs to Mama and Papa's room where I'd stored my clothes. I changed out of my wrinkled jeans and T-shirt and pulled on a clean pair of jeans and a dark green sweater that complimented my coloring.

I stuck the letter from Benjamin in the top drawer of the dresser, underneath my socks. It would stay there until I could figure out a safer place for it. I had no idea what I was going to do with the information my uncle had passed on to me, but for now, I didn't want it falling into the wrong hands.

In the soft sunlight of a new day, the letter seemed like a bad dream. I wanted to read it again, just to make sure I'd understood it, but first I needed to seek God's council. Before I went downstairs, I prayed, "Father, I'm asking You to show me the way. Give me wisdom. I don't know what to do. Thank You for Your guidance."

Remembering Sam's comment about a chill in the air, I grabbed a light jacket from the closet and put it on. When I went downstairs, he was still sitting in Benjamin's rocking chair. He stood up as I entered the room.

"Wow, you really do clean up quick." An odd look flitted across his face. "Please don't take this wrong, but you sure look like. . ."

I sighed. "I know. My uncle Benjamin. I saw a picture of him last night."

"It's just the coloring. I don't want you to think you look like a middle-aged Mennonite man."

"Oh, thanks. Because that's certainly not the look I was going for."

He laughed and walked to the door, holding it open for me. "Then you've succeeded. Ready for breakfast?"

I searched for my purse and found it next to the couch. "I don't usually eat much in the morning. Sometimes I grab an energy bar on the way to the office or some coffee cake from Starbucks."

His expression registered confusion.

"Oh, Starbucks is..."

His hearty laugh stopped me in my tracks.

"Grace, I know what Starbucks is. I may have lived in Harmony most of my life, but I do get to the city quite a bit. Besides, we actually do have television out here." He shook his head. "You're still in America, you know. This isn't a foreign country. I was just wondering how anyone can get their day started without breakfast. It's the most important meal of the day."

Now it was my turn to laugh. "Yes, I know. My mother tells me that all the time. And sorry about the Starbucks comment. It's just so different here. Sometimes it feels like I'm living a long way from civilization."

He pointed toward the door, his gray eyes twinkling. "Just the reason I want to introduce you to Harmony. I think you'll be pleasantly surprised."

I stepped outside to a chilly morning. I tugged my Windbreaker closed and locked the door.

Sam trotted down the steps in front of me. "There is a lake behind us," he said. "On the other side of the tree line. You'll find that it's cooler living near the water. We'll warm up fine in a couple of hours." He pointed up the road toward his house. "My place is even closer to the shore. Believe it or not, it's a little colder in my backyard than it is in yours."

I pushed back a desire to ask him if I could see the inside of his fabulous house, but I was afraid he'd misunderstand my intentions. Besides, running into "Sweetie" wasn't something I looked forward to.

On the way to the restaurant, Sam told me some of the history of Harmony. Founded in the late 1800s by a group of German immigrants, it was once called Bethel. In the early 1900s it was changed to Harmony because of another Kansas town that adopted the original name.

"Although at one time, most of the residents lived under Old Order rules, now the population is largely Conservative. There are a few, like Ben, who still live under the old traditions, but along with the conservative Mennonites are those who are much more liberal."

"I noticed two churches here," I said. "We just passed Harmony Church, and on the other side of town is Bethel Mennonite Church."

Sam nodded. "Bethel serves the conservative Mennonites. Harmony members are either more liberal Mennonites—or not Mennonite at all. Harmony Church is nondenominational." He turned to smile at me. "That's where I attend. I'm not Mennonite and never have been. But the pastor there, Marcus Jensen, was raised Mennonite."

I stared out the window of Sam's truck. Main Street bustled with activity. The shops were open and people meandered down the sidewalks, stopping to visit before proceeding on to their destination. Most wore clothing I would associate with Mennonite culture, but quite a few were dressed just like Sam and me.

"How do the two churches get along?"

"Surprisingly well," he said. "For the most part, Harmony's name fits the town. Of course, that wasn't always the case. Although this was before my time, back when your family lived here, the church's bishop was a man named Amil Angstadt."

"My dad mentioned him. I guess he's the reason my parents left Harmony."

Sam nodded. "From what I've heard, he ran this town with an iron fist. He died about ten years after your father left. That was about a year after your grandparents moved away. Some people thought they'd come back, but they never did." He smiled at me again. "I understand they didn't want to leave behind a granddaughter they'd grown to love."

"They stayed away for me?"

He shrugged. "That's what Ben told me. I believe he exchanged a few letters with his parents."

"I—I didn't know that. He certainly never wrote to my father."

"Ben wouldn't talk about his brother much. That was a closed subject."

The mention of my uncle's name brought back the memory of that awful letter. "Sam, have you ever heard of a man named Jacob Glick?"

Sam frowned. "Jacob Glick? Sounds familiar. I think Sweetie mentioned him once. Some really unpleasant man who used to live here. If I remember right, he moved away a long time ago, but I'm not sure. I could ask my aunt if you'd like."

"No. That's okay. Just forget it." I didn't want Myrtle Goodrich involved any deeper in my life than she already was.

I turned away to look out the window again. I could feel Sam's eyes on me, probably wondering why I'd asked about Glick. I really didn't want to think about him now. I was in Harmony, and I wanted to experience it without the specter of Glick or my dead uncle hanging over me. I tried to concentrate on the shops and people we passed, putting the letter out of my mind. But its presence hung on me like a heavy coat—not so easily shed.

Sam pulled up in front of Mary's Kitchen. The old two-story redbrick building looked as if it had existed almost as long as the town. Wooden beams held up the sloping porch roof. The second story windows were thin and topped by stone carvings that resembled intricate valances. Four white rockers sat on the front porch, two each in front of the wide glass windows that framed a bright red wooden door. Signs in the windows read OPEN and No Shoes, No Shirt, No Service. A menu was posted in one window and flyers from both of Harmony's churches in the other.

"There aren't any wimpy city breakfasts here," Sam said with a chuckle. "I hope you're hungry."

Surprisingly, I was starving. There was something about the country air and the wonderful aromas drifting from the restaurant that stirred up memories of Mama Essie's big Saturday breakfasts. We'd drive to Mama and Papa's house every weekend and gorge on homemade pancakes with lots of butter and maple syrup. And spicy link sausages with crusty edges. Without warning, my mouth started to water. "I don't think you need to worry about me. This morning I feel like I could eat my breakfast *and* yours."

Sam laughed and jumped out of the truck. I started to put my hand on the door latch, but before I had a chance to flip the handle, my door swung open. He stood waiting for me to get out of the truck. Add being a gentleman to his other great qualities. I flashed back briefly to my last several dates in town. Not one of my escorts had opened the car door for me. In fact, now that I thought about it, none of them had opened any doors for me. After I exited the truck, he hurried up the steps to the diner and held that door open, too. I could certainly get used to this kind of treatment.

"Hey, Sam!" several patrons called out when we stepped inside. Burnished wood floors and wooden booths reminded me of an old diner in Fairbury that had never left behind its '70s motif. A few tables sat against the front window. Stainless-steel legs with yellow laminate tops and matching chairs held the obligatory salt, pepper, sugar, and orange plastic container with nonsugar sweeteners. Cerulean blue walls were covered with photographs. Many of them looked pretty old. Without closer inspection, I assumed they were pictures of the town down through the years and of the people who had called Harmony home. Some of the portraits looked to be from the 1800s or early 1900s. Scattered among lots of smiling faces, several dour looking families frowned upon the easygoing patrons enjoying their food.

Sam pointed to a table for two next to a wall near the window. "How's this?"

I nodded and sat down on one side of the table while he took the other chair.

"Mary! You got customers!" An older man in overalls who sat in a nearby booth hollered toward the back of the restaurant.

A long wooden counter that matched the booths held large glass containers filled with slices of pie and cake. An old cash register sat underneath one of the café's hanging lights, which consisted of large, white, round globes positioned around the interior of the room. Most of them were glowing even though the intense daylight that streamed through the front windows made their attempt to provide proper illumination completely futile. Steam rose from two coffeepots sitting on a warmer behind the counter, and overhead someone had mounted a couple of dead fish on the wall. Next to the stuffed fish, two large chalkboards contained the day's specials. A hallway next to the backward L-shaped counter led to restrooms and a door that had to be the entryway into the kitchen. An old metal step stool pushed against the door held it open. A couple of minutes later, a rather harried-looking young woman came out carrying plates of hot, steaming food.

"If you yell a little louder, Harold, they can hear you in Council Grove."

The chastised Harold greeted her good-natured ribbing with a raucous laugh.

"Just tryin' to keep you on your toes, Mary," he said with a grin. "Didn't want nobody starvin' to death due to your pokiness."

The woman plopped a large plate in front of him. "I don't think you have anything to worry about." She jabbed at the man's large belly. "You could live on what you've got stored up for quite some time."

The other two men sitting with Harold exploded with laughter. I noticed that one of the Mennonite families sitting nearby joined in the merriment. The overall feeling inside the restaurant was one of cozy familiarity.

After serving the rest of the plates in her hands, Mary headed our way. Her quick smile for Sam faded when she saw me. But she fixed it back into place so fast most people wouldn't have noticed.

"Howdy, Sam. Who's this pretty lady? You're not stepping out on me, are you?" She placed her hands on her hips and locked her gaze on me. She had long dark hair pulled back in a ponytail. Long lashes framed deep brown eyes set in a heart-shaped face.

Sam flushed a nice shade of pink. "Now Mary, you be nice." His smile seemed a little tight. "This is Ben Temple's niece, Grace. She's here to take care of his estate."

I saw a flicker of relief in her expression. "Nice to meet you, Grace," she said, extending her hand. "I'm Mary Whittenbauer. I own this joint." Her grip was stronger than I'd expected.

"Most people call me Gracie. Nice to meet you. I hear you fix a mean breakfast."

"Well, Hector Ramirez, my cook, is responsible for most of the meals here. I tell people I taught him everything he knows, but he says it's the other way around."

She looked at Sam. "You havin' the usual?"

He nodded.

Mary pointed to one of the chalkboards on the wall. "That's our menu. What sounds good to you, Gracie?"

I picked the regular breakfast with scrambled eggs, sausage, hash browns, and toast. I said yes to coffee and watched Mary saunter back to the kitchen.

"I take it you two date?"

Sam looked at the tabletop like he saw something interesting there. "We've dated some, yes. It—it's not that serious though."

"Sounds like Mary thinks it is."

His eyes bored into mine. "Let's talk about something else, okay? I'm not comfortable..."

"I'm sorry. It's not my business anyway." My eyes strayed to the photographs on the wall next to us. "Tell me about these pictures."

Sounding a little more relaxed, Sam launched into a few stories about the families that had settled in Harmony years ago. Many of the original settlers still had descendants who lived in the small town. He confirmed my suspicion that as a rule, Old Order Mennonites didn't go in for having their pictures taken. They believed capturing your likeness on film was akin to creating a "graven image" and that excessive attention to one's outside appearance could lead to vanity and self-worship. Their lives revolved around aspects they considered to be really important. Faith and family were at the top of the list. However, there were a few scattered pictures of people dressed in clothing that identified them as members of the Old Order community. Sam explained that down through the years, a few pictures had turned up here and there. Some families who really wanted keepsakes had pictures taken in secret, not letting the rest of the community know. I thought back to the photograph I'd found back at Benjamin's. It tickled me to think of Papa Joe as a rebel—even back then. I was certainly grateful he'd had at least one portrait taken. I wondered if there were more somewhere. Maybe a little digging would uncover others.

I was so engrossed in Sam's stories I didn't even notice that Mary had returned with coffee. I looked down to see a cup in front of me. I picked it up and took a sip. Its deep, rich flavor was exactly what I needed.

"You're probably used to that froufrou Starbucks coffee," Sam said. "The only flavors you can add here are cream and sugar."

I laughed. "Who told you I drink 'froufrou' coffee anyway? For your information, Starbucks has regular coffee, too."

He raised his cup. "Point taken. Sorry to make assumptions."

Before I had the chance to admit that I liked many of the flavored lattes and Frappuccinos that probably fit his "froufrou" description, the front door of the restaurant opened and a large man with a dark, bushy beard walked in. He wore the kind of straw hat I'd seen in Benjamin's closet and on some of the other men in Harmony. His black pants and blue shirt reminded me of Benjamin's clothes. However, he also wore a blue Windbreaker not much different than the one I had on.

"Abel!" Sam called to him.

The man raised one of his meaty hands and a wide smile spread across his broad face. "Hello there, Sam."

Sam waved him over, and the man approached our table. His size was intimidating, but he radiated affability.

"Grace Temple," Sam said, "I'd like to introduce you to Abel Mueller. He's the pastor of Bethel Church."

Pastor Mueller's huge fingers enveloped my hand. "Grace Temple? Is this Benjamin's niece?"

I nodded. "One and the same."

He kept my hand nestled in his and covered it with his other hand. "We're glad you're here, Grace. I'm so sorry your family wasn't notified when Benjamin became so ill. I tried and tried to convince him that you would want to know, but he forbade me from contacting anyone."

I had to admit that Pastor Mueller had taken me by surprise. In my mind, I'd lumped him into my preconceived idea of Mennonite leaders—grumpy, judgmental, and humorless. But this man was far from that. "It was Benjamin's choice, I guess. Not much you could do about it."

"Thank you. That makes me feel a little better." He finally let go of my hand.

"Emily and Hannah meeting you for breakfast?" Sam asked.

Pastor Mueller grinned. "Yes, as soon as they're through picking out fabric from Ruth's place. Spring is in the air, so new dresses are on the horizon."

"Why don't you have a cup of coffee with us until they get here?" Sam said.

58

The pastor looked at me. "If Grace doesn't mind."

"No. Please do."

He grabbed another chair from a nearby table and pulled it up to ours, easing his large frame onto the padded seat. His eyes scanned the room. Mary stood talking to a family seated near the kitchen. The pastor waited until she looked his way and then stuck one of his fingers in the air. The restaurant owner nodded. Seemed as if Mary knew what everyone wanted before they asked for it. In Wichita, I visited the same Starbucks almost every morning, and each time the workers behind the counter acted as if they'd never seen me before.

"So, how long will you be in Harmony, Grace?" Pastor Mueller asked.

"Two weeks. I have to get back to work. And please, call me Gracie." I took a sip from my coffee cup.

"Gracie, it is," he said with a smile. "And what kind of work do you do?"

"I'm a graphic designer. I work for an advertising agency."

The pastor's eyebrows shot up. "An artist, huh? I have a lot of respect for those to whom God has given artistic talent. I'm afraid that's something He neglected to bestow upon me."

"I've always loved to draw. I began when I was pretty young. My mother says I started drawing bugs when I was two years old."

He chuckled. "Bugs, huh? Glad you moved on to other things." He took a sip of coffee and then put his cup down. "What are your plans while you're in Harmony?"

"I need to find a way to let people know my uncle's house is for sale. How should I go about that?"

"Well, if you don't mind, I'd like to spread the word in town first before you put anything in a newspaper outside of Harmony. We have a few young couples that would love a chance at that property." He looked at Sam. "I'm thinking about Kenneth and Alene Ward. They've asked about Ben's place several times."

Sam nodded. "I think they'd buy it gladly."

"I'm not sure why," I said. "The house isn't bad, but there are much nicer places around here."

Pastor Mueller smiled. "Your uncle owns somewhere around thirty acres of the land surrounding that house. When your grandparents lived there, it was farmed for wheat and corn, but Benjamin let it all go after they left. An industrious young couple could bring the land back."

A chill ran through me. Farming meant digging and turning over the soil. A good chance my family's secret would be uncovered. The very thing my uncle had feared.

"You won't have any trouble selling Ben's property," Sam said. "I'll help you get the word out. Maybe we can make some flyers and post them around town."

I nodded dumbly, but my mind was still focused on the body hiding somewhere under a few feet of dirt. Then another thought struck me. "Pastor Mueller, how did my uncle survive? Financially, I mean. Without any crops. . ."

"First of all, please call me Abel," the gregarious man said. "Pastor Mueller is a little too formal for me."

"Thanks."

"Your uncle's income source is easy to spot as you walk up and down our streets," he continued. "He made all the wonderful rocking chairs scattered all over town. And the birdhouses and feeders. You'll see many of them in Ruth's store when you visit." He shook his head. "Benjamin never lacked for work. He was a skilled craftsman."

"I didn't see any kind of workshop on his property."

"Most of the time, he worked in the basement," Sam said. "Have you been down there?"

"No. I thought about it last night, but without electricity. . ."

"Too spooky?" Abel laughed. "I can understand that."

At that moment, Mary showed up at our table with plates for

Sam and me. She set his down carefully in front of him. A pile of pancakes topped with butter and a plate of sausage. She shoved my plate toward me without as much care. I looked up to see her giving me a rather frosty stare. Was she warning me? I had no idea why she saw me as a threat to her relationship with Sam. I wasn't going to be around long enough to cause her any problems. But maybe I was misinterpreting her actions.

She refilled our coffee cups. "Anything else here?"

"Thanks, Mary," Abel said heartily. "Emily and Hannah should be along soon. We'll need a round of your wonderful pancakes."

"You got it, Abel." She shot one more pointed look toward me and headed to another table. I glanced at Sam to see if he'd noticed, but he was busy pouring syrup on his plate.

"Abel, would you say grace?" he said after placing the syrup pitcher back on the table.

I bowed my head as the pastor thanked God for our food and the day He'd given us. I silently added a couple of requests of my own, said "Amen," and picked up my fork. The eggs were fluffy and delicious, and the sausage reminded me of Mama Essie's. The coffeemaker behind the counter chortled as it created another round of the fresh, robust brew. I usually try to keep myself down to one cup of coffee a day, but I decided to relax my rule this morning. Mary's breakfast was made to be eaten with the accompaniment of her great coffee.

"So what do you think of Harmony so far?" Abel asked, looking at me.

I quickly swallowed a mouthful of food. "I haven't seen much of it yet. Sam's going to show me around a little." I put my fork down and frowned at him. "This town hasn't had a good effect on my family, you know. I have to say that I came here expecting to find something much different than what I've seen so far."

Abel smiled. "You mean a place full of religious zealots and judgmental people?"

61

I nodded.

"Gracie," he said with sincerity in his voice, "if you could see Harmony as it was thirty years ago, that might be exactly what you'd have found. Except for a few people, like your father, who stood up against the tyranny in this town, everyone took their orders from a man who certainly didn't follow the real tenets of our faith. Amil Angstadt was a bully who thought his brand of religion was the only way to heaven. You see, Mennonites believe salvation comes through the grace and the sacrifice of Jesus Christ. But Angstadt taught that the price our Savior paid for us wasn't enough. That what you wore, what you did or didn't do, or even who you spoke to paved your way to heaven."

I shook my head at him. "But isn't that the same thing you do? I mean, making these women wear these long dresses and odd caps. Not using electricity. None of these things produce righteousness. That comes from the inside. Not the outside."

I saw Sam's eyebrows shoot up. Maybe I was being too direct, but after seeing the havoc this man's religion had played in my family, I didn't care.

To my surprise, he smiled widely. "First of all, we use electricity. I know your uncle didn't, but he held to some of the old ways that most of us don't. And as far as what produces righteousness, you're exactly right. I agree with you completely."

"I'm confused. Then why. . ."

"Gracie, we don't *make* anyone wear certain clothes or do anything else. You see, we live this way because we want to. There isn't a single person in my church who has ever been compelled to do anything except follow the teachings of Christ: to love Him with all their hearts—and to love their neighbors as themselves." His forehead wrinkled, and then he chuckled. "You know, I haven't had to explain our ways for a very long time. I guess we're rather isolated here." He took a sip of his coffee and then set the cup down in front of him. His eyes sought mine. I saw compassion and kindness in them. Even though I hadn't been prepared to like him, I did. Very much.

"Living a simple life isn't done so we can earn brownie points with God," he said in a soft voice. "It's a lifestyle we adopt because we truly believe it's helpful for us." He held out his open hands. "Take television. Don't even have one. When there's a storm, sometimes I'll come here and Mary will turn the set on so we can get updated weather forecasts. Or if something of national importance happens, I may go to a neighbor's house and watch a news channel for a bit so I can keep abreast of the situation. While waiting for whatever information I need, I've seen snatches of several of today's. . .what are they called. . .sitcoms?" He pulled on his beard. "I think our community is better off without them."

"But there are good things on TV, too," I said. "Shows that spread the gospel."

"I know that. I believe television can be a wonderful way to touch the world with the Good News. But the rest of it. . . Well, we would just rather live without its leaven. Please understand though—it's not a rule of the church or anything like that. It's a suggestion. Just as with many of our other choices. Like what we wear." He leaned back in his chair and folded his arms across his chest. "Let me ask you a question. Some of the schools in Wichita have adopted dress codes. Do you know why?"

I nodded. "Because it stops kids from wearing gang colors. Also, it helps to cut down on the attention to clothes and refocuses it back on schoolwork."

"That's exactly right. In wearing modest, simple clothing, we believe it helps us to focus our lives on God and His service and away from worldly concerns. It's as simple as that." He shrugged. "But please understand—we only ask that our members dress modestly. They choose their outfits. I don't visit everyone's house in the mornings and approve their choices." He chuckled. "Not even for my Emily. She says I have no taste."

I stabbed another sausage with my fork. "Okay, I understand the clothing thing. But why did my uncle turn his back on our family? Sam says you don't actually ban people."

"He's right. If we discovered a church member was involved in some kind of serious error, we would reach out in compassion to him, but we wouldn't turn him away unless there was no other choice. In my entire life I've never seen it happen. I'm not saying I haven't watched people leave the faith, but they always left on their own accord." He hesitated and gazed intently at the table-top for a moment. "I've heard that Amil Angstadt used what at one time was called The Ban, but trust me—when he died, the practice died with him. I visited your uncle many times, trying to convince him that he needed to reach out to his family. He refused to even discuss it with me. I have no idea why."

But I was pretty sure I did. "Abel, I appreciate everything you've said. I had some wrong ideas. I guess it isn't your religion that was the problem in my family. It seems that following the wrong leader caused most of the destruction."

He nodded. "I believe that to be the truth."

I finished the coffee in my cup and glanced toward the front counter. Mary leaned against the back wall and glared at me. I changed my mind about raising my cup to indicate I wanted more coffee. Fortunately for me, Sam noticed I was out and waved to her. She picked up a pot, carried it over, and silently filled everyone's cup. She left the table with a backward glance at me. Let's just say that the small town charm evident in the café didn't carry over to its owner.

"I—I do have another question," I said to Abel while I tried to ignore Mary's obvious distaste for me, "but I'm not sure you can help me. You weren't in Harmony when my parents lived here."

He shook his head. "No, I wasn't. But I have learned a lot about those days from some of the folks who lived through them. Ask away."

"Do you know anything about a man named Jacob Glick?"

A loud gasp from behind me revealed an older woman standing next to a girl who looked to be around fourteen or fifteen. They were dressed almost exactly the same, in long pastel dresses covered by a white pinafore. Both wore caps with ribbons that hung next to their faces.

Sam sat closest to the older woman whose face had gone horribly pale. He reached out and caught her as she staggered.

"Emily!" Abel cried out. "Are you all right?"

She nodded vigorously and pushed away from Sam, steadying herself. But the look of fear in her wide eyes told me a different story.

This woman was terrified of Jacob Glick.

Chapter Six

I hope Emily's feeling better." Sam glanced over to the table where the Muellers sat, waiting for their pancakes.

"Yeah, me, too."

Emily Mueller's hurried explanation of a sharp pain in her side left me with more questions than answers. I didn't want to think she'd lied to me, but her reaction seemed to be more a response to the name of Jacob Glick than to some kind of physical pain.

Eventually she regained her composure, even managing to paste a smile back on her face before Abel ushered his family to their own table. Sam and I accepted an invitation for Sunday dinner tomorrow after church. The request for our presence hadn't come from Emily. I had to wonder if she was as happy as her husband to welcome us to her home.

I watched the Muellers as I finished my breakfast. Although Emily wouldn't look my way, her daughter, Hannah, seemed fascinated by me. I wasn't quite sure why. There were other non-Mennonite people in Harmony. What was so special about me?

The girl's head covering and simple dress couldn't hide her natural beauty. Tendrils of golden blond hair trailed from beneath her cap, and her large sky blue eyes were framed by flawless skin.

A lack of makeup certainly didn't hurt her stunning looks. A teenage boy, eating breakfast with his family at a nearby table, kept sneaking glances at her. I didn't blame him a bit.

As if reading my mind, Sam said, "Hannah Mueller seems quite taken with you. Probably because Abel introduced you as an artist. You'll see some of Hannah's paintings at Ruth's. Harmony has a few artisans, including Joyce Bechtold. She painted your uncle's birdhouses." He lowered his voice. "Although she'd never admit it, I think Joyce hoped someday Ben would become more than just someone she worked with. In all those years, he never gave her any kind of encouragement." He grunted and looked past me, as if viewing something I couldn't see. "I saw him stare at her once when he didn't know I was watching him. I could have sworn I saw something in his face. . .a tenderness." He shook his head and refocused his attention on me. "Must have been my imagination. If he was interested in her, why wouldn't he have said something? Except for loving God, finding the right person to share your life with is the most important thing in the world."

Was that how he felt about Mary? She kept looking our way, as if checking up on us. Obviously, her relationship with Sam wasn't that secure—in her mind anyway.

I waited while Sam went up to the register to pay our bill. Mary said something to him that seemed to upset him. She tried to grab his arm, but he gently wrestled it away from her. As he turned to walk back to where I sat, the look Mary shot me was one of pure anger. Her expression shook me. I certainly wasn't after her boyfriend. In fact, I had no intention of starting a relationship with anyone in Harmony. Not even a man as nice as Sam Goodrich.

"Let's take that tour," he said when he reached the table. I stood up and was headed for the front door when he put his hand on my shoulder. "Wait a minute," he said. "I just thought of something." He pointed at some pictures against the far wall of the restaurant. "There are some old pictures of Harmony here. I think your Jacob Glick might be in one of them."

I followed him to a grouping of black-and-white photos. Sure enough, they appeared to be photographs of the town down through the years. I began to scan them. Sam pointed to a shot taken of a dry goods store on what must have been opening day. The proprietors stood proudly in front of their business. Off to the side stood a bearded man in dark clothing. He stared straight at the camera. His fierce expression chilled me, and I shivered involuntarily.

"Amil Angstadt," Sam said. "I'm sure he had no idea he would show up in the picture, but there he is. Sweetie showed me this photo years ago, but she won't talk much about him. Pretty scary, huh?"

I nodded my agreement. So this was the man who had caused so much pain in my family.

"Here," Sam said triumphantly, pointing to a picture a few spots away. "Ever since you mentioned this Glick person, I kept thinking I'd seen the name somewhere. This is a picture of the church building in 1980. That's Glick standing in front."

I looked closely. Sure enough, someone had written "Jacob Glick" in the margin of the photograph.

"Glick wasn't actually a part of the church." I jumped at Abel Mueller's voice coming from behind me.

"Then why is he shown in front of the building?"

"He worked around the church," Abel said. "I have some old memoirs written by people who attended Bethel down through the years. They refer to him as a church custodian. Appeared to be a rather solitary fellow. No family. Not well liked. He was asked to leave town—more than once."

"And why is that?"

Abel shrugged. "According to what I've managed to glean though some old letters and diaries, Glick was very interested in finding a wife. Mennonite women are encouraged to marry within the faith. Since he refused to join the church, church leaders rebuffed his efforts. He finally gave up and left town. And that was the end of Jacob Glick."

I wished with all my heart that a bus out of town *had* signaled the end of Glick, but unfortunately, unless my uncle had taken leave of his senses, a rock in the side of the head had been his actual means of departure.

Glick was an unusually unattractive man. I assumed his looks hadn't helped him in his quest for companionship. Dark hair, bushy eyebrows that had grown together, and an unusually long nose worked together to produce a rather frightening visage. His beady, black eyes held an odd hint of wildness to them. This was a man most women would run *from* instead of toward.

"Not what you'd call a good-looking guy is he?" Abel asked.

I shook my head while Sam snorted his agreement.

Abel cleared his throat. "I don't mean to pry, but is there some reason you're interested in Mr. Glick? I mean, he's not part of your family. He wasn't even part of the church."

Wishing I'd come up with a reason for asking about Glick sooner, I blurted out the only thing that came to my mind. "I found his name on something at my uncle's. I was just curious. It's no big deal." Well, at least I hadn't out-and-out lied. I wasn't sure about the "big deal" part, but maybe that would prove true, as well. I decided to change the subject before I was asked more uncomfortable questions. "Sam said Old Order Mennonites didn't believe in having their pictures taken. Is that why there are no pictures of the church members or the families here?"

Abel nodded. "Yes, but there are a few. Ida Turnbauer told me that the cousin of one of the church members was a photographer. It seems a few folks contacted the man privately and had family pictures taken. They weren't normally shown to anyone outside of the family, but I know they were treasured mementos." He pointed to a grouping of family photos showing people dressed in the same kind of clothing depicted in the picture at Benjamin's.

"Why are these here? I would think the families would have kept them."

"Most of them did. These were either left behind when the families moved away or donated by relatives who still live in Harmony." He directed our attention to one of the photographs. A very handsome young man stood next to an older man and woman. "That's Levi Hoffman. He owns our candle shop. Lived here all his life." He motioned toward the other photos. "The rest of these folks moved away. Levi's the only one who still lives in Harmony."

I glanced around at some of the other pictures on the wall. "Kind of sad that there aren't more images of the early Mennonite settlers. Wouldn't they help to keep their memories alive? Help people remember what they accomplished?"

Abel chuckled. "I understand your point, Gracie. But we have no photographs of Christ, and He changed the world. I'm not sure how important pictures really are."

I wanted to tell him how special the portrait of my family hanging in Mama and Papa's room was to me, but I kept my mouth shut.

I looked closer at the face of Amil Angstadt. There was something burning in those eyes—and it didn't reflect the heart of the loving God I'd come to know. A rush of emotions churned inside me. The depth of my feelings surprised me. Being in Harmony, the place where my parents had grown up and fallen in love, was affecting me in ways I hadn't anticipated. It made their experiences so real. I could almost sense their fear and heartache.

While I fought to bring my feelings under control, I studied Jacob Glick again—the man who was buried somewhere on property that now belonged to me. I had a strange urge to blurt out the truth to Abel. I felt strongly that he had the heart of a pastor and would want to help me. But I had to remind myself that I really didn't know him—or anyone in this town. Besides, until I'd prayed more about it, I couldn't risk sharing anything with anyone. I turned around and ran right into Sam. I put my hands on his chest to balance myself.

"Oh, s–sorry," I stammered. Still touching him, I looked up into his eyes. What I saw there made my toes tingle.

"Th–that's okay," he said in a husky voice.

I forced myself to step away from him. Without planning it, my gaze swung toward the back of the restaurant where I'd last seen Mary. She was still there—staring at me. But I saw more than just jealousy in her face. There was hurt.

"We'd better get going," I said more forcefully than I meant to. I was almost to the door when I remembered Abel. I looked back to find him watching me. "It was nice to meet you. I guess we'll see you tomorrow. . .about one?"

He nodded. "See you then, Gracie."

Mary watched as Sam and I walked toward the front door. I thought he'd at least say good-bye, but he seemed to have completely forgotten about her. Although I'd never been in love, I knew the signs. This woman was head over heels for Sam Goodrich, but he didn't reciprocate her feelings. I felt sorry for Mary. I hadn't come to Harmony to cause anyone pain. Maybe two weeks was too long to stay—and then I remembered Uncle Benjamin's secret. I was trapped here until I could find a way to resolve my family mess.

Sam and I stepped out into a bright spring day. "Let's start on this side of the street. Then if there's time, we'll hit the other side." He shrugged. "If not, we'll come back next week. There's no rush."

I nodded and followed him to Ruth's Crafts and Creations. The little store was housed between the restaurant and Menlo's Bakery. At Sam's recommendation, we decided to save the bakery for last. Good idea since I was so stuffed I couldn't even think about food.

A bell tinkled above the door when we walked into the sunny yellow building with cream-colored trim. A gray-haired woman with a wide red face looked up from something she was working on behind her counter.

"Why, Sam Goodrich. It's been a month of Sundays since you've come to see me. What's going on?" She fastened her inquisitive expression on me. "Well, goodness gracious. Who is this?"

Sam put his hand on my elbow and gently guided me toward the counter. "Ruth Wickham, meet Grace Temple, Ben's niece."

The woman's hands flew to her ample chest. "Oh my. Grace, I'm so happy to finally meet you. I'd heard you were coming. I wish Benjamin had let someone contact your family so you could attend his service."

A thought struck me. "Is—is my uncle buried near here?"

Ruth's round face softened into a smile. "Yes dear. In the cemetery outside town." She pointed her chubby finger at Sam. "Sam can show you where it is." She wiped her hands on the calico apron she wore over jeans and a bright red sweatshirt. "I've got some lovely flowers in the garden out back. You come by here whenever you want, and I'll give you a nice bouquet to put on his grave."

"Thank you."

She waved her hand at me. "It's nothing. As persnickety as Benjamin was, we thought a lot of him. Such an honest and ethical man. You should be proud of him, Grace."

"Please call me Gracie," I said. I realized as I said it that Sam kept introducing me as Grace. In fact, I couldn't remember him calling me Gracie once.

"Gracie it is," Ruth said. "Now let me show you around some." She came around the corner and took my arm. "I've got several of your uncle's birdhouses and feeders over here." She sighed heavily. "I can hardly believe there won't be any more."

"Joyce can still paint birdhouses for you, Ruth," Sam said. He reached up and ran his fingers along the smooth side of a beautifully carved house. "I guess no one makes a house quite like Ben, though."

"No. No they don't." Ruth put her hands on her hips and stared at the birdhouses displayed on her shelves. "Benjamin took pride in everything he did. Never rushed the job. Never sacrificed quality for speed, yet he met every order on time." She brushed at her eyes with her hand. "Aren't many men like Benjamin Temple anymore." A quick smile chased the sadness from her face. "Except you, Sam. I swear, if I didn't know better, I'd believe you two were related."

Sam's easygoing expression faltered for a moment, and something dark crossed his features. I wondered what was behind it. Why did he live with his aunt? Where were his parents? He'd mentioned living in Harmony for most of his life. My curiosity was aroused. Sam Goodrich was an interesting man. I found myself wanting to understand him.

Besides my uncle's creations, Ruth's shop was filled to the brink with handmade items: beautiful quilts, dried flower arrangements, pottery, and bolts of cloth. On one wall, I discovered several framed paintings. Most were landscapes; several were of horses. Each one was striking, painted by someone with remarkable natural talent. And every single painting was set into a carved frame that highlighted the scene perfectly. One particular picture really caught my eye. It depicted a man plowing a field, with a storm brewing in the sky behind him. Dark clouds boiled with moisture. The farmer's urgency to beat the impending rain showed in his taut muscles and stalwart expression. I realized the style was familiar.

"These are outstanding," I said. "I believe my uncle has two paintings by this artist hanging in his house. Who. . ." I leaned in and saw the signature. *H. Mueller.* I couldn't hold back a gasp.

"Hannah Mueller painted these?"

"Hannah painted all of them," Ruth said, bustling up next to me, "and the pictures in your house. She's a very talented young lady. Hard to believe she's only fourteen. You know, painting used to be frowned upon by many in the Mennonite community. This kind of art was considered useless."

I shook my head. "That's a shame. I'm glad Hannah's family doesn't believe that."

Ruth smiled. "Well, you can still see influences from those beliefs in Hannah's work. You'll notice that most people are either seen from a distance or their faces are turned away. Landscapes are the prevalent theme, and almost every picture is of local life and community."

"I don't understand."

Ruth shrugged. "I've seen some paintings I wouldn't allow into my house, haven't you? I guess it's just an attempt to keep the subject wholesome and free of vanity. Like it says in Philippians: 'Finally, brothers, whatever is true, whatever is noble, whatever is right, whatever is pure, whatever is lovely, whatever is admirable—if anything is excellent or praiseworthy—think about such things.'"

An image from a lurid art show I'd accidentally stumbled upon during a downtown art crawl in Wichita flashed through my mind. It had left me feeling disgusted. "I—I see what you mean, Ruth. Painting the kinds of things that honor that verse makes sense."

She nodded. "Abel and Emily see Hannah's painting as a gift. They encourage her, but they also make certain she uses it in a way they believe will please God. I think she does that admirably. She's never had any formal training, you know. Unfortunately, the school she attends has no art teacher."

"Her technique is very advanced. I'm surprised." I leaned in closer and inspected the painting a little closer. "Are these for sale? How much for this one?"

"The watercolors are twenty dollars, and the oil paintings are thirty."

"That's not enough. These are worth much more. Goodness, the frames alone. . ."

"These frames don't set Hannah back a penny," Ruth said, chuckling. "They're donated by a very talented man who loves to help other people." She smiled at Sam.

"You?" I said to him. "You carved these frames?"

He shrugged. "No big deal. Something I do while I watch TV."

"Well, it *is* a big deal. They're beautiful. You could sell them." I fumbled in my purse and pulled out my pocketbook. "Here," I said to Ruth. "I won't give Hannah less than fifty dollars for this painting. And it's worth much more."

Ruth put her hand up to her mouth. "Oh, she will be so thrilled. We haven't sold many." She noticed the surprised look on my face. "Not because people don't love them," she said. "It's because Hannah gives them away to everyone. The only people who pay for them are out-of-towners, and we don't get that many. Of course, there is one person in town who's bought quite a few." She crooked her thumb at Sam.

I grinned at him. "So let me get this straight. You give her frames—and you buy the paintings and the frames back?"

He flushed just as he had at the restaurant. "I never had brothers or sisters. Helping Hannah kind of fills the void, I guess."

Ruth chuckled and looked at him fondly. "You're a good man, Sam Goodrich. You know that? I'm proud to know you. I really am."

Sam turned an even deeper red, causing Ruth and me to laugh. He shook his head and walked over to a display of colorful plates, feigning disinterest in our attention.

Still giggling, Ruth grabbed a bag and some newspaper from under her counter. While she wrapped up the painting for me,

I poked around the shop a little more. I found lots of wood carvings and a table full of embroidered towels and pillowcases. I grabbed four of the pillowcases—two for me and two for my mother. A nicely decorated box of homemade fudge called my name, and I added it to my selections.

On the other side of the room sat a table with the most artistically designed stationery, cards, and envelopes I'd ever seen. "These are lovely," I said to Ruth. "Where did you get them?"

She toddled over to see what I meant. "Oh, you mean Sarah's paper." She picked up a sheet of stationery with green and yellow leaves that wrapped around the top and one side. Each leaf was intricately designed. "Sarah Ketterling is one of our few Old Order residents. She and her father live on a farm outside town." She fingered the eye-catching design. "This is called wood-block printing. Do you know anything about it?"

A faint memory from one of my college classes flashed through my mind. "I've heard of it, but this is the first example I've seen. She carves the design into wood, right? And then rolls paint across it. Then the paper is put on top and the design is transferred."

Ruth smiled. "That's the basic idea, but it's a little more complicated than that. I have these patterns in right now, but I sell out pretty quick. People love this stationery. I also have several customers from outside Harmony who order it regularly." She ran her hand over the paper again. "Sarah's about your age. A lovely young woman." She sighed. "But her father keeps her on a pretty tight rein, so I don't get to speak to her often. Her father, Gabriel, was very close to Bishop Angstadt when he ran the church here. He's never cottoned to Abel Mueller—thinks he's too liberal." She touched my arm. "Even though Benjamin was part of that Old Order group, he wasn't too thrilled with Gabriel's brand of parenting. He and Ida Turnbauer tried talking to him more than once. Never did any good. Just made him mad."

"Well, Sarah is very talented. A real artist." I picked up a package of the green leaf stationery, along with some matching envelopes. "I'd love to learn more about this process."

"Gabriel won't let you anywhere near his daughter," Sam said. "In fact, when Ruth sells her work, she has to give the money to him. He won't allow the proceeds to go directly to Sarah."

"He sounds like an awful person. Why doesn't Sarah just leave?"

Sam shook his head. "She's afraid of him, Grace."

"I'm not so sure she isn't more afraid *for* him," Ruth said frowning. "Gabriel used to be a different person before his wife ran off with another man. He always had a good word for everyone. I liked him. But after his wife left, he completely changed. I think Sarah feels responsible for him—as if it's her job to look after him."

Anger churned inside me. "I'm sorry for him, but what about *her* life? She must be extremely unhappy."

"I don't believe he realizes what he's doing to her," Sam said. "He thinks he's protecting her against the world. The same outside world that stole his wife. Of course, Angstadt's early influence in his life has only reinforced his suspicion and fear. One of the bishop's main teachings was that worldly influences cause nothing but spiritual pollution. I guess in his mind, that justifies his treatment of Sarah."

"That preacher left a trail of confusion behind him, that's for sure," Ruth said, shaking her head. "Thank God Abel Mueller came to this town. The difference is night and day."

"If you've spent enough money, we should get going," Sam said. "I didn't think we'd be spending our whole day here."

"Now you let Gracie alone, Sam Goodrich," Ruth said good-naturedly. "She can buy anything she wants."

I took the stationery up to the counter and put it with the painting, the pillowcases, and the fudge. "I'd really better get out of here. I won't have any money left."

"Well, before you leave, I have to show you my pride and joy." Ruth's eyes sparkled as she directed my attention to something silver inside the glass case under the counter.

Sam grinned. "She shows off her pride and joy to everyone who steps foot in this place."

"Now, Sam Goodrich," Ruth shot back, "you just hush."

"Oh my goodness. What is it?"

Ruth smiled. "This is the one thing I won't sell. I let it stay in the store so folks can enjoy it. You see, I live alone. Keeping it in my house just for my tired old eyes doesn't make much sense."

She slid the door behind the case open and lifted out a silver piece that looked like a vase with handles and a top. Under the silver cover decorated with floral finials sat a glass container. The silver itself had been beautifully decorated with rosettes and laurel leaves. Leaves ringed a square-shaped stand, and on the front, a silver flower encircled a crest.

"I've never seen anything like it," I said. "It's beautiful."

"Believe it or not, it's a chestnut vase." Seeing the surprise on my face, she beamed. "That's what it was designed for, but near as I can tell, my ancestors actually kept sugar in it." She touched it lovingly. "It was handcrafted in the 1700s by a rather well-known designer and given to one of my relatives as a gift. It's been handed down for generations. When I'm gone, it will go to my daughter. It's very valuable."

"Does your daughter live here?"

"No, she lives in Kansas City with her husband. But she visits when she can. Next time she comes, I'll introduce you."

"I would like that, but I'm only going to be here a couple of weeks."

Ruth's forehead wrinkled. "That's right. I forgot. For some reason it seems as if you're already a part of us." She carefully put the vase back behind the counter. "Well, it's too bad. Carolyn would have loved you."

She rang up my purchases on a cash register that looked about twenty years old. My total was a lot smaller than it would have been for the same items in Wichita.

"Why don't you leave this stuff here and come back for it later, when you're finished looking around town?" Ruth said. "That way you won't have to lug it around or let your fudge melt inside Sam's truck. It doesn't seem hot outside, but you know how steamy the inside of a vehicle can get when the sun beats down on it."

"Thanks. I will."

Sam stood at the front door, holding it open. "Come on, woman," he said with a grin. "We've only made a little dent in our tour."

"He's getting a little pushy, don't you think?" I said to Ruth, who laughed and waved good-bye.

Back out on the sidewalk, Sam guided me to the next store. Harmony Hardware was exactly what the sign declared. A small hardware store with items you would find in most other shops just like it. However, among the hammers, nails, and other tools, there were handmade wooden spoons and oil lamps. Obviously it was geared to accommodate all of Harmony's citizens. I recognized the outside of the building as the place where Amil Angstadt's had had his picture snapped unawares so many years ago.

Sam introduced me to Joe Loudermilk, a small man with a ready smile and an offer of hot coffee.

"Joe's got the pot going all day," Sam said. "Don't you, Joe?"

"You bet." He lowered his voice and gave me a secretive smile. "Get 'em in for coffee, and they're buyin' stuff they forgot they needed. Works every time."

"Well, I don't want coffee, but I need some things to help Grace live a little better out there at Ben's house." Sam said. "Why don't you give me a good flashlight—and a couple of those battery-powered lamps?" He turned to me. "These will give you a lot more light than those old oil lamps."

"Great idea, but what if I hear another monster clumping around outside?"

"I have a plan that should keep you safe from monsters. We'll have to stop by my place on the way home, though."

I was thrilled to know I was going to get to see the inside of his house, yet disturbed that he called my uncle's house *home*. It certainly wasn't *my* home.

Sam paid for the lamps and flashlight even though I offered. His argument that he could use them after I left took the wind out of my protests, and I finally agreed.

We visited two more stores on that side of the street: a secondhand store that had lots of great items, and a clothing store that carried some of the traditional garb worn by many of Harmony's populace. The proprietors at Cora's Simple Clothing Shoppe were friendly and welcoming, even though my basic questions and ignorance about their practices made it obvious I wasn't Mennonite. They showed me different garments and explained that originally, wearing certain kinds and colors of clothing was an attempt by the Mennonites to show their separation from the rest of the world. But eventually it was determined that although keeping oneself removed from carnality was a positive thing, removing themselves too far from the people Christ called them to love wasn't productive. They showed me dresses in lovely fabrics and styles, along with many skirts and blouses that, although plain, were no different than clothing being sold in regular stores across the country.

"Dressing modestly is our aim," Cora Crandall, the store owner, said. "Quite a few of the women love the traditional prayer coverings while some wear nothing on their heads at all—except in church." Her white cap and peach-colored dress accented her dark skin and large brown eyes. Her husband, Amos Crandall, towered over her and exuded friendliness. I immediately liked this couple.

"Many people believe that the scriptural admonition of a head covering in church isn't relevant for today," Amos said. "Others feel it is. So each person wears what they feel comfortable with. There are no rules set in stone."

I thanked them for their insight. I came incredibly close to buying a lovely apple green dress with small flowers, three-quarter-length sleeves, and a gathered waist. The lace around the collar was light and delicate. Unfortunately, I couldn't think of a single place to wear it. I held it for several minutes before reluctantly putting it back on the rack.

Sam and I spent the rest of the morning visiting the other side of Main Street. I met the owners of the leather and feed store. Paul and Carol Bruner carried everything needed for horses and cattle. Dale Scheidler ran the farm implements store with his brother Dan.

Then we got to Nature's Bounty, a small shop that sold dairy products, fruits, and vegetables.

"I sell a lot of my fruit here," Sam said. "Although most of it is marketed in Council Grove and Topeka."

The store was rather crowded with people buying milk, cheese, and fruit. Sam pulled me aside. "That's Joyce Bechtold," he whispered. "She's the woman who painted the birds on Ben's houses and feeders. We should come back when she's not so busy. I know she wants to meet you."

Joyce was a lovely woman with curly hair the color of molasses, cut to just above her shoulders. She had soft brown eyes and laugh wrinkles. I whispered to Sam, "Is she Mennonite?"

"No, as a matter of fact, she's not. She attends my church."

I wondered if that had anything to do with my uncle's lack of interest in her. Too bad. Even from across the room, her graciousness and kind attitude toward others was obvious. As she finished helping a customer, her eyes swung over to where Sam and I stood. When she saw me, her eyes widened and her complexion grew pale. I saw Sam nod slightly to her.

"Let's get going," he said gently.

When we were outside, I grabbed his arm. "Joyce seemed shocked when she saw me. Why?"

Sam sighed. "She knew you were coming, but none of us knew how much you looked like Ben. It's rather startling."

"You didn't seem surprised when you first met me."

He blushed. "Guess I was just thinking about how pretty you are."

I stared at him, but I couldn't come up with a snappy comeback. All I could think about was that he'd said I was pretty. I tried to change the subject quickly. "I—I get the feeling Joyce really cared for my uncle."

"Yes," he said quietly. "She really did."

Next to Nature's Bounty was Keystone Meats. I started to open the door when Sam caught me by the arm.

"We don't really need to go inside. John Keystone. . ."

"Don't be silly," I said lightheartedly. "We've made the rounds of all the other stores. I want to check out this one, too."

I swung open the old screen door on the whitewashed building with the bright red–painted letters and stepped inside. Unlike Joyce's store, there weren't any customers standing around. In fact, Sam and I were the only ones. My first impression was that there wasn't anyone at all in the store. Then a man came from behind the meat counter. He was tall and slender, probably in his early thirties. His long, aquiline nose and dark eyes enhanced his well-sculpted good looks and tanned skin. Longish black hair only added to his overall attractiveness. I felt my mouth go a little dry.

"Hello, Sam," he said in rich, deep tones. "What do you want here?"

"John," Sam said, acknowledging the man with a nod. "This is Grace Temple, Benjamin Temple's niece."

"Hello," I said slowly. The tension between the two men was palpable. What was this about?

John wiped his hands on the white apron he wore over jeans and a dark blue shirt. He stuck out his right hand, and I took it. He held it a little longer than was necessary, but I didn't pull it away. His eyes locked on mine and for a moment I felt transfixed. A door slammed behind us, breaking the moment.

"Well, here you two are. I was beginning to wonder if you'd left town." Mary sashayed up next to us, a fake smile plastered on her pretty face. Before Sam or I had a chance to respond, she turned her full attention to John.

"I need some ground chuck and twelve rib eyes for tonight, good lookin.' Is that possible?"

He spread his arms apart. "Anything for you, gorgeous." He whirled around and disappeared through a door behind his counters.

"So, Gracie. Have you met everyone in town yet?"

"Of course she hasn't, Mary," Sam said in measured tones. "There are almost five hundred people living in Harmony. We couldn't possibly meet all of them in a couple of hours."

Mary's right eyebrow shot up. "Oh, has it only been two hours? Seems like much longer."

Frankly, I was getting tired of Mary's jealous digs. "Maybe we should go, Sam. I'd like to take a nap sometime today. I didn't sleep well last night."

"Sure. No problem." He walked to the door and pushed it open, waiting for me to exit first. The door slammed loudly behind us.

"Look, Sam," I said when we were a few feet away. "I don't want to be a source of contention between you and Mary. Maybe it would be better if we. . .well, if you and I didn't see each other again."

"No!" His explosive response startled me. He blew a deep breath out between clenched teeth. "I. . .I should explain, I guess." He pointed toward a bench in front of the meat market. "Let's sit down a minute."

I lowered myself down on the bench and waited. After a little pacing, he finally sat down next to me.

"Mary and I... I mean... We're kind of engaged."

My mouth dropped open in surprise. "Kind of engaged? How can anyone be *kind of* engaged? Either you're engaged or you're not."

He hung his head and stared at the ground. "I don't know how it happened. To this day, I swear I don't remember asking her to marry me. But somehow she got the idea that I did. Now I don't know how to get out of it. I—I don't want to hurt her."

I let out an exasperated sigh. "You can't marry someone because you don't want to hurt her feelings. That's ridiculous."

"I know, I know. I've been trying to fix this thing for months. But every time I even begin to bring up the subject, she starts crying and I back off."

I put my hand on his arm. "The longer you string her along, the worse it will be. You've got to tell her. Let her get on with her life."

"I know. I know you're right." He put his hand over mine and looked into my eyes. "Thanks."

"You're welcome." I pulled my hand away, my own words ringing in my ears. In two weeks I would be gone. It wasn't fair to either one of us for me to allow feelings to build up between us. Of course, maybe Sam wasn't interested in me at all, but when I looked in his eyes, I could almost swear I saw something stirring there.

I decided to change the subject. "You and John Keystone don't get along very well. Is there a problem?"

He shrugged. "Keystone's only been in Harmony a little over a year. He came here with an attitude. I'm not the only one he doesn't like. No one's been able to forge a friendship with the guy—except Mary."

It seemed odd that someone with no roots in Harmony would move here and start a business, but John Keystone wasn't my problem. I had other fish to fry. I pointed to the last shop on the street. Hoffman Candles. Now there was something I could get into. "I love candles. Let's finish our tour—and then to the bakery."

Sam nodded and stood up. He swept one hand toward the candle shop and bowed slightly. Then he followed me to the white clapboard building with large windows and dark blue shutters. He ushered me into a room that contained a hodgepodge of aromas. Shelves with different kinds and sizes of candles shared space with interesting holders made of wood and metal. Some were freestanding while others were made to mount on the wall. I'd never seen so many different types of candleholders before and mentioned it to Sam.

"Levi Hoffman makes the candles, but the holders are created by Harmony residents," he said. He pointed to a set of burnished metal holders. "These were built by Cora and Amos's son, Drew."

"Wow. They're very good. He's very skilled."

"Yes, he is."

I heard something in his voice that made me look up at him. Sam smiled. "Drew has Down syndrome. Cora and Amos have done an outstanding job with him. They don't treat him as if he has a disability. He's a great kid, and he's achieved so much more than most people expected."

I nodded but didn't say anything. Grant, my boss, had a son with Down syndrome. I'd watched his struggles with Jared and felt great compassion for the Crandalls.

"Who's that out there?" A voice rang out, breaking the silence.

"Levi, it's Sam. I've brought Ben's niece to meet you."

A curtain hanging in the back of the store parted, and a man stepped out. He couldn't have been much older than my father, but his hair was almost completely white. With his bushy beard and chubby body, he looked like a real-life Santa Claus. His eyes twinkled, and he broke out into a big smile when he saw us. Although he had certainly changed since the picture in the café, I could still see traces of the handsome young boy in his face.

"So this is Gracie?" he said in a deep voice. "I've been waiting for her. Abel stopped by a little while ago and told me you were making the rounds." I held out my hand, but instead of taking it, he wrapped me in a robust hug.

"Nice to meet you," I said, my words muffled by his shoulder.

He let me go and then stared at me with interest. "My goodness. She's the spitting image of Ben. I can hardly believe it."

"I know," Sam said. "It's a little disconcerting."

"Well, I think it's wonderful."

I was getting a little tired of being talked about and not addressed directly. "Were you and my uncle close?"

Levi stepped back a few paces. "No one was really close to Ben," he said, a note of sadness in his voice. "But I cared for him." He walked over to a nearby shelf and picked up two tall wooden candleholders. "He made these."

He held them out, and I took them from his hands. They were oak, stained dark. Each one had carved round balls at the top where the candle was supposed to sit. Then they straightened out for about six inches before the bottom spread out into a carved base. I looked closely. The carvings were of birds and flowers.

"They're beautiful, Levi."

"Please, I want you to have them. Let's find some candles to go in them. What would you like? Sandalwood, vanilla, rose, lilac. . ."

"I'd love lilac," I said, "but let me pay for them."

"Pshaw. This is a gift. For the niece of my friend." The candlemaker's eyes flushed with tears. "I'll put them in a bag for you."

"Thank you very much. I'll treasure them."

Levi had just pulled some paper from a stack on a table and was wrapping the candles and the holder when the door swung open behind us. A tall, grim-faced man dressed in dark clothes, a white shirt, and a large black hat stepped inside the store. Behind him trailed a young woman also dressed in black. Her long dress dusted the floor, and even though it was spring she wore full sleeves. Her head was covered with a stiff bonnet, not the light prayer covering I'd seen on other women in town. She kept her eyes downcast as if she were carefully watching her black laced-up shoes. Her attire was almost too morose for a funeral, yet the overall spirit emanating from the pair made that destination a definite possibility.

"Hello, Gabriel," Levi said. "Have you brought me some new candleholders?"

The man stepped in front of Sam and me as if we weren't even in the room. He put a large box on the counter in front of the store owner. "No other reason I'd be here, Levi." His voice was sharp and raspy.

The store owner looked down into the box and carefully lifted out several metal holders. They were actually quite stunning. Intricately formed and freestanding, curved pieces of wrought iron formed the legs that held them up. Other pieces of metal had been twisted into designs that ended up creating a place to hold a candle.

"Why, they're beautiful," I said. "You made these?"

The man swung his gaze around and fastened his angry eyes on me. Even through his black beard I could see his lips locked in a sneer. "I'm sorry. I don't remember addressing you," he spat out.

"Now Gabriel, you mind your manners," Levi said evenly. "This is Gracie Temple. Benjamin's niece."

The man's eyes traveled up and down my body. "Doesn't look like anyone Benjamin Temple would cotton to. He wouldn't have approved of anyone this worldly." His eyes flashed with anger. "Would have been mighty ashamed to call something like this family."

I could feel my blood start to boil. "Now you look here. . ." Sam put his hand on my shoulder, and I caught myself before I said something I would probably regret. I stood there stoically, determined not to start an argument with this man. It was obvious it wouldn't do any good.

Assuming I wasn't going to rise to his bait, Gabriel turned back to Levi and resumed his transaction. I couldn't help but glance over at the girl who stood by the front entrance. So this was Sarah Ketterling. Although she'd kept her head lowered throughout her father's rude behavior, she looked up long enough to find me staring at her. Her lovely dark eyes were full of pain and embarrassment. Her light complexion turned even paler and she turned quickly toward the door.

"I'm going to wait outside, Papa," she said in a soft voice. She slipped quietly out of the store. Gabriel didn't appear to hear her.

"Wait here," I whispered to Sam. I crept to the old screen door and opened it slowly. Then I stepped out onto the wooden side-walk where Sarah stood with her back toward me, her thin body leaning against a light pole.

"Sarah," I said as gently as I could so as not to scare her. "I wanted to tell you how beautiful I think your stationery is. I bought some of it this morning. You're very talented."

The girl swung around, her eyes wide. She glanced nervously toward the entrance of the candle shop. She reminded me of a frightened fawn with large brown eyes and long dark lashes. The hair under her bonnet was almost black, sharply framing her delicate features.

"Th–thank you," she said in a voice so low I could barely hear her. "It–it's wood-block print. I love to do it."

"It's wonderful," I said with a smile. "I'm an artist, too, although a lot of what I do is on the computer. But I love all kinds of art. I paint and I've done some sculpting. I've never had the chance to learn wood blocking though. I wish you would teach me."

Her eyes swung past me and back to the shop behind us. "I'm afraid Papa wouldn't allow me to give lessons. I—I don't see many people."

I reached out and touched her arm. "Maybe you could ask him? I'd pay you for the lessons, of course. I'm staying at my Uncle Benjamin's house. If you could show me even once. . ."

"Sarah won't be showing you anything." Gabriel's harsh voice broke through the calm morning air. "I'll thank you to leave my daughter alone."

With that, he grabbed Sarah by the arm and pulled her toward him. Then he stomped down the sidewalk, his daughter scurrying behind him like some kind of pet dog. I was so furious with him— with his treatment of Sarah—that tears stung my eyes. How can anyone call himself a father and behave that way?

I swung around, grabbed the door, and pulled it open, once again almost running into Sam. Twice in one day. This had to stop.

"Sorry, Grace," he said. "Gabriel's been like this ever since his wife left. His problems have nothing to do with you. Don't take it personally."

Levi made a clucking sound with his tongue. "He locks Sarah in the house with him. She hardly ever goes out. I think he's afraid of losing her like he did her mother. It's a sad situation."

"Well, Abel convinced me that regular Mennonites aren't like Gabriel," I said sharply as I approached the counter. "But these Old Order people really take the cake. I guess this is what my mom and dad had to deal with."

Levi chuckled as he slid my candles and their holders into a paper bag. "Gabriel's not typical at all, Gracie." He pointed at Sam. "Why don't you introduce her to Ida Turnbauer?" He smiled at me. "Ida lives right down the road from you. She's Old Order. You'll find her to be a wonderful and loving woman."

"Good idea," Sam said. "We'll stop by sometime in the next

couple of days. You'll love Ida. She's a doll." He smiled at me. "You know, people are people, Grace. No matter what group you belong to, some members are gracious and loving, but some are mean, just like Gabriel. That holds true for everyone: Mennonite, Baptist, Pentecostal, Methodist, or any other label you want to use."

I nodded. "I get your point."

"My friends," Levi said, holding out my package. "I'm afraid I must tend to some hot wax that won't wait. I'm sorry to rush you. I'd love to spend some time getting to know you better, Gracie. Maybe we can plan to get together soon?"

"Why don't you and Grace come to my house for supper tonight?" Sam said.

I took the bag from Levi's outstretched hand.

"That would be wonderful," he said, giving Sam a wide smile. "Gracie, would that work for you?"

"Sounds great."

"How about six o'clock?" Sam said.

Levi shook his finger at Sam. "Try and stop me. I hope your aunt serves some of that fantastic applesauce she makes." He rubbed his round stomach. "It's worth the trip, Gracie."

"We'll let you get to your wax," Sam said. Then he turned to me. "I'll go to the hardware store and pick up your lamps and flashlight. Why don't you go to Menlo's and wait for me? After I introduce you to the Menlos, we'll pick up your packages from Ruth's."

I nodded, thanked Levi again for the gift, and set out for Menlo's. By the time Sam got to the bakery, the lovely German couple and I were already friends. Sam and I spent almost an hour listening to them talk about their family and laughing at their funny stories. Finally, Sam made our excuses and we left.

Sam went to the truck to wait for me while I hurried to Ruth's to pick up my earlier purchases. Although she didn't seem to be around anywhere, my sack was on the counter, ready to go. As

I came out of her store, I saw John Keystone standing by his window, watching me. I waved, but he just stared at me. The odd expression on his face made me feel uneasy, and for a fleeting moment I felt strongly that'd I seen him somewhere before. But that was impossible. I would have remembered if I'd met him in Wichita or Fairbury. I rejected the odd feeling and made my way to the truck. As I climbed inside, I noticed Mary standing outside the restaurant with a cup of coffee, glaring daggers at us. I felt confident I'd made some friends today, but Mary Whittenbauer, John Keystone, and Gabriel Ketterling certainly weren't among them.

Sam backed the truck into the street, and we headed down Main toward Faith.

"So, did you have a good time?" he asked.

"I did. Harmony is an interesting place. I just wish I'd come here while my uncle was alive."

"I know. Me, too." He handed me a small sack sitting on the dashboard. "Better put your cherry turnover inside one of your other bags. If you leave it in my truck, I can't ensure its safety."

I laughed and grabbed the bag. "Thank you. I love these. I'll try to save it for breakfast, but I can't promise anything."

"Besides being a nice man, Mr. Menlo is a skilled baker. Cakes, pies, all kinds of pastries. He sells sandwiches, too." Sam smiled. "But these turnovers are my favorite."

We rode in silence the rest of the way. My uncle's letter kept running through my mind. Visiting downtown Harmony had been a welcome distraction, but now I had to face reality again. What were my options? Should I destroy the letter and act as if I'd never read it? Or should I bring it out in the open and let the chips fall where they may? One minute the first choice felt right, and the next minute the second seemed the only alternative. As I considered my options, a new possibility occurred to me. Maybe Benjamin's letter would be enough to prove my father's innocence.

In a way, it was a record of Benjamin's testimony—revealing his belief that Glick's death was an unfortunate accident. Could this be my way out of this awful situation? Even if it worked, it would pull my dad into a whirlwind. Did I really want to do that?

I was so lost in thought I didn't realize that Sam had pulled up in front of Benjamin's house. "Hey, you should wait until you get inside to take your nap," he said gently, pulling me out of my reverie.

"I–I'm sorry. Guess I was somewhere else."

He looked around and smiled. "Nope, still Harmony." He held his hands out for my packages. "Let me carry these in for you."

He grabbed my bags as well as the sacks from the hardware store. Once inside, he put batteries in the lamps and showed me how to use them. Sure enough, they outshone the oil lamps by far. I felt relieved to have them.

"But what about the monster question?" I said, teasingly. "What do I do if Godzilla visits after dark?"

He walked over to the front door. "Sweetie told you about the flowers during the day, right?"

I nodded.

"She and Ben used those flowers as a way for him to let her know if he needed anything. She took care of him for several weeks before he died. Cleaned his house. Fixed meals. Washed his clothes. She'd walk down our driveway several times a day looking for that pot."

"That won't help at night when Godzilla wants to eat me."

"No, it won't. But I have an idea." He smiled, seemingly pleased with himself. "Walkie-talkies. Sweetie and I use them when I'm out working in the orchards. She can call me into supper or tell me when she wants something. I'm going to give you one tonight, and I'll keep the other. That way, if you need me, all you have to do is scream."

"Oh, great. Hopefully, there won't be any actual screaming."

He laughed. "I hope not. It might disrupt my snoring."

"Just don't saw logs too loudly. I'd hate to have to compete."

"Don't worry. I'll keep it to a dull roar. Now you go get that nap you've been planning." He put his hand on the doorknob. "I'll pick you up about a quarter to six. Oh, and bring your cell phone and charger along. We'll charge up your phone, but I don't want to mislead you. Those things are spotty at best out here. Sweetie and I use walkie-talkies because we gave up on cell phones and needed something we could count on."

"Okay," I said, stifling a yawn. My lack of sleep was catching up to me. "I'll see you tonight."

"One last thing. I hope you don't mind that I invited Levi to join us. I did it for two reasons. One was because he's a great guy, but the other is that he's lived in Harmony his whole life. He knew your family. I thought maybe you'd like to talk to him about them." He frowned. "Sweetie was born here, too, but she won't talk much about her life before I came to live with her. I have no idea why." He hesitated a moment. "You know, I don't say this to many people. I love Harmony, but there's something. . .an undercurrent." He shrugged and laughed. "I sound goofy. Maybe I need a nap, too."

Sam was right. There were definitely undercurrents. So deep they threatened to drown my family. I smiled at him. "I'm glad you invited Levi. I'm sure we'll have a wonderful time. And thanks for the tour. I really enjoyed it."

"You're welcome."

I watched as he walked down the steps, got in his truck, and drove away. So Myrtle didn't want to talk about the past. Did she know something? She and my uncle Benjamin were obviously good friends. She was the person who kept his house clean while he was ill. If they were that close, had he told her his secret? I closed the door and leaned against it. The information I'd gotten about Glick interested me and confirmed Benjamin's sentiments.

Glick sounded like the kind of man who might have had enemies. Could his death have been something else besides an accident? Uncle Benjamin believed Glick had died accidentally—by my father's hand. But I knew my dad. He would never walk away from a severely injured man. If he'd hurt him badly, my father would have gone for help.

In the truck, I'd wondered if I should ignore the entire situation or just tell my dad the truth and let him decide how to proceed. But as I stood here, contemplating those choices, I added two more items to my list of possibilities. What if Glick really had been murdered by someone other than my father? Someone Glick had harmed in some way. Should I keep digging? Attempt to find the truth and bring this decades-long mystery to a close?

Of course, the letter could simply be the incoherent ramblings of a dying man, and Jacob Glick might be alive and well—totally oblivious to the mystery his disappearance had caused. If that were true, my decision to walk away from my uncle's strange missive would be the right one.

I might be confused about how to proceed, but one thing I wasn't confused about. I had no intention of spending my life guarding this family secret the way Benjamin had. I needed to choose a course—and quickly.

I ran up the stairs to get the letter and read through it again. Maybe this time I'd see something I hadn't noticed before. Something that would guide me in the right direction. I pulled the dresser drawer open and rifled through my socks.

The letter was gone.

Chapter Seven

I spent the next two hours attempting to convince myself I'd simply misplaced the letter, but I finally faced the fact that it was gone and that someone had broken into the house and stolen it. After making certain no one else was in the house, I checked the front and back doors. The locks were still intact. How had my burglar gained access? A quick check of the front porch revealed a key hidden under the doormat. There was no way to know if someone who knew the key's location had used it to enter—or if the intruder had simply stumbled upon the simple hiding place. I dropped the key into my pocket. At least now, getting into my uncle's house wouldn't be quite so easy.

I sat in the rocking chair on the front porch for over an hour, trying to decide what to do next. I'd lost the only piece of evidence I had that might prove my father's innocence. What did the theft of the letter mean? Had someone else discovered our family secret? Or were they trying to hide the truth for other reasons? And why take the letter now? Benjamin's place had been vacant for almost a month. Why not break in and steal it before I arrived in Harmony? My visit wasn't a secret. Try as I might, I couldn't make sense of it. A tension headache began to nibble at my temples, and I rubbed them, trying to chase away the pain.

My eyes wandered to the flowerpot sitting near the porch railing. Myrtle! Maybe she saw something. Unfortunately, it was a long shot. Sam had mentioned that they'd both been working in their orchards. Myrtle may not have been in a position to notice anyone coming or going from Benjamin's house. I decided to check with her tonight though. Couldn't hurt.

I rocked back and forth awhile longer and stared at my car. I had an almost overwhelming desire to pack up and go home. Confusion combined with a growing sense of fear gathered strength in my mind. Finding the letter was bad enough, but knowing it had found its way into someone else's hands made everything much worse. Who had it and why? Was I in danger? Unfortunately, I had no answers to these questions.

My plan for a quick nap had been chased away by this strange turn of events. As I got up to go inside and change my clothes for supper, I realized that whoever had the letter had obviously been aware of my itinerary. Sadly, that fact didn't narrow the list of suspects much. Almost anyone could have done it. Except Sam. At least I could be certain he wasn't involved since he'd been with me all day.

I went inside and climbed the stairs to Mama and Papa's room. As I picked out a fresh white blouse and a pair of khaki slacks, my fingers brushed against one of the long dresses hanging in the closet—a dark blue and cream calico print. I pulled it out and looked closer. The lace around the collar was slightly yellowed with age and the material was thin beneath my fingers. But even after all these years, there was a feminine quality about it that appealed to me. On a whim I took off my sweater and jeans and pulled the dress over my head. Then I took one of the white caps hanging on a nail inside the closet and placed it over my hair. I closed the closet door and turned to look at the old mirror attached to the dresser. I couldn't help but gasp. The Gracie who looked back at me was a stranger. I even felt a little different. I ran my hands over the material, thinking about Mama Essie. She'd stood in this very spot, looking at herself in these clothes. I wished she were still here. Her sweetness and wisdom had always helped to lead me in the right direction.

As I stared at my reflection, I wondered what she would do in my place, but the answer to that question wasn't hard to discern. Above all, Essie loved her family. There was nothing she wouldn't have done for them. She would have met this challenge head-on, fighting for the truth in an effort to protect her son. She would never have believed that my father had killed another human being. As I removed the dress and put on my own clothes, I knew what I had to do. If I was even a little unsure about my father's innocence before, I was totally convinced of it now. The theft of the letter made it clear there was a secret hidden beneath the seemingly calm surface of Harmony, Kansas—a truth someone wanted to keep hidden. I intended to find out what it was.

I gathered my fresh clothes together and put them in the downstairs bathroom. Then I headed for the basement door. I remembered Sam's instructions about turning on the generator so it would pump water for my bath. I grabbed one of the flashlights purchased in town and walked gingerly down the rickety stairs. Thankfully, there were small windows in the basement walls so the flashlight wasn't necessary.

The basement held several surprises. As Sam had said, Benjamin used this space for his carpentry work. There were eight rocking chairs lined up against the back wall. Six were painted—two were not. About twenty birdhouses in various stages of assembly were stacked up on a large workbench. Another corner of the room held a variety of old trunks and ancient, unused furniture. A quick search through one trunk revealed several beautiful quilts and other handmade items carefully packed away. In another I found a set of china, beautifully decorated with small pink flowers, and silver candlesticks wrapped in cheesecloth. These treasures must have belonged to Mama Essie. They were certainly part of the family heirlooms my father wanted me to rescue.

I finally figured out how to start the generator and hurried back upstairs to take a bath. Although I was used to showers, I had to admit that soaking in the tub felt good. Unfortunately, the knowledge that someone had been inside the house made me uneasy, so I didn't tarry long.

I was ready to go by five thirty. As I sat waiting for Sam, something I'd seen while searching for the letter from Benjamin popped into my head. I got up and went over to the secretary where I'd first found the family Bible. I opened a long drawer underneath the desktop and took out a key attached to a blue ribbon. Maybe this was the key to the third bedroom upstairs.

I still had some time before I had to leave, so I hurried upstairs to check. Sure enough, the key fit and the door clicked open. I pushed it in slowly until the contents of the room were revealed. Unlike the other rooms, everything was covered with dust. Not wanting to get dirty after my bath, I ventured in only as far as the dresser that sat near the door. I carefully opened the cover of an old Bible lying on top of the grime-covered piece of furniture. The name *Daniel Temple* was scrawled on the inside cover. As I'd suspected, this had been my father's room. Why had Benjamin kept the other bedrooms clean and in pristine condition but allowed this one to sit without any attention? There was only one reason I could think of. He'd closed off this room because he wanted to forget his brother. Why? Resentment? Even hate?

Looking around the neglected room, I began to wonder if the letter was actually an attempt to point the finger of blame at the wrong Temple brother. Could Benjamin have killed Jacob Glick? I left the room and climbed down the stairs to wait for Sam.

A new possibility swirled through my mind while I sat staring at the front door. Perhaps the isolation Benjamin had surrounded himself with hadn't come from some noble attempt to protect his family. Maybe it had actually been nothing more than the act of a desperate, guilty man who hated his brother and wanted one last chance to destroy him. But if this were true, how in the world could I ever prove it?

I suddenly felt the need to get out of Benjamin's house. I stepped out onto the front porch while thoughts of the missing letter, the abandoned room, and new suspicions about my uncle created a cacophony of fear inside my brain.

Chapter Eight

I want to make a quick stop before we go to supper," Sam said as he shut the truck door after I slid into the passenger seat.

"A quick stop? I can see your house from here. There are no stops between here and there."

He jogged around the front of the truck and climbed inside. "I'm aware of that," he said with a grin. "We're going the other way."

We drove out of the driveway and turned left—away from the big red house. There were two old homes that sat down the road about a quarter of a mile from Benjamin's. Sam pulled into the dirt driveway of the closest one and turned off the engine. "This is Ida Turnbauer's place. I want to introduce you."

"But she doesn't know we're coming. It's rude to just stop by without calling first."

Sam laughed. "Maybe that's true in the city, but out here you could have company stop by almost anytime. And besides, you can't call Ida anyway. No phone. I want you to meet her. I'm afraid you have some wrong ideas about folks like her."

I started to protest again when an elderly woman stepped out onto the porch and began waving us in. She had on a long, dark blue dress, and her head was covered with a white bonnet.

100

"Too late now," Sam said innocently. "We're trapped."

I sighed and shook my head.

Sam reached over and put his hand on my arm. "Grace, Ida loves company. She's always ready for a visit. Trust me."

"Okay, I get it. I'm not in Wichita. The rules are different here."

He nodded. "Most of your rules don't even exist in Harmony. Besides, we're only staying long enough to say hello. I promise."

We got out of the truck and walked up to the porch where Ida stood sporting a wide smile. "This must be Grace," she said as we approached. "I wanted so much to walk over and greet you when you first arrived, but I know city folk do not like unannounced company."

Her face held evidence of past beauty. She spoke with an accent, her words slightly guttural. Proof of German descent, just like my grandparents. I instantly felt drawn to her and a little embarrassed to be counted among "city folk."

"I–I'm happy to meet you."

"My goodness," she said as I stepped up next to her. "You are the spitting image of your uncle." She took my face in her hands. I could feel the calluses on her fingers as her faded blue eyes sought mine. "Bless you, child. I know it meant the world to Benjamin— knowing you would come and take care of things after he died. I wish there had been time for him to see you before the end."

I wanted to tell her that my uncle had had all the time in the world to "see me" if he'd wanted to, but I kept quiet.

A tear slid down the old woman's wrinkled face. "Ach, your uncle was a good man," she said softly. "I hope you believe that. No matter what anyone else tells you, you hang on to that, ja?"

She let go of my face and grabbed Sam's arm. "I have some brewed tea and warm cookies inside. You two come and sit a spell with me."

Sam leaned over and kissed her cheek. "Can't do it right now,

Ida. Sweetie's waiting supper, and you know how she gets if I'm late."

Ida smiled. "I know how she gets. But you two will come back, ja?"

Sam looked at me, and I nodded.

"How about Monday afternoon?" he said.

"That would be wonderful. I will look forward to it. I just might make one of those strawberry pies you are so fond of."

"Well, in that case, we'll definitely be here." He turned to look at me. "Ida makes the best strawberry pie in Kansas."

"I'm not so sure about that," I said teasingly. "My grandmother made a mean strawberry pie herself."

The smile slipped from Ida's face. "*Made* pie?" she said. "You do not mean Essie has passed away, do you?"

"Why yes," I answered. "It's been almost five years now."

Ida clasped her hands to her chest. "Ach, no, no." She toddled over to the white rocker that sat a few feet from her front door. Gracious, did everyone in Harmony have white rocking chairs?

"My uncle didn't tell you? I don't understand. . ."

She sat down slowly and covered her face with her hands. "I do not either. Surely he knew."

"I'm sure he did. My father sent him a letter."

Ida lowered her hands. Tears stained her weathered cheeks. "Your uncle was very tenderhearted. Maybe he did not want to cause me pain."

One look at her face made it clear that if that had been his intention, he'd failed miserably. "Were you and my grandmother close?"

Ida nodded. "Ja, we were best friends growing up. I loved her dearly."

"Then why. . ."

"Did I not try to get in touch with her in all these years?"

I nodded.

Ida sighed and stared out at the wheat field across from us. A gentle breeze caused the knee-high, green stalks to sway gently as if caught in some kind of synchronized dance. "It's hard to explain," she said. "I was so hurt when she decided to leave that it was easier to put her out of my mind." She turned her gaze back to me. "I know that does not make much sense. Her leaving had nothing to do with me. I realize that now. But I turned it into something personal, and now it is too late." She shook her head slowly. "She sent me a letter not long after she and Joe moved to Nebraska. I—I never opened it." Ida reached up and wiped a tear away from her eye. "Perhaps it is time I did."

"You kept it all these years?" I said.

She reached over and patted my arm. "Yes. I just could not bring myself to read it."

"So your silence toward my grandmother had nothing to do with some kind of banning?"

Ida's eyes widened. "Of course not." She scowled at Sam. "Ach, what have you been telling this child?"

Sam shrugged. "Didn't come from me."

"Oh. Benjamin. I should have known." Ida shook her head. "Benjamin had his own ways, Grace. In our faith, if someone is caught in sin and they are not repentant, they may be forbidden to participate in some of the ceremonies in the church service, but they are not asked to leave the fold. And we still talk to them. Understand that any action the church takes is not seen as a punishment; it is an attempt to help them get straight with God. But actually excommunicating someone? I saw it a couple of times when I was a girl. One had to do with a man who would not stop beating his wife and child, and the other was a woman who flagrantly carried on an adulterous affair with a man in our community. The elders counseled all of them and only asked them to leave the church after they refused to change their ways. Thankfully, the wife beater left his family behind and the church was able to help restore them." She stared into my eyes. "My guess is that any other church would have done the same thing. You must understand that what happened under Bishop Angstadt was done through his own attempt to control his members. It was not godly nor would the Mennonite Church have approved it—if the area leadership had known about it. Benjamin's attitude toward your family may have originated through Bishop Angstadt, but he held on to it all those years without any help from anyone else. When the bishop died, anyone approving of The Ban died with him." Ida stared down at her feet for a moment. "I want you to know that I tried talking to your uncle many times on the subject, but he wouldn't budge." She looked up at me and frowned. "I often wondered if there was something else behind his stubborn refusal to contact his family. Something he would not tell any of us."

Her sentiments echoed what Abel Mueller had told me. That made at least three people who'd confirmed that after Amil Angstadt died, Benjamin's silence toward my family had been his decision alone—perhaps for the reasons he'd written in his letter—or perhaps for other reasons yet to be uncovered.

"Ida, I'm sorry to break this up," Sam said softly, "but we've really got to be going."

The old woman nodded. She reached for my arm, and I helped her to her feet. "Grace, you leave this big strapping man at home Monday and come by on your own, ja? Maybe we could read your grandmother's letter together?"

"Hey, how come I get cut out of the loop?" Sam said playfully. "What happens to *my* strawberry pie?"

Ida and I both laughed. "I tell you what," I said to Ida. "Why don't I come by around one o'clock and Sam can join us at two? That way everyone gets what they want."

Ida clapped her hands together and a smile lit up her face. "Ach, that would be wonderful. And we promise to save you some pie, Sam."

"In that case, try to stop me." He leaned over and kissed the old woman on the cheek. "Unless you both want Sweetie to come here after us, we've got to get going."

I said good-bye to Ida, and we got back in the truck.

"So do you still think Old Order Mennonites are mean, judgmental people?"

"No, you and Abel were right. I came here with the wrong impression. I'm beginning to understand that as a whole, Mennonites live the way they do because they're trying to protect their community." I glanced at the houses and fields around us. "You know, as much as I love the city. . ."

"You're beginning to appreciate a simpler lifestyle?"

I laughed. "Don't put words in my mouth." But he was right. Outside of the situation with my uncle, Harmony was beginning to grow on me. It must have been very difficult for Papa and Mama to leave here—even with the church problems they faced. The knowledge that being with me meant more to them than their friends and hometown roots touched my heart. I worked to swallow the lump that tried to form in my throat.

"Well, here it is," he said as we pulled into his driveway and he turned off the engine.

Although I'd seen his house from the road, I found it even more striking up close. Deep red with creamy white trim, a large porch, and two turrets—it portrayed all the beauty and elegance of the Victorian period. As Sam held out his hand to help me down from the truck, I couldn't tear my eyes from it.

"I think this is the most extraordinary house I've ever seen," I said. "Where did it come from? I mean, it's different from any other home around here."

After I hopped down, Sam shut the truck door behind me. "This house has an interesting history. A man who owned most of the land in this area built it in the late 1800s. When a group of German Mennonites began to buy nearby plots, he fought to drive them out. But in the end, he converted to their ways. Gave away a lot of his land to the settlers. When he died, he left the rest of it, along with his house, to the community."

"How did you and um...Sweetie end up with it?"

Sam chuckled at hearing me finally use his aunt's nickname. "Well, these simple people weren't quite sure what to do with a house like this. They couldn't see it as a church building, and no one wanted to move into it. It sat empty for many years. Believe it or not, eventually Amil Angstadt used it as his parsonage."

I snorted. "Now that *is* hard to believe. I thought he was so rigid and uncompromising. Surely he would have seen this house as ostentatious."

He grunted. "I've found that judgmental people generally are more focused on other people than they are on themselves. Goes back to that 'board in your own eye' thing Jesus talked about. Angstadt found a way to accept something for himself that he never would have allowed for folks in his congregation."

I nodded my agreement with his assessment. I'd known a few people whose lives were caught up in trying to decide what was right or wrong for everyone else. On the Internet I'd even stumbled across Web sites totally devoted to judging different ministries. They were disturbing to say the least and always left me feeling as if I needed a shower.

"So how *did* you end up with it?"

"Well, when Angstadt died, the church elders were left to decide what to do with the remaining congregation. Some members left the church altogether, happy to be out from underneath his thumb. Harmony Church was started by ex-members of Angstadt's group who wanted a fresh start." He shrugged. "I think even folks who were close to Angstadt were glad to have the chance to begin again. Those who remained wanted nothing to do with his house. My aunt was a young woman then. She and her father owned one of the few non-Mennonite farms in the area.

My grandmother died when Sweetie and my mother were pretty young. Her father, my grandfather, was severely injured when his tractor flipped in the field one day. Sweetie spent about a year trying to run their farm alone while she cared for him. Eventually he died. Sweetie sold their farm and bought this house and the land. It took almost every penny she had. With the little that was left, she began planting fruit trees and berry patches. Over time, this place became very productive."

"But hard for one person to run."

Sam nodded. "I came to live with her just in time. Together I think we've done a pretty good job." He cocked his head toward the house. "Now, let's get inside before I end up being the main course at supper."

We were almost to the front porch when the screen door flew open and Sweetie stepped out waving a big spoon at us. "Well, it's about time," she screeched. "Didn't I say six o'clock?" She turned around and went back inside, the door slamming behind her. We could hear her mumbling something about learning to tell time.

Sam looked at his watch. "It's four minutes past six." He shook his head. "Sweetie takes being on time very seriously. Unless *she's* late."

"Wow. I'm sorry we upset her. Should we apologize?"

He chuckled. "I guarantee you that by the time we start eating, she will have forgotten all about it. Don't worry about her. She never stays mad for long."

I noticed a black and silver Suburban parked in the driveway. "Is that Levi's car?"

"Yep. Which means we'd better get inside before Sweetie puts the food on the table. Levi can shovel it down faster than almost anyone I know."

I hesitated for a moment. Standing on Sam's porch, I felt safe for the first time since I'd found the letter. An almost overwhelming desire had been building in me all day. I had the urge to grab Sam by the arm and tell him everything—the whole truth. I desperately wanted an ally, someone I could trust. But I still had doubts running through my mind. Benjamin had kept this secret for thirty years, and here I was ready to blurt out the truth after only a day. And I didn't really know Sam that well. What if he decided to take things into his own hands? What if he insisted on calling the authorities? Could I really risk my dad's future with someone who didn't know him or care about him the way I did? That little bit of doubt forced me to shove the whole situation to the back of my mind, where it sat like an uncomfortable ache, waiting to turn into a full-scale migraine. I prayed that by the time supper was over, I'd know what to do.

Sam led me through a wonderful wood-paneled entry hall and into the dining room. The furniture was gorgeous—and certainly not what I'd anticipated from Sweetie. The walls had been painted a lovely shade of deep red with white wainscoting almost halfway up. Crown molding accented the ceilings. Long windows let in plenty of light, overpowering the soft glow from the brass chandelier that hung over the table. The furniture in the room perfectly fit the Victorian styling. A massive Victorian sideboard sat against one wall. It matched the mahogany dining-room table and chairs.

I was so stunned I froze in my tracks.

"Not quite what you expected from a couple of hick farmers, huh?" he whispered in my ear.

"I don't think you're a hick farmer," I hissed back. "But where...?"

"Some of the furniture came with the house, but the lion's share of the decorating was done by my aunt. She's spent years trying to bring back the original style of the house."

A gentle push sent me toward the table where Levi sat waiting. I could hear Sweetie rummaging around in the kitchen. I sat down in the chair Sam pointed to and smiled at Levi.

"Quite a place isn't it?" he said. "I've watched it change little by little over the years, but I'm still impressed every time I come here."

I made a mental note to remind myself about not judging a book by its cover. I'd certainly done that with Sweetie—or Myrtle—or whoever she was. One thing I knew: There was a lot more to this woman than a loud voice, coarse mannerisms, and a nosy attitude.

Sam said something about helping his aunt bring in the food and disappeared. Levi and I made small talk about the weather for a few minutes before they came back carrying a large platter of fried chicken and bowls of mashed potatoes and creamed corn. Another trip to the kitchen resulted in big, fluffy rolls straight from the oven, along with strawberry preserves and a bowl of homemade applesauce. Levi's face lit up when he saw it.

I sipped my delicious brewed iced tea until everyone sat down. Sam said grace and then began to pass plates of food around the table. I quickly discovered that Sweetie was more than a crack decorator; she could hold her own in the kitchen as well. Her flaky fried chicken had a buttery taste along with just a hint of spice. I had to admit that she may have even surpassed Mama Essie's skill in chicken frying. In fact, she could give the Colonel a big run for his money. And the applesauce had so much flavor I had no desire to sample the canned variety ever again. Levi filled his bowl with the flavorful sauce.

"So, Gracie, what do you think of Harmony so far?" Levi asked. "I hope your little run-in with Gabriel Ketterling hasn't soured you on the whole town."

I swallowed a scrumptious mouthful of mashed potatoes and gravy. "No, not at all. I like almost everyone I've met. Sam introduced me to Ida Turnbauer right before we arrived here. She's a lovely woman. Nothing like Gabriel."

"So that's why you're late for supper," Sweetie said, glaring at

Sam. "I swear, boy, you can't get from A to B without a few Cs and Ds thrown in, can you?" She shook her head, but I caught the hint of the smile she tried to cover up by holding a chicken leg up to her mouth. Her love for her nephew was obvious.

Sam held up his hands in mock surrender. "Sorry, Sweetie." He looked at Levi and me with a big goofy grin on his face. "I take after my aunt. I just can't keep my nose out of other people's business."

Sweetie's face turned pink. "I got no idea what you're talkin' about. I don't go stickin' my nose where it don't belong. Goodness gracious."

Levi chuckled. "Now Myrtle. You and I may not be churchgoing folks, but I know a whopper when I hear it. You need to repent to these two young people right now."

Sam and I laughed, and after a few feeble attempts to defend herself, Sweetie gave up and joined in.

"Okay, okay," she sputtered as the laughter wound down, "I guess I am a little interested in what goes on 'round here." She wiped her eyes. "My mama said I was a curious child, and I seem to have grown up into a powerful curious adult."

"*Curious* being a nicer word than *nosy*?" Sam asked with a wink.

She shook her head. "You'd better watch it, boy. I got apple pie in my kitchen, and it ain't gonna shake hands with your gullet if you don't knock it off."

"My abject apologies for casting aspersions on your veracity," Sam said mockingly.

Sweetie looked at me, her face screwed up into a frown. "I got no idea what he's talkin' about sometimes, but I know I heard somethin' like an apology in that mess, didn't you?"

I nodded my agreement. "It didn't make sense to me either, but I think it's safe to assume he's sorry."

"Well, in that case, I guess you can have pie—after you finish your supper," she said to Sam.

"That won't be a problem." He loaded up his fork with potatoes. "As usual, you've outdone yourself, dear aunt."

"Yes, this is absolutely delicious," I said. "You're a terrific cook."

Sweetie blushed again and mumbled something about people bein' silly, but I could tell she was pleased.

Levi had just started to tell me some of Harmony's history when there was a loud, insistent knock on the front door.

"Now, who in the world would come botherin' folks at suppertime?" Sweetie sputtered as she got up from her chair.

I guess the idea of visiting neighbors whenever you felt like it actually did have some rules attached: Never drop by during supper.

We could hear Sweetie open the front door and say something to whoever was outside. Then the door closed and footsteps neared the dining room. Sweetie came into the room followed by Ruth Wickham. Her normally red face was a couple of shades darker than usual.

"Ruth's got somethin' important to say to us," Sweetie said. Her expression made it plain she still wasn't happy about her meal being interrupted.

Ruth stepped up next to the table, wringing her hands.

"Why, Ruth," Levi said. "What's the matter? Is something wrong?"

She nodded. "I–I'm not in the habit of accusing anyone of stealing," she said haltingly. "But as hard as it is, I have no choice."

"Stealing?" Sam said. "What in the world are you talking about, Ruth? What's been stolen?"

A tear slipped down her cheek. "My—my chestnut vase is gone. I'm—I'm sorry, Sam. But as far as I know, there was only one person who could have possibly taken it."

To my horror, she fastened her gaze on me. "Gracie Temple, you give me back my vase. Right now."

Chapter Nine

"I'm really sorry about this," Sam said again.

We were seated in the living room. It was as beautifully decorated as the dining room with the same crimson walls and white wainscoting that matched the fireplace mantel. But I couldn't focus on the decor. I was far too upset.

Sam sat across from me on a plush brocade love seat that matched the couch where I waited to be exonerated. I'd told Ruth she could search Benjamin's house and my car if it made her feel better and had given her my keys. Levi had gone with her.

"It's not your fault," I said. We were beginning to repeat ourselves. Sam had apologized, and I'd assured him he wasn't to blame at least four different times.

"When they don't find anything, Ruth will acknowledge her mistake and everything will be back to normal." His eyes kept darting from me to the hallway that led to the front door.

I didn't respond. It would never be "back to normal," whatever that was. My previous feelings of being charmed by Harmony and its residents had vanished like smoke in the wind. I was sorry about Ruth's chestnut vase, but I had the distinct impression that I was her prime suspect because I didn't live here. I'd only been

112

accused of stealing one other time in my life. That was when a girl in high school told several people I took her favorite CD. When she found it in her boyfriend's locker, she didn't even bother to tell me she was sorry she'd accused me. But I made sure everyone who knew me found out the truth. I only learned when I got older that it would have been better to keep silent about it, letting God be my defense.

I realized that I needed to do that now, so I quietly put the situation in His hands. There was nothing I could do about it anyway. The truth is, people believe whatever they want no matter how much we try to defend ourselves. I looked over at Sam. His dark brown shirt made his sun-bleached hair look almost white. He flashed me a quick smile that I'm sure was supposed to comfort me, but I related more to the nervous tapping of his left boot on the hardwood floor. The sound stopped suddenly, and I looked up to see his eyes fastened on mine. Something that felt like electricity traveled up my spine.

"I didn't take it, you know," popped out of my mouth before I could stop it.

His eyes widened. "There was never any question in my mind, Grace."

"But you didn't see what was in my sack when I left Ruth's."

"It wouldn't have made any difference. I know you're not a thief. But you might be interested to know that I actually did look inside your bag. It's just like the one from the hardware store. I mixed them up when I went looking for the lamps after we got back to your place. Believe me, if the chestnut vase had been there, I would have seen it."

I felt a quick stab of relief. At least one person knew I was innocent. I felt certain Ruth had already tried, convicted, and sentenced me. I didn't think she was intentionally trying to frame me, but I had to admit that having Levi go with her made me feel more comfortable.

I looked at my watch. "They've been gone a long time."

"It's only been about thirty minutes. It's taking longer because they can't find anything."

The clatter of dishes from the kitchen highlighted another problem. Sweetie was fit to be tied. Her supper had been ruined. Was she angry with Ruth—or with me? With Sweetie it was hard to tell.

The sound of a car door slamming told us that Ruth and Levi had returned. I waited for them to come inside and tell me they'd found nothing—followed by an effusive apology from Ruth. But no one entered the house. A moment later we heard a second car door slam, followed by the sound of someone starting up a vehicle and driving away.

"What's going on?" I asked Sam.

"I don't know, but I'm going to find out." He'd just stood to his feet when the front door creaked open and we heard the sound of footsteps in the hall. Levi walked into the room, and the expression on his face made my heart sink so low it felt like it hit my shoes.

"What's going on, Levi?" I hated the squeaky sound my voice made, but I couldn't seem to control it.

He came over and sat down next to me, taking my hands in his. "Gracie, we—we found the vase in your basement. It was in a trunk, hidden under some old quilts."

I tried to say something but didn't seem able to form anything coherent. All that came out of my mouth was "But. . .but. . .but. . ." I looked over at Sam, whose mouth hung open—the color drained from his face.

Levi squeezed my hands. "Ruth isn't going to press charges. Folks in Harmony don't call the authorities very often. We like to handle these things ourselves. But she did ask that you stay out of her store from now on."

After another squeeze, he got up and walked toward the entryway. At the doorway he stopped and looked back at me.

"Gracie, Ruth isn't angry with you. You'll find that most people in Harmony are very forgiving. We work hard to deserve our name." He shook his head. "I must admit that I find it hard to understand how this happened. You certainly don't seem like the kind of person who would take something that doesn't belong to you. Whatever's going on, I want you to know that I'm here for you. If I can do anything to help you—anything at all—you come see me. Anytime, night or day." With that, he turned and left the room. A few seconds later we heard the front door close.

I tried to hold back my tears, but I couldn't. I covered my face with my hands and sobbed. Until that moment, I had no idea how much I'd begun to like this town and these people. But now I was marked as a thief—for something I hadn't done.

I felt Sam sit down next to me and put his arm around my shoulders. I leaned into him and cried until I couldn't cry any more. He handed me a handkerchief from his pocket. I took it and wiped my face.

"Sam, I swear. . ."

He reached over and touched my lips with his fingers. "Don't even go there." He reached under my chin and pulled my face up to his. "I think it's about time you told me what's going on, don't you?"

"What. . .what do you mean?"

His eyebrows knit together in a frown. "Oh, come on, Grace. Your uncle had some kind of secret. He leaves his property to a niece he's never met. You're asking questions about Jacob Glick, a man who left Harmony years ago. And you've had something weighing on your mind ever since this morning. I know you didn't take that vase. That can only mean one thing. Someone is trying to frame you. My guess is they're hoping this accusation will make you leave town." His eyes sought mine, and I couldn't look away. "So tell me what this is all about. You can trust me. You know that, don't you?"

As I stared into his face, I was aware of two things. One: that I really could trust him. And two: that he was going to kiss me. Both of those realizations forced my heart from my throat and back into my chest where it belonged. His kiss was tender and sweet. And when he pulled back, I could still feel the pressure of his lips on mine. I kept my eyes closed for a few seconds afterward just savoring the moment. When I opened them, he was smiling at me.

"Look," I said, keeping my voice low so Sweetie wouldn't overhear us. "I'll tell you what I know, but you have to promise that you won't take matters into your own hands. This situation is very serious, and it has to do with my family. I have to decide what to do about it without pressure from anyone else. Can you live with that?"

"Of course. All I want to do is help. I'm not planning to cowboy up and 'take care of the little lady.' I know you can handle yourself just fine."

"We need to go somewhere else. Someplace where we can talk without being overheard."

Sam stood up and took my hand. Then he led me toward the front door. First he stopped by the kitchen where Sweetie was still banging pots and pans around.

"We're going out to the barn for a while," he said in a voice loud enough to be heard over the racket. "Sorry about supper. It was great." He rubbed his stomach with the hand that wasn't holding mine. "I'm still hungry. I don't suppose we could have some leftovers when we get back?"

Sweetie's expression didn't offer us much hope of anything—let alone remnants of her abandoned meal. But she finally nodded. "You go do whatever you need to do, boy. I'll heat you up somethin' when you're done."

She wiped her hands on her apron and shot me a look that took me by surprise. It wasn't so much anger as it was fear. Was she afraid her nephew might be getting involved with someone she didn't trust? We stared at each other for a moment longer until Sam pulled me away.

The barn sat about one hundred yards from the house and was painted the same color. As we approached, a small tricolored dog ran around from behind the structure. He looked like a cross between a Jack Russell terrier and a rat terrier. His big ears stuck straight up, and his short legs moved so quickly he almost appeared to be flying.

"Hey, Buddy!" Sam called. He knelt down as the little dog jumped up into his arms and licked his face. "Grace Temple, meet Buddy Goodrich. The third member of our little family."

After Sam set the small, wiggly dog back on the ground, I dropped to my knees and got an almost identical welcome. Buddy had big brown eyes that stared deeply into mine. It was as if he were trying his best to read my thoughts.

"Hi there, Buddy," I said after he'd finished handing out wet doggy kisses. His stump of a tail wagged so hard his whole backside quivered. I looked up at Sam. "I figured you'd have some kind of big farm dog."

"Buddy's a stray. We kind of picked each other. I'm probably not the kind of owner he had in mind either—but our relationship works just fine." He pointed toward the barn, and I followed him inside with Buddy hot on our trail.

Sam sat down on a hay bale, and Buddy jumped up next to him, laying his head on Sam's lap. I plopped down on a bale across from him. A quick glance around the barn revealed stored farm equipment, bags of seed and fertilizer, and a couple of horses. One was dark and shiny, while the other, a pinto, matched Buddy's colors. Although I'd never owned a horse, a friend back in Nebraska had kept several. She'd had a pinto pony almost exactly like this one. I breathed in the barn's sweet, earthy mixture of hay and horses. The setting sun sent its rays through the open windows and bathed our surroundings in a golden glow.

"Now, what in the world is going on, Grace?"

Even though I'd decided to tell him the truth, for just a moment, fear nipped at my heels. Benjamin had spent his life guarding this secret, even from Sam who had been his friend for many years. Could I really trust this man who sat waiting to share my family's strange secret? One day in this town and my life was in chaos. Up was down and down was up. I sighed and stared into Sam's eyes, silently asking God to show me if I should spill my guts.

"Look," he said quietly, noticing my obvious reluctance to take the dirty Temple laundry out of the bag, "if it helps any, I'm going to tell you what Ben told me. Once when he meant to talk to me—and one time when he didn't. Maybe it will help."

I nodded. "Go on."

Sam sighed and stared at something above my head. "About two weeks before he died, I stopped by his house. Sweetie had made up some food for him although he wasn't eating much. I was trying to talk him into a bowl of her chicken and rice soup when he suddenly stopped me. 'Sam,' he said, 'I need you to make me a promise. I want you to help my niece when she comes to Harmony. It won't be easy for her.' I tried to get him to tell me more, but he wouldn't say another word."

"Did you promise him?"

"Yes I did. I figured it was the least I could do for a dying man. Someone I considered my friend." Sam smiled. "I have to say that I was certainly pleased when you opened the door yesterday. I had this image of Ben in a dress that I couldn't get out of my mind. The truth was much better than my imagination."

"Thank you." I rubbed my hands over my upper arms. The gentle spring air was beginning to chill. "Now tell me the thing you overheard that you weren't supposed to."

Sam stared down at the hay-covered floor. "This happened a

few days before Ben died. He was getting weaker but refused to go to the hospital. I'd come by to see if he needed anything and to try once again to convince him we should contact your father." Sam took a deep breath and let it out slowly. "But he was adamant that we not call him. Abel and I debated the situation more than once. It was a difficult decision."

I waved my hand at him. "Look, I have no idea what I would have done in your situation. Hindsight is twenty-twenty. I'm not angry with anyone in Harmony for abiding by my uncle's last wishes. It wasn't your fault."

"Well, thanks for that. Now that I know you, I wish we'd gone a different direction. But what's done is done, I guess."

"Getting back to your story. . ."

"Oh yeah. Sorry." He fixed his gaze over my head again. "Anyway, I'd actually walked out the front door and gone to my truck when I realized I'd forgotten to give Ben the flowers Sweetie had sent over for him. I grabbed them and went back into the house. Ben was still sitting at the kitchen table where I'd left him. As I approached the door, I heard him praying. He was asking God to protect you and to forgive him, and he was crying." Sam acted as if he were brushing the hair out of his eyes, but I could tell he was moved emotionally remembering Benjamin's distress.

"Is that it?"

He shook his head. "No. Suddenly he rose to his feet and walked over to the kitchen window. Then I heard him say something like, 'You will not have the last word, Jacob. You hear me? We will be rid of you. Somehow. Someday. You may have imprisoned me, but another one will take my place. Maybe I couldn't defeat you, but I'm praying *she* can.' And with that, he staggered back to his chair and collapsed." Sam lowered his gaze, and his stormy eyes fastened on mine. "I backed out of the room and left the flowers on the table in the hall. I never told Ben that I'd overheard him. When you first asked about Jacob Glick, it didn't mean anything to me.

But when you brought him up again at the diner, I remembered Ben's words and realized they may not have been the crazy ravings of a dying man. He could have been referring to Glick. I just didn't know why—or what it had to do with you."

Could this be the sign I'd asked for? I felt a peace settle over me. I had my answer, and now it was time to share the burden I'd carried alone over the last twenty-four hours. I took a deep breath and just let the story tumble out. I told Sam about the letter, what it said, and how it had been stolen. I also explained that I was becoming convinced someone else was concerned about keeping Glick's death covered up, because there were secrets even my uncle didn't know.

"My father would never kill anyone," I said finally. "Nor would he leave someone fatally injured and just walk away. I believe he fought with Glick—but I also believe someone else killed him. To be honest, I suspected my uncle for a while. I wondered if he was trying to blame my father for his own misdeed. But after thinking about it, I realize it doesn't make sense. No real Christian who knew he was going to die would leave behind such an awful accusation. He'd care more about the hereafter than the here and now. Benjamin even wrote about being afraid of carrying a lie into the next life. And he sure didn't take that letter from my dresser, nor did he try to frame me by stealing Ruth's chestnut vase. Someone is extremely interested in keeping the truth about Jacob Glick buried. Literally and figuratively."

Sam, who hadn't moved a muscle since I'd begun my discourse, just stared at me with his mouth open.

"S—say something," I said finally. "You're scaring me."

He shook his head as if trying to clear his brain. "I—I had a few ideas about what you were going to tell me, but I must admit they didn't come close to the reality. The only thing I got right was that Ben was talking about Jacob Glick." He looked down at his scuffed leather boots. "Wow. I don't know what to say." He swung his gaze back to me. "So you're saying there's an actual body buried on your property? Someone who's been there for thirty years?"

"That's about the size of it."

He stood up, waking Buddy who looked at him accusingly before he put his head back down and dozed off again. Sam paced back and forth a couple of times. Then he stopped. "We've got to call the sheriff, Grace. We can't fool around with this."

I jumped up, too. "You promised you'd let me make the decisions about what to do, remember?"

"Yes, but I'm pretty sure having a buried body on your property is illegal," he said sarcastically. "Especially if the person was murdered."

"Listen, Sam. That body's been there for thirty years. Another two weeks isn't going to make a difference. I want some time to try to figure out what really happened to Glick."

"And if you can't?"

"Then we'll decide what should be done. I agree that we'll probably have to call the sheriff. I have no intention of living here for the rest of my life, guarding the body of some guy I don't even know."

It felt good to say "we." Bringing someone else into the mess my uncle left behind lifted a weight. But that still didn't bring me the answers I needed.

Sam sauntered back over to his bale of hay and sat down. He reached over and scratched Buddy behind the ears. "Wait a minute. This might be easier than you think. If you never mention the letter, no one will know who killed Glick. They won't be able to prove Ben knew anything about it even though they might suspect him. He can't be hurt by this anymore. Maybe we could just accidentally uncover the body, call the police, and act dumb."

I sighed. "You're forgetting my dad. Trust me. He'll try to take responsibility for Glick's death."

"But why would he connect the remains to Glick? Your father thinks he moved away years ago. It might never occur to him that the dead man is someone he knew."

"Benjamin packed a suitcase to make it look like Glick left town and buried it with him. It won't be hard for the authorities to figure out who the body belongs to. Look, Sam. In the time I have left here, let's see what we can find out about Jacob Glick. There are still people in Harmony who knew him. I think we might be able to figure out what really happened if we talk to the right person. And in the process, we'll probably find out who took Ruth's vase and planted it at my place. Until then, everyone's going to think I'm guilty."

Sam stared at the floor for several seconds. Finally, he raised his hands in surrender. "I might be making the biggest mistake of my life, but okay." He pointed his index finger at me. "But if we can't solve this thing. . ."

"Like I said, we'll probably have to call the sheriff."

"Probably?"

I reached for a strand of hair and twirled it around my finger. "Just what kind of man is he?"

Sam's eyes widened, and then he laughed. "He's a jerk. I know it's not nice to say things like that, but folks in Harmony try their best to keep him out of their business. He doesn't like religious people, and he sees our little town as a hotbed of crazy zealots."

I snorted. "Oh great. That's encouraging."

"Sorry. Just being honest."

"Well, let's keep that prospect in the background for now." I looked at my watch. "It's getting late. Let's see if we can talk your aunt into having pity on us. I'm starving. Then I need to get back to my uncle's and get a good night's sleep. We have a lot of work to do. . ."

Sam held his hand up like a cop stopping traffic. "Whoa right there, little lady. I might have promised not to interfere in how you handle your family secret, but that doesn't mean I'm going to stay quiet about everything you do."

I frowned at him. "What are you talking about?"

He stood up again. Somehow, Buddy knew this time Sam intended to leave. The small dog jumped down and waited at his master's feet. "You heard noises outside Ben's place last night. Today someone's been inside your house twice. There's no way on God's green earth I'm letting you stay there another night. I'll drive you over so you can get whatever clothes and supplies you need, but then you're coming back here. And you're staying with us until we know beyond a shadow of a doubt that you're safe." He folded his arms across his chest and glared at me.

My own stubbornness raised its ugly head and met his expression with one of my own. I desperately wanted to inform him that he wasn't about to tell me what to do. But to be honest, the idea of staying at Benjamin's alone gave me the heebie-jeebies. "Don't get used to pushing me around," I growled at him. "However, in this case, I think you're right." I nodded toward the house. "What will Sweetie say?"

"Sweetie won't say a word. She trusts me. If I say you need to stay with us, she'll go along with it."

Great. Just what I needed. A hostess forced into extending hospitality. I sighed. "Let's see if she'll feed us, and then you can give her the news. I'm sure she'll be overjoyed."

He chuckled and pointed toward the large barn door. Buddy and I headed out, but when I turned around, Sam wasn't behind us. He stood in front of one of the horses, petting its head and speaking softly to it. I waited while he said good night to both of the beautiful animals, admiring his tenderness with them. Sam Goodrich was different than any man I'd ever known—except my father. Was that why I was drawn to him? I made an inner vow to keep a little distance between us—physically and emotionally. It would be hard. His long blond hair glowed in the dusky light, and the muscles in his arms moved as he stroked the horses. The remaining sunlight caught the light golden hairs on his arms. His lean body moved with an unusual grace. I suspected it came from working on the farm. I couldn't call him cover-model handsome, but his looks were appealing, even though I got the feeling he wasn't aware of it. More importantly, Sam Goodrich was an honorable man. To me, there was nothing more attractive than a man with a virtuous heart. And there weren't enough of them around. I ran through a short mental list of the men I'd dated in the past year—every one a polished professional. Yet none of them held a candle to this Kansas farm boy.

Sam checked the padlocks on each stall and faced me with a smile. "Sweetie and I rescued Ranger and Tonto from a man in Council Grove who abused them. When we brought them here, they were sick, skinny, and afraid of people. They've come a long way."

"Ranger and Tonto? Like on *The Lone Ranger*?"

"You're too young to remember that show," he said with an amused grin.

"So are you."

He ambled over to where Buddy and I stood waiting. "When I was a kid I watched reruns. I used to pretend the Lone Ranger was my father—and Tonto was a wise uncle I could go to when I needed advice."

I stepped outside so Sam could close the barn door. Dusk was giving way to darkness. The light above the barn door created a safe, golden circle for Sam, Buddy, and me. I'd told Sam my secrets. Was it time to ask him to reveal his? I took a deep breath and dove in. "I hope you don't think I'm being nosy, but where are your parents? Why do you live here with your aunt?"

"You're not being nosy. It's a natural question." He leaned against the barn door and crossed his arms. "My mother died when I was young. I never knew my father. Sweetie is my mother's only sister. She applied to be my guardian, and here I am."

"I'm sorry."

He shook his head. "Don't be. Sweetie's been a wonderful substitute parent. I had a great childhood, and there's no other place I'd rather live than on this farm. I love Harmony and the people who live here." He smiled at me, but it didn't quite reach his eyes. "Really, don't feel sorry for me, Grace. I don't." He leaned down and petted Buddy on the head. "Now, let's see what kind of mood Sweetie's in. I swear, my belt buckle feels like it's hitting my spine."

I nodded and followed him and Buddy back to the house. I was glad I'd asked about his parents, but I'd noticed that he hadn't told me how his mother had died or why he'd never known his father. Maybe I was splitting hairs. I guess he'd tell me when he was ready. Right now, Sweetie's fried chicken and mashed potatoes called my name.

By the time we reached the porch, we could tell by the aroma that she had decided to have mercy on us. Sure enough, when we walked in the door, she yelled at us from the kitchen to "sit down at the table before I change my mind and throw this food in the trash." A few minutes later, we were eating.

At first Sweetie didn't say anything to me directly. She made sure I had some of everything on the table. After my second helping of mashed potatoes, she finally addressed me.

"So how do you imagine that silly vase of Ruth's found its way to your place?" Her tone was sharp and confrontational, but there was no condemnation in her expression. I got the feeling she was testing me.

After swallowing the bite of biscuit and strawberry preserves in my mouth, I met her fixed gaze, refusing to look away. "I have no idea. Someone put it there, and I intend to find out why."

After a brief staring contest, she lowered her eyes and nodded slowly. "Good for you. You might find it a little uncomfortable in town for a while, but sometimes you just gotta stand up straight and do whatcha gotta do. Backin' down from a fight ain't never the right way to go. You gotta face your adversaries with your head held high."

"Sweetie, I want Grace to stay here with us," Sam said. "Someone broke into Ben's place and left that vase there to implicate her. It's not safe."

His tone didn't invite discussion, and to my utter amazement, Sweetie didn't offer any. The disagreeable look on her face was either due to my extended visit—or because she had indigestion. I couldn't be sure, but to her credit she nodded.

"I'll put clean sheets on the bed in the south bedroom."

"Sw–Sweetie," I said with a gulp, "did you see anyone at Benjamin's house today while Sam and I were in town?" I patted myself mentally for finally spitting out the silly name.

She frowned so hard her two eyebrows became one. "What kind of a fool do you take me for?" she snapped. "If I'd seen someone snoopin' around your house, don't you think I woulda told you already? For cryin' out loud. . ."

"Now, Sweetie," Sam said in a soothing voice, "I intended to ask you the same question. Grace just got it out before I did. We're not saying you'd forget to tell us if you saw someone. But sometimes we don't realize until later how important some little detail might be in a situation like this."

"Well, I didn't see nothin'. I was workin' today. Not gallivantin' around town."

"Thanks," Sam said. "That's all we needed to know. And thanks for this great supper. No one cooks the way you do. Not even Hector down at the café."

Sweetie's face relaxed, the storm seemingly abated for now. Sam certainly knew how to control his aunt. She stood up. "You two ready for some of my apple pie?"

I was so full my stomach wanted to scream "No!" but I found myself nodding along with Sam. It was as if my head had no actual connection to my brain. Within a few minutes we were eating the best apple pie I'd ever tasted, covered with cream. I'd had apple pie and ice cream before, but never warm pie with pure cream ladled over it. It wouldn't be the last time.

Finally, when there was no way to put another bite of food into my body, Sam and I left to pick up my things from Benjamin's. As we approached the house, a clap of thunder exploded overhead, and I jumped.

"Hope you're not afraid of storms," Sam said. "In the spring, we get them all the time. Sometimes one right after the other. The farmers look forward to the rain—as long as it's not too much."

"No, I love rain. I just didn't realize we had a storm coming in."

As if on cue, thick sheets of rain began falling on us. Sam parked as close to the door as he could, but we still got soaked before we hit the front porch. It didn't take me long to gather what I needed. Before we left, I carried a lantern to the basement. I wanted to look inside the trunk where the vase had supposedly been found. It was still open, and except for a quilt that had been moved to one side, it looked just as it had when I'd gone through it the first time.

"The trunk was unlocked?" Sam had followed me down the stairs.

"Yes."

"And where was the letter?"

"That was upstairs, in Mama and Papa's room." It made me nervous to think that someone had not only been in this basement, but also in the main room and the upstairs. The entire house felt tainted somehow.

Sam closed the chest. "I don't like leaving the house un-protected." He shook his head. "In Harmony, we don't usually worry about locking our doors. I don't think I've ever thought about someone breaking in and stealing something as long as I've lived here. But now I'm uneasy. This house is way too accessible."

I reached over and put my hand on his arm. "Look. Whoever broke in was here for a specific reason. To get that letter and to plant the vase. I don't think anything else is missing, and I doubt they'll be back—especially since they know we'd be watching for them."

He stared at the closed trunk. "Maybe you're right," he said thoughtfully, "but some new locks and dead bolts wouldn't hurt." His face creased in a deep frown. "Grace, how could anyone know about that letter? I mean, I doubt seriously that Ben told anyone else about it. If he had, they could have gotten it before you came to town."

"I've wondered about that myself. I don't know the answer."

He turned toward me. "I might. I think the noises you heard last night were more than squirrels. I think someone was watching you and saw you read the letter." He reached over and put his hand on my cheek. "You need to consider the idea that whoever is behind this may not take kindly to your probing and prodding around for information. I'm beginning to wonder if you might actually be in some danger."

Although I already shivered from the chilled rain outside, his words made me feel even colder on the inside. Seeing my distress, he opened his arms, and I leaned into him. In the circle of his embrace, I felt safe. But I couldn't shake the feeling that right at that moment, someone else in Harmony had very different intentions—and my safety was the least of that person's concerns.

Chapter Ten

After a hot shower and clean clothes, I felt more like myself. I crawled into bed and gazed around the room Sweetie had prepared for me. Although only a guest room, it matched the rest of the house in charm and decor. Deep purple violets adorned the wallpaper. The thick oak furniture was delicately carved. A gorgeous lavender and gold Victorian rug lay in the middle of the gleaming wood floor. Flowers and vines decorated its edges. A fireplace with a thick oak mantel held a large basket of silk lilacs. I tried to imagine lying in this tall bed and snuggling down into the soft, stuffed mattress while snow fell outside and a fire crackled in the fireplace. Even though it wasn't winter, it made me feel warm and comfortable. Over the bed hung a beautiful painting of children playing in a meadow full of flowers. I pulled myself up so I could see the signature. *H. Mueller.* Still another painting by Hannah. After hearing that Sam regularly bought her work, I felt confident I'd find more of the young girl's paintings throughout the house.

I lay back down in the bed, pulled the thick, handmade quilt up to my chin, and stared up at the decorated ceiling tiles. The glow from a bedside lamp made the room seem so cozy and safe that the tension from the day's earlier events began to lessen. I listened to the rain pelting the roof overhead and prayed for guidance. One of my favorite times to talk to God was after climbing into bed at night. Everything is dark and still, and His presence seems so real. Although no voice boomed out of heaven with the answers to my problems, a solid sense of peace washed over me, reminding me that I am never alone and that my Father is never surprised by any turn of events. Nor is there anything He can't handle.

After praying, my mind wandered back to the intruder at Benjamin's. The rain had successfully washed away any clues, such as footprints or tire tracks—not that they would have helped us anyway. If my visitor had left something behind that could identify him, it would likely be inside the house, and I hadn't noticed anything that didn't belong.

My silent musings drifted back to Sam's embrace in the basement. Since then, he hadn't tried to kiss me again, and I wondered why. Did he regret that first kiss the way I did? We had no future. It was pointless to stir up yearnings that could never be fulfilled. Keeping ourselves in check was the only sensible thing to do. I let out a deep sigh that seemed extremely loud in the silent room. Then why couldn't I get that kiss out of my mind? And why did I get butterflies in my stomach every time I looked at him? Obviously, I knew the answers to my own questions—and they weren't acceptable. "Stop it, Gracie," I whispered. "Get control of yourself." I had no intention of creating any additional problems in my life. I already had more than I could handle. In two weeks, come hell or high water, I intended to head back to Wichita, leaving Sam Goodrich and Harmony far behind me.

I forced myself to stop thinking about Sam. My priority right now lay in another direction, and I couldn't allow errant feelings for some good-looking fruit farmer to interfere.

I turned out the light and listened to the rain for a while. Sam had asked me to go to church with him in the morning. At first I'd said no because I knew Ruth would be there. Finally, he'd convinced me that if I didn't go, I would look guilty. Reluctantly, I'd agreed, but I was having second thoughts now. How would people treat me? Was the story all over town? Even as a part of me dreaded confronting the accusing looks and whispers, my stronger, more independent side rose up in indignation. I hadn't done anything wrong, and I had nothing to feel embarrassed about. My parents had drilled several strong beliefs into me down through the years. One of them had to do with only playing to an audience of One—and that His opinion was the only one that mattered. I knew He wanted me to be kind and forgiving, yet He didn't expect me to accept condemnation.

I thought about Mama Essie and Papa Joe and how much courage it took for them to walk away from the town and the people they loved because they knew Amil Angstadt was leading his congregation away from the Bible as well as the tenets of their faith. I figured if they could stand up for what was right in such a big way, I could certainly attend church knowing my conscience was clear and the charges against me were false.

I flipped over on my side and had just started to drift off when I heard the door to my room open slowly. I turned over to see who it was. The light in the hallway illuminated the empty doorway. I kept staring but no one appeared. Great. What now? Ghosts? Suddenly, something hurtled toward me, and a scream escaped my lips. A hairy face sought mine, and a wet tongue licked my forehead. Buddy!

"You scared the snot out of me," I hissed accusingly.

Seemingly unfazed by my brief bout of hysteria, Buddy settled down next to me. I'd just put my arm around him and snuggled closer when the ceiling light suddenly clicked on. I turned my head toward the door. Sam stood there in a dark blue T-shirt that read ROCK CHALK JAYHAWK and matching sweatpants that had JAYHAWK printed down the side.

"KU fan?" I teased.

His tousled hair and "deer in the headlights" expression made it clear he'd been sound asleep. "I thought I heard you scream."

Even though I wore a T-shirt and sweatpants myself, my usual sleeping attire, I pulled the covers up closer to my chin. "You did. I was just attacked by a vicious beast."

As if on cue, Buddy lifted his head and stared sheepishly at his perturbed owner.

"Buddy," Sam grumbled. "What are you doing here?"

I quickly ran my hands through my hair, trying to rid myself of bedhead. "He's attempting to sleep—just like me." I smiled at him. "Thanks for running in to save me, but I'm fine. I can handle monsters this cute and cuddly." I stroked the little dog. "Please don't make him leave. Having him here makes me feel better."

Finally, the stricken look on Sam's face softened, and he shrugged. "Fine, he can stay, but only if you promise there will be no more screaming unless you're being mauled by something a little more dangerous than Buddy."

"You got it. Now if you don't mind?"

Buddy's mouth opened in something close to a doggy grin. Then he put his head down again.

"Boy, loyalty means nothing in this house," Sam said accusingly. "Good night."

"Good night." I watched as he closed the door. It felt great to know he was looking out for me. And having Buddy in the room only added to my feeling of security. "Thanks," I whispered into the darkness, "for two angels named Sam and Buddy. I know You're watching over me. Please help me to uncover the truth. I'm counting on You." Once again, I cuddled up next to Buddy and promptly fell asleep.

It seemed like only minutes passed before I awoke to Sam's voice saying, "Time to rise and shine, sleepyhead!"

I sat up in bed and looked at the clock. It was a little after eight. Buddy stood up, yawned, and then jumped down off the bed and ran toward his master.

"Sure, *now* you pay attention to me. When you want food and you need to go outside." He grinned at me. "Sweetie's making breakfast."

"Be down as soon as I get dressed."

He nodded and closed the door. I could hear Buddy's nails clicking on the wooden floor in the hall. I rolled over on my back and gazed up. The specter of accusing stares and angry murmurs from the citizens of Harmony floated like fuzzy visions across the ceiling. But the words of Jesus whispered louder. *"Peace I leave with you; my peace I give you. . . . Do not let your hearts be troubled and do not be afraid."*

I spent a few minutes thanking God for the day before me. Then I put myself into His capable hands. I rolled out of bed, grabbed my clothes, and made my way to the bathroom, as my slippers made a *slap, slap, slap* sound on the floor.

It took me about twenty minutes to scrub my teeth, change my clothes, apply some makeup, and run a brush through my hair. I'd brought one of my few dresses along. I usually wore slacks to church, but I hadn't been certain what to expect in Harmony. Although my simple light aqua frock was modest and thankfully hung below my knees, the apple-green dress that I'd seen in Harmony popped into my mind. I really wanted it but was worried that the Mennonite shop owners might think it was inappropriate for someone not of their faith to purchase it. How could a simple dress make me feel so insecure? I stared at my reflection in the mirror. "You can buy any dress you want, Gracie. Get the dress. You don't have to wear it here. Wear it in Wichita."

Having a quick talk with myself made me feel better. I would buy the dress. But I'd probably wait until right before I left town.

I picked up my T-shirt, sweatpants, and slippers and went back to the bedroom where I put them away. Then I made my bed and went downstairs. Sweetie and Sam were already sitting at the table. The smell of fresh-brewed coffee tickled my nose as I entered the kitchen. Sweetie got up when she saw me.

"My waffles are gettin' cold, girl," she said, her tone accusatory.

I glanced over at Sam who rolled his eyes and shook his head. I was beginning to learn that Sweetie's nickname smacked more of irony than reality. This woman was about the sourest person I'd ever met.

"Sorry," I said softly. "I got ready as quickly as I could. I'd never purposely be late for one of your delicious meals."

My statement seemed to take the wind out of her sails. She paused with a plate of waffles in her hand. "Th—that's okay," she said finally. "I'll have them to you lickety-split."

Sam gave me a thumbs-up when his aunt wasn't looking. I remembered the scripture that promised a gentle answer would turn away wrath. Wow. Obviously it worked.

Before long, I was full of waffles, bacon, and coffee. When Sam announced it was time to go, I got up and followed him to the front door. Sweetie stayed behind.

"Doesn't your aunt ever go to church?" I asked when Sam closed the front door behind us.

He shook his head. "She used to when she was younger, but I guess something happened that changed her. She encourages me to go, and she reads her Bible and prays. She just won't step foot inside a church building." He shrugged. "I used to try to get her to tell me why, but I finally gave up. Whatever her reasons, she's determined to keep them to herself."

I thought about Sweetie as Sam's truck jiggled down the dirt road toward Harmony Church. I'd met quite a few ex-church members like her—people who used to be part of congregations but had left for various reasons. Sometimes they'd pulled out because the church didn't seem to be meeting their needs. And sometimes it was because they'd been hurt. I couldn't help but wonder what would happen if more churches took care of the people already inside its borders instead of concentrating so much on bringing in new bodies. Numbers are great. I have no problem with large churches as long as they care for their members. But I'd seen firsthand what happens when people are neglected. I thought about a friend of mine who belonged to a small singles' group at his church. Because of work, he missed several meetings in a row. "Wow, Gracie," he'd told me. "Not one person ever called to ask me if I was okay—or to tell me they missed me." I could still see the look on his face. He quit going to that church. A simple phone call—a little concern—would have made a huge difference in his life. Jesus' admonition to Peter, "Feed my sheep," slipped into my mind. Unfortunately, some of His sheep seemed to be starving.

Sam turned into the parking lot at Harmony Church, forcing me to put my thoughts on hold. "Here we are," he said as he pulled into a space. "Are you nervous?"

I looked out the window at the people headed for the large brick building. Not one of them stared at the truck or seemed interested in who was inside. "A little bit." The scripture about God's peace came back to me. "I'll be fine. Let's go inside."

I waited for Sam to open my door, and then I climbed down carefully, keeping my skirt in place. He was incredibly handsome in his black slacks and gray striped shirt.

"You look really nice this morning," I said as I stepped out of the truck.

"And you look absolutely beautiful," he said in a low voice.

I felt the blood rush into my face and had to turn away so he wouldn't notice. He took my arm and escorted me toward the front entrance. Several people stepped up to introduce themselves as we entered. Sam told them who I was, yet no one acted as if they'd heard about my supposed thievery. I'd started to relax until we almost ran smack-dab into Ruth and her companion—Mary Whittenbauer. Their expressions made it obvious they'd been talking about me. Mary already had it in for me. Combining forces with Ruth made for a poisonous mix.

Sam's grip on my arm tightened, and he steered me right toward the two women, even though I pulled away from him and tried to go the other way.

"Hello, Ruth. Hello, Mary," he said, his voice a little too loud for my liking.

Ruth's mouth dropped open. Mary just glared at him.

"G—good morning, Sam," Ruth said after she regained her composure. "Gracie."

"Good morning," I mumbled. I fought a quick rush of embarrassment and had to remind myself that I had nothing to be humiliated about. "Good morning, Mary," I said a little more forcefully.

"Good morning, Gracie." She fired her words back at me like small, potent bullets.

I felt Sam tug on my arm, but I wasn't quite finished. A small fire of indignation burned in my gut. "I'm looking forward to today's sermon," I said with a smile. I directed my gaze toward Ruth. "Maybe the pastor will preach about the ninth commandment, Ruth. Do you know it by any chance?"

"Let's go," Sam said gruffly. This time he didn't try to gently lead me away from the women. Instead, he yanked me so hard I almost toppled over.

"Let go of me," I hissed once we were out of earshot.

He stopped in his tracks and faced me. His eyes flashed with anger. "Do you feel better now that you put Ruth in her place?" He shook his head. "Don't you know that you don't fight wrong with more wrong? It never works."

"She had it coming. Bearing false witness is a sin."

"So is not turning the other cheek," he said in a tight, controlled voice. "God is all about love and forgiveness, Grace. With your name, you'd think you'd have figured that out by now."

As we made our way to our seats, an internal struggle was going on inside me. Self-righteousness screamed that I'd been wronged, while humility whispered that no one was more wronged than Jesus—yet He had forgiven the world. Of course, humility won, quickly followed by conviction and its close friend, repentance.

Sam sat silently beside me. As the music ministers began taking their places on the platform, I turned to him. "You're right," I whispered. "I'm sorry. Hope I didn't embarrass you."

He let out a big sigh. "I'm not embarrassed. I overreacted, too. You only said what I was thinking. But we can't pay back evil for evil. It always blows up in our faces."

"I know. I'll apologize after the service."

"You pray about that. If you feel the need, I'll go with you." He put his hand on mine. "You're a wonderful person, Grace. You don't deserve to be in the spot you're in. I hope I'll be able to help you."

"Me, too." My eyes drifted past Sam. Two rows up, Mary turned around and glowered at us. I quickly looked away. "Mary may be more of a problem than Ruth," I said softly.

Sam grinned down at me. "You could be right. We usually sit together in church."

I turned toward him in surprise. I wanted to tell him that ignoring Mary to sit with me wasn't wise, but before I could get the words out, the praise and worship music began. I took one more quick look at Mary, but she'd turned her head toward the platform. As much as I resented her talking to Ruth about me, I felt uncomfortable knowing my presence caused her pain. By the time the music came to an end, I'd made a firm decision. Sam and I would have to talk about the reality of our relationship. That there wasn't one—and never would be. He and Mary would have to sort out their own problems. I couldn't be in the middle anymore.

As the singers and musicians left the platform, a man came up and stood behind the pulpit. I figured him to be somewhere in his middle forties, although with his receding hairline, he could have been younger. He towered over the retreating musicians by quite a bit. His thin frame and rather large nose put me in mind of drawings I'd seen of the fictional character Ichabod Crane. When he opened his mouth to speak, a rich voice rolled out. I sighed deeply as he introduced his sermon topic—"Walking in Love." In other words, God had my number. I could almost feel the target on the top of my head. By the time Pastor Jensen finished, I'd been properly spanked. I'd learned long ago that God disciplines his children through His Word. When a sermon reaches into your heart and shines a light on your wrong attitudes, it is the Holy Spirit bringing His loving conviction.

I was convicted all right. I glanced over at Mary. My visit to Harmony had disrupted her life. Perhaps it wasn't my fault, but my reaction to her situation *was* my responsibility. When the sermon came to a close and we were dismissed, I asked Sam to wait for me in the truck. I knew he'd offered to go with me if I decided to talk to Mary, but I felt strongly that this was something I had to do alone. He gave me an odd look but headed for the exit. I caught up to Mary just as she scooted out of the pew where she'd been seated.

"Mary, may I speak to you privately for a moment?" I put my hand on her arm and held on.

"I—I don't know. . ." Her expression reminded me of a fox I'd found caught in a trap once when we lived in Nebraska. It had taken quite awhile for him to trust me enough to let me open the trap and free him. I kept the light pressure on her arm.

"Please."

She sighed, and resignation registered on her face. "I suppose it would be okay." She pointed toward a small alcove to my left. I released her arm and followed her there. As she walked in heels higher than I'd be comfortable with, her dark, silky hair bounced in rhythm to her full but rather short skirt. I tried not to think about the appropriateness of her outfit for a church service. It wasn't my job to judge her. Especially now. When we reached our destination, she turned and folded her arms across her chest, her red mouth pursed in a pout. "What do you want, Gracie?"

I prayed silently for the right words, clearing my throat to give me a second to hear from God. "We seem to have gotten off on the wrong foot, Mary," I said finally. "I'm not sure why, but I'd like to clear it up if at all possible." I gazed into her deep brown eyes and saw the hurt and insecurity there. A wave of sympathy washed through me. "I'm not interested in Sam romantically," I said gently. "He's a wonderful man and has been a good friend since I arrived in town—but that's all. Whatever's going on between you two has nothing to do with me. Please understand that I'm not your problem—or your enemy. In fact, I'd like to be your friend if you'll let me. Like Pastor Jensen said, we're a family. We should act like one."

Instead of the warm reaction I'd hoped for, her mouth tightened and she stepped away from me. "I honestly don't know what kind of game you're playing, but I know Sam Goodrich. He has feelings for you. It's obvious. Maybe you don't return them, but that doesn't change a thing. We're engaged—at least we were until you showed up."

Well, I guess the soft-answer-turning-away-wrath thing doesn't work all the time. This certainly wasn't the reaction I'd prayed for. "Look, Mary," I said slowly, "surely you realize that if your relationship with Sam is secure, my presence won't interfere with it in any way. If you two are meant to be together, no one will be able to come between you—on purpose or accidentally."

"How dare you!" she huffed. Her face flushed an angry red. "I couldn't care less about your opinion on any subject. I understand stealing fiancés isn't the only kind of theft you're interested in."

My good intentions flew out the window. Anger coursed through me in a torrent. "Look here, you little. . ."

"That's enough, Grace."

Sam's stern tone caught me off guard. I turned around to find him standing behind us, Ruth at his side.

"But she said. . . ," I sputtered.

"This is all my fault," Ruth said, interrupting what promised to be a scathing report of the injustice leveled against me.

Her words stopped me cold. "Wh–what?" I managed to get out between clenched teeth.

Ruth reached over and took my hands in hers. "I said, I guess this is all my fault." She glanced up at Sam and shook her head. "Sam told me that you couldn't possibly have taken the vase. I've known him ever since he came to live here, and if there's one thing I can count on in this life, it's the truthfulness of Sam Goodrich." She squeezed my hands. "I can't say I understand how my vase got into your trunk, Gracie. To be honest, it will take a leap of faith for me to believe you had nothing to do with stealing it. But I trust Sam. And I didn't actually see who took it. Those two facts have to outweigh my suspicions. I have no choice but to give you the benefit of the doubt." She smiled at me. "Could you possibly find it in your heart to give me another chance?"

"Of course, I can. I'm not a thief, Ruth. Really. I would never take something that doesn't belong to me." I swung my gaze toward Mary. "Not on purpose anyway."

Ruth hugged me. "Let's just put the whole situation behind us, okay? You're welcome in my shop anytime. Maybe we need to have a cup of coffee together this week and get to know each other a little better."

"I–I'd like that."

A quick glance at Mary made it clear her anger was now not only directed at me but at her friend, as well. She mumbled something I didn't understand and stomped away, stopping to speak to a couple exiting a pew several rows away from us.

"Don't worry about Mary," Ruth said. "I can handle her. She gets pretty angry sometimes, but she usually finds a way to move past it." She put her arm around my shoulder. "I'm going to walk you back to Sam's truck." She frowned at him. "I just said some nice things about your willingness to be honest, Sam Goodrich. You need to do that now." She glanced toward Mary and then back at Sam. "You understand me, boy?"

He nodded, his face pink. "Yes ma'am," he mumbled.

Ruth guided me away from Sam and Mary. When we were out of listening range, she let me go. "Sorry to rush you off like that, but Sam owes Mary a frank talk. It should have happened a long time ago." She sighed and shook her head. "Mary pushed and prodded him into this so-called *engagement*. At first, Sam was too nice to tell her he wasn't certain about it. Finally, I think he just gave in. Sometimes when you live in a town this small, you can start thinking that your choices in life are limited to what's here. I think in the back of Sam's mind, he figured he might as well hook up with Mary because there would never be anyone else." She smiled at me. "Since you've come to town, he's started rethinking that attitude."

I started to protest, but Ruth pointed toward the doors of the church. "Let's talk outside. Esther Crenshaw is on her way over here, and she's the biggest gossip in town."

Over my shoulder I saw a woman with curly brown hair wearing a bright red dress and a large flowered hat making a beeline toward us. Ruth quickly pulled me out the door, and we hurried to Sam's truck where we stood on the side not facing the church. Esther followed us outside but stopped to talk to someone else, seeming to forget us completely.

"Listen, Ruth," I said when we'd safely escaped Esther's attention, "I have no romantic interest in Sam. He's a nice man, and I think we're building a friendship—but that's all it is. For goodness' sake, I've only known him for two days. That's not enough time to fall in love."

Ruth's round face crinkled as she laughed. "Oh, Gracie. My husband and I fell in love on our first date. I knew he was the man for me, and he knew I was the woman he wanted to spend his life with. We were married almost forty years before he died. And every single year was happy." She reached over and patted me on the shoulder. "Love isn't something you buy at the store when you're ready," she said gently. "It's a gift that can arrive all of a sudden—without warning. It can come at the most inconvenient time—and it almost never looks the way you expect it to." She reached up and touched my face lightly. "The worst thing you can do is not take the gift when it comes. It may never come your way again. Believe me, I know."

I stared at the older woman, unable to find the words to respond to her. Sam couldn't possibly be the man for me. Everything about him was wrong. Wrong kind of man. Wrong profession. Wrong town.

"I understand what you're saying," I said, trying to sound convincing, "but honestly, Sam and I are not a couple. Nor will we ever be. We're not a good match."

She smiled. "Maybe not. Sorry. Guess I shouldn't stick my nose into other people's business."

"It—it's fine." I cleared my throat and tried to offer her my most sincere expression. "Look, I want you to understand something. For reasons I can't explain right now, I'm convinced someone took your vase and placed it inside my uncle's house just so they could cast a bad light on me personally. I know that doesn't make sense to you now, but I hope to prove it before I leave Harmony."

Ruth's forehead puckered. "You don't have to prove anything to me, honey. But if someone was actually trying to set you up..." She shook her head. "You know, Benjamin Temple was the loneliest man I ever met. Now don't get me wrong—I adored him. His honesty, his compassion. But there was something bubbling below the surface of that man. Now you come to town and things start heating up." She studied me for a moment. "You be careful stirring that pot, Gracie. If it boils over, people can get burned."

Was she warning me or threatening me? Truth was, I had no idea who was my friend—and who was my enemy. Could Ruth have planted the vase at Benjamin's house? Maybe she put it there herself. And what about Mary? She had a good reason for wanting me out of town.

I looked around at the people heading toward their cars. Nice people. Friendly people. But someone in this town hid a dark secret, and I had no intention of leaving until I uncovered it. "Here he comes," Ruth said suddenly.

I looked past her and saw Sam coming our way. His face was set in stone without a hint of a smile. No sign of Mary.

"Let's get going," he said brusquely as he approached the car. "We don't want to be late for dinner at Abel's."

He opened the truck door for me, and I climbed inside. He slammed it shut and rounded the front of the truck toward the driver's side. A determined-looking Ruth blocked his way. The window on his side was rolled down, which made it easy for me to hear their conversation.

"Did you talk to her?" she asked in a firm voice.

"Yes I did." By the look on his face and the tone of his voice, it was obvious Mary hadn't taken it well.

"Good. Now you both can move on."

Sam grunted. "Not necessarily. She's pretty angry. I think I'll have to make myself scarce for a while."

"Nonsense. She'll come around. I'll speak to her. Trust me."

Sam leaned down and gave Ruth a kiss on the cheek. "Well, if there's anyone who can settle her down, it's you. But I'm not sure even your powers of persuasion will work this time."

Ruth's light, musical laugh drifted through the air. "Oh ye of little faith." She stepped out of Sam's way, and he slid into his truck. Then she leaned on the open window and frowned at me. "You be careful, Gracie. And remember what I said." With that she turned and walked away.

"What did she say?" Sam asked as he turned the key in the ignition.

"She told me I might be getting ready to bite off more than I can chew." I sighed. "I'm beginning to wonder if she's right."

"Phooey." Sam backed the truck up, being careful to avoid distracted churchgoers involved in animated conversations in the parking lot. "You can't give up now. You must be on the right track. You certainly caught someone's attention."

I had to agree with him on that point, but as we drove to Abel Mueller's, Ruth's admonition kept ringing through my mind. *You be careful stirring that pot, Gracie. If it boils over, people can get burned.*

Chapter Eleven

T his chicken is delicious, Emily," I said, taking another bite. "And this stuffing. I've never had anything like it."

"It's called *bubbat*," she said with a smile. "The raisins add a nice flavor, I think."

"It's wonderful. And these rolls." I picked up a round roll with another round knob on top of it. It looked like a little snowman without arms and legs.

"Zwieback," Hannah said. "Mama makes it all the time. She's a great cook."

"She certainly is." I smiled at Emily. "I'm amazed. How did you put together a meal like this so quickly? Doesn't your church let out about the same time as Sam's?"

"I cook Sunday's dinner on Saturday," Emily said with a small laugh. "We don't like to work on the Sabbath. So you see, all I had to do was heat everything up."

"Well, you're the best heater-upper I've ever met."

Hannah giggled, and Abel laughed warmly.

Thankfully, dinner was relaxed and enjoyable. Whatever had caused Emily to react so violently to me in the diner wasn't evident today. I'd been a little nervous on the way over, wondering if Abel and his family had heard about my supposed criminal activity. Sam had assured me that even if Ruth had wanted to tell Abel, there wouldn't have been any opportunity. Two different churches, two different schedules, not enough time. Hopefully, now that Ruth had removed me from the top of her suspect list, the rumor wouldn't go any further.

I glanced over to find Hannah's brilliant blue eyes fastened on me. She seemed intrigued by the new guest in the Mueller house. I was very interested in her, too. A girl with so much natural talent needed encouragement and training. Her chances of receiving it in Harmony were slim to none.

Abel's house felt cozy and welcoming. Not much different than my folks except for the lack of a TV or DVD cabinet. The Muellers had electricity, and a quick peek into Emily's kitchen revealed modern appliances. What Abel told me at the diner appeared to be true. His day-to-day existence wasn't much different than mine except for an effort to keep life simpler and free of outside distractions.

The dining room where we gathered to eat was spacious and homey. The large oak table with twelve chairs spoke of big dinners and lots of guests. Our small group assembled at one end. A large painting of Bethel Church hung over the carved oak buffet pushed up against the wall. On the other side of the room, I spotted another painting. A girl with a white prayer cap sat under a tree and gazed out at a lake graced by a family of swans. The figure was in the distance with her face turned away. I remembered Ruth's comment about Mennonite paintings not showing features or figures close up. Even so, there was something achingly sad about the image. The young girl had wrapped her arms around her knees, almost in a fetal position. I started to ask about the origins of the work when Abel spoke up and redirected my attention.

"Hope you saved some room for dessert," he said energetically. "My wife makes the best peach cobbler in Harmony."

"Oh, I didn't realize cobbler was a Mennonite dish."

Abel's eyes widened and he let out a belly laugh, his beard bouncing up and down. "Oh, Gracie. Emily made you some special dishes passed down from her mother and grandmother because she thought you might enjoy them. But we eat the same things you do. Emily makes a mean pizza, and I'm partial to Chinese food. We even drive to Topeka once in a while to eat at the Chinese buffet." He wiped his face with his napkin, still grinning. "And I doubt very seriously that the Mennonites can take credit for cobbler."

Hannah seemed particularly amused by my gaffe. I smiled at her. "I'm sorry. I guess I have a lot to learn about the Mennonite way of life."

"There's not much to learn," Emily said softly. "We're really pretty normal."

"I keep confusing the way things are with the way they used to be when Bishop Angstadt ran the church."

The smile quickly left Emily's face, and the tense look I'd seen when I first met her returned. Amil Angstadt seemed to be a sore subject to almost everyone who lived here.

"As I explained to you in the café, Harmony *is* a much different place now," Abel said. "During Bishop Angstadt's day, I doubt that our little town would have deserved its name. There was a lot of unhappiness in Harmony back then."

"My folks don't talk about it much," I said. "They believe in forgiveness, so I guess that makes them unwilling to dredge up the past. But there's still some anger and mistrust even if they don't acknowledge it."

Abel nodded. "I understand. In Philippians, Paul talks about forgetting what lies behind. But over the years, in counseling folks in the church, I've discovered another truth: that sometimes we try to bury things that aren't dead."

"What do you mean?" Sam asked.

"Well, in Paul's mind, his past had been dealt with. It was dead. He could look forward and knew that looking back would simply stop him from achieving everything God had called him to do. But sometimes people try to bury things they *haven't* dealt with. And when that happens, the past won't stay silent. It manifests in other ways—interfering with your life and not allowing you to move forward."

Abel's wise admonition appeared to be pointed in a specific direction. I noticed that he looked at Emily several times while he spoke.

"You've just described Benjamin Temple," Hannah said in her light, girlish voice. "I think something awful happened to him. He always seemed so sad."

Hannah had been so quiet throughout dinner that hearing her speak startled me. I smiled at her. "You're very perceptive."

"Benjamin isn't the only one," she said matter-of-factly. "It doesn't take much perception to know that Harmony is a town full of secrets. You haven't been here very long. Just wait."

"Hannah!" Emily's sharp tone startled me. She turned my way, her face flushed. "I must apologize for my daughter. She is at an age where a little drama goes a long way."

"Well, what about John Keystone?" Hannah shot back. She gave me a conspiratorial wink. "That man's hiding something all right."

"Hannah, that's enough. This family does not gossip." The seriousness in Abel's deep voice caught his daughter up short. It was obvious that when Abel stepped in, Hannah knew she had overstepped her boundaries.

"There certainly *is* something wrong with that man," Emily murmured under her breath.

Abel frowned at his wife. "I'm sorry, Gracie. For some reason, Emily has taken a dislike to our town's butcher. I have no idea why."

Emily didn't respond, but the look on her face displayed

something fiercer than dislike. What was that about?

I glanced over at Hannah. Just what secrets could she be privy to? Perhaps talking to her privately might reveal something that would help me find out what happened to Jacob Glick. It was a long shot since she wasn't even alive when Glick lived in Harmony, but I knew from past experience that many times children overhear things they aren't supposed to. Most parents would be mortified if they were aware of everything their children repeated outside their homes.

Hannah didn't respond when her father rebuked her. Instead, she pouted. Typical teenage reaction. I tried not to smile.

I had every intention of bringing up Glick's name again. After Emily's reaction at the diner, I was certain she knew something. But it felt wrong to do it now. The Muellers had graciously welcomed us to their home. Using them for information at the dinner table seemed somewhat impolite. I suddenly realized that I'd been plotting the best ways to use my hostess and her fourteen-year-old daughter for information. My stomach lurched at the prospect. Finding the truth was important, but at what cost? What lines would I cross to protect my father?

I tried to deal with my guilty conscience as Emily and Hannah cleared the dishes. When they'd finished, Emily brought out cobbler and ice cream.

"Why don't we eat our dessert on the porch?" Abel said. "Hannah, get everyone fresh coffee, will you?"

Sam and I picked up our bowls, napkins, and forks and followed him and Emily out of the dining room toward the back of the house. At the end of the hall, Abel opened a door and we stepped out into a large screened-in porch lined with pots of colorful flowers and plants. Lovely white wicker furniture with dark blue cushions and small white flowers sat against powder blue walls. A white ceiling fan turned lazily, moving fresh spring air through the room.

"Oh, this is charming," I said. "If I lived in this house, I think I'd spend every minute I could right here."

For the first time since I'd met her, Emily's expression completely lost its haunted look. She smiled widely and her eyes twinkled with life. "That's exactly what I do." She set a pot of coffee on a small, nearby table and opened the lid to a large cream-colored trunk that sat in front of a set of matching love seats. "All my sewing supplies are kept in here. I sit in this room almost every day and sew for hours." She sighed happily. "It makes me happy. When it's nice, I love to listen to the birds singing. But I especially enjoy rainy days. I feel so safe and cozy in this special place." She put her hand over her mouth and giggled. "I sound silly, don't I?"

When she laughed, I got a quick glance of the beauty she had once been—before some kind of sadness chased away much of her vivacity. Her dark eyes sparkled and her cheeks took on a rosy hue.

"I sound a little unhinged, I know. But this room is very important to me." She smiled at her husband. "Abel built this porch. He said I needed a room of my own."

Emily clearly loved the big, burly man who stood next to her. Although he blushed from the attention his wife gave him, it was obvious her joy pleased him. These two were still crazy about each other even after many years of marriage and a teenage daughter. I wondered if I would be as blessed someday as they were now.

I glanced over at Sam who'd settled down in one of the padded chairs. His expression as he gazed at me made me feel warm inside. I quickly glanced away and had started to sit down when I noticed something in Emily's chest. I put my bowl of cobbler on the floor next to my chair. "That material," I said, picking up a large, folded piece of apple green–colored cloth with small, white and yellow flowers. "I saw it in the dress shop."

Emily took it from me and smiled. "Why, yes. I made a dress out of this."

"You made it?" I knew dresses didn't just grow on trees and fall on the ground for people to pick up, but I'd never really known anyone who made clothing. My grandmother used to, when she lived in Harmony, but she only did it because it was seen as her duty. When my grandparents moved to Nebraska, she'd informed my grandfather that unless he wanted to run around naked, he'd better learn to buy his clothes from a store. Thankfully, he did just that. Mama Essie had also detested baking bread. Although she was a wonderful cook and baked all the time, she never made another loaf of bread after leaving Harmony. "For goodness' sake," she'd quip. "Why spend all that time on something when it's right there on the shelf?"

Of course, there were lots of things on grocery shelves she could have substituted for homemade—but bread was the only thing she ever skimped on. Papa Joe explained it to me once, after he made me promise not to tell Mama. Seems that when she was a girl, her mother had been especially hard on her when it came to bread making. In fact, she'd informed her daughter that if she couldn't bake a good loaf of bread, no man would ever marry her. And no matter how hard she tried, Essie's bread-making skills stayed woefully inadequate.

Then she met the handsome Joe Temple who didn't seem to know that rule. If she couldn't even find the oven, he didn't care. He told me he fell in love with the beautiful Mennonite girl with the reddish gold hair and flashing green eyes the first minute he laid eyes on her. Thankfully, my great-grandparents approved the union. Although marriages weren't actually arranged in their community, they had to be agreed upon by the parents. Joe and Essie weren't allowed to date, but they were allowed to attend church functions together and to sit next to each other at supper when the two families would meet for fellowship. Essie, on the other hand, wasn't completely sure about Joe. She'd laugh when telling the story about how one day she watched him pick up a baby bird that had fallen out of its nest. He climbed the tree with one hand while holding the bird in the other, and carefully put it back where it belonged. Joe had no idea that he'd been seen by anyone—and he never mentioned it. Yet he would stop by that tree frequently to check on the little bird's progress. Essie figured that if he could care that much about a baby bird, he would care even more for her. She was right.

Emily's voice startled me out of the past and brought me back to the present.

"This shade is perfect for your coloring. Perhaps you'd allow me to make a dress just for you?"

"Oh, my," I said quickly. "I—I can't allow you to go to all that trouble. I'll just buy the one in the store."

Emily's eyes ran up and down my body. "Nonsense. That dress is for someone larger than you. It won't fit right." She gave me a sincere smile. "It isn't any trouble, really. Sewing makes me happy. Please allow me to do it."

I swallowed the lump that tried to form in my throat. Here I'd been planning to use this woman for information, and all she wanted to do was to bless me.

"I would absolutely love it, Emily. I don't know how to thank you."

"No thanks are necessary. If you have time before you leave, I'll take some measurements and we'll talk about how the dress should look. I know our styles aren't very hip."

Abel burst out laughing. "Did you just use the word *hip*? And where did you learn that word, my dear?"

"Well, goodness gracious, Abel," Emily sniffed as she closed the trunk and rose to her feet, "we don't live in a barn. I *do* know a little bit about the world."

Abel's hearty chuckle filled the room. I looked over at Hannah who grinned at her parents' antics.

"I'm sure you do," Abel said with a broad smile. "I'm just

trying to imagine the conversation you had where this word was used." He stroked his beard and gazed at the ceiling. "I know. Perhaps it came from the widow Jacobs. She probably showed you her new support stockings. Or was it eighty-year-old Fred Olsen commenting on his newest pair of 'hip' overalls?" He sighed dramatically. "It's so hard to figure out. There are so many hip people in Harmony."

Emily lifted her flushed face toward her husband as the rest of us laughed. "You're very, very funny—you know that? Actually, it was one of the children in my Sunday school class. They told me I was a 'hip' teacher. Now what do you think of that?"

Abel leaned down and kissed the top of his wife's head. "I think they're absolutely right," he said gently. "You're the hippest person I know."

Emily turned on her heel while mumbling something about taking the material she held into the bedroom, but I could see the smile on her face as she left the room.

Still chuckling, Abel encouraged us to eat our cobbler while it was warm. The crunchy topping was perfect for the warm peaches dusted with cinnamon. The ice cream tasted homemade. It had a rich, creamy goodness that store-bought ice cream couldn't begin to match. Sam and I finished our desserts, and Hannah took our bowls and refilled the coffee cups. A sense of peace settled all around me, and I realized I was really enjoying my time in the Mueller's house. However, a glance at the clock on the wall reminded me that I really needed to call my parents. I'd originally planned to call them from Sam's, but it was later than I'd suspected. I was afraid they might be worried. I asked Abel if I could use his phone, and he led me to a small alcove at the end of the hallway where a built-in shelf held their telephone. I got my calling card out of my purse and dialed the necessary numbers to have the charges billed to my home phone. After a couple of rings, my father's deep voice boomed through the receiver.

"Hello?"

"Hey, Dad! It's me."

"Snicklefritz! It's about time. We've been concerned about you."

"I know. Sorry, Dad. Benjamin's place doesn't have a phone. I knew you'd be wondering about me—even if it's only been two days."

His warm laugh drifted through the phone. "I know it doesn't seem long to you, honey. But to parents, two days feels like an eternity. Now tell me what's happened so far. How do you like Harmony? Who have you met? Are people being nice to you?"

"Whoa. Too many questions. Why don't I just start from the beginning?" I told him about my arrival in his old hometown, but of course I left out the most important things: the letter, the theft, and the fact that I wasn't staying in Benjamin's house. My father seemed most interested in the people in Harmony. If I mentioned someone he knew, he'd stop me and ask about them. He knew Emily and wondered how she was. When I told him she was married to the pastor who'd called him about Benjamin's death and that they had a daughter, he seemed very pleased. He was interested to hear that I'd met Levi Hoffman but even more excited that I planned to spend some time with Ida Turnbauer.

"Ida and your grandmother were such close friends," he said. "I always liked her. An honest woman and a wonderful Christian. She encouraged your mother and me when we told her we were leaving Harmony. One of the few people who did. Please tell her we said hello."

"I will," I promised. "She certainly was shocked to find out that Grandma had passed away. Uncle Benjamin didn't tell her."

"I wanted to contact Ida when Mama died, but Papa said no. He still had some resentment toward a few folks in Harmony. I guess Mama tried to explain their leaving to Ida, but she wouldn't listen. That church. . ."

"Actually, it wasn't the church, Dad." I proceeded to explain the situation to him.

"Goodness," he said after taking a deep breath I could hear clearly through the receiver. "I guess I blamed everything on the church. Perhaps that wasn't completely fair."

"I'm finding out that most of the bad things that went on here came from Amil Angstadt. A lot of people disagreed with him, just like you and Mom."

"Well, more of them should have stood up to him. That man caused a lot of grief and confusion." I recognized the sharp tone in his voice. It meant *this discussion is off-limits. Move on to something else.* Life in Harmony had certainly left my father with some unresolved feelings.

I changed the subject and started telling him about Benjamin's house and the things I'd found there. I debated telling him about his old room, but when he asked about it, I knew I couldn't lie.

"He left it like it was when I moved away?" He repeated his sentence twice as if he couldn't believe what he was hearing. "I—I don't understand."

"I don't either, Dad. Maybe it's best not to try to figure it out. I—I mean, at least he kept all your things. M—maybe that means something."

With everything that had happened, I was certain Uncle Benjamin had truly loved my father, even if his decisions made it look otherwise. But my main proof was contained in the missing letter, and I couldn't tell my father anything about that yet. I could only pray that someday, when the truth came out, Dad would know that his brother cared deeply for him. After sharing with him that there seemed to be interest in the house and land, I informed him that we'd need a moving truck to cart all the family heirlooms to Nebraska.

"That's not a problem. I'll rent some storage, and we can put everything there until we decide what to do with it. When do you want me schedule the truck?"

I named the last Saturday before the Monday I was supposed to be back to work.

"Can't you put the sale of the house in someone else's hands and leave sooner? Maybe you could come here for a few days before heading back to Wichita. Mom and I miss you."

"I miss you, too, Dad. I'll visit you guys the first free weekend I have after I go home. I promise. But I really think I need to spend the next two weeks here. There's a lot to do, and besides, I really like Harmony. Since I'll probably never be back, I'd like to hang around as long as I can."

The silence on the other end of the phone told me that my father was having a hard time accepting my sentiments about a place he still held in a negative light.

"It's really different now," I continued. "The people are very nice, and the pastor isn't anything like Angstadt. He's more like Pastor Buchannan at your church."

"Well, I must admit that even though we only spoke briefly, Pastor Mueller seemed like a very nice man. I—I'm glad things are going well for you there. I'll have to take your word about the positive changes in Harmony. If you say things are different. . ."

"I do."

I promised my father I'd call him again in a couple of days. Now that I was at Sam's, it would be much easier to contact him. However, not telling him the truth about where I was really staying made me feel a little guilty. It suddenly hit me that I'd only been in Harmony a couple of days and I was already collecting secrets of my own.

I started to say good-bye when I decided to take the plunge and ask him the question I really wanted to. I prayed it wouldn't make him suspicious.

"By the way, Dad," I said as casually as I could, "do you remember a man named Jacob Glick?"

The deep intake of breath from my father was matched in stereo from behind me. I whirled around to see Emily Mueller standing a few feet down the hall, the same look of terror on her face that I'd seen at the diner. I told my dad I had to hang up, and I'd call him back. I didn't hear any response, but I knew I had to speak to Emily right away. I quickly put the phone down. I'd have to square things with my father later.

"Emily," I said in a low voice, "I need to know about this Glick person. I can't tell you why, but it's very important. Please, please, tell me the truth. Why does he frighten you so much?"

She lifted a trembling hand to her face and pushed back a stray strand of hair that had escaped from her bun. We studied each other for several moments before she spoke in a sharp whisper. "I don't understand why you feel the need to dredge up Jacob Glick. Why can't you just leave the past buried? It won't do anyone any good to talk about him."

My mouth almost dropped open at the use of the word "buried." "Listen Emily, as I said, I can't tell you why I need to know about him. But it's very important. People's lives could be adversely affected if I don't find out the truth." I frowned at her and took a step closer. "If you know anything...please, please, help me. I promise it will stay between us. You have my word." Even as I gave her my promise, I wondered if I'd be able to keep it. Eventually the truth about Glick was going to come out. Keeping Emily insulated from the fallout might be impossible.

I could actually see her internal struggle play out on her face. Finally, she grabbed my arm and started pulling me toward a door in the hallway.

"I'm taking some measurements for Gracie's dress," she called out loudly enough for her husband to hear. "Stay out of the bedroom."

"All right, dear," Abel yelled back. "I'm going to take Sam outside to see the garden. Hannah's with us."

Emily waited until we heard the door to the porch slam shut. Then she opened the bedroom door and guided me inside. It was a lovely room with lace curtains and dark mahogany furniture. A homemade spread covered the bed. Emily sat down on top of it, still clutching the material for my dress. She pointed to a spot next to her. I took a seat, curious yet almost apprehensive about what she was getting ready to share.

"Growing up in a Mennonite home was wonderful," she said slowly, measuring her words carefully. "We had no distractions like television or video games. We just had each other. I played with my brothers and sisters all the time—and we knew each other. I mean, really knew each other. And I read. A lot. I especially loved the classics. Dickens was a favorite. And *Little Women*. But then Amil Angstadt came to Harmony." Her eyes shone with tears. "Everything changed. I lost all my books. We were only allowed to read the Bible and certain religious books approved by the church. Children were supposed to work—to be productive. Playing was discouraged. It was worse on the girls. Bishop Angstadt made us feel that unless we were being prepared for marriage, we were useless. And he insisted that all engagements come through him for approval. I cared deeply for one young man, but the bishop forbade me to see him. It broke my heart to tell this man we couldn't marry." She sighed and wiped away a tear that slid down her cheek.

"Why didn't someone stand up against Angstadt?"

She shook her head. "Mennonites are taught to be respectful and submissive to authority. Many of the adults were confused. They were torn between their responsibility to the church and their concerns about what was happening. Some people did leave. Like your parents. Others met secretly, trying to find a way to change things, but they were faced with resistance by certain members who felt they were trying to personally attack Bishop Angstadt." She sighed so deeply her body trembled. "It was a terrible time for everyone."

"I–I'm sorry you had to go through that," I said gently. "But what does this have to do with Jacob Glick?"

"I swore I would never mention that man's name again." Her voice shook with emotion.

I held my breath and waited for her to continue. I could see my questions were causing her distress. After reading my uncle's letter and remembering something Abel had said at dinner, I had a pretty good idea what she was getting ready to tell me. On the one hand, I wanted to hear it. On the other hand, I dreaded the words I feared were coming, but I couldn't do anything to stop her. I had to know the truth. This was too important to me—and to my father. Finally, she took a deep shuddering breath and looked into my eyes. The raw pain I saw in her face shook me.

"Jacob was hired to do maintenance work around the church. Although he wasn't actually a member, he was almost like the bishop's second in command. Anyone wanting to see Bishop Angstadt had to get through Jacob first. He was always at the church. He even lived in the basement." She cleared her throat and stared at the material in her hands for a few moments. When she looked up, her face was pale—almost ghostly white. "No one else knows what I am about to tell you. I vowed I would never say anything, but I'm afraid you're going to keep digging until it comes up in a way I—I can't control."

I put my hand over hers. "Emily, please understand that unless it was absolutely necessary, I wouldn't put you through this. Glick may be involved in something that could seriously hurt my family unless I find out everything there is to know about him. I realize it seems unfair to ask you to tell me your secrets when I can't tell you mine, but if you could only trust me a little."

She smiled slightly and nodded her head. "I hope I can, Gracie. Because what I'm about to tell you could damage my family, as well."

Once again, something rose up inside me that wanted to stop her. To stop this entire thing. To go home and forget that Harmony, Kansas, existed. But somehow I knew that the secrets buried in Harmony were meant to come out. That the truth would set people free. Something Abel had said at dinner floated through my mind. *But sometimes people try to bury things they haven't dealt with. And when that happens, the past won't stay silent. It manifests in other ways—interfering with your life and not allowing you to move forward.* I suspected this was true for Emily. Maybe today would be the day she would take a step forward from her past. I prayed it was true.

I squeezed her hand. "I understand. Please. . ."

She grabbed my hand back with such force I almost yelped in pain.

"I—I was only seventeen. My—my mother sent me to the church to pick up some hymnals that were torn and needed mending." Her voice trembled and tears fell down her cheeks. "J–Jacob was there. He—he told me the hymnals were in the basement. I—I followed him down there."

She took a breath and held it. Without realizing it at first, I held mine, too. Even before she spoke, I knew what was coming. Then in a rush of words she said "When I got down there, he led me to a room—his room. And then he. . ."

I put my fingers on her lips to stop her. Neither one of us needed to hear the rest. I opened my arms, and she leaned against me and sobbed as if her heart would break. After several minutes, she gently pushed me away.

"After it happened," she said haltingly, "I ran to a special spot near the lake. I liked to go there sometimes to think. . .you know, to be alone."

I could only nod, afraid to trust my voice at that moment.

"I sat there for a long time, looking at the water, wondering what to do. Finally, I got up and went home. I made the decision to never tell anyone." She sighed. "You see, I was afraid. Afraid of what people would think about me. Afraid that my parents wouldn't love me anymore. Afraid Jacob would tell lies about what happened." She shook her head. "I couldn't stand that." She patted her prayer covering with trembling fingers. "I never went back to my favorite spot again. It always reminded me of. . . of. . ." Emily straightened her back and stared at me with a frank expression. "I'm certain I'm not the only one Jacob molested— or tried to molest. There were complaints, but Bishop Angstadt always protected him."

"The picture in the dining room. That's you, isn't it?"

She nodded slowly. "I loved to paint when I was a girl, but it was frowned upon in our community. I painted that picture at school after the. . .incident. When the year was out, I snuck it home and hid it in our attic. I should have thrown it away, but for some reason I didn't. I brought it with me when Abel and I married. Even though I hid it, he found it and insisted we hang it in the dining room. He said he was proud of my talent. I couldn't tell—tell him. . ." She wiped her wet face. "I don't know why I kept it in the first place. Maybe because it was the last thing I ever painted. I don't know. It was a stupid thing to do."

"So Abel has no idea what it represents?" I couldn't keep the incredulity out of my voice. "You've kept it to yourself all these years?"

Emily grasped my arm with her small fingers. "Yes. I hate that painting. Every day it mocks me. Reminds me of what Jacob took from me." Her fingers tightened on my skin. "I've wanted to say something—to tell Abel the truth, but I couldn't. Not in all these years. If only I'd told someone what happened after Jacob. . .um, left, but I was still too ashamed. And afraid. Of course, the longer I waited, the harder it became to confess. Now, I just want the whole thing to go away."

"But like your husband said, these kinds of situations don't just fade away by themselves." I tried to keep my voice soft and nonthreatening, but there was a sense of fury building inside me. Against Glick and men like him. And against toxic secrets that people hide inside themselves, ruining their lives. Was the church to blame for some of this? Are we too afraid to be honest with each other?

As if reading my mind, Emily said, "Please don't blame anyone in the church—except Bishop Angstadt. There were many people who cared about me. I alone made the decision to keep this secret. No one forced me to." Another deep sigh escaped through her lips and shook her thin body. "I realize now that I could have told my parents. They would have believed me. And they would have done something. Maybe the truth would have even stopped Jacob from hurting another young woman. I live every day with the guilt of my decision and wonder how much damage my cowardice caused."

"This secret has been kept too long, Emily," I said matter-of-factly.

She smoothed her hand over the apple-green cloth in her lap. "It's too late now, Gracie. I will not allow Abel and Hannah to be hurt by something that happened so long ago."

"But don't you realize that Abel already suspects there is something you haven't told him? Didn't you understand that his admonition about buried secrets was directed at you?"

Her head shot up and she stared at me with wide eyes. "No. He's never said anything..."

"Look, I'm not married, but I've watched my mom and dad through the years. They know instinctively when something is bothering the other one. It's a kind of radar."

"You know," she said in a dreamy voice, "after what happened, I made up my mind that I would never marry. The young man I told you about earlier begged me to marry him after Bishop Angstadt died, but I turned him away. I was convinced no man would ever want me—and I would never want another man. But then Abel came to Harmony. There was something about him. He brought out feelings in me I'd never had before. It—it was as if we were meant to be together. Although I rebuffed him at first, I finally realized I couldn't live without him."

"Oh Emily," I said with a smile. "I've only known your husband a short time, but if I've ever met anyone you could talk to about something like this, it would be Abel. Don't you know that about him?"

She was silent for a few moments. Then she nodded. "Yes. Yes, he probably is. But I just can't ruin his image of me." She turned her head and stared at me, her eyes wide and shiny. "I lost myself a long time ago, Gracie. The only time I feel real is when I see myself through Abel's eyes. If you take that away from me, I'm afraid I won't exist anymore."

"But don't you know that when God sees you, He only sees His dear and precious daughter? Isn't the reflection we see in His eyes the true image of who we really are?"

She smiled sadly and patted my hand. "I know in my heart that what you say is true. But my mind is still full of shame and sorrow. I will not allow Jacob Glick to spread his hateful venom to Abel and Hannah. I will not."

She spoke the last three words carefully and with absolute conviction. I had no response. She obviously blamed herself somehow for the awful thing Glick had done. She needed help—some kind of intervention. But I wasn't the one to provide it. She needed her husband's support and counsel. Suddenly, something else she'd said popped into my head.

"You said you were still afraid—even after Glick left town. That doesn't make sense. If he was gone, why would you still be afraid of him? He couldn't hurt you anymore."

Emily pushed her hair back again, tucking it under her cap. She straightened her back and closed her eyes. In a voice so soft

I could barely hear her, she said, "That's easy to answer. There was a new evil in Harmony. Something we'd never experienced before. I could feel a dark cloud hanging over the town. Our first murder. Our first murderer. I had no way of knowing if Jacob Glick would be the only victim."

Chapter Twelve

I sat silently on the bed while Emily got up and looked out the window. "Abel is showing off his roses," she said in a monotone. "He's so proud of them."

I finally overcame my shock enough to speak. "Emily. . .you know that Jacob Glick is dead?"

She came over and stood in front of me, her hands folded tightly together as if she didn't know what to do with them. "I didn't see him die, nor have I ever heard anyone else admit it."

"Th–then how. . ."

She sighed, picked up the material for my dress, and sat down next to me. "I really do need to take some measurements. You look to be about Hannah's size. Of course, you're much more womanly than she is."

I grabbed her arm. "Emily, how do you know Jacob Glick is dead?"

She smiled sadly. "A few days before he. . .disappeared, I overheard him talking to Bishop Angstadt. They were in the hardware store, looking for new door latches. I was in the next aisle. Mama needed a pot to replace the one I'd accidentally scorched, and I'd found some on the bottom shelf. I was crouched down, looking them over. That's why they didn't see me."

"What does this have to do with Glick's death?"

She reached over and patted my hand. "Don't worry, Gracie. I'm getting there." She smoothed the dress material with her hand. "Jacob knew something about the bishop—something he wanted to keep quiet. I'm certain it's the reason Jacob was free to do almost anything he wanted without fear of retribution. It's also why I was afraid Bishop Angstadt wouldn't help me if I went to him about what Jacob did to me." She shook her head. "I have no idea what it was. Neither one of them mentioned details. They simply referred to it as the bishop's 'secret.' Bishop Angstadt was clearly frightened. When Jacob demanded that he find him a wife, the bishop mentioned three women he might be able to deliver as marriage candidates, because he believed he had some kind of influence over them or their families."

"Who were they?"

"Kendra McBroom, the daughter of one of the church's elders. Her parents thought the sun rose and set on Bishop Angstadt."

"Who else?

An odd look crossed her face. "Are you sure you want to know?"

"Yes. Tell me, please. It's important."

"Beverly Fischer."

She said the name so matter-of-factly, for a moment it didn't register. "My—my mother?"

She nodded.

I felt my throat go dry. This wasn't welcome news. It gave my father a motive for murder. If he'd found out that Angstadt planned to auction off the woman he loved to a lowlife like Glick, he would have gone ballistic. At least now I knew what their fight was about. Then something occurred to me. "My grandparents would never have allowed it."

She shrugged. "Bishop Angstadt acted as if he could convince them. Of course, he might have simply been trying to placate Jacob. I don't know."

I almost laughed. At one time, Marvin Fischer may have allowed the bishop too much influence into his life. But if he'd tried to touch his daughter, Angstadt would have seen another side to my grandfather. When his family was threatened, Grandpa Fischer was like a pit bull with a bad attitude. "You said there were three women?"

"Yes. The last was a young woman who was trying to run her family's farm single-handedly. Her mother was dead and her father an invalid. Even though several people in the community had tried to help her, no one believed she could possibly succeed. Bishop Angstadt thought she would marry Jacob if she were offered enough cash to help run the farm and pay for an operation that might restore her father's health. Jacob seemed pretty happy about that idea. I think he was interested in this young woman above the others. He insisted that the bishop approach her. Of course, this meant the bishop would be out a great deal of money. I'm sure the prospect didn't appeal to him."

"But where would Angstadt get that much money? I can't imagine a Mennonite minister being paid enough to handle something like that."

Emily shrugged. "There were a lot of things about the bishop that didn't make sense. I overheard my father telling my mother that some property had been signed over to the church when someone in the community died. The proceeds were supposed to go to restoring the church building. But as far as I know, it never turned up. It's possible Bishop Angstadt intended to use that money for Jacob's bride. It's also possible that's what Jacob had on him. But that's only conjecture. Gossip wasn't acceptable in our community—especially when it was about our leadership." She took a deep breath and let it out slowly. "I don't believe in gossip either, but if there had been more honesty in the church, a lot of bad things might have been averted."

I nodded my agreement, but my mind was still working on Angstadt's agreement with Glick. Actually, blackmail gave the old Mennonite bishop a pretty good reason for wanting Glick dead. Although I had my doubts that Angstadt would go that far beyond his faith, I began to understand that my father was only part of a long list of people who'd wanted Jacob Glick removed from their lives. A thought struck me that made me go cold inside. "Emily, who was the third woman?" Even though I knew the answer before she said it, I was still shocked when she spoke the name out loud.

"Myrtle Goodrich. Sam's aunt."

I stared at her while I tried to sort this information out in my mind. Sweetie? Had Angstadt actually approached her? Was Sweetie involved in his death? I had to shelve these thoughts for now. I couldn't deal with them and concentrate on my final questions for Emily.

"Let's get back to how you know Glick is dead," I said.

She shrugged, her face expressionless. "I wasn't absolutely certain until today. But I suspected it because Jacob had Bishop Angstadt in his pocket and the bishop was preparing to give him the one thing he wanted more than anything in the world. There's no way he'd leave Harmony right before his dreams of companionship came true." She sighed and shook her head. "So many people hated Jacob. It didn't take much to figure out he'd finally been dealt with. After a few months, I began to believe that whoever killed him had no intention of hurting anyone else. They'd killed Jacob for a reason, and now that he was gone, they had no need to hurt anyone else. I was very young, and the idea of one human being murdering another was very frightening. I guess my fear came from the suspicion that a murderer lived in Harmony." She shivered involuntarily. "It still bothers me. It's like finding a spot on your favorite dress that won't come out.

Eventually you learn to live with it, but you don't like it. Harmony is...well, it's not a place where murder...belongs." She frowned at me. "Does that make sense?"

I nodded. "Actually, I think I understand exactly what you mean."

The sound of voices drifted down the hall. Emily paled. "Stand up and let me measure you."

I stood to my feet while she took a tape measure out of her pocket. She held it up to my neck and measured to the end of my shoulder. Then she wrote the figure down on a small pad of paper on the dresser. Next she wrapped the tape around my chest.

"Emily, did you ever tell anyone about your suspicions?"

Her eyes flew toward the bedroom door. "Shhh. No, never. After Jacob disappeared I felt nothing but intense relief. Not just for me, but for any other girl he might have hurt. I decided to leave well enough alone."

After writing down my chest measurements, she measured from my shoulder to my bustline and then from my shoulder to my waist. While she worked, I thought about the information she'd given me. I wasn't sure how much it helped, but at least it had opened up some new possibilities. Emily tugged on the tape measure she'd wrapped around my waist.

"Thank you for being honest with me," I said. "Hopefully, it will lead me to the truth."

She pulled the measuring tape to just below my knee, and then she stood up and stared at me, her features tight with emotion. "What I told you today is in confidence, Gracie. If at all possible, you must keep it to yourself."

"Sam is aware of the situation, and I trust him, Emily. What you overheard between Glick and Angstadt is very important and could help us immensely. I need to tell him about that, but I won't reveal anything personal about your...situation. Can you accept that?"

She studied my face for a moment. "I—I suppose so." She grabbed my arm. "But if at some point you feel you must bring me into whatever you're doing, will you come to me first? My husband deserves to know the truth before anyone else in Harmony."

I reached out and took her hands in mine. "Okay, but I sure wish he'd heard this from you before I did. Please—please, consider telling him everything you shared with me. I suspect keeping these secrets has cost you dearly. Isn't it time Jacob Glick stopped interfering in your life?"

A small groan rose from somewhere deep inside her. "I understand what you're saying, Gracie. I really do. But I'm so afraid. I love my life. What if the truth ruins it?"

"Jesus said that the truth would set you free, didn't He?"

"Yes. Maybe you're right, I don't know. But it must be my decision." She carefully put the tape measure back in her pocket and picked up the pad of paper, which she placed on top of the material. "I'll begin working on your dress tomorrow. It will be so pretty with your lovely auburn hair."

"Thank you." I turned to open the bedroom door. "Everyone will be wondering what happened to us."

"Wait a minute," she said. I stopped with my hand on the doorknob. "I've told you what you wanted to know. Are you going to tell me why it's so important to you? And how you've discovered that Jacob Glick is dead?"

I hesitated. "Not yet. But as soon as I can. . ."

"It's okay," she said, wrapping her arms around herself in a hug. "Believe me, I know what it's like to be forced to keep secrets."

The sorrow on her face touched me. "Why don't we pray that God will bring us both to a place of freedom, Emily? A place where we won't have to keep secrets anymore."

She hugged herself a little tighter. "I've lived with this so long. . ."

"Too long, I think." I took a deep breath and pushed the door open. "Ready?"

She nodded. "Thank you, Gracie. Telling you helped a little bit, I think. Even though I didn't want to."

I fixed a smile on my face and followed her down the hall to the sun porch. Abel, Hannah, and Sam were laughing at something Abel had said. Obviously their conversation was more lighthearted than the one Emily and I had just shared.

"Well, there you are!" Abel bellowed. "I was just telling Sam about the time Mabel Samuelson brought her sweet plum pudding to the church dinner but accidentally used salt in her recipe instead of sugar." He wiped a tear of laughter from his eye. "No one said a word because they didn't want to hurt her feelings. Until Teresa Harker's boy, Jonathon, spit his out on the table and said the pudding 'sucked big-time.'" Abel chuckled. "You remember that, Emily? Mabel was so embarrassed, but everyone at the table started laughing and it turned out to be one of the best church dinners we ever had."

Emily smiled at her husband. "Yes, I do remember. I also remember that Mabel's older son, Michael, had to do extra chores for teaching Jonathon that phrase."

Sam grinned at me. "What took you two so long? Abel and I were beginning to think you'd come out of there with your dress already made."

"Oh, you know. Girl talk." I looked at the clock on the wall. It was already after three. "Are you about ready to go?"

Sam stood up. "Well, if we don't get out of here soon, I'll probably fall asleep."

Abel snorted. "Are we really that boring?"

"That's not the problem," he said. "My stomach is so busy digesting Emily's fantastic food, the rest of my body is almost useless."

"I'm glad you enjoyed it," Emily said. "You and Gracie will

have to come back soon. We love having you here."

I turned around and gave her a hug. "We will. Thank you so much for your hospitality." Emily clung to me for several seconds. When we broke apart, there were tears in her eyes. I felt a deep connection to her and a desire to help her rid herself of the demons from her past. My dislike for Jacob Glick had grown to a smoldering fire. No one had the right to take his life, but something inside me couldn't mourn for him.

Abel and Emily escorted us to the front door with Hannah bringing up the rear. After saying our last good-byes, as Sam and I walked to his truck, the front door of the small yellow house swung open, and Hannah came running out, calling my name. I stopped to wait for her.

"I—I just wondered if sometime we could paint together or do something. . ." The words tumbled out so quickly I really had to concentrate to understand her. Her china blue eyes were wide and her cheeks flushed a delicate pink. Such a beautiful child. For a moment, I saw Emily in her. Was this how she looked when Glick violated her? My heart ached at the thought.

"Of course," I said, trying to keep my voice steady. "I'd love it. Maybe one afternoon this week? After school?"

Hannah nodded enthusiastically, and a smile erupted on her face that only added to her loveliness. "That would be wonderful. Will you call me?"

I barely got out the word "Absolutely" before she wrapped her arms around me.

"Oh, thank you, Gracie. I can hardly wait." With that she turned and ran back to the house, her pale blue skirt flapping around her long legs. She turned once to wave at us before closing the front door behind her.

"Hannah hasn't had anyone in her life who could help her with her art," Sam said. "Ida told me Emily was a pretty good artist as a young girl, but she gave it up. Lost interest in it, I guess. Seems strange to me—with a daughter like that." He shrugged. "But what do I know? I'm just a man. I don't pretend to understand women."

I swallowed the lump that rose in my throat and tossed him a sideways smile. "We're not that hard to figure out. We're just like you—only smart."

He swung the truck door open for me. "Funny. If you all are so smart, why do you hang around us?"

I climbed into the seat, holding my skirt. "Because God took one look at Adam and said, 'Wow. This guy's going to need all the help he can get.' And here we are."

He raised one eyebrow and cocked his head sideways. "I don't remember those words from the Bible."

"I'm paraphrasing, but that's exactly what He meant."

Sam laughed and closed the truck door. Then he got in and started the motor. "Did you talk to your dad?"

I slapped my forehead. "Oh man. I hung up on him. I need to call him back."

"It will only take a few minutes to get to my place. You can call him from there."

I nodded and stared out the car window. As Sam backed up, I noticed a car parked in front of a detached garage near the back of the property. "Is that Abel's car?"

"Yes. You're wondering why all the chrome is painted black?"

I nodded. "I noticed a few cars like that when I came into town. My father mentioned something once about Mennonites who still affiliated themselves with the old ways but felt cars were a necessity in today's world. They paint their bumpers dark so their cars won't look too 'flashy.' He called them 'black bumper' Mennonites. I just assumed Abel was more progressive than that."

"Harmony is a town full of all kinds of people, Grace. You've seen that. Old Order, modern Mennonites, conservative

Mennonites, non-Mennonites—even some folks who don't go to any church at all. Yet for the most part, everyone gets along. They care about their neighbors." He backed out of the driveway and pointed the truck toward Main Street. Then he stopped and turned toward me. "This is a special place, you know? It's not perfect, but there's something. . .unusual here. As cliché as it sounds, I feel like I found myself in Harmony." He grinned. "I know. I sound like a throwback from the sixties."

"Well, kind of."

He laughed. "Get ready to think I've really gone over the edge, but here goes. Ida Turnbauer told me that after Angstadt died, a bunch of the women got together and prayed that God would protect Harmony from the kind of divisive spirit that ruled this town during his reign. That God would bless this town with peace and make it a special place where people truly feel at home and treat each other like family. She believes He answered that prayer."

"Maybe you need to talk to Mary and John Keystone. I don't think they've heard this story."

"I didn't say people can't get angry and upset. I just said it won't rule. We've had our share of spats and problems, but I've been here since I was a kid, and I've never seen them go unresolved. Eventually peace comes." He put the truck in gear and started down the dirt road.

"Well, that's very interesting, but what does that have to do with Abel's painted bumpers?"

"Oh yeah. Almost forgot. Well, Abel painted his bumpers black as a way to bridge the gap between the modern Mennonites and the few Old Order folks who live here. He saw it as a compromise. Abel cares more about not offending someone than he does about how good his car looks. I think it's a great example of humility, and it goes a long way toward keeping the spirit of peace alive in Harmony."

I smiled broadly at him. "Oh, now I understand your truck. You're trying to be the humblest, most peaceful person in Harmony."

He burst out laughing. "Oh man. You're brutal." His hands caressed the old, cracked steering wheel. "Actually, I just like this truck. We're comfortable together. I realize it's an eyesore, but I don't care. I'll trade her in one of these days." He reached out the window and adjusted the side mirror. "You know, I used to own Levi's Suburban. His old station wagon broke down, and he needed transportation. He asked about this truck, thinking I might be willing to sell it since I had two vehicles. But I just couldn't let it go so I sold him the Suburban instead."

"You chose this truck over that nice Suburban?"

"Yep. I sure did." He winked at me. "Now don't tell me you're ashamed to be seen in this fine vintage vehicle."

"Heavens no. I drive a Volkswagen. That proves I have no ego whatsoever."

We both laughed. As Sam's truck shook and jiggled down the uneven road, I gazed out the window at the passing houses. Families were out in their yards playing together. Happy dogs ran around with toys in their mouths while being chased by children who screamed with delight. Old people sat in rocking chairs on their front porches, watching their antics while mothers and fathers cleaned their yards and prepared barbeque grills for dinner. Sam was right. There *was* something about Harmony. Something I'd never felt before—even in Fairbury. Sometimes I had the strangest sense that I'd been here before—that I knew this place. It was a passing feeling—one that came and went so quickly it was almost like a quick flash of lightning. I suppose it was seeing Mama and Papa's house—talking to people who knew my family. Whatever it was, the sensation left me feeling slightly unsettled.

My mind drifted back to Emily and my discussion with her. What was I going to do about her revelations? What should I tell

Sam? I'd promised Emily I'd do my best to keep her secret, yet I didn't want to lie to Sam. I settled on a compromise.

"Sam, do you trust me?" I asked more sharply than I meant to.

He frowned at me. "Yes. Why?"

"Emily told me some things I think will help us find the truth about what happened to Glick, but I can't tell you all of it. Some of it is very private—to Emily. Will you respect that and not push me for information I can't share?"

"I suppose so. If that's what you need me to do."

"Thank you." I began to recount the conversation Emily overheard as a child, leaving out her past involvement with Glick. I hesitated before actually naming names.

"I guess we need to find out just what Glick had on the good old bishop," Sam said. "We also need to uncover the names of the three women being dangled as bait."

"I—I know who they were."

Sam glanced over at me. "So tell me."

"A woman named Kendra McBroom."

He nodded as he turned onto Main Street. "Kendra married a man over in Clay County. I don't remember his name, but she has a sister who still lives here."

"Sam, my mother was one of the women."

He didn't reply, but he slowed down and pulled over to the side of the road. We were parked right in front of Levi's candle shop. All the shops on Main were closed except for the café.

"Your mother?" His voice quivered with surprise. He stared through the windshield at the almost empty street. "That could explain the fight your father had with Glick. If he'd found out about it. . ."

"But how?"

A look of confusion crossed his face. "What if Angstadt went to your grandparents and told them he wanted their daughter for Glick?"

"I don't think so. First of all, my grandparents would never have agreed to it. They fully supported my parents' relationship. Besides, I'm pretty sure Glick had someone else at the front of the line. I'd think if Angstadt had approached anyone, it would have been her."

"You mean Kendra?"

I shook my head slowly and stared at the dashboard. "No. From what Emily told me, Glick favored one woman over the rest."

Sam waited silently. Even before I could get my next words out, his eyes grew wide. "It's not. . .not. . ."

I put my hand on his. "It's Sweetie, Sam."

His face hardened. "I don't believe it."

"Look, it's hard for me to accept, too." I didn't tell him that I couldn't see Sweetie as a romantic figure. She must have changed a great deal over the years.

"Tell me everything Emily said about my aunt," he said, his voice hot with anger.

"Emily said Sweetie was trying to run the family farm by herself and that her father was disabled. Angstadt mentioned some operation that might help him—but that Sweetie couldn't afford it. He believed that if he offered her enough money to save the farm and pay for her father's surgery, she might agree to marry Glick."

Sam focused an icy stare out the window. "That's true about the operation. My grandfather's broken bones weren't set correctly. He developed a pressure ulcer that restricted his blood flow, and he died. If he'd had surgery to put those bones where they belonged, his life might have been spared."

"That's awful Sam. I can't imagine what your aunt went through. I'm so sorry. I hate the thought of dragging her into this situation and making her relive what must be the most painful time of her life."

His hands gripped the steering wheel so tightly his knuckles turned white. Finally, he released his hold. "There's nothing for you to be sorry about. You didn't cause this situation. Besides, now we really are in this together. You don't have to fight this battle alone."

I smiled at him. "I was never alone. God has been with me from the beginning. But even before the moment I told you about the letter, I believed He sent you to help me. After I told you the truth, I *knew* He had."

Sam turned in his seat and pulled my face to his. His kiss was gentle but determined. Before I realized it, my arms were wrapped around his neck and we were locked in a tight embrace. When his lips left mine, I looked into his eyes and almost gasped at the raw emotion I saw there. I pulled back and straightened up in my seat.

He scooted back behind the steering wheel. "I—I keep apologizing to you. I don't know what came over me. I shouldn't have. . .I mean. . ."

"It's okay." I felt something bold rise up inside of me. "I wanted you to kiss me, Sam. It's not just you."

He ran a trembling hand through his hair. "Look, I know we've only known each other a few days. . ."

"Two days," I interjected. "Two short days."

"Well, they don't feel short to me. I feel like I've known you all my life."

The sincerity in his voice made my breath quicken. I gazed into his eyes. I had to fight to slow my breathing and catch my breath. What was happening to me? I'd never felt anything like this before. "I–I'm not sure if I can concentrate on this situation with my uncle if I'm thinking about you all the time. Can we agree to put our feelings on hold until we find a way out of this dilemma? My dad's future hangs in the balance."

Sam's eyes ran over my face as if he were trying to memorize it. "Yes. Of course." His voice was low and husky. He ran his finger down the side of my face. "But once we figure this thing out. . ."

I smiled. "We'll talk."

Sam started the truck. As we pulled out in the street, I noticed someone near the entrance of the café staring at us.

Mary Whittenbauer stood with her arms folded, her expression full of naked anger. If looks could kill, I'd be breathing my last.

Sam's attention was focused on a passing horse pulling a buggy. In his attempt not to startle the horse, he missed seeing Mary. As we drove by, she and I locked eyes. And what I saw there gave me chills that even a warm day like today couldn't drive away.

Chapter Thirteen

What's wrong?"

"It's that obvious?" I couldn't remember anyone ever hating me with the kind of passion I'd witnessed on Mary's face. The experience shook me to my core. "Mary was standing outside the café. She saw you kiss me."

"Oh great," he mumbled.

"Maybe the next time you decide to get romantic, you shouldn't do it right in front of your girlfriend."

He gave me a withering look. "First of all, Mary isn't my girlfriend. To be honest, right now, she's not even my friend. Secondly, I'd like to draw attention to your use of the words 'next time.' I assume that means there will be a 'next time'?"

Before speaking I carefully measured my words. "It would be dishonest of me to say that I don't want you to kiss me again. But besides trying to stay focused on the business at hand, we've got to remember that I'll only be here two weeks. Do you really see any kind of a future for us?"

"You make it sound impossible—as if we're both immovable."

"But aren't we? You have a farm. You can't leave it—or Sweetie.

And I'm a graphic designer." I waved my hand toward the small businesses lined up along Main Street. "Do you see any advertising firms in Harmony? I have a great job in Wichita that I can't walk away from. Besides, I'm just not a small town girl. I need the excitement of the city."

His expression grew pensive, and his lips tightened into a thin line.

I waited for him to say something, but he stayed silent. I stared out the window and watched downtown Harmony pass by me while I tried to drive the picture of Mary's face out of my head. I'd tried to make peace with her. Of course, I'd also assured her I wasn't interested in Sam. At the time, I'd meant it. But what she saw today made me look like a liar. I wasn't sure what to do. Should I leave it alone or try once again to soothe her hurt feelings? My last attempt had been a disaster.

I forced myself to think of something else. There wasn't anything I could do about Mary right now. I tried to focus on the uniqueness of Harmony as we drove down Main Street. I'd never seen a town with so much personality. Every building was painted a different color—and each one had its own design. Whether expressed through brightly colored or plain exteriors, or store names painted with individual flare and imagination, the individual buildings somehow added up to a complete picture. A desire to paint Harmony welled up inside of me. I hadn't painted anything in a long time—ever since I'd started working for Grant. Perhaps Hannah and I could come down here together. It would be a great way to teach her the mechanics of painting. Not that she hadn't picked up most of it through pure talent and instinct. The problem was finding the time.

"What did you tell your father?" Sam said, interrupting my thoughts.

"What?"

"Your father. What have you told him?"

I sighed. "I'd just asked him about Glick when Emily inter-rupted us. I'm sure he's wondering what's going on."

We reached Faith Road, and Sam turned the truck toward his house. "You know, it would be helpful if you could get his side of the story."

"Without spilling the beans?"

He nodded.

"I guess I'll do what I'd originally planned. Just tell him I've heard stories about Glick and was wondering if he knew him."

"You don't think he'll find that the least bit suspicious?"

I shrugged. "Why would he? I've already brought up other people I've met."

"Yeah, but you haven't met Jacob Glick."

I slowly blew air out between pursed lips. "Well, in a way I have. It's like he's haunting me."

"Don't be silly. People aren't really haunted by ghosts."

"Well, he won't go away, and he follows me wherever I go. What do you call that?"

"Point taken." Sam pulled into his driveway and parked next to the house. "Listen, I know I need to question Sweetie about Glick, but I can't just go in there and ask her if he tried to buy her for his wife. Obviously, if he approached her, she didn't accept his offer."

"Maybe. Or maybe her father died before she had the chance to act on it."

Sam vigorously shook his blond head. "I can't accept that. She would never consider it. I know her. She's not that kind of person."

I reached out and took his hand, wrapping my small fingers around his large, strong ones. "Sam, if Sweetie could save *your* life, what would she be willing to do?"

His face took on a stricken look as he considered my question.

"I rest my case," I said gently. "None of us know what we'd do to protect someone we love. Besides, this happened years ago, and people change."

"I don't want her to think I don't trust her."

"Why would she think that? We'll just ask her if she knew Glick. Give her a chance to tell us on her own what we need to know."

Sam shook his head. "We can't keep asking everyone about Jacob Glick. It looks weird. We need a cover story."

The curtains in the front window moved slightly. Sweetie was probably wondering why we hadn't come inside.

"What if we say we found something of Glick's and it got us to wondering about him."

Sam frowned at me. "But that's a lie."

"Well, you come up with something better," I said with exasperation.

His forehead wrinkled in thought. "What about the truth?" he asked after a long pause.

"The truth? What truth? We can't tell what we actually do know—and we have no idea what we don't know. . ."

"Could you repeat that?"

I slapped him lightly on the arm with my free hand. "Seriously, what are you suggesting?"

"That we simply tell people we've heard some interesting things about Glick and we're curious about him."

"And if someone asks what we've heard?"

He smiled angelically. "We say we can't tell them. That's the truth."

I let go of his hand and pushed myself back against the truck door. "You know, that may actually be a rather brilliant idea. People who have nothing to hide will probably accept it as simple curiosity. But someone who had something to do with his death will see us as a. . .as a. . ."

"I think the word you're searching for is 'threat.'" Sam rubbed his hand over his face. "Suddenly my brilliant idea doesn't seem so brilliant."

"Nonsense. We don't have a lot of time, and we need to flush out the truth. This could do it." I grinned at him. "Besides, no one is going to try to hurt us as long as we're together. You're a rather intimidating fellow, you know."

He snorted. "Sure. I can lug around baskets of fruit with the best of them. If it comes down to that. . ."

"Listen. I think it's evident that whoever killed Glick did it out of anger. We're not hunting a serial killer. Sure, someone is trying to keep me quiet, but so far, all they've done is steal a letter and plant a stolen vase in Benjamin's house. If they'd really wanted to harm me, wouldn't they have done it by now?"

Sam stared at me glumly. "It's not like I work for CSI or something. And yes, before you ask, I've seen *CSI*. Truth is, I'm a simple farmer. I have no idea what the person we're looking for is capable of. I have every hope that whoever hit Glick on the head with that rock didn't mean to kill him. But that doesn't mean he isn't determined to keep his involvement quiet—and that he's not willing to do whatever it takes to accomplish that goal."

"I understand, but after finding out more about Glick, I'm convinced his death was a crime of passion—totally unplanned. I mean, who cooks up a scheme to murder someone out in the open where there could be witnesses? And no one *chooses* a rock as a weapon. It was used because it was handy."

The curtains in the front window moved again. Sweetie was getting antsy.

"Well, I'm glad you've got this all figured out," Sam said caustically. "But just in case your skills as a profiler are lacking in any way, I think I'll keep an extra close watch on you."

I stuck my hand out. "Agreed."

He shook my hand but didn't let it go right away. Finally, I pulled it back. "Sweetie's been watching us ever since we got here. If we don't get inside, she'll probably come out and drag us in by our hair."

As if she'd heard us, the front door flew open, and Sweetie stepped out on the porch. Buddy ran out from behind her. When he saw Sam's truck, he raced toward us, barking happily.

"I think this is Sweetie's way of telling us our time is up," Sam said. "Let's go. I want to show you something."

We got out of the truck and headed for the porch where Sweetie stood glaring at us with her hands on her hips. Today's overalls were cut off at the knee, and she wore a red T-shirt without stains or tears. I fought the urge to ask her if this was her special Sunday outfit.

" 'Bout time," she shouted. "I thought maybe you two was plannin' to move in there permanently."

"Well, we would," Sam said, "but you'd have to bring our food out to the truck, and I wouldn't want to inconvenience you."

"Wouldn't inconvenience me none, 'cause I'd let you both starve to death."

Sam quickly climbed the stairs and pulled his aunt into a big bear hug. "Now, Sweetie. You know you love me too much to let me waste away."

She pushed him away laughing. "Boy, you are a mess. A really big mess."

Sam leaned over to pet Buddy, whose joy at welcoming us home caused him to wag his stumpy tail so hard he could barely stay on his feet. "At least someone is glad to see us." Sam was quickly rewarded with a sloppy kiss.

He clumped back down the stairs. "Grace and I are going down to the lake," he told his aunt. "We'll be back in a while."

She nodded. "Supper at seven. I'm sure you stuffed yourself at Abel Mueller's house. I'm just makin' a fruit salad."

He smiled at her. "Perfect choice, Sweetie. Thank you."

"Shoot, I was gonna make fruit salad anyway," she grumbled as she went inside the house.

"I've been wondering about the lake," I said as I followed him around the side of the house. Buddy trotted after us, stopping once in a while to investigate a weed or a patch of dirt. We walked through the orchards. The apples and peaches were visible but still small.

"We'll start harvesting next month," Sam said. "It's a big job. I hire some of the boys in town to help." He stopped and pointed toward some land to the south of where we stood. "Those are our blackberry and strawberry fields." He smiled widely. "We have some empty fields on the north. We're thinking about planting pumpkins."

"It's wonderful, Sam." I could tell he was proud of what he and his aunt had accomplished. The orchards were beautiful. The trees looked strong and healthy and the fields lush and green. I breathed in the scent of wet earth and growing things. It was intoxicating. The city had its smells, too. Unfortunately, they weren't anything like this.

"The lake is this way." He pointed toward a row of cottonwood trees that stood about fifty or sixty yards away from the last row of fruit trees.

"Man, if your house is closer to the lake than Benjamin's, it must be quite a hike from his back door."

"It is. Ben's property is bigger than you think."

We trudged on until we reached the cottonwoods. A worn dirt path wound between them. The tall trees reached toward the sky, their thick gray trunks furrowed with age and nature. Puffs of cottony seeds sailed gently on the air like small dancers in an impromptu spring ballet. The white fibrous masses reminded me of large feathery snowflakes. I stopped in my tracks to watch the magical performance. Sam paused beside me as if he understood my captivation. However, Buddy ran ahead, oblivious to my sudden enchantment. When we finally exited the trees, Sam grabbed my hand and pulled me up next to him. A large azure blue lake lay before us, lined with cottonwoods and wildflowers. The flowers grew unchecked and added splashes of color against the green grasses, creating a soft patchwork blanket that surrounded the clear blue lake. A long dock stretched out before us, the wood aged and ripened by years of sun, rain, and snow. Sam guided me toward it.

"It's absolutely beautiful here," I said, awestruck. "I—I've never seen anything like it."

Buddy ran to the end of the dock and sat down, gazing out at the water as if he also found it captivating.

"I love it out here," Sam said softly. "It's so peaceful. I come here a lot just to think."

"If I was going to be in Harmony longer, I'd paint it."

"Let's sit here." He pointed toward the edge of the dock where Buddy waited for us. "I like to take my boots off and dangle my feet in the water."

I settled down next to Buddy who leaned up against me. We were becoming fast friends. I reached down to untie my shoe, and he quickly kissed me on the cheek. I found the gesture endearing and kissed the top of his head. "Thanks, Buddy. I love you, too," I whispered.

Sam put his boots and socks behind him, rolled up his jeans, and let his feet dip into the still water of the lake. "Brrr. It's a little chilly this early in the spring."

I swished my toe around, creating a small ripple. "You promise fish aren't going to nibble at my toes?"

His laugh was deep and warm. "I'm not promising anything. But if you catch one, make sure he hangs on until we can pull him out. Sweetie fries a mean catfish."

"Oh great. I didn't get a pedicure just to become fish food."

Sam frowned at me. "A pedicure, huh? You really are a city girl."

I giggled. "Oh, sorry. How do you country folks do it? File your nails down with a rock?"

He snorted. "Ha, ha. No, we use clippers. Believe it or not, they work just fine." He held his feet up to show me. "See? My toes don't look like they should belong to the Wolfman or anything, do they?"

Actually, he had fine feet. Large, well-formed, with light golden hair that snaked up toward his ankles. I noticed an odd spot on the side of his right foot. "You've got a nice scar there. What happened? Did you step on a rake?"

He shook his head. "No. Unfortunately, once in a while we get hunters who like to set traps around the lake. Hunting isn't allowed in this area, but it doesn't keep everyone out. I check the shoreline as often as I can for traps." He wiggled his foot. "I found one the hard way."

"You and I have more in common than I thought." I told him about living in Fairbury and the fox I'd released from a trap.

"Wow, Grace." His forehead furrowed with concern. "You took a real chance there. Most wild animals don't understand that you're trying to help them. They can be very dangerous, especially when they're in pain."

I reached over and ran my hand down Buddy's back. "I couldn't leave him there, Sam. I just couldn't. I took the risk knowing what could happen. Fortunately, it turned out okay."

"Well, I won't be taking you with me to check for traps, that's for sure."

A family of Canada geese swam past us, the little goslings struggling to keep up. Their soft gray feathers ruffled in the gentle breeze that moved across the deep blue water. A group of ducks squawked loudly from the other side of the lake. From their frantic bobbing, I could tell they'd found a school of small fish. As my eyes drifted a little to their right, I couldn't help but gasp. "Oh my goodness. I don't believe it!"

Sam turned his head my way. "What is it you don't believe?"

"That—that looks like a whooping crane!"

"It *is* a whooping crane. We've got all kinds of wildlife out here. Several kinds of owls, eagles, hawks, raccoons, skunks, possums, foxes, deer—almost anything you can think of."

"Wow. It's just incredible. I could sit out here forever."

"I understand, but unfortunately you need to call your father and we both need to talk to Sweetie."

"Maybe you should do that by yourself. She might feel uncomfortable with me there."

He sighed and swirled his right foot in a circle. The water rippled around it. "I don't know. It might seem strange if I approach her alone. Why don't we start a conversation tonight about the town and its history? We'll slide Glick's name in and see what happens. Hopefully, she'll open up and tell us something helpful." He stopped moving his toes and fixed his gaze on the duck family that had eaten its fill and was now gliding across the lake. "Maybe we should just tell her the truth. I mean, about your uncle and all. She might be a great help to us."

I hesitated a moment before answering him. I didn't want to offend him or make him think I didn't trust his aunt, but ever since our first meeting, I'd had the odd feeling she was hiding something. "Look, Sam. I don't think that's a good idea. I—I know you're not going to like this, but..."

"You think she's a suspect?"

I put my hand over my eyes to shield them from the sun and turned to look at him. "I don't know. I just think we need to keep our..."

"Investigation?"

"It sounds silly when you actually say it, but yes. We are searching for the truth, so I guess it is kind of an investigation. Anyway, I think we need to keep it quiet for now."

"I trust Sweetie with my life," he said in a somber voice.

"And I trust my father with *my* life," I responded gently. "But here I am, asking questions that could end up implicating him in a possible murder."

Sam cleared his throat and stared at his bare feet. "Okay, okay," he said finally. "But it would be nice if we could bring someone else into this who knew Glick. We're shooting in the dark here."

"Who would you suggest? Emily's already told us what she knows. She can't help us any further even though she suspects Glick is dead. . ."

"You didn't tell me that," he said sharply. "Why does she think that?"

"Well, think about it. If Glick was finally about to get himself a wife, why would he leave town? Emily told me she's suspected he's been dead all these years."

"But then why. . ."

"That's all I can say about that for now, Sam. Please don't ask me any more about Emily." I patted his arm. "I'll tell you everything when I can. Just trust me when I tell you that Emily has helped us as much as she can."

"Okay." He stared at the water for a few moments before suddenly snapping his fingers. Buddy took it as an invitation and moved next to him.

"Fickle dog," I said teasingly while I scratched him behind the ear.

"I know exactly where we can go," Sam said. "Levi."

"Will he keep what we tell him secret?"

"Absolutely. Levi was here when Glick lived in Harmony, and he knew Angstadt very well. He used to be one of his elders but got so disgusted with the way things were being handled he left the church. He was also really good friends with your uncle. In fact, I think Levi was one of the people Ben trusted the most."

"Well, if you think it's a good idea, it's okay with me. He doesn't appear to have any real connection to Glick. If we're going to bring anyone else into this situation, it should be someone who has no motive to want Glick dead."

He nodded. "Okay. I'll set up a meeting." That settled, he pointed at a spot to my right. "Look. You can see your dock from here."

"I have a dock?"

"Just like this one, only not quite as long."

I followed his finger. Sure enough, off in the distance, I could see another dock stretching out into the lake. It was almost hidden by the natural grasses that grew out of the water. I stared at it for several seconds, feeling unsettled for some reason. "I have the strangest feeling I've seen this lake before," I said. "It started when we first came through the trees, and it's even stronger now."

"But didn't you say you've never visited Harmony?"

"Yes. I've never been here. I have no idea why it seems so familiar."

He smiled. "Déjà vu. You've been somewhere else that reminds you of this place. Have you spent much time at any other lake?"

"Yes. Near Fairbury where we used to live. My dad took us camping and fishing there."

"That's probably it."

"Does this lake have a name?"

Sam laughed. "Well, the early Indians who settled here called it Trouble Lake."

"What an odd name. Not very fitting for this beautiful, peaceful spot."

"Actually, it is. The Indians believed that when they came here and bathed in the water, their troubles were washed away."

I gazed out on the tranquil scene. "Wow. That's inspiring. Maybe if I floated for a few hours. . ."

Sam grinned. "I'm afraid you'd only get waterlogged."

"That's probably true." I glanced at my watch. "I've really got to call my dad. It wasn't fair to drop Glick's name and then hang up on him." I reluctantly took my feet out of the water and began pulling on my socks. "When we talk to Levi, let's start off asking him what he knows about Glick. If we don't get what we want from that, then we'll drop the bombshell. But only after he promises to keep what we tell him to himself."

Sam slid his socks on. "Okay, but I really think we can trust him with the whole story, Grace. I just hope he can point us in the right direction. I sure think it's worth a try." He finished pulling on his boots and stood up, holding out his hand to help me to my feet. Buddy ran halfway up the dock and turned around to look at us as if he was wondering why we were so slow.

"The idea of actually telling someone else is a little scary," I said. "But we only have two weeks. I guess we have no choice."

Sam nodded. "Let's get you to a phone. And don't forget our strategy at supper."

I followed him and Buddy back to the house. Were we making a mistake telling Levi about Benjamin's letter? I couldn't see any other option. At the end of two weeks, I would have to do something. If I couldn't discover some information that would help my father, the situation could head in a terrible direction. One that I didn't want to face.

Sam led me to the back of the house and opened a door into a screened-in porch. It reminded me a lot of Emily's. He laughed at the expression on my face.

"Look familiar? This is where Emily got the idea for her porch. She fell in love with this one and told Abel. He came out and looked at it and built a similar one for her."

"Does Emily spend a lot of time here?" I couldn't see Emily and Sweetie as close friends.

"Oh, she probably drops by a couple times a month at least." Sam checked a large potted plant near the corner windows. Then he picked up a nearby watering can and added some moisture to the huge green fern. I almost laughed. I had a fern in my apartment that looked like some kind of sickly cousin to this one. And I'd thought mine was pretty healthy. Obviously I'd been deluded. "Sweetie and I hire some of the teenagers from the church to help during harvest—and for a few other chores around here. Abel and Emily drop by to make sure they're working hard." He flashed me a big grin. "Sweetie and Emily actually like each other very much. Emily loves this house, and Sweetie loves to show it off. I guess when people find something they have in common, anyone can forge a friendship."

"I guess so." Spending time in Harmony had begun to change the way I looked at people. I was beginning to see that I didn't have everything and everyone all figured out after all. I watched Sam examine some of the other plants and couldn't help but once again compare him to the men I knew in Wichita. Sam was intelligent, compassionate, courteous—and he really listened when I talked. My last date had spent the entire evening talking about himself. The only chance I'd had to speak came when he occasionally took a breath, and even then I'd felt he was just waiting for me to finish so he could launch into another boring story about his supposed success as a copywriter at another advertising agency in town.

"You'd better call your dad," Sam said after inspecting several of the pots scattered around the room.

I nodded. "My dad and your aunt in one day. It's a lot to face."

"Well, at least it should be interesting," he said as he opened the door into the main house.

I walked past, brushing against him as I stepped up into the kitchen. He smelled of aftershave and the outdoors. My mind went back to our kiss in the truck, and I felt my cheeks grow hot. I hurried ahead of him so he wouldn't see how much he affected me.

"Why don't you use the phone in the study?" he said. "It's down the hall and to your left."

Without turning around or acknowledging him, I followed

his instructions. The first door on the left opened into a beautiful room lined with tall oak bookshelves. Against the back wall, long windows looked out on the orchards. Two leather, high-backed chairs sat near a wood-burning fireplace in the corner of the room. An intricately carved wood mantel above the fireplace held several framed pictures. I moved closer so I could see them. In the first, a young boy held the hand of a handsome woman who smiled at the camera. I realized with a start that the boy was Sam and the woman was Sweetie. Sam's long blond hair almost covered one eye. Although he smiled for the camera, his eyes held a deep sadness. The picture must have been taken not long after he came to live with his aunt. I stared at Sweetie's picture. I guessed her to be in her late thirties. Curly amber-colored hair cascaded down to her shoulders. Her large dark eyes held the guarded look I'd come to know. The next picture was a head shot of an achingly beautiful woman with sandy hair and bright blue eyes. Sam's features were unmistakable. His mother. I stared at her for several seconds. A quick look through several of the other framed photographs showed no shots of her with a man. Where was Sam's father?

The rest of the pictures were of people I didn't recognize, although I suspected that a portrait of an elderly couple was of Sam's grandparents. The very last picture caught my attention. A young woman with blond hair piled up on her head smiled at the camera. Although I almost couldn't believe it, I realized it was an earlier photo of Sweetie. She had to have been in her late teens or early twenties. She was breathtaking. In her large, luminous eyes I detected no hint of the hardness that would change her. I saw only happiness. This picture must have been taken before her father's accident. Had that loss changed her into the gruff, suspicious woman she had become? Or could it have been something else? Had Jacob Glick's touch of evil driven the hope from her life?

I found the phone on top of a large mahogany desk. I slid into the leather chair behind the desk and dialed my dad's number. He answered on the first ring.

"I'm sorry I had to hang up so fast, Dad," I said quickly. "We were having lunch at the pastor's house and. . ."

"Why in the world did you ask me about Jacob Glick? Where did you hear that name?"

My dad's sharp tone startled me. I thought back quickly to my conversation with Sam. I needed to sound nonchalant without actually lying to my father. "I've been hearing lots of names, Dad. His was just one of them. It seems he wasn't a very nice man."

I waited quietly for my father to respond but was greeted with total silence. "Dad?" I said finally. "Are you there?"

"Is that man back in Harmony? Has he approached you, Grace Marie?"

My dad had called me by both my given names—a sign that at that moment he was as serious as he could possibly get. And he'd asked if Glick had come back to Harmony. He had no idea the man was dead. My knees felt weak. If I hadn't already been sitting down, I think I would have collapsed. I trusted my father, but a little corner of my brain had held on to a small pocket of fear—fear that my father had been someone else once. Someone I didn't know. I knew now, beyond a shadow of a doubt, that he was completely innocent of Glick's death.

"N–no, Dad. He's not here. I guess he left not long after you did."

"Well, thank God for that. He was a terrible man. He's the only person I ever hit, Gracie. I'm not proud of it. I don't believe in violence. Never have. But that man. . ."

"What did he do?"

"It doesn't matter. I don't want to talk about it."

"I'm twenty-three years old, you know. Not a baby."

"I know that."

My dad's stern voice didn't welcome any further challenge.

But with what was at stake, I took a chance and pressed on. "Someone told me he was a little too friendly with the girls in Harmony. For you to hit him, he must have made a move on Mom."

My dad's exasperated sigh echoed loudly through the receiver. "Why in the world is this important to you? If Jacob is gone, who cares what he did or didn't do?"

If I could tell my father what Glick had done to Emily Mueller, he'd probably tell me whatever I wanted to know. But I couldn't do that. "Look, I'm just interested, that's all. Sam's been showing me around town, and I'm learning all kinds of things about Harmony—past and present. Jacob Glick is just one of the people whose name came up. Why are you so defensive?"

He sighed again. "I don't know. Jacob is a part of the past I'd like to forget. I suppose if it's important to you, I can try to remember whatever I can. I haven't thought about the man in over thirty years."

"Well, it's not *important* really. I'm just curious."

"Okay, okay. He was the maintenance man for our church, but he spent most of his time skulking around town, following young girls, and being a general nuisance. He bothered your mother on more than one occasion, even though he knew we were seeing each other." He paused for a moment as if gathering his thoughts. "There were rumors that he'd been extremely inappropriate. You know, actually grabbing some of the ladies in town. I have no idea if that's true. My parents didn't discuss unpleasant things in front of my brother and me, so what I know is only through rumors."

"But why did you get in a fight with him?"

"The night before your mother and I left Harmony, we were supposed to meet in a small clearing in the trees behind my house. Even though our parents and a few other people knew we were going away to get married, we didn't want too many people involved. If Bishop Angstadt found out, he would have

196

exerted great pressure on our families to stop us. When I arrived at the spot where I was to meet your mother, I found Jacob hiding behind a tree, watching her. He'd been bothering her for months. She'd had to rebuff him more than once. I'd warned him to stay away from her. When I confronted him, he told us he knew what we were planning and he intended to tell Angstadt. I guess everything just boiled up inside me. I hauled off and slugged him so hard I bruised my knuckles."

"Your—your knuckles? You hit him with your fist?"

He snorted. "Of course I did. What did you think I'd hit him with?"

"Not a rock," I mumbled to myself, not realizing my father could hear me. He hadn't hit him with a rock at all. That meant. . .

"A rock?" Dad said. "Of course not. I only wanted to stop him from bothering Beverly. I wasn't trying to kill him, Gracie. Goodness gracious. You sure get some funny ideas. Must be all that television. . ."

"Okay, Dad. I get it." I didn't have time for another lecture on the evils of television. Boy, he and Abel were like twins when it came to that subject.

"All right," he said. "I told you about Jacob Glick. Now, who's Sam?"

I launched into a narrative about Sam and Sweetie, leaving out that I was staying with them.

"You say this Sweetie person has been in Harmony for a while?" He sounded puzzled. "I don't remember anyone with that name. It's certainly not a name I'd likely forget."

"Her real name is Myrtle, Dad. Myrtle Goodrich."

"Oh my goodness gracious. Myrtle Goodrich. Wow. She's still there? I figured she'd left after her father passed away."

I told him about the farm and the house she'd renovated. I also explained that she'd taken Sam in when he was a boy.

"Well, that's very interesting," he said softly. "I always felt so sorry for Myrtle. I didn't really know her very well, but the whole town was aware of her plight. I'm really happy to hear she's made something of herself and overcome her past." I heard him move the phone away from his mouth and say something I couldn't make out. Then he laughed into the receiver. "Honey, your mother is pestering me to give her the phone. I'm going to hand you over. You call us back again in a couple of days, okay?"

"Okay, Dad. I love you."

"I love you, too, Snicklefritz."

I talked to my mom for another ten minutes before we finally hung up. I put the receiver down and stared at the phone for quite some time, trying to turn over the information I'd gotten from my dad. He'd hit Glick with his fist. My father hadn't killed Glick at all—on purpose or accidentally. I felt as if a major weight had been lifted off me. I started to get up to find Sam, when the door to the study swung open and he came inside.

"Are you finished?" he asked.

I nodded and motioned to him to close the door. He latched it and came over, sitting down in a chair near the desk. I told him everything I'd learned from my father.

"So you see," I said when I'd finished, "my father not only doesn't know Glick is dead, but he couldn't possibly have killed him. Dad didn't hit him with a rock, Sam. Someone else did that. Someone else killed Jacob Glick."

Sam studied me for a moment. "And you believe your father told you the truth?"

I nodded. "I know him better than I know myself. I'm convinced of it."

He shrugged. "That's good enough for me." He sat forward in the chair and put his head in his hands. "Glick never made it from the spot where your father hit him. So if we can figure out who met Glick in the clearing after your father and mother left and before Ben found him, we've got our murderer." He straightened up and frowned at me, his face creased with concern. "Since we know your father didn't accidentally kill Glick, I think the person who hit him with that rock probably intended to kill him, Grace. They probably saw your dad hit him—and then when your parents left, they picked up a rock and finished him off. I suspect Glick was a little woozy after being punched in the face. Most likely, that made it much easier to approach him."

"That makes sense," I said, thinking it over. "The problem is that no one we've talked to actually saw who hit him. I'm beginning to think our only chance at finding the truth is to discover the identity of the person who took my letter and planted Ruth's vase at Benjamin's. That person must be the real killer."

Without warning, a side door to the library opened and Sweetie stepped in, holding something in her hand. "I can't help you with Ruth's vase, and I can't help you figger out who killed that stinkin' varmit Jacob Glick. But I can tell you exactly who stole your letter." She walked over and slammed the papers she held in her hand onto the desktop right in front of me. "It was me. I took your blasted letter."

Chapter Fourteen

I had no intention of ever talkin' 'bout this. I'd hoped it was dead and buried. . .just like that miserable old letch Jacob Glick."

Sam and I sat quietly at the kitchen table. Sweetie had refused to explain her surprising admission until she was ready. She'd ordered us into the kitchen where we sat waiting while she scooped out three bowls of fruit salad and shoved them in front of us. The salad looked and smelled delicious, but my appetite had vanished. From the somber expression on Sam's face, it was evident he felt the same way.

After her comment, Sweetie stared at me as if I might want to respond, but for the life of me, I couldn't think of a single thing to say. Her shocking revelation seemed to have affected my ability to voice anything coherent, so I simply nodded. She took it as a sign to continue.

"I barely knew Jacob. I only seen him when I went to town. Didn't go to that church where he worked or nothin', so there weren't much call for me to run into him." She sighed and shook her head. "Whenever I did cross his path, that man always gave me the willies. He had a look in his eyes that was. . .well, *lustful* is the best word I can come up with. I tried to keep my distance from him. My daddy told me not to ever give him a reason to approach me." Her features softened, and for just a moment I saw a quick flash of the young woman I'd seen in the pictures on the mantel. But instantly her expression hardened, and Sweetie was back.

"But...but what does this have to do with why you took Grace's letter?" Sam's harsh tone caused his aunt to glower at him.

"I'll get to that, boy. You need to hush up and let me tell the story my way. It's the only way you're gonna get it. You understand?"

"Whatever." Sam shrugged, then jabbed a forkful of salad and shoved it into his mouth.

"Anyways," she continued, "I kept to my daddy's advice, but every time I seen Jacob in town, he'd watch me with those sharp, beady eyes of his. After a while I got kinda used to it. And then my daddy had his accident. I didn't make it to town much 'cause I was takin' care of him after he came back home." She stared at the tablecloth as if she could see the past woven into its design. "Several of the nearby farmers helped me, tryin' to take care of our fields. Some folks from town came with food and medical supplies." Her voice caught. "Your grandma and grandpa were there for me almost every day, Gracie. Along with Levi and the Turnbauers. Good people. But then that Angstadt fellow started comin' around. Not too often, but even a little of that man was too much for me. I always felt like he was checkin' me out, you know? Pretending he wanted to help—but like he had another motive hidin' behind his fake smile."

She paused for a moment before she rose from her chair and grabbed the iced-tea pitcher from the counter. She refilled her glass and Sam's. I hadn't even touched mine. When she finished, she sat back down with a grunt.

"Well, Daddy just got worse and worse. The doc from Council Grove came out to check on him. He's the one who told me Daddy's bones hadn't set quite right. Unless he had an operation to fix them proper, he could die. Had to do with the way the blood flowed through his body. I didn't have no money, and I couldn't figger out a way to get it quick enough. I thought about sellin' the farm, but that would take time—time Daddy didn't have."

"We know about the deal Angstadt offered you," I said gently. "He'd give you the money for the operation if you'd marry Jacob Glick."

Sweetie's eyes grew wide. "Now how in tarnation did you hear about that?"

I started at the beginning, from reading the letter, to deciding to tell Sam the truth. I finished with the conversation Emily had overheard between Glick and Angstadt when she was young. The only thing I left out was Glick's awful attack on Emily.

"My, my. You two have been busy little beavers, ain't ya?" The touch of amusement in her tone seemed in stark contrast to the seriousness of the situation. She leaned back in her chair, folded her arms, and stared at us. "So you want to prove that Daniel Temple didn't kill Jacob." She snorted. "Shoot, I coulda told you that. Daniel was one of the nicest boys I ever met. He wouldn't harm a hair on no one's head. Not even that low-life Jacob's." She shook her head slowly. "No, Daniel didn't kill Jacob."

"Do you know who did?" Sam asked solemnly.

To our amazement, Sweetie laughed. "Now boy, set your mind to rest. I didn't kill Jacob. If'n I had, wouldn't nobody ever find his body, and all this trouble wouldn't be happenin' now." She reached over and touched Sam's hand. "No, I didn't kill that varmint, boy, and I don't know who did. Wish I'd seen it though. I'd like to help Daniel out. That boy was always nice to me. Always respectful. After Daddy got sick, he'd come with his parents and work on my farm until he was about ready to drop. Never asked for nothin'. Willin' to do anything he could to help. Him and his brother, Benny. They was both special."

I was beginning to get exasperated. Sweetie was taking her

own sweet time and still hadn't explained why she took my letter. I tried to think of a way to hurry her along.

"Guess I better get to what happened that night and why I snuck in and took that letter," she said as if she'd recognized my growing frustration.

I settled back in my chair and waited. Hopefully, we were rounding third base and heading toward home. My stomach growled lightly, and I picked up my fork. The first taste of Sweetie's fresh fruit salad convinced me I could actually eat and listen at the same time.

"Angstadt came to our house two nights after the doctor told me Daddy needed that operation. He told me he would pay for it if I'd marry that snake in the grass Jacob. I was appalled and told him to get outta my house. I didn't tell Daddy nothin' about it. But in the next few days he started gettin' worse and worse." She sat forward in her chair and clasped her rough, work-worn hands together as if she were getting ready to pray. Her knuckles turned white, and the end of her fingers grew red with exertion. She stared at them instead of us. "I—I know what I'm about to say sounds awful, but I just couldn't let my daddy suffer that way. I decided to take Angstadt up on his offer." She looked up at us, her face a mask of pain. "There wasn't nothin' else I could think of to do. The idea of lettin' that man. . .well, let's just say that I loved my daddy more than I loved my own life. It's as simple as that. If either one of you ever loves someone that much, maybe you'll understand." Her expression hardened, and she set her jaw. "After Jacob died and then my daddy passed away, all I wanted was for the whole situation to fade away. I tried to put it out of my mind." She looked at Sam, and the tightness in her face softened. "Then Sam came into my life. I vowed he would never find out that I'd almost sold myself to someone like Jacob Glick. I woulda done anything to keep my decision secret." She sighed. "I didn't want Sam to be ashamed of me."

"So that's why you took my letter?" I asked. "Because uncovering Glick's death would bring all of this to light?"

"That's a big part of it, Gracie girl. But there's more."

Again, I nodded at her to continue. Sam stared at his aunt as if he didn't know her. I understood his shock at finding out Sweetie had kept secrets from him and had my letter all this time, but I was pretty sure some assurance from him would mean a lot to her right now. Her eyes kept flicking toward him, but the look on his face offered little encouragement.

"You see, after I told Angstadt I'd accept his offer, he arranged a meetin' between Jacob and me. We was to get together by the lake. When I came up to the spot where he was supposed to be, I seen he weren't alone." She looked at me. "Daniel and your mama was there, and your daddy was yellin' at Jacob. Seems I wasn't the only girl he had his eye on." She stared at her hands again. "I was standin' behind the trees watchin' when Daniel hauled off and hit Jacob. That nasty man fell down on the ground, but he sure weren't dead. And your daddy didn't hit him with no rock the way the letter says. I couldn't believe it when I read that. What in the blue blazes was Benny thinkin'?"

"What did my father do after he hit Glick?" I asked.

"He and Beverly left. Jacob got up on his feet and stood there cussin' up a blue streak." Sweetie pointed her fork at me. "He was fine, Gracie. Your daddy left him alive. Believe me."

"What did you do then?" Sam asked.

Sweetie ran a hand over her face. "I ran. I chickened out. I hated Jacob, and for some reason, seein' Daniel stand up to him made me want to do it, too." She blew out a long breath between clenched teeth. "But when I got home and was faced with Daddy's pain, I went back, hopin' Jacob was still there."

"And was he?" I asked.

"Oh, he was there all right. Deader than a doornail, his head all busted in." She rubbed her palms together. "All I could do was look at him and think about the money for Daddy's operation. I wasn't sad Jacob was dead. I was just feared my daddy's chances were all gone."

"So you really don't know who killed him," I said with a sigh.

"Nope. But as I told you, it sure weren't Daniel Temple. And I know one other person who didn't do it."

"And who's that?" Sam asked. Thankfully, the tension in his face had eased somewhat. At first I'd thought he was angry with his aunt, but I realized now that he'd just been worried. Afraid she'd killed Glick. Afraid he'd lose the only parent figure he had left.

"Benny Temple. You see, I watched him find Jacob's body. And I watched him bury him. I figgered it was because he thought Daniel had killed him. Weren't no other reason for him to be hidin' Jacob's body."

My mouth dropped open. "You knew Benjamin buried Glick and never said anything?"

"You got that right, missy," she retorted. "I was glad that piece of human scum was dead and gone. And I was determined to keep Benny's secret."

"That's why you took my letter? To protect my uncle?"

She nodded slowly. "That was part of it, surely. But that's not the only reason. You see, I thought Benny saw me that night. After he started buryin' Jacob, I tried to get outta there, but I stepped on a big dry twig, and it cracked real loud. I ran away as fast as I could, tryin' to stay amid the trees so Benny wouldn't see me, but I could hear someone followin' behind me most of the way. It musta been him. And I could swear he looked at me kinda funny after that night. I was feared he thought I killed that nasty old man instead of his brother. I was worried he'd tell folks I did it."

"You never asked him about it?" Sam said incredulously. "In all these years?"

"Nope. Never did. And Benny never brought it up neither. It

were our secret. Anyway, until she came to town." Sweetie crooked her thumb my way.

"But how did you know about the letter?" I asked.

"Because Benny said somethin' about it. Toward the end, he'd sleep a lot. I'd come up to check on him and find him thrashin' around on the couch, mumblin' stuff. One day I found him havin' one of them nightmares. When I tried to wake him up, he grabbed my arm with all the strength he had left and started shoutin' your name, Gracie. He kept yellin', 'The truth's in the letter! The truth's in the letter!'" Sweetie's eyes locked on me, her face puckered in a fierce scowl. "I was sure he was talkin' about Jacob. I couldn't let him bring all that back. I didn't know if he named me as Jacob's killer. Or maybe your daddy. I had no idea what kinda 'truth' was in that letter." She sighed. "Too many lives could be ruined by diggin' up things that are better left dead. I respected your uncle, but in this case, I thought he was all wrong."

"But don't you realize that this letter could clear my father?"

Sweetie leaned back in her chair. "You ain't thought this out, Gracie girl. That letter says your daddy *did* kill Jacob. Even if he didn't mean to."

"You could testify," Sam said. "You can clear Mr. Temple."

Sweetie looked at him as if he'd lost his mind. "And how am I supposed to do that? I can't come forward now, thirty years later, and tell someone I kept quiet about it all this time. Ain't no one gonna believe me. Especially since I probably have more motive than anyone else for killin' him." She shook her head. "Nope. That won't work. I won't do it."

"Then what do we do now? What do we do with the letter?" I could hear the hint of hysteria in my voice, but I was tired and confused. It seemed now that the letter actually made things more complicated. Benjamin had been wrong all these years. He'd assumed his brother was guilty of murder—even if it was accidental. But now we knew that my dad wasn't guilty of anything except maybe giving Glick a well-deserved punch in the face. And the only person who could back that up wasn't willing to do so.

"I wish I'd found that letter before you did and destroyed it," Sweetie said harshly. "It's nothin' but trouble. It should disappear just like Jacob. If it goes away, our problems go away. We can get back to normal."

"Aren't you forgetting the body buried on Grace's property?" Sam asked.

Sweetie shook her head vigorously. "I got a solution to that problem, too. I buy your land, Gracie. I been wantin' to expand anyway. Nobody will think nothin' about it. Jacob stays right where he belongs, and we all go on with our lives."

For just a moment, I saw a ray of hope, but it quickly became clear that Sweetie's plan was flawed. "But Jacob Glick *was* murdered by someone," I said. "We can't just ignore that."

"Anyone living in Harmony coulda bashed in that old coot's head," she said with contempt. "You can't investigate the whole town in a few days, girlie. Besides, maybe the person who killed him already moved away—or died themselves. You could be wastin' your time."

I wrapped a strand of hair around my finger while I thought about Sweetie's theory. "But what about Ruth's vase? Someone took it and planted it in Benjamin's house. Why would anyone do that unless they were afraid I was getting too close to the truth?"

"Was probably Mary," Sweetie said triumphantly. "I heard tell she hates your guts. She did it so you'd get upset and leave town."

"No," Sam said. "It wasn't Mary. I already thought of that. I asked Hector where she was Saturday. She never left the café."

I frowned at him. "You didn't tell me you'd checked up on Mary's whereabouts."

He shrugged. "I just wanted to be sure it wasn't her. I didn't say anything since I was pretty sure she wasn't involved. No point stirring up any more bad feelings between the two of you."

Sweetie's jubilation over her hypothesis had taken a swift nosedive. She scrunched up her face while she considered this revelation. Finally, she clapped her hands together. "Maybe Ruth took it herself. She and Mary are tighter than two thieves. They probably planned it."

"I don't believe that," I said. "I haven't known Ruth long, but she seems like an honest woman who would never accuse an innocent person of a crime."

Sweetie started to make a snide comment, but Sam jumped in before she got it out. "You're absolutely right, Grace. She wouldn't." He flashed his aunt a warning look, and she shut her mouth.

I leaned forward and caught Sweetie's attention. "Even if we really believed no one would ever find Glick, *we* know he was murdered. And it's not right."

"Even though we might never find out who killed him?" Sam asked.

"Yes. I realize he was a bad person, but he was also someone's son. Maybe someone's brother." I directed my next comment to Sweetie. "Maybe someone's nephew. How can we just leave him in the ground?"

"I understand what you're sayin'," Sweetie said, raising her eyebrows, "but if you can't figger out who knocked him off, this thing could blow up in your face and hurt a lotta people. I say you two do your investigatin', but if you don't find nothin', I buy the land and we leave well enough alone."

"I don't know. You might be right," I said.

"You sound hesitant," Sam said. "Is that really what you want to do?"

I exhaled slowly. "I don't know. It's confusing. I don't want to cause my family trouble, but if we just walk away, it's like Glick will haunt us the rest of our lives. He'll never be put to rest."

Sweetie's rough laughter told me she didn't understand. But

Sam's worried expression mirrored my own. He knew I was right. I was beginning to understand how my uncle felt. Sometimes, doing the right thing is more complicated than it should be.

Sweetie stood up. "Well, since we're bein' all honest and everything, I have somethin' you should see."

Sam and I followed her out of the kitchen toward the study. I had my uncle's letter clasped tightly in my hand, and I had no intention of losing it again. Sweetie swung the study door open and motioned us inside. Then she crossed over to a painting on the far wall. Probably another one of Hannah's. She grabbed the left side of the picture and pulled. To my amazement, it swung out, revealing the door to a safe in the wall.

"I had no idea this was here," Sam said to his aunt. "Why didn't you tell me?" He sounded slightly offended.

"I don't gotta tell you everything, boy." She reached over and patted him on the shoulder. "Wasn't 'cause I don't trust you. Just felt it was better if you didn't know nothin' about it." She quickly turned the dial. I could hear the tumblers fall into place. "I found this after I moved in. Don't know who first put it here, but Amil Angstadt was usin' it—that's for sure. It's also for certain his flock knew nothin' about it." She swung the heavy door open to reveal a deep interior full of papers and a large metal box. She pulled the box out and carried it over to the desk. Sam and I shot each other questioning looks and trailed behind her. Sweetie was turning out to be full of surprises.

"So what is it?" Sam asked.

"When Angstadt came to see me, he asked me how much my daddy's operation was gonna cost. I told him it was five thousand dollars. He offered me ten thousand. It was enough for the operation and to get our fields in shape. I figgered I could save the farm and get Daddy healthy again so when he was ready, he could take up where he left off."

"Ten thousand dollars was a lot of money back then," I said.

"Where in the world would Angstadt get that much?"

Sweetie's eyes were burning coals of hate. "I don't know, but I'm certain he coulda helped my daddy without askin' me to sell myself to Jacob Glick." The timbre of her voice rose. "He was supposed to be a Christian man—no matter what group he belonged to. And he let my daddy die. When Jacob disappeared, he refused to help me. Said he was no longer bound to the bargain 'cause Jacob wasn't in the picture. Yet he had all of this." She flung the top of the box open to reveal stacks and stacks of bills.

"You—you said you found this here?"

She nodded. "After I bought the house, I found the safe. I was gonna crack it open but realized the number was written on the back of an old tapestry that hung here. Evil thing it were. Hell and all its demons torturin' souls. Just like somethin' Angstadt would have. I threw it out and put up an old print that belonged to my daddy until Sam brought home one of Hannah's paintings while I was workin' on this room."

Sam ran his hands over the money. "How much is in here?"

"A little over twenty thousand dollars." Her expression grew tight. "And I ain't never spent one stinkin' dollar of it. I kept it here all these years just 'cause I could. I hope that rotten scoundrel knows I got his money." Her voice trembled with emotion.

"Sweetie," I said softly, "he probably doesn't know. And even if he did, I don't think it matters to him anymore."

"Well, it matters to me. It matters a great deal to me." Tears coursed down her face. "That so-and-so minister watched my daddy waste away when he coulda saved him. After Angstadt dropped dead, I sold daddy's farm and bought this house just to spite him." She looked around the room. "'Course once I realized it weren't the house's fault, I started to love it here. I fixed it up my way. Ain't no part of that man here no more." She gazed down at the box. "'Cept his cursed money. The thing he loved most in the world."

Sam and I just looked at each other. Sweetie had imprisoned

herself with hate for a man who'd died years ago. A wave of compassion swept through me. Sweetie's gruff exterior housed a broken soul.

"Why don't you put it back now, Sweetie?" Sam said gently. "We'll talk about it later."

She slammed the lid shut and picked up the box. "I'll put it back, but there ain't no reason to talk about nothin'. I ain't gonna spend it. And I ain't gonna never get rid of it. It will sit in that safe until it rots away. Just like that no-good preacher." She pointed at the letter still in my hand. "You might as well put that letter in the safe, too. No one can get to it there. I ain't gonna bother with it anymore. You have my promise."

I wordlessly handed her the letter, which she carried along with the box to the open safe door. Once they were safely ensconced inside, she shut the door and twirled the knob. Then she swung the painting back against the wall.

"I know it's early, but I'm plumb tuckered out," she said yawning. "If you two don't mind, I'm gonna take a bath and watch a little TV in my room till I nod off." She pointed her index finger at Sam. "You gotta help me in the orchard tomorrow, boy. We gotta repair the irrigation lines. Them rabbits been chewin' on 'em again."

"Yes ma'am," he said. "I'll be up at the crack of dawn." He leaned over and gave his aunt a kiss on the cheek. She reached up and put her arms around his neck, giving him a quick hug. "You're my blessin', you know," she whispered. "The good Lord mighta been sleepin' when my daddy died, but when He woke up He felt bad and sent you to me." With that she turned on her heel and headed for the door.

"Sweetie," Sam said before she had a chance to make her escape, "you shouldn't have worried that I'd be ashamed of you, you know. That would never happen. Never."

The elderly woman didn't respond. Nor did she turn around.

She hesitated for a moment and then walked out of the room.

"Wow," I said when the study door closed.

"Yeah, wow," Sam echoed.

"I know where the money came from."

Sam gaped at me. "How could you know?"

I told him about the church member who died and left some land to the church when Angstadt was still running things. "Emily wondered what had happened to the money. It never showed up. Now we know."

He nodded. "And we also know what Glick had on Angstadt."

We stood for a moment staring at the door as if Sweetie was going to burst in at any moment with some new revelation. Finally, Sam shook his head and suggested we sit out on the back porch. After stopping by the kitchen for some iced tea, we made our way to the porch. Sam sat beside me in a wicker love seat that looked almost exactly like Emily's. We watched the sunset for a while without speaking. I wasn't certain what he was thinking, but I kept trying to process Sweetie's surprising disclosure with all the other information we'd managed to gather.

Finally, Sam broke the silence. "So now what?"

I shook my head. "I wish I knew. Frankly, I don't think anything's changed. Just because Glick's killer didn't take the letter, we're still dealing with someone who doesn't want me to uncover the truth."

"Has it occurred to you that stealing that vase from Ruth's in broad daylight was really risky?" Sam asked with a deep frown. "He could have easily been caught."

"Yes, I thought about that. It smacks of desperation."

He nodded slowly. "It certainly does. It also means that whoever did it was watching us in town yesterday. He knew you'd been to Ruth's."

"And he knew I'd be back to pick up my purchases. How could anyone possibly know that?"

212

"I have no idea." Sam let out a deep sigh. "I'm still processing the fact that Sweetie had your letter and has been keeping twenty thousand dollars in a hidden safe."

I placed my hand on his arm. "She's still the same person she was before she told you about the letter and the money." I stared out the window at the remnants of the sun as it slipped behind the reddish-bronze horizon. "I can't stop thinking about the pain she's been through. If I had to watch my father die. . ."

"You know, you and Sweetie both know what it's like to have to fight for your father. You two have a lot in common."

His words jarred me. Sweetie seemed so odd—so different than me. Yet when it came down to our hearts, we *were* a lot alike. I tried to put myself in her place. Would I have made the same decision she had? I wasn't certain and prayed I'd never have to find out.

"At least we know who *didn't* kill Glick," I said slowly. "Now we just have to figure out who did. Sounds like the entire town of Harmony is suspect."

Sam chuckled. "This is starting to remind me of a mystery novel I read once. A man was killed by an entire group of people on a train. Each one struck a blow that could have been the fatal one so no one would know who the actual murderer was."

"*Murder on the Orient Express* by Agatha Christie," I said. "Great book. Great writer."

"Yes, she was," he agreed. "Do you remember how Hercule Poirot figured it out?"

"Not a clue."

"Me either."

We both laughed, and Sam scooted closer to me. A chill ran up my spine along with a message of caution. The light in the room grew dim and with it, my resistance.

"You do realize that Sweetie knows exactly where Glick is buried, don't you?" Sam said.

"Yes, but until we find out how he got there, I don't want to know where he is. It's too creepy."

Sam didn't answer. Somehow talking about the location of Glick's grave made everything seem way too real.

"I sure hope we find out something useful from Levi," Sam said after a long pause.

"Me, too. If he can't help us. . ."

"We might be out of options. At least he doesn't have a dog in this hunt."

"A dog in this hunt?" I said with a smirk. "Is that some kind of colloquial farm boy saying?"

He laughed. "Sorry. I forget you city girls don't understand our country phrases."

"I'm starting to learn some of them, and I have to admit it worries me."

Sam chuckled again. "Well, don't get too concerned. I'm pretty sure it takes a lot to drive the city out of someone like you."

"Not as much as you might think," I said softly.

Sam was silent for a moment. Before I realized what was happening, he leaned over and kissed me. Just like the time in the truck, I didn't have the power to fight back. My mind told me to stop, but my heart urged me on. After a long, sweet kiss, he leaned back.

"Sometimes I'm almost grateful to Jacob Glick," he whispered.

"Grateful? To that awful man? Wh–what are you saying?" The soft light of sunset highlighted Sam's strong profile. I had the strangest urge to touch his face—to run my fingers across the stubble on his firm chin.

"I'm not grateful for the evil he did, but I'm grateful he's kept you here so I could get to know you."

"It—it would have been better if I'd come here for another reason, b–but I know what you mean. I—I wouldn't trade the time we've had together for anything." My voice had an odd squeak to it that I couldn't seem to control.

He started to lean toward me again, but I held my hand up to his chest to stop him. "I—I think we need to get back to planning our next step. It would be easy to get sidetracked, and we can't afford that right now."

He let out a ragged breath. "You're always the voice of reason, aren't you? Just so you know, it's really beginning to get on my nerves."

I couldn't hold back a giggle. "Sorry, but someone's got to keep us grounded. You certainly don't seem capable of it."

"You got that right." He leaned across me, his hair brushing against my face. The musky smell of his shampoo made me almost forget my former admonition. I started to protest his attempt to kiss me again, but a small click and a flash of light confirmed that his target had been the lamp next to me. It provided just enough light to chase away the darkness but kept the warm ambience created by the soft glow of dusk. As he moved back to his side of the seat, I fought the urge to grab him and throw caution to the wind. The depth of my feelings toward this man didn't make sense. What was happening to me?

"I'm supposed to be at Ida's tomorrow at one o'clock," I managed to croak out.

"I'll meet you there at two. After I fix the irrigation system."

"From the attack of the vicious bunnies?"

He laughed. "Yeah, and the vicious mice. There are quite a few wild animals that like to nibble on our irrigation lines. Fixing them is a constant chore."

"Do you think Ida might have any information that could help us?" I asked, guiding the subject away from crazed crunching critters.

Sam stretched his legs out in front of him and yawned. "Maybe. You don't plan to tell her about Glick do you?"

"No. Levi's it unless we're pointed specifically to someone

who might know the whole truth."

"Except the person who knows the whole truth might just be the killer. I doubt seriously that whoever it was ran around sharing that information with anyone else in town."

"You've got a point. Should we talk to Levi after we leave Ida's tomorrow?"

"I'll call him. See if he can meet with us around five." He grunted. "I'd suggest we all go to the café for dinner, but I may never be able to set foot in there again."

"That's not practical, Sam. Maybe you should give Mary a chance to react normally to you. You two can't avoid each other forever. Harmony's too small for that. Besides, you have just as much right to eat in the café as anyone else."

He sighed. "You might be right, but I want to give her some time to settle down. She's way too upset right now."

The look Mary had given me this afternoon made me wonder if he wasn't making a wise choice after all. "Why don't we get some sandwiches and dessert from Mr. Menlo? We could meet Levi in the park. I'd love to spend some time there. It's so beautiful."

"Yes it is," he agreed. "The churches keep it up."

"Together?"

He grinned. "Yes, together. I told you Harmony is a special place. The churches get along great. In fact, Abel and Marcus are good friends."

"It *is* a special place," I said quietly. "In more ways than one."

Sam started to say something but then hesitated.

I looked at him questioningly. "What?"

"Well, you may think this sounds crazy."

I shook my head. "Listen, Sam. With what I've been through the past few days, nothing sounds crazy."

"Okay, here goes." He took a deep breath and slowly let it out. "Harmony is almost like a person, you know? With its own personality. But it's been hiding something. A secret. When you came to town, it's like the town. . .like the town decided to use you to uncover those secrets. You know, so it could heal. I feel like you were meant to come here. Meant to find that letter. Meant to finally bring the truth to light." He turned toward me. "Does that sound nuts?"

Although he tried to keep his tone light, I knew he was dead serious. And the funny thing was that the same odd thought had been flying around in my mind lately, trying to find a place to roost.

We said good night and went off to bed, but I couldn't sleep. I lay in bed and stared at the ceiling for quite a while, wondering if God really had led me here. If what was happening was more than coincidence. If my life and the small Kansas town of Harmony were tied together in some kind of divine destiny. Finally, with Buddy curled up next to me, I drifted off to sleep.

Chapter Fifteen

I awoke to a cloudy, overcast morning. A quick glance at the clock told me I'd slept later than I'd planned. I roused Buddy, found my slippers, and headed downstairs to a silent kitchen. A note on the table told me that Sam and Sweetie were already out in the orchards and that Sweetie had left breakfast for me in the fridge. Sure enough, I found a plate with scrambled eggs, ham, and a couple of biscuits covered with plastic wrap. I popped it into the microwave and checked the coffee. It was still hot. I poured a cup while I waited for my breakfast to heat up. The trick is to heat food up slowly in a microwave. That way it doesn't taste like it's been nuked. Years of living alone had forced me to learn the intricacies of microwave cooking. Not really something to be proud of.

I took my coffee cup, stepped out into the enclosed porch, and looked out the windows for Sam and his aunt. Buddy ran to the door and whined to go out, so I opened it. I finally spotted Sam kneeling on the ground near the edge of the orchard and remembered Sweetie's directive about repairing the irrigation lines. After Buddy finished his business, I watched as he ran over to Sam and enthusiastically jumped up on him. Sam put down his tools and hugged the little dog while Buddy licked his face.

I didn't see Sweetie anywhere and figured she was somewhere deep within the orchard. When I heard the microwave ding, I went back inside and took my plate out. Sweetie's culinary skills translated very well to any meal, and this was no exception.

After breakfast I took a shower, dressed, and bundled up my dirty clothes. I scouted around downstairs until I found the laundry room and tossed my dirty things in to wash. I'd just stepped out into the hall when I heard Sam call my name.

"Back here," I yelled. He came around the corner wearing a black T-shirt that highlighted his flaxen hair. When I looked into his eyes, I was reminded of prairie storm clouds. I felt my heart skip a beat or two.

"Man, it's about time. How late do you city girls sleep?"

"Look you, I'm usually out of bed by six in the morning every weekday and in the office by eight. I suppose you get up earlier."

He leaned against the wall. "I get up by five, and I'm out in the orchards by seven. I imagine you're still drinking coffee and putting on your makeup."

"Okay. You got me beat. So what are you doing now?"

He pushed off the wall and turned toward the kitchen. "Came in to get another cup of coffee. Hope you didn't drink it all."

"Nope. I'll join you if it's okay." I followed him to the kitchen. "I'm washing some clothes. Hope Sweetie doesn't mind if I use her washing machine."

Sam pointed at the kitchen table, so I sat down while he poured us both a cup of coffee. "She won't mind. As long as you don't break anything."

"I actually have washed clothes before. I think her appliances are safe."

"Then you should be okay." He pushed my cup in front of me and sat down on the other side of the table. "So, yesterday was quite a day, huh?"

"Yeah, that's an understatement." I stared through the window, making sure Sweetie wasn't on her way back. "What do you really think about that money?" I kept my voice low just in case she was in the vicinity. "I mean, it belongs to the church, doesn't it?"

He shrugged. "You're guessing about its origin. Truth is, we don't really know where it came from. It's in Angstadt's house, so for now, it's Angstadt's. Of course, his being dead makes it a little difficult to return."

"Even though we can't prove this money is the missing money Emily told me about, this house originally belonged to the church. Doesn't that fact make it clear it should go to them?"

Sam leaned forward, wrapped his hands around his cup, and stared into it. "I honestly don't know," he said after a brief hesitation. "I don't think Sweetie would give it to them. I told you before that she doesn't go to any church." He sighed. "At least now I understand why."

"But Sam, she's judging everyone by Amil Angstadt, and that's not fair. I came to Harmony with a negative opinion of the Mennonite church here—but I was wrong. Dead wrong. Just because Angstadt was a bad apple, that doesn't mean the whole barrel is rotten."

Sam cracked a smile. "Are you trying to put this into fruit terms so I'll understand it?"

I chuckled. "Not on purpose. Maybe you're rubbing off on me."

"You're becoming fruitier?"

"Sadly, that seems to be the case. But back to the money. . ."

"Look, Grace," he said, the smile leaving his face, "I'm not going to pressure my aunt about that money. I had no idea everything she'd been through. Now that I know, I'm going to let her decide what to do. I'm not Holy Spirit Jr. She and God are going to have to work it out between them. My job is to love her—and support her no matter what she does."

I didn't argue with him; this wasn't the time for it. Sam loved his aunt deeply, and finding out how Angstadt and Glick had tried to manipulate her had caused him pain.

"Okay. Let's just leave that alone for now." I glanced at my watch. "Wow, I can't believe it's almost noon. I have to be at Ida's by one."

"I'll make us some sandwiches."

"Oh my, no. I just finished breakfast. And Ida plans to stuff me with strawberry pie."

"You're right," Sam said, frowning. "Maybe I'll just eat half a sandwich. . ."

I laughed. "You'd better be careful. I would hate for you to drop over from starvation."

"Very funny." He winked at me. "I'll have you know I'm a growing boy."

"I'm surprised you don't weigh five hundred pounds the way Sweetie cooks."

He shook his head. "Working out in the orchards keeps me fit. God help me when I get too old to do it anymore. My only hope is to marry a gal who can't find her way around a kitchen."

He gazed at me with a serious, fixed stare, and any humorous retort I might have tried to sling back died in my throat. I quickly dropped my gaze to my coffee cup and took a sip.

"Do you want me to drive you to Ida's?" he asked, his voice a few notches lower than normal.

"N—no. It's just down the road. I'd like to walk." I stood up and pointed toward the porch. "Think I'll go down to the lake for a while before I head over to her house. There are some beautiful flowers growing along the shore. Thought I might pick some to take to her."

Sam smiled. "She'd love that, Grace. How nice of you to think of it. I'll eat a little something and get back to work. See you at two."

"Okay." I headed out the kitchen door onto the porch and

then out the back door. The overcast sky added a chill to the air. My sweatshirt wasn't enough to protect me from the cold that nipped at me. As I broke through the trees, the beauty of the lake struck me again. Trouble Lake. If only I could jump in the water and leave all my troubles behind just as the Indians had done so many years ago. It was hard to believe that I'd only been in Harmony four days. It felt as if I'd been here forever. Wichita seemed far away—almost like someplace I'd only dreamed about.

I gathered some of the lovely wildflowers that lined the water's edge, winding my way around until I reached the dock behind Benjamin's house. Even though it was smaller than Sam's, it looked sturdy and inviting. I walked out to the edge and looked back toward the big red house. It was barely visible above the tree line, but I could see Sam's dock clearly. I turned to walk away when I noticed someone standing at its edge. It was Sam. He stood there, staring into the water. He remained motionless for several minutes. Finally, he took something from his pocket and stared at it. Then he suddenly threw it into the water and walked back toward the house. What in the world had he tossed into the lake?

I turned and headed toward Benjamin's house, wondering if Sam was keeping a secret from me. And if so, what? I was so wrapped up in my thoughts I didn't pay much attention to my surroundings until I entered the grove of trees between the lake and the house. I'd no sooner stepped into the clearing when I stopped dead in my tracks. Was this where Jacob Glick was buried? Was I standing on his grave? Talking about a dead body on your property is one thing. Being faced with the reality of it is quite another. Sweat broke out on my forehead and my knees felt like rubber. I looked back, trying to get my bearings. Although not obvious from the road, Benjamin's house actually sat on a small hill.

As I stared at the lake, that odd feeling of déjà vu came rushing back. Even though it made no sense, I knew I'd definitely been here before. I'd looked at Trouble Lake from this very spot. No, wait a minute. Something wasn't quite right. I walked through the clearing to a grassy knoll right above the tree line. Now I knew where I'd seen this view of the lake. In Emily's heartbreaking self-portrait. This was where she'd sat all those years ago, after Glick's heinous crime, frightened and wondering what to do. I looked around, saddened to think of a young Emily sitting where I stood now, terrified and alone, afraid to tell anyone what had happened to her. And now, years later, Glick's body lay hidden beneath layers of earth. Was this some kind of divine justice or just a bizarre coincidence? I thought about Paul's admonition to the Galatians, that a man will reap what he sows. Jacob Glick had sown evil, and his end had been violent and deadly. A deep sadness washed through me for Emily and, oddly, for Glick himself. If only he'd chosen a different path and given God a chance to make something good of his life. Of course, it was too late for him, but it wasn't for Emily.

Without warning, a sudden gust of wind moved quickly through the trees. The rustle of their leaves seemed to whisper to me, "Beauty instead of ashes. The oil of gladness instead of mourning." I knelt down in the soft grass and prayed for Emily—that she would find a way to exchange the ashes of her past for the beauty God had waiting for her. Too much evil had occurred here. It was time to vanquish it. I knelt before the Lord for several minutes, praying until I felt a release. Trying to shake off the odd sensations that surrounded me, I got to my feet and almost ran out of the grove and into the sunlight. I hurried past Benjamin's silent house and made my way to the road. As I approached Ida's house, I noticed the old woman waiting for me on her front porch. She rocked slowly back and forth in her rocking chair but stood to her feet as I approached.

"I'm so happy to see you, my dear," she said with a delighted smile.

Her friendly expression helped to banish the disturbing remnants of the past that tried to cling to me. "I picked these for you." I held out my armful of flowers, grateful to be out of the clearing and in the presence of this sweet woman who radiated friendliness.

She clapped her hands together and then took them from me. "Ach, wildflowers. I love them so. My husband used to pick them for me. After he died, I would go once in a while to gather them, but as I got older, it became harder and harder to make it down to the lake." She pulled open her screen door. "Come inside and sit while I find a vase."

The inside of her house reminded me of Benjamin's. Homey but simple. I sat down in a lovely chair with quilted upholstery. The open windows picked up the spring breeze and moved it through the house, fluttering Ida's sheer curtains in a slow spring dance.

She left the room for a few minutes but tottered back with the colorful flowers arranged in a cut-glass vase. She put them on a dark wooden table next to the couch and sat down beside them. The floral scent wafted through the room, carried by the gentle air currents. Even though it was still early afternoon, I suddenly felt sleepy. The peaceful quiet of Ida's home made me compare it to my own. Seemed like the television was always on—or music CDs. But now I could hear the wind moving through the trees, the birds singing in different tones and voices, and Ida's clock ticking away the seconds of a lazy April afternoon.

"I thought we would read your grandmother's letter first, dear," Ida chirped in a voice that quivered with the sound of age and contentment. "I baked a strawberry pie this morning. And the coffee is on. It should be ready soon."

"That sounds lovely," I said. "Please, read the letter."

She reached into the pocket of her long, dark blue dress and pulled out an old envelope, faded and yellowed with age. Carefully opening the brittle seal, she reached in and pulled out the folded pages inside.

"I was foolish to leave this unopened all these years," she said, her words heavy with the accent of her heritage. "Herman, my husband, passed away about three months before your grandmother and grandfather decided to leave Harmony. Essie and I were so close. I felt she had deserted me." She shook her head slowly. "It was selfish of me. I should have understood. They had finally freed themselves from their commitment to the church and wanted to spend time with you. Benjamin was old enough to fend for himself and encouraged them to go." She wiped a tear from her wrinkled cheek. "Poor Benjamin. Essie was confident he would follow them someday. But as soon as they left, he shut himself in that house and refused to have anything to do with anybody. I asked him about his parents frequently, and all he would say was that they were fine. About two years after they left, I finally questioned him about why he had not left Harmony to be with them. I will never forget what he said. Or the look in his eyes. They were so dark and cold. 'They have made their bed, Ida,' he said. 'I have made mine. And that is the end of it. I have no need of anyone but my God.'" She made a clucking sound with her tongue. "Never could figure out why he cut them off." She looked at me with sadness in her face. "Did Essie and Joe ever try to contact him?"

"I honestly don't know a lot about it. No one talked to me much about Uncle Benjamin. But I did hear Mama Essie say something once about trying to talk to him. He told them he wanted nothing to do with them—or my father. Papa Joe made plans to come here and try to reason with Benjamin, but then Mama died and Papa Joe started having problems with Alzheimer's. He never did make that trip."

"But now you are here," she said. She smoothed her skirt and smiled at me. "You came here for them. In their place, ja?"

"I—I never thought about it that way. Of course, I was too late for Uncle Benjamin."

"I am not so sure about that, child. God has a whole different sense of time than we do. What looks too late for us is sometimes right on time for God." She held the letter to her chest. "Why, just think about your grandmother and me. She left Harmony in 1990. You were jus a toddler." She shook her head. "Bishop Angstadt pitched a fit, he did. Your grandparents were leaders in the church, you know. When they started to doubt his leadership, things began to fall apart for him. Others in the church began to leave. He died a couple of years after your grandparents moved away. Even if Benjamin could not leave because of his loyalty to the bishop, his death should have made his way clear. I guess the bishop's beliefs about The Ban overcame Benjamin's loyalty to his family. It's a shame."

"One thing I don't understand, Ida. Wasn't there anyone keeping an eye on Angstadt? Someone from your denomination or something?"

"Bishop Angstadt himself was an overseer, but there were no other congregations except ours in this area. And those whose job it was to watch over him were far removed from Harmony. They assumed everything was fine. None of us complained. Perhaps we should have." She lifted her hands in surrender. "It is hard to explain now, child. But at the time we thought we were doing the right thing. Criticizing our bishop was looked upon as an awful sin."

"Seems to me that following your 'old ways' led to a lot of heartache. Yet you still cling to these same principles. I don't understand. . ."

"Now let me stop you there, child," the old woman said with a smile. "I *do* embrace many of the old ways, but it is only because I want to. I love my life—the way it is. Of course, not all my choices are made out of the desire for simplicity. For example, I certainly have nothing against electricity. If it didn't cost so much, I might put it in." She sighed. "But you know something? I love the glow of a lamp at night. And I love sitting in front of a fireplace in the winter and snuggling under the quilts my mother made." She shrugged. "I must admit that I am not a fan of really hot days, but I can harness my old horse, Zebediah, and ride my buggy into town. I sit in the cool café and visit with my neighbors." She put her hand to her mouth and giggled like a schoolgirl. "Now this must stay between you and me, ja? Sometimes, I strip down to my underwear and soak my feet in a tub of cool water. Good thing I can see anyone who turns into my driveway. That way I am able to get decent before they see me in my altogether." She pointed her finger at me. "And is there anything as wonderful as a cold glass of lemonade on a blistering day?" She clapped her hands together. "How can we enjoy the good things in life if we don't understand what it is like without them?"

Ida's simple delight in her lifestyle made sense to me. "I think I understand. If someone had tried to tell me a month ago I'd be envious of people like you, I'd have thought they were crazy. But now. . ."

"You're beginning to like us, ja?" she said laughing. "I'm so glad. If nothing else, you have made some friends here. Maybe someday your mother and father will come back for a visit. I am afraid they have some bad feelings toward Harmony. But this town is special—and very resilient. Even someone like Bishop Angstadt could not break its spirit."

"Sam told me that a long time ago you and some of the other women in Harmony prayed that this would be a peaceful place."

She nodded slowly. "Ja, we certainly did. And our Lord has honored that prayer all these years. I would like your father and mother to see the work He has done here."

"Maybe they will. I intend to tell them about Harmony and what it's become. I think it would heal them to come back for a visit."

"I agree, child. You are very wise." Ida's eyes twinkled with an inner joy that drew me to her.

"You know, you remind me a lot of Abel Mueller. Do you mind if I ask why you don't attend his church? I mean, it's Mennonite and all. Is it because you think he's doing something wrong?"

Ida's eyebrows shot up. "Ach no, child. That is not it at all. Pastor Mueller and I have talked about the reason I am still with our small group, and it has nothing to do with him." She sighed and looked out the window. "Truth be told, I would love to go to Bethel." She swung her gaze back to me. "I will tell you the real reason, but it must stay between us. Is that something you can abide by?"

"Of course."

"It is because of Sarah Ketterling. We have developed a fine friendship, and I just can't desert her, Gracie. The poor child is so isolated. At least Gabriel lets me talk to her. And he even allows her to visit me from time to time. I am afraid if I start attending Bethel, he will forbid our relationship."

I told Ida about running into Sarah in town and my desire to learn wood-block printing from her.

Ida nodded slowly. "I wonder if Gabriel would allow her to teach you if you met here in my home."

"I—I kind of doubt it," I said. "He wasn't very nice to me. Told me my uncle would be ashamed of me."

Ida's face flushed crimson. "That man had no business speaking to you that way. He is so filled up with hate, he can't love anyone." She shook her head. "Your uncle would be so proud of you, Gracie. You are such a lovely young woman. Good and kind—and full of love. Do not listen to Gabriel. I knew Benjamin better than most folks. He was a troubled man—but he was a good man."

She turned her attention to the old letter and unfolded its yellowed pages slowly. "Now, let us read this letter before that handsome, young Sam Goodrich breaks in, looking for a piece of my pie."

I nodded and settled back in my chair. Listening to a letter from my grandmother written twenty years ago gave me a lump in my throat. How I wish I could talk to her one more time. Feel her hug my neck or call me her "little gift of grace."

" *'My dearest friend, Ida,'* " the old woman read in her age-crackled voice. " *I know our leaving has caused you pain. I am so sorry. When we drove away from Harmony for the last time, all I could think of was you. I know you have felt alone since Herman's passing. In the past few years, our friendship has grown even stronger. Surely you realize how much I treasure it—and you. But I cannot allow Grace to grow up without her Mama Essie and Papa Joe. When we visited Daniel and Beverly, my heart broke when we had to leave. Gracie cried for us as we walked away. I cannot bear it, Ida. Can you understand that, my friend? If I could have both of you, I would. Joe and I talked about asking you to come with us. But I know you do not want to leave your home, and I respect that. Can you respect the yearning in my heart for my beautiful grandchild? I wish you could see her, Ida. She has the most beautiful green eyes and bright red hair. She looks so much like Benjamin. Joe and I are hopeful that he will join us soon. My little gift of grace will love her handsome uncle—I am sure of it. And oh, Ida, if you could only see Daniel and Beverly. What a lovely home they have made for themselves. They are so much in love, even today. It is such a blessing to be near them.*

" *I know Bishop Angstadt was angry about our decision, but I have come to realize that the love of God I read about in the Bible is not the kind of love I see in him. I will not speak ill of anyone, Ida, but I will ask you to remember that Mennonites are dedicated to following God's love and living in peace with everyone. It is because of my love for Him and*

His ways first, and the love of my family second, that I have embraced the decision my husband made to move to Nebraska. This does not mean that my heart is not broken because I had to leave Benjamin and you behind. Maybe someday soon I will be able to come to you—to greet you once again with a holy kiss. I pray for this.

" 'Please take care of yourself, my dearest friend. And if you can find it in your heart, please forgive me for any pain I have caused you. I want you to know that I will love you every day I live. And if I never hear from you again in this life, I will wait for that kiss in the fields of heaven where we will take off our socks and shoes and dip our toes into God's holy waters. I love you today and forever.

" 'Your loving sister in Christ, Essie Temple.' "

Ida lowered the letter with trembling fingers. Tears coursed down her face, and I realized with a start that my face was wet, too. As we looked at each other, I was filled with a desire that seemed to speak straight from my heart. I rose to my feet and walked up to Ida. Then I leaned over and kissed her lightly on the cheek. "This is from Essie," I said, trying to keep my voice from breaking.

The old woman's breath caught, and she reached up and put her arms around my neck. I hugged her back while we both cried. When I straightened up, my shoulder was damp with her tears.

"Oh, my dear Gracie," she whispered. "My dear, dear Gracie."

I sat back down and tried to compose myself. I couldn't help but compare this letter to the one my uncle had left for me. The first letter brought fear and confusion. This one had delivered healing and love. Ida reached into her pocket and took out a hankie, which she used to dry her face. Not having a tissue handy, I wiped my tears with my sleeve. Finally, I started to giggle. "My goodness, if Sam finds us like this, he'll think we've lost our minds."

A grin erupted on Ida's face, and we soon found ourselves wiping away tears of laughter instead of sorrow.

"My goodness," she said once she managed to stop. "What joy you've brought to my home today. I am so grateful and happy I read Essie's letter with you. It made it even more special."

"She always loved you, Ida." I followed that statement with a rather loud, high-pitched hiccup.

Ida chuckled. "I think it is time for something to drink, ja? Coffee or lemonade?"

"Lemonade, please." I tried to stop the next hiccup before it got past my lips. My attempt only made it worse, culminating in a sound that was a cross between a hiccup and a squealing pig.

Ida hurried off to the kitchen, probably afraid I might actually implode before her eyes. She was back almost immediately with a tall, cold glass of homemade lemonade. I swallowed half the glassful in only a few seconds. When I pulled the rim away from my mouth, we both waited in anticipation. Thankfully, my embarrassing bout was gone. Peace reigned once again in my body.

"I–I'm sorry," I said. "I guess laughing and crying at the same time makes me hiccup. I have no idea why I can't hiccup like a normal human being. It's humiliating."

Ida's eyes filled with tears once again even though she smiled. "Your grandmother sounded exactly like that. I used to tease her about it unmercifully."

"You're right. I'd forgotten." Sometimes at family gatherings, my father and grandfather would purposely pester my grandmother until she got the hiccups. She would scold them for it, but somehow it just made the situation funnier. Mama Essie had a way of wrinkling her nose when she was amused that reminded me of a young girl. I fought against the emotions the memory brought. There had been enough crying for one afternoon.

"You know," Ida said in a dreamy voice, staring out the nearby window. "Growing up Mennonite wasn't bad at all. Oh, there were challenges as a young girl, but the positive things always outweighed the negative."

"Tell me about it, please. My father never talked much about his childhood."

"Well, school was the hardest. I grew up in Pennsylvania. We moved to Harmony when I was ten. In Pennsylvania we had our own community school. But when we moved here, I had to go to regular school in Sunrise, a town about ten miles from here. That was hard. We looked different than the other children. And we weren't allowed to participate when they stood for the Pledge of Allegiance."

"I don't understand," I said, frowning. "What's wrong with the Pledge?"

"We were taught that our allegiance was only to God and His kingdom. Not to any government."

"Oh. Did the other kids tease you?"

She nodded. "And not just about that. The way we dressed, the way we wore our hair, and the buggies we rode to school in. There was always something, it seemed. As a child, your heart cry is to fit in. Yet we never did."

"Do those memories make you sad?"

Ida smiled. "No, child. When I was young, it seemed as if my life was very hard. But now, I'm grateful. I would not want it any other way. Being raised the way I was taught me what is really important in this life. Goodness, God has blessed me so much. I could never repay His kindnesses to me. Why, look at the blessing He has given me through you. I know we are going to be very great friends."

I started to remind her that I wouldn't be here long, but I couldn't get the words out. Of course, driving to Harmony for weekend visits wasn't impossible. This town had grabbed a piece of my heart, and I knew I'd have to return whenever I could.

We sipped our lemonade in satisfied silence. I could look out

Ida's front window and see Benjamin's house. The sight of the silent, deserted structure reminded me of a question I wanted to ask her.

"Ida, did you happen to notice any cars at Benjamin's house on Saturday?"

"Let's see." Her forehead wrinkled in thought. "I did see one automobile there. I can't quite remember what time it was."

"Do you know who it belonged to?"

"Why, certainly. It was Sam's."

Disappointment must have shown in my face, because Ida frowned and reached for my hand. "I'm sorry, my dear. That doesn't seem to be the answer you were looking for. Were you hoping I had seen someone else?"

"It doesn't matter. It's not important." I had no intention of telling her about the vase. I felt certain she would believe in my innocence, but I didn't want her to worry about me.

I heard the rumble of Sam's truck on the dirt path that led to Ida's house. The old woman rose to her feet.

"Sounds like I need to cut some pieces of pie," she said happily. "It is so nice to have company. I—I certainly wish you lived here, Gracie. It would be wonderful to have you close." With that, she headed toward the kitchen.

"Let me help you," I called after her.

She turned around and smiled. "Not necessary, child. You stay there and let Sam in, ja? I'll be back lickety-split."

I got up and opened the front door. Sam came bounding up the steps. "Hey, there," he said when he saw me. He looked like he'd just stepped out of the shower. His hair was still damp and he'd changed into a clean shirt.

"Hey, yourself. I hate to tell you this, but Ida and I ate all the pie."

He stopped cold and gaped at me. "I hope you're kidding. . ."

I tried to keep a straight face but found it impossible. His shocked expression made me laugh.

"You are in so much trouble." He flashed me a crooked grin. "I will get you. Somehow. Someway. Somewhere."

"Wow, watch out. I'm shaking." I opened the screen door for him, and he stepped inside. Before I knew it, he had his arms around me in a big hug. He smelled of bath soap and cologne. Startled, I pushed him away. He stepped back quickly and tried to smile, but I could see the hurt in his eyes.

"Sorry. I'm just glad to see you."

"No, I'm sorry," I said. "I shouldn't have done that. You—you just surprised me."

"Forget it," he said brusquely. "I understand."

He walked away from me before I could say anything else. Regret coursed through me. He'd obviously showered and dressed for me. And in his mind, I'd just rejected him. I chided myself for shoving him away. Why had I reacted that way? For some reason, an uncomfortable tension grew inside me that had nothing to do with Jacob Glick or the stolen vase. There was a war waging in my soul. A war I couldn't afford to acknowledge.

I sat down in Ida's chair and listened to Sam and Ida teasing each other in the kitchen. They had a wonderful friendship based on mutual trust and admiration. I wasn't sure I had that in my life. I had friends, sure, but after spending a few days in Harmony, they were beginning to look more like acquaintances. Maybe it had to do with living in a small town. Whatever it was, I couldn't seem to put my finger on the difference.

"Here we are," Ida called out. Sam followed behind her, carrying a tray with three plates of pie and three cups of coffee. Ida wrinkled her nose and laughed. "I told this man I could carry that tray by myself, but he would not let me do it. Thinks I am an old lady, I guess."

"That's not it," Sam said, winking at me. "I just need the exercise so I can keep up with you."

I smiled at him. Thankfully, the friction between us seemed to have disappeared. Ida moved the flowers off the table next to the couch and pulled it over so it sat between us. Sam put the tray on top of it while Ida carried the vase over to a long table against the wall.

"Did you see the flowers Gracie brought me?" she asked Sam.

"They're beautiful," he said, smiling.

She fingered them for a moment and then leaned over to smell them. When she turned around, her eyes were moist. "They remind me so much of Herman. Thank you again, Gracie."

"I'll bring you flowers after Grace leaves," Sam said. "Wish I'd thought of it myself."

Ida tottered back over to the couch. "Pshaw. Men don't understand flowers. Women do though. And my Herman." She reached over and tousled Sam's hair. "You show your concern every time you drop by to see if I need anything. And when you fix things that are broken." She looked at me. "This man completely replaced my roof when it got weak and water began to leak in. He also built new back steps and fixed Zebediah's barn when it started to rot. I could not ask for a better neighbor."

"Oh hush," Sam said good-naturedly. "You know I only do those things so you'll feed me."

Ida chuckled as she took the pie plates and coffee off the tray. She handed me the tray, and I set it down next to my chair.

"This table is not very big, but it will hold our pie," she said. "Now before we eat, will you say grace, Sam?"

We bowed our heads while Sam prayed over the food and asked God's blessings on his friend. We all said, "Amen," and dug into our yummy-looking dessert. It was topped with a rich whipped cream, and the strawberries were encased in a flavorful gelatin. All this was supported by a flaky piecrust that practically melted in my mouth.

"This is delicious," I said after taking my first bite. "My goodness, you definitely would give my grandmother a run for her money."

"I almost forgot," Sam said after swallowing a big bite of pie. "Did you read the letter?"

"Yes, we did," I said. "It was wonderful. We both cried, and I got the hiccups."

Sam laughed. "Oh, great. Don't show it to me. I don't want to cry, and people laugh when I hiccup. I make this strange squeaky sound. Can't control it."

"Thanks for the warning," I said. "I'll try to keep you happy."

Sam gave me a strange look and shoved another piece of pie in his mouth.

"You two young people talk like you have known each other all your lives," Ida chirped. "Gracie, didn't you just arrive here on Friday?"

I nodded. "Yes, I did. But for some reason, it seems like a lifetime ago."

Ida raised her eyebrows. "My goodness, are we so boring?"

"No, not at all." I sneaked a quick look at Sam who returned my gaze with an overly innocent look. "I—I guess it's just that I've been learning so much about the town and its people. And about my family. Things I never knew."

"I understand that." Ida sat her plate down and picked up her cup. "There is a lot of history in Harmony. Many people have come and gone. In fact, few people are left from Bishop Angstadt's days. Most of the old folks have passed—and the young ones have moved away. Only a handful of us left. But the town has changed. People stay now. Things are better. More peaceful."

I was certain she believed what she said, but I knew Harmony still had ghosts. Ghosts that needed to be exorcised. "Abel told me he has diaries and memoirs left behind by past residents. He seems to be an expert on Harmony history."

An odd look crossed Ida's face. "Well, he does have some information, but. . ."

"But there's nothing like actually being there?" Sam finished for her.

Ida sat her cup down and folded her hands. "People only write down what they want people to know in their memoirs. They tend to leave out the unpleasantness—especially their own failures and disappointments." She smiled at us. "Now mind you, I am not saying Abel is misrepresenting anything, but he just has written words. He cannot see the hearts behind the words."

"You're probably the best source of information in town," Sam said. "People should come to you when they want to research Harmony's past."

"Well, I do not know about that, but folks have come around from time to time to ask about past incidents and residents."

I caught Sam's eye, and he gave me a little nod.

"Ida," I said, trying to keep my tone light, "do you remember a man named Jacob Glick?"

She frowned at me. "Jacob Glick? Now why would you ask me about him?"

"I—I ran across his name somewhere. Seems like an interesting man."

The old woman grunted. "Interesting? About as interesting as a snake in the grass." She screwed up her face in a grimace. "The bishop's sidekick, that's what he was. But there was no pretense of godliness in that man. Evil intentions. Evil thoughts." She shook her head. "Herman and I kept our eyes on him. We were determined to keep him away from the young women in our town. Herman confronted him more than once, but Jacob slithered back to the bishop who always protected him."

"That must have been frustrating," Sam said. "Why did you and Herman stay here? Why didn't you leave?"

"Because she felt she had to protect people," I said softly. "Just

237

like she's trying to protect Sarah now."

Ida's head bobbed up and down. "Ja, ja, that's one reason. But we also felt Harmony needed us." She stared past us. "You know," she said dreamily, "too many people are looking for a place where they feel comfortable. But life is not just about comfort. It is about being in a place where you are needed. Comfortable or not, we all have a special place where God wants to use us. A place where someone is waiting just for us. I belong to Harmony. I belong to the people He sends to me. I may not know why—but I know it's important to His plan." She refocused her attention to us. "And I intend to be in the center of His will. That is my calling, you see. Even if He only has me here for one person—it is His plan, not mine that counts."

Sam nodded as though he understood. I just shook my head. I also believed God had a plan for everyone's life, but I had no idea what mine was. Sometimes I worried that I'd completely missed it. Maybe I was so far off track I'd never find my way to that place Ida talked about.

"I—I suppose other people felt the same way about Glick that you did," I said, trying to shift the conversation back to the dead man buried on Benjamin's property. "I mean, he had enemies, right?"

"Oh my, yes. Most of the parents who had young girls. And to be honest, even though Bishop Angstadt protected Jacob, I got the feeling he did not like him any better than the rest of us. He certainly seemed relieved when he left town."

"What made Glick leave?" Sam asked.

"It was strange timing," Ida said slowly. "The last time I laid eyes on the man, he looked like the proverbial cat that had swallowed the canary. Happy as a lark. Never could figure out why."

"I'll bet a lot of people were happy to see him go," I said. Sam and I had hoped Ida would point to someone who specifically wanted Glick gone. But it seemed that everyone in Harmony wanted him out of town. This wasn't getting us anywhere.

Ida rose to her feet. "More coffee?"

"Sounds great," Sam said.

"Let me help you with that." I started to get up when she waved her hand at me.

"You two sit still." She picked up the tray and headed to the kitchen. "I'm not so old I cannot fetch three cups of coffee."

As she toddled away, she mumbled something that I couldn't completely understand. But before she got much farther, a couple of the words brought me to full alert.

"Ida," I said, a little louder than I meant to. "What did you just say?"

Sam shot me a concerned look, but I held my finger to my lips, signaling to him to be quiet.

Ida stopped and turned around. "I am sorry, dear. It is nothing. I—I just said that it is odd so many people are interested in that terrible Jacob Glick."

Sam got to his feet and crossed over to where the elderly woman stood, still holding the tray. He gently took it from her. "What do you mean? What people?"

Ida looked back and forth between Sam and me, a look of confusion on her face. "I guess I should not have said *people*. Just one person who asked me all kinds of questions about Jacob. I had almost forgotten about it. It was awhile ago."

"And who was that?" I asked.

"Why, it was John Keystone, the butcher. He visited me not long after he moved to Harmony. Wanted to know about the early days of our little town, but our conversation kept angling back to Jacob Glick. I found it odd at the time. He said he was doing some kind of family research." She shrugged and headed toward the kitchen, leaving Sam and I to stare at each other with our mouths hanging open.

Chapter Sixteen

Sure didn't expect that," Sam said after we climbed into his truck and waved good-bye to Ida.

"Me either. Why would John Keystone ask about Glick? Could he possibly know something about his death?"

Sam shook his head as he turned onto the main road. "How could he? He was a baby when Glick died. Besides, he only moved here a year ago, and he barely knew Ben. It doesn't make sense."

"He said it had something to do with family business. What could that mean?"

"I don't know, but he must have been referring to *his* family. I remember Abel saying Glick had no relatives."

"So John was talking about his own family," I repeated. "Glick was a predator. We can't assume all his victims lived here. John's interests may have nothing to do with anyone in Harmony."

"You could be right. But what if he lied? Maybe he was just trying to keep Ida from getting suspicious about his questions."

"But why? Who is Glick to John Keystone?"

Sam just shrugged.

My brain kept trying to wrap itself around this new twist. What information was John fishing for? I thought back to Saturday.

John's meat market was right across the street from Ruth's shop. He easily could have slipped in and stolen the vase after Ruth left. But why would he want to cause trouble for me? I was no threat to him.

"Could Mary have overheard me asking about Glick and told John?"

"They're pretty good friends," he said slowly. "I think she'd tell him whatever he wanted to know." He frowned. "But was Mary even in the room when you mentioned Glick?"

"She was there all right. Every time I looked her way, she was shooting me dirty looks."

He sighed. "Well, Abel's pretty loud. Even if Mary didn't hear you, she easily could have heard him. And he mentioned Glick very clearly."

"I—I don't know what to make of this." I stared at him. "Can you ask Mary if she talked to John about me? And if Glick's name came up? I have to know if John had any reason to take Ruth's vase."

"Oh man. You don't know what you're asking. Mary would like to take off my head and serve it as the main course for supper. Besides, even if she did mention our conversation, it doesn't mean John had any reason to frame you for theft."

I patted his arm. "I know that. I'm just trying to follow the trail to see where it leads—even if it's a dead end. Talking to Mary might be difficult, but you've got to mend fences with her anyway. Surely you're not planning to avoid the café for the rest of your life."

"Well, actually that was the plan," he said with a smirk. "It may be the safest alternative."

The silly look on his face made me laugh. "I think you can come up with something better than that."

His only answer was a grunt.

We passed Ben's house and reached Main Street. I looked at

my watch. Four fifteen. We were supposed to meet Levi at four thirty. A little early for supper, but he had something else planned around six. We had just enough time to pick up sandwiches. "You know, even if we find out that John knows of my interest in Glick, we still have no idea what that means."

"I agree. That's why we have to confront him."

"Confront him!" I tried to keep a note of hysteria out of my voice, but I failed miserably. "Since coming to Harmony, I've taken a long-held secret and blabbed it to so many people I'm surprised my family skeletons haven't danced their way onto the front page of the local paper!"

Sam cast a disapproving look my way. "First of all, we don't actually have a local paper. Secondly, if we did, I hope we could come up with something better than your exploits. Besides, just who have you blabbed to? Me? Sweetie found out on her own. You didn't tell Emily the truth."

"But I more or less confirmed her suspicion that Glick was dead. And as far as Sweetie goes, she found my uncle's letter because of me. Because of my carelessness."

"Now hold on there," Sam said sharply. "You weren't careless. Sweetie was overly nosy. There was no way for you to know her part in all this or that she was actually spying on you. That's not your fault."

"I guess you're right, but it sure feels like this situation is spiraling out of control."

"This situation has been out of control for thirty years. We're the ones who need to bring it back under control. You've convinced me that discovering the truth is our only hope."

Of course, he was right. Every moment I'd spent in Harmony had only proved that secrets buried in emotional graves eventually turn deadly. The truth had to come out. I was also well aware of the fact that at the end of my two weeks, if I still didn't have the answers I needed, I would have to tell my father everything. Now that I knew he hadn't actually caused Glick's death, I certainly felt better about that possibility. However, just because I knew my father wasn't involved didn't mean the authorities would believe it. As of now, he was the only person we knew about who'd fought Glick the night he died. And then he'd left town. No matter how you sliced it, Dad looked guilty. The only outcome that would absolutely protect my father was handing over the real killer. I prayed God would help Sam and me find him before it was too late.

We were nearing the bakery. "So what are we going to tell Levi?" I said.

"I don't know. I guess we'll tell him the truth."

"Will he keep our conversation secret?"

"If we tell him to, yes." He pulled up in front of the bakery.

"I hate passing this burden on to someone else."

"I do, too." He turned off the engine. "But we've got to have more information, and he's the only person I can think of who might be able to give it to us." He smiled at me. "Don't worry. I've known him all my life. If there's anyone in Harmony we can trust, it's Levi Hoffman. He's been like a father to me."

I nodded. "Okay, okay. Guess I'm just getting a little antsy. Seems like we take off down one rabbit trail and another pops up. I just hope this journey we're on has a satisfying conclusion. We're dragging a lot of lives behind us."

Sam reached over and turned my face toward his. "You've got to have some faith, Grace. God brought you here for a purpose. He won't desert us now. The results of this journey, as you called it, aren't on your beautiful shoulders. They're on God's strong ones."

I gazed into his eyes and saw the sincerity there. "Exactly what I've been telling myself. But you might need to remind me several times a day. Think you can live up to the challenge?"

He laughed softly. "I'll try." He learned over and kissed me on the forehead. "Now, let's go pick out some sandwiches."

We exited Menlos' a few minutes later, loaded down with sandwiches, pop, and cookies warm from the oven. Mrs. Menlo gave us paper plates, napkins, and plastic utensils—something I hadn't thought about. She also stuck three pieces of baklava into our sack.

We got back in the truck, and Sam drove while I balanced our meal on my lap. I'd passed the city park on my way into town, but this was my first chance to actually scout it out. We turned onto a dirt road that wound around the small lake. A group of geese glided smoothly across the shimmering crystal water. Several small ducks quacked noisily as a woman and her daughter threw pieces of bread to them.

We passed a lovely stone water fountain surrounded by whitewashed wooden benches. Water gently danced down the four-tiered stone fountain. "It's beautiful," I said to Sam. "Looks expensive. Where did it come from?"

He slowed the truck down, backed up, and pulled over to the side of the road. "We've still got a few minutes. Get out and I'll show you something."

I followed him down a stone path leading to the fountain. It was even more beautiful close up. I peered over the edge of the bottom tier. The floor of the fountain was layered with coins dropped in by people with wishes in their hearts.

"I left my purse back in the truck," I said. "I want a penny to throw in."

I turned to go back to the truck when I felt Sam's hand on my shoulder. "Here." He reached into his jean pocket with his other hand. "I've got change from the bakery." He pulled out several coins.

I took a penny, thought a minute, then threw it into the sparkling water.

"You really think that will help?" he asked with a smile.

"I don't actually wish when I throw coins in a fountain. I pray. I just prayed that God's will would be done in Harmony—and in my life."

"Pretty dangerous prayer," Sam said in a quiet voice, the sound of water splashing lightly in the background.

"How so?"

"What if God's will isn't your will?"

"I'm not sure I understand what you mean."

He cocked his head to one side and raised both eyebrows. "A real prayer of consecration—saying not my will but Yours. It means your life may take a turn you hadn't planned on. Are you ready to accept that?"

I stared into the water. Had I really meant what I prayed? Or was I trying to fit God into *my* plan? Doubt flooded my mind. "I—I don't know. I guess I'll have to think about that."

Sam laughed easily, his blond hair blowing gently in the afternoon breeze. "You'd better decide pretty fast. You may have to face that question sooner than you imagine."

I squinted up at him, not quite sure what he meant. The look in his eyes caused a strange tickling sensation to run down my spine. I swallowed hard. "We—we better get going. Levi will be here soon."

"I told you I wanted to show you something." He grabbed my hand and led me around to the other side of the fountain. He pointed to a plaque attached to the front of the structure. It read:

HARMONY, KANSAS
WHERE LOVE REIGNS
1 CORINTHIANS 13:8—LOVE NEVER FAILS
DONATED BY THE MENNONITE WOMEN OF HARMONY

"Oh my," I said. "How wonderful."

"The women I told you about—the ones who got together

after Angstadt died? One of them, Kendra McBroom, had a brother who was a stonemason. The women worked hard to save enough money for his materials, and he donated his labor. They gave this fountain to Harmony as a symbol of their prayers, asking God for His blessing on the town. Your grandmother was one of them, you know."

"I—I didn't know that. No one ever told me."

He nodded. "Your grandparents were well loved in this community. I've heard stories about them ever since I came to live here. Wish I could have met them."

"They were very special people," I agreed. "But I didn't realize just how special until I came here. Funny how sometimes we see those we love through fresh eyes when we see them through the eyes of others."

Sam nodded. "I wish people would see my aunt through my eyes. She's an amazing woman. Just because she comes wrapped in a rough exterior, people sometimes miss how beautiful she really is."

His voice cracked with emotion, and I reached over and slid my arm through his. We stood for a few moments, watching the water dance from tier to tier.

"Levi just pulled up to the shelter," Sam said finally. "We'd better get going."

Sure enough, Levi's Suburban was parked next to a picnic table at the farthest point of the lake. We got into the truck and drove to where he waited. He waved as we approached. Sam carefully carried the sack from Menlo's to the table, and within a few minutes I was chomping away on the best chicken salad sandwich I'd ever tasted.

Sam laughed at my sounds of satisfaction. "I take it you approve of your simple supper?"

"Harmony could have restaurants on every street the way people cook here. I've never had so many delicious meals."

Levi nodded and patted his rounded stomach. "I used to be skinny," he said with a sigh. "But eventually I gave in. Life is too short to miss out on all this great food."

Sam raised his eyebrows and tried to look serious. "Life might actually last a little longer if you said no once in a while."

Levi sighed deeply. "But it wouldn't be as enjoyable."

I laughed. "We haven't even told you about the baklava Mrs. Menlo gave us."

"Oh mercy," he said. "She makes the best baklava in town."

"Well, I'll just add that to my growing list. The best strawberry pie, the best peach cobbler, the best baklava. I see a trend here." I put my sandwich down and wiped my mouth with my napkin. "When do I get something healthy?"

"Now wait a minute," Sam said. "We did have fruit salad the other night. That was very healthy."

"One healthy meal. Great. It's a wonder I can still fit into my clothes. Beginning immediately, I'm cutting down."

Levi chuckled. "My goodness, you're barely there as it is. If you lose any more weight, we won't be able to see you."

I reached over and patted him on the arm. "I knew I liked you the first minute I saw you. Now I know why."

Sam and Levi laughed. The conversation turned to weather forecasts, crops, and harvest. As they exchanged information, I glanced around me. Several families ate together in the lush park. A small playground on the other side of the lake entertained a handful of happy children who shrieked with laughter as they begged their parents to push them higher on the swings or run faster as they clung to the merry-go-round. A man wearing jeans and a T-shirt pushed a little girl, who wore a long dress and a prayer covering on her head, on the swings. And a man with a beard and a large straw hat played ball with a father and his son who both wore jeans and T-shirts. My eyes wandered over to the fountain erected by the praying women of Harmony, and

I got a lump in my throat. God had so clearly answered their prayer. Could what Sam said be true? Would my foray into the past actually bring healing to this community? Or would it tear a fabric in the peace that hung over this place like a comforting quilt? I silently cried out to God, asking Him to bind me to the prayers of my grandmother and the other women who had lifted up this town to Him. *Show me the truth, Lord. Use this situation to help Harmony.*

"Did you hear me, Grace?" Sam's voice cut through my thoughts.

"I—I'm sorry. What did you say?"

He frowned at me. "You okay?"

"Yes. Sorry. I just drifted away for a minute. This really is a beautiful park. I guess it's owned by the city?"

"Actually, the church owns it," Levi said. "They donated the land for the city's use. Both churches worked together to put in the facilities and the playground equipment. And they maintain it together."

"That's amazing," I said. "Unfortunately, there aren't a lot of churches that cooperate like that."

Levi shrugged. "I guess Harmony is unusual."

"You said something to Sweetie about not being a churchgoer," I said. "Yet I understand you used to be an elder at Bethel. I don't mean to be nosy but. . ."

"But what happened?" Levi sat his sandwich down and wiped his mouth. "Let's just say that I've had all the religion I can stand."

"Jesus felt the same way," I said gently. "He told us to strive for. . ."

"I know. Relationship not religion. Abel has told me that more than once." He rubbed his hands together and smiled at me. "Maybe one of these days I'll give in and go back to church. I have to admit that Abel and Marcus Jensen aren't anything like Amil Angstadt." He shook his head. "I'm sorry. Amil Angstadt was the old bishop at Bethel."

"I—I know who he was, Levi. He's one of the reasons Sam and I asked to talk to you this evening."

His eyebrows shot up as he looked at Sam. "I figured you two had some specific reason to meet with me. Why in heaven's name would you want to talk about Bishop Angstadt? That man's dead and buried. Best to leave him where he is."

"Levi," Sam said slowly, glancing around to make sure no one was near enough to hear us, "something odd has happened. Grace and I need your help. We want to ask you some questions about your old bishop. And about a man who worked for him. Jacob Glick."

Levi's eyes widened. "Jacob Glick? My goodness. I haven't heard that name in many, many years. Why would you want to know about him? He left Harmony a long time ago. And good riddance, by the way."

Sam reached over and knitted his fingers through mine. "We have something to tell you, Levi. But first we need you to promise you'll keep it between us."

"You can tell me anything—you know that, Sam." Levi stared at us quizzically.

Sam shook his head. "You need to consider our request more carefully than that. What we're going to share involves a very serious crime."

Levi's mouth dropped open. "You and Gracie. . ."

"No, not us," Sam said quickly. "Someone else. A long time ago."

Levi wrapped up the remainder of his sandwich and pushed it to the side. "Listen, you two," he said evenly, "whatever you say to me will stay right here. You have my word. Although I can't imagine. . ."

"Jacob Glick didn't leave town," I blurted out. "He's dead. And buried on my uncle's property."

Levi looked as if I'd just slapped him in the face. "Wha—what? What are you talking about?"

In slow, measured tones, Sam told Levi the whole story—everything that had happened since I'd arrived in Harmony. He carefully left out Sweetie and Emily's involvement. Levi finally lost his shocked expression, but the gravity of our situation wasn't lost on him.

"Goodness gracious," he said finally. "All this time. . ." He shook his head. "Ben kept this secret all these years?"

I nodded. "Yes, but he was wrong about what happened. Someone besides my father killed Glick. We need to know who it was. You seem to be the only person left in Harmony who worked closely with him and Angstadt. And Sam said we could trust you to keep this quiet until we find the truth."

"And if you don't uncover the murderer?"

Sam and I looked at each other. "Then we call the authorities," I said. "We can't keep this buried the way my uncle did. It's got to come out."

Levi stared down at the table for several seconds. "Sorry. I'm trying to digest everything. It isn't easy."

"I know it's a lot to take in," Sam said. "Can we ask you some questions about Glick?"

Levi nodded.

"What did you think of him?" I asked.

"He was a terrible man," Levi said. "He and Bishop Angstadt were almost always together. I never could understand it. As an elder, I took my concerns about Jacob to the bishop on several occasions." He took a deep breath and let it out slowly. "There were accusations about his behavior toward several young women. Yet every time I mentioned it to the bishop, he dismissed me, saying I had wrong information. Or he'd accuse me of spreading gossip. It was very frustrating."

"You were aware of his inappropriateness with some of the women?" I asked. "Do you remember who he approached?"

Levi grunted. "Almost every female in town was bothered by

that lecherous man. Didn't matter how old they were, but he liked the young ladies best. Many of them too young, if you know what I mean. That man was shopping for a young wife." He picked up his pop can and took a drink. Then he wiped his mouth. "I remember specifically his interest in your aunt, Sam. And Kendra McBroom. She left Harmony a long time ago."

"What about Emily Mueller?" Sam asked.

Levi's face went blank. "I—I don't remember anything about that." He frowned. "Emily was only a child when Jacob lived here. I would hope he never approached her."

"What about the parents of these women?" Sam asked. "Did any of them know about Glick's proclivities? Was there anyone you can think of who might have had a reason to kill him?"

Levi hesitated for a moment. "I'm really trying to remember, but it's so long ago. . ."

"I know," Sam said. "Take your time."

Levi stroked his white beard and stared off into the distance. Finally, he shook his head. "I just don't remember anything that will help you. The thing you must understand is that the bishop worked hard to protect Jacob—to keep him from suspicion."

"Well, he didn't succeed," I said. "Someone killed him."

"Give me some time to ponder on this. Maybe I'll remember something helpful." He folded his arms and looked at me. "You said he was killed on your property?"

I nodded. "Yes. Somewhere just inside the tree line."

"Seems like a stupid thing for a man like Jacob to do," Levi said. "Isolating himself. Standing out in the open with all those trees surrounding him. Anyone could have been hiding there, watching him. Waiting for a chance to get rid of him. You know, there was no love lost between that man and at least half of the folks in Harmony. When he disappeared all those years ago, I assumed his leaving was a result of his lechery. Guess I was right, but I just envisioned the wrong kind of departure."

"Angstadt couldn't protect him from everything," I said. "Although I suspect he was relieved when he realized Glick was gone for good."

Sam opened his mouth to say something but stopped when a commotion from Main Street caught our attention. A fire truck with a large tank in its bed bounced down the street while several men ran behind it. A couple of them grabbed the back of the truck and held on while the rest scrambled for their cars.

"What in the world...," I said.

Levi jumped to his feet. "There's a fire."

Sam stood up, too. "Stay here, Grace," he said.

As he and Levi sprinted toward their vehicles, I quickly gathered up the remnants of our abandoned supper and stuffed everything except the opened pop cans back in the sack.

"Sam, wait for me!" I yelled, running as fast as I could for the truck before he took off. I quickly threw the sticky pop cans in a nearby trash can.

Sam honked his horn impatiently before I reached the passenger door. "I want to help," I said breathlessly as I climbed inside.

He just nodded and threw the truck into gear. We sped down the access road toward Main Street. As we neared Main, Sam slammed the brakes on at the sight of Abel Mueller waving him down.

Sam rolled down his window as Abel hurried up to us. "It's Ben's house," he yelled. "Sweetie called it in."

"My uncle's house?" I said incredulously. A house that had stood for three generations was burning? How could that be?

"Thanks, Abel," Sam said. "We need to get there as fast as we can."

"Emily and I are coming in my car," he said pointing to the church. His black car with its painted bumpers sat near the front door. Emily waited in the passenger seat.

Once again, Sam put the truck in gear and tried to navigate down Harmony's main road. People ran out of their businesses, jumping into cars and buggies. It looked as if the whole town was turning out. I recognized many of them: Mr. Menlo, Amos Crandall from the clothing store, and Paul Bruner from the leather and feed store. Joe Loudermilk locked the door of his hardware store, ran down the street, and got into a car with Dale and Dan Scheidler from the farm implements store. Even John Keystone joined the frantic, disorganized race.

"I don't understand how this could have happened," I yelled to Sam, trying to be heard over the rattling of the truck on the uneven dirt road. "There isn't any electricity in the house. Nothing to catch fire."

Sam shook his head. "I checked everything the last time we were there," he said loudly, trying to be heard while he kept his eyes on the road. So many people were pouring into Main Street we looked like part of a badly organized, last-minute parade. "The propane, the generator downstairs—everything was turned off. I have no idea what could have started it."

"Is that tanker truck the only fire truck in Harmony?"

He nodded. "Sunrise has a volunteer fire department. They'll come if we need them, but they're ten miles from here." He glanced over at me, his face tight with concern. "If the fire is spreading quickly, they won't make it in time. We have fire hydrants in town, but none outside of town. This kind of fire is always a worry."

I found myself praying that the house wouldn't burn down. All I'd wanted to do when I got to Harmony was get rid of my uncle's property. Now, only four days later, the prospect of losing the house where my family had lived all those years deeply saddened me. I tried to stop the tears that slid down my face, but I couldn't. That house meant something to me now, and I didn't want to see it destroyed.

It seemed like it took forever to get to Benjamin's. We hadn't even turned onto Faith Road by the time the large plume of smoke was clearly visible above the tree line. When we finally pulled up, the little house was surrounded with vehicles and people. Several of the men from town were hauling a long yellow hose from the tanker truck.

"The truck only holds about three hundred gallons of water," Sam shouted. "We'll use that along with a bucket brigade from your well."

As Sam parked the truck, I could finally see the fire. Flames danced from the corner of the house where the kitchen was located and licked up toward the roof. If the roof went, the house would most likely be gone.

I jumped down and followed Sam toward the people forming a line from an ancient metal water pump located about fifty yards behind the house. Ruth Crandall and Mary Whittenbauer ran toward the pump, carrying stacks of metal buckets. I was so shocked to see Mary that I froze in my tracks. Sam kept going. He quickly took his place in line, trying to stretch the line from the pump to the fire. I jogged up next to him, but was quickly pulled out of the line by Joyce Bechtold.

"Only men in the line!" she yelled at me. I started to protest, but she grabbed my shoulders. "The buckets are too heavy, Gracie," she yelled. "You won't be able to pass it without spilling it." She pushed me toward a large truck that had a hand-painted sign attached to its side. It read HARMONY HARDWARE. "Here," she said, handing me a stack of buckets from the back of the truck. "Carry these to the pump. That will be a big help."

I took the stack from her hands and ran past the growing group of men that stretched from the pump almost to the house. As I set them down next to the water pump, I noticed a man frantically filling buckets and sending them down the line. I was shocked to see Gabriel Ketterling moving water through that old pump faster than it had probably ever flowed before. He glanced my way but didn't acknowledge me at all. Without thinking, I reached out and put my hand on his arm. Startled, he gazed up at me, his face locked in his usual scowl.

"Thank you."

For a few seconds, his expression softened and he gave me a brief nod. The he went back to his work. I ran back to the hardware truck. By now, several women were carrying buckets. I started to get another stack when Joyce grabbed me again.

"Stand at the end of the line," she shouted. "When four buckets are empty, pick them up and run them back to the pump. Do you understand?"

I nodded yes and took off toward the house. Water from the pumper truck was flowing freely on the fire, and the line from the pump was complete. I was shocked to see all the people who'd left their homes and businesses to help. Some I'd met. Most were strangers. Some wore clothing just like mine. Most wore plain clothing. All of them worked together as if they'd been doing this all their lives. Abel Mueller stood next to Marcus Jensen. Sam and Hector from the restaurant passed a huge bucket of water between them. A young man with Down syndrome moved the bucket down the line and turned to wait for the next one. I could feel the tears streaming down my face, but I didn't care."

"Quick," a deep voice hollered. "Take these to the pump!"

I held out my hands for a stack of empty buckets and looked up into the soot-streaked face of John Keystone. His hair was wet and combed back from his face, and his usual smirk had been replaced with a frown. As I stared at him, a sudden revelation hit me so hard I almost stumbled as I ran back toward the pump. I remembered the odd sensation I'd had when I'd met him on Saturday. Now I knew where I'd seen him before. And the realization shocked me. I dropped off the buckets and ran back to the end of the line, passing Cora Crandall and Emily Mueller. They hurried toward the pump, their arms full of empty buckets, and their long skirts flapping against their legs. If the situation hadn't been so serious, I would have found it humorous.

As I reached the beginning of the line, I realized that the roaring flames were down to a flicker. Our efforts were paying off. My earlier tears of gratitude were turning into tears of relief. Between all the running, crying, and breathing in smoke, I was beginning to feel light-headed. By the time I got back to John, things around me began to spin.

I reached over to pick up the empty buckets stacked next to his feet when I felt myself sway. Strong arms reached out and caught me before I fell. I felt myself lowered to the ground.

"Take a big breath, Gracie," a deep voice said. My eyes, which had closed for a moment to stop the world from turning around me, flew open. John was a few inches from my face. "Are you okay?"

"We need more buckets. . ."

He shook his head and smiled. "No. The fire's under control. The pumper truck can finish the job. I think we need to get you into the shade."

"I feel so foolish."

"Don't be ridiculous," he said brusquely. "You have nothing to feel foolish about." He helped me to my feet, keeping his arm around me, and gently guided me over to a nearby tree where he helped me to sit down."

"Here's some water, Gracie," a soft feminine voice said.

Sarah Ketterling knelt next to me with a cup of water in her hands. Wondering where it had come from, I noticed Mary and Ruth filling Styrofoam cups from the restaurant with water from the pump. They handed them out to the tired and thirsty volunteers.

"Thank you."

Sarah's lovely eyes were full of concern. "Are you feeling any better?" she asked.

I nodded as I finished the water. "Yes. Guess I just got carried away a little. I had no idea I'd react this way about my uncle's house."

Sarah smiled at me. "You mean *your* house, don't you?"

I started to protest, but as I gazed at the old house, I realized she was right. It was my house now. And I didn't want it to burn down. "I—I guess you're right."

"Sometimes we don't realize how much something means to us until we're faced with losing it," John said in a low voice. A look passed between him and Sarah that I didn't know how to interpret.

Sarah's pale face turned pink, and she rose to her feet. "I need to check on Father. I'm glad you're feeling better." With that she turned and walked away. John watched her for several seconds before he turned his attention back to me.

"If you're feeling okay," he said brusquely, "I'd better help the guys clean up the mess."

"Yes, I'm fine. And thank you, John. Thank you so much."

He raised an eyebrow, and his face took on the same expression I'd seen when I first met him. "I don't know what it is about this town," he said with an air of disgust. "It gets in your blood somehow. Even if you don't want it to." He shook his head. "Wish I could figure it out."

With that he walked away, leaving me to ponder his words. I should have found them strange, but somehow I completely understood. I started to get up when a sharp voice startled me, and I sat back down with a *thump*.

"Well, there you are." Sweetie stood in front of me in her ever-present overalls. Usually streaked with dirt from her orchards, this time soot decorated the old, worn denim. Streaks of black across her face told me she'd been pretty close to the fire. "I been lookin' all over for you."

At that moment Sam walked up next to her. His T-shirt clung

to his chest and sweat dripped down his face. "It's really not too bad, Grace," he said. "The kitchen will have to be rebuilt, but the rest of the house is okay. A little smoke damage here and there. It will stink inside for a while, but it could have been far worse. Thank God it was called in before it got too bad."

"Abel said you saw the fire and got help, Sweetie," I said. "Thank you so much."

She grinned widely. "Well, I called it in, girlie. But Ida alerted me to the fire. She saw it from her house and ran down the road to my place to tell me. She fell before she got there, but I spotted her layin' on the road thrashin' about. 'Course, by the time I got to her, I could see the smoke."

"Is she okay?" My voice trembled with concern for my new friend.

"Sure, sure. She's back at her place restin'. I took care of her after I called the fire department in Sunrise and Joe Louder-milk. He contacted the rest of the men in our volunteer fire department. I told him to tell Ruth and Mary about the fire. I knowed those two women would alert the whole town. And they sure as shootin' did."

"But what about Gabriel Ketterling? No one called him."

"Nope. He was just drivin' by in his buggy and saw the flames. Him and Sarah pitched in right away.

I shook my head slowly and struggled to my feet. "I can't believe all these people turned out to help me," I said. "If it hadn't been for everyone here. . ."

"If it hadn't been for Ida," Sam interrupted. "This is a terrible time for your house to catch fire with everyone still in town or out in the fields. If she hadn't seen the smoke, it probably would have burned to the ground before anyone had a chance to call for help."

Abel ambled up to us. "Just wanted to tell you that we're going to clean things up tonight and start fixing the kitchen tomorrow. We'll have things as good as new in no time at all."

"How—how much will it cost, Abel?" I said. "I don't have much money, but I'm sure my dad will be happy to. . ."

"Gracie Temple!" Abel said loudly. "Do you still not understand Mennonites? This is what we do. You don't owe anyone anything—except a promise not to leave an oil lamp burning when you're not around."

"That what started the fire, Abel?" Sweetie asked.

"Yep. Too near the curtains from what we can figure. Just got too hot and started a blaze." Before I could say anything, he patted my shoulder. "Don't worry about it, Gracie. If you're not used to having oil lamps, accidents can happen."

Someone called his name, and he turned and walked away. Sweetie followed him.

"I didn't leave any oil lamp burning," I hissed to Sam.

"I know that," he said in a low voice. "Keep your voice down. Obviously someone started the fire on purpose. I think they wanted to burn down the whole house. They just didn't count on Ida and her determination."

"But why burn down the house? It doesn't make sense."

"I have no idea, but my guess is they want you out of Harmony. Seems to me if someone wanted to physically hurt you, they wouldn't be stealing family heirlooms and setting fires when you're not home."

"You've got a point."

"Look, you've been through a lot today," Sam said. "I'm going to have Sweetie drive you home. I need to stay here." He looked up at the sky. "It doesn't look like rain, but we can't take a chance. We need to make sure the house is protected from any surprise storms."

"Thanks, but I'll drive my car. It's been sitting ever since I got here."

Sam started to protest, but I put my fingers on his lips. "This isn't open for debate. I want to check on Ida. I'll go straight to your place after that."

"All right, but if you start feeling woozy again, you either come and get me or go on to the house, okay?"

I nodded solemnly. "I promise."

With a final look of warning, he joined a group of men talking about what to do next to fix my uncle's house. Correction: *my* house. That concept was going to take some getting used to.

I felt a hand on my shoulder and turned to find Joyce Bechtold standing behind me. "I hope you'll forgive me for ordering you around earlier," she said. "I'm usually not so aggressive." Her face belonged to a beautiful woman who had lived with laughter, but her eyes held shadows of pain. Perhaps some of what I saw was planted there through years of unrequited love for my uncle.

"Please don't apologize. I had no idea what to do. I needed someone to tell me, and I'm grateful for your help."

Her well-used laugh lines fell into place as she smiled. "Thank you, Gracie. I wouldn't want to offend you. Your uncle spoke of you quite often. Especially toward the end of his life. He wanted so much to see you. I—I wish he would have reached out to his family before the end. I never understood his reluctance, and although I asked him about it, he never seemed to be able to explain his reasons."

I nodded but couldn't come up with a response. Not one she would want to hear anyway.

She hesitated for a moment as if she wanted to say something else. Finally, she took a step back. "I guess I'd better go. I left the shop unattended, and I'm fairly sure I left the lights on and the door unlocked. All I could think about was Ben's. . . I'm sorry. I mean your house."

I reached out and touched her arm. "No, that's fine. It's hard for me to call it my house, too. He'll always be a part of it."

She nodded silently. Sadness emanated from her.

"Joyce, I wanted to ask you about the birdhouses."

She raised her eyebrows. "You mean the ones I painted with Ben?"

I smiled at her. "Kind of. Actually, he left quite a few of them unpainted in the basement. I'd really like you to have them."

"Oh dear, Gracie. I—I mean, I could paint them for you, and you could give them to Ruth. . ."

"No no. I don't want to sell them, Joyce. I really want you to take the houses. You can do whatever you want with them. Keep them, sell them. I don't care. I know my uncle would want you to have them. And if there's anything else. . .something you gave him or a memento you'd like to have, please let me know. I realize you were close to him."

A tear slid down her face. "Not as close as I wish we'd been. I'm afraid he kept a wall around himself. I feel blessed to have glimpsed behind it a few times, but in the end, that emotional barrier was too strong for us. I wish. . ."

She didn't need to finish the sentence. I knew what she wished. "As soon as things settle down some, will you come by?"

She smiled through her tears. "Thank you, Gracie. Your uncle would have absolutely adored you. I hope you know that."

As she walked away, Gabriel Ketterling's words rang in my head. *Would have been mighty ashamed to call something like this family.* I wondered which statement was true. Would I ever know the answer?

I jogged over to Sam's truck, found my purse, and grabbed the sack of baklava from Menlo's. Then I hurried to the other side of the house where my car had been parked since I'd arrived in Harmony. As I pulled out onto Faith Road, I passed John Keystone. He was getting something out of his car, but his thoughts seemed to be focused in another direction—on the beautiful Mennonite girl waiting in her father's buggy. Sarah sat with her head bowed and her eyes downcast. She appeared to be oblivious to John's fixed gaze. As I drove past, he saw me and quickly redirected his concentration back to the task at hand. Strange. John Keystone was obviously attracted to Sarah, but there was very little hope for romance there. Gabriel would never allow someone like John anywhere near his daughter. Frankly, I was surprised by his attention. I would have thought someone like Mary would be a more likely match.

As I drove down the dirt road toward Ida's, I turned to my earlier conjecture about John. I felt certain I was right. But now what to do with my suspicion? I needed to confront him, but I really wanted Sam with me. Even though I'd seen a softer side to the butcher, I didn't want to be alone with him when I asked the question I had to ask.

I turned into Ida's and parked near the porch. Zebediah stood near the fenced area behind the house. I took a minute to pet him before going inside. He moved his face next to me and closed his eyes while I stroked his soft face. His gentleness touched me. He was used to being cared for. I couldn't help glancing at my car as I made my way to Ida's front porch. I couldn't pet it or have deep feelings about it. Maybe Ida had a point. If I lived in Harmony, I would definitely have a horse.

I stopped cold at the bottom of the steps. *If I lived in Harmony?* Where had that thought come from? Man, a few days here and I was turning into Fannie the farmer. I shook off the silly thought and bounded up the stairs. The door was open, the screen door closed. Instead of knocking, I called out Ida's name. I heard her holler at me to come in. When I stepped into the living room, I found her curled up on the couch with a pillow, a comforter, and a book in her hand.

"Are you okay?"

She struggled to right herself. "Ach, I am fine. My goodness. An old woman takes a tumble and everyone thinks she is ready to be put out to pasture."

Regardless of her protests, I'd noticed a slight wince when she'd sat up. "I don't think you're ready for the pasture, but I do think you should take it easy for a couple of days. Are you sure nothing's broken?"

She waved her hand at me. "I am absolutely certain. I bruised my hip, but everything is still working just fine. I feel so silly, falling like that." She reached down and stroked her legs. "Getting older is not any fun, you know? God keeps me strong and healthy, but our bodies do start to wear out. And there is not much we can do about it." She smiled at me, her face full of joy. "But with every day that comes, I know I am getting closer to going home. And I can hardly wait. Zebediah and I will ride the beautiful trails of heaven—both of us young and vibrant again."

For just a moment, in the look of bliss on her face, I could see the beautiful young girl she was once, and the woman she believed she would be again. It brought a lump to my throat. I sat down in the chair across from her.

"So you believe Zebediah will go to heaven?" I asked gently.

Ida straightened her comforter and put her book on the table next to her. *The Pilgrim's Progress* by John Bunyan. One of my favorites. "I certainly do. I do not believe God would give us so much love for animals if we would never be with them again. The Bible says they have souls. I know there is more than just body and instinct inside them." She smiled at me. "I realize they do not go to heaven the same way we do. But since nothing is impossible for Him, I am convinced He can bring our beloved pets back to us. There have been a few animals in my life. . ."The old woman's voice shook with emotion. "Forgive me, dear," she said in a quiet voice. "Herman and I never had children. Some of our pets became like our children. I recently lost a dog I had for quite some time. I have not had the heart to replace him. It still hurts too much. And Zebediah? My goodness. What an old and dear friend he is. I cannot imagine my life without him."

"I understand." Ida's remembrances of beloved pets struck a little too close to home. I'd grown up with dogs, but after we lost Eddie, a darling little Jack Russell, I'd vowed I'd never have another one. When I moved into my apartment and discovered that dogs weren't allowed, I'd felt relieved. My cat, Snicklefritz, was the only companion I needed. Of course, I'd been certain I could never get as close to a cat as I had a dog. My assumption had proved false. Silly cat had found a way into my heart. I was suddenly filled with a longing to see him.

"How is your house, Gracie? I tried to watch the attempt to put out the fire from my window, but unfortunately I could not stand long enough to see much."

"It's going to be fine." I shook my head. "I can hardly believe the way everyone came together to save it."

"That is the way it is in Harmony. We are a family." She adjusted her slightly askew prayer covering over the gray braids piled on top of her head. "Let me see if I can get us some tea."

"I really don't have time," I said gently. "But let me make you something before I go. Have you eaten?"

"No, but I will get to it." She winced again. "I am fine, child. Just a little sore."

"You get comfortable," I said with a smile. "I'll brew some tea, get you some supper, and make sure you have everything you need before I go."

Ida's face flushed. "Oh dear. You really do not need to put yourself out so."

I got up and went over to where she sat. Taking her hands in mine, I said, "Ida, you saved my house. Sweetie saw you even before she noticed the smoke. If you hadn't tried to get help, the house might have burned to the ground. My family and I owe you so much."

"Goodness, anyone would have done the same..."

I shook my head. "No. Not everyone would have done the same thing. Most people wouldn't have risked themselves the way you did."

"Ach, child. I am just happy help arrived in time."

I gave her a quick hug. "Now for that supper." I'd started toward the kitchen when she stopped me.

"Gracie, how did the fire start?"

Not wanting to worry her, I said, "Ummm. . .I guess I left an oil lamp burning."

Ida's face wrinkled in a deep frown. "I do not understand. I leave lamps burning all the time. They have never started a fire."

I shrugged. "I guess the lamp was too close to the kitchen curtains. Anyway, that's what I was told." I took a deep breath and tried to keep my tone light. "I don't suppose you saw anyone at the house late this afternoon did you?

She shook her head. "I must admit that I fell asleep reading and spent the entire afternoon napping on this couch—until I smelled something burning." She raised one eyebrow. "Why? Surely you do not suspect. . ."

"No. No reason. Just wondering."

I left the room quickly before she could ask any more questions. I didn't want to alarm her by telling her I thought someone had purposely started the fire, but I had to know if she'd seen anything.

I put some water on for tea. Inside Ida's small refrigerator, I found cold cuts and cheese. There was bread in the bread box. I made a sandwich and sliced an apple. Then I poured a cup of hot tea and carried everything into the living room. Ida had pulled the small side table in front of her, and I set her supper on it.

"Ach, that looks perfect," she said, smiling. "What a blessing. Thank you so much."

I told her to wait a minute and ran out the front door to my car. I grabbed the sack from Menlo's that I'd transferred from Sam's truck. "I have a special treat for you," I said as I reentered the living room. "I hope you like baklava."

Ida's face lit up. "Oh ja. I absolutely love it."

I pulled the gooey desserts out of the sack and put them in front of her. "Three pieces. Is that too many? I can put some in the refrigerator."

She slapped playfully at my hand. "You leave them right where they are," she said, grinning. "I intend to make short work of every one."

I laughed at her enthusiasm. "I have to go, but I'll be back later to clean this up and help you get ready for bed."

Ida's bright smile slipped from her face. "Oh no, Gracie. I am just a little sore. I can get around just fine."

I leaned over and hugged her. "No arguing. I'm going to keep an eye on you for the next few days until I know you're okay. Since I can't call to check on you. . ."

She held her hand up to stop me. "I have learned my lesson this time. If I had a telephone I could have called for help right away instead of having to run down the road to Sam's. I would have been a better help to you and would not have this awful bruise on my hip. I intend to get one installed right away." She shook her head. "Honestly, I have never had anything against telephones. I simply did not think it necessary. I was wrong." She grabbed my hand. "I hope you can forgive me for being so stubborn."

I laughed. "Listen, I've changed my way of thinking in so many ways since I arrived in Harmony. I can't get a signal on my cell phone here. Not having it ring twenty times a day was hard on me at first. But now I find myself enjoying the peace and quiet. I have no intention of being a slave to my phone when I go home. Peace and quiet are much more precious to me now."

She patted my arm. "Thank you for that. Maybe a nice place in the middle of the road will be good for both of us, ja?"

I hugged her again. "Ja," I said softly. "Now, is there anything else you need before I go?"

"There is one thing I would like. Could you go into my bedroom and get my cane? It is in my closet. It will help me get around a little more safely."

"Of course." I followed Ida's finger, which was pointed toward a hallway near the kitchen. I easily found her bedroom. The sparse room held an old iron bed and an antique dresser. The closet door creaked as I opened it. A wooden cane was lying against the wall just inside the closet. I grabbed it and was headed out the door when I took a second look at the bedspread on Ida's old bed. I recognized the familiar pattern. It was one of Mama Essie's, but it was so old and faded, it was only a shadow of the glorious quilt it once had been. I ran my fingers over it. I could see places where the pattern had become worn and the quilt pieces had been patched and mended. I thought back to the trunk with quilts in the basement of Benjamin's house. As soon as I could get back inside, I intended to give Ida a new quilt. I smiled to myself as I pondered the joy it would give her.

I closed the door to the bedroom and delivered the cane to Ida. After assuring her I would be back by nine o'clock, I left. As I drove past Benjamin's house, I saw that there were still quite a few men working. Gabriel was helping Sam nail plywood and plastic sheeting over the exposed areas of the kitchen. The burned areas had been removed. A quick look revealed that Gabriel's buggy was no longer parked on the road, meaning Sarah must have gone home. John's car was gone, too. I glanced at my watch. Almost seven thirty. Although I'd planned on waiting for Sam, my chance to talk to John today was fading fast. After a brief argument with myself, I decided to swing by the market just to see if he was there, although I doubted it. By now he should be home, and I had no idea where that was.

I turned my car toward downtown Harmony. As I neared the market, I began to feel a little apprehensive. When I pulled up in front, I noticed the lights were on. John's car sat in front. I stayed in my own car for a while trying to decide what to do. In my rearview mirror I noticed Ruth leaving her shop. She headed down the sidewalk toward the restaurant. I jumped out of the car and called her name.

"Oh Gracie," she said as I hurried up to her, "I'm so glad the men got the fire out. They were weatherproofing it when I left. Tomorrow we'll start repairs. I want you to know that I have some kitchen things for you if you need them."

"Thank you, Ruth. I can't thank everyone enough for their kindness."

Her face crinkled as she smiled. "We always pull together in Harmony." She closed her eyes and breathed deeply. "Can you smell the honeysuckle blooming? Every spring I wait for its aroma." She sighed and opened her eyes. "I love it here."

I reached out and put my hand on her arm. "Ruth, I need to ask you a favor."

She nodded. "Of course. What is it?"

"Are you going to supper?"

"Yes. Can I get you something?"

"Thank you, but no. I—I..."

She put her arm around me. "What is it, child?"

I cleared my throat. "I know this sounds odd, but if my car is still in front of John Keystone's store when you leave the restaurant, will you come looking for me?"

Ruth's gaze swung toward the meat market, and she frowned. "All right," she said slowly. "But why..."

"It's probably nothing, Ruth. It's just that John is a little... well, different. I need to talk to him about something, and Sam is busy at the house. I will just feel better if someone is watching out for me."

"Maybe I should come with you."

I smiled at her. "No, that's not necessary. Really. If you'd just check on me when you leave—if my car's still there—that's enough."

"Okay. I'll do it. You know," she said quietly, "I think most people have John all wrong. There's something about that man that touches me. I don't think he's as angry as he is sad. He reminds me a lot of Gabe Ketterling." She shook her head. "Maybe it's my imagination. Maybe he's just mean. But I've found that hurting people tend to be difficult because they're afraid to love. What's that phrase?" She thought for a moment. "Oh yes. Hurting people hurt people. It's really true."

"I think you're right, Ruth. Thanks. I'll try to keep that in mind."

The older woman laughed lightly. "Sorry. I've drifted off track here, haven't I?" She grabbed my hand. "You go on. I'm only getting a bowl of chili so I won't be long, but I will wait around until you leave. And if it seems to take too long, I'll come across the street and pretend I desperately need a pound of hamburger."

I hugged her. "Thanks, Ruth. I appreciate it."

I'd turned to leave when I noticed Gabriel Ketterling's Appaloosa horse and buggy tied to a hitching rail a few yards from the entrance to Mary's café. No one was inside.

I hurried across the street to the market. Even though the lights were on, the door was locked. I knocked loudly, praying the whole time I wasn't making a huge mistake. A few seconds later, John stomped out of his back room, a scowl on his face. When he saw me, his eyebrows arched in surprise, and his already annoyed expression deepened.

"I'm closed," he shouted at me through the glass window next to the door.

"I need to talk to you, John. Please!"

With a thoroughly disgusted look, he unlocked the door and held it open. I stepped inside. "I–I'm sorry to bother you," I said quickly, "but I really need to speak with you. I wouldn't come by this late unless it was important."

He pointed to a small table with two chairs that sat against the far wall. "You're right. It *is* late, Grace. I just came back to make sure I'd locked everything up after running out so quickly this afternoon."

As he finished his sentence, I heard a noise that seemed to come from his back room. It sounded like a door closing. "Is someone here? I didn't mean to interrupt. . ."

"No," he said sharply. "There's no one here. Now what do you want? Is it about the house?"

"Well, I did want to thank you for everything you did. But that's not why I stopped by."

His features locked into a frigid stare. "Okay, then why are you here?"

I took a deep breath and met his direct gaze. "I'm here because I want to know why Jacob Glick's son is hiding out incognito in Harmony."

Chapter Seventeen

Although I'd figured John was related to Glick after realizing how much he looked like the picture in the restaurant, I hadn't been certain he was actually his son. He could have been his brother—or even a cousin. It was his age that made me suspect the relationship. John's reaction told me immediately that I'd hit a nerve. Big-time.

"How—how...," he sputtered, his face pale and his eyes wide.

"It's the photo in the café. You have your father's distinct features. Please don't take this the wrong way, but they look good on you. On your father...well, let's just say they didn't work as well for him."

John didn't respond at first. Finally, he cracked a small smile. "Well, thank you for that. You can imagine my shock when I first saw that picture."

The tension in the room eased considerably. Out of the corner of my eye, I saw a dark figure hurry across the street. Sarah. She glanced quickly toward the market and then slipped into her buggy. She certainly hadn't come from the café. Was it Sarah I heard leaving through the back door when I arrived? I'd already noticed John's interest in her, but could she actually have feelings for him, too? The bad-tempered John Keystone and the quiet Mennonite girl? Interesting to say the least.

"So why are you here?" I asked. "It seems strange that you would come to Harmony and not tell anyone who you are."

He jumped to his feet and began pacing the floor. "If your father was Jacob Glick would you want people to know?" After crossing back and forth several times, he stopped moving and put his hands over his face. When he brought them down, his features were twisted with distress. "After I arrived and began finding out just who my father really was, I felt disgusted and ashamed. I planned to leave this place and never come back. I wanted to walk away from him and from his embarrassing legacy."

"But you didn't leave."

John shook his head and threw his hands up in mock surrender. "I have no idea why. I just—I just. . ."

"Couldn't go?" I finished for him. "Must be something pretty powerful that holds you here."

A shadow passed the window. Sarah Ketterling's buggy. We both watched her drive away. John turned back to me, and our eyes met.

"Yes," he said softly. "Something holds me here." He came back to the table and slumped into the other chair across from me. "Something about this town. Something about these people." He placed his palms down on the tabletop—his fingers splayed. Instead of looking at me, he stared at his hands. "I—I never really had a home. My mother did her best. Raised me alone. She was always at work. I had no brothers or sisters. She'd told me that my father died when I was young. When she passed away a little over two years ago, I found her diary tucked away in a box. She wrote about my father—Jacob Glick. She'd gotten pregnant, and he'd abandoned her." He finally swung his gaze up and met my eyes. "I wanted to know why. That's all. The diary mentioned Harmony—and that he'd moved away without telling anyone where he was going. I thought Harmony would be the starting point in my search for him. But the opposite happened. Everything ended here. I couldn't find a trace of my father after he left town." He shrugged. "It didn't make any sense. Was he still living somewhere in the area? Had he moved far away? Had he died? Why did the trail go cold? I've looked everywhere for answers, but there are no records to be found. No work records, no social security records, not even a death certificate. I wanted to know why, so I left my practice, contacted a farmer friend in Council Grove, and offered to sell his meat in Harmony. He accepted, and here I am."

"You left your practice? What kind of practice?"

He laughed rather harshly. "I'm a doctor—a family physician. At least, that's what I used to be."

"And what have you discovered about your father?"

He blew air out between clenched teeth. "Well, let's see. I've learned that he was a womanizer, a possible child molester, and an all around terrible person. Seems that his only interest in life was finding an acceptable wife—no matter what the cost."

"But what about your mother? Why didn't he marry her?"

John spit out a curse word. "Sorry. I'm assuming it was because my mother wasn't good enough to marry. You see, she was black."

I'd thought I couldn't dislike Jacob Glick any more than I already did. I was wrong. He was not only a rapist and a child molester. He was a bigot. I thought about the fair-haired, fair-skinned beauties he'd chased in Harmony, and I felt sick to my stomach."

"I–I'm sorry he treated your mother so shamefully. But you can't take it personally. You're not responsible for his behavior."

He shrugged. "I know that somewhere in my mind, but in my heart..."

"Your heart knows the truth, too, John. You're not your father."

He brushed his dark wavy hair out of his face. "Thank you for that, Gracie."

"So you've never discovered your father's current whereabouts?" I tried to keep my tone light, but guilt ate at my conscience.

He grunted. "Not a clue. Everyone who was around during the time he lived here told me he suddenly left town. Back when I cared where he was, I searched for him. But as I said, I couldn't find him in any public records. It's like he disappeared off the face of the earth."

More like under the earth. "John, I have to ask you something. Please don't be offended. Do you have any reason to want me out of Harmony?"

He stared at me curiously. "You? No, of course not. Why do you ask?"

I shook my head. "Strange things have been happening to me. I get the very distinct feeling that someone in this town would like to see me head back to Wichita. And the sooner the better."

"I can assure you it's not me. But I must admit I've been wondering why you're asking questions around town about my father. Mary told me you were very interested in his picture. I realize your parents knew him, but it seemed odd to me that after all these years anyone would care anything about him."

"I do have a reason, but I can't explain it right now, I'm sorry, but I'm going to have to ask you to trust me. Just for a few more days."

John's eyes narrowed and he frowned at me. "Do you know where he is?"

I didn't answer him. I had no idea what to say.

He sighed and shook his head. "He's dead, isn't he?"

"Again, I'm sorry. You've waited a couple of years to find out the truth about your father. Can you wait just a little longer?"

He shrugged. "I guess so. It's not like I care that much anymore."

I heard his words, but the look in his eyes betrayed him. John cared, all right. He cared very much. My stomach turned at the realization that I would have to confirm his suspicions that his father was gone. It wasn't something I looked forward to.

He cocked his head to the side and frowned at me. "You mentioned some strange occurrences. You mean like Ruth's vase disappearing? And the fire?"

I nodded. "Exactly like that."

"Are you saying the fire was deliberately set?"

"It's possible, but please keep this to yourself. I don't want the person who did it to suspect I know the truth. Everyone except my firebug friend thinks I left an oil lamp burning too close to the kitchen curtains."

A scowl marred John's handsome features. "Maybe you did."

I explained to him about the battery-operated lights Sam had purchased for me.

"Sounds to me like you need to be very, very careful."

I saw something flicker in his eyes. Was that a warning? Could John be the person who had been trying to get me to leave Harmony after all? Something inside me said no. Maybe it was a gut reaction. Or maybe it was the still, small voice of God. I wasn't certain, but I decided to listen to it. "I'm staying at Sam's house. He knows what's going on and is keeping an eye on me."

"Look, Gracie," John said earnestly, "I won't tell anyone about our conversation—if that's what you want."

"Yes it is. For now anyway."

"Fine, but I would also ask you to keep my secret. At some point I may tell people who I really am. I haven't decided, but I'm certainly not ready yet."

"All right, although there aren't a lot of people left who knew Glick. You have nothing to worry about." Even as I said the words, I thought about Emily. How would she feel about it? Although I'd just agreed to keep John's secret, once the truth came out about

Glick's murder, John's identity would most probably be revealed, as well. "I will have to tell Sam, but we'll keep it to ourselves."

He snorted. "I'm sure Sam will find it extremely amusing."

"No he won't. He's not like that at all. Not sure why you two have such animosity for each other."

John shook his head. "Maybe it's my fault. Just seems like he's got it all. People who care about him. Folks who respect him." He sighed. "It's probably my own jealousy."

I noticed the clock on the wall. "I'd better go. It's getting dark. The men working on my house are probably finished for the day."

"*Your* house?" He grinned. "You'd better watch out. Harmony will pull you into its web, too, if you're not careful. A warning from someone who knows."

I smiled back at him. "I have no intention of leaving my life in Wichita behind. I have everything I want there."

John chucked. "Okay. Whatever you say. I'll be at the house that isn't really yours early tomorrow morning. A bunch of us are determined to get you fixed up as quickly as possible."

"I—I don't know what to say. Thank you. I can hardly believe how supportive this community is. I still feel funny about not being able to pay for materials."

"Mennonite community, Gracie. Helping their neighbors is big here. Anyway, the church usually pays for most of the materials. They have a fund set up just for that." He ran his hand through his hair. "The first year I moved here a storm came through and a farmer outside of town lost his barn. The next day he was flooded with volunteers who cleaned up his property and built him a barn twice the size of the first. And they wouldn't let him invest anything except his own time and sweat. It was amazing."

"This place is pretty awesome."

"Yes it is." He crossed his arms and shook his head. "Something else that's pretty awesome: Gabriel Ketterling showed up today to help, and he plans on working with us again tomorrow. This is the first time I've seen him join in anything. I think his love for Ben originally sent him to your house, but his decision to come back. . . Well, it's a surprise. Funny thing is, I think he enjoyed being around people again. I actually saw him smile a couple of times."

"So all it took was catching my house on fire? Maybe I should have done it a long time ago."

"You know what?" he said seriously. "I know you're kidding, but there's truth in what you just said. He responded to being needed. And then he responded to being around other people. Your little accident may have actually been the best thing that's happened to Gabriel in many, many years." He smiled widely at me, erasing almost every reminder of his father, whose photograph had displayed features locked in deep-seated anger and hate. "I think you're good for Harmony, Gracie Temple."

I crooked my thumb toward the restaurant across the street. "Will you tell that to your friend, Mary? I think she would disagree with you."

He waved his hand at me. "Don't worry about Mary. She knows Sam wasn't the man for her. She's known it for a long time. If she could be honest about it, I think she'd tell you the same thing. Right now her pride is hurt. If she could have been the one to break it off, she wouldn't be so mad. It'll pass. Trust me."

"I have a feeling it won't pass until after I'm gone."

He shrugged. "Well, she was there to help during the fire. She didn't have to be."

"I—I guess so. I assumed it was just something she'd do for anyone."

"That might be true—but thanking her might not be a bad idea."

My gaze swung once again toward the clock on the wall. I stood up. "I appreciate the suggestion. I'll try to find a way to tell her how grateful I am for her help. Hopefully, it will go better than the last time I attempted to make things right between us."

John stood to his feet again and stepped over to the locked front door. He turned the lock and held the door open. "I'm glad we got the chance to talk, Gracie. And thanks for keeping my secret."

"You're welcome." I stepped outside onto the boardwalk. The air had cooled considerably and the myriad of stars overhead had begun their nightly spectacular display. I took a deep breath and let it out slowly. The scent of honeysuckle wafted around me like a sweet perfume. As I crossed the street, I replayed parts of my conversation with John in my head. Although I still didn't trust him completely, I doubted he was the person who took Ruth's vase or set Benjamin's house on fire. I also knew now why Emily was so uncomfortable around him. Subconsciously, when she looked at him, she saw his father. Someday when the truth came out, I wondered if her reaction to him would be better or worse. There was no way to tell. I slowly walked up the steps to the café and stood at the door for a few moments, screwing up my courage. Finally, I pushed it open. Ruth sat at a nearby table with her back to me. Just my luck, Mary stood next to her. The two were engaged in a conversation. I had a strong urge to hurry out before the women saw me, but I wanted Ruth to know I'd escaped John's market unscathed.

I walked up quietly and touched Ruth on the back. She cranked her head around and smiled at me. "Oh, Gracie. There you are. I take it everything went okay?"

"Yes, very well. Thanks, Ruth."

I patted her on the back and turned to go.

"I—I guess some of the men will be working at your place tomorrow."

Mary's statement was said as fact, but I responded as if it were a question. "Yes. I mean, that's what I heard. I'm very appreciative."

Although nothing in her expression softened, her next words took me by surprise. "I'll bring lunch by around one fifteen. Have to get through my midday rush first."

"Wh—why, thank you, Mary. I'm sure they'll be happy to hear. . ."

The rest of my sentence was useless since she turned and ambled off as soon as I opened my mouth. She engaged a couple at the next table in a discussion about the weather. But it was progress. I shrugged at Ruth whose cheery response would have been more appropriate if Mary hadn't walked off and left me standing there with my mouth open.

"Oh wonderful!" she said, rather breathlessly. "I knew she'd come around!"

I nodded without much conviction, thanked Ruth again, and left the café. I headed back toward Benjamin's house, but just as I got to Faith Road, I saw Sam's truck coming my way. I stopped and rolled down my window.

"We're done for the day," he hollered, trying to make himself heard over the noisy truck engine. He pointed in the direction of his house. "Let's go home."

"I've got to check on Ida first," I yelled back. "I'll be there shortly."

He nodded, put the truck in gear, and took off down the road while I turned my car the other way and drove to Ida's. It only took a few minutes for me to find out she was feeling better and didn't need any help. After promising to check on her again the next day, I drove back to Sam's.

When I turned into the driveway of the magnificent red house, I couldn't help but wonder if I'd ever have a home like this. Until I'd seen this place I'd never thought much about what my own home might look like someday. Frankly, I'd always imagined it as much more modern. Most of my designer friends were into clean lines and contemporary styling. They'd laugh at me if they saw this house I'd fallen in love with.

I parked behind Sam and got out of the car. He sat on the front porch steps waiting for me.

"No rain predictions tonight or tomorrow," he said as I reached him. "But just in case, we have everything buttoned up tight. Tomorrow we'll start making actual repairs." He got up and put his hand on my shoulder. "The refrigerator, the stove, and the table are ruined. Sorry. But they can be easily replaced."

"I don't know why I'd do that," I said, more sharply than I meant to. "Whoever buys the property can bring in their own furniture and appliances."

"I guess you're right." Sam's tone was soft, but there was something in his voice that made me realize my attitude was inappropriate.

I grabbed his hand as he took it from my shoulder. "I'm sorry. I have no idea why I snapped at you. I guess I'm just tired. It's been a long day."

He smiled. "Yes, that it has. Let's grab something to drink and sit on the back porch. I have a few things to tell you."

"I have something big to tell you, too."

A few minutes later we were comfortably settled in the beautiful enclosed porch. I almost emptied my entire glass of iced tea in one gulp. I hadn't realized I was so thirsty. Sam got up and refilled our glasses. Then he sat back down next to me in the love seat. The only illumination in the room came from the kitchen behind us. I suddenly became aware of how tired I really was. Sam yawned deeply. Although my weariness was probably more emotional than physical, I realized that he had to be absolutely exhausted.

"I need to tell you what I found out today," I said. "But we can get into it more tomorrow. I'm sure we could both use a good night's sleep."

Sam closed his eyes and leaned his head against the back of the seat. "Sounds good. Go ahead and tell me your big news."

I took a deep breath. "John Keystone is Jacob Glick's son."

His eyes shot open like they were hooked to an electric circuit that had just been switched on. He sat up straight. "He–he's what? What did you say?"

He looked so shocked I laughed. "I said John is Glick's son."

He turned to stare at me with his mouth open. "How. . .I mean. . .how. . ."

I patted him on the leg. "Okay, settle down. How did I find out?"

He nodded dumbly.

"It was the picture of Glick. I know he's not an attractive man, but he has such distinct features. His narrow aquiline nose. His long face and bushy eyebrows. His coloring. John Keystone is a lot better looking than Glick, but the features are the same. When I met him, I kept thinking I'd seen him somewhere before. Today I finally put it together."

"But—but there are other people in Harmony who actually knew Glick. Why didn't they put two and two together?"

"I don't know. Maybe it's my artistic side. I study shapes and contrasts. I remembered the structure of Glick's face and matched it to John's."

"Well, Emily was an artist, and she's known him longer than you. Wonder why she didn't see it?"

I shrugged but didn't say anything. If she had noticed the similarities between father and son, I was certain her mind had blocked it.

He shook his head slowly. "His son. That's incredible." He frowned. "But you're just guessing, right?"

"No. I talked to John. He admitted it."

"Grace Temple!" Sam exploded. "You confronted him? I hope you weren't alone."

I nodded. "Sam, it's all right. He. . ."

He grabbed me by the shoulders. "It's not all right at all. What if he'd attacked you? He could have killed you."

"Ouch," I yelped. "You're hurting me. Let me go!"

Sam released me and jumped to his feet. "I'm sorry, but that was stupid. This means John was the person who took the vase and set the fire."

I sighed deeply. "Yes, Sam, that's it. You've figured it all out. You're Sherlock Holmes in the flesh. You see, as a baby John Keystone crawled to Harmony all by himself. He grabbed a rock and hit his father on the head, killing him. Then he crawled back to Council Grove, where his mother lived, climbed into his crib after washing off all the incriminating evidence, and waited until adulthood to come back to Harmony in case a graphic designer from Wichita showed up to accuse him of murder."

"Okay, that doesn't actually make sense," Sam said sheepishly. "So why does John want you out of town?"

"He doesn't. He's not even aware Glick is dead. Now if you'll just sit down, I'll tell you the whole story."

He came over and plopped down next to me. I filled him in on everything I'd learned. When I finished, he was silent for a while. "Wow. I sure wouldn't want to find out my father was someone like Glick."

"I think it's the reason he's been so defensive."

Sam laughed softly in the semidarkness. "I wouldn't have characterized it quite so nicely, but I guess I can understand his attitude. I have to say he really pitched in and helped today."

"You said you had something to tell me?"

Sam shook his head. "You kind of stole my thunder. My news isn't as startling as yours."

I reached over and ruffled his hair. "I'm sure it will be quite interesting. Go ahead."

"You're talking to me like a child again."

"Sorry. Tell me what happened today, or I'll beat you senseless."

He snorted. "That's much better." He turned toward me. I could see the outline of his face illuminated by the kitchen light.

"This may not mean a lot to you, but if you'd lived around here as long as I have, you'd find what I'm about to tell you nothing short of amazing. Gabriel Ketterling worked with us all day. I heard him tell Mary he'd hang in there until the work was completed. Even better than that, he seemed to enjoy being with us. He even laughed a couple of times."

I started to tell him that John had mentioned the very same thing, but before the words popped out of my mouth I sucked them back in. Male ego being what it is and all. "Now that *is* big news."

"Don't make fun of me. This is a major step for him. When I left, he and Abel were sitting on your front porch talking. They'd been at it for almost an hour."

"Oh Sam. That *is* wonderful. Really." I'd been teasing him up to now, but knowing that Gabriel and Abel had spent that much time together was encouraging. I thought about Sarah and how much it would mean to her if her father began to reenter the community. "I'm going to pray over this situation," I said quietly. "Wouldn't it be wonderful if. . ."

"Yeah," Sam said before I finished. "It would definitely be wonderful."

"Hey, you spent some time around Mary today. How did that go?"

"Surprisingly well. It's not like we had an emotional moment when we wrapped our arms around each other and forgave everything, but she was civil to me. I'd say it was a step forward."

"She'd better keep her arms to herself." The sentence burst out before I realized what I'd said. I'd spoken in jest, but my words were still badly chosen.

"Why?" Sam said in a low voice. "Do you really care if someone else puts their arms around me?"

"I'm gonna plead the fifth here," I said lightly. Being so near him in the semidarkness, I felt my resolve to keep some distance begin to melt. Time to change the subject. "Hey, we need to talk about our discussion with Levi before the whole fire thing erupted."

Sam leaned back in the seat and sighed. "Oh yeah. With everything else, I kind of forgot."

"Basically we got nowhere. Levi doesn't know anything that can help us."

"So what now?" Sam asked. "I have no idea where to go from here."

"Me either, but someone set that fire, Sam. We find our firebug, and we find our answers."

"Did you check with Ida to see if she noticed anything?"

"Yes, but she slept all afternoon and didn't see anyone at the house."

Sam sighed deeply. "Well then, I have no idea what to do next."

"Me either. I guess we think about it for a while. To be honest, my mind is exhausted."

Sam yawned. "My mind and my body are in agreement. They're both ready for bed." He stood up and held out his hand. I reached out for him, and he pulled me up. Before I knew it, his lips were on mine. I was too tired to resist.

"You know this is only going to make it harder when I leave," I whispered when his lips left mine.

"I don't care." His voice was heavy with emotion. "I only know that right now I want to kiss you more than I care about what happens next week. Can you understand that?"

I didn't trust myself to answer. As if my hands had a mind of their own, I reached up and pulled his face close to me. Although our second kiss was as tender as the first, a feeling of sadness washed through me. I pulled away from him and walked toward the door to the kitchen.

"I—I've got to go to bed. I'm so tired I can hardly stand it."

Sam stepped around me and swung the door open. Light flooded in, and I saw his eyes sparkle with unshed tears. I quickly turned my head. Seeing his pain hurt me deeply inside.

"I'll be going out early in the morning to Ben's," he said in a controlled voice. "I won't see you before I leave. In fact, I may not see you much at all in the next few days."

"I understand. Good night." I'd wanted to say so much more, but instead I fled to my room, confused by the emotions coursing through me. Ever since coming to Harmony, my thoughts and feelings had been jumbled and confused. In Wichita I'd felt that I knew who I was—what I wanted. But here. . . Here everything was different. It was like someone had torn me into little pieces, gathered them up, and thrown them into the air. As they drifted back to earth, all the parts that were Gracie fell into a different picture—one I didn't recognize.

In the hallway outside my room I found Buddy waiting for me. I opened the door, and he ran up on the bed, turned around a couple of times, and curled up in a ball. I changed my clothes, crawled into bed, and pulled him up close to me. Then I stared up at the ceiling for quite a while, feeling strangely unsettled. Besides my jumbled emotions about Sam, something else nagged at me. Something I'd missed. I chewed on it for quite some time without success. Eventually I fell into a troubled sleep.

Chapter Eighteen

The next few days passed quickly. As Sam had predicted, I hardly saw him. When he came home late at night, he was so tired he didn't feel much like talking. I spent the large part of each day giving Sweetie a hand in the orchards. We pruned the trees, which was difficult work, and placed small balls of nitrogen around the bottom of the trunks to fertilize them. By the time we came in for supper, I was exhausted. After we ate, I'd sit in the rocking chair on the front porch and wait for Sam to come home. Usually, I fell asleep before he finally pulled into the driveway.

I'd gone over to my uncle's several times, but each time I'd been told there was nothing I could do there. It didn't take me long to realize that God was doing a special work, and I needed to leave the men alone so He could complete it. In only a few days, Gabriel Ketterling seemed like a different person. Sam and John had bonded as if they were old friends. It wasn't unusual to hear them all laughing together. By Wednesday afternoon I'd completely abandoned my daily visits. Even Mary seemed to realize that something unique was happening. She'd drop off lunch and leave immediately, hardly speaking to anyone.

Thursday afternoon I picked up Hannah and we drove downtown. I brought along a couple of sketch pads that I'd thrown into the car in case I found time to draw while I was in Harmony. I remember thinking my short vacation would be boring and I'd need something to do. Boy, I'd sure missed the mark there. Together Hannah and I sketched the outside of the café, Menlo's Bakery, and Ruth's shop. Hannah wanted to add someone sitting on the empty bench in front of the café, so I roughed in a figure we could detail later, talking to her about how to add dimension to her drawing. I also taught her about using proper perspective. She soaked up my words like they were water and she was a dry sponge.

We had a wonderful time even though we were interrupted so many times it was a miracle we got anything done. Mrs. Menlo brought us warm macadamia nut cookies straight from the oven, along with a cup of coffee for me and a glass of chocolate milk for Hannah. Ruth ran across the street to see what we were doing. She oohed and aahed over our sketches until Esther Crenshaw stuck her head out the front door of her shop and hollered, "If you don't mind, Ruth, I'd rather not live the rest of my life waiting for you to check me out!"

Hannah and I giggled as Ruth jogged back across the street yelling, "Esther, why don't you just keep your silly wig on? I'm not on the earth just to serve you, you know!"

Two of Hannah's friends stopped by to find out what she was up to. Hannah introduced Leah, a vivacious young girl with milk chocolate brown hair, rosy cheeks, and a glint of mischievousness in her deep doelike eyes. The second girl, Jessica, hung back and stared at me as if she'd never seen anyone like me before. Her dishwater hair hung in thin strands below her dingy prayer covering. One of the ribbons from her cap was missing, and the ill-fitting dress she wore stretched tightly across her chubby body. Leah's face sparkled with life while Jessica's features seemed lost and faded in her sallow skin. Hannah treated both girls with the same enthusiasm, which seemed to help Jessica come out of her shell a little. The two girls stayed only a few minutes. A rather large woman I'd never seen before stepped out of the café across the street and called for them to hurry up if they wanted pie. That was all it took for the girls to say good-bye to Hannah and take off across the street as if the pie would disappear if they didn't eat it right away.

Almost everyone who strolled down the boardwalk stopped to watch us and ask questions. Our venture proved to be a great way to create a successful social occasion, but we didn't get as far with our sketches as I'd hoped. We made a date to meet again on Saturday morning to finish what we'd begun. I hoped some of Harmony's business owners and residents would be at home with their families so we could get some work done.

Friday night when Sam walked in the front door, he informed me that they would probably be finished with the house by Saturday afternoon. I sat at the kitchen table across from him while Sweetie fixed him a late supper.

"I want to do something special to thank everyone," I said. "Do you think we could have some kind of dinner or something?"

Sweetie, who overheard us talking, interrupted Sam's attempt at a response. "How 'bout some of the women and I get together and plan a big picnic in the park Monday evening? There's plenty of room there, and folks could bring their families."

"Oh, that sounds wonderful. Do you think the men would enjoy it?"

Sweetie's coarse laugh broke loose. "I think anytime them hungry men get a chance to chow down, they receive it with gusto."

"I think it's a wonderful idea, Grace," Sam said. He cranked his head around and looked at Sweetie who was busy making him a sandwich. "Hey, be sure to get Levi involved in the party, will you? He helped us out at the house the first day and a half, but then he dropped out. Said he's not feeling well. I'm a little worried about him."

"Sure," she said. "I'll call him first thing in the morning. Make sure he's okay. You know, Levi's not as young as he used to be. Maybe he started feelin' bad tryin' to keep up with all you young men."

Sam shook his head. "Maybe, but Abel's about his age and seems to be doing okay." He shrugged. "Hope we didn't do anything to offend him."

"Oh, pshaw," Sweetie said with a wave of her hand. "Levi and I are two ducks in the same pond. You can't offend us for nothin'."

I raised an eyebrow and smiled at Sam. Sweetie got offended at least four times a day at something or someone.

"I'd sure like to see Gabe come to the picnic and bring Sarah," Sam said, changing the subject. "She could use a friend." He yawned loudly. "I almost forgot to tell you," he said to me when he'd finished. "Gabe's been asking about you. Something about taking some kind of lessons from Sarah? Said he told you no when you first asked, but he's changed his mind."

I clapped my hands together. "Oh, how wonderful! She does the most beautiful wood-block prints. I've heard of the technique, but I'd never seen it done. I'd love it if she'd teach me before I leave. Of course, I'd pay her for her time."

He nodded. "Honestly, Gabe and Sarah could use the money. They don't have much. But I don't think he's got money on his mind as much as he finally wants to reach out to people." He yawned again. "I've had a really bad attitude about him for years. Turns out I really like the guy."

"He's had some tough breaks," Sweetie said. "Tends to make a body careful. That girl's all he's got left. I think he's feared he might lose her, too, and have nothin'."

"Well, he's sure changed."

Sweetie stopped what she was doing and stared hard at her nephew. "Folks don't usually change in a couple of days, Sam. He might be a-comin' out of his shell, but I wouldn't take it as some kind of miracle transformation. He's still got a lotta bitterness inside him. God help any man that tries to touch his daughter."

Sam shrugged. "I don't know about that. I just know he's talking to us and seems to really be enjoying our company."

"All I can say is I hope you're right." She turned back to her meal preparations while I thought about her mention of some man trying to approach Sarah. I had to wonder just how close John and Sarah had become. It was clear they'd been intentionally hiding their relationship. What would happen when Gabriel found out?

"Well, it will be interesting to see if Gabe accepts the invitation for Monday night," Sam said. "It's a purely social invitation. If he and Sarah show up, I'd say we've come a long way this week."

I laughed. "I can hardly believe you're calling him Gabe. Was that your idea or his?"

"Actually, Abel started it. But Gabe seemed to like it. And honestly, it fits him."

"So, do I have any hope you'll call me Gracie someday?"

Sweetie plopped a huge ham sandwich in front of Sam with a side of homemade potato salad. His eyes widened and he sighed with pleasure. "I love the name Grace. God's grace has always been important in my life. Does it bother you?" Without waiting for an answer, he bowed his head, said a quick prayer, and took a big bite of his sandwich.

"I guess not. It's just odd to be called Grace instead of Gracie."

Sam chewed and swallowed. "Why? It's your real name, isn't it?"

I nodded. "Yes, it's my real name." I thought about informing him that there was nothing wrong with the name Gracie, but it was obvious Sam was lost in sandwich heaven and wasn't in a listening mood. Besides, for some reason I liked hearing him call me Grace.

"You seem to be getting along with John, too," I interjected.

Sam chewed silently. I couldn't interpret the look on his face. Finally, he said, "Turns out we have more in common than I thought." He shook his head. "I think we'll end up being pretty good friends."

I started to ask him what he meant about having something in common with John when Sweetie interrupted me.

"I need to drive into Council Grove in the morning." She pointed a finger at Sam. "I'll drop you off at Benny's before I head out. What time do you figger you'll be done?"

He shrugged and swallowed. "Like I said, sometime in the afternoon. But don't worry about me. I'll walk."

"Okay. I'll check on you when I get back. I'm gettin' some groceries for Ida, too. I'll run them to her place and then swing by to see how you all are doin' before I come home. And on the way home, I thought I might stop by Bernie's in Sunrise and pick up some of them chocolate milkshakes you like so much. How many men do you think will be a-workin' tomorrow?"

Sam chuckled. "If word gets out about those milkshakes, we'll have all the help we can use—and more. How many milkshakes can you carry?"

She grinned at him. "I'll have 'em put the shakes in them big carryout boxes. It'll keep 'em from fallin' over on the way home. You figger twenty will be enough?"

"I think that would be perfect. Between Mary and you, I'm liable to actually gain weight working on Grace's house."

There it was again. *Grace's house.* Seemed like everyone was beginning to see Benjamin's house as mine. Even me. I could have corrected Sam's choice of words, but since he'd been working so hard to save the house, it didn't seem important. The effort being made to repair the fire damage meant the world to me. In fact, every time I drove past the house and saw the men laboring in the afternoon heat, tears sprang to my eyes.

"I take it these chocolate milkshakes are something special?"

Sam snorted. "I'll bet you don't have anything like them in Wichita."

"I don't know. Wichita has lots of places with great shakes."

Sam pointed his fork at his aunt. "Pick up one for Grace, will you? She needs to experience a Bernie's milkshake for herself."

Sweetie brought us both a slice of apple pie and ice cream. "I'll do it. You got a treat a-comin', girlie."

I winced at hearing "girlie" again. I kept hoping that particular moniker would eventually fade away, but it appeared it was going to follow me around, much like "Snicklefritz." However, with a mouthful of Sweetie's warm, delicious pie, I had to admit it didn't sting quite as much. As soon as we finished eating, Sam headed to bed.

When Buddy and I woke up Saturday morning, Sam and Sweetie had already gone. I made some toast, took a shower, and headed downtown to meet Hannah. All the way into town, that odd sense that I'd forgotten something persisted. I hadn't mentioned it to Sam, because at this point it was nothing more than a feeling. But I couldn't shake it. When I pulled up in front of the meat market, I found Emily and Hannah waiting for me.

"Good morning," I called out as I got out of the car and grabbed the sketch pads. "Wonderful weather, isn't it?"

They both agreed. I'd just begun to tell them about the picnic when I heard the sound of hoofbeats coming toward us. I turned to see Ida's buggy racing down the street. She came from the direction of the church.

"Whoa, Zebediah," she hollered as she pulled up next to us. Ida pointed at me. "Gracie, I need your help."

I put the sketch pads down on the bench and hurried over to the elderly woman whose face was red with emotion. "What in the world is going on? Are you okay?"

She shook her head. "It is not me. It is Levi. Something is wrong. You have got to find him."

Emily came up behind us. "What are you talking about, Ida? What's wrong with Levi?"

Ida shook her head. "I do not know, but I am afraid for him." She took a deep breath and tried to calm her trembling voice. "I was at the cemetery—putting flowers on Herman's grave. I saw Levi there—which is not unusual because his folks are buried there. But he was wild-eyed and talking out of his head. Something about God's judgment and how he had to find forgiveness. I tried to talk to him, but he just stared at me like I was not there at all."

"Where is he now, Ida?" I asked.

"I don't know. But he said something about washing away his troubles. Could he be talking about Trouble Lake?"

"That lake is huge," Emily said, her eyes wide with fear. "He could be anywhere."

"He asked me if the men were working at Benjamin's today," Ida said. "I told him yes. Then he asked if Sweetie was home." Her eyes filled with tears. "I told him Sweetie was in Council Grove. I should not have done that. I I just was not thinking. He must be there."

"I'd be glad to check on him," I said hesitantly. "But I don't think he's actually in any danger."

"Levi can't swim," Emily said quietly. "Never learned how. The water around the end of Sam's dock is very deep. If he jumps into the lake from there. . ."

"And there is something else, Gracie," Ida said. "Remember when I told you Sam was the only person at Benjamin's last Saturday?"

I nodded.

"Well, I did not know Levi was driving Sam's other car. It was not the truck I saw at Benjamin's in the early afternoon. It was that other car. The big one. The one Levi drove today."

I turned to Emily. "I'm going to Sam's. Will you find someone to drive over to my house and get him? Maybe Abel should come, too. We might need his help."

293

"I'm coming with you," Emily said, her face set with determination. She ran up to Ida's buggy. "Ida, please get Mary. Tell her to go to Benjamin's house and get the men over to Sam's as quickly as possible." She ran toward my car while she called out to her daughter. "Hannah, you stay with Ida until we get back. Do you understand?"

"Yes Mama." Hannah may have understood her mother's instructions, but her confused look matched the jumbled thoughts careening around inside me.

I jumped into my car as Emily slid into the passenger seat, pulling her long skirt in after her. Although I was trying to understand Ida's revelation about Levi being at my house on the day the vase was planted there, I was also struck by the sudden forcefulness of Emily's attitude. The timid woman I knew was gone, and someone else had taken her place.

As I pulled out onto Main Street, I looked in my rearview mirror and saw Hannah helping Ida from her buggy. A second glance revealed the young girl patiently guiding the older woman toward the café.

As we sped down the street, I didn't say anything to Emily, but she saw me glance sideways at her.

"Gracie," she said finally, "do you remember me telling you about a man I cared about when I was young? The one who asked me to marry him?"

"Yes. Was Levi that man?"

She nodded. "When I turned him down, after Jacob disappeared, Levi changed. He quit going to church. He was friendly to people, but. . .I don't know. It was like something in him died. He never acted quite the same. Around me, he was especially reserved. And when I married Abel, he almost stopped acknowledging me at all." She sighed. "It wasn't so noticeable that anyone else would see it. But I did."

"You never talked to him about it?"

"No. I couldn't tell him what had happened to me." She stared out the car window, silent for a few moments. When she turned toward me, her eyes were wet. "If Jacob Glick hadn't attacked me, I would have married Levi. I turned him away because I cared for him, not because I didn't. In my mind, I couldn't be the kind of wife he deserved. It wasn't until I met Abel that I had the courage to give love a chance." She smiled sadly. "Abel's the first man I ever trusted completely, but Levi was the first man I ever loved."

Keeping one hand on the steering wheel, I reached over and touched her shoulder with the other. "Emily, if you trust Abel so much, why won't you tell him the truth? You've spent too many years bound by the past. God wants you to be free. Please talk to your husband."

She patted my hand. "Let's take care of Levi first. Then we'll tackle my marriage."

"Fair enough." I put my hand back on the steering wheel and concentrated on driving as fast as I safely could. When we reached the intersection of Main and Faith, I almost turned toward Benjamin's. I really wanted Sam's help. But not knowing what kind of situation we faced with Levi, I drove on to Sam's. I'd been looking in my rearview mirror ever since we'd left downtown Harmony. There was no sign of Mary's truck behind us. I prayed she'd reach the men soon.

As we approached the big red house, I felt relief that Levi's car was parked in the driveway. If we hadn't found him here, it would have been almost impossible to locate him since the lake was so large and surrounded by thick clusters of trees.

Emily and I jumped out of the car and ran around the side of the house toward the tree line. Buddy came running up behind us, barking wildly. We must have been a sight. Me in my jeans and T-shirt, Emily in her prayer cap and long dress, and Buddy frantically bringing up the rear. As we cleared the trees we saw

Levi standing at the end of the dock, staring down into the water. A quiet approach was out of the question, thanks to Buddy. Levi swung around and saw us coming toward him. As we got nearer, he held his hand up.

"Stop right there," he yelled. "Don't come any closer. I don't want your help. Just go away." His eyes were locked on Emily. It was as if I weren't there at all.

"Levi," Emily called back. "What are you doing? Tell me what's wrong."

He glared at her, his face pale and twisted. "What's wrong? I guess that's the big question, isn't it? What's wrong?" He laughed bitterly. "Perhaps you could answer that question better than I." Tears streamed down his round cheeks. "I loved you. I—I still love you, Emily. You're the only woman I ever wanted. In all these years. But you rejected me. And after everything I did for you. . ."

Emily took a small step closer to him. I had no idea what she thought she could do. If Levi jumped into the water, there was no way we could get him out. He was too big for us.

"I didn't reject you, Levi. I loved you. I—I just couldn't marry anyone then. It wasn't you at all. It was. . ." Her voice trailed off.

"It was because of Jacob Glick," Levi said angrily. "Because of what he did to you."

Emily's whole body shuddered. "You—you knew? How. . . ?"

"Because Jacob told me. In fact, he boasted of it." Levi spit the words out as if they were bitter. "I was at the church one afternoon, painting one of the classrooms because the bishop had asked for my help. When Jacob came in and found me there, he became angry. He didn't like anyone, even Angstadt, working in that building. He acted like he owned the place. He started taunting me, calling me names. I tried to ignore him, but then he asked if I was the boy who was sweet on Emily Kruger. I—I said yes. That's when he said. . .it." Levi made his hands into fists and shook them several times in the air. "I—I can't even repeat what he said. It was vicious and disgusting. I ran out of the church, but I couldn't forget his words. I had to know what he meant. That night I followed him down to the lake. I saw Daniel Temple and his girlfriend, Beverly, running away from the clearing behind the Temple's house like the devil was chasing them. I hid in the trees. Jacob was there all right. Rubbing his jaw. Mad and yelling at no one."

"You were there," I said slowly. "I should have realized it. You admitted as much to Sam and me. You mentioned Jacob standing in the open with trees all around him. We never told you exactly where it happened. You knew because you saw him. I knew I'd missed something."

He shook his head. "I didn't even realize I'd said that. I was so panicked after you told me you knew about Jacob."

I took a step closer to Emily. Levi didn't seem to notice. "So you confronted him that night, Levi?"

He looked down at the dock, his body shaking with sobs. "I confronted him all right. He told me what he did to you, Emily. And he was proud of it. Laughed as he said horrible, vile things."

"And that's when you picked up a rock and hit him?" I tried to keep my voice steady. I didn't want to spook him.

He nodded slowly. "It—it was in my hand before I realized it. I just wanted him to quit talking about Emily—to stop saying those things. I—I didn't mean to kill him." He looked up at us, his eyes pleading for understanding.

"I believe you, Levi," Emily said. "No matter what happens, Abel and I will stand with you. You know that, don't you?"

He ignored her and looked at me. "I'm sorry about the vase and the fire. I wasn't trying to hurt you. I just wanted you to leave town. I couldn't risk anyone knowing about Jacob. If I'd known that you already knew the truth, I never would have done those things. Especially the fire. I'd hoped the house would burn down and you'd leave town. Maybe no one would ever dig up the land and find the body." He shook his head. "I set the fire and then drove into town to meet you and Sam. I figured that since most people were still at work, by the time help arrived, the house would be gone." A sob ripped through him. "And then you told me about Ben's letter. I couldn't believe it. I didn't know what to do. Here I'd caused you all this trouble for no reason. Decades of carrying the guilt of murder and trying to keep the past hidden. I—I just can't do it anymore. It's too much to bear."

"But even if the body had been discovered, why would anyone have suspected you?" I asked gently.

He shrugged. "As long as Jacob stayed buried, my sin was buried. I've spent years trying to pretend it never happened. Th–that it was just a bad dream. If Jacob was found, I wouldn't be able to do that anymore. It would be obvious to everyone that he'd been murdered. I would never be able to allow someone else to take the blame. The pressure of what I've done was already too much. That would be beyond comprehension. I'd have to admit to everyone, even myself, that I'm a cold-blooded murderer." He blinked several times and looked at Emily. "I—I wrote a note that explained all of this. It's in the back room of the store. I knew it would be found after—after. . ."

"Oh Levi," Emily said, her voice catching.

"Did you know it was Benjamin who buried the body?" I asked gently. I knew I had to keep him talking until Sam arrived.

He nodded and refocused his attention to me. "When I realized he was dead, I went down to the lake for a while, trying to figure out what to do. When I finally went back to the clearing, I found Ben digging a grave. I couldn't believe it. At first I wondered if he'd seen me kill Jacob. Then I realized he must have thought his brother did it."

"And you let him continue to believe that all these years?" Emily asked.

"Yes. I know it was wrong, but I was frightened. Scared to go to prison. At first what happened seemed like the answer to everything. Jacob was gone. Everyone believed he'd left town. I thought it was an answer from God. But down through the years it ate at me. And as I watched Ben distance himself from his family, I knew it was my fault." He shook his head. "I was a coward. I just stood by and let it happen. You know, I always told myself that the truth would come out someday. There were just too many people involved. Daniel and Beverly. Ben." He focused his attention to me. "And Sweetie. . . That night, when I found Ben planting Jacob in the ground, I noticed her watching him from another spot in the trees. But she suddenly took off toward the lake. I tried to follow her, to see if she was all right, but she ran too fast. I've always wondered if she saw me. In all these years she's never said a word."

"She didn't see you," I said. "She thought it was Benjamin who chased her."

Levi's eyes grew large. "She never asked him about it?"

"No. But she's been afraid all these years that he thought she'd killed Glick."

"So many lies," Emily whispered, tears falling down her cheeks. "So many secrets."

"And so much hurt," I finished for her. "Hurt that didn't have to happen."

"It's all my fault," Levi said, his voice breaking. "If I'd only told the truth." He stepped closer to the edge and stared into the water. "I wonder if it's true—that this lake will wash your troubles away. I—I pray it will wash everyone's troubles away." He took another step. His voice was monotone, and he moved as if he were in a trance. Fear that he would actually jump wiggled inside me. I was trying to figure out a way to rush him—to keep him from jumping in when Emily spoke up.

"Levi Hoffman, you will not take the easy way out this time! Do you hear me?" Her sharp tone caught the distraught man's attention. "You've caused all this pain because you didn't tell the truth. It's time now for you to be a man and take your punishment. If you jump into that lake, the people who need to ask you questions—who need to understand—will be cheated again." Her voice softened a little. "The man I loved would never allow that to happen."

Levi gazed blankly at her. He blinked several times—but then he took another step back toward the edge of the dock.

"Levi, if you really love me, then I want you to come to me." She held out her hands to him.

Levi looked back at the water once more, but then a sob broke out from somewhere deep inside him and he ran unevenly up to us, throwing his arms around Emily.

Thankfully, I heard the slamming of car doors behind us. Sam and Abel had finally arrived. Now, even if Levi jumped into the water, they could save him. I felt my body relax for the first time since Ida had driven into town.

Still holding Levi in her arms, Emily began to lead him back to land. Buddy and I followed her. As we stepped off the dock, Sam and Abel came crashing through the trees, running toward us. Gabriel and Mary were right behind them.

"What's going on?" Sam asked when he got to us.

"I'll explain after we get Levi inside," I said. For some reason, my voice quivered and I lost my balance, almost falling. It was as if my legs were made of rubber. Sam grabbed me and put his arm around my waist.

"It's over, Sam," I said as uncontrolled tears rolled down my cheeks. "It's finally over."

Chapter Nineteen

So what will happen to Levi now?" Ruth asked as she passed around the plate of fried chicken. "I suppose there will be a trial?"

"I doubt it," I said. "Levi admitted to the sheriff in Council Grove what he did all those years ago. I suppose they'll transfer him to a larger city and sentence him."

A sudden shout drew our attention away from the fantastic food brought forth from the good folks of Harmony for the community picnic. My idea for a simple get-together to thank those who'd worked on my uncle's house had turned into a huge event. No one even remembered the original reason for the gathering. Everyone was having a wonderful time sharing a mild spring night with their family, friends, and neighbors.

Another boisterous bellow rang out. The women gathered at the table laughed at the antics of the men who'd put together a baseball game with odd rules and even stranger equipment. Sam had hit a softball past a package of unopened bread that lay on the ground. Abel and Gabe insisted that John had moved the bread when they weren't looking and discounted John's assertion that this signified a home run. However, the argument became moot when Buddy picked up the package in his mouth and began running around their designated playing field. Watching Abel and Gabe run after him while Sam, John, Drew Crandall, and his father yelled enthusiastic comments at the playful dog brought gales of laughter from the rest of us. The men's careful inclusion of Drew, the young man with Down syndrome, into their exploits was touching. He was having as much fun as the rest of them, laughing at Buddy's attempt at disrupting the game. Finally, Sam, who pretended not to be interested in the bread at all, sucked Buddy into his clutches and grabbed the shredded loaf from his mouth. The men were now in a game of keep-away with one another.

"Can't tell the difference between those men and little bitty boys," Sweetie said around a mouthful of potato salad.

"That's for certain." Emily was able to smile tonight after a couple of days of emotional upheaval. Levi's admission that he'd killed Jacob Glick because of his love for her had shaken her deeply. She finally told Abel about the rape. As I'd suspected, he wasn't really surprised. His knowledge of Glick, as limited as it was, and his wife's reaction to the mere mention of the man's name, had caused Abel to suspect the truth years ago. References to Glick had occurred a few times in the past because of Abel's interest in the memoirs and diaries left behind by early Harmony residents. Each time, Emily's reaction had been similar to the one I'd witnessed Saturday at the café. It didn't take a detective to realize something was wrong. Not feeling he should confront Emily before she was ready, Abel had spent a long time praying for his wife. His prayers, along with his undying love and support gave her the strength to finally bring her shameful secret out into the open. When seen in the light of God's love, the darkness vanished, as did the humiliation and guilt. This revelation allowed her to accept God's redemptive power to heal her pain.

She'd finally removed that sad painting off the wall in her

dining room and replaced it with one of Hannah's delightful landscapes. In fact, she and Abel had destroyed the self-portrait together and thrown the remnants on the fire. Now that it was finally vanquished, along with the fear of losing her family, she'd even promised to pick up a paintbrush again. Hannah was understandably delighted, as was Emily's devoted husband.

In an odd twist of fate, although Levi Hoffman may have wanted to protect Emily when they were younger and failed, in admitting his part in Glick's murder, he'd actually helped to set her free. I could only hope he'd find some comfort in that knowledge.

"Well, I can hardly believe what's happened," Ruth said. "Seeing Gabriel and John out there having fun with the other men—why it's nothing short of a miracle."

"Here's another miracle," Emily said with a smile. "Sunday morning we had some very special visitors."

Ida, who sat beside me, reached over and hugged my arm. "That is correct. Gabriel, Sarah, and I came to church together."

"That's wonderful," I said, kissing her on the cheek. "Just a visit or. . ."

"Not sure," Ida said. "I do not want to push Gabriel. I think it could be a mistake. I just told him I would be going every Sunday I could and would love it if we could ride together. We will have to wait and see what happens."

"Did the investigators fill that hole back up after they dug Glick out of the clearing?" Ruth asked.

I shuddered. "No. Something to do with possibly needing more evidence. They've got crime scene tape all around it. I don't think they'll keep it like that for long. Not with Levi's confession. I'm just staying away. It gives me the creeps."

" 'Twas a might more creepy when Jacob was actually there," Sweetie said. "You should rest better now that that mean old thing is gone."

I sighed and speared a piece of watermelon with my fork. "I guess I do. Honestly, I'm not sure how I feel about any of this. It's just too fresh, I guess."

"Ruth told me you stopped by her shop to get some flowers for Ben's grave," Joyce said. "How did the visit with your uncle go?"

"It was good. I'm glad I went." I smiled at Ruth. "And thank you so much for the lovely flowers. They look so pretty next to his headstone."

I looked around at the people sitting at the large picnic table. "I haven't had the chance to ask anyone before this, but who picked the inscription?"

"Why, Ben did, child," Joyce said. "Who did you think chose it?"

I was pretty sure I knew the answer to my question before she said it, but I had to ask. After I'd found Benjamin's headstone and read the inscription, I could only stand in front of it and weep. Under his name and the dates of his birth and death, these words had been inscribed: 'TIS GRACE THAT BROUGHT ME SAFE THUS FAR, AND GRACE WILL LEAD ME HOME. I couldn't miss the capitalization of the second *grace*. Unless the engraver had made a mistake, my uncle had sent me a final message. He'd trusted me to find a way to lay his pain to rest. Being able to complete the task he'd left for me brought me great peace.

"So did you get. . .what do they call it. . .closure?" Emily asked.

I smiled. "You know, I think I did. I sat down and had a nice long conversation with my uncle. Told him everything that had happened since I came to Harmony. He may not have heard me, but it made me feel better."

"He certainly left a lot behind for you to deal with," Ruth said.

"I know. But now I understand it, and I'm at peace with it."

"I'm sure your father was happy to know you'd put flowers on his brother's final resting place," Emily said.

"Yes—yes he was."

The call I'd made to my dad had really thrown me for a loop. Telling him what Benjamin had tried to do for him was harder than I'd anticipated. I was glad to be free from our awful family secret, but I hadn't fully anticipated how deep the emotional impact would be for my father. When I explained that his estrangement from his brother hadn't been because Benjamin had rejected him but because he'd been trying to protect him, Dad broke down. Then I cleared up another mystery thanks to something Sweetie told me while we were planning the picnic. A few weeks before Benjamin died, she'd asked for the key to my father's old bedroom so she could clean it. Benjamin refused. He'd told Sweetie that he missed his brother so much he couldn't bear to have anything touched or changed. In fact, sometimes he'd pretend Daniel was still living in the house, just on the other side of the closed bedroom door. It shook me deeply to listen to my father cry. Of course, once he got control of his emotions, he went another direction. He chewed me out. Royally.

"Gracie, you should have told me what was going on the first night you got there," he'd said sternly. "I hate that you went through something like this alone. I would have been there for you. You should have known that."

After assuring him it would never happen again, and being pretty confident that I would never run up against a situation quite like this one again if I lived three lifetimes, we'd hung up. After putting the phone down, I'd had a good, long sobfest myself. Not sure exactly why, but I think it had something to do with relieving tension—and hearing my father cry. Not something I wanted to experience again for a long, long time.

"All kinds of changes going on in Harmony," Ida said, pulling me back into the present. "I am getting a telephone!"

"Now that really *is* something," Joyce said with a smile. "What made you decide to do it?"

The old woman shook her head. "After Gracie's fire and Levi's situation, I saw that I could have gotten help for my friends much faster if I had a telephone. I do not intend to let that happen again."

I smiled at her, feeling a great sense of relief. Now if she ever needed help, she'd be able to call someone.

"You know," Sweetie said, "all this goodwill has made me do some thinkin'. I—I was ponderin' the idea of goin' back to church myself." She grinned at Emily. "Don't think it will be your church, though. I don't cotton to dresses, and those caps you wear would just look silly on my old head."

Emily laughed good-naturedly. "Actually, you could wear what you want and still be welcome at Bethel. But you should go where you feel most comfortable."

"I should say you'd be welcome at Bethel!" Abel loudly proclaimed. He and Sam had finished their game and run up to the table. "We can't tell you how much we appreciate what you did for us."

I looked over at Sweetie who wrinkled up her face in a frown. "Now Abel, I told you to be quiet about that."

He shook his head. "Sorry, Sweetie. I think all the blood must have rushed from my head out there with Sam chasing me all over the place. I forgot you didn't want anyone to know."

"Know what?" Ruth asked. "You might as well tell us now, Abel. You know we'll keep needling you until you cough up the truth."

Abel looked over at Sweetie who glared at him. "Sorry, Ruth. It's Sweetie's story to share, and she doesn't seem open to it."

Sam raised one eyebrow. "Well, I know what it is, and I'm not afraid of retribution."

"I told you, boy, I can cut off your food supply if you irritate me," his aunt said forcefully. She waved her hand at the group gathered around the table. "It ain't no big thing, but I'd surely appreciate it if it wouldn't go no further than this group." She shook her finger at Abel. "And that goes for you especially, Abel Mueller. You're a pastor. I shouldn't have to worry about you spreadin' gossip."

Abel bowed at the waist and made a motion as if he were doffing his hat. Actually, his large straw hat was sitting on the bench next to his wife. "My humble apologies for divulging your secret." He straightened up and shook his finger back at her. "But you make it sound like you did something wrong, Sweetie. It's not like you stole Ruth's chestnut vase or something."

Everyone at the table laughed. It was nice to find humor in something that had been so painful only a short time ago. Sweetie guffawed louder than anyone else.

"Well, here's the story," she said when the laughter finally died down. "After I moved into the red house, I was workin' to fix it up. I found an old safe that belonged to that Amil Angstadt character. There was twenty thousand dollars in it. I found out that years ago, a member of Bethel sold some land and donated the proceeds to the church. Seems it never made it to its final destination though." She shrugged. "So I gave the money to Abel—for fixin' up damaged houses and such. You know, like what happened to Gracie here."

Emily reached across the table and took Sweetie's calloused hand. "You're a good woman, Sweetie Goodrich. I'm proud to know you."

Sweetie blinked several times and her eyes got big. "Why. . . why, thank you, Emily. Can't say I heard that too much in my life."

"I remember that money," Ida said. "That property belonged to Mason Guttenberg. After he died, his wife decided to go back to Pennsylvania to live with her parents. Viola wanted to do something in Mason's memory and told folks she was going to sell their land and give part of the proceeds to the church. Funny thing was, we never heard anything else about it. We all wondered what happened to the donation, but then the bishop died, Viola and the kids moved on, and it was forgotten." She smiled at Sweetie. "God used you to put it where it was supposed to go. Praise the Lord!"

Sweetie turned three shades of red. She probably didn't hear herself described as a vessel of the Lord very often.

I could only wonder why Angstadt never gave that money to the church. Was that the secret Glick had held over his head, or was it something else? Did the minister plan to do the right thing someday? The fact that none of the money was ever spent made me hope his intentions were honorable. He'd been a harsh and judgmental man, but was he a criminal? Unfortunately, I would never have the answer to that question in this life.

At that moment, Marcus Jensen and Amos Crandall walked up to the table. "Pastor Mueller," Marcus said with a grin. "I've been sent over here to challenge you to a game of horseshoes. I hear you're pretty good, but I think I'm better. Are you game?"

Abel looked at Emily whose light, lilting laugh made me feel happy inside. "It's fine. You go on. Have fun."

"How 'bout you, Sam?" Amos asked.

"Thanks, Amos, but I have something I need to talk to Sam about," I said. "He'll sit this one out."

Marcus smiled and patted Sam on the back. "Sounds important, Sam," he said in a jovial voice. "I think you'd better tend to it. Catch up to us later if you want to. Abel will probably need the help."

"Pride goeth before destruction, Pastor Jensen," Abel said, winking at us. "I think you're in for a whoopin', as my mother used to say."

The two took off toward the area where the horseshoes had been set up. We could hear their good-natured ribbing as they walked away.

Hannah's friends Leah and Jessica ran up to the table and grabbed her arm. "Let's watch the men play horseshoes, Hannah," they said between giggles.

Hannah looked at Emily who nodded her permission. The three girls ran toward the horseshoe area, laughing and teasing each other.

"Come with me, Mr. Goodrich," I said to Sam. "I think you're in for a whoopin', too."

"Yikes," he said, grabbing Sweetie's hand. "Save me from this vicious woman."

She shook her hand free and laughed at him. "Boy, I think you been in need of straightenin' out for a long, long time. Gracie's got my blessin'!"

"See, there's no help for you here." I grabbed his other hand and pulled him away from the table.

We held hands and strolled over to the fountain. In the dusky glow of evening, lights flickered on and highlighted the fountain and the benches. The sounds of people and children laughing and playing echoed behind us. The aroma of freshly cut grass combined with the sweetness of honeysuckle created an atmosphere so special I wanted to remember the sights, sounds, and aromas forever.

Sam swung my hand back and forth as we walked. I felt a peace inside me that I'd never known before. I wanted to savor it, so I slowed my steps down to a stroll. As if he felt the same thing, Sam matched my unhurried gait with his own.

"Abel's talking about having a funeral for Glick," he said. "He hasn't mentioned it to John yet. He's not sure how John will feel about it."

"Wow. Not sure if that's a good idea. Glick caused a lot of heartache in this community."

"I know, but Abel says funerals are for the living, not the dead. The idea of John burying his father alone doesn't sit too well with either one of us."

I considered this. "You've got a point. Maybe a small, private funeral for John and a few friends." I sighed. "I like John. He shouldn't feel bad about Glick. We don't get to pick our fathers."

As we reached the benches, Mary walked past us. She carried a large box full of pies.

"Boy, that smells good," Sam said. "Need some help?"

She smiled. "Thanks, Sam. But I've got it. These won't last long. You two better get back soon so you don't miss out."

I nodded. "Good point. We'll do our best."

After flashing us another smile, she took off toward the food table.

"Well, that's an improvement," I said.

Sam nodded. "I think we're going to be okay. We had a talk the last day I worked on Ben's house. She finally admitted that she knew we weren't right for each other." He stopped walking and turned to look at me. "You know, after only knowing you a few days, I realized that I'd almost made the biggest mistake of my life. I'd picked someone to marry because I didn't think I had any other choices. I was willing to give up passion for—for convenience, I guess. After Mary and I ended up engaged, I bought her a ring." He laughed. "Funny thing, I could never bring myself to give it to her. With my lightning-fast mind, you'd think I'd have figured out why. But anyway, after you left the other day to pick wildflowers for Ida, I got that ring out of the drawer where I kept it and. . ."

"You threw it into the lake," I finished for him.

His eyebrows arched in surprise. "How did you know that?"

"I saw you. Of course, I didn't know what you'd tossed into the water. I have to admit that I wondered about it."

He grinned. "Did you think I was getting rid of evidence? I couldn't have killed Jacob Glick you know. I wasn't even born. . ."

I put my fingers up to his lips. "Oh hush. I don't know what I thought, but I couldn't have been too suspicious. I actually forgot about it until you just brought it up." I frowned at him. "You could have gotten your money back for the ring, you know."

"For some reason I really needed to pitch it, Grace. I don't know if you can understand that."

I gazed into his eyes. "I understand it completely."

His face flushed slightly, and he guided me to one of the benches. He sat down and pulled me down next to him. "Before you start in on whatever you wanted to say, can I tell you something?"

"Of course."

He took my hand and covered it with both of his. His head hung down as he stared at the ground. "I—I told you that John and I had a lot in common. Do you remember that?"

"Yes."

He hesitated for a moment. "Th–the truth is that I have no idea who my father is. When my mother got pregnant with me, she wasn't married." He breathed in deeply and let it out. "John didn't know who his father was until after his mother died. He was born out of wedlock, too. I may never know my father, but the thought that he might be someone as awful as Jacob Glick makes me feel sick to my stomach."

I squeezed his hands. "Why didn't you tell me this earlier?"

He swung his head up. "I was afraid you'd think less of me. It's embarrassing, Grace."

I shook my head. "Look, I want to be understanding, I really do, but I don't see why in the world you should be embarrassed. It had nothing to do with you."

His face flushed. "It sounds like my mother was loose or something. But she wasn't. She might have made a mistake, but she was a wonderful mother. She did everything she could for me. And she took me to church." He cleared his throat. I could tell this was difficult for him. "And she didn't abort me. She could have."

"I don't believe for one moment that your mother was loose, as you put it. You're the most wonderful man I've ever known. I'm certain your mother had a lot to do with that. We've all made

311

mistakes. It we didn't, we wouldn't need Jesus, would we?"

He shook his head.

"Have you ever thought about trying to find your father?"

"I've toyed with the idea. I get the feeling Sweetie knows something she hasn't told me. But to be honest, this thing with John made me even more reluctant. Obviously, finding your biological family doesn't always turn out like a fairy tale. There's not always a happy ending."

I had no answer to that. His conclusion was probably true.

Sam got up and walked over to the plaque attached to the fountain. "Remember how I told you that Harmony is a special place?" he said evenly. "I believe that even more now. Since—since you came here."

"What do you mean?"

He turned toward me. The seriousness in his expression startled me. "I truly believe you were meant to come here, Grace. There were hurtful secrets buried below the surface of this town. God used you to bring them out."

"Anyone could have..."

"No," he said firmly. "Not anyone. Ben couldn't do it. He kept the truth buried for years, letting it cause devastation and pain."

I got up and went over to him. "But it wasn't the truth. It was all a lie. Benjamin protected a lie. If the real truth had come out when Glick died, I'll bet things would have been different for a lot of people. For my family, for Emily, Sweetie..."

"And Levi."

I nodded. "Yes, Levi, too. Spending all these years harboring guilt and bitterness is almost worse than being in a physical jail, isn't it?"

"Yes, I believe you're right." He put his hand under my chin and kissed me lightly. "I still believe coming to Harmony was your destiny." He ran his finger down the side of my face. "I want to spend the rest of the week with you. Sweetie said she'd hire some help in the orchard so we can have every possible minute together."

"Thank you, Sam, but that's not necessary."

He frowned. "I don't understand. I know you have to figure out how to get your possessions out of the house, but I can help. Sweetie really wants to buy the land so we can expand the orchards. She'll give you a good price. . ."

"Sam, I'm leaving in the morning. I'm not waiting until the weekend."

He stepped back from me, his face drained of color. "I—I don't understand. I–I'm not ready for you to go."

I sat on the edge of the fountain and looked into the water. "Do you remember when you first showed me this fountain?"

"Of course. It was only a few days ago."

"I told you I prayed for God's will in my life. You warned me that I'd asked for something dangerous. You called it a prayer of consecration. You said it meant that my life might take a turn I hadn't planned on. You asked me if I was ready to accept that."

Sam's beautiful gray eyes locked onto mine. "Yes, I remember."

I could feel the tears that filled my eyes, but I was powerless to stop them. "I wasn't then, but I am now. Since I came to this town my life has been in constant upheaval. I kept thinking how different the world is in Wichita. At first I wanted nothing more than to get home to it."

He took a step toward me. "You said 'at first'?"

I nodded and a sob broke past my lips. "Then all of a sudden, the idea of going back didn't seem so appealing. I finally realized it wasn't the life I wanted anymore."

"I don't understand. What are you saying?"

I reached up and touched his lips with my fingertips while the sound of dancing water played in the background like gentle music. "I'm leaving in the morning so I can go back to Wichita and pack up my things. I've already called my boss. He's willing to let me do freelance work for him. I'm moving to Harmony because. . ."

Sam's kiss cut off anything else I might have wanted to say. His arms held me close, and I could feel his body tremble. In my entire life, I'd never been kissed the way Sam Goodrich kissed me then and there. When he let me go, it took me a little while to speak.

"There is one thing I need from you, Sam," I finally whispered. "One thing you must promise me."

"Anything," he said in a husky voice. "I would do anything for you. Name it."

I smiled and wiped a tear from his face with my finger. "I can tell you in one word."

He cocked his head to one side. "Tell me."

I couldn't hold back the laughter that bubbled up from inside of me. "Electricity. You've got to help me get electricity."

Laughing and kissing might not seem to go together, but somehow it worked for us.

"You have my word," he said with a grin. "I'll even make sure you have a phone."

"Oh thank you."

From behind us I heard someone call our names. We turned around to see Abel standing a few yards away.

"I'm attempting to save you both a piece of pie," he yelled. "You'd better get over here before it's too late!"

Sam grabbed my hand, and we started walking toward the kind Mennonite man who had become my friend.

"Hey, we're trying to schedule one more game of horseshoes before it gets dark," he said. "What time are you two going home?"

I smiled at Abel and squeezed Sam's hand. "Why, Abel," I said, "we have all the time in the world. You see, Sam and I are both already home."

He stood and watched us as we walked back toward the picnic area. He didn't say anything, but I could hear his hearty laughter floating past us on the gentle spring air.

DISCUSSION QUESTIONS

1. While working and living in Wichita, Gracie Temple believed her life was everything she'd always wanted. Yet she struggled with a nagging sense of unrest. What caused this feeling?

2. Gracie arrived in Harmony with many preconceived ideas about the people who lived there. Why? Was she wrong, right, or a little of both?

3. Did you like Harmony, Kansas? Would you want to live there? Why or why not?

4. Several people in Harmony had long-held secrets. What happens when we bury hurts down deep inside? Do you have anything you've never told anyone? After reading how keeping a secret affected Emily's life, have you changed your mind about staying silent?

5. How do you feel about the way some of the Old Order and Conservative Mennonites live? Do you understand their desire for a "simpler life"? Or do you think it's unrealistic?

6. Do you believe two different churches could really live in harmony in a small town? Why or why not?

7. How did Gracie change from the beginning of the book until the end? Would you have made the same choice she did about whether to stay in Harmony or go back to Wichita?

8. When did you figure out who killed Jacob Glick? Were you surprised?

9. What do you believe motivated Amil Angstead? Do you think he was an evil man? Or was he just a man who thought he was right?

10. Do you know anyone like Sweetie or Levi who quit going to church because they'd been hurt? As Christians, what can we do to help people like them?

11. What is the main theme of this book? Finding out that God's will for your life may be different than what you thought it was? Not judging people negatively who may look or live differently than we do? That "secrets buried alive never die"?

Simple Deceit

DEDICATION

Sometimes in life, God sends us friends who are so special they can never be replaced. When they leave us, they leave a hole in our lives that stays empty. My friend, Judy Roberts, was such a person. I miss you so much, Judy. But I can still hear your sweet voice saying, "Can you feel my love?" And the answer is, "Yes. Now and forever."

ACKNOWLEDGMENTS

My thanks to the following people who helped me to create *Simple Deceit*. First of all, my thanks to Judith Unruh, Alexanderwohl Church historian in Goessel, Kansas. You are the voice that whispers in my ear while I write.

To Sarah Beck, owner of Beck's Farm in Wichita, who has been so much help to me. The only bump in our road happened when I asked her how someone would go about destroying a fruit orchard. She admits that my question made her a little nervous—LOL!

To Gordon Bassham who answered all my real estate questions.

Thanks again to my friends Penny and Gus Dorado for being willing to help me with my Mennonite research.

Thank-you to Alene Ward for her constant encouragement, for editing under extreme pressure, and for creating Sweetie's Christmas quilt. I can hardly wait to see it finished!

I want to acknowledge a few other writers of Amish/Mennonite fiction for their support and encouragement: Cindy Woodsmall, Kim Vogel Sawyer, and Wanda Brunstetter. Thank you for being more than just great authors. You are also wonderful, gracious people.

As always, my thanks to the folks at Barbour. You guys are the best!

To the readers who are willing to take a chance on me. I appreciate you all so much.

As always, to the Mennonite people who have given our country such a rich heritage of faith and taught us to respect the things in life that are really important.

Lastly, and most importantly, to the One who never gives up on me. I will always believe.

Chapter One

There are five words guaranteed to strike terror into the heart of any human being. No, it's not "Step up on the scale," although this phrase is certainly a contender. And it's not "Can we just be friends?" which might actually run a close second. Of course, I'm ruling out all scary medical conditions that elicit remarks like "Let's run that test again." I'm talking about day-in, day-out, non-life-threatening situations that we all face but hope every day when we roll out of bed that today won't be *that* day.

Unfortunately, today was *that* day.

"License and registration please, ma'am."

I fumbled through my purse, looking for my driver's license. The setting sun pierced through the windshield like some kind of spotlight on steroids, almost blinding me. My hands shook as I flipped open my Garfield wallet. I flashed a smile at the basset hound–faced man who watched me through narrowed eyes. He was obviously not amused.

"I—I know it's here," I said a little too loudly. A quick thumb through all the cards jammed into the dividers revealed my debit card, an old library card, several business cards belonging to people I couldn't remember, and my only credit card. The credit card had never been used because my father had convinced me that the first time I pulled it out of my wallet, I would end up on the street, overcome by high interest rates and personal degradation. I found a reminder card for a dental appointment I'd completely forgotten, an expired coupon for Starbucks, an expired coupon for a Krispy Kreme doughnut, and a card from a video store that had gone out of business two years earlier. No license.

The officer's breathing became heavier and created steam in the frigid November air. I was reminded of one of those English horror movies where the thicker the fog, the sooner the intended victim bites the dust. The cold seeping into my car through my open window did nothing to dispel the beads of sweat forming along my hairline. Where was that stupid license? Could it have fallen out inside my purse? But why would I have taken it out of my wallet? Another quick look revealed a bank envelope with the cash I'd withdrawn before I left Wichita. I tore it open like an addict looking for drugs. Sure enough, my fingers closed around the small piece of plastic that would surely save me from being hauled to jail.

"Here it is!" I declared with gusto. "I had to show it to the bank when I withdrew cash from my account. I forgot it was still in the—"

"And the registration, ma'am?" The officer's cold expression and stern tone made it clear that finding my license hadn't ignited elation in the man's obviously stony heart. However, this time I was prepared. My father actually checked my glove compartment every time I went home to Fairbury, Nebraska. He was almost paranoid about making sure my registration was where it was supposed to be. Between that and the "credit cards are straight from hell" lectures, I knew where my car registration was at all times.

This balanced out the fact that I had almost no credit. Even my car was a gift from my parents. At least the rent on my old apartment had been in my name. My one accomplishment as an adult.

I pulled the registration out of the blue plastic folder in my glove compartment and handed it to the waiting officer. If I'd expected him to congratulate me on this show of responsibility, I would have been disappointed.

"Wait here."

Like I was going to take off and let him chase me? I was pretty sure his patrol car had more power than my Volkswagen Bug, even if it *is* cute and perky.

While he ran my license, no doubt hoping I'd pop up on some Most Wanted list, I tried to figure out what crime I'd just committed. I always drove under the speed limit, even if it meant everyone raced around me, many times blaring their horns like I was breaking the law instead of abiding by it. I hadn't passed anyone in a no passing lane. In fact, I hadn't passed anyone at all for quite some time. I'd stopped at every stop sign and slowed down to a crawl in every small town I'd driven through. Why in heaven's name had he pulled me over?

In my mind I quickly ran over my exit from Wichita. I'd spent the last two and a half months there, working with my boss at Grantham Design to set up a way to freelance for him while training his newest in-house designer. I'd cleaned my apartment and finished out my lease so I wouldn't lose my deposit. All my utilities had been turned off, but I was pretty sure utility companies don't contact the police if you fail to end your business with them correctly.

I glanced at my watch. Almost six o'clock. I'd told Sam I'd be back to Harmony by sunset, but there was no way I'd make it. Being gone so long had been necessary, but I'd missed him and Harmony more than I'd anticipated.

I glanced in my rearview mirror. The officer was heading my way with a flashlight in his hand. What now? Was he going to go through my car? If he thought he'd find drugs or alcohol, he'd be disappointed. About the only exciting substance in my car belonged to my cat, Snicklefritz, who was sleeping peacefully in his carrier. If the officer wanted a real fight on his hands, all he had to do was try to wrestle Snickle's catnip toys away from him.

I know the smile I gave the officer was goofy, but I couldn't help it. I felt goofy even though I had no idea why.

He leaned in and handed me back my license. "Ma'am, do you know your right taillight is out?"

I breathed a sigh of relief. "No. No, I didn't, Officer. It was working when I left Wichita."

His frown deepened. "And how do you know that, ma'am?"

His deep, throaty voice and slow drawl didn't help to dispel my nervousness.

"Well. . .I mean, I guess I don't. It's just that I took my car to Jiffy Jump before I left town, and they checked everything out. N–not that you're mistaken or anything. I mean, I guess it went out after I left. I–I'll get it fixed right away."

His raised eyebrows confirmed what I already knew. I sounded guilty. And slightly insane.

"Just where are you headed, ma'am?"

"I'm going to Harmony. I recently moved there. You see, my family used to live in Harmony, and—"

"You have anything to do with that body they dug up a few months ago?"

"Why, yes. In fact, the body was found on my property. Well, it was my family's property when it was buried there. Then, of course, it went to my uncle, who—"

He snapped his notepad shut so forcefully the sound made me jump. "Ridiculous goings on," he growled, giving me a look obviously designed to frighten me. It worked. "You should have called me the minute you knew someone had been killed. People like you, thinking you can handle things outside the law. You're lucky you weren't charged with aiding and abetting. If I'd had anything to do with it. . ."

Okay. That did it. Maybe it was being stuck in Wichita for so long, or maybe it was simply my desire to get home to Harmony, but this man had jangled my last nerve.

"Excuse me, Officer," I said, sarcasm dripping from my words like warm honey. "We weren't sure the man had actually been murdered until someone admitted to it. And then we called the authorities immediately. If you'll check with your superiors. . ."

His rough laugh silenced the rest of my sentence. He leaned over and put his face up close to mine. Too close for my liking. "The pastor of that crazy Mennonite church called the sheriff in this county once you all had finished playing detective. Do you know who the sheriff is, little lady?"

I felt myself bristle at his *little lady* comment. "As a matter of fact, I do," I retorted. "His name is Patrick Taylor."

"And have you ever met Sheriff Taylor?" The officer's voice dropped an octave and his frown intensified.

I don't know what made me glance at his badge, which was partially hidden by his jacket, but something inside me knew. It was a sinking feeling followed quickly by a wave of nausea. The name on his badge was Taylor, and for the first time I realized he wasn't with the police. He was with the sheriff's department. "N–no, I never met him in person. After Abel Mueller called him, the FBI took over the case. I dealt with them directly."

A grin spread across the man's face that could only be described as evil.

"Y–you're Sheriff Taylor, aren't you?"

The sheriff spat on the ground and slowly put his notepad in his pocket. "I'm lettin' you off with a warning, little lady, but you'd better have that light fixed right away. If I see you again and it's not workin', even your little Mennonite friends won't be able to save you."

I put my hand over my eyes in an attempt to shield them from the sun and gazed up at him. Was he serious? I remembered something someone had said once about Pat Taylor—that he had a bad attitude toward the residents of Harmony. That he thought they were all a bunch of religious zealots.

"I'm sure I don't know what you mean, Sheriff. I assure you that I can take care of my own problems. Thank you for the warning. I will make sure the light is fixed as soon as possible."

Sheriff Taylor glowered at me for a few more moments. From what I could see of his expression, my assurances to take care of my taillight hadn't endeared me to the ill-tempered law officer one little bit. "Be sure you do," he said finally. "I'll be keeping my eye on you. That uncle of yours tried to subvert the law." He leaned down until his face was just inches from mine. "Blood ties are strong, Miss Temple. Stronger than you could ever imagine. Don't you forget it."

With that, he turned on his heels and strode back to his patrol car. I sat there with my mouth hanging open. He was already inside his vehicle by the time I could come up with a response to his outrageous statement. But as his odd comment rolled through my mind, I had the strange feeling that Pat Taylor had known who I was from the first moment he pulled me over. I found the idea unsettling.

I waited a couple of minutes, hoping he would leave first, but his cruiser didn't move. Finally I put my car into gear and pulled back out onto the highway. The sheriff's car slid right into line behind mine. I kept my speed low, hoping he would pass me, but he kept a steady distance between us. I had at least thirty miles to go before I reached the turnoff to Harmony. Surely he wasn't going to follow me all that way. I slid my favorite Rich Mullins CD into the player. His music always calms me, and I needed that now. I tried to concentrate on the words and forget that I was being tailed by the sheriff from you-know-where.

As Rich began to sing about another hour in the night and a mile farther down the road, I could feel the tension leaving my body. I was so into the song that I forgot all about my new law enforcement buddy. When I finally checked my rearview mirror again, he was gone.

A few minutes later, I spotted the road to Harmony. The sun had set behind the trees, so I could finally see my way clearly. I looked at the clock on my dashboard. Almost six forty-five. I'd planned to be at Sam's by six thirty for supper. Myrtle Goodrich, his rather persnickety aunt whom everyone called "Sweetie," had to be fuming. It would take another forty-five minutes at least for me to get there. Unfortunately, I couldn't blame everything on my impromptu visit with Sheriff Taylor. I'd left town later than I'd meant to.

I slowed down some and fished my cell phone out of my purse. Once I reached Harmony, it was virtually useless. But maybe I could get Sam while I was still a good distance away. I punched in his telephone number and was gratified to hear ringing.

"Hello!" A voice screeched through my small phone. "Is that you, Gracie Temple? Where in tarnation are you? My meat loaf is gonna dry up and turn to dust if you don't get here pretty soon."

"Sweetie, how did you know it was me? What if you'd just yelled at some innocent person?"

"Pshaw. Ain't no one else missin' right now. You're the only one would be callin' me right at suppertime. No one else in this town, specially someone I'd call a friend, would take a chance on rilin' me up like that."

She was probably right. "I'm sorry, but I'm going to be late. It'll be another hour, maybe a little less, before I get to town. You and Sam go ahead and eat. If there's anything left, you can warm it up when I get there."

Sweetie's voice softened just a little. "Nah, I'll just spoon some juice over it. Me and Sam would rather wait for you, Gracie. Been kind of lonely here without you."

"I missed you, too, Sweetie. Is Sam nearby?"

"Sam!" She yelled so loud I almost dropped the phone.

After some odd crackling noises and a thud, I heard Sam's voice. "Where are you, Grace? I've been sitting on the porch watching for your car, and I'm slowly freezing to death."

I explained my late departure from Wichita and briefly described my meeting with the Morris County sheriff. "I'll tell you more about it when I get there," I said. "I don't like talking on my cell phone while I'm driving."

Sam's warm chuckle drifted through the phone. "You're on the county road leading to Harmony, Grace. Do you see another car anywhere?"

I had to admit that I seemed to be completely alone. "I know, but I just feel uncomfortable when I'm not focused on my driving the way I should be. I guess it's not such a big deal right now, though."

He sighed. "Boy, I've missed you. I can't believe it took so long to get everything tied up in Wichita."

"I know. Between my landlord and Grant, I wondered if I'd ever get out of there. But the lease is settled, and I got my deposit back even though they tried to keep half of it."

"Half? Why?"

"Because Snickle tore up part of the carpet with his claws."

"But Snickle is declawed."

I snorted. "Yeah, that kind of took the wind out of their

argument, and they forked everything over."

Sam laughed. "Glad that's behind us. But what about Grant? What if he fires this second guy? Will he expect you to go back and train a third designer?"

My old boss, Grant Hampton at Grantham Design, was having a tough time replacing me. After spending almost a month in Wichita training his first pick, I'd been persuaded to come back and work with the second. Since I really needed the freelancing work he'd promised me, I was kind of between a rock and a hard place.

"He promised I wouldn't have to teach my job to anyone else. I think we're safe for a while. Four trips to Wichita in the past six months is more than enough."

"I can hardly wait for you to get here, Grace. To be home for good."

Home for good. Those words were music to my ears. "Hey, I'm working on a project that I can't wait to tell you about. Believe it or not, I think it will actually help Harmony."

"That sounds great, but right now all I want to do is put my arms around you and hold on for the rest of our lives."

I couldn't respond for a moment. My heart felt like it had lodged in my throat. "Hey, I'm going to hang up now," I finally croaked out. "I'll see you in a little while."

"I love you, Grace."

"I love you, too, Sam. Bye."

I clicked off the phone and dropped it into my purse. Then I settled back in my seat and clicked the CD to Rich's song about Kansas. As he sang about the prairies calling out God's name and our sunsets resembling a sky set ablaze with fire, I watched the incredible countryside pass by me, perfectly portrayed in his lyrics. I'd always thought of myself as a city girl, but the last few months had shown me that I belonged out here where God's creation outshines anything man can possibly fashion. Gratitude for His awesome power and tender provision overwhelmed me, and a tear slid down my cheek. I whispered a prayer of thanks. "You led me to Harmony, Father. And I found my life there. I'm so thankful. . . ."

I wiped my face with my sleeve and checked the mirror to make sure my mascara hadn't run. I didn't wear much, but I had no intention of seeing Sam for the first time in months looking like a raccoon.

Rich had just started to sing the first song again and Snickle was beginning to let me know he was ready for freedom when I pulled into Harmony. I slowed down because of slick spots on the road that led through the center of town. A recent ice storm had left its mark. Sam had explained to me that while most small towns had the resources to clear their main streets, there were no funds for that kind of thing here. For the most part, residents just waited until the ice melted. The Bruners, who run the local feed store, donate coarse salt that clears off the wooden boardwalks, but there's not much they can do about the streets. Snow can be scooped up with plows, but ice is another matter.

The sun had set, and the old-fashioned streetlights had flickered on, lighting up the wooden boardwalks and all the interesting buildings that sat side by side, no two structures alike. Each business had its own personality—and paint color. Harmony was certainly colorful—literally and figuratively. I loved its quaint style and unique presence.

No one was in sight, although I could see cars parked in front of Mary's Kitchen, the only restaurant in town. I'd heard about small towns that figuratively roll up their sidewalks after dark. Harmony certainly fit the bill. Most of the population consisted of Conservative Mennonite families who spent their evenings at home. Children did not run wild and parents did not carouse.

Family time was sacred, and evenings were spent having dinner, doing homework, and reading the Bible before early bedtimes. A good way to live, in my opinion, even though I actually enjoy staying up late. I love the peaceful quiet of the country and like to spend time sitting out on my front porch at night, watching the sky become christened with God's flickering jewels. There would be none of that tonight, though, and perhaps the rest of the winter. I had no intention of having someone find me frozen solid to my wooden rocking chair.

I passed the old cemetery where my uncle Benjamin was buried and had just driven past the huge Bethel Mennonite Church building on the edge of town when I noticed something in my rearview mirror. A figure stood near the front door of the church, holding a large object. I pulled over to get a better look. All the inside lights were off in the church except for the pastor's office. Sure enough, Abel's dark blue car with its black-painted bumpers sat off to the side of the building. The frigid temperature caused me concern. Was it Emily, Abel's wife, trying to get inside? Had she been locked out?

I turned the car around while trying to calm Snickle and drove back. I pulled into the circular drive in front of the building. My headlights shone on a figure in a dark cloak, her hood hanging over her face. The woman seemed startled to see my car and froze for several seconds while I drove up closer. Just as I opened my car door, she set her package down and backed slowly down the steps. A strange, plaintive wail rose through the quiet Harmony evening. I ran up next to a large basket and pulled back the thick blanket on top. A tiny baby reached out its little fingers toward me.

"Hey," I yelled to the woman who watched me from the driveway. "What are you doing? This—this is a baby!"

With that, she spun around and began to run toward the thick grove of trees that lined the edge of the church's property. Not knowing what else to do, I pounded on the church door as loudly as I could and then took off after her. Unfortunately, the grass was slick with ice that had melted and refrozen. Although it impeded my progress, it also caused the woman her own problems. A few yards before the tree line, I reached out and grabbed her cloak. She spun toward me as I tried to secure her with my other hand. Suddenly pain exploded in my head and everything went black.

Chapter Two

"Gracie, can you hear me?"

I slowly opened my eyes. "Please. Get that light out of my face." My voice sounded far away. "Wow. My head hurts. What happened?"

"You knocked yourself out." I'd recognized the first voice as Abel's, but this was someone else. I squinted through the throbbing and discovered John Keystone leaning over me. He flicked a small flashlight back into my eyes and caused an explosion of pain to shoot through my head.

"Would you stop doing that?" I pleaded. "It isn't helping." I glanced around the room and realized I was in the pastor's office.

"I carried you in here," Abel said gently. "I heard a commotion outside, and when I got to the door, I found. . ."

"A baby?" I finished.

"Yes, a baby." He stepped closer and frowned down at me. "What do you have to do with this, Gracie? Did you see who put this child near the door?"

I struggled to sit up over the protestations of both men. "Hey, I just got hit on the head. It's still attached. I'm all right." I shook

335

my head slowly at Abel so as not to cause myself further agony. "I saw a woman put the basket there, but then she ran away. I was trying to catch her when she clobbered me."

"I don't think she actually hit you," Abel said, handing me a glass of water, which I gratefully took. "I think you slipped on the ice and hit your head on the ground."

I rubbed my offended noggin. "Well, maybe so. I didn't see her slug me, and we both fell when I grabbed her." I looked up at Abel with one eye closed. "I don't suppose you saw her, did you?"

"I'm sorry, Gracie. I didn't. She was gone by the time I reached you. Did you recognize her?"

"No. She was wearing a long dark cloak, you know, like the one Ida wears. She had the hood pulled over her face."

John wiped the side of my face with a warm, wet cloth. There was dirt and dried grass on the fabric when he took it away. "I hope you're not telling us that the baby is Ida's," he said with a grin. "She's in her eighties or nineties, isn't she?"

Abel chuckled.

"Very funny. No, it wasn't Ida." I glanced toward the basket. "How's the baby?"

"She seems fine. I'm grateful you knocked loudly enough for me to hear you. I usually leave by the side door. If she'd been left outside all night. . ."

"I think the mother was trying to get your attention. Did you hear anyone else at the door?"

Abel rubbed his beard. "To be honest, I did hear something, but I thought it was the old pipes acting up again, so I ignored it. But when I heard a loud banging and you yelling, I came downstairs."

I sighed. "That was definitely me. Banging, yelling, and falling on my head."

Abel chuckled. "I missed the falling-on-your-head part. Sorry."

I grabbed John's arm and pulled myself up. "Look, I've got to get home. Snickle needs to get out of his carrier. The last time I looked, he had his legs crossed. Besides, Sam and Sweetie are waiting dinner for me."

"I think you need to rest awhile longer," John said, his handsome face twisted in a frown. His dark eyes showed concern.

"What do you know?" I said teasingly. "You sell meat."

He laughed. "My advice comes not as a butcher but as a doctor."

"You *were* a doctor."

"It wasn't so long ago I can't tell pretty girls to take it easy after they knock themselves silly."

"Do I have a concussion?"

He shook his head. "I don't see any signs of one, but it wouldn't hurt for you to drive into Sunrise tomorrow and see the doctor there."

"How about this," I said, trying to ignore the pounding in my head. "I'll drive to Sam's very slowly. When I get there, I'll take some aspirin. After dinner I'll go home and lie down. If I don't feel better tomorrow, I'll call the doctor in Sunrise and make an appointment. Will that satisfy your doctor/butcher sensibilities?"

"Yes, I suppose that will have to do. But I really don't think you should ever use the words *doctor* and *butcher* together. Puts a bad image in people's minds."

"I see what you mean." I grabbed my coat and held my hand out to John. "Thank you for checking me out and cleaning me up. I owe you one."

After shaking my hand, he picked up the cloth again and wiped my other cheek. "There. Now you're presentable." He smiled at me. "I'm just glad you're back, Gracie. Harmony missed you."

"Thanks.

I shook my finger at Abel. "If I were you, I'd call Emily. Your

337

wife is a wise woman. And I'm sure she knows how to change a diaper. From the smell of things, that's going to get more and more important as the evening wears on."

He nodded. "She's on her way. She's great with babies."

"Maybe you should call someone else, too. You know, like Child Services."

Abel's mouth tightened. "What if this little girl belongs to someone in our congregation? Perhaps the mother will regret her action and come back." He stared at the now-whimpering baby. "No. Maybe I can find a way to restore this family."

I reached out and patted his arm. "I guess the person who left this child here trusted you to make the right decision. I'm confident you will."

His face relaxed and he smiled at me. "Thank you for the vote of confidence. Have I told you how happy I am you're home?"

I grinned at him. "No, but you've had your hands full."

"Go see Sam. I'll talk with you tomorrow."

John stood up. "I'll walk you downstairs to your car."

I didn't want to admit it, but I felt a little woozy. I appreciated his offer and gladly accepted it. I waved good-bye to Abel, but his attention had turned to the baby, who had started to fuss.

"I know he wants to find the mother," I told John as we walked down the stairs. "But what kind of woman would desert her baby like that? I think it might be better if Child Services was called in. It's possible the woman who gave birth to that baby isn't capable of raising her."

John was quiet for a moment. "Maybe," he said finally. "My mother kept me even though she wasn't married. Her own parents had no faith in her ability to be a responsible parent, but she was a wonderful mother. I knew every day of my life that I was loved. Some kids don't have that. Maybe this little girl's mother is scared, afraid she won't measure up. I hope Abel finds her and she decides to give things a chance. She might surprise herself."

I looked at him and smiled. "Well, that's awfully upbeat and hopeful. Not what I'm used to hearing from you. What happened to the grumpiness and negativity we've all come to love?"

We reached the bottom of the stairs and John stopped. "I don't know," he said quietly. "I guess it's the company I keep. It's turning me into a pussycat."

Maybe it was the bump on my head, but "You're talking about Sarah Ketterling, aren't you?" popped out of my mouth before I could stop it.

John's eyebrows shot up. "How—how do you know about. . . about. . ."

"John, the way you two look at each other, I mean, it doesn't take a genius to see how you feel."

"Who else knows?"

I shrugged. "No one that I know of, except Sam. We haven't told anyone. We'd never do that."

John's worried expression made me feel the need to reassure him. "Seriously, I don't think anyone else is aware of it. Maybe I'm just overly observant." Actually, it hadn't been that hard to figure out. I'd seen the Old Order Mennonite girl leaving John's store late at night. And every time she walked past him, the longing in his eyes was clear. They'd obviously been successful in keeping it from Gabe, Sarah's father. To say he wouldn't approve was an understatement. In the past few months, he'd started to come out of a rigid shell of protection he'd erected around his daughter and himself. If he found out about John and Sarah. . . Well, it would be a disaster.

"You know, I'm sorry Gabe's wife ran off with some guy, but it's not my fault. And it's not Sarah's. How long will she have to pay for her mother's mistake?"

I patted his arm. "I don't know," I said softly. "But if you and

Sarah are to ever have a chance, you'll have to tell Gabe. Hiding the truth never turns out well in situations like this."

He gave me an amused look. "Is this one of those 'The truth will set you free' speeches?"

I laughed. It hurt. "Ouch. And yes, it is."

"You're still taking lessons from Sarah, right?"

I nodded. That hurt, too. "Yes. Wood-block printing. She's very talented. It's a new art form for me, and I'm enjoying it very much. I'm not as good as Sarah, but I'm getting better." John's distracted look made it obvious he wasn't interested in my wood-block printing skills. "Why?"

"Has she ever. . .I don't know. . .said anything about me?"

"For goodness' sakes, John. This isn't high school."

His face turned red. "Never mind. Sorry I asked."

"It's okay. I'm just teasing you. No, she's never said a word. But she wouldn't. I'm sure she's as committed to keeping your secret as you are."

"If she told anyone, it would be you, Gracie. She considers you her best friend."

It was my turn to blush. "I didn't know she felt that way. Wow. That means a lot to me."

"Thanks for getting me to talk about this," he said. "I've never spoken to anyone about Sarah. It feels good to finally get it out." He walked me toward the door. "So how are you feeling right now?" he asked, steering the conversation in another direction."

"Yes, I know. I really am feeling better, but I have an awful headache. The sooner I get to Sam's, the sooner I can gulp down a handful of aspirin."

John started to say something, but I held up my hand to stop him. "Just kidding. I won't do that, I promise. Just a couple. To start."

"How about four to start and two more every four hours until morning?"

"You've got a deal. Am I released?"

John ran his hand through his thick black hair. "I suppose. But do you promise to call me if you're not better when you wake up?"

"Yes, I promise. And thanks, Doc."

He chuckled. "No one's called me that for a long time."

I smiled at him as I buttoned up my coat. "Maybe they should."

He didn't respond, just patted me on the back.

After saying good-bye, I pushed against the big front door of the church. The cold slapped me in the face, and I gasped involuntarily. Watching for ice, I walked carefully to my car. Jarring my head in another spill was the last thing I needed. I wasn't angry at the runaway mother because of the bump on my head, but I was frustrated and sad that someone was so desperate for help that they'd leave their baby on the steps of a church. My joy at coming home was overshadowed by concern for the abandoned baby and her mother. At least the woman had brought her child to Abel. If anyone could help, it was the Muellers.

Pain shot through my skull as I got into my car. A sharp yowl reminded me that Snickle had surpassed his level of tolerance inside his carrier. I spoke soothingly to him and tried not to think about my headache as I drove through downtown Harmony. A dozen cars and a couple of buggies sat outside the old redbrick building that housed the restaurant. Ruth Wickham of Ruth's Crafts and Creations was just locking up, probably on her way to Mary's Kitchen. She waved enthusiastically when she spotted me. Three other people walking down the wooden sidewalk stopped and waved, too. Cora and Amos Crandall owned Cora's Simple Clothing Shoppe. They sold most of the garments worn by the Mennonite population in Harmony. I waved back at them. Their son, Drew, put his hand up and laughed at me.

Drew has Down syndrome, but his parents' patience and love have done wonders for him. A sweet, gentle young man, he holds a special place in the hearts of everyone in town. Of course, Harmony is like that. As Sam reminds me constantly, it's more a family than a town. Although it might be a really small town by anyone's standards, it was still the most interesting place I'd ever been.

Ruth waited until the Crandalls caught up to her. They were most likely having dinner together before going home. Even though Ruth lives alone, she doesn't have much time to feel lonely with friends like the Crandalls who go out of their way to include her in their lives. I glanced up and down the street, but it seemed that almost everyone else had already gone home.

I drove past shops and businesses owned by people who were no longer strangers, but friends. Besides Ruth's Crafts and Creations and Cora's Simple Clothing Shoppe, there was Menlo's Bakery, Bruner Leather Goods and Feed, Scheidler's Farm Supplies, Nature's Bounty, and Keystone Meats. All the stores belonged to people I had come to know and care about. I noticed that the sign for Hoffman's Candles had been taken down. I wondered where Levi was tonight. He'd been accused of a long-ago murder, but many folks in Harmony hoped someday he'd come back. I was one of them. But for now, someone else occupied his old store.

I thought back to my first introduction to Harmony. Expecting my visit to be uneventful, instead I'd been greeted by a dark family secret that turned my world upside down. God not only brought me through it but had opened up a new life for me. Now I looked forward to some peace and quiet. I'd had enough excitement to last a lifetime. All I wanted was to settle down and see where my relationship with Sam would go. That was stimulation enough for now.

A few minutes later, I turned onto Faith Road. To the left was

Sam's, and to the right was the house where my father had grown up and where my uncle had died. I remembered wondering why an uncle I'd never met had left me his house. All I'd wanted to do was sell it and leave this little town in the dust. Now I couldn't wait to get back to the place I called home.

As I turned toward Sam's, I could see the beautiful red Victorian house aglow with lights. Homecoming lights—for me. In spite of my sore head, my eyes immediately filled with tears of happiness. I bounced down the dirt road until I pulled into the driveway. Sam's old truck sat in the curved driveway, and I parked behind it. After grabbing my purse and Snickle's carrier, I got out of the car and almost ran toward the large wraparound front porch that graced the Queen Anne–style house. Sam wasn't on the porch, but the frigid temperature was explanation enough for that. I thought about knocking on the door, but I was too excited to wait a second longer. I pushed the door open and hurried down the hall toward the kitchen. I almost ran into Sam, who'd stepped out into the hall. He laughed and grabbed me, immediately putting his lips on mine.

"Mmm. . .mumph. . .mucca. . ."

"For cryin' out loud, boy, let the girl speak."

At Sweetie's admonition, Sam finally stopped kissing me. His gray eyes sparkled. "Did you say something?"

I smiled up at him. "Yes. I said, 'I'm so glad to be home!' "

Wrong thing to say. Or the right thing. Depends on how you look at it. "Mmm. . .mumpha. . .moley moo."

This time when he unlocked our faces, I laughed and wrestled out of his arms. "Give me a chance to unwind a bit. I'm tired, hungry, and injured."

Sam frowned at me. "Injured? What are you talking about?"

I took off my coat and handed it to him. "Get me some aspirin and some food, and I'll tell you all about it."

Sweetie shook her finger at Sam. "You go get the aspirin outta the medicine closet, boy," she ordered. "I'll take care of the food part." She guided me toward the dining room. "You park yourself at the table while I serve up this supper that's been waitin' around all night."

A few minutes later, after I'd swallowed four aspirin, we were chowing down on thick slabs of rich meat loaf, creamy mashed potatoes, homemade applesauce, and flaky rolls that almost melted in my mouth. A far cry from the fast food and frozen meals I'd been living on for months. Within minutes, my headache began to subside.

"It's delicious, Sweetie," I said. "I've missed your cooking so much."

"Looks like you ain't been eatin' too good in Wichita. You're skinny as a rail."

"I've lost ten pounds. If you don't mind, I'd rather not put them back on. I've got to exercise self-control if I'm going to live in Harmony. Too much good food. Too many great cooks."

"Wait a minute," Sam said. "You lost that weight while you were by yourself. That doesn't say much for your cooking skills."

"You're right about that," I said, grinning. "The truth is, I'm a terrible cook."

Sam's mouth dropped open in disbelief. "You can't cook? You never told me that before."

"Does this mean you don't love me anymore?"

Sweetie grunted and adjusted her graying bun. "Gracie girl, this boy has been so poky-faced while you been gone, he didn't even eat much of *my* food. I don't think your cookin' abilities are too important to him." She sighed as she looked at her nephew. "He certainly missed you. I'm glad to see him smilin' again."

Sam brushed a lock of blond hair off his face and stared at me innocently. "I have no idea what she's talking about. Were you gone? I didn't notice. . . ."

I laughed and pointed my fork at him. "You'd better watch it, bub. I can head back to Wichita anytime."

He tossed me a lopsided grin. "No, you can't. No apartment anymore, remember? Seems to me you're stuck here now."

"Speaking of being stuck here, I'm almost afraid to ask. Did you get the problems with my electricity figured out?" Although my Mennonite uncle's house had been wired for electricity, there had been a lot of problems with it. I never knew from one day to the next if it was going to work.

"The furnace is in, the electricity is on, but it's a work in progress, I'm afraid. I'll have to keep tweaking it. When summer comes, we'll have to add a couple of air conditioners."

I breathed a sigh of relief. "I'm more concerned about freezing my toes off than I am about air-conditioning right now. Thanks for taking care of things for me. Sorry to put all this on you, but with having to go back and forth so much. . ."

Sam waved his hand at me. "No apology necessary. It's worth it. I'm just glad you're here."

"Me, too. You have no idea."

A tiny meow and the sensation of something rubbing against my leg reminded me that Snicklefritz was glad to be home, too.

"Snickle will be glad to get settled down in his own house tonight," Sam said. "Just remember what we said about keeping him inside."

I swallowed a bite of mashed potatoes. "That won't be a problem. He's always been an indoor cat. I don't think he has any desire to go outside."

"You might be surprised, Gracie," Sweetie retorted in her low, raspy voice. "Animals is animals, you know."

Sweetie wasn't crazy about cats. Of course, this meant Snickle gravitated to her like white on rice. What is it about cats that makes them hound the people who dislike them the most? Sam and I thought it was kind of funny.

"It's especially important that you keep an eye on him, Grace," Sam said. "Without claws he's a sitting duck for coyotes or other animals."

"I know, I know. You've told me that a hundred times."

"I think you might be exaggerating just a little."

"I had him declawed so he wouldn't tear up my furniture," I retorted. "Guess I should have realized I'd end up someday as Gracie of Sunnybrook Farm."

Sam snorted. "That's ridiculous. You don't have a farm."

"All right, you two," Sweetie said. "Let's quit talkin' about that mangy cat."

As if on cue, Snickle took that moment to jump into her lap. Sweetie shrieked and waved her fork around, which caused a piece of meat loaf to sail up into the air and land on the floor a few feet away. Snickle jumped down and made a beeline for the tasty morsel, scarfing it up before any of us had a chance to react.

Sam burst out laughing. "Hope meat loaf is okay for cats."

Sweetie stood to her feet, her face beet red. She beat one hand against the bib of her overalls. She reminded me of King Kong defending himself against his attackers on top of the Empire State Building. "You hope my meat loaf's okay? That cat did that on purpose. He planned it!" She pointed her fork at Snickle, who gazed at her interestedly while he chewed and swallowed the last juicy morsel of Sweetie's main course. "It's a good thing you're goin' home tonight, cat. If you was around here much longer, I'd. . ."

"You'd what?" Sam asked. "You wouldn't hurt an animal if it set fire to your hair. I couldn't even get you to put out traps for the mice and rabbits that chew our irrigation lines. You talk big, but you have no intention of hurting that cat."

Sweetie gave her nephew a fierce frown. "Them mice weren't flippin' my meat loaf in the air, neither."

Snickle chose that exact second to rub up against Sweetie's leg. Her complexion deepened, and I began to worry she was having a stroke. After glaring at my poor cat, she seemed to surrender and plopped back down in her chair. "Now just what caused that bump on your head, Gracie? That cranky old Pat Taylor better not have anything to do with it. You need to start fillin' us in on the details, girlie."

Since the baby was the more important story, I decided to get my meeting with the sheriff out of the way first. I quickly recounted my run-in with the fussy lawman, first assuring them that he had nothing to do with my injury. "He let me off with a warning, but I got the feeling he would have rather executed me on the spot." I pointed my finger at Sam. "You're the one who told me he hates everyone in Harmony. I guess you're right. He was especially upset about Jacob Glick's body. Seems he thinks we should have called him in sooner."

Sam shook his head. "That would have been a disaster. Frankly, if there'd been a way to keep him out of it altogether, I would have been happier about it. That man makes me uncomfortable. He used to come to town and park himself in the diner. Then he'd watch everyone, like a snake looking for its next meal. Even came around here a few times, poking his nose in our business, like he wanted to make sure we were doing everything by the book. Some of his questions were weird, though. Personal stuff." He speared another piece of meat loaf and held it up in front of him. "I was very relieved when he stopped hanging around so much."

"You must not be the only one who thinks that," I said. "I heard folks in Harmony try to solve their problems without bothering him. I certainly understand how they feel. I know it sounds crazy, but it was almost like he knew me. And when he said he was going to keep an eye on me. . . Well, it seemed, I don't know, like a threat."

"I don't like the way that sounds," Sam said after swallowing the food in his mouth. "I just don't trust the guy. And you're right about people here trying to keep him out of their business. Of course, there have been a handful of times when there wasn't much choice. He'd either come or send a deputy, but it was clear he wasn't happy about it."

Sweetie, already stirred up by Snickle's antics, exploded. "That man's a sharp-tongued, nasty-minded, side-winding snake in grass who—"

"So something really interesting happened when I got into town," I said quickly, hoping to pull Sweetie's attention away from her newest source of contention, Sheriff Pat Taylor. As I told them about the abandoned baby and my subsequent fall, Sam's mouth dropped open.

"Grace, are you sure you're okay? I can drive you to the emergency clinic in Sunrise. You should probably get X-rays."

I grinned at him. "Are you trying to tell me I should have my head examined?"

"It's not funny. Head injuries can be serious."

"Thanks, Sam, but Abel called John, and he came over and checked me out. I'm fine. Just a headache and it's already better. Between the aspirin and the good food, I'm recovering nicely, thank you."

"John Keystone is not a real doctor," Sweetie sputtered. "For cryin' out loud. He sells meat. You're not a side of beef."

"But he *was* a doctor," I said gently. "He examined me thoroughly. No sign of a concussion. Just a nice bump on the head. Really, I'm fine."

"What about the baby?" Sam asked. "Is it okay?"

"She seemed fine. She needed to have her diaper changed, but other than that, she looked healthy and well fed."

Thankfully Sweetie's attention turned from my welfare to the baby's. "Oh my goodness gracious," she said in a tight voice. "And no one knows who the mother might be?"

"No. Abel's wondering if it could be someone in his church. He wants to keep the baby for a while to see if the family comes to get it." I shrugged. "I told him he should contact Child Services if he doesn't find the mother soon. I wouldn't want to see him get in any trouble."

I noticed that Sam had little to say about the abandoned baby. He seemed to be concentrating on his food.

"It's wrong to leave your child behind and take off," Sweetie said. "Seems to me that mother ain't much of a mother."

"We don't really know what's going on," I said. "Hopefully Abel and Emily will find the right solution."

Sam finally broke his silence. "One thing I know. Abel Mueller will do everything in his power to make things come out right."

I nodded my agreement.

"Changing the subject," he said, "you mentioned something on the phone about some project that would help Harmony. What's that about?"

"It's a developer. A new client of Grant's. He's thinking about building a retirement community down the road a few miles from here. He's in negotiations to buy land he needs from some farmer. He believes Harmony adds charm to the area and his residents will find the town an appealing attraction."

Sweetie slapped her hand on the table. "We don't need to be overrun by no fancified, rich retired folks who have nothin' better to do than to come down here and gawk at us. Retirement community. What a daft idea."

I cleared my throat. If Sweetie couldn't find anything to be upset about, she'd turn something as innocuous as a small retirement village into the invasion of the Huns. "There will only be sixty homes in the development. I hardly think a hundred people over fifty-five constitutes being 'overrun.'"

She scowled at me. "We like Harmony the way it is. Don't need no hoity-toity strangers changin' things. Besides, we only have around five hundred folks livin' here now. Another hundred? My lands, girl! That's a huge amount for this little town to support."

Sam held his hand up. "You know, this explains some of the rumors I've been hearing. Seems that your developer friend has already visited several people in town. Convinced them that his project will change their lives—bring more business in. Between the folks who actually live in the community and their friends and family members, several of our business owners are seeing dollar signs, especially during the holidays. I hope it's true. Ruth could use the business, and so could Gabriel and Sarah. You know they're working hard to get Levi's candle shop off the ground."

I put my fork down and frowned at him. "I knew Eric was in town, but Grant said he was just here to spread the word about a town meeting tomorrow night. I figured he'd save all the details until then."

Sam shrugged. "When a stranger comes to Harmony and starts asking residents to attend a meeting, there are going to be questions. I doubt he had much choice."

"You're probably right. Still, I wish he'd waited for me to get back. I could have helped him."

"I believe he's been here almost two weeks now," Sam said. "But only during the day, I guess. I doubt he's driving back and forth from Wichita. He's probably staying in Council Grove. No other hotels nearby."

"So what exactly do *you* have to do with all this foolishness?" Sweetie asked me, still eyeing Snickle, who had curled up next to her feet.

"I'm going to be working on this project with Eric. You know,

350

helping to get things set up. Designing the brochures and promotional material for the community. It's my first freelance job for Grant, and I'll be making pretty good money. If this project works out well, Eric promised Grant even more business down the road. That means more work for me." I grinned at Sam. "Makes it possible for me to pay for all that fancy electricity that's powering my house. Also means I might actually have food through the winter."

"Like we would let you starve." Sweetie sniffed. "You don't need no hoity-toity developer to take care of you. You got us."

I smiled at the woman who had become like a second mother to me. When I'd first come to Harmony, I'd seen her as a nuisance—someone to avoid like the plague. Now she was one of the most important people in my life. "Thank you, Sweetie. I know that." I reached over and covered her hand with mine. "I feel the same way about you."

She scowled at me and moved her hand away, but not before giving my fingers a little squeeze. "Land's sakes. No need to get all sloppy about it."

"Okay, but thanks anyway."

She cleared her throat and grabbed another roll. Sweetie didn't express her feelings very often, but when she did, it didn't last long.

"Hope this big-time developer's not plannin' on breakin' ground now. Bad weather will be comin' down on us soon enough. Not a good time for buildin' anything."

"No, he intends to get started in the spring. He wants to get the planning out of the way—and get the community behind the idea."

"So tell me about this Eric," Sam said. "I still haven't met him. Haven't been to town much, and every time I do manage to get there, he seems to be gone. How old is he? Should I be jealous?"

"Eric Beck's around thirty years old, wealthy, and quite handsome." I laughed at the stricken look on his face. "And no, you

351

shouldn't be jealous. Of anyone. Ever. I've discovered I have a thing for farm boys with gray eyes and long blond hair, and Eric is definitely a city guy. All the way."

"Sounds like a slick showman with a tricky streak," Sweetie said sharply.

I sighed. "Well, he isn't. He's a very nice man who truly believes his retirement village will be a blessing for everyone." I shot her a disapproving look. "You might want to reserve judgment until you actually meet him."

Aware that she'd been chastised, she murmured something under her breath and reached for the jelly. Hopefully the storm was over for a while.

I turned toward Sam and rolled my eyes. He shrugged. We were both used to his aunt's outspokenness, but sometimes she went too far.

"Do you know whose land he's looking to buy?" Sam asked.

"A Rand McAllister. I don't know him."

"Rand McAllister?" Sweetie squawked. "Why, that land of his ain't worth nothin'. Rand is as lazy as the day is long. Spends his time drinkin' in the shed behind his house if you want my opinion. And the way he treats his poor wife and child. . ."

"Sweetie, that's enough."

Since Sam rarely raised his voice, especially to his aunt, Sweetie's jaw dropped and she stared openmouthed at her nephew.

"I'm sorry," he said, his eyebrows knit together in displeasure, "but you've had something bad to say about every single person who's been mentioned at this table tonight. Two weeks ago after church, you asked me to tell you if you were being too critical, remember? Well, I'm doing that now."

Sweetie studied the tablecloth for a moment. Then she nodded. "You're right, Sam. I'm sorry."

Hearing that Sweetie wanted to change her disparaging

comments toward others was my first shock. The second was hearing her apologize.

Sam smiled at her and winked at me, but his joy was short-lived.

"But Rand really is a snake in the grass," Sweetie said in a low voice. "Have you seen the way he treats his family?"

The smile slid from Sam's face. He started to say something but apparently changed his mind. Finally, he let out a deep sigh. "Look, let's not roast anyone else over the coals tonight. But the truth is, Rand really is hard to like." He looked at me quizzically. "You've met his daughter, Jessica, right?"

"I hadn't realized he was her father. Yes, I've met her. I must say she doesn't seem like a very happy girl. She's good friends with Hannah Mueller."

Sweetie geared herself up to say something else, but a quick look from Sam made her clamp her jaw shut. Time to steer the conversation in yet another direction. I was beginning to feel like a cop directing traffic.

"You mentioned Gabe and Sarah. How are they doing? When I was here last, things were moving pretty slow."

"They've been busy," Sam said. "Sarah is selling her stationery in the new shop as well as at Ruth's. Gabe is getting the hang of candle making. It was touch and go there for a while, but he seems to be doing okay now."

Sweetie snorted. "Don't know what some of them scents was, but boy, they stank to high heaven."

Sam laughed. "Yeah, I think Gabe got a little carried away with new kinds of candles. His creativity left a lot to be desired. He might enjoy the smell of hay, but somehow it doesn't translate well in a candle. Smelled like. . .like. . ."

"Don't need to finish that sentence, boy," Sweetie said with a grin. "I think Gracie gets the idea."

I took a sip of coffee and leaned back in my chair. Sweetie's great dinner and the long ride home had made me really sleepy. I was ready to go home and climb into bed. I'd sold most of my furniture during a previous trip to Wichita and spent the last two and a half months in a sleeping bag on the floor of my apartment. Snuggling under the quilts on a nice, soft bed sounded like heaven.

"Did they finally come up with a name for their store?" I asked.

Sweetie smirked. "Yep, they sure did. Ketterlings' Candles and Notions. Lots of imagination, huh?"

"I like it. It's simple but appealing."

"Sweetie's suggestion was Wick It Ways," Sam said with a chuckle. "Great name for a business owned by an Old Order Mennonite family, huh?"

"Gabe Ketterling has a sense of humor, you know," his aunt said, bristling.

"Yeah. You should have seen the look on his face when Sweetie suggested it." Sam guffawed. "You'd think someone had painted racing stripes on his buggy. Funniest thing I ever saw."

Sweetie stood to her feet and started gathering the dishes. "You're gettin' a little big for those britches of yours, ain't ya, boy? How 'bout I skip cuttin' you a piece of my coconut cream pie?"

Sam's eyes widened. "Never mind. I take it all back."

"I thought you might." Sweetie looked my way. "How about a piece for you, Gracie girl?"

"I'll take a rain check," I said, stifling a yawn. "I don't think I can keep my eyes open much longer. Think I'll head home."

"Your eyes been tryin' to close all night," she said. "You go on home and sleep till you feel rested up. There'll be time for pie tomorrow."

"I'll walk you to the door," Sam said. "The heat's on over there, and we put some food in your fridge."

"You're too good to me."

He grinned. "That's probably true."

"Don't you forgit that blame cat of yours," Sweetie interjected. "I don't want that varmint gettin' into my kitchen." She glared down at poor Snickle, who patted her sneaker with his fluffy paw.

I went over and scooped him up. Then I planted a kiss on Sweetie's cheek. "I happen to know that your bark is worse than your bite. If Sam and I weren't in the room, you'd be cuddling with this darling little kitty."

Sweetie's mouth opened and closed like a fish gasping its last breath, but no words came out.

I slid Snickle into his carrier and followed Sam to the front door, leaving his aunt still trying to find the words to defend herself. When we stepped out onto the porch, we were greeted with barks of joy from Sam's small dog, Buddy. Part Jack Russell and part rat terrier, he wore a constant smile and acted as if every moment of his existence was nothing but pure joy. I set the carrier down and knelt next to the excited little animal.

"I missed you so much, Buddy." He licked my face and nuzzled up against me. A plaintive meow from Snickle redirected Buddy's attention. My cat, who'd hissed at every dog he'd ever seen, had fallen in love with Buddy. Anytime they were together, they played like two siblings.

"You and Snickle can get together soon," I said, scratching the small dog's head.

Sam took the carrier and loaded it into the backseat of my car. "Goodness," he said, gazing at the interior. "This thing needs a good cleaning."

The floor of the backseat was full of cat toys, snacks, water bottles, and maps. "You try driving back and forth from Harmony to Wichita every couple of months. I started leaving things in the car I'd need for the next trip."

Sam grabbed me and pulled me into his arms. "Throw it all

away, Grace. No more trips. No more being apart."

He kissed me soundly.

"Now this I could get used to."

He laughed. "You'd better. It'll be happening a lot."

With his promise ringing in my head, I started to get into my car. Suddenly the face of Pat Taylor popped up in front of me. I stopped and called out to Sam. "Will you take a look at my taillight? I should probably get it fixed right away. I certainly don't want Sheriff Taylor tracking me down. I think he plans to throw me into the slammer the next time any part of my car malfunctions."

Sam walked around to the back of the car. "It's not broken," he called out. "Start your engine and turn on your lights."

I slid behind the wheel and put my key into the ignition. After the engine turned over, I clicked my lights on. Then I stuck my head out the door. "What's going on?" I yelled back to Sam.

"Step on the brake," he hollered.

I put my foot on and off the brake several times.

"Okay, that's enough." He came around the side of the car and leaned into my window. "It's working now," he said with a frown. "Maybe there's a short in it somewhere. I'll look at it again sometime in the next few days."

"Thanks. And thanks for putting honest-to-goodness heat in my house. Man, I'm freezing. Sure glad I don't have to warm the house up with that old cast-iron stove of my uncle's. It would take forever."

Sam kissed me on the nose. "As long as everything's working, you should be fine. Why don't you call me in the morning when you get up? I don't want to wake you."

"Sounds great. I feel like I could sleep for at least a week."

He kissed me once more before I drove out onto the dirt road that led to my house. My house. I still wasn't used to it. Funny how putting your future in God's hands can take you down paths you couldn't have found on your own. I'd never aspired to live in any small town—especially one like Harmony, Kansas. Founded by German Mennonites in the 1800s, it was an enigma—a town that shouldn't exist in today's modern world. But it does. Strolling down its streets is like being inside a Norman Rockwell painting. Every time I come home to Harmony, it's as if I've crossed the border into a place of safety—a place where evil can't come. Or at least, where it can't stay. Evil has visited this town—but it hasn't made its home here. Harmony has a way of finding it and rooting it out. I firmly believe the prayers and faith of the unique people who live here have made this a very, very special spot.

As my house came into sight, I thought about my neighbor Ida Turnbauer. Ida lives about a quarter of a mile down the road from me. I wanted to stop by and say hello, but it was late and she usually turned in early. I'd call her in the morning. I laughed remembering how funny she was when she first got a phone. Raised Old Order Mennonite, she'd never used one until a few months ago. At first she couldn't get the hang of it and kept hanging up on people when they called.

I turned into my dirt driveway and pulled up next to the house. Sam had installed lights in the yard and on the porch. Being out in the country and not having streetlamps means it gets incredibly dark on nights when there's no moon or it's hidden behind thick clouds.

My once stark white house had been painted a pale yellow. Cream-colored shutters adorned the front windows. The white wooden rocking chair my uncle made sat on the porch, waiting for spring.

I'd started to turn off my car lights when I thought again about my taillight. Odd. I felt certain it was working when I left Wichita, and Sam hadn't found anything wrong. Maybe there really was a short in the electrical system. Still, for some reason my run-in with Sheriff Taylor made me feel uncomfortable. Did he really stop me because of my taillight, or was it something else?

With a sigh, I scolded myself for being ridiculous and turned off the engine. Then I grabbed Snickle and one of my bags from the backseat and headed toward the house, grateful for the lights and warmth that awaited me. I put my bag and the pet carrier down on the front porch, found my key, and opened the door. As soon as we stepped inside, Snickle began meowing. He knew he was home and wanted out. I opened the door of the carrier, and he took off for the kitchen as I followed behind him. A can of cat food and a bowl of water would go a long way toward calming my travel-wearied feline.

I'd just reached for the light switch when something outside the kitchen window caught my attention. A light moving in the darkness. I crept cautiously up to the glass and pulled the curtain all the way to the side. Someone with a flashlight was skulking around in the trees behind my house.

Chapter Three

I can't find anything, Grace. I've gone over the whole area—from your back door to the lake."

"Well, someone most certainly was out there. It's almost ten o'clock. Why would anyone be prowling around in the dark like that?"

Sam sighed and sat down at the kitchen table. We both watched the row of trees that lined the back of my property. Nothing stirred.

"Maybe it was the reflection of the kitchen light on the glass," he said helpfully. "It could easily look like a flashlight."

I crossed my arms and scowled at him. "Well, that might be a possibility, except that the kitchen light wasn't on." He opened his mouth to speak, but I held up my hand to stop him before he headed a direction he shouldn't go. "And no, there wasn't any light on in the living room that could have shone on the window. I already checked that out."

He shook his head and didn't respond.

"You don't believe me, do you?" I hated the petulant tone in my voice, but Sam's attitude left me feeling slightly defensive. I'd looked forward to finally coming home, but having a run-in with Morris County's sheriff and discovering an abandoned baby had already left me shaken. Seeing someone lurking in the dark behind my house was the cherry on top of an already disturbing sundae.

"Of course I believe you, Grace," Sam said in clipped tones. "I was just trying to offer alternative explanations to what you saw. If you tell me someone was out there, then that's good enough for me. I just can't figure out who would be hanging around outside in twenty-degree weather. Sometimes kids like to run around near the lake, and since Jacob's body was dug up last spring, quite a few people have come by to get a glimpse of the spot. But that's during the day, not at night when you can't see your hand in front of your face. And as far as this being kids, you know what Harmony's like. I'm sure by this time of night everyone's children are accounted for and in bed. No one has a reason to be out there for any. . .any. . ."

"Disreputable reason?"

Sam ducked his head for a moment. I suspected it was to hide a grin, but I didn't find the situation the least bit funny. His inability to take me seriously made me angry. When he looked up, his expression was composed. "Yes, disreputable reason. What would anyone want behind your house this late and in these temperatures?"

"I have no idea, but I know what I saw. Tomorrow when it's light, I'm going to look around."

Sam stood up. "I searched all through there once, Grace. But if you feel it's important to go over the area again, why don't you call me first and we'll do it together?"

I frowned at him. "You don't think there's anything to this, so I'll check it out myself, thank you."

Sam came over and wrapped his arms around me, nuzzling my neck. Goose bumps crawled down from my scalp and broke out all over my body.

"Okay, maybe I'll wait for you after all," I said, my voice husky.

He lifted my face with his hand and looked in my eyes. His stormy eyes seemed to peer into my soul. His gentle kiss gave me double goose bumps. If he didn't leave soon, I was going to be one big, strange-looking lump.

"If I don't get out of here, people will think there's a disreputable reason for my visit," he said when he finished kissing me.

"You—you'd better take off." I gently pushed him away. "We'll take this up again tomorrow."

"The person with the flashlight or the kissing?"

I smiled up at him. "Both." I reached out and took his hand. "Sam, I'm sorry I've been so snarky. I'm just ready for my life to be peaceful—without all the drama of the past several months. Then I come home and find someone creeping around outside. Forgive me."

He let go of my hand and grabbed his coat from the back of the kitchen chair. "Don't worry about it. I understand, and believe me, I'd feel exactly the same way." He studied me for a moment. "You know you can come back to my house if you'd feel safer."

I'd taken up residence in his home for a while when it appeared someone in Harmony meant to harm me. Sweetie's impeccable restoration to the home's original Victorian glory had produced an incredible interior as well as an eye-catching exterior. You'd never know she had the talent to design and furnish a house by just looking at her. She's eternally dressed in old, ratty overalls from her homeless haute couture collection. I almost said yes to Sam's proposal just so I could snuggle into my favorite bedroom. Decorated with purples and reds, it's one of the most beautiful rooms I've ever seen. I'd loved every moment I'd spent in it. But I finally had my own house, and I had no intention of allowing anyone to chase me out.

"Thanks, but I'll stay here," I said with as much conviction as

I could muster. "I'm sure I'll be fine. And now that I actually have a phone, I can call you if I need help."

He chuckled. "Remember when we had to use walkie-talkies to communicate with each other? Seems like a lifetime ago."

I shook my head. "To you maybe, but not to me. I still thank God every time I walk past that beautiful telephone."

"Well, I'd better get back before Sweetie comes looking for me. You call me if you see anything else, Grace. Do you want me to take one more quick look before I go?"

"Oh, would you? I'd feel so much better."

He smiled. "Sure. If I see any cause for concern, I'll come back to the house. If not, I'll just head on home, okay? And we'll still take another look in the morning when it's light if that will make you feel better."

I grabbed his arm. "Yes, it would. Thank you, Sam. I want to enjoy this house without feeling like someone's out to get me. There's been enough of that."

He nodded slowly, his expression grave. "I'm sorry. I should have been more understanding." He started toward the front door but turned back before putting his hand on the knob. "I know you're tired and want to sleep late and putter around in the morning, but why don't we go to lunch at the café? Mary's been asking about you, and I know there are other people who would like to say hello."

"I'd love to. Mary sent me the sweetest note before I left Wichita. Believe it or not, I think your ex-girlfriend and I are going to be great friends."

He brushed a lock of hair out of his eyes. "I'm glad. She's been pretty nice to me lately. It didn't happen overnight, but I don't get a knot in my stomach anymore when I see her."

I laughed. "That's a huge improvement over a few months ago. Why don't you come by around noon, and we'll drive into town together? I'll probably run over and visit with Ida first, so if I'm not home when you get here, check for me over there."

After assuring me he would, he left. I went back to the kitchen and sat in the dark, gazing out the window. True to his word, he headed out toward the trees once again with his flashlight. The moon was only a sliver tonight and clouds passed quickly in front of it, plunging us into inky blackness. The beam from Sam's light bounced around for several minutes, disappearing for a while when he stepped past the tree line. Finally, he reappeared and strode quickly toward the front of the house. I heard the engine of his old truck start up and listened as he drove away. Obviously he hadn't found anything this time either. I felt a little guilty for making him look twice, but his thorough searches comforted me. Whoever had been out there was obviously gone. I'd probably never know the identity of my late-night visitor, but it was a mystery I felt no strong desire to uncover as long as it never happened again. The light had been suspiciously close to the place where Jacob Glick was once buried, but I had to agree with Sam. It didn't make sense to think someone had been out there in the dark and the cold trying to find a grave that had been empty for months.

I fixed myself a cup of hot tea and sat at the table for another thirty minutes until I decided to turn in.

Before leaving the kitchen, I set Snickle up with food, water, and a new litter box. He seemed happy to be home and purred as he christened his box. Then I grabbed my suitcase and headed upstairs to my bedroom. It had originally been my grandparents' room, and although I'd kept the original furniture, I'd added some of my own touches to make the space belong to me. Buttercream wall paint created a warm glow. A large overstuffed chair with a matching footstool sat in the corner where the old potbellied stove had once been. I'd found the chair at a church rummage sale. The lovely dark green patterned upholstery had called to me. A friend helped me to move it to my apartment, where it had never really looked right. But it fit perfectly here. Funny how things turn out. The chair was like an omen for change, although I hadn't recognized it at the time.

The faded quilt that had originally been on the bed had been bundled up and placed in a trunk in the basement for safekeeping. I'd covered the bed with the quilt Mama Essie, my grandmother, had made just for me. I'd always been afraid to use it—afraid it would be damaged—but it belonged here. On this bed. In this room. Mama Essie would be pleased to know I'd finally taken it out of mothballs.

I stared at the large picture on the wall. A portrait of an Old Order Mennonite family in their simple garb—the men and boys in wide-brimmed black hats. Although Old Order Mennonites were discouraged from having their pictures taken, Papa Joe, my grandfather, had bucked tradition for this one photograph. I smiled at Mama Essie, young and beautiful, and Papa Joe, strong and manly with a twinkle in his eye. My father and my uncle, both young boys, gazed stoically at the camera. This was the only early family picture I had and the only photograph of my uncle, Benjamin Temple. My red hair and freckles had come from him. As had my dimples.

I unpacked my clothes under the soft, golden glow of a single lamp on the dresser. All the light in the house came from a few well-placed lamps. Sam had said that later on he could wire the house with ceiling lights, but for now, this would have to get me by. After living without electricity, I felt like every outlet in the wall was a blessing.

I reached down and flipped on the electric heater. The downstairs had heat in the living room and in the kitchen. But the bathroom still needed to be set up with an air duct and a vent. The upstairs would be last to receive attention. At least we were on the right track. To be honest, I kind of liked the warm luminescence of the heater in the room. I'd considered leaving the old potbellied stove until the central heating system was completed, but Sam showed me where the metal had rusted through. Besides, it took up so much space that once it was gone, the bedroom seemed much larger.

After preparing for bed, I checked all the doors and windows before retiring for the night. Everything was locked tight, and there were no more odd lights outside that I could see. I fell asleep with Snickle curled up next to me.

When I woke up the next morning, it was almost ten o'clock. I took a quick bath, got dressed, and headed over to Ida's house.

As I pulled up next to the plain white house, Ida's old horse, Zebediah, trotted up to the fence near my car. I got out and went over to pet him. Zeb nuzzled my face with his soft muzzle.

"Hey, Zeb," I said quietly, "I missed you. How are you?"

He shook his head up and down. Then he whinnied softly.

"Good." I stroked his face a few more times before heading toward the house. I'd just reached up to knock on the door when it swung open. Ida stood there with a big smile on her face.

"*Ach*, my Gracie is home!"

I leaned into an exuberant hug. I hadn't realized how much I'd missed the elderly woman until I had my arms around her. She'd been friends with my grandparents and had known my father when he was a boy. She'd also been close to my uncle most of his life. And now she'd become my dear, treasured friend.

"It is so cold out here," Ida said. "Come inside where we can warm up."

Stepping inside Ida's house is like walking back in time. Wooden floors with handmade rag rugs and old furniture polished to a high sheen decorate the living room. Light and heat come from the fireplace, which was crackling and blazing, sending warmth throughout the room. Additional light comes from oil lamps scattered around the house. An old hurricane-style lamp flickered from a wooden table near the couch. The day had dawned dark and overcast. The light from the fireplace and the lamp pushed against the gloom and gave the room a comfortable ambience.

Ida lives without electricity as her choice—a throwback to the Old Order way in which she was raised. Although she has no belief that electricity in and of itself is evil, she prefers to live in the quiet—without the noise and interruptions that can spring from modern technology. I have to admit that Ida's simple life holds great appeal to me.

"So you are here to stay, *ja?*" she asked. Traces of a German accent added a guttural tone to her voice. She pointed me toward her couch.

"That's the plan. I've surrendered my apartment and have a promise from my boss that he won't call me back to Wichita again."

"I think that man asked too much of you," she huffed as she sat down next to me, smoothing out her dark blue dress and black pinafore. "But you were so good to help him anyway."

I smiled. "I don't know how good I was. I needed the money."

Ida reached for a ceramic teapot that sat on the coffee table in front of us. She poured hot tea into a lovely china cup decorated with small red roses and handed it to me. "I heard you were supposed to be back last night, and I so hoped you would stop by today. I kept an extra cup on the table just in case." Her sweet smile warmed me even more than the tea possibly could, although I was grateful for it. It promised to be a frigid day. A brisk winter wind had chilled me inside and out.

"I should have called to let you know I was coming. To be honest, I completely forgot about your new phone."

The old woman laughed. "You are not the only one. Every

time it rings I almost jump out of my skin. I cannot get used to that loud noise."

"Maybe you have the ringer set too high."

She wrinkled her nose. "Ach, I did not know it could be adjusted."

I got up and walked over to the black phone that sat on a small table between the living room and the dining room. The instrument had a large keypad so that the numbers were easy to read. I picked it up and checked the side. Sure enough, the ringer had been turned up all the way. Not sure how good Ida's hearing might be, I reset the tone level to medium.

"Try this," I said, putting the instrument back on the table. "It won't be as loud. There's an even softer setting, but you don't want the ringer to be so quiet you can't hear it if you're in the next room. Of course, if this is still too loud, we can certainly try it."

She clapped her hands together. "Thank you, Gracie. I know I made the right decision to have a phone, but when it jangles, I begin to regret allowing it inside my peaceful home."

As I sat down next to her, I gently reminded my friend about a couple of situations that might have caused less stress on her and others if she'd had a phone. She nodded as I talked.

"Ja, ja. I know you are right. Thank you for bringing these things to my remembrance." She reached over and grasped my hands in hers. "Now tell me everything that has happened to you since we have been apart."

I briefly described my time in Wichita and finished up by telling her about the baby left on the church's doorstep.

Ida's already pale complexion turned even whiter. "Ach, no. A baby? Some poor unfortunate mother left her baby alone in the cold? What could she have been thinking?"

"Well, Abel's car was outside and his office light was on. She knocked on the door, so I'm pretty sure she believed the baby would be taken care of right away." I shook my head. "It really is a tragedy. A child should be with its mother."

"That's the truth," Ida said. She adjusted her prayer cap, tucking in one long gray braid that threatened to come free of its pins. "But it sounds as if more needs to be done than to just deliver the child back to her. She must need help. Someone to guide her. If she does not get the support she needs, perhaps she will remain unprepared to deal with her situation."

"You're right," I agreed. "I'm sure Abel and Emily would be willing to provide some counseling. If anyone can help her, they can."

Ida nodded, took a long sip of her tea, put the cup down, and scooted up closer to me. "Gracie, I have heard that a man is in town who wants to build some kind of new development here. Mary told me that you know something about this, ja?"

"Yes, it's a small retirement community. It will be a couple of miles from town, but I believe the people who live there will visit Harmony and bring some much-needed revenue to our businesses." I smiled at her. "It's a win-win situation."

She frowned and gazed into my eyes for several moments without saying anything. "Win-win situation?" she repeated hesitantly. "And what does this mean?"

From time to time, Ida and I have a slight communication problem. Talking to a person who never watches television or reads large newspapers means that many phrases and concepts are foreign. Obviously "win-win" was one of them.

"It means that there is no downside to the situation," I assured her. "This project should be positive for everyone."

She looked down as if studying her black leather shoes. "Ach, I wonder."

I reached over and touched her arm. "What is it about this that concerns you, Ida?"

"I—I do not know. I cannot explain it. It is a feeling. A stirring inside my spirit that tells me something is wrong."

"Please don't worry about it," I said, trying to reassure her. "If there was any chance the project would hurt Harmony, I wouldn't allow it to happen. I hope you believe that."

She grabbed my hand. "Ach, dear one. I trust you completely. It has nothing to do with you. Perhaps it is just my upbringing. My parents were very suspicious of English ways. They fought hard to keep them from contaminating our community. The idea of bringing strangers into Harmony concerns me. But I am most probably overreacting." She squeezed my hand. "You know about the prayer that went out many years ago by the women of this town—believing that Harmony would be a special place of peace and blessing? I would hate to see anything war against the wonderful miracle God has granted to us. I do not know much about the outside world, but I have been told that there are not many locations left that are like our Harmony." She gazed at me with tear-filled eyes. "You will protect us, ja? Make certain nothing ever comes here that does not belong?"

"I promise you, Ida. I'll do everything I can to protect this town. It's my home now, too, you know."

She smiled at me and nodded her head. "Ja, I do know. And how happy that makes me. I almost feel as if my Essie has returned to me. She was my very best friend in the whole world. Now her beautiful granddaughter has taken that place."

Ida had lost her close friendship with my grandmother when she'd moved to Nebraska to be near me when I was a child. It had fallen on me to tell Ida that Mama Essie had passed away several years ago. That news had caused the old woman pain. I was pleased to know that my presence would help to return some joy. Ida had become very important to me as well. She had begun to fill the empty place my grandmother's death had left in my heart.

We talked about other things that had happened in the community while I'd been gone, although Ida's uneasiness about the new retirement facility kept nagging at me. I'd hoped everyone would see what a blessing the development would be for Harmony.

It was almost noon by the time Sam's old truck rattled up the driveway.

"Oh dear," Ida said. "You must go so soon?"

"We're going into town for lunch. Why don't you come with us?"

She shook her head. "Ach, no. I am afraid the cold does not like my old bones. I believe I will stay here in front of the fire. Besides, you two young people do not need an old woman tagging along with you."

I started to protest, but she shook her head and smiled at me. "Bless you, dear. I know your invitation is sincere, and I appreciate it. Another time, ja?"

I reached over to hug her. "Another time, ja," I repeated softly.

Sam knocked on the door and then pushed it open so Ida wouldn't have to get up and let him in.

"A couple of fine-looking women," he said, grinning at us. "I'm here to take at least one of you to lunch. Both of you if you'll let me."

"Ach, you two young people," Ida said, waving her hand at him. "You are too good to me. When a warmer day comes, we will all go to town together. But that day is not today."

"Ida already turned me down," I told Sam. "I guess we're on our own."

"Oh well. Guess you'll have to do," he said, smiling at me. "Are you ready?"

I hugged Ida one more time and then grabbed my coat.

"Gracie," Ida said before I made it out the door, "will you please let me know if Abel finds that baby's mother? I will be praying hard for her and her child."

"I will, I promise. Hopefully it will be soon." I waved good-bye and followed Sam to the truck. We decided to leave my car at Ida's for now and pick it up after lunch. Leaving the warmth of the old woman's house for the bone-chilling air outside hit me like a slap in the face.

"I swear it's colder now than when I left the house," I grumbled as I climbed into the truck. "I hope the heater in this thing is in operating order." I knew the air-conditioning was useless. I could only hope the heat was a different matter. Sam started the engine, and a blast of hot air spat out of the vents on the dashboard.

"Wow," I said happily, "at least something in this old heap actually works."

Sam grunted. "Hey, everything works. I have no idea what you're talking about."

"What about the air-conditioning? I sweat so much this past summer I thought I'd drown us both."

"The air-conditioning works fine," he said as he pulled out onto the street. "It's called a window. I can't help it if you didn't want to roll them down because you'd mess up your hair."

As we bumped down the road, I was reminded of something else the old truck was missing. Shock absorbers.

"Before you say anything else derogatory about this fine vehicle, it might please you to know that I'm thinking about buying another truck—for backup."

I laughed. "Backup? I thought this incredible specimen of automotive excellence was perfect. Why would you need backup?"

"Well, to be honest, it broke down while you were gone. We almost couldn't get it going again." He stroked the steering wheel like it was a beloved pet. "What if Ida needed help or we had an emergency?"

"Well, there's my car."

He burst out laughing. "I'm afraid your little bitty Slug Bug couldn't haul much fruit or farm equipment." He shook his head. "Thanks for the offer, but I think I'll have to pass."

I frowned at him. "You didn't say you needed to haul anything in it."

"Well, you may not have noticed, but I grow fruit. Lots of fruit. Of course I need something I can use on the farm."

"Okay. I get it. And by the way, what in the world is a Slug Bug?"

He turned to stare at me. "You mean you don't know about the game?"

"Obviously not. What are you talking about?"

"When you're out on the road and someone in the car sees a Volkswagen Beetle, they're supposed to slug another passenger and call out, 'Slug Bug!' "

"Oh, lovely," I said in a sarcastic tone. "So you plan to start hitting me whenever you see my car?"

"No." His mouth tightened slightly. "My mom and I used to play it. We didn't hit each other hard. It was just a game to pass the time. We traveled a lot."

Sam didn't talk much about his mother, so I was surprised to hear him mention her. She'd died when he was a boy. That was why he'd come to live with his aunt.

"Sounds very entertaining if not a little painful. Your mom must have been a lot of fun."

His mouth relaxed and he smiled. "Like I said, we didn't hit each other hard. More like a tap. And yes, she was fun. In fact, sometimes you remind me of her."

"Thank you, Sam. That means a lot to me."

We were quiet the rest of the way to town. I hoped someday he'd reveal more about his mom. I knew so little. Just that she'd died in a car wreck and that she'd never been married. I blew air out slowly between pursed lips. What was it about men that made it so hard to get to really know them? Put two women together and within fifteen minutes they'll be privy to each other's entire life story. But men. . . . It takes a lot of trust and effort to get them to open up.

By the time we pulled up in front of Mary's Kitchen, I felt warm and toasty. I could only hope the café wasn't cold. When we entered the quaint seventies-style restaurant with its polished wooden floors and cerulean blue walls, I was thrilled to find that I could take my coat off and still be comfortable.

"Gracie!" someone yelled out. I turned to see Eric Beck waving at me from a table in the corner of the room. He sat across from a thin, rather rat-faced man who glared at me like I'd come into the diner just to annoy him.

I pulled on Sam's arm and guided him over to where Eric sat. In his expensive suit he looked out of place at the old table with its yellow laminated top and stainless steel legs.

"I heard you were in town," I said, smiling. "Sounds like your plans are public knowledge now."

His warm laugh highlighted the kindness in his face. Eric's dark, wavy hair brought out his light blue eyes and perfect white teeth. "Yes, I'm afraid the cat's out of the bag. I discovered that Harmony residents aren't a shy bunch. Nor are they willing to let a stranger keep any secrets."

I nodded. "I could have told you that." I patted Sam's shoulder. "Eric, this is Sam Goodrich. I guess you two haven't met yet."

Eric held out his hand and Sam shook it. "No," he said. "As a matter of fact, I don't think I have. You must not come to town much."

"Haven't lately," Sam replied. "Been kind of busy at my place. Nice to meet you."

"You, too, Sam. I suppose you both know Rand McAllister."

He motioned toward the other man sitting at the table, who glowered at us but didn't say anything.

"Yes," Sam said, ignoring Rand's obvious distaste for our presence. "Nice to see you again, Rand."

Sam's greeting was acknowledged with a grunt.

I ignored the ill-mannered man and directed my attention to Eric. "So is the town meeting still on for tonight?"

He nodded. "Yes. Six o'clock in the empty building next to the hardware store. I'm renting it as a kind of base of operation while I'm here. The church down the street is loaning us some chairs, so we should have plenty of room for everyone who wants to come. I'm just trying to hash out the final details with Rand. Hopefully we'll have everything settled before the meeting."

There was a slight hesitation in Eric's voice that caused me to glance at Rand. As far as I knew, the deal had been agreed upon weeks ago. What still needed to be "settled"? The look I got back was toxic. I pulled once again on Sam's arm.

"Excuse us, Eric," I said, ignoring Rand, who'd fastened his beady eyes on me. "I'm starving. If we don't eat soon, I might pass out right here. We'll see you tonight. If you need any help. . ."

"Thanks, Gracie," he said. "But I'm set. I used the flyers you made to announce the meeting, and I think the whole town knows about it. We should have a great turnout."

I told him good-bye, not even bothering to acknowledge Rand. I was beginning to think Sweetie had described the man pretty accurately. I said the same to Sam when we sat down. We were well enough away from Eric and his unpleasant luncheon companion that I was confident we couldn't be overheard.

"I agree he's not a very nice person," Sam said. "I have no idea why he acts that way, but he's been contrary from the first day he arrived. I think someone in his family left him some land, and he felt he had to move his family here. He's not a farmer, even though he makes a halfhearted attempt to grow wheat. Almost every year some of the other farmers have to help him harvest it. Rand always has some kind of injury, you know. Something that keeps him from doing his own work."

"Why do people help him if they know he's just lazy?"

"Because he has a wife and daughter. You know how people are around here, always looking out for each other. His wife and daughter go through enough just living with the man. No one wants to see them go hungry."

The front door of the restaurant slammed shut loudly, and I turned to see Sheriff Pat Taylor saunter into the room. His gaze swung around until it rested on me. My stomach knotted. He watched me for several seconds. Then he ambled over to an empty table and sat down.

"Sheriff Taylor is here," I whispered to Sam. He started to turn his head to look. "Don't look," I hissed. "I don't want him to think I care one way or the other."

"No, we wouldn't want him to think he has any effect on you." Sam's exaggerated tone made me feel a little silly.

"He has every right to be here, I know that. It's just that. . . I don't know. . . I feel like I'm under surveillance."

Sam raised his right eyebrow. "So you think the sheriff of Morris County drove all the way to Harmony for lunch because he's interested in *you?*"

I started to say something when Sam shook his head. "I will admit it's a little strange. He hasn't been around here for months. Now suddenly he stops you on the highway then shows up in town the next day."

"Well, now I *am* worried. I thought you were going to tell me I'm imagining things."

"I'd love to, but to be honest, that guy makes me nervous. There's something. . . not right about him."

Before I could respond, a woman's voice rang out, interrupting our conversation.

"Well, there you are!" I looked up to see Mary Whittenbauer standing next to our booth, holding two glasses of water. "I've been wondering when you'd stop in." Her wide smile quelled any fear that there was still some animosity between us.

Mary had once considered herself to be engaged to Sam, even though Sam wasn't certain just how their "engagement" happened. Her negative reaction to me when I first came to Harmony only deepened as Sam and I became closer. However, a few months ago, Sam and Mary had finally talked honestly to each other. It had become clear to both of them that their relationship had no future. From that point on, Mary and I had started to mend our broken fences. The letter she sent to me in Wichita expressed her heartfelt desire to be friends. Although I'd forged a relationship with Sarah Ketterling, I really wanted a friend who was a little more like me. Someone I could talk to about everything. There were things I hesitated to bring up to Sarah because of her Old Order lifestyle.

"Got in last night," I said, smiling back at her. "A little later than I'd planned."

"I'm so glad you're back." Mary's sweet, heart-shaped face lit up. "I know just how to celebrate. Lunch is on me. Anything on the menu. The both of you."

Sam and I thanked her profusely and placed our order.

"Boy," Sam said after she left, "she sure has done a one-eighty." He sighed with relief. "Must be God."

"She's probably come to her senses and figured out she missed a bullet when she dumped you."

Sam raised an eyebrow. "Dumped me? She didn't dump me; I—"

"Save it, Romeo." I grinned at him. "Men and their egos."

He chuckled while I glanced toward the sheriff. Although he seemed to be perusing the menu, his eyes kept darting my way. I started to say something about it to Sam when the sound of a chair hitting the floor, followed by a string of shouted obscenities, got my attention. I turned around to see Rand standing over Eric like he was getting ready to hit him. The chair he'd been sitting in lay on its side.

"You'd better come up with what I asked you for, or you ain't gettin' nothin' from me," he snarled. "And don't you come 'round my place again, botherin' me with your highfalutin ways. You hear me, boy?"

Sam got up and walked slowly toward the table where Eric still sat. "That's enough, Rand," he said in a calm voice. "I think you need to leave. Maybe you and Eric should take this up again after you've settled down some."

I glanced over at Pat Taylor, who watched the confrontation with an amused look on his face. Why wasn't he intervening? Why allow Sam to put himself in the middle of this tense situation?

Rand took a step toward Sam, his hand knotted in a tight fist. "Don't you poke your nose in my affairs, Sam Goody-goody-rich. Everyone knows you ain't nothin' special. You ain't even got a real daddy."

I could see Sam's shoulders tense through his shirt, but he held his temper. Mary came out from behind the counter and advanced toward the two men. As if he sensed her, Sam held his hand up. She stopped where she was.

"I'm asking you nicely to leave," Sam said again, his voice steady. "If you refuse, we can take this a step further."

I guess the sheriff had finally had enough, because he hauled himself out of his chair and stood between the enraged man and Sam. "I believe this man invited you to vacate the premises," he said to Rand. "Isn't that correct?"

I couldn't see his face, but whatever Rand saw in the sheriff's expression made him take a step back. After glaring at him for several seconds, Rand finally grabbed his coat and scurried toward the door. It slammed loudly behind him.

I hurried over and stood next to Sam. His face was tight with anger. I was shocked to see the fury in Pat Taylor's expression. No wonder Rand had run out the door. I put my hand on Sam's arm.

Eric stood up and shook Sam's hand and thanked him profusely, his relief evident. He turned toward the sheriff and stuck out his hand, but Sheriff Taylor abruptly turned on his heel and walked back to his table, completely ignoring all of us. Eric watched him for a moment then shrugged.

"I have no idea what got into Rand," he said to Sam. "We were talking about closing our deal, and he suddenly doubled the price we'd agreed on." His wide eyes shifted back and forth between Sam and me. Then he ran a hand through his hair and stared at the door Rand had slammed shut when he left. Eric was obviously shaken by the strange little man's outburst. "We've already offered him much more than it's worth. It's a fair deal. Honestly."

Several people had left their tables and were watching us with interest. Dan and Dale Scheidler, two brothers who owned the farm implements store, stood peering over the top of their booth. A family I didn't know had also turned around to observe the proceedings.

Mary stepped up to the table then turned to look at her surprised customers. "You folks go on back to your food. There's nothing more to see."

Harold Price, an elderly man who ate most of his meals in the diner, called out from a table where he sat alone. "Another satisfied customer, Mary?"

His comment broke the tension and several people laughed, including Mary. "I guess that's it, Harold. Funny thing is, he ordered the same thing you're eatin'."

Laughter broke out once again, and all the diners went back to minding their own business. Sheriff Taylor seemed content to drink his coffee and ignore everyone.

"What happened here?" Mary asked Sam quietly. "I don't

allow fighting in my restaurant."

"It was Rand," he said, trying to keep his voice down. "Seems he tried to improve his deal with Eric."

Mary grimaced. "He's not gonna blow this deal for the whole town, is he? Truth is, I would love to get some new customers. We get by here, but sometimes it's just by the skin of our teeth. Bringing in some of these well-to-do retirees and their families could really help. I might actually be able to buy some new equipment. My grill is on its last legs, and the refrigerator is making noises no appliance should ever make."

Eric sighed. His encounter with Rand seemed to have shaken him up. His usual ruddy complexion had paled somewhat. "I think it's a last-minute attempt to blackmail me. I'll just have to let him know it won't work."

"Maybe you'd better wait awhile," Sam said. "Don't confront him now. Let him cool down. I don't trust him."

"Thanks, you're probably right. I'm going to finish this delicious cheeseburger and these fabulous fries before I go looking for him." He slapped Sam on the back. "Thanks again for coming to my rescue. Guess I just froze. His reaction completely took me by surprise. He's been real easy to work with up until today."

Mary chuckled. "Rand McAllister? Easy to work with? He must have a twin, then. That man never has a kind word for anyone." She smiled at Eric. "He was nice to you because you offered him money. Now he's figured out he might be able to milk you for a little more."

Eric sat down slowly. "Well, he can't. I have investors, but between this and another project we're involved in, the group is spread pretty thin. To be honest, if Rand acts up too much, I'm afraid they'll walk away."

"I sure hope that doesn't happen," Mary said. "People in this town are really counting on this boost to our economy. Lots of small towns dry up and blow away without the kind of help you're offering. Not only will your retirees want to shop and buy here, but what better place to send the grandkids for some swimming or fishing?"

Eric bobbed his head toward the table where the sheriff sat. "What's his deal? I appreciate his help, but he acts like I did something to offend him."

"It's not just you," Sam said. "It's everyone. To be honest, I'm surprised he bothered to get involved at all." He noticed Eric's puzzled expression. "He has a problem with Harmony. Thinks it's full of religious nuts."

"That's too bad."

"Eric, you're still planning to hold the meeting tonight, aren't you?" I asked.

"Yes." He shrugged. "I'll get it straightened out by tonight. Like I said, when Rand figures out I won't give in to his demands, he'll cave. If that doesn't work, I know someone I can call. He'll pony up a little more. It's not what Rand asked for, but maybe if he feels he got one over on me, he'll sign the contract. He'd be stupid not to, since he stands to make a lot of money free and clear."

I patted him on the shoulder. "I hope he does, Eric. If you need anything, please let us know. Sam and I will do whatever we can to help."

He reached up and grabbed my hand. "Thanks, Gracie," he said earnestly. "I really appreciate it."

I let go of his hand and headed back toward our booth. Sam said something else to Eric that I couldn't hear and then followed after me.

"Wow," I said when he slid into the other side. "Rand put on quite a show. You don't think he's really dangerous, do you?"

"I honestly don't know. I haven't spent enough time around

him to have much of an opinion. I sincerely hope not, but that temper of his. . ."

"Should we be worried?"

"I told Eric I'd go with him to see Rand if he wanted me to. He thinks it will be okay, but he promised that if he felt uncomfortable about it, he'd call me."

I smiled at him. "That was very nice of you. You know, you really can be a rather pleasant fellow."

"Well, thank you, ma'am," he drawled.

Mary suddenly appeared next to us, carrying two large platters, which she plopped down in front of us, a big grin on her face.

"I'm pretty sure I know what a chicken salad sandwich looks like," I said. "And this isn't it. It looks more like steak to me."

She chuckled. "Look, you guys, I appreciate that you both ordered something cheap after I told you lunch was on me, but I really wanted to fix you a nice meal. I know you both love my rib eyes, so I took it upon myself to change your orders." She whirled around on her heels. "I've got two large Caesar salads along with some buttery garlic bread in the kitchen. I'll be right back."

Two huge sizzling steaks sat in front of us, covered with mounds of sautéed mushrooms. On the edge of each plate, stuck into whatever room was left, was a gigantic baked potato slathered in butter, sour cream, and chives.

"Wow!" Sam said, his face glowing with the promise of enough food to feed a family of four. "That was such a nice thing for Mary to do." He gave me a silly, sloppy, sideways smile. I recognized it. Sam had slipped into meat utopia, a place where men live in ecstasy and women live in fear of never fitting into their jeans again.

"I appreciate the sentiment," I whispered, "but I'm not looking to welcome back that ten pounds I lost."

"Whatever you can't finish. . ."

I waved my fork at him. "No way. I don't want to have to roll you out of here."

Sam laughed and then prayed over our food. With a big smile, he speared his steak with his fork and cut off a big chunk with his knife. After stuffing it into his mouth, he closed his eyes and let out a long, slow breath.

"You look ridiculous," I told him in a tone that should have brought conviction. However, my first bite completely explained his reaction. Mary's cook, Hector, sure knew how to grill a steak. I'd taken my third bite by the time Mary returned with our salads and hot garlic bread.

"Now you two enjoy yourselves," she said, covering every open surface left on our tabletop with food. "And for dessert—"

"Whoa." I shook my head. "I doubt I can get all this down. As generous as your offer is, nothing with sugar or chocolate will pass through these lips today."

"What kind of dessert?" Sam asked, happily smacking his mouth.

I started to chastise him when I noticed that Eric was heading for the door.

"Hey," I said softly, "he's leaving. Should you ask him again if he wants you to tag along when he talks to Rand?"

Sam quickly wiped his face with his napkin and hurried over to catch Eric right before he pushed the front door open. Mary and I stared at them, but we couldn't really make out what they were saying. The radio was playing the Marty Robbins song "El Paso." All I could hear was something about "a handsome young stranger lying dead on the floor." A chill ran through my body.

"Does Sam really think Rand might hurt Eric?" Mary asked.

"I don't know. Most people don't really know Rand, and they're not sure just what he's capable of."

Mary nodded. "He's eaten here quite a bit. Sometimes with

his family. Sometimes alone. I can't get him to talk. I gave up a long time ago. I just take his order and bring him his food." She leaned over close to me. "He doesn't tip," she said softly, shaking her head.

"Why is it I don't find that the least bit surprising?"

Harold's loud voice interrupted Mary's response. "Hey, Mary. Could I get another cup of coffee sometime in this century?"

"Just keep your shirt on, Harold," she shot back. "I have some real customers here."

The elderly man laughed loudly.

"Better get going," Mary said with a smile. "Hey, after you've gotten settled in, why don't we get together for dinner?" She waved her hand in a semicircle. "I'll close early and we'll have the whole place to ourselves. I'm a pretty good cook. While we eat, we can visit and get to know each other a little better."

I smiled warmly at her. "I would love that, Mary."

"You can call me in a couple of days and let me know what night would work for you." The coffeeless Harold loudly cleared his throat. "Knock it off, Harold," Mary hollered. "Or I'll pour that coffee in a place you won't appreciate."

Her comment brought another guffaw from Harold. She winked at me and took off toward the kitchen. She'd just disappeared through the swinging door when Sam reappeared at the table.

"He says he'll be fine, but I gave him my number and told him to call me anytime I can help." He scooted back into the booth and picked up his fork again.

"I hope he's right. There's something about Rand that bothers me. His daughter doesn't look well cared for. And she always seems a little. . .I don't know, frightened. I hope he's not abusing her."

Sam stopped cutting his steak and frowned at me. "Believe me, Gracie, if something like that was going on, someone here would have noticed it. Jessica and Thelma attend Abel's church.

And Jessica goes to school in Sunrise. If there were bruises or anything. . ."

"If they're where they can be seen." I noticed Sam's startled look. "I had a friend in school once whose dad beat her. No one knew about it until one day in gym class. When she undressed for the showers. . . Well, it was obvious something was horribly wrong. The gym teacher immediately notified the principal, and he called in the authorities."

"That must have been awful for that girl."

I nodded. "It was. But things turned out for the best. After it was discovered that her mother knew about the beatings and did nothing to help, Caroline was put into foster care. She got placed with a wonderful family who loved her and eventually adopted her. She went to college and married a super Christian man. They just had a baby."

"You stay in touch with her?"

"Yes. We call each other several times a year. She lives in Michigan."

"That's great, but I really don't think Jessica's being abused."

"You know some abuse isn't physical, right?" I said.

Sam chewed another bite of steak but didn't say anything. He seemed focused on his food.

"I mean, someone like Rand could easily be verbally abusing his wife and daughter. That would explain Jessica's demeanor. The only time I've seen her smile is when she's around Hannah Mueller and their friend Leah."

He nodded at me but appeared to be thinking more about his steak than about what I was saying.

"Sam, did you hear me? Maybe Rand is. . ."

The front door of the restaurant blew open. I'd been watching the skies darken and could tell the wind was picking up by the amount of dust swirling around in the street. Abel Mueller struggled to close the door with one hand while holding on to his hat with the other. Harold jumped up to help him. Together they pushed the door shut.

I started to call out a greeting when I noticed Abel's expression. In the seven months I'd known him, I'd never seen him look so upset. He glanced quickly around the room until his gaze settled on me. The way he looked at me sent a shiver down my spine. By now, Sam had also noticed Abel. He looked back and forth between us a couple of times. Finally, he waved Abel over to our booth. After hesitating a moment, the Mennonite pastor walked slowly toward us.

"Hey, Abel," Sam said when the big man came up next to us, "what's going on? You look like you've seen a ghost."

"Is everyone all right?" I couldn't control the way my voice trembled. "I just saw Ida. . ."

"No. No, Gracie. I'm sorry. As far as I know, everyone's fine." He took off his wide-brimmed black hat and held it in front of him. His eyebrows knit together in a frown. "I—I know this is going to sound odd, but I need to talk to you." He glanced quickly at Sam. "Alone. I don't mean to alarm you, but it's very important."

For the life of me, I couldn't begin to figure out what Abel would need to say to me that Sam couldn't hear, but I could tell the kind pastor was truly upset.

"Why don't you stay here and finish your lunch," I said to Sam, who seemed as surprised as I was by Abel's strange request. "Abel and I can move to another table." I looked up at him to see if he agreed. He nodded silently, still grim-faced.

I pointed toward an empty table that sat all the way across the room. "Is that okay?"

Once again Abel nodded. I followed him, trying to avoid the prying eyes of customers who wondered why the pastor of Bethel Mennonite Church would call me aside for a private meeting.

Even Harold looked interested. Abel and I sat down, and I scooted my chair around so that my back faced the rest of the room.

Abel suddenly scanned the room as if he hadn't noticed we were being watched. "Oh my," he said. "I didn't realize. . . Maybe we should go to my office where it's more private." He nodded for several seconds. "Yes. That would be better, Gracie. I should have thought of it sooner. It's just that. . . It's just that I was so shocked. . ."

"Abel, you're scaring me," I said, trying to keep my voice soft but firm. "I don't want to go to your office. Please just tell me what you came to say. You said everyone is okay. No one is ill? No one is dead?"

He laid his hat on the table and studied it. Finally he cleared his throat. "This has nothing to do with anything like that, Gracie." He reached into his pocket and took out a folded envelope, which he handed to me. "I found this stuck in the door at the back of the church about thirty minutes ago when I arrived to prepare my Sunday sermon. I felt the right thing to do was to bring it to you. I saw Sam's truck in front of the restaurant and hoped you were here with him."

Frowning, I reached over and picked up the envelope. *Pastor Mueller* was written in block letters on the outside. Inside was a folded piece of notebook paper. I opened it up and read it.

Dear Pastor Mueller,
    The baby left at the church belongs to Gracie Temple. I saw her put it there.

                                      A Very Concerned Citizen

Chapter Four

I had no idea that emotional shock can hit you just like a physical punch in the gut. I couldn't speak. Couldn't seem to catch my breath. Who in the world could do something like this? I'd come home to Harmony—my place of safety. A place where I was loved. A place where I belonged. And now this?

"You know it's untrue, don't you, Abel?" I finally croaked out. "You know the baby's not mine?"

Abel looked past me, unwilling to meet my gaze. "Gracie, I'm a pastor. I may not be *your* pastor, but I still have a pastor's heart toward you." He finally looked into my eyes. "If you tell me this isn't true, I will believe you."

"It isn't true, Abel. I've never had a baby. And if I did, I wouldn't abandon it. Ever. How could you. . ." I didn't finish my sentence because in a flash of clarity I knew the answer. I was outside the church when the baby was found. Abel hadn't seen anyone else there. I'd been gone for almost three months, and I'd come back to town thinner than when I'd left. I put my hand over my mouth to hold back an inappropriate desire to giggle. If a deserted baby weren't involved, this would actually be rather

387

funny. But the look on Abel's face dispelled any urge to laugh.

"Then that's that," he said. He picked up the letter and put it back into the envelope. "I intend to get rid of this. We won't talk about it again."

I reached over and put my hand over his. "Abel, I swear to you as your Christian sister that there isn't a shred of truth to this. Someone is playing a really cruel joke, and I intend to find out who it is. Maybe you should keep the letter for now. It might lead us to whoever wrote it."

He pushed it back over to my side of the table. "You keep it. I don't want it."

"Thank you. If I discover the truth behind this lie, I'll let you know. Will you do the same for me?"

"Yes, of course." He smoothed his unruly salt-and-pepper hair with his hand before placing his hat back on his head. "I'm sorry if this caused you pain. That was not my intention. I felt I had to show it to you. To keep it from you, or to talk to someone else about it before I spoke with you, made me feel. . . uncomfortable."

I smiled at him, although it took effort. "That's because in many ways you really are my pastor, even if I don't go to your church. And besides that, you're my dear friend. I know you love me."

"Yes," he said gently, his dark, compassionate eyes locked on mine. "Yes, I do." With that, the gentle giant of a man got up and left the restaurant. I stayed where I was, trying to figure out what to do next. Life really is full of surprises, and some of them aren't pleasant. Who in the world could be behind this? A small flame of anger began to burn inside me. Starting a rumor like this without proof was irresponsible, even though so much circumstantial evidence pointed to me. I glanced over at Sam, who looked at me oddly. I folded the letter up, stuck it in my jeans pocket, and went back to our table. I looked around the room to see if people were still watching, but everyone seemed occupied with their own business. I guess they'd all moved on.

"What was that about?" he asked as soon as I slid into my side of the booth.

"I—I really don't want to talk about it right now. Let's wait until we can go somewhere more private."

Sam put his fork down and stared at me. "Is everything okay?"

I shook my head. "No. No, it's not. Someone has made an accusation about me that isn't true. I'll tell you about it later. Right now, let's finish this wonderful meal."

Sam didn't pursue it, but I could tell he was curious. I tried to eat the rest of my lunch, but my steak was cold and everything else seemed tasteless. After a few more bites, I gave up.

Sam finished most of his food but left a few bites of steak and about half of his potato on the plate. We waited for Mary to come back by so we could thank her for the meal.

"Why, Sam Goodrich," she said when she saw his leftovers. "You always lick your plate clean and ask for more. And Gracie, didn't you like the steak? Was there something wrong with it?"

"Oh no, Mary," I said, trying to sound reassuring. "It was fabulous. I just couldn't finish it. Besides, I'm trying to watch my weight."

She reached over and patted my shoulder. "I can tell you've lost quite a bit. You stick to your guns, Gracie. Losing weight is tough, I know. If I didn't run around this place all day long, I'd weigh a ton." She turned her attention to Sam. "What's your excuse?"

Sam grinned and patted his stomach. "Maybe I'm watching my weight, too. Did that occur to you?"

Mary threw her head back and laughed. "Absolutely not. I've never seen anyone who can pack it away like you and still stay lean." She shook her finger at him. "If you ever retire, you'd better watch out. You'll be as big as Harold over there."

"I can hear you, you know," Harold said.

"I know," Mary shot back. "That's why I said it."

"How's he doing?" Sam asked quietly as Harold chuckled.

"Better," Mary said in a soft voice. She swung her gaze to me. "Harold lost his wife early in the year. He started hanging out here almost every day. I think facing a quiet house is too much for him. He likes our noise."

"It's nice of you to care so much about him."

Sam started to say something, but I waved his comment away. "I know, I know. Harmony is just one big family." The edge of irritation in my voice caught Sam and Mary's attention, and they both looked at me strangely. "Sorry." I sighed. "This hasn't been a great day."

"You just got back," Mary said. "You're not allowed to have a bad day yet."

"You'd think so, wouldn't you?" I did my best to smile at her even though I didn't really feel much like smiling. "It's not your fault. You're one of the bright spots. Thank you again for the wonderful lunch."

"You're very welcome. Let me wrap that steak up for you. It will make a great sandwich tomorrow."

I thanked her again before she sailed toward the kitchen.

"Where do you want to talk?" Sam asked.

"I don't care. My house or yours."

"Let's make it mine," he said. "I have something I want to show you. It was too dark for you to see it last night."

"Okay." I watched the kitchen door, hoping Mary wouldn't take too long. I was ready to leave the restaurant behind. Mary's plan to present us with a pleasant meal had been ruined by Rand McAllister and that awful letter. While I waited, I examined the pictures lining the walls of the restaurant. Old photographs of former and present Harmony residents. Pictures of the town down through the years. Not many depictions of its German Mennonite roots, but their influence was still strongly felt. I realized that the photograph of Jacob Glick was gone. Good. Emily and Abel Mueller didn't need to see it, and neither did I. The man had caused enough sorrow. Having to look at him was too much to ask of anyone who'd been affected by his evil. I noticed that more of Hannah Mueller's paintings were hanging on the walls. Since we'd started painting together, her technique had improved. Her work had taken on a professional quality far beyond her young years. She had the talent to go far, but living in Harmony certainly put limits on her ability to make an impact beyond the town's borders.

I gazed out a nearby window. The OPEN sign was in the window of Keystone Meats. John had originally come here to find out who his father was. No son wanted to discover the things John had. Jacob Glick's legacy was best forgotten by everyone, including his biological son, John. Some folks thought he would take off after realizing his father was a scoundrel, but he stayed. I knew part of the reason was his fondness for Harmony, but what drew him more were his feelings for Sarah. Many folks in Harmony hoped he'd pick up his practice again. Since the nearest doctor was in Sunrise, about ten miles away, the idea of having a doctor here was certainly appealing. Next to John, the closest medical professional we had was old Widow Stegson. Clara lived alone on a run-down farm outside of town. Some of the kids called her "the witch." Her storehouse of herbs and medicinal concoctions was widely known to make people sick rather than cure them.

I wanted to run over to Ruth's shop and say hi, but that would have to wait. I had to tell Sam about the note before he heard it from someone else. I knew Abel would never discuss it, but whoever wrote the note could easily spread the story.

"Here you go." Mary's voice cut through my thoughts. She handed me something wrapped in tin foil. I reached out and took it. Then I slid it into my purse.

"Thanks again. And you're right. This will make a great sandwich. I really appreciate your generosity."

"Don't be silly," she replied. "It wasn't much. I just wanted you to know I'm glad you're back. You call me in the next couple of days, and we'll get that dinner set up, okay?"

I put my hand out. She took it. "Deal."

We left the restaurant and headed back to Ida's to pick up my car. Sam kept glancing my way during the drive, but I ignored him. For some reason telling him about the letter made me nervous. I tried to reassure myself that he would probably think the whole thing was ridiculous and laugh it off. So why were frantic little butterflies flitting around inside me? Abel's reaction had left me shaken. He'd seemed relieved when I denied the accusation. Had he actually believed it might be true?

We stopped at Ida's to get my car. Sam followed me to my house, where I dropped it off and then got back into his truck. I didn't say much on the way to Sam's. My mind was filled with a faint but distinct dread.

"Before we get to the house," Sam said, interrupting my thoughts, "here's what I wanted to show you." He slowed the truck down and pointed at some land on the north side of his property. The previously undeveloped plot was now cleared. "We'll plant our first pumpkins after the spring rains. By September we'll have lots of big orange pumpkins sitting out there."

"Oh, Sam. How wonderful. I know this is something you and Sweetie have wanted to do for a long time. Good for you."

He nodded, a look of satisfaction on his face. "It will be a lot of work, but I already have several stores in Council Grove expressing interest."

I reached over and hugged him. "I'm so excited. Maybe I can help out some. I'd love to be more involved in what you do."

"I'd like that, too," he said, kissing the top of my head as I rested it against his shoulder. "We'd better get going." He put the truck into gear and drove up to the house. "Sweetie's not here," he said as he pulled into the driveway. "She took some food over to Alma Ledbetter's house. Alma's recovering from knee surgery and can't get around very well."

I was grateful Sweetie was gone. It would make it easier to talk to him. We went inside, and I followed him into the kitchen.

"I'll make some coffee to warm us up." Sam took my jacket and laid it over the back of one of the kitchen chairs. "Have a seat."

I scooted into one of the wooden chairs that sat around the large oak table. While the rest of the house maintained an authentic Victorian charm, the kitchen was more updated. Gleaming stainless steel appliances, parquet floors, and shiny pots and pans that hung from hooks over the butcher-block kitchen island made it clear that this kitchen belonged to someone who knew a thing or two about cooking. Sweetie shone in this room. She loved to cook, and those who knew her loved to eat her food.

Sam finished filling the coffeemaker with water and pressed the button to begin brewing. Within seconds, the smell of freshly made coffee began to fill the room. He came over and sat down across from me at the table.

"Okay, so what's going on?"

"Abel found this note stuck in the door of the church this morning." I took the crumpled envelope out of my pocket and shoved it toward him.

Sam smoothed it out and withdrew the notepaper inside. As he read it, the color drained from his face. "I—I don't understand."

"I don't either. It doesn't make any sense. Why would anyone make up a cruel lie like this? What would they have to gain?"

His focus stayed on the note, and he didn't look at me. "I have no idea. Why would someone suspect it was true?"

"I've been gone for almost three months. I came back to town thinner than when I left. And I'm the one who first found the baby. I guess one of Harmony's more pious citizens decided to add up all those coincidences and come to the erroneous conclusion that I had to be that poor child's mother."

Sam finally raised his head. The look on his face chilled me. I reached over to take his hand.

"Sam. Please don't make me deny this charge. Surely you know me better than this. If you don't. . ."

He pulled his hand away, folded the note, and jammed it back into the envelope. "If I don't know you better than what?" he said, his tone sharp. "Is that some kind of threat?"

"A threat?" I said incredulously. "What are you talking about?"

"Look, Grace, I've got some work to do in the orchards. I'll drive you home first."

"Why are you acting like this? Of course that baby's not mine. I think you'd have noticed if I was pregnant, even if I've been gone for a while. Besides, you know me. If I'd been pregnant, I would have told you. And I would never, ever abandon my baby. Never."

His face flushed a deep red. "I really don't want to argue about this right now. Please. We'll talk later. I—I just can't do it now. I mean it."

I grabbed my purse from the table and my jacket from the nearby chair. "Fine. Take me home, please."

Rage and hurt coursed through me. I could feel angry tears forming in my eyes. How could Sam believe this? It was ludicrous. Suddenly I felt as if I didn't really know him. Maybe I never had. If this was all it took to cause a division between us, how could we ever hope to sustain a real relationship?

I hurried out the door to the truck, unable to hold back my emotions. As I fled down the stairs, I ran right smack into Sweetie.

"For cryin' out loud, girlie," she screeched. "Watch where you're goin'. You almost knocked me into the middle of next week. Why are you. . ." I pushed past her, mumbling an apology. She turned around and watched me get in the truck. As I slid into the passenger seat, I saw her grab Sam before he could get past her. He tried to wrestle away, but she hung on like her life depended on it. Aunt and nephew exchanged a few words; then she let go of him and he got into the truck. As we pulled out of the driveway, I looked back at Sweetie. She hadn't moved, just stared at us as we drove away.

Sam was silent until he pulled up into my driveway. "Look," he said quietly after turning off his engine, "I'm sorry." He reached over and wiped away the tears on my cheeks. "I'm not upset at you, and of course I believe the baby isn't yours. I know we have to talk this out, and we will. I just need you to be patient with me for a little while."

"But I don't understand. What's wrong? Why did this upset you so much?"

He shook his head and gazed out the window. "I'll explain it to you, Grace, I promise. I just need a little time to get my thoughts together. I'm as shocked as you are at my reaction." He turned to look at me, his eyes full of concern. "Give me some space, okay? Just a couple of days. When I'm ready to talk, I'll tell you everything. Hopefully I'll be able to explain myself. Can you do that for me?"

I sniffed, wiped my face with my coat sleeve, and nodded. I really didn't trust myself to say anything at this point. Selfishly, I felt slighted because this attack was on *me*, not Sam. I'd expected his support, and now here I was trying to console him.

I quickly kissed him and got out of the truck, not even looking back as I ran into the house. A few seconds after I closed the door behind me, I heard his truck start up and rumble out of the drive-way. It occurred to me that we were supposed to check out the woods once more to see if we could find signs of my late-night intruder. It would have to wait. At that moment, I didn't care much. Last night seemed like it had happened weeks ago.

I went to the kitchen, dropped my purse on the table, and looked out the window. Everything was quiet. No signs of life except for a couple of squirrels chasing each other up and down the trees. I marveled at their agility. How could they run and jump so high and so fast and not fall?

I heard a long, drawn-out meow from behind me. Snickle stood in the middle of the kitchen stretching his body. Must have just awakened from a nap.

"Hard life there, bud," I said. "Wanna trade?"

He answered me by flicking his tail and running out of the room.

"Good answer."

I checked the clock. The town meeting was scheduled for six. It was a little past three. Plenty of time for a nap, although I was probably way too upset to sleep. First I washed some dishes that had been sitting in my sink, soaking. When I had enough power in the house, my next purchase would be a dishwasher. Washing dishes by hand was for the birds.

I'd finished the dishes and was on my way upstairs, trying once again to sort out Sam's strange reaction to that awful note, when I heard loud knocking. I gazed down at the door like I could see who was on the other side. I didn't get many visitors. In fact, I never had visitors. The only person who ever came over was Sam. Maybe he'd come back to talk. I rushed down the stairs, hoping it was him. When I swung it open, I found Sweetie stand-ing there. She looked flustered.

"Hi there, Gracie girl." She wiped her hands nervously on the front of her coat even though they looked perfectly clean. "I need to talk to you. Can I come in?"

"Oh, sure. Sorry. I thought you were someone else." I opened the door wider so she could get past me. She made a beeline toward the couch. I sat across from her in the rocking chair.

"The place looks great," she said, giving the room the once-over. "Still looks the way Benny had it, but I can see your touches, too. I like that you kept some of Benny here."

"Me, too. Maybe someday I'll do more decorating, but it didn't seem right to change everything right away."

Sweetie nodded and nervously cleared her throat. "Listen, Gracie, I want to talk to you about Sam. About why he acted like he did today."

"He told you what happened?" I could hear the sharp edge in my voice, but the idea he'd talked to his aunt before we'd really had a chance to talk upset me.

She shook her head slowly. "Now don't go gettin' your knickers in a knot. I could tell he was upset when he came home. I forced it outta him." She slid off her winter coat and put it on the couch next to her. "Glad to see you got some heat in here. Feelin' a mite warm. Hope you don't mind if I shed this thing for a few minutes."

"Of course not."

Sweetie kept looking at me and then glancing away. I'd never seen the woman so uncomfortable.

"Sweetie, why are you here?" I asked finally. "What is it you want to say?"

She cleared her throat a couple more times. "I want you to know somethin', Gracie. I—I need to tell you. . ." She stopped and stared at the floor. Suddenly her head shot up. "This is stupid. For cryin' out loud, I can't figger out what's wrong with me." She cleared her throat a fourth time, making me wonder if she was coming down with something. "Gracie Temple, I love you. I love you like you was my own daughter. I ain't used to tellin' anyone that 'cept Sam, so it's a little hard for me. I know it shouldn't be, but it is."

My irritation for the woman melted away. "I love you, too, Sweetie. You know that, right?"

"Yeah, I guess I do. That's one of the reasons you mean so much to me. Most folks don't cotton to me at all. They think I'm some kinda hillbilly, redneck numbskull. But you have a way of lookin' past the way I act on the outside and seein' the real me on the inside. That's one of the reasons I care about you so much. And it's one of the reasons I'm so grateful you love Sam." She grunted. "When he was runnin' around with Mary, I was plumb worried. Now understand, Mary and me is friends. I like her. But she weren't right for Sam. I knowed that as well as I knowed my own name."

"Thankfully Sam and Mary figured that out themselves."

"Yep. Better it were them than if someone else had tried to tell them. I figger it would have been me eventually, but it never came to that, thank the Lord."

"You didn't come here to talk about Mary and Sam, did you?"

"Nope." She rubbed her hands together like she was cold. "I know you can tell this is hard for me to say. I know lyin' is a sin, but I been makin' Sam lie 'bout somethin' ever since he was a boy. Now he's payin' the price for it. Actually, you both are. I gotta make this right."

"I don't understand. What are you talking about?" A cold thread of fear wound around my insides. I'd always valued Sam's honesty, and I hated deception.

Sweetie took a deep breath and locked her eyes with mine. "It's Sam's mama. She didn't die in no car wreck. She's alive. When he

Simple Deceit

was a little boy, she just went off and left him, Gracie. Dumped him off in front of a church—just like that poor little baby you found last night."

399

Chapter Five

At first, I couldn't seem to find a response to Sweetie's shocking statement. Finally I managed to say, "Why did you lie? Why did Sam lie—to me?"

She cleared her throat again. I knew she did it out of nervousness, but it was beginning to get on my nerves. "One day Bernie told Sam they was goin' out to eat and then to the movies. She never had much money, so Sam was pretty excited. Kept him outta school even. Sure enough she took him to a burger joint for lunch and then to a movie. After that she drove over to the church where Sam had been goin' with a neighbor boy. She told him to wait there for her while she ran a quick errand." Sweetie wiped away a tear. "That's the last time he saw his mama. A couple hours later she called the church and told them to call me. That's how he came to stay in Harmony."

My mind went back to the conversation we'd had about the abandoned baby the night before. Sam had been strangely silent and changed the subject without much discussion. Suddenly his reaction made sense.

"I know tellin' a fib is a sin, Gracie, but how could I let that little boy tell folks the truth?" She shook her head. "I told him to tell everyone his mama died in a car crash to save him from embarrassment. Maybe it was right, maybe it was wrong. But now it's caused this problem between you, and it just ain't right. Sam reacted so bad to that note because it reminded him of what happened to him so long ago. I think he sees some of his mama in you—the good parts. But this thing with the baby. . . Well, it just hit too close to home. Stirred up some kinda feelin's he ain't dealt with yet." She wrung her hands together. "You just gotta wait it out, Gracie. I know he'll come around. If you wanna be mad at someone, be mad at me. I'm the one who caused this unholy mess."

Frankly, at that moment I was somewhat angry with both of them. But the picture in my mind of Sam waiting for his mother, wondering where she was, overcame my bruised feelings and evoked deep compassion. "Sam did tell me once that I reminded him of his mother."

She nodded. "I thought so. You see, there was lots of good things about my sister, Bernie. She was so pretty, and when she laughed, it sounded like sunshine. She loved animals, and she had a good heart. Saw things really deep, you know? Had a way of findin' the good in folks—same way you do."

"Her name was Bernie?"

She nodded. "Bernice. We called her Bernie ever since she was small. She just weren't no Bernice. Just like I weren't no Myrtle."

I frowned at her. "You make her sound like a good person. But she left her son. That's certainly not a good thing to do."

"I know that. This may sound silly to you, but I believe she left Sam at that church because she loved him. She was hooked on drugs back then, and she didn't think she could take good care of the boy. She thought I'd make a better mama than her." Sweetie covered her face with her hands for a moment. When she brought them down, I could see her anguish. "I hope she was right. I been tryin' my best all these years. I sure love that boy like he was my own."

"So what you're saying is that when I showed him that note, he thought maybe I actually *had* left my baby—just like his mother left him?"

Sweetie held up her hands in surrender. "I know it sounds nuts, Gracie, but yeah. I think that's exactly what happened. That boy loves you so much it almost hurts. But this situation made him think of his mama. I think he's afraid you're gonna hurt him like she did." She eyed me carefully. "I know Sam seems all growed up and well-balanced, but he ain't never healed from the pain his mama caused by leavin.' All these years, I been hopin' he'd get over it. But I can see now that he's still hidin' his hurt inside." She ran her weathered hand over her face. "This is all my fault. Not lettin' him deal with the truth. Now I mighta cost him the best thing that's ever happened to him in his whole life. You, Gracie girl."

"It's not your fault," I said, shaking my head. "But I wish Sam would have told me the truth. It makes me feel like he doesn't trust me. Surely he doesn't think something like that would change the way I feel about him."

Sweetie stood up and walked to the window, where she looked out toward the dark clouds that hung over Harmony. "Gonna start snowin' soon." Her voice sounded far away, even though she only stood a few feet from me. As if on cue, big fat snowflakes began drifting past the windows. After a few seconds, she whirled around to face me. "No matter who did wrong, you have to decide if you can work through it. Is Sam worth enough to you to put out the effort it will take to ride out this storm?" She crossed her arms and studied me. "I ain't tellin' you it will be over tomorrow. Sometimes storms blow through with big winds and lots of fury—then suddenly they're gone." She waved her hand toward the thickening snow. "And sometimes they park themselves right over you and take their sweet time movin' along. You gotta have your feet planted firm, Gracie, so the storm don't knock you over." She walked back to the couch and picked up her old coat. "It's like that story about the man who built his house on the rock and the man who built his house on the sand." She shook her head and laughed. "I realized a long time ago that both those men had the same storms. Life ain't always gonna be as smooth as a baby's clean behind. Sometimes there's gonna be somethin' nasty that's gotta be dealt with. I used to blame God for what happened to my mama and daddy. And what happened to my sister. But down through the years I figgered somethin' out. I was lookin' in the wrong place. It ain't God sendin' the storm. It's God who gives us the rock."

I couldn't hold back a smile. "You're a pretty smart woman, Sweetie Goodrich. There are a lot of religious experts who haven't figured that out."

She snorted. "I quit puttin' much stock in them experts a long time ago. Only PhD in religion comes from the Holy Ghost, and He ain't much interested in what kinda title you got after your name. Shoot, them rotten ole Pharisees thought they were experts, too. I think God's more interested in open hearts willin' to listen to His voice." She peered closely at me, her expression grave. "Now I just got one question for you."

"You want to know if I'm willing to stand on the rock and see this through?"

"That's it, Gracie girl. Do you love Sam enough to ride out this storm?"

I got up and went over to where she stood. Then I wrapped my arms around her. "Yes," I whispered. "I'll stand on that rock as long as it takes. We'll make it through this storm—as long as that's what Sam wants."

She squeezed me hard and then shook herself loose. After

sliding on her coat, she walked to the door but turned around to gaze at me once more before stepping outside. There were tears in her eyes. "Don't you worry about that, okay? That boy loves you so much he don't know his up from his down. When he's ready to talk, he'll come to you. Trust me. I been around him a long time now. He has to deal with stuff in his own way."

"Okay. I won't push."

She nodded and walked out the door. I was left standing alone in my house, wondering if I'd just promised Sweetie something I couldn't do. Did I really love Sam enough to weather this storm? I'd had such high hopes for us—for my life in Harmony. But things weren't turning out the way I'd expected. Had I missed God?

I puttered around the house for a while, too tense to settle down for a nap. Originally, I'd planned to go to the meeting tonight with Sam, but since he said he needed some time to himself, I had to assume I was going alone. Although I hated to drive my little car in the snow, at least the meeting wasn't far and if I had any trouble, I'd be easily found.

I wasn't in the mood to cook anything for dinner, so I made a quick sandwich with the leftover steak from lunch. I'd just taken my first bite when the phone rang. I quickly swallowed and reluctantly left my makeshift dinner on the kitchen table while I hurried into the living room. As soon as I picked up the receiver, I knew who it was.

"Hello? Gracie, are you there?" Ida's plaintive voice reached me before I had the chance to say "Hello" myself. I'd tried a couple of times to encourage her to wait until the person she was calling answered before she said anything. Obviously we still had some work to do.

"I know," she'd responded with a chuckle. "I just get so nervous I forget."

"I'm here, Ida," I said.

"Oh, Gracie, honey, it is snowing so hard I would hate to take Zebediah out tonight. Can you give me a ride to the town meeting in your automobile?"

"I'd love to. I'll pick you up about twenty till six. Is that okay?"

"Oh yes. Thank you so much. Umm. . .so we will hang up the phone now, ja?"

"Yes, that's fine. See you later." The silence that followed led me to believe that she was waiting for me to end our call. Ida would never be rude. The idea of hanging up on me probably horrified her. I gently put the receiver down.

At five fifteen I went outside and started my car after knocking off the snow that covered it. I wanted the interior to be warm for Ida. In Wichita, the police frowned on allowing cars to run unattended. They quickly became targets for car thieves. Here in Harmony, I could start my car in the middle of Main Street and leave it running and unlocked, and the only person who would touch it might be someone who felt the need to move it out of the way for other drivers. The kind of security the small town offered was wonderful but hard to get used to.

I went back inside and waited until twenty-five till six. Then I drove over to Ida's. I was surprised by her request to ride into town with me. Most of the time, our Old Order Mennonite citizens avoid town meetings and elections. Their belief about keeping themselves separate when it comes to worldly systems of government means they don't take social security payments or accept Medicare. Medical problems are usually taken care of by the community through homespun remedies. However, doctors are certainly consulted when necessary. Because of a lack of health insurance, larger bills are taken care of either by the local community church or through the district's overseeing body. Sam told me once that since he'd come to live in Harmony, he'd noticed that those who lived by the Old Order or Conservative Mennonite teachings seemed to be healthier than most. I'd wondered if the lack of smoking, drinking, and junk food contributed. Sam had laughed and said most of Harmony's Mennonite community would agree with my assessment—after adding one other reason. The most important one. Prayer.

Getting close to Ida's was somewhat complicated. The snow had piled up and my little car skidded and slid all the way up to the house. Zebediah was nowhere to be seen. I felt confident he was huddled inside his stable, out of the unpleasant weather. As I clomped through the deepening snow, gusts blew ice particles into my face. I struggled to reach Ida's front door. Right before I reached out to knock, it swung open.

"Ach, child," Ida cried. "I would not have asked you to drive me to the meeting if I had known the weather would turn so awful."

I stumbled inside, and Ida closed the door behind me. "It's not really as bad as it looks," I assured her. "There's only a couple of inches on the ground. It's the wind. It's really picked up in the last thirty minutes." I looked down to see the snow from my boots melting onto the homemade rug near Ida's door. "I'm afraid I'm making a mess."

"Do not worry," the old woman huffed. "That rug is only made of old rags. You are worth much more to me than it is."

As she reached for her long, heavy black cape, I said, "Are you sure you want to go out in this?"

"Ja," she replied. "Usually I do not go to town meetings. They seem to be about things that do not concern me. But this time. . ." Her voice trailed off as she tied the cloak under her chin. She pulled the hood up and peered out at me. "I told you that I have a bad feeling about this new building project. Please understand that this is not about the people who will come. I am sure they will be an asset to our community. But there is something else. Something that disrupts my peace. I have learned over many years to listen when that happens. I want to hear this plan for myself. Perhaps my peace will return. I must find out."

I nodded at her, but I truly believed the old woman's attitude toward Harmony was the real cause of her disquiet. Many years ago, a man who held the position of bishop in the Mennonite Church had caused a lot of disruption in the town. Ida was one of the women who had prayed Harmony would never see that kind of confusion again. Ida believed strongly that Harmony existed as a special place of refuge from the rest of the world. Although I felt the same thing, to Ida it was more than a feeling. It was absolute reality. I was certain the new retirement village was no threat to the residents here, but obviously she had some concern that it might be. I could only hope that tonight's meeting would quell her fears.

I held the door open for her, and we leaned into each other as we fought the wind. I got her into the car, and we headed toward town. The main streets were snowy but passable. The wind actually helped by pushing the snow into drifts on the side of the road. The real problem was blowing snow that made visibility very poor. I wondered if the weather might affect other citizens trying to make it to the meeting. By the time we pulled up to the building Eric had acquired, it was clear that Harmony residents were out in force.

I started to park on the other side of the street, but a man I didn't know came running out of the building, pulling on his coat. He motioned at me to wait and jumped inside a truck parked near the front door. He backed out into the middle of Main Street and waved me into his parking place. After turning off my engine, I looked in my rearview mirror and saw him pull into the spot where I'd started to park. I chuckled to myself at the thought of anyone in Wichita doing something like that. Battling over parking spaces, especially in the winter, seemed to bring out the killer instinct in people. Frankly, I'd rather walk a block in a blizzard than fight with someone over something so trivial. But today, with Ida in the car, the man's kindness wasn't trivial at all. It was a true act of kindness.

I told Ida to wait for me to come around and help her out, but by the time I reached her, the same man who had given up his parking space was already assisting her from the car and guiding her through the blustery wind toward the front door of the building. When we got inside, I caught him by the arm.

"Thank you so much," I said, a little out of breath from fighting the wind. "That was so thoughtful."

"You're welcome. Usually I wouldn't park so close to the door. I was already in town doing business and just got back to my truck." I gauged him to be in his forties or fifties. Graying brown hair, dark green eyes, and an engaging smile. His warm and easy manner made me feel immediately comfortable in his presence.

I held out my hand. "I'm Gracie Temple."

He took my hand and shook it firmly. "Temple. Any relation to Benjamin Temple?"

I nodded. "He was my uncle. He left me his house when he passed away."

He let go of my hand. "I'm Bill Eberly. I own a farm between here and Sunrise. I knew your uncle. We were friends when we were younger. Unfortunately, we didn't see much of each other for many years before he died. Ben kind of kept to himself."

"Yes, he did." I couldn't tell if Bill knew the reason my uncle had been afraid to encourage close friendships or if he was just being nice. Whatever the truth, it would have to wait. Eric had taken his place behind a podium set up at the front of the room, and people were beginning to find their seats. I excused myself to Bill and escorted Ida to a row near the podium so she could hear. As I got closer, I was able to see Eric more clearly. His face was pale, almost devoid of color, and his usual friendly smile was missing. I waved at him, but he seemed to look right through me.

Ida tugged at my sleeve after we sat down. "Is this the man you are working with?"

I nodded.

"This man does not look happy. I wonder why."

All I could do was shrug. It wasn't hard to figure out that Rand was probably involved in some way. I felt sorry for Eric. Having to deal with Rand was a lot for anyone to handle, let alone someone as young and easygoing as Eric.

Slowly the noise and discussions ceased, and the crowd waited for the information they'd come for. I looked around the packed room. John Keystone was here, as were the Crandalls and the Scheidler brothers. I saw Ruth, who smiled at me from across the room. Joe Loudermilk from the hardware store was in deep conversation with Paul Bruner. Gabriel and Sarah Ketterling stood in the back against the wall. I waved at Sarah, who lifted her slender fingers in acknowledgment. I wanted to visit their store so I could see how things were coming along, but I guess it would have to wait until tomorrow. I couldn't ask them to open up tonight, especially with the weather turning bad. I was really looking forward to renewing my lessons in wood-block printing. I gazed across the aisle and saw Abel. I nodded to him and he smiled at me. Emily hadn't come with him. I assumed she was at home taking care of the baby—unless they'd found the mother.

The door in the back of the room opened and closed. I glanced back to see Grant walk in. He'd mentioned coming to the meeting when I was in Wichita, but with the weather I'd figured he'd probably changed his mind. I tried to catch his eye but couldn't. He stood against the back wall looking uncomfortable and out of place in his dark gray suit and long black coat.

Once again the door opened. A few people in the back groaned. The frigid wind cut through the room like an icy knife. It was Sam. For some reason, I turned my head away, afraid he'd see me. My reaction didn't make any sense, but I couldn't chase away the feeling that there was a barrier standing between us that had never been there before. It made me uncomfortable.

Eric pounded on the podium with a small gavel even though it wasn't really necessary. All eyes were on him as the room fell deathly quiet. Just before he spoke, Sam slid into the seat next to me. He stared straight ahead toward the front of the room and didn't acknowledge my presence.

"Ladies and gentlemen," Eric began. "I want to thank you for coming out today." He stared down from his place behind the podium. A few people around us looked at each other. The atmosphere in the room, which had been charged with excitement when we first came in, was so quiet I could hear the people around me breathing. It was easy to see that Eric was under some kind of stress. A light buzz of whispered conversation began to build.

Eric cleared his throat and glanced around the room. Finally he opened his mouth. "I–I'm sorry to report that I don't have good news for you."

The noise in the room increased, and Eric banged the gavel again. "Please, if you could keep it down. I need to explain the situation. I'm still hopeful we can work something out." The hum of voices stopped, but not before a man's voice was heard clearly above the din.

"Told you we couldn't trust no city slicker."

Eric's eyebrows knit together in a frown. "I'm afraid the problem isn't with me. As many of you know, Rand McAllister promised to sell me his land for a fair price. Unfortunately, today he increased what he was asking to an amount I simply can't agree to. I've spent the better part of a day trying to reason with him, but to no avail." He glanced at his watch. "We were supposed to meet an hour ago to try to come to some kind of final understanding, but he didn't show up. I don't know where he is."

"So there's still hope you two might be able to work this out?" Mary's voice cut through the crowd.

Eric shrugged, his face etched with apprehension. "Honestly, I don't think so. Rand's last offer was way above anything I could possibly match. The fact that he didn't bother to show up to meet with me indicates he has no intention of being reasonable."

A few irate shouts exploded from the gathered residents. Joe Loudermilk loudly called out, "Rand McAllister would sell his mother for a few bucks. He couldn't care less about this town."

A man in the front row stood up. I recognized my pastor, Marcus Jensen from Harmony Church. "I know several of you felt this venture would help to undergird your businesses, but it seems to me we were all doing okay before this proposal came along." He turned and smiled at the crowd behind him. "I mean, don't get me wrong, I think it would be great to welcome a few new people into our community. But do we really need to get this upset if it doesn't pan out?"

Paul Bruner from the leather and feed store jumped to his feet. "Small towns are dyin' all over the state, Pastor. Are we makin' it? Yeah, I guess so. But some months we just barely get by." He pointed his finger at Eric. "This man came here and started tellin' us we could do better for our families and our town. I don't want to move away from here just so my kids can have some of the things other kids have. But if that's what I have to do, I may just pack us all up and go to Council Grove or Topeka."

"I'm sorry, Paul," Eric said. "I thought this deal was done. I guess I should have waited until all the papers were signed before

I shot off my big mouth. But Rand seemed so set on this venture, it never occurred to me that he would back out."

One by one, three other men shot to their feet. But a hush fell over the room as Ida slowly stood up. The sight of this elderly Mennonite woman clothed in black seemed to quiet even the most outspoken citizens. The men sat down, deferring to one of Harmony's most respected residents.

"I am not used to talking to large groups," she said, her voice strong but quaking with age. "However, I love this town, and I would like to ask permission to speak." She turned and looked over the crowd. "Is there anyone here who would be offended if I addressed this assembly?"

No one voiced an objection. Several people offered their encouragement.

"Thank you." She turned back to Eric. "Mister Beck, I have no reason to believe your plan was anything more than a good business proposition. One that many of our citizens felt would be a help to our town. I do not fault you for this." She turned back toward the crowd behind her. I held on to her arm as she teetered a little. "That being said, I have had misgivings about this venture since I first heard word of it. You see, many of you were content with your lives until the idea of gaining more money and possessions was held in front of you. I realize that some of you may be experiencing hard times. But in my whole life, I have never seen anyone in Harmony go without assistance when they were in need. Neighbors have helped neighbors as long as I can remember. And the church has reached out whenever someone could not make it on their own. Perhaps we are not what the world would call wealthy in goods or in monetary treasures, but in truth we are very rich, ja?" She smiled. "There are not many towns that have what we have." She looked at Eric. "Now this man comes and our town is in turmoil. There is division. Our sights are set not on what we have, but what we do not have."

Once again she faced the crowd. The room was eerily quiet. "Harmony is an exceptional place. I implore all of you to remember what makes us this way. It is not money, and it is not possessions. It is a sense of community. It is the feeling of family. It is love. Above all, it is God's blessing, ja?" She shook her head. "If this new development is built, then I will pray God's blessings on it. If it is not, then I will pray God's blessing on our town anyway. It is not this proposal I am afraid of. It is the darkness in our souls. The Good Book asks what good there will be if a man gains the world but loses his soul in the process. This is my fear. That Harmony's soul is at risk." She fastened her eyes on Eric. "That is all I have to say, Mr. Beck. I am sure you are a good man who truly believes he is doing what is best for our town. I disagree with respect, and I thank you for giving me time to speak." She grasped my shoulder and slowly sat down.

There was silence for several seconds, and then someone in the back began to clap. Soon many in the room joined in. A glance around told me that not everyone agreed with Ida's sentiments. Mason Schuler, who owned a local dairy farm, stood up.

"First of all, I want to say that I appreciate what Mrs. Turnbauer just said. There's a lot of truth in it. But she can't speak for all of us. I love Harmony as much as anyone else, but I have two teenagers who want to go to college. My desire to see more money come into this town has nothing to do with wanting to be rich or with buying a bunch of stuff. Bonnie and I honestly want to offer our kids the chance to make something more of their lives."

A few other residents asked to be heard. Each one basically said the same thing—that Harmony needed the influx of money. That losing the retirement village would hurt the town and its citizens.

Eric listened patiently to each person but didn't address their questions until the last person sat down. Then he stepped closer to the podium and stared out at the crowd. His first few words were so soft several people shouted for him to speak up. I was struck by the hurt on his face and couldn't help but remember when I first met with him and Grant about the project. He was so excited about building a place where people could spend their retirement away from the big city but were close enough to necessary services. Council Grove had a hospital and Sunrise had an emergency clinic. Although Sunrise was ten miles from downtown Harmony, from Rand's place, it was only six. As Eric learned more about Harmony and began to realize that his development could also help the town, his enthusiasm only grew. Now he stood in front of the people he thought he would be helping without a clue whether he could deliver on the promises he'd made. I felt sorry for him, but I had to admit that I was a little concerned about my own future as well. If this project fell through, hopefully Grant would be able to send other work my way. I'd been counting on this job to see me through the winter. I had a little money saved up, but paying for electricity and heat in my uncle's old house wouldn't leave me with much to live on.

Eric stepped away from the podium and got closer to the crowd so they could hear him more clearly. He wiped a thin sheen of sweat from his forehead and stared at me. I smiled in an attempt to encourage him. Out of the corner of my eye, I saw Sam watching me. It was my turn to ignore him.

"Look, I know some of you are disappointed that I don't have better news tonight," Eric said loudly. "You have my promise that I'll try to keep this deal alive. I'll find Rand and attempt to talk some sense into him. If there is any way to save the project, I'll do it. We might as well dismiss now. After I speak to Rand, I'll schedule another meeting."

Mary spoke up again. "If Rand doesn't want to sell his land, can't you find another location to build this place of yours? There's lots of acreage out here. I can't believe there aren't folks willing to sell for the right price."

"That's a good idea," Eric acknowledged, "and we did talk to several landowners in the area. Rand was the only one who had what we needed and was willing to sell."

"So let me get this straight," she said. "If you can find something close to the size and location of Rand's farm, you'll continue with the project?"

Eric considered her question for a moment. "It's possible. Just remember that I have several investors. The final decision isn't up to me. It's up to them. It would have to be a pretty good plot of land. Trust me, it's not that easy to find."

Mary sat down. The crowd murmured among themselves, but no one else addressed Eric. He dismissed the group and hurried off the platform, stopping at the end of the row where I sat. He motioned to me. I excused myself and scooted past Sam.

"Gracie, Grant and I would like to talk to you. Can you meet us in the restaurant for dinner?"

I started to explain to him that I had to drive Ida home first, but I felt a hand on my shoulder. It was Sam.

"You go ahead," he said. "I'll take Ida home."

I looked past him at Ida. "Is that all right with you, Ida?"

"Ja, ja. You go to Mary's," she said. "But don't stay in town too long. If it keeps snowing, you might have a problem getting home."

"We won't keep her too long, I promise," Eric said, smiling at Ida. "And if it gets too bad, I'll drive her. My truck has four-wheel drive."

Ida pointed at him. "I will trust you to take care of her, young man. She is precious to me."

I leaned over and kissed her on the cheek. "I'll be fine. You go home and get warm."

She nodded and Sam took her arm, guiding her toward the back of the room. Several people stopped them on their way, wanting to tell Ida how much her comments meant to them. By the time I got my coat and purse, Ida and Sam had left the building. Sam had basically ignored me. Self-pity simmered inside me. He'd told me everything was okay. That he loved me. But his actions tonight sure didn't show it. Just then Eric touched my arm.

"Are you ready?" he asked.

I nodded and followed him toward the door. Before I could reach it, someone grabbed me. I turned to find Ruth staring at me oddly.

"Gracie, I'm sorry to bother you, but I need to speak to you for just a minute. It's important."

"Well, I was on my way to a meeting," I said hesitantly.

"We'll see you at the restaurant," Eric said. "You go ahead."

Ruth took his comment to heart and immediately pulled me to a corner of the room that was empty. In several other areas, residents had formed small groups and were deep in discussion. I looked for Abel, but he was already gone. I'd really wanted to ask him about the baby.

"First of all, I'm so glad you're back," Ruth said. "I missed you so much." She gave me a quick hug, but I could tell her heart wasn't in it.

"What's wrong, Ruth? I can tell you're upset."

"Oh, Gracie," she said, her round, red face even more flushed than usual. "People are talking. I mean, I know it's not true, but I just think you should know. Not that it matters what people think, but talking behind someone's back, well, I mean. . ."

"Ruth," I said sharply. "What in the world are you talking about? Spit it out."

She took a deep breath. "It's about that baby someone left on the church's doorstep."

"What did you hear?" I felt my heart sink.

She reached for my hand. "The story is circulating that the baby is yours, Gracie. Everyone's talking about it. Well, almost everyone. I told Esther Crenshaw to shut her trap, and so did Cora and Amos."

"And where did Esther hear it?"

"I have no idea. Esther spreads gossip like wildfire, but she won't tell where the spark started. I guess she thinks it makes her look innocent of spreading her nasty rumors."

I glanced around the room. Sure enough, quite a few of the people who hadn't left were looking my way. Why hadn't I noticed it before?

"Look, Ruth, there's no truth to—"

"Don't you dare deny this stupid lie to *me*, Gracie Temple. I wouldn't believe it if that baby crawled up here, grabbed your leg, and called you Mama. You would never desert your child. We may not have known each other for long, but I know you well enough to be sure of that. You're one of the most honest, thoughtful, and good-hearted people I've ever met."

Her sentiments touched my heart, and I hugged her tightly. "Thank you," I whispered. "At least you and Abel believe in me."

"Abel? What does he have to do with this?"

"He got a letter from someone claiming the baby was mine. He had to ask me if it was true."

Ruth crossed her arms and frowned at me. "You've only been in town less than a day. Someone's already written a letter accusing you of something awful, and Esther has hold of this little nugget of poison." She shook her head. "Something doesn't seem right here. I mean, even Esther can't spread a story that fast." She patted my arm. "You need to be on the lookout. It's like someone is out to get you, Gracie."

I tried to smile at her. "I'm sure it's just Esther and some of her

417

silly friends trying to stir up something interesting in Harmony."

Ruth chuckled. "Seems to me Harmony's already pretty interesting, even without your illegitimate baby."

"Shhhh," I hissed, looking past her. "Don't ever say that."

"Oh. Sorry." Ruth reached over and squeezed my arm. "You'd better get going. It's starting to snow pretty hard. You call me if you need to talk, okay? In the meantime, I'm going to threaten Esther within an inch of her miserable life. If anyone can get her to shut up, it's me. That woman's afraid of me for some reason." She grinned. "Might be because I told her once that if she didn't keep her gossipy comments to herself, I was going to tell Marvin Upshaw that Esther's brown curls aren't really hers." She covered her hand with her mouth, reminding me of a little girl with a secret. "Esther wears a wig, you know. She doesn't think anyone suspects. I think everyone in town knows her hair isn't real. But as long as Esther doesn't know we know. . ."

"You have some control over her?" I finished. I grinned at her. "You're pretty crafty, you know that?"

Ruth giggled. "Let's just keep that between us, okay?"

"You've got a deal."

I left Ruth and made my way to the front door, looking straight ahead. If people were talking about me, I didn't want to know it. I stepped outside to find thick, fat snowflakes filling the sky. In the dark, lit by streetlamps and carried about by the wind, their sparkling dance seemed almost magical. I stood for a moment in the cold, letting the flakes drift down on my face and coat. There's something so special about snow. As I let it fall on me, I felt a sense of peace in the hushed quiet of a winter's night. It was as if God was caressing me with His love.

"Beautiful, isn't it?"

I turned to find Marcus Jensen standing next to me. "It reminds me of the scripture that talks about Jesus washing us as white as snow." He smiled. "Snow covers up the ugly things. It has a way of making everything seem clean."

I nodded. "I feel the same way."

He pointed toward the diner. "Are you going to Mary's, or were you planning to stay here for a while?"

I involuntarily shivered from the cold. "No. I think I've had enough. I'll be satisfied to sit in the restaurant, drink a hot cup of coffee, and watch the snow where it's a little warmer."

He laughed and held out his arm. I took it, and he guided me across the street. Right before we reached the steps to the diner, he stopped.

"Gracie, I'm your pastor. If you ever need someone to talk to. . ."

I peered at him through the flakes that drifted between us. "I know that, Pastor. I don't think I. . ." My stomach did a flip-flop. "Pastor, if you heard a rumor about that baby dropped off at Abel's church. . ."

He chuckled and patted my shoulder. "Gracie, I am talking about that, but probably not for the reason you think. I know that baby isn't yours. I'm just concerned about you. About having to face these kinds of silly stories."

"How did you hear about it?"

He shook his head and sighed. "You know that Esther Crenshaw is one of my parishioners. Much to my chagrin."

"Well, you could certainly give her a message from me."

"I've probably given her your message already. Although I suspect it was presented in a more charitable fashion than what you might be prone to employ."

Even though I was upset, I smiled at the kindly pastor. "I have no doubt about that."

"Let's get inside and warm up. But my offer holds. Come see me anytime. I mean that."

"Thank you. I know you do."

As we entered the restaurant, I seriously considered taking Pastor Jensen up on his offer. Between this ridiculous baby rumor and the way Sam had reacted to it, I definitely needed someone to talk to.

"Gracie, over here!"

I spotted Eric and Grant sitting at a table near the back of the room. Probably hiding. I pushed my way through the crowded restaurant. It looked like most of the town had decided to eat at Mary's after the meeting. I could hear angry discussions as I passed tables and booths packed with concerned Harmony residents.

I was almost to the table when I spotted Pat Taylor sitting alone only a few feet from where Eric and Grant sat. I must not have hidden my shock well, because he tipped his hat at me and grinned. Why was he here? Had he been in the meeting? It seemed he was popping up all over the place. Feeling unsettled, I nodded his way and kept going. Funny to see him alone at a table that could easily seat four people. Every other table was full, with family and friends eating together. Either no one was brave enough to approach him—or if they had, he'd sent them packing. Nice man.

"We already ordered," Grant said apologetically when I reached them. "Sorry, but I'm starved, and it looks like it's going to take a while to serve everyone."

I shook my head, slid my coat off, and sat down. "Don't worry about it. Honestly, I'm not hungry anyway."

"Quite a town you've moved to, Gracie," Grant said with a hint of sarcasm. "The physical description you gave me is accurate, but I thought you said this place was peaceful."

"I thought it was, too. Frankly, ever since I hit the edge of town, everything's been topsy-turvy. I have no idea why."

"I hope we can still work this thing out," he said. "I do have a couple of other jobs I can send your way, but to be honest, I can't pay much for them."

"I understand."

Grant had never had a robust complexion, but tonight, under the lights in the restaurant, he looked pasty and haggard. I knew he was worried about losing the work this venture promised, as well as the additional future work Eric had alluded to. The investment group behind the project had their fingers in many other pies. For both our sakes, as well as the town's, I hoped Eric would find a way to keep the deal with Rand.

I noticed Grant staring past me. I turned to see Cora and Amos Crandall walk in the door with Drew. As they waited for a table, I couldn't help but compare Drew to Grant's son, Jared. Drew's happy nature was controlled and appropriate. Amos and Cora treated him with kindness but applied gentle correction when it was needed. Actually, their attitude toward Drew was one of normalcy. Not that they didn't allow him to be himself, but they also expected him to display proper behavior. They didn't give him a pass because of his disability. Jared, Grant's son with Down syndrome, was much less disciplined, often running through the office, grabbing people, and running off with items from their desks. He reminded me of a playful puppy. Grant seemed uncomfortable correcting him—almost as if he was embarrassed by his son.

"So what should I do now?"

Eric's plaintive question forced me to refocus my attention on the situation at hand. Problem was, I had no answer for him, and Grant just stared at him blankly.

"Coffee?" I hadn't seen Mary come up behind me.

"Oh yes, please," I answered. "Right now a cup of your coffee is exactly what I need."

"Are you okay? You look stressed." She poured coffee into the cup that sat next to my silverware.

All I could do was shake my head. "You have no idea."

"Sorry to hear it," Mary said. "I guess everyone's skating on the edge a bit." She patted my shoulder. "Don't let it get to you. Everything will work out. It always does."

"From your mouth to God's ear," Eric said under his breath.

"Your food will be out shortly, Mr. Beck," Mary said with a smile.

"Please, call me Eric." He pointed toward Grant. "And this is Grant Hampton."

"Nice to meet you, Grant," she said. "Someone told me you're Gracie's boss. Is that right?"

Grant nodded. "For now anyway."

Mary's eyebrows shot up, but she didn't ask him what he meant. She turned her attention back to me. "What are you hungry for, Gracie? We're backed up some, but I'll push you to the front of the line so you can eat with your friends."

My appetite was almost nonexistent even though I hadn't finished the sandwich I'd made at home, but I ordered a bowl of chili.

"She's very pretty," Grant said after Mary walked away.

I nodded. "Yes, she is."

"By the way, where is Sam?" Grant asked. "I thought I'd get the chance to meet him tonight."

My voice caught. "He—he took my friend Ida home so I could come here. I'm sure you'll meet him later."

I tried to sound nonchalant, but Grant knew me well enough to know something was wrong. He stared at me for a moment but let it go. I was grateful. The last thing I wanted to do right now was talk about my love life. "So why did you two ask me to meet with you?" I glanced toward the big windows at the front of the restaurant. If anything, the snow had thickened. "I need to get going soon. If it snows much more, my little car won't stand a chance."

"We thought since you know the residents better than we do,

you could help us navigate this situation," Eric said. He leaned in and lowered his voice. "I truly don't believe Rand is going to come around. I didn't want to say that at the meeting, but it isn't just the money. For some odd reason, he's taken a real dislike to me." He sighed and shook his head. "I don't think I'm a snob, but Rand has convinced himself that I think I'm better than he is. There were signs of his attitude early on in our relationship, but I convinced myself it was my imagination. I mean, I don't see myself as better than anyone else. I try to treat everyone with respect." His blue eyes sought mine for reassurance.

"You're not the least bit stuck-up," I said, trying to match his quiet tone. "From what I've heard, Rand is convinced everyone is out to get him."

"I hope you're right. I'd feel terrible if I'd done something to make him feel uncomfortable."

"Oh, come on," Grant said, shaking his head. "The man's obviously a fruitcake. This isn't your fault."

Eric's eyes swept the room. The cold expressions tossed his way were everywhere. He sighed again. "Anyway, I want to save this project if at all possible. I'm going to scan the property maps again. Look for another location as close to Harmony as I can find. I may need your help with that, Gracie."

"I'll be glad to do anything I can."

"I want you to keep working on the advertising campaign we started," Grant said to me. "I'll make sure you get paid for your time, no matter what happens."

Eric clapped Grant on the back. "And I'll make sure you get paid for your work so far—even if this project is scrapped. Even if I have to pay you out of my own pocket." His expression turned serious. "I have no intention of allowing people who trusted me to come out of this with a loss of any kind. I intend to find a way to follow through with the development—if it's humanly possible."

His earnestness touched me. I hoped his good intentions would be enough. Weariness began to overtake me just as Mary made it to the table with our food. Across the room, I noticed Hannah and her friend Leah taking orders.

"Mary, do you need help? I used to wait tables on the weekends while I was in school. I'd be happy to put on an apron and do what I can."

She set the bowl of chili in front of me and slid Grant and Eric's plates to them. Then she leaned down and studied my face. "I appreciate your offer more than you know. But I'm going to say no. The girls and I are on top of it. You look so tired, Gracie. I think you could use some rest."

"I'm sorry," Eric said. "I should have realized you were tired. Let's eat and head out of here. Maybe I shouldn't have asked you to meet with us tonight."

I shook my head. "It's fine. I was concerned about you, and I wanted a chance to see Grant."

"The snow's really getting deep," Mary interjected. "You all need to get on the road." She frowned at Grant and Eric. "Hope you two are staying in town."

"I've got a hotel room in Council Grove," Grant said. "Think I'll leave before it gets any worse." He smiled at Mary. "Can I get a box for my hamburger and fries? I'd like to take it with me."

"Here." Mary held her hand out for his plate. "I'll wrap it up in tinfoil first and then put it in a box. That way you've got a fighting chance of keeping it warm."

"Thanks, Mary," he said, holding out his plate.

"What about you?" Mary's question was directed at Eric.

"I'm at the same hotel," he said. "But I'm going to eat here. My truck has four-wheel drive and does great on snow."

"Well, my Bug doesn't have four-wheel drive, and when it

sees a flake of snow it immediately drives straight for the nearest ditch." I quickly slurped down a couple of spoonfuls of chili and reached for my coat.

Eric frowned and took hold of my arm. "Listen, Gracie. I don't think you should take a chance with your small car tonight. Why don't we both finish our dinners, and then I'll take you home on my way to the hotel? You can pick up your car later."

I started to say no. If I could count on Sam to drive me back to get my car when the storm moved out, I would have said yes immediately. Eric noticed my hesitation.

"I'll come back by in the morning when it's light and drive you back into town. I can easily pull your car to your place if necessary. I've got a strong bumper and solid chains in the back bed. My cousin has a small car, too. I'm always pulling him out of snowdrifts."

I decided to take him up on his offer. He seemed eager to help, and to be honest, I hate driving on snow and ice. Without giving it further thought, I agreed.

"Great," he said with a smile. "Now let's enjoy the rest of our meal."

A few minutes later, Mary returned with Grant's food. He thanked her, put a big tip on the table, and left. I watched as he made his way through the restaurant. He walked slowly past the Crandalls, his eyes locked on Drew. By the way his shoulders slumped, I knew he was discouraged. It wasn't just because of the business deal he stood to lose. He and Evie must be having a tough time with Jared. It seemed to go in waves. I felt bad for them both.

"So this is the town you gave up your job for?" Eric said, interrupting my thoughts.

"Believe it or not. Of course, when I left, things weren't all stirred up like this."

"I guess you have me to thank for that."

Eric ran his hand through his thick dark hair. I was struck once again by his boy-next-door looks. A slightly turned-up nose and steely blue eyes that made women turn their heads when he walked by. But Eric seemed totally oblivious to how good-looking he was.

"Don't be silly. This deal is good for everyone. If I'd thought for a moment it would hurt Harmony, I would have said something. I still believe in this project."

He grew silent and his forehead creased.

"What are you thinking?" I asked. I immediately regretted my words. An old boyfriend told me once that men hate to be asked what they're thinking. "Most of the time we aren't thinking anything," he'd told me. "So quit asking." We broke up not long after that.

"I can't help but think about your friend—the older woman who spoke at the meeting."

"Ida? Oh, goodness. I'm certain you noticed the way she dresses. She's Old Order Mennonite. They don't like change. I wouldn't worry too much about her. Most everyone else disagreed with her."

As I said the words, I felt disloyal to Ida, but I truthfully felt her allegiance to the "old ways" meant she would never be supportive of anything that could disrupt the status quo in Harmony.

"I don't know," he said. "Quite a few people seemed to respect her opinion." He stopped eating and seemed to scrutinize me for several seconds. "You know, I'm not so sure she's wrong, Gracie."

I put my spoon down. "What do you mean? You're not rethinking this project, are you?"

"No. Not really. It's just that I understand the idea of protecting things that are important to you. I wouldn't want our development to harm this little town in any way. You really do have a special place here."

"But that's just the point, isn't it? We need some money coming into the community to keep Harmony going. Your development is just right. Not too big so as to change the complexion of the town, but big enough to undergird many of our businesspeople." I found myself speaking with more passion than I thought I had. Several of the speakers at the meeting had made sense. And the same was true in my situation. Without the work from this project, I was in a heap of trouble.

Eric shrugged, but I saw the first spark of hope in his face since the meeting. "I pray you're right. All I can do is keep going forward. First thing tomorrow I'm going to try to find Rand. If I can save the deal with him, I'll do it. If I can't, then we need to look for new property."

"You said at the meeting that Rand's was the only property that would work for your project."

He polished off the last bite of his cheeseburger before answering me. "That's right. But I'll look again. And now that the word is out that we could lose the development, maybe someone else will be willing to sell." He scanned the room until he saw Mary and waved his hand, trying to get her attention. "I think we need to get going. Even my truck has its limits. Let's get you home. I'm tired, and I'm afraid the forty miles in front of me will be slow going. It hasn't stopped snowing since we got here."

I scooped up the last spoonful of chili while he and Mary settled the bill. I tried to offer to pay for my own meal, but he wouldn't hear of it.

"I asked you to have dinner with me," he said, his sky blue eyes twinkling. "Besides, just having you to talk to is worth a hundred bowls of chili."

Mary laughed. "Now that is a compliment, Gracie. Especially when it's *my* chili."

I smiled at both of them. "Now on that, I have to agree. It was delicious, Mary. Thank you."

"You're welcome. And don't forget to call me about that dinner. How about Monday night? It's pretty slow here Mondays. I can close early."

"Sounds great as long as we're not both snowed in."

She glanced out the window at the thick, fast-falling flakes. "Boy, you've got that right." She took Eric's money and started to rummage around in her apron pockets for change.

"Hey, just keep it," Eric said. "Best cheeseburger I've had in a long time. It was worth much more than you charged me."

Mary flashed Eric a coquettish grin that lit up her heart-shaped face. Even in the harsh, yellowish hue of the restaurant lighting, I was struck by her looks. Her long black hair glowed, and her dark eyes with their long, thick lashes sparkled. I felt washed out next to her. Her perfect, pale complexion was free of the freckles sprinkled across my nose. Most of the time I tried to hide them with makeup, but by the end of a long day, like today, they seemed to emerge from under their temporary camouflage. Some people in Harmony probably wondered why Sam ended his relationship with Mary to start one with me. A sudden flash of insecurity exploded inside me, and Mary's chili seemed heavy and indigestible.

"I said, are you ready?" Eric's voice caught my attention. Mary had already walked away, but I was still staring at her.

"Sorry. I guess I really am tired. Yes, I'm ready to go."

I pulled on my coat and followed him to the door. Several customers stopped eating to watch us leave. I knew most of them, but some were strangers. I had no idea if their stares were for Eric or for the low-life baby deserter. Either way, they irritated me. By the time we made it to the front porch, my blood was boiling.

"You okay?" Eric asked.

I nodded. "I love Harmony, but one negative aspect of living in a small town is that everyone knows your business—or they think they do, anyway. It's really starting to bug me."

"Sorry if I've added to your stress."

I turned to look at him. He seemed so concerned for me it stirred something deep inside. I needed Sam, but he wasn't here. I was suddenly grateful Eric had come to Harmony.

"No. I'm glad you're here. I just wish I could come up with a solution for you."

"That's not your job, Gracie. Please don't worry about it." He pointed across the street to his huge black truck. "Let's get you home before you turn into a very lovely popsicle."

He held out his arm and I took it. The street was icy, and Eric kept me upright more than once when my feet almost slipped out from underneath me. As we approached his truck, I realized for the first time that it was a Hummer. I'd seen them, but I'd never known anyone who had one. Eric held the passenger side door open for me and helped me climb up into the seat. It was made easier by a metal step that gave me a head start. Then he closed the door and went around to the driver's side door. When he got inside I said, "Wow. This is a Hummer. I've never been inside one before."

He started the engine and the heat came on almost immediately. "Your seat heats up, too. If you get too hot, let me know."

"Again, wow." I couldn't help but compare Eric's Hummer to Sam's old broken-down truck.

"Don't be too impressed," Eric said. "It's not brand new. I bought it from a guy in Kansas City who'd lost his job and had no way to pay his mortgage. I think I paid more for it than it's worth. I just had a new alarm installed, and now sometimes the engine won't start. Most of the time I can fix it by wiggling a few wires around." He grinned. "Real high-tech stuff."

"Well, I still think it's nice." We weren't even out of town yet, and I was already warm and toasty. Eric's heater was much better than the one in Sam's old truck.

We were silent the rest of the way home except for my occasional directions. I assumed Eric was thinking about his project. My thoughts centered around Sam. I had an internal battle going between my selfish side and the other part of me that loved him no matter what. But I had to wonder if it was enough. Would I be debating our relationship if I felt certain we were meant to be together? I was hurt by his request to spend a few days alone. I wanted to understand, but in truth, it just felt like rejection. I suddenly realized that Eric was turning onto the unpaved road that led to my house. Of course, now it was buried under so much snow I was amazed he found it. Especially since there were ditches on both sides.

"How in the world did you locate my driveway?" I asked. "Is there some kind of special Hummer radar that sees under snow?"

He laughed. "No. The snow dips down on both sides of your driveway. I assume those are ditches. It's not that complicated."

"Boy, you're good. Sorry I wasn't watching."

He stopped the car and put it into park. "It might also have something to do with the super-duper headlights this thing has. Of course, any small animals caught in their beam are now permanently blind."

"So when I see bunnies and squirrels running into each other, I'll have you to thank?"

He grinned widely. "Yes, ma'am. Happy to serve."

"Well, thanks again. I'm definitely glad I didn't have to take my little car out in this. Not only would I have probably ended up in a ditch—the snow would have buried me in seconds. I might have been missing until next spring."

Eric shook his head. "I doubt that. You're the kind of girl someone would look for right away. You'd be missed."

I felt my face flush, and it wasn't because of the heated seat. "Um, thank you." My hand fumbled for the door handle.

"Let me help you up your porch steps," Eric said, turning off the engine and jumping out of the truck. He came around to my side and opened the door. "I would hate for anyone to find your frozen body during spring thaw."

I laughed and thanked him, holding on to his arm while we tramped through the snow. Once we reached the door, I fumbled around in my purse until my fingers closed over my keys. "I'd ask you to come in," I said as I unlocked the door, "but I know you need to get to Council Grove."

"You're right. Maybe some other time. I'll be back in the morning, and we'll fetch your car." He turned to leave but stopped halfway down the stairs and looked back at me. "Thanks, Gracie. For everything. Most of all for just being there."

The light from my living room bathed his face in a soft glow. The sincerity in his handsome features made me catch my breath. "You're very welcome. I'll see you tomorrow."

I watched as he followed the path we'd made through the snow all the way back to his truck. Then I closed the door and leaned against it. Was I having feelings for Eric? Was I comparing him to Sam? Emotions tumbled around inside me like numbers in a bingo basket, and I couldn't hold back a sob. I wanted to go back in time somehow—grab Sam and hold on to him as hard as I could. But after the way he'd ignored me tonight, I was beginning to wonder if he had already slipped away.

Chapter Six

I'd hung up my coat and put a kettle on for tea when a knock on the front door startled me. Who in the world would be stopping by on a night like this? As I hurried toward the insistent pounding, hope sprang up in my heart that Sam had come to apologize. To talk out our situation. I flung the door open expectantly. Eric stood there looking cold, wet, and extremely embarrassed.

"I'm so sorry," he said, shaking his head. "I can't get my stupid truck started. Can I come in for a while? I'll try it again in a little bit."

I held the door open. "Of course. Get in here before you freeze to death. Have you been out there all this time?"

When he came inside, I could see him trembling.

"Yes. I really didn't want to bother you."

"Oh, for crying out loud, Eric," I scolded. "I think it would have bothered me more to find your corpse in my front yard."

In spite of his obvious discomfort, he laughed. "Stupid Hummer. I had my eye on a Jeep. I should have bought it instead."

I helped him off with his overcoat. "Take off your boots and set them on the small rug in front of the door."

432

He leaned over and pulled off his boots. His socks were soaked. He frowned. "Seems as if I have defective boots as well as a defective vehicle."

"I think you'd better remove those socks, too. I'll get you a dry pair that will make your feet feel better."

"That would be quite an accomplishment since I can't feel them at all." As he slowly pulled off his socks, he reached out a hand and placed it on my shoulder for balance. His toes were bright red.

"Oh, wow. Come over here and sit on the couch. I'll get a fire going." My uncle's unused fireplace had originally been covered by a bookcase. Sam had shown it to me when he was working on the heat and electricity. He'd cleaned it out so I could use it. Benjamin had relied on a cast-iron stove to heat the living room, but with the new gas heating system, I'd had it removed. I guided Eric to the couch and covered him with one of Mama Essie's quilts. Then I took some logs out of the wooden bin Sam had made for me, placed them in the holder, added some kindling, and lit one of the long matches kept on top of the mantel. "While the fire gets going, I'll make you something hot to drink." I smiled at him. "Are you a coffee, tea, or cocoa kind of guy?"

He chuckled. "Hot cocoa in front of a fire sounds like a slice of heaven. Are you sure you want to go to all that trouble?"

"I'm sure. You stay cozy. I'll be back in a few minutes." Before I left the room, I moved his coat, socks, and boots near the fire to dry.

As I prepared our cocoa, my emotions swung back and forth between being glad Eric was here—and being uneasy Eric was here. We were just acquaintances through work—nothing more. Why did I feel guilty? I stirred the powdered cocoa into the bottom of a pan along with the sugar and a little milk, making a paste. Since my electricity was still a little iffy, Sam had told me to wait on a microwave. However, I had to admit that I'd grown to enjoy my hot chocolate prepared the old-fashioned way. I even liked popcorn popped in a pan on the stove better than the microwave stuff.

I added the rest of the milk and stood next to the pan, stirring it so it wouldn't burn. What if Sam drove by and saw Eric's truck here? What would he think? Had Ida looked out her window and seen Eric's giant Hummer next to my house? Would she think we were up to something? I shook my head. Why was I worried? Wouldn't my real friends know better? I couldn't hold back a harsh laugh. Sure, just like they knew I'd never drop off my baby on the church steps.

The milk started to bubble, so I removed it from the burner and turned off the heat. As I poured the hot chocolate into two cups, I made up my mind. Sam and Ida—in fact, the entire town of Harmony—would just have to think whatever they wanted. I couldn't control them. And I couldn't live my life worrying about what they thought or didn't think.

I found some marshmallows in the pantry, plopped them into the cups, and carried them out to the living room. Eric appeared to be comfy on the couch. Snickle sat on his lap, looking as happy as that spoiled cat could possibly look.

"Oh, Eric. I'm so sorry." I glared at my furry feline friend. "You get down off of there, Snickle, or I'll put you in your carrier."

"No, please," Eric pleaded. "He's a great cat. I think we're bonding."

"Are you sure?"

"I'm certain. He's purring, and if I could purr, I'd join him." He frowned at me. "What did you call him? Did you say 'Snickle'?"

"Yes. It's short for Snicklefritz. It's my father's pet name for me. I decided to give it to the cat as a way to discourage my dad from using it for his daughter. Especially in public."

Eric grinned. "Snicklefritz. I like it."

I held one of the cups up in the air. "If you want this hot chocolate, you will promise right this minute that you will never call me that."

He laughed and put one hand over his heart. "I give you my word, I will never, ever call you Snicklefritz. Even under pain of torture."

"Well, I'm not sure just who would want to torture you to find out my nickname, but I'll accept your promise anyway."

I put his cup on the table in front of him and sat down in the rocking chair. "I must say, you look pretty comfortable."

He sighed. "I am. This has been a very stressful day. Dealing with Rand, the meeting, the truck not starting. This is the first moment of peace I've had."

"I'm sorry everything has turned out so badly. I wish I could do something to help you."

"Thanks, but you're doing that right now." He took a sip from his cup. "Wow. That's delicious. My grandmother used to make cocoa that tasted like this. Now she makes the instant stuff just like everyone else."

I smiled. "If I had a microwave, I'd probably be doing the same thing. But I really do think this is better."

Eric put his cup down and his expression grew serious. "Gracie, do you mind if I ask you a personal question?"

"Go ahead. My life is an open book."

"I know it's none of my business, but I noticed you and Sam at the meeting. Things seemed, I don't know. . ."

"Strained?" I finished for him.

"Well, yes. Is everything okay? My altercation with Rand. . . It doesn't have anything to do with what's going on between you two, does it?"

"No, Eric. It has nothing to do with it." The fire crackling in the fireplace, the snow falling outside, and a nice hot cup of hot chocolate helped to lower my defenses. I really liked Eric and felt I could trust him. I slowly began to tell him about the baby, the accusatory note, and Sam's reaction. By the time I finished, his features were locked in a deep frown.

"I don't want to interfere in your life," he said gently, "but I have to say I find Sam's reaction strange. I mean, what does this poor baby have to do with you? Surely he believed you when you told him the child wasn't yours."

I was silent for a moment. Finally I said, "Yes. He believed me."

"Then I don't understand. . ."

As the truth tumbled out, I wanted to stop it. On one hand, telling Eric about Sam's mother didn't feel right. Sam would be furious if he knew I'd betrayed his confidence. Yet on the other hand, the pent-up emotions inside me seemed to have a life of their own. I couldn't seem to quit talking. When I finally finished, Eric was silent. "I'm sorry. Maybe I shouldn't have told you about this. I didn't mean to dump my problems on you."

He rubbed Snickle under the chin. The silly cat acted as if he'd never been given an ounce of attention before. "I'm glad you confided in me," Eric said finally. "It's just that. . ." He cleared his throat before speaking again. "I was engaged about a year ago. She was the woman I thought I was meant to be with, you know. My soul mate. Then about two weeks before the wedding, I found out she was adopted and that her birth mother had died of AIDS. Thankfully Michelle didn't contract it." He shook his head. "Her brother actually told me. Michelle didn't. I asked her why she'd never told me. I didn't care about her past. The thing that bothered me was that she didn't trust me. For some weird reason she thought if I knew about her mother, I would think less of her or something."

"But that's ridiculous."

"Of course it is. She was the one with the hang-up about it, not me."

"So what happened?"

"We broke up." His voice trembled slightly. Obviously it was still a very painful subject. "And it had nothing to do with her mother. It had to do with her lack of confidence in me. I mean, how can two people share a life together if they don't trust each other? What about all those situations that come along in life when trust is the only thing that gets you through? How could we make it past those moments?"

I tried to blink away the tears that spilled down my cheeks. Eric was right. Sam hadn't trusted me, not with the truth about his mother and not when he first read the note about the baby. I'd promised Sweetie that he and I could make it through this. But now I wasn't so sure. Even though Sam had assured me he loved me, instead of talking to me about his feelings, he'd tuned me out. How could two people build a life with each other if they couldn't honestly discuss their problems?

Eric sat up straighter and put down his cup. "Oh, Gracie. I'm so sorry. I wasn't talking about you and Sam. I'm sure you have a much stronger relationship than Michelle and I had. You two will be fine. I certainly didn't mean to make you cry."

"It's not you. Really. You only said the same things I've been thinking." I stood to my feet. "More cocoa?"

"No. Thank you." Eric moved Snickle, who didn't seem happy about it. Then he pushed back the blanket and got up. "I think I'd better try to get out of here before it gets any worse out there. It will be a long drive back to Council Grove. I hope the highway is open."

"But what if your truck doesn't start?"

"Like I said, this has happened before. The engine almost

always turns over after it sits for a while." He shook his head. "I can't believe I shut it off in the first place. I know better." He gave me a sideways smile. "I guess I had you on my mind and forgot everything else."

He grabbed his socks and had started to pull them on when my grandfather clock began to chime. Eleven o'clock. With the roads so bad, he probably wouldn't get to his hotel until after one or two in the morning.

"Listen, Eric," I said. "Why don't you just sleep on the couch? The idea of you getting stuck in the snow worries me. I'm not as concerned about the highway being closed as I am about the road that leads to the highway. It's several miles of dirt road, and it's probably impassable. You shouldn't try it. Even in your monster machine."

He stopped pulling on his sock and straightened up. "Look, Gracie, as much as I appreciate the offer, I can't do that. It wouldn't look right. The last thing you need is to add another problem between you and Sam. If he knew I spent the night here. . ."

I held my hands up. "I'm getting a little tired of worrying about who might believe what about me. We're not doing anything wrong. It isn't safe for you to leave. I want you to stay. Please."

Eric shook his head. "No. I appreciate what you're trying to do, but I can't do it. I just can't."

I watched silently while he finished putting on his socks and shoes and then pulled on his coat. He walked over and put his hands on my shoulders. His crystal blue eyes gazed into mine. His looks reminded me of drawings of Prince Charming in the storybooks I'd loved as a child. Almost perfect features, from his thick dark hair to his strong chin, full lips, and long dark lashes.

"I'm so glad we're friends now," he said softly. "And I won't allow anything to ruin that relationship. I have to leave. Not just for our friendship, but for you and Sam. Do you understand?"

I nodded but didn't say anything. I didn't trust my voice.

He zipped up his coat without complaint, but I knew it couldn't be completely dry. Going outside in a wet coat wouldn't feel good. I was grateful his truck was so warm.

When he reached the door, I jumped up and followed him. "If the truck starts and you don't get stuck somewhere, will you at least call me when you reach your hotel? I want to know you're safe."

He stopped with his hand on the doorknob and hesitated. "Yes. I'll call you. I promise."

"Do you have my phone number?"

"Grant has it, right? I can get it from him."

"All right." I reached out and put my hand on his arm. "Eric, be careful, okay?"

"I will. Don't worry." He took a deep breath and flipped up the hood on his coat. Then he opened the door, stepped outside, and pulled the door behind him without looking at me. I stood on the other side and leaned my head against the thick, rough wood. I couldn't deny that Eric had sparked strong emotions inside me. How could I love Sam if I had feelings for Eric? I stood there trying to sort out my thoughts while Eric tried starting his Hummer. After several attempts, the engine finally roared to life. I listened as he backed out of my driveway, turned onto the road, and drove away.

I finally picked up our dishes and took them into the kitchen. Usually Snickle followed me everywhere I went, but instead he stayed curled up on the couch. Probably hoping Eric would return. For just a moment I agreed with him, but I quickly dismissed the thought. I loved Sam. I knew that. Now that I was alone, my head and heart were in agreement. Surely tomorrow, in the light of day, everything would be the way it was supposed to be. Eric as my friend and business acquaintance—and Sam as my boyfriend. We had problems, but we would work them out. Still, Eric and Michelle's failure to escape the kind of situation Sam and I faced made me a little uneasy. Before long, exhaustion quickly took over, and all I really wanted to do was put this day behind me. I pushed thoughts of Eric and Sam out of my head.

After cleaning up the kitchen, I trudged upstairs, changed my clothes, and crawled into bed. The space heater hummed in the quiet room, creating an almost hypnotic sound. I'd almost fallen asleep when a loud noise made me sit upright. There it was again. Now what? I got out of bed and hurried down the stairs, Snickle right behind me.

When I got to the door, I turned on the new porch light Sam had installed and peeked through the window. Eric stood there, his arms wrapped around himself. I quickly pulled the door open.

"G–G–Gracie," he said through chattering lips, "I slid off the road about a mile from here. I—I didn't know where else to go."

I reached out and pulled him inside. "Oh, Eric. There are other places closer than mine. Why would you walk all the way here?" He shivered so badly I was afraid he'd fall down, so I led him over to the couch.

He shook his head. "Wh–where could I go? Everyone here hates me. I didn't want to ask for help from someone I didn't know. I walked past Sam's house, but I was afraid he'd find out I'd been at your place. I—I didn't want to cause any more trouble between the two of you." He laughed shakily. "And I really thought your place was much closer. If I'd realized how far it actually is, I'd have taken my chances with Sam."

I knelt down and pulled off his shoes and socks. The dry ones he'd worn earlier were still on the arm of the couch. I put them back on his feet. "That's ridiculous. It's dangerously cold out there."

"I know. You don't need to berate me. I've already bawled myself out." He smiled at me as I pulled off his coat. "You know, we just did this. I guess I should have listened to you and stayed in the first place."

I shook my head. "You think?"

"Are you mad? Maybe I shouldn't have come back."

I handed him the quilt. "Yes, I'm mad at you, but only because you could have really gotten hurt. Ever hear of frostbite?"

He grinned at me while I tucked the quilt around him for the second time. "So you're not mad at me for inconveniencing you; you're mad because you care about me?"

I started to answer him when he reached up and put his hand behind my head, pulling me close to him. As he kissed me, a voice in my head yelled at me to stop him—to walk away. But I didn't. After a few seconds I pushed away from him and took a few steps back. "Please, Eric. Don't do that. Not now."

He sat up straighter, still keeping the quilt wrapped tightly around him. I could see he was still shaking, so I grabbed a few more logs and put them on the fire, which had died down to glowing embers.

"Not now?" he repeated softly. "Does that mean there might be a chance in the future?"

As I turned to face him, I realized for the first time that along with my sweats I wore an old, thin T-shirt—with nothing on underneath. I instantly felt exposed and embarrassed. The only thing handy was a blue shawl draped over the back of the rocking chair. I quickly wrapped myself in it. "No, I don't think so. I love Sam, and I intend to see if we can work things out. With God's help, I believe we can. Anyway, I'm going to try as hard as possible to make that happen."

I pulled the rocking chair closer to the couch so I could see him clearly. The look on his face told me I'd hurt him. "Look,

Eric. I'm sorry. If Sam wasn't in my life, I'd definitely be inter-ested. I like you. I like you a lot. You're a good man. Any woman would be blessed to have you in her life—but not me. Not now."

He ran his hand through his hair, gazed into the fire, and sighed. "You don't need to be sorry about anything. It's my fault. I know you have strong feelings for Sam." He turned back to look at me, his eyes searching mine. "I apologize. It's just that. . .well, if you were free. . ."

"But I'm not. Not right now. Look," I said, getting to my feet, "let's get you situated for the night. We'll find your truck tomor-row and figure out a way to get it out of the snow. Tonight I want you to stay here, get warm, and stay warm. I don't want any fingers or toes falling off in my living room."

He gazed at me for a moment with the firelight flickering on his face. His expression made it hard for me to breathe. I was definitely attracted to this man, and the immature, fleshly part of me wanted to find out where this relationship could lead. But that still, small voice that spoke to me from the core of my being told me that Sam was the man for me. I knew better than to ignore it.

"You're right," Eric said finally. "Leaving body parts lying around your house is definitely not my intention." He started to get up, but I came over and gently pushed him back down. "I don't want you to leave this couch unless you have to. What do you need?"

He sighed and sank back down. "My insides are freezing. I thought maybe you'd let me make some hot tea or something."

"Or some hot chocolate?" I said with a smile.

He chuckled. "You're reading my mind."

"You stay here. I'll be right back."

"Um. . .Gracie. . ."

I raised my eyebrows. "What is it?"

Even in the low light I could tell he was embarrassed. "It's these pants. They're. . .well. . .I waded through the snow."

Realization dawned on me. "They're wet."

He nodded. "Well, frozen anyway. But I think they're defrosting."

I laughed. "I have some clean sweats downstairs. I'll get them."

Eric's forehead furrowed. "I don't think. . .I mean, you're so tiny. I doubt. . ."

"Don't worry. They're an old pair that used to belong to my dad. I kept stealing them because they're so comfortable. He finally gave them to me. He's larger than you are. They'll fit perfectly."

He sighed with obvious relief. "Thank you. I'm really cold."

"Follow me. You need to get out of those wet things. I'll bring you a clean sweatshirt, too."

I showed him the bathroom, ran down the stairs, and got the sweats and one of the extra-large sweatshirts I liked to sleep in. I found another one and pulled it over my T-shirt, leaving the shawl on top of the clothes basket. When I got upstairs, I knocked on the bathroom door and handed the clothes to him when he stuck his hand out.

While he changed, I made more hot chocolate. My fingers shook as I poured the milk. I'd kissed Eric. Should I tell Sam, or should I keep quiet? We weren't actually engaged, nor had we promised not to date other people. Somehow it was just assumed. But was that fair? I banged the cups down on the counter when I realized I was arguing with myself. I felt tired, confused, and guilty. Tomorrow would be soon enough to sort this all out. I couldn't think straight tonight. I heard Eric leave the bathroom and go back into the living room. I hoped the couch would be comfortable. There were two more bedrooms upstairs. One that had belonged to my uncle and another one that was my father's when he was a boy. I had no intention of offering either one to Eric. I couldn't possibly sleep with him in an adjoining room.

Even putting him up on the couch bordered on being inappropriate. Unfortunately, there wasn't any other choice. Eric's truck was out of the picture, and my car was still in town. Not that my Bug had a chance of making it through the huge snowdrifts the wind had created. The only other mode of transportation within a reasonable distance was Zebediah. I was pretty sure he wouldn't take kindly to being hauled out into the middle of a snowstorm. Of course, Eric probably wouldn't be too thrilled either to be stuck on the backside of an old horse in weather like this. Even though our situation wasn't funny, the image that popped into my mind made me giggle.

I stared out the window toward the trees where I'd seen the light the night before. It felt more like a month ago. I'd been so upset. Now the whole thing seemed almost unimportant.

I waited until the cocoa was ready and took it to Eric. I was a little disappointed to find out that he looked better in my sweats and sweatshirt than I did.

"Didn't you make yourself some?" he asked after taking a sip.

"No. I really don't need any more sugar tonight. However, I definitely need some sleep. If you have everything you need, I think I'll head to bed."

"I'm fine, Gracie," he said, smiling. "I'm warm, comfortable, and exhausted. I'm sure I'll sleep like a baby." His gaze swung around the room. "This is quite a house. Sure has a lot of character."

"If by character you mean it's old and needs a lot of work, you're right. It's been in my family a long time."

"I can tell. It must be difficult for a woman alone. Being responsible for a house like this, I mean."

"Yes, it is." I started to mention that Sam did most of the work, but I choked the words back. It suddenly occurred to me that if something happened to Sam and me, I would have to face taking care of the house and property by myself. The thought shook me. "Well, think I'll get myself upstairs. You know where the kitchen is if you're hungry or thirsty." I pointed to the wood bin. "If the fire gets low again, just toss a couple of logs on it. You should be fine."

As if to emphasize my words, a big gust of wind shook the house. I glanced out the window to see the snow being driven almost sideways.

"Thanks, Gracie," Eric said, yawning. "If I sleep too long in the morning, will you wake me up? I'll need to find someone to pull my truck out of the ditch."

"Sure. With all the farmers around here, we shouldn't have too much trouble locating someone with a tractor." Sam had a tractor, but I had no intention of asking him for help.

"That's great. Good night."

"Good night, Eric." I checked the bathroom and found Eric's wet clothes lying on the edge of the tub. I grabbed some hangers and hung them up. If they weren't dry in the morning, I'd toss them in the dryer downstairs. Hopefully that wouldn't trip the breaker. Sam's warning about not putting a lot of stress on the electricity flicked through my thoughts. Trapped in a blizzard without electricity wasn't on my list of things I wanted to experience.

I went upstairs, crawled into bed once again, and lay there staring up at the ceiling. Eventually I fell asleep, the winter wind pounding the house with its fury.

I dreamed I was lost in the woods. Every time I thought I'd found my way out, snow covered my path. I could hear Sam calling my name, but I couldn't respond. For some reason no sound would come out of my mouth. I wanted him to find me—to rescue me. His voice got stronger and louder. I knew he was close. If only I could call out loud enough. . .

"Gracie? Gracie, are you awake?"

I opened my eyes. Daylight. I sat up and found Eric standing over me.

"I'm sorry to wake you," he said. "But the power's out. It's probably my fault. I put my clothes in the dryer downstairs and poof. Everything went off. I flipped all the breaker switches, but nothing happened. I thought you'd want to know."

I ran my hand through my messy bed hair and tried to focus. "No, you did the right thing. If you'll give me a minute, I'll come down. Maybe I can get it going."

He nodded and left the room. Stupid dryer. I should have told him not to use it while my space heater was on, but it hadn't occurred to me he'd take it upon himself to dry his clothes. Probably trying to save me the trouble. I certainly couldn't be upset with him.

I closed the bedroom door and changed into jeans and a sweater. Then I checked the heater. Sure enough, it wasn't working. The upstairs would be an icebox before long. I hurried downstairs and found Eric sitting at the kitchen table, still wearing my clothes.

"I made coffee. I see you do it the old-fashioned way." My aluminum coffeepot sat on one of the burners. Good thing the stove was gas. An oil lamp burned on the table. The sun was up, but the clouds and snow kept much light from filtering in.

"Thanks. I'll take a look at the breaker box, and then I'll make us some breakfast." I grabbed a flashlight from under the sink and headed downstairs. Eric had removed his clothes from the inside of the dryer. They lay on the top. I felt them. They were still pretty damp. We'd have to dry them in front of the fire. I had no intention of restarting the dryer if I got the electricity back on.

I shone the light from the flashlight against the far wall. The door to the breaker box was still open. I checked all the breakers. They seemed to be okay. Sam had taped a list of the different switches and what they were for on the wall next to the box. Not all of the switches had actually been installed yet, though. There were only three. I flipped them all. Nothing. I waited a few minutes and tried again. Still nothing. With a sigh I gave up, grabbed Eric's clothes and some hangers, and tramped back up the stairs.

As I approached the first floor, I heard voices. With a sinking feeling I jogged up the rest of the way and entered the living room.

Eric held my front door open, and Sam stood on the porch, looking daggers at him.

Chapter Seven

The three of us stared at each other for what seemed like an eternity. In truth, it couldn't have been more than a few seconds. I suppose the correct reaction would have been for me to begin explaining the situation to Sam as quickly as I could. But that isn't what happened. For some reason, the absurdity of our circumstances struck me as incredibly funny, and I began to laugh. Not laugh as in "tee-hee," a ladylike giggle. I mean full-scale, stomach-holding, tears-down-the-cheeks guffawing. I tried to stop, but I couldn't. Sam and Eric both looked at me like I'd lost my mind. And I wondered it myself. Needless to say, neither one of them appeared to find the situation the least bit humorous.

"Sam, it's not what you think," Eric said, keeping a wary eye on me. I'd sunk into the couch, trying hard to control myself. I'd moved past the maniacal cackling that had kicked off this odd episode, and I'd started making little explosive noises created by laughter combined with weird hiccups that forced their way past my tightly locked lips.

"I think it's exactly what I think," Sam snarled. "Where's your truck? And where's Grace's car?"

Eric quickly explained the entire thing, from dinner at Mary's to the reason he'd stayed the night. He specifically detailed exactly where he'd slept—on the couch. As he talked, Sam's frown only deepened. Finally he held his hand up in front of Eric's face.

"Okay, that's it. Get your clothes. I'll take you to your truck. If it won't start, we'll figure out what to do from there." He pointed at me. "You stay here. I'll be back." With that, he turned and walked back to his truck.

Eric looked at me, his eyes wide. "Are you okay?"

His question sent me into another spasm of giggles. I tried to say something but couldn't. Finally I nodded enthusiastically. It was the best I could do. Eric seemed to be evaluating me, probably trying to gauge the level of my nervous breakdown. Then he quietly left the room to change into his clothes and face the angry man who awaited him outside.

While he was in the bathroom, I began to get some control back and tried to figure out why I'd acted so crazy. Yesterday I had two men interested in me. Today, even Snickle had deserted me. He peeked out from underneath a chair, his eyes as big as Eric's had been. For some reason, knowing I'd scared him with my behavior finally snapped me out of it. It took some coaxing, but I finally got him to come out. I was petting him when Eric came back into the room.

"Are you sure you're okay?" he asked.

"I really am," I said sheepishly. "I don't know what came over me. I'm so sorry. You must think I'm deranged."

He smiled tentatively. "Maybe a little."

"It's really not the least bit funny. I think it's all the pressure of the last couple of days. I guess I just reached the end of my patience with everything. Sam included."

Eric slid his damp coat on. He would be uncomfortable for a while, and I felt bad for him. "Listen, Gracie," he said, wincing slightly, "this is completely inappropriate, I know. But if things between you and Sam don't work out. . ."

"To be honest, Eric, right now, I can't think that far ahead. My ridiculous reaction just proves I need some time to myself. When the roads are passable, I might drive home to Nebraska and stay with my folks for a while. I don't seem to be accomplishing anything here."

He frowned. "But you'll come back, right?"

"I don't know. Maybe. Maybe not." I looked around the room. "I'd need to sell this place so I'd have something to live on for a while. I guess I can find someone in Harmony who'd be interested. . . ."

Eric put his hand on the doorknob. "Before you try to sell this house, let me know first, okay? I might be able to help you."

"Okay. I will. Promise. Now you'd better get out there. I don't think either one of us wants Sam to come back."

"That's an understatement." He gave me a rather sickly smile. "And if no one ever hears from me again, will you please tell my family what happened?"

"I think you're safe. Sam would have to get rid of both of us."

He chuckled and opened the door. But before he stepped out onto the front porch, he paused and looked back at me. "Thanks, Gracie. I know this sounds ridiculous, but I had a really good time last night. And it was because I spent it with you."

After the door closed, I sat on the couch for a while, thinking. It seemed pretty clear that Sam and I were finished. If he hadn't trusted me before, there was no hope he'd believe the truth now. My mind kept wandering back to the first time I'd come to Harmony. Sam and I had developed feelings for each other so quickly. In retrospect, our relationship must have been built on emotion—not day–in, day-out reality. Neither one of us was perfect, and we obviously didn't have the kind of bond that can overcome challenges. Unfortunately, life is full of challenges.

My previous hysterical response turned to tears of frustration. Eventually I cried myself to sleep. I awoke to the sound of a male voice. I let loose with a small scream before I realized it was Sam.

"H–how did you get in?" I gently pushed Snickle off my lap and sat up.

"The door was unlocked."

I tried to pat my hair into place, wondering why I should even care what I looked like. Sam had obviously come to tell me we were through.

"What happened to Eric?" I shivered from the cold and wrapped the quilt around me. The fire in the fireplace was low, and the house was freezing.

"I took him to his truck and pulled him out of the ditch. He's on his way to Council Grove."

"Good. I'm glad he's okay. You didn't. . . I mean, he's not. . ."

"Did I beat him up? Is he injured?" Sam shook his head. "No. He's fine."

"Good. Thank you." I stared up at him. "Nothing happened, you know. Everything was absolutely innocent. I know you don't believe that, but I want to say it anyway, just because it's true." I gave him a moment to respond. When he didn't, I pointed my finger at him. "Why don't you just say what you have to say? I already know what's coming. Let's just get it over with, okay?"

Sam brushed back the bangs that hung down over his stormy gray eyes. Then he sat down in the chair across from me. Snickle promptly jumped off my lap and went to his. Disloyal cat.

"Okay. Here goes." He began stroking Snickle, not looking at me. "I've been a stupid fool. I should have told you about my mother from the beginning. But you need to understand that I never set out to lie to you. Sweetie and I have been telling people my mother is dead for a long time. Not because we wanted to deceive anyone, really. Just because it saves a lot of questions and pain. Honestly, it never occurred to me to tell you. I guess because I thought I'd dealt with it and it wasn't important to me anymore." He laughed harshly. "I seem to have been wrong about that." He finally swung his gaze back to me. "When you showed me that note, I don't know, it brought it all back. The abandonment. The confusion. The hurt. It had nothing to do with you, Gracie. You thought I was afraid you'd done the same thing my mother had—abandoned her child. But that's not it. It has to do with finally facing how angry I've been at my mom for not trying to find another way. I know she thought she was doing the best thing for me, and I'm grateful to Sweetie for the life she's given me. But I loved my mother. I believe we could have found a way to deal with her problems together."

"I'm sorry, Sam. You've always acted as if losing your mother didn't bother you that much anymore. But of course, I didn't know the whole story."

He shrugged. "Hey, I'm as surprised by my response as you are. Even more. I thought it was all behind me, too."

"So where does this leave you and me?"

"You mean how do I feel about finding you and Eric here? Knowing he spent the night and seeing him in your clothes?"

I started to explain, but he stopped me.

"I don't want to hear it, Gracie. Eric tried to tell me the whole story again in the car. I told him to be quiet or I'd kick him out and leave him stranded in the snow."

"So we can't talk about it? Are we finished? It's over? I mean, we're over?" Even though I'd already suspected it, the reality hit me with a finality that made my heart feel as if it would break.

Sam rose from his chair and came over to where I sat sobbing. He reached for my hands and held them. "No, Grace. That's not what I meant. I mean you don't need to explain last night. I know nothing happened. Eric got stuck here, and you gave him a place to stay. That's it." He let go of one of my hands and pushed back the hair from my face. "You silly girl," he said, a tear escaping his eye, "when you started laughing like that, I realized two things. How much stress I've put you under, and how ridiculous it was to think you and Eric were. . .involved." He took my face in his hands. "I know you, Grace. I know your heart. I was stupid to ever let anything come between us. And you have my word it will never happen again. Never. If you can forgive me for the mistakes I've made, then. . ."

Before he could finish, I kissed him. Then I cried a little. And then I kissed him again.

"I take it that means I'm forgiven," he said with a crooked smile.

I laid my head on his chest and cried until I couldn't cry anymore. Except this time it was from relief.

"Why don't you get cleaned up?" he said softly. "I'm going to see if I can get your electricity back on. Then we'll attempt to get your car back here."

I sat up, still sniffling. "I doubt we'll even be able to find it."

"It's stopped snowing, and everyone's trying to dig out. But if we decide to let the car sit for a while, I'll take you wherever you need to go, okay?"

"Okay." I got up and started toward the bathroom.

"Grace?" Sam called out.

I turned around and found him standing near the couch, still smiling at me. "I love you."

"I love you, too," I choked out. Then I fled to the bathroom before another round of tears began. When I closed the door, the room was pretty dark. I raised the window shade. Sure enough, the snow had come to an end. The world was covered in glistening white. The beauty outside my window certainly wasn't evident inside my bathroom. I looked in the mirror and was horrified to find a disheveled woman with a runny red nose, pink eyes, and hair that looked like it hadn't been brushed anytime during the current century. Besides the way I looked, my behavior over the last few hours had left me feeling drained. I'd gotten nervous giggles before—most people have. But launching into bizarre and uncontrolled hilarity was a new experience. Funny, though. I felt better now. Not just because Sam and I were okay, but because I felt released from the tension that had held me in its grip since I'd come back to Harmony.

I closed my eyes and prayed quietly. "Lord, I don't know if You sent the laughter—or the tears. But I feel better. Allowing myself to worry so much isn't much of a testament to my faith in You. I'm sorry. I truly believe You led me to this place, so I intend to trust You to complete what You started. I'll do a better job of casting my care—if You'll help me. Show me what You want me to see through everything that's happened. I know You love Harmony and the people who live here. Let Your perfect will be done. And use me to bring that about. Thank You."

I took a deep breath and shook myself. Like Sweetie said, God doesn't send the storm, but without faith in Him and in His goodness, I would certainly end up tossed around. . .and wet.

After attempting to fix my makeup and hair, I finally felt presentable enough to face Sam. As I left the bathroom, the light suddenly flickered on. I opened the door to the stairs and yelled, "The lights are back!"

"Great!" Sam hollered. "Let me work on this switch just a few more minutes. I want to make sure the connection is tight."

"Okay." I decided to run upstairs and change my clothes. When I came downstairs he was standing in the kitchen, drinking a glass of milk.

"Say, I'm starving," he said. "You have anything here to eat?"

"Well, like I told you, I'm not a great cook, but I can rustle up some bacon and eggs."

"Sounds wonderful. If you'll do that, I'll make the coffee."

"It's a deal."

The chilly kitchen warmed up quickly, and before long we were eating. We talked about the snow and how Buddy had jumped around in it as if it had been sent just for him to play in.

"He's not that tall," Sam said, chuckling. "He almost disappeared."

Sam told me that Sweetie had gone out first thing in the morning to clear the driveway as if the storm had been a personal attack on her. By the time we finished, I felt like things were almost back to normal between Sam and me. I knew we needed to talk more about what had happened, but I wasn't quite ready to do that yet, and it appeared that Sam felt the same way. Right now, laughing and talking together felt good. Like medicine to my bruised soul.

Finally we decided it was time to brave the outdoors. Sam's truck started right away. I wanted to make a comment about the old vehicle being more dependable than Eric's Hummer, but I kept my mouth shut. The less said about Eric the better. At least his huge truck had made some deep tracks we could use to get out of the driveway. Once we got to Faith Street, I realized the road was in pretty good condition.

"This isn't so bad," I remarked.

"I stuck a plow on the tractor and went up and down between my house and Ida's," Sam said. "See the snow piled up on the side of the road? That was on the street before I moved it."

"Shouldn't we check on Ida before we go into town? I'd like to know she's all right."

"Already did that. Brought some wood in for her fire and fed Zebediah. Shoveled most of the snow out of his stable and fired up the old woodstove in there so he'd be warm."

"Wow. You have been busy. What time did you get up this morning?"

He shook his head. "Way too early. I'm tired. But at least I'm not hungry now."

I smiled. "Well, if you're happy eating breakfast all day, I'd be glad to cook for you anytime."

He grinned. "Hey, I'll just keep Sweetie nearby. That way there's no pressure on you."

"You're a funny, funny man."

"I know."

I scooted up closer to him, and not just for warmth. We turned onto Main Street. That road was pretty snow packed. We bounced and slid, almost getting stuck several times. Finally we pulled into Harmony. The town sat silently, no one outside. However, several cars were parked on the street. Most of them still covered with snow. I saw Gabe and Sarah's buggy in front of their store.

"Gabe and Sarah are in town?"

"Doesn't look like they went anywhere. Probably stayed the night in the shop rather than try to get home in the storm."

"I'd like to check on them."

Sam nodded. "You go ahead. I'm going to see if I can dig your car out."

I glanced over to see my poor little Bug almost completely covered. I balled up my fist and lightly punched Sam on the arm. "Slug Bug."

He shook his head and laughed. "Boy, I'm going to be sorry I told you about that game, aren't I?"

"You betcha."

I got out of the truck and waded through the snow toward the candle shop. Gabe and Sarah's horse had been unhooked from the buggy. He'd probably been moved to a nearby stable, out of the cold and snow. When I opened the front door, a wonderful aroma greeted me. Sarah sat in a chair near the front counter. She smiled when she saw me. "Gracie! I'm so happy you're home."

I hugged her. "Me, too. Did you get stuck here last night?"

She grabbed my hand. "Yes. The snow was too much for Molasses."

I laughed. "Your horse's name is Molasses?"

She winked at me and lowered her voice to a whisper. "Papa says she's as slow as molasses but just as sweet. Sometimes I think he worries more about that horse than he does me."

"I doubt that's true. By the way, where is he?"

"Where is who?" a deep voice bellowed from behind me. I turned around to find Gabe standing in the doorway that separates the store from the workroom. "Is that Gracie Temple? It's been so long, I almost forgot what you looked like."

My relationship with Sarah's father had improved greatly since we first met, but I had no plans to hug him. Something like that could set us back to where we started. I was really glad to see him, though.

"Well, you weren't missing much. I saw you at the meeting, but maybe you didn't see me. I sat in the front."

Gabe walked over to the counter next to Sarah and put the candle he held in his hand on the glass top. "I guess I did spot you sitting next to Ida Turnbauer." His frown made it clear something bothered him.

"Did you hear what she had to say?"

He nodded, and the lines in his face deepened. "Yes, I did."

Sarah and I glanced at each other. She rolled her eyes.

"You didn't agree with her?" I asked.

"Oh, I agreed with her. I just don't think it was proper for her to speak."

Even though I like Gabe, I could feel my blood pressure ratchet up a notch. "Because she's a woman?"

He raised his eyebrows and stared at me with amusement. "No, not because she's a woman, although I do believe a man should speak in a situation like that if one is available. But Ida is a widow. She has no man to intercede for her."

I wanted to go off on a mini tangent and let him know that the only time a man would ever talk for me would happen after I completely lost the power of speech, but I reined myself in. "So you're not upset because she's a woman. So what are you upset about?"

"I don't think Mennonites should get involved in disputes that have to do with the governing of a town. It isn't our place."

"But this isn't about governing anything. It's about building something that will benefit the town."

He raised his eyebrows again. "And how will this wonderful new development benefit me?"

I swung my hand around the room. "People will come here to buy candles. To buy Sarah's stationery and note cards. You'll make money."

He crossed his arms over his chest. "Money. That's what it always comes down to, isn't it. Man's greedy desire for money."

I sighed. Gabe and I had been over this ground many times before. Unfortunately, neither one of us intended to budge.

"Money is the root of all—," he started.

I shook my finger at him. "Not money. The *love* of money. You know that, Gabe. We've been over and over this. Sometimes I think you—"

"Stop that right now," Sarah said sharply. "You two do this every time you get together. If I didn't know how much you liked each other. . ."

"Now who said I liked this skinny little redheaded girl?" Gabe growled, shooting me his fiercest expression.

"You did, Papa," Sarah said softly. "You said Gracie reminded you of your sister, Abigail. You said—"

"That's enough," Gabe barked. His expression softened as he gazed at his beautiful daughter. "I see I can't say anything to you in confidence ever again. You love to tell all my secrets."

"How you feel about Gracie isn't any secret." She fastened her large, dark-chocolate brown eyes on me. "And I know you like Papa. Isn't that right, Gracie?"

"I'm sure I have no idea what you're talking about," I quipped, grinning at Gabe.

He shook his head and held up the candle he'd brought with him into the room. "Now that my daughter has restored peace between us, I'd like to show you one of my newest creations."

I moved over to where he stood behind the counter and examined the soft buttercream-colored candle he referred to. "This isn't your hay candle, I hope. I heard it smelled like—"

"It would be advantageous for you to stop right there," he said. "This town. You make one small mistake and you never hear the end of it."

Sarah laughed. It was a light, airy sound that made me feel good. "Oh my. It took us a week to get the smell out. I had no idea a little candle could stink that badly."

"Well, I think I can safely say this candle won't cause the same reaction." He held it up near my nose. "What do you think of this?"

I breathed deeply. "Why, it's honeysuckle. Oh, Gabe. It's perfect. Beautiful."

"Is it good enough for you to forget all about the hay-scented candle?"

"Actually, yes. And I intended to get quite a bit of traction out of that."

"I'm sure you did." Gabe rolled the candle around in his hands for several seconds before putting it down. He cleared his throat.

"You said you love the smell of honeysuckle. That you would miss it in the winter."

"Yes, I did. You didn't. I mean you didn't. . ."

"Make this candle for you?" Sarah finished gently. "Yes. Yes, he did. And he named the scent Honeysuckle Grace."

"You did that for me?" My words came out in a whisper as I forced back tears. This man had been so harsh and unyielding when I'd first met him. He kept Sarah with him at all times, never allowing her out of his sight. And he had no love or trust for any human being. But over the past several months, he'd changed. And now he'd made me a candle. It was too much, and tears coursed down my cheeks.

Gabe looked horrified. "My goodness, girl. It's just a candle."

Sarah came around from the other side of the counter and put her arms around me. "Gracie, is something wrong?"

I clung to her. "It's just. . .it's just that things have been so messed up since I got back. I almost forgot how much this town means to me." I looked past Sarah's shoulder at her father. "How much everyone here means to me."

At that moment the shop's front door opened, and Sam came inside to find me bawling. "For crying out loud, it's only been a few minutes. What happened?"

I tried to explain but couldn't get the words out. Sarah patiently tried to tell him my tears were about the candle, but Sam only looked more confused. He shook his head. "I don't know. Earlier today she was laughing like a maniac. Then she bawled like a baby. Now she's at it again. I guess I just don't understand women at all."

"This is why men must band together," Gabe said with a sigh. "We need to have rational people around us."

I let go of Sarah. "You two stop it," I said sharply. "I just thought the candle was a sweet gesture. Since I got back, I haven't had too many *sweet* moments."

Sam came over and put his arm around me. "I guess that's true. I'll tell you what. From here on out I will shower you with sweet moments. Would that make you feel better?"

"I can't promise anything"—I sniffed—"but it's a good start."

"Can I change the subject now, or are you going to start blubbering again?" Gabe asked. "I have something I want to talk to Sam about."

I shrugged. "Depends on what you say."

Gabe looked at me carefully. "I'm not sure the odds are good enough. . . ."

I pushed Sam away. "Honestly, change the subject, I don't care." I grabbed Sarah's arm. "I want to see what you've been doing since I left. Will you show me?"

Sarah nodded enthusiastically. "I have a worktable set up in back. Come with me."

I followed her to the back room, leaving Sam and Gabe to their conversation. The room behind the curtain was warm and cozy. A fire burned in a big potbellied stove that sat in the middle of the space. A long workbench sat against one wall where candles cooled in their various molds. The aromas were intoxicating. Homemade curtains covered the windows, the fabric decorated with small flowers and finished with lace. Sarah's touch was evident. She led me to a corner of the room where a wooden table had been set up for her wood-block printing projects. Several blocks lined the back of the table. Two rollers sat next to them as well as a couple of small paint trays. Sarah reached across the table to some shelves that had been attached to the wall. "Papa made these cubbies for me so I could stack my paper and cards here." She pointed to one section. "This is all my blank paper and card stock. And over here," she said, moving her finger to the right, "is all my finished work." She motioned to me to follow her over to another table a few feet away. "And this is where everything dries. I wanted to show you three new patterns I've designed." She pointed to a lovely sheet of stationery with a flowering vine that crept up one side. "It's a passion flower," she said softly. "I've only seen it in pictures, but it's really beautiful, isn't it?"

The dark blue color of the flowers intermingled with the green vines. The design was set against a cream-colored paper. The effect was striking. "It's beautiful, Sarah. I love it."

She smiled and pointed me to the next row of drying paper. "And I'm certain you know what this is." The light yellow paper was edged with honeysuckle.

"I'm sure I don't have to tell you how much I like this," I said. "You won't keep much of it in the store."

We looked at the third design, which was a combination of deep red and purple flowers against a dark blue background. The paper itself was light blue. Sarah had outlined the flowers in a way that made them seem three-dimensional. "This must have taken hours to design and print," I said. "It's absolutely incredible. Put me down for the first order."

She laughed. "I already have twelve orders. Papa brought several people back here so he could show them my work."

I hugged her arm. "That's wonderful. I'm really not surprised, though."

Sarah pointed toward a small table with two chairs. "Why don't we sit down for a minute? I'd like to talk to you if you don't mind."

"Of course I don't mind. You're my friend."

Sarah sat across from me, folding her long blue dress under her. Her dark hair matched the black apron over her dress. White ribbons on the sides of her prayer covering touched her smooth, unblemished skin. Her natural beauty had no need of makeup. I envied her in this respect. Although I didn't use much makeup myself, I was certainly too insecure to go out in public au naturel.

"This is where Papa and I have our lunch," she said. "Sometimes we go to Mary's, but Papa doesn't like to spend money in restaurants."

That sounded like Gabe. "Where did you and your father sleep last night?" I looked around the room. There didn't seem to be any place to bed down.

"Oh, Papa brought the blankets in from the carriage. We always carry some in the winter. And John Keystone brought us a couple of cots he keeps in his shop. When he first moved here, he actually lived in the back of his store for a while. Now he has a nice little house outside of town. Papa and I were quite comfortable." She flushed at the mention of John's name.

"I saw John briefly when I got into town. He seemed to be doing well."

She cast her eyes down and wouldn't look at me. "Oh? I'm pleased to hear that."

I didn't say anything. Sarah had never confided in me about their relationship. Not directly anyway.

She raised her head and looked toward the door to the shop. "I—I wonder if I could talk to you, Gracie. About something. . . personal." She swung her large, doelike eyes back to me. "I haven't really had any friends for such a long time. Papa has kept me away from everyone except the people in our small church group for the past several years. He's afraid I'll leave him—like my mother did." She reached up to wipe away a tear that slid down her cheek. "I could never cause my father that kind of pain. I know how much it hurt him. I wonder if being abandoned by the person you love isn't the worst thing that can happen to a person." She let out a deep sigh. "You know, I've wondered for many years if she left because of me. Perhaps I was too much trouble. It hurts me to think that might be the reason." She gave me a sad smile. "I realize I don't know much about the world. I'm sure there are things much worse that people must bear."

I reached over and put my hand on hers. "There may be," I acknowledged. "But losing a parent is right there at the top." I squeezed her hand. "Your mother left because she was unhappy with herself, Sarah. Not with you. Perhaps not even with Gabe. She may have gone away with another man, but there was something wrong inside her. A healthy person doesn't walk away from their family. You should never, ever blame yourself for her choices."

"It's hard not to. In all these years, I've never heard a word from her. If she cared about me, I would think she would contact me, don't you?"

I didn't know how to answer the beautiful Mennonite girl so full of grace, dignity, kindness, and pain. I thought carefully. At that moment, the idea of having about ten minutes alone in a room with her so-called mother for some real "come to Jesus" justice sounded very appealing. But that probably wouldn't set well with someone like Sarah who believed in peaceful solutions. "I have no idea why you haven't heard from her. But wondering about things you can't control or situations you have no direct knowledge of is useless." I smiled at her. "There is one thing I do know. Missing out on being with you should be the greatest regret of her life. You're a wonderful person. Any mother would be proud to have you for a daughter."

Another tear coursed down her face. "Oh, thank you, Gracie. You're so kind. And such a dear friend." She hesitated and looked toward the door again. "I'm so torn. I need some advice, and you're the only person I feel safe enough to confide in."

I knew where this was going, and to be honest, I wanted to get up and run away. Instead I gave her a smile of encouragement.

"There's a. . .situation," she said, almost whispering. "And I'm afraid Papa will be very upset if I tell him about it." She shook her head. "He was so angry for so many years. I'm afraid. Afraid if I'm honest with him, life will go back to the way it was before. When he had nothing to do with others, and I had to stay inside all the time." She stared deeply into my eyes. "I can't cause him more pain, Gracie. Yet I can't continue to deceive him either. I don't know what to do." She took a deep breath. "You see, I am in love. I am in love with John Keystone."

From behind us came a strangled sound—more of a groan, really. Sarah's face turned deathly white. I turned around to find Gabe standing in the doorway, his expression one of incredible rage.

Chapter Eight

No one moved for several seconds. Then Sarah stood up. "Papa...," she whispered. She swayed suddenly, and I jumped up to catch her before she fell. I lowered her gently to the floor and put her head on my lap. Gabe seemed rooted to his spot by the door.

As I called Sarah's name and stroked her cheek, Sam came into the room. He had to gently push Gabe out of the way. "What in the world?" he said when he spotted Sarah and me. "Is she okay?" he asked as he hurried to my side. "Is she sick?"

I shook my head at him. "No. She's not sick. She's afraid."

Sam raised his eyebrows in surprise. "Afraid. Afraid of what?"

I met Gabe's fixed glare. "Of her father. This poor girl is afraid of her father."

Sam stared at Gabe, too. "Gabe. I don't understand. What's going on?"

Gabe looked back and forth between the two of us. "What's going on is that I allowed my daughter to come in contact with the world," he snapped. "I see I have made a terrible mistake."

I pulled Sam down to the floor and transferred the unconscious girl to his arms. Then I rose to my feet and approached her furious father. "Listen to me, Gabriel Ketterling. Sarah is terrified of hurting you. She loves you more than anything in the world. She certainly didn't set out to cause you pain. Please don't turn this into something that will create even more destruction." I tried to take his arm, but he pulled away from me.

"What part did you have in this?" he railed at me. "Did you encourage her to chase after that. . .that ungodly man?"

"Gabe," I said as soothingly as I could. "Sarah just now told me about her feelings for John. You heard her."

"So you had no idea this betrayal was going on behind my back?"

"Betrayal? What are you talking about? Sarah didn't betray you. This isn't about you. It's about her—and John."

He took one step closer to me and peered directly into my face. "I asked you a question, Grace Temple. Did you know about this?"

I looked back at Sam, who still held Sarah. She had begun to moan and blink her eyes. There was no way out. I had to tell the truth. I turned to meet Gabe's eyes with mine. "I suspected it, Gabe."

He took a couple of steps away from the door. "I want you to leave. Now. You and your boyfriend. And you're not to ever come around here again. Ever. And let me make this very clear so you understand me." His whole demeanor was menacing. "You are never to see my daughter again. I mean it."

"Papa. Papa, please. . ." Sarah's plaintive wail shook me. She struggled to get to her feet with Sam holding her tightly. "This is all my fault. Gracie had nothing to do with it. Please don't take it out on her."

"Take your hands off her," Gabe shouted at Sam. "And follow your girlfriend out of my shop. And out of my life." He rushed over to Sarah and pulled her out of Sam's arms. She almost tripped and fell, but Gabe caught her and guided her over to the table, helping her back into her chair. Sarah seemed helpless against her father's control over her.

Sam stood next to me. "Let's talk about this," he said to the enraged man. "You're being irrational. We're your friends. You're important to us. And Sarah is an adult. She has the right to make her own choices."

Gabe let go of Sarah and advanced toward us. For a moment I was afraid he intended to hit Sam, but Sam held his ground and refused to be intimidated. I prayed there wouldn't be a fight. Gabe's anger showed no sign of the passivity his faith embraced. Would physical violence be next? He stopped about two feet away from us, his face twisted with contempt.

"I don't need your advice on anything. My daughter and I are not your business. Not anymore. And we were never friends. Friends don't bring pollution into your life." He focused his attention on me. "If you'd been my friend, you would have told me about John Keystone. You wouldn't have allowed that. . .that disgusting heathen to put his hands on my daughter!"

His last few words were screamed at us. Sam took my arm and began to pull me out of the room. At first my concern for Sarah made me fight him, but I could see that Gabe was coming unglued. Sobbing, Sarah waved at us to go. I decided to leave for her benefit, but not before I made sure of one last thing.

I pointed my finger at Gabe. "I want you to know that I will be checking up on Sarah whether you like it or not. If you lay one hand on her, so help me. . ."

With that, Sam pulled me from the room. We got our coats and made our way out the front door. I couldn't help but notice the Honeysuckle Grace candle still sitting on the counter. Emotion hit me like a punch in the gut as we stepped outside and closed the door behind us. The snow that covered Harmony sparkled like millions of little diamonds. But the hurt in my heart dulled the beauty before me. I'd lost my friend. No, I'd just lost two friends.

"We've got to warn John," I said to Sam. "He needs to know what's coming."

He shook his head in disgust. "Great. All we need is for him to go tearing in there to save Sarah." He put his arm around me. "Are you okay?"

"Yes, I'm fine. I'm just worried about Sarah. And Gabe, too."

He sighed. "You want to tell me what happened? I mean, I realize your suspicions about John and Sarah turned out to be correct. But what set Gabe off?"

"Sarah told me she loves John. She'd never told anyone before. Wanted someone to confide in. Wonderful result, huh? The first time she shares her heart, Gabe goes crazy and bans her from ever talking to anyone again."

"He didn't actually tell her she couldn't talk to anyone."

I stamped my foot in frustration. "I know that. I'm just trying to make a point."

He hugged me. "I know. Sorry. Let's see if John is in his store."

We hurried as quickly as we could through the snow to John's, but the windows were dark, the door locked. "He must have made it home," Sam said. "Good thing. It would be best if he stayed out of town until Gabe calms down."

"Calms down? I don't think that's going to happen anytime soon. Let's check Mary's. If he's not there, we need to call him."

"I agree. How about a hot cup of coffee? I'll use Mary's phone."

We walked across the snow-covered street to the restaurant. Sure enough, it was open. I wondered if Mary had spent the night in town, too. When we stepped inside, it was obvious several Harmony residents hadn't made it home. Many of them were wearing the same clothes they'd had on the night before. The

Crandalls sat together at a table against the back wall. Cora waved and smiled as I approached their table.

"Have you all been here the whole night?" I asked.

Amos nodded. "Our place is too far away, and our car is too old to make it through that much snow. So Mary put us up. Some of us slept in booths, and the rest of us slept on the floor. Ruth and Carol gave us blankets to keep us warm."

Cora laughed. "Ruth's beautiful quilts were certainly more comfortable than Paul and Carol's horse blankets. But we were all warm and overly fed."

As if on cue, Mary came out of the back room with plates of food in her hands. She dropped them off at a nearby table, laughing and joking with the people who sat there. She turned and spotted us. "Hey, you guys back already? This is getting to be a habit."

"Just couldn't stay away, Mary," I said. "I see you have some captive customers."

"Tried to get them to leave, but they kept whining about the snow and the bad roads." She grinned. "Bunch of big babies."

Her comment brought laughter from the assembled "babies."

"You two hungry?"

"Thanks," Sam said, "but we already ate. Maybe we could give you a hand."

"I appreciate the offer, but I've got lots of help taking orders and getting food to the tables." As if on cue, Ruth came out of the kitchen carrying some trays, along with Pastor Jensen and his wife, Wynonna.

"I see what you mean. But if there's anything else I can do. . ."

"Not unless you can cook."

"Unfortunately, it's not one of my strong points. But if Hector can tell me what he needs, I'm more than willing to try."

Mary picked up some dirty plates from one of the tables and cocked her head toward the kitchen. "Follow me. If you can flip pancakes and make toast, it would be a big help."

"I'm going to round up some of the men and see what we can do about getting Main Street cleared," Sam said.

"And maybe you could make that call?"

Sam understood I was talking about John and nodded.

"I'll take care of it." His grim expression made it clear he didn't look forward to telling John about the dramatic scene we'd witnessed between Gabe and Sarah.

Mary looked at us oddly but thankfully didn't ask any questions.

"And while you big men are working to clear the streets, be careful not to run over my car, okay?"

Sam hugged me. "I'll try, but it's so small we might not be able to see it."

He tried to give me a quick kiss, but I pushed away from him. "Sorry, bub. No more of that until I know my Slug Bug is safe."

"I'll do my best, but when a guy can't get a kiss, it throws everything off. Not sure what will happen now."

I gave him a quick shove. "Get out of here. I've got to flip pancakes. That's real work."

Sam grinned at me and waved good-bye. I waved back and followed Mary to the kitchen. I'd never been in the back room and was surprised to see how big it was. A large grill took up most of one wall. Hector was busy pushing a large pile of bacon around with a spatula. Several eggs crackled on the hot grill. He greeted me quickly, but it was obvious his concentration was on the work at hand. On the other side of the kitchen, rows of shelves held all kinds of pots and pans. Nearby, a huge refrigerator hummed away, and a large dishwasher whirred softly as it cleaned the dirty dishes. I noticed a door near the refrigerator and asked Mary where it led.

She put her tray on the counter. "Follow me," she said. She swung the door open to reveal a walk-in freezer full of different kinds of frozen foods. "A lot of what we keep in here is meat. Some folks like to buy a side of beef because it's cheaper, but they don't have anyplace to put it. I let them store it in my freezer as long as I have the room." She pointed to some large chest freezers in the back.

"Wow. I had no idea so much went on back here. You could feed a small army from this place."

She closed the door. "Harmony isn't a big town, and there's not a lot to do. Eating out is special to folks. You'd be surprised how many people come through here in a week."

"I guess I would."

She handed me an apron slung over a nearby chair. "I need you to put this on. And you either need to put your hair in a net or pin it back."

"I've got a scrunchie in my purse. What if I put my hair in a ponytail?"

"That'll work. And you'll have to wash your hands thoroughly." She pointed to a dispenser on the wall. "Hot water. Use lots of soap, and dry thoroughly. Then put on gloves." She pointed to a box of plastic gloves. "You've got to put on fresh gloves if you touch anything new or if the gloves get dirty. And rewash your hands every time."

"Boy, lots of things to remember."

"It's not that bad. We just work hard to keep everyone healthy."

Hector pushed some plates onto a counter next to the grill. "Order up," he said.

"You get ready, and then Hector will tell you everything you need to know. And thanks, Gracie. I appreciate your help."

She grabbed the new plates and left the kitchen. I found my scrunchie, pulled my hair back, thoroughly washed my hands, and put on my gloves. I spent the next two hours following Hector's orders. I flipped pancakes, made toast, held out the plates for him to fill with hot, steaming food, and listened to Hector's stories about growing up in Mexico. The minutes flew by, and I had a wonderful time. I could hardly believe it when Mary told me Sam was looking for me.

"We're all caught up, Gracie. Thanks," she said, smiling. "How'd she do, Hector?"

He laughed and pointed his spatula at Mary. "You should hire this little gal full-time. She did a great job, and she didn't get bored by my stories. *Ella es muy buena trabajadora.*"

"He says you're a very good worker. Seems you've made another fan," Mary said as she held out her hand for my apron. "I guess we'll just have to add Hector to your list of conquests."

There was a tone in her voice that took me by surprise. I looked carefully at her but couldn't detect anything unfriendly in her face. I decided she must be joking and shrugged it off.

I thanked Hector and left the kitchen. The main room had emptied to only a few people. Sam stood near the kitchen door.

"Where'd everyone go?" I asked him.

"We were able to clear enough of Main Street so folks had a chance to get home. 'Course the side streets are still bad, but almost everyone decided to chance it. A few of the guys followed behind some of the cars just to make sure everyone made it home safely."

I looked out the window to see the street definitely looking better. The cleared area was just a little bigger than one lane. "What if two great big vehicles meet each other going opposite directions?"

"Then someone better turn around. Leave it to you to find the fly in the ointment."

"How in the world did you guys accomplish all this?"

He shrugged. "Besides a few of us who have our own snow-plows, Joe has a couple of small plows, and Paul keeps one in the storage shed behind his store. It's not in great shape, but it does the job. Boy, it's a lot of work, though." He rubbed the side of his face. "I'm really tired. Do you think we could sit here a bit and grab a sandwich before we head home?"

I had to admit that all that cooking had made me a bit weary as well. And all that food had stirred up my appetite even though we'd had a fairly substantial breakfast. We sat down at a nearby table. I glanced around to see if we were in earshot of anyone else. "What did John say when you called him?"

Sam shook his head. "I couldn't reach him. The phone just rang and rang. Either he's not home or the storm has caused some trouble on the lines."

"Oh, Sam. What if he comes to town not knowing what's happened?"

"There's nothing I can do about it, Grace. We'll try him again from my house. Maybe we'll get through."

Just then Mary came out of the kitchen. "I thought you two were leaving."

Sam explained his need for food, and before long we were eating. Sam had a hot roast beef sandwich, but I had a stack of pancakes. Watching those light, puffy rounds of dough brown and sizzle on the grill had given me a real desire for a stack of my own. I wasn't disappointed.

"This is your second breakfast," Sam noted. "What's for dinner? Cereal?"

I waved my fork at him. "Maybe. What business is it of yours, bub?"

"Absolutely none," he replied with his mouth full of roast beef. "Your dietary dilemma is your own."

"Oh, thanks."

Mary walked over to the table with a frown on her face. "Have you heard the weather report?" she asked.

We both shook our heads. She aimed the remote control in her hand toward the small TV mounted on the wall near the counter. A man from the Weather Channel had a big map behind him with a large white and pink mass displayed in the middle of the country. And Kansas was in its path. A few minutes into the broadcast, the weariness in Sam's face turned to concern and he stopped eating. When the forecast was over, Mary lowered the volume.

"Looks like we're in for another round," she said.

"Worse than this one," Sam said. "I'm afraid the work we did on the streets will only last a few more hours before it's completely covered up."

"What do we do?" I asked.

"You all get out of here as soon as possible," Mary said. "I don't mind being an impromptu boardinghouse for one night, but I'm not looking to do it again."

"We need to get the word out," I told them. "What about all the people without TVs? How will they know what's coming?"

Mary smiled. "That's nice of you to think of them, but this isn't our first big storm. The Mennonite people take care of each other. A warning will be passed around faster than you can imagine."

I wanted to feel reassured by her words, but I didn't. "Sam, at least call Abel. Okay?"

"Sure. Can I use the phone again, Mary?" he asked.

"You can use the phone whenever you want. You don't have to ask." She took off toward the kitchen.

Sam went to make the call while I thought about being snowed in at home. With the electricity being so unreliable, was it a good idea? I didn't need to worry. When Sam came back, he told me he'd reached Abel, and sure enough, as Mary had said, the news was already being spread throughout the Mennonite community that a big snow was coming. He assured Sam that everyone would be fine.

"Now that we've taken care of that," Sam said, pulling on his coat, "let's get out of here. I'll take you to your house to get Snickle and some clothes, but you're coming home with me. I don't want to worry about you alone in that old house, not sure if you have electricity. There's some wood for the fire, but not enough to last out a long period if it comes to that."

I breathed a sigh of relief. "Thanks. I was hoping you'd offer."

"I've already called Sweetie to tell her you're coming. She's thrilled." He shook his head. "She comes off like a tough old bird, but she's more tender than most people think. And she loves you, Grace. Very much."

"I know she does, and I love her, too."

He held out my coat. I quickly took a couple more bites of my pancakes then stuck my arms in my coat sleeves and grabbed my purse. Before we left, Sam checked with the few remaining customers, making sure they had a way home or a place to go. When he was satisfied everyone was okay, we left the restaurant.

Sure enough, my Volkswagen was uncovered from its snowy tomb. "Can I drive it home?" I asked. "I really don't want to leave it here."

"Okay. I'll follow behind you."

As I walked toward my car, I noticed Gabe's buggy was gone. "So Gabe and Sarah got out okay," I said. "Did you see them go?"

"Yeah, I sure did. Gabe didn't acknowledge me, and Sarah looked absolutely miserable."

"Can we drive past John's on the way home and tell him what's going on?"

Sam shook his head. "That storm could hit anytime. We just can't. Not now. As soon as it's possible, I'll try to get over to his place."

I didn't like not being able to talk to John about Gabe and Sarah, but it didn't seem like there was much choice. I tried to open my car door but couldn't get the key to turn. Sam fetched some deicer out of his truck and sprayed it into the lock. A few seconds later, I was able to open my door, and soon we were on our way.

Even though Sam and the men had made the main road better, it certainly wasn't ideal. I slipped and slid so much, it felt as if my little car had skate blades instead of tires. I got stuck twice. One time I was able to get myself out; the second time Sam had to help me.

Finally we made it to my house. It didn't take long to pack a few things, but it took a little longer to catch Snickle and put him back in his carrier. Sam and I chased him around the house for at least fifteen minutes before Sam finally trapped him in the bathroom. As he carried Snickle out, the very offended feline hissed to let us know he wasn't happy to be imprisoned again.

"I hope he doesn't drive Sweetie up the wall," I told Sam as he deposited my cat in his carrier. "Being trapped for a day or two with your aunt when she's unhappy isn't a pleasant prospect."

Sam chuckled as he snapped the carrier door shut. "Around my house, that's pretty much life as usual." He handed the carrier to me while Snickle yowled with unhappiness. "Although I must admit, she's trying to change. Now when she begins to lose her temper or say something nasty about someone, she'll usually catch herself and stop." He grunted. "Makes for some rather quiet moments while she searches for something positive to say. Sometimes she just gives up, goes out on the back porch for a while, and stomps around. 'Course even though the porch is enclosed, it still gets pretty cold out there, so she doesn't stay long."

"Hey, she's trying. That's the most important thing. I respect that."

"You know what? I do, too. I'm proud of her."

"Have you told her?"

He snorted. "No, because then she gets upset and tells me I'm imagining things."

I laughed.

Sam checked around the house to make sure everything that should be off was off and everything that should be on was on, and we left. I felt bad leaving my home once again, but the idea of being snowed in alone, without heat, made me feel even worse.

I watched my house grow smaller in the rearview window as I drove away. Even though I was excited to be staying once again in Sam's big, beautiful house, I'd grown to love my simpler home with its history and old-fashioned character. I forced myself to focus on the next few days. Maybe the storm wouldn't be as bad as predicted. Maybe I'd be able to go home tomorrow. That prospect made me feel a little better. After some more slipping and sliding, we finally made it to Sam's place. I could see the road up ahead, past the big red house, and wondered just where Eric had gotten stuck. Neither Sam nor I had mentioned him since *the incident*. Of course, Eric would be back to Harmony sooner or later to work on his real estate deal, so at some point, Sam would have to face him. Hopefully things would be peaceful between them.

Sam got out of his truck and came over to my car. He took Snickle out of the backseat and grabbed my suitcase while I got the extra tote bag full of Snickle's "supplies." I giggled when I realized that his "box" would most probably end up on the back porch. Maybe the next time Sweetie got upset, her bout of bad temper would be cut even shorter. Even though I cleaned his box out every day, a litter box doesn't always remind one of springtime flowers.

As we walked through the snow up to the front porch, Sweetie waited to greet us. She grabbed me before I crossed over the threshold.

"I knowed you two would get everything sorted out," she whispered in my ear.

I gave her a quick hug. "Thanks for talking to me about his situation," I said softly. "It really helped."

She glanced toward Sam, who was already to the kitchen door. "Let's keep our little discussion between us, okay? I'm not sure how he'd take my comin' to you like that."

I didn't answer her, but I felt uncomfortable keeping secrets from Sam. At some point, I'd have to find a way to tell him about Sweetie's visit. But for now, it was enough for us to be back together. That little bit of information could wait for a while.

As Sweetie closed the door behind us and I followed Sam to the kitchen, I wondered if Sweetie's ecstasy at finding out Sam and I were back on track had caused her some kind of temporary blindness. She hadn't said a thing about Snickle. When we all reached the kitchen, though, her vision cleared.

"You brought that cat over here?" she shrieked. "Why can't that thing stay in Gracie's house? Put out some food and water. He'll be fine."

Sam leaned up against the table, Snickle's carrier at his feet. "And if the electricity goes out? Cats may be adaptive, but they're not part of the polar bear family. Wouldn't you feel bad if we'd left him there and Gracie went home to find a frozen Snickle?"

He said it tongue in cheek, but Sweetie didn't find it very funny. "Sounds like some kinda dessert," she mumbled. "Frozen Snickle."

I had to bite my lip to keep from laughing.

Sam shot his aunt an amused look. "Why don't you go unpack?" he said to me. "I want to check the weather report and see if there's an update."

"Does it matter which bedroom I take?" I directed my question to Sweetie, who grinned like the cat who ate the canary, the

Snickle controversy seemingly behind her.

"Well, let's see. I could set up a cot in the basement. 'Course it gets a little cold down there." She rubbed her chin like she was thinking. "I don't know."

"You're very funny," I said, smiling at her antics. "Think I'll take the purple room." Sweetie knew how much I loved it. I grabbed my suitcase and hurried up the stairs to the most gorgeous room I'd ever slept in. Purple violets on the wallpaper accented a beautiful lavender and gold oriental rug. Intricately carved oak furniture with a Victorian design completed the room perfectly. It was cozy, spacious, and absolutely stunning.

When I swung the door open, I found a fire burning in the fireplace and an extra quilt lying at the foot of the four-poster bed. I pulled it out and ran my hand over it. Sweetie's Christmas quilt. She'd shown it to me once when I was here for dinner. Her mother had made it for her when Sweetie was a young girl. Unfortunately, Sweetie's mother died before she could give it to her. In fact, the Christmas after her mother's death, Sweetie's father had given her the quilt. It was almost as if her mother had reached down from heaven and given her daughter a special Christmas gift. The beautiful reds and greens were so bright, the quilt looked like it had been made yesterday. In the middle was a Christmas wreath. It was the most beautiful quilt I'd ever seen.

I folded it back up. Putting the quilt on the bed was Sweetie's way of telling me she'd planned for me to stay in this room all along. I took my clothes out of the suitcase and placed them in the drawers of the huge dresser that sat against one wall. Then I unpacked my toiletries in the bathroom down the hall. I spent a few minutes enjoying the room before I headed back downstairs.

I could hear the TV in the den, so I knew Sam was watching the weather. I started to join him, but the cold outside seemed to have seeped into my bones. A hot cup of raspberry tea called my name. I'd just reached the door of the kitchen when I saw Sweetie bent over, talking to herself. I started to say something when I realized she wasn't alone. At her feet lay the much-hated Snicklefritz. He was on his back, purring to beat the band while Sweetie stroked his stomach and talked baby talk to him. I almost laughed out loud, but I held it in. No sense in embarrassing Sweetie and setting this love fest back several months.

I crept down the hall and then turned back toward the kitchen, this time stepping loudly and even emitting a couple of coughs. By the time I reached the doorway, Sweetie stood near the stove. Snickle sat nearby, staring at her with an expression that clearly demonstrated his displeasure at being suddenly deserted.

"Hope Snickle isn't bothering you," I said. "I guess Sam let him out of his carrier."

Sweetie shrugged. "Is that mangy cat in here? Had no idea it was already loose." She waved a large spoon at me. "You'd best keep that big rat catcher outta my hair. That's all I gotta say." With that she went back to stirring whatever she had on the stove.

"Okay, I'll try. Any chance for a cup of tea?"

"Sure. You want raspberry?"

"Sounds wonderful. I'm going to check on Sam, and I'll be back in a few minutes. Do you want me to take Snickle with me?"

"Nah, that's okay. Silly cat would probably just run back in here. He loves to irritate me."

"Okay. Thanks, Sweetie. I'm really sorry to cause so much trouble."

She turned to look at me, and her expression softened. "Shoot, Gracie. You ain't no trouble a'tall. I'm glad you're here." She gave Snickle a dirty look. "Me and this cat will find a way to get used to each other. Some way. Don't you worry none about it."

I gave her a smile and went to find Sam. Sure enough, he

had parked himself in front of the TV in the home's large study. Wooden bookshelves lined the walls, and a beautifully carved fireplace mantel held the only pictures I'd ever seen from Sam's childhood. Several of Hannah's paintings hung on the walls. Although this room was decorated in a heavier style than the other rooms in the house, it was still one of my favorites. Sam sat behind a huge mahogany desk, watching a flat-screen TV mounted on a nearby wall. I barely got out "What's going on?" before he shushed me.

The forecaster was pointing right at Kansas. "This system is likely to dump another ten to twelve inches on an area already reeling from a recent storm. And it could get even worse, folks. Should the system stall over northeast Kansas, some areas could see record amounts of snowfall. Unfortunately, it isn't just the amount of snow that's a concern with this storm. It's the strong winds and the possible subzero temperatures. Blizzard conditions could exist over a large part of the state. To call this storm dangerous is an understatement."

Sam picked up the remote control and turned the sound down. "Good thing you're here. This is starting to look pretty bad." His taut expression told me he was worried.

"Sam, that forecaster said something about temperatures below zero. Could that affect your trees?"

"When they're dormant, they can stand pretty cold temps, but if we hit several days below zero, we could be in trouble."

"Isn't there anything you can do?"

He nodded slowly. "We can put out smudge pots and light our burn barrels, but I don't know if it will do any good. I can only raise the ground temperature a few degrees. Hopefully it will be enough to protect the roots of the trees."

"And if you can't get it warm enough?" I was suddenly hit with a wave of apprehension. The tone in his voice was one I hadn't heard before.

"It means we lose our trees, and we'll have no crop next year."

The idea of something like that happening had never occurred to me. "Well, I'm going to pray that God will protect your trees. Psalm 91 says, 'He will call upon me, and I will answer him; I will be with him in trouble, I will deliver him and honor him.'" I smiled at Sam. "I believe that."

He stared down at the floor for a moment before raising his head to return my smile. "Guess I need to put my faith to work, huh? I have to admit that owning a farm can make a person start thinking everything depends on however the weather decides to turn. Thanks for reminding me who is really in charge."

"You're welcome." The grim weather forecast made me think of Ida, all alone in her old house. "Sam, what about Ida? We should have checked on her before we came here."

He clicked the TV off. "You're right. I didn't realize it was going to be quite this bad. I'm going to head over there now before the storm hits."

"I'll go with you."

He shook his head. "I'd rather you stay here. If she decides she'd like to come with me, I'll need room in the front seat for her and her things."

"But you could put her stuff in the truck bed."

"Can't you feel that wind? It's already blowing pretty good out there. I don't want to take the time to tie anything down, and I doubt lightweight items would stay in the truck very long."

Sure enough, a blast of air shook the house. The storm was moving in quickly. "All right. But don't take too long. I swear, if you're not back in thirty minutes, I'm coming after you."

Sam rose from his chair. "That little Slug Bug of yours wouldn't last a minute in a big wind. You'd be blown away just like Dorothy and her house." He pointed his finger at me. "You stay put. And I mean it."

I followed him to the coat closet in the hall. He quickly kissed me and left.

"Where in blazes is that boy goin'?" Sweetie asked as she came out of the kitchen. "Don't he know how bad it's fixin' to get out there?"

I explained our concerns about Ida.

"Oh my. I shoulda thought about her myself, but I thought Sam just stopped by there yesterday."

"Well, he did, but now it looks like the storm may be worse than we originally thought. He's going to try to bring her here."

She nodded. "That's a good idea. This house is built to last. Not so sure about her little place, although Sam has done a good job of keepin' things tight and weatherproof." She wiped her hands on the apron she wore on top of her overalls. "Your tea is ready. Why don't you come in and keep me company? I'm makin' a roasted chicken for dinner."

I'd just sat down at the kitchen table with my cup of tea when the phone rang. Sweetie was cutting potatoes, so I grabbed it for her.

Before I could say hello, a frantic male voice blasted through the receiver. "Sweetie? Sweetie, is that you?"

"No, this is Gracie. Sweetie's busy. What—"

"Gracie. Gracie, this is John Keystone. I need your help."

"John, I thought your phone might be out."

"It was. It's only been up a few minutes, and I'm not sure how long the connection will hold. Gracie, I need to talk to Sam. Right now."

"John, he's gone to check on Ida. He's not here. What's wrong?"

There were several seconds of silence on his end of the phone. I could hear his heavy breathing. Finally, when he spoke, his voice was shaky with emotion. "Look, Gracie, I know about what happened between Gabe and Sarah."

"We tried to call you right away, John, but—"

"That's not important now," he said, cutting me off. "Gabe is at my place. Sarah's missing."

I felt my body turn cold. "What do you mean, missing?"

"She and Gabe had an argument, and Sarah took off in the buggy. Gabe thought she might have come here and had a neighbor drive him over. Gracie, we need help looking for Sarah. Sam was the first person I called."

"Oh, John. The storm's moving in really fast. If Sarah is caught in it. . ."

"I know," he said, his voice tinged with desperation. "That's why we don't have a moment to lose."

I thought for a moment. "Do you have any idea where she might have gone?"

"No. Gabe thinks she could be on her way to your place or to town. I'm hopeful we'll find her on the road. But if not. . ."

"I'll call Sam and tell him to hurry home. He should be back by the time you get here."

"Could you also call some other people and ask for help? The more folks looking for her the better."

"Of course. I'll start calling as soon as we hang up."

"Okay, Gracie. Thanks, and—"

As a major gust of wind hit the house, I lost the phone connection. I called John's name several times, but the line was dead. I clicked the receiver, hoping the problem was on John's end. No such luck. I put the receiver down and explained the situation to Sweetie.

"Oh my lands," she said. "That little girl don't stand a chance in one of them rickety buggies. Not in this wind. And when the snow starts. . ." As if on cue, the scene outside the kitchen windows turned white. The snow was so thick and the wind so strong that it created an instant whiteout.

I began to feel panic rise inside me. "Sweetie, what are we going to do? I can't contact anyone else for help, and I can't call Sam."

She popped her chicken in the oven, took off her old apron, and came over to the table. "Well, I may not be the spiritual one in this family, but I believe we should pray, don't you?"

"I think that's a great idea." Sweetie being the one to initiate prayer was something new, but I was grateful. We certainly needed God's protection working for Sarah. We joined hands and thanked Him that His angels had charge over her. We also asked that she would be found quickly. When we finished, I felt a calm assurance drift over me.

After our prayer, I got up and went to the front door. At this point, I had two choices. Either I could wait for Sam to come back, or I could get in my car and go after him. But when I opened the door and looked outside, I knew my car didn't stand a chance. This wasn't a snowstorm; this was a bona fide blizzard. I watched the snow shriek and swoop past the house, carried by wild winds. I couldn't even see the road. Visibility was almost nothing. I'd put my trust in God to deliver Sarah, but thinking about her out there, alone in this storm, brought tears to my eyes.

I'd just decided to go back into the kitchen when I heard the sound of a motor. Through the blanket of blowing snow, Sam's truck became visible. He pulled up as close as he could to the house. His door opened and he got out, fighting against the wind, almost falling down twice, until he reached the porch. It took the both of us to get the outer door open and then hold it so the wind wouldn't break it off its hinges.

"Where's Ida?" I asked as soon as he got inside and closed the door behind us.

"Snug as a bug in a rug," he said. "She doesn't want to leave.

She's nice and warm, has plenty of food, and wants to be near Zebediah."

"What about Zeb? Will he be all right?"

Sam nodded and started to take off his coat. "I closed him inside the stable and started a small fire in the stove. As soon as things die down some, I'll go back and check on both of them again."

I grabbed him before he could completely remove his coat. "Better leave it on. Something awful has happened." I quickly filled him in on John's frantic call. As I talked, Sam's expression grew more ominous.

"It's awful out there, Grace. Sarah is in real danger. We need more people than just Gabe, John, and me out there searching for her. Have you checked the phone again? Maybe it's working."

Sweetie walked out into the hallway. "It's still deader than a doornail, son. Sorry."

Sam stared at both of us for a minute. I could almost hear the gears grinding in his head. "You said John and Gabe are on their way over here?"

"Yes. Knowing Sarah is in danger seemed to pull them together. John sounded so frightened. And I'm sure Gabe is beside himself."

Sam sighed deeply and shook his head. "All I can do is wait for them and hope they find her on the road coming here. If they do. . ."

The sound of a vehicle pulling into the driveway stopped Sam from finishing his thought. He flung the door open. John's SUV had pulled up next to Sam's truck. The driver's side door opened and John got out. He shut the door behind him with great difficulty and made his way to the front porch. Sam held the door open and struggled to close it once John was inside.

"Did you get anyone else to help us?" were the first words out of his mouth.

"The phone lines are down," Sam said. "There's just me. I take it you didn't find her on your way over here."

John's look of panic made my insides churn. "No. No sign of her." He stared wide-eyed at Sam. "What are we going to do?"

Sam buttoned up his coat and hurried to the closet to find his wool hat. He pulled it down over his ears. "We're going to go look for her. Let's take your car. It's much sturdier than my truck. We'll figure out which way to go when we get in the car."

I pushed my way past him and opened the closet door. "I'm coming with you."

"No," Sam said forcefully. "I want you to stay here. The phone might come back on. You can start calling for help."

I finished pulling on my coat and put the hood up. "Sweetie knows how to use the phone. You have no idea what you're going to find out there or how much help you'll need. I'm strong."

Sam started to say something else, but Sweetie spoke up from behind us. "You listen to that girl, son. She can help. I'll man the phones. If the line comes up, I'll start callin' everyone in this here county. Now you all get a-goin'."

I could tell Sam wanted to argue, but I had no intention of letting him leave without me. Sarah was my friend, and I was determined to find her.

Without another word, the three of us fought our way back to the SUV where Gabe waited for us. Sam held on tightly to my arm. The force of the wind almost knocked me down several times. But it wasn't just the wind. The snow hit my face like tiny needles, making it impossible to keep my eyes open. By the time I climbed into the car, I felt exhausted.

Once everyone was inside, Sam asked, "Where would she have gone, Gabe? If she didn't go to John's or Ida's or my house, what places are left?"

Sam and I sat in the backseat with John and Gabe in the

front. I couldn't see Gabe's face, but the snap of his head told me something had occurred to him.

"She told me once that she always feels safe and calm when she's in church," he said. "Maybe she'd go there."

"In this storm?" I asked incredulously. "Surely she knows Abel wouldn't be there. The church wouldn't be open."

"But it wasn't snowing when she left. We had no idea a blizzard was on its way."

John put the SUV into gear and started down the driveway. "Actually, that could be good news. If she made it to town, someone would have seen her and taken her in. Let's hope that's what happened."

We drove slowly down Faith Street. Even though the SUV was massive, it rocked back and forth when hit by strong gusts of wind.

"Watch out the windows," John said loudly. "If you see any thing that doesn't look right, whatever it is, yell. I'll stop and we'll check it out."

It was almost impossible to even make out where the road was supposed to be, let alone a buggy. But we all kept our eyes peeled as John drove slowly. Finally we reached Main Street. The only way I could tell was by the street sign, which flapped violently in the wind. John turned carefully. I prayed silently that God would let us see the buggy, that it wouldn't be totally covered by snow. We'd gone about a quarter of a mile when I thought I saw something odd several yards from the road. At first I wasn't certain. It looked like a small hill covered with snow. But then a gust of wind blew past it and uncovered something round. A wheel!

"Stop! Stop!" I hollered. "Over there. I think it's the buggy!"

John put the SUV in park. "Where?" he shouted. "I don't see—"

"Yes!" Gabe yelled. "Over there."

We all got out of the car and fought our way through the blowing snow. Sam held on to me, but once again I struggled to stay upright. I put my hand up to shield my eyes, but it didn't help. Finally we reached the buggy.

Gabe was yelling something, but I couldn't hear him over the wind. We started trying to clear the snow off the buggy, which lay on its side. Was Sarah still inside? Was she alive?

All four of us pushed the snow away, but Sarah wasn't there. During a lull in the wind, I heard Sam say something about the horse.

Gabe checked the harness. "It's been undone," he shouted over the howling wind. "Sarah must have let her loose."

I knew that horses usually try to find their way home when they get away from their owners. So at least Sarah had the presence of mind to unhook Molasses. But what happened after that?

Gabe began digging through the snow like a madman. If Sarah was anywhere near. . . I pulled on Sam's arm. "There!" I shouted. About thirty or forty yards from us, something lay in the snow. It was almost completely covered, but there was a strip of black showing through. Sam grabbed Gabe and John and pointed. Then he motioned for me to stay where I was. This time I didn't argue. I tried to watch the men, but every time the wind blew, I had to put my head down and wait for it to stop. The next time I looked up, I saw John lift something out of the snow and start back toward me. Sarah! As they got closer, I could see her still, white face. Tears streamed down my cheeks. Was she alive? Were we too late? Sam grabbed me and pulled me to the SUV. The wind, which had died down long enough for me to see Sarah in the snow, suddenly regained strength. If Sam hadn't taken my arm, I would have fallen backward.

John gently laid Sarah's body in the backseat. Then he scooted in, putting her head on his lap. Gabe ran around to the other side and got in. Sam pushed me toward the passenger door and helped me into the front seat. Then he got behind the wheel. I turned around in my seat, wanting to see if Sarah was breathing. Thankfully I could see her chest rise and fall—slowly.

"It's going to be almost impossible to get her to Sunrise," Sam said to the two worried men. "The storm is getting worse. Where do you want me to go?"

"Drive back to your house," John said in a controlled voice that belied the distraught look on his face.

"Wait a minute," Gabe barked. "I'm her father. I'll decide what we do."

"Gabe," John said in a no-nonsense tone, "you've forgotten I'm a doctor. We don't need to go to Sunrise. I can help her." He stared at Gabe intensely. "I know you disapprove of Sarah and me. And I know you probably blame me for this, but we have to put our differences aside now. Sarah needs us. Both of us. I'm going to ask you to trust me. I know that sounds crazy with everything that's happened, but I know what I'm doing. I'm actually an excellent doctor. And whether you believe this or not, I love your daughter. Very much."

Both men kept their eyes locked on each other for what seemed like minutes. I could feel the thick emotion between them. Finally Gabe broke the staring contest.

"All right. But when Sarah is well. . ."

"When Sarah is well, we'll talk. I promise."

Gabe fell silent, and John apparently took it as a sign of his agreement.

"There's a blanket in the back of the car. I want you to lean over the seat and get it." Gabe did as John asked without hesitation.

Sam, who'd been struggling to turn the SUV around on the slick, snow-packed road, finally got us going in the right direction.

491

I watched carefully, trying to help him navigate in zero visibility. I could hear John giving Gabe instructions in the backseat to elevate Sarah's legs. When I turned around to check on them, Sarah was fully covered by a thick, heavy blanket. John had his hand on her wrist while he looked at his wristwatch. He kept saying Sarah's name, trying to get her to wake up.

Suddenly I felt the SUV slip, and we went into a spin. It happened so fast, all I could do was grab the handgrip over the door with one hand and put my other hand on the dashboard. Thankfully Sam didn't panic and brought the large vehicle under control.

"Sorry," he said. "I'm doing the best I can."

"It's fine, Sam," John said soothingly. "You're doing great, and so is Sarah. Just getting her into a warm car is helping to bring up her temperature. Gracie?"

I cranked my head around again, still shaken by the unexpected slide. "Yes?"

"When we get to Sam's, we need to take Sarah into bed as soon as possible. I need you and Sweetie to get these clothes off her. She needs something warm and dry. Can you do that?"

"Yes."

"Maybe I should take off her shoes now and rub her feet," Gabe said.

John shook his head. "No. That's one of the worst things you can do. If the tissue is damaged, rubbing it will make it worse. We need to get her warm—outside and inside. Gracie, is there a room with a fireplace?"

"Yes. She can stay in my room."

"Okay. Thanks."

"Is there anything we can do for her now?" her father asked. I could hear the apprehension in his voice.

"We're doing everything possible," John said. "Her respiration is good. I think she'll be fine. I just can't tell about frostbite until

I can get a better look at her."

"John?" Sarah's voice was so soft at first I almost mistook it for the sound of the wind rushing past the car. "Are you really here?"

I turned around again. Man, I was going to have the mother of all neck aches by the time we got back to Sam's. Sarah's eyes were open. They looked almost black against her pale skin. "What happened?" she asked weakly.

"You went out in the buggy," John said, gently stroking her face. "That was a foolish thing to do, Sarah. You could have been seriously hurt."

"I–I'm sorry. It's just that Papa. . .Papa said I couldn't see you anymore. I'm so sorry. Papa will be so mad."

"Sarah, I'm here," Gabe said. "And I'm not mad. I'm just grateful. Grateful you're alive."

Sarah raised her head to find her father holding her feet, tears on his face. "Papa. Why. . .why are you here? Oh my. Please forgive me. It was wrong of me to leave in anger. I just wanted time to think. I had no idea the storm would come up so quickly."

"There is nothing to forgive, daughter. I'm so thankful to the Lord that He kept you safe. I shouldn't have been so harsh with you. This is all my fault."

"No," she replied in a weak voice. "I made the decision. I took the buggy. No one else is to blame."

"Okay," John said. "Let's not worry about whose fault this is right now. Let's just be grateful we found you. I want you to be quiet and rest. We'll be at Sam's soon, and we'll get you warmed up and feeling like yourself again."

"I would love some hot tea. I'm so cold."

"I'm sure we can find you some tea. Now rest."

She closed her eyes again. Within seconds her breathing deepened. Although she was still abnormally pale, at least she'd started to lose the corpselike pallor she'd had when we found her.

It took us forty-five minutes to make a trip that should have taken ten, but we finally made it back to the house. Sweetie held the door open as we struggled to get up the steps.

"Land sakes alive," she said when she saw Sarah. "You found her. Is the child all right?"

"We need to warm her up, Sweetie," I said when we got inside. "We're taking her to the purple room. Can you stoke the fire in there? And make her some hot tea?"

"You bet."

I led John up the stairs with Sarah in his arms. Gabe followed behind us. Sweetie added some logs to the fireplace while John carried Sarah to the bed.

"You two go downstairs while I get these wet things off her," I told them. "I'll call you when she's situated."

They nodded and left the room. Sarah helped me remove the heavy, wet garments. Sweetie, who had the fire blazing, took them from me.

"I'll get this stuff washed and dried," she said.

I got a heavy flannel nightgown from the dresser drawer and helped Sarah into it. Throughout the entire process, she didn't say a word. I removed the quilt on top of the bed that had gotten wet from melting snow and unfolded Sweetie's beautiful Christmas quilt. Before long, I had Sarah under the covers, dry and warm. I got a towel from the bathroom and undid her braids. Then I dried her hair and brushed it out. With her long black hair, pale skin, and dark eyes, she reminded me of a picture in one of my books as a child. She was the spitting image of Snow White. As I finished brushing her hair, she grabbed my hand. Her grip was weak and her fingers were still cold.

"Thank you," she said in her small voice. "I'm so grateful for everything you're doing for me. I'm so sorry to have caused all this trouble."

I put my hand over hers. "It's no trouble, Sarah. This is what friends do." I noticed she flinched when I touched her skin. "Does your hand hurt?"

She nodded and her eyes filled with tears. "They both sting. And my feet." She wiped a tear that snaked down her cheek. "I hope Molasses made it back to her stable. I had to release her. I couldn't get the buggy right side up. I hoped she would find her way back and alert Papa there was a problem."

"I'm sure she's fine. But Sarah, why didn't you stay in the buggy? Why were you in that field?"

"I thought I could make it to your house," she whispered. "But I got so turned around. When the wind blew, I couldn't see anything. I'm still not sure how you found me."

"God led us to you. I'm convinced of it. There's no other explanation."

Another tear ran down her cheek. "He is too good to me. I don't deserve. . ."

"I don't believe God loves us because we deserve it. I think He loves us because that's just who He is. I find comfort knowing His love isn't based on my goodness. . .or lack of it."

She brushed a strand of dark hair that fell across her face. "You're right, Gracie." She gave me a quick smile. "Your name fits you. You seem to really understand the grace of God. Sometimes I have a hard time comprehending how God can love me so much no matter what I do."

I wanted to explain to Sarah that having a father who'd spent so many years being bitter toward people and God would certainly make it difficult for her to grasp the concept of unconditional love and forgiveness, but I held my tongue.

"Do you think Papa will ever forgive me?" The plaintive tone of her voice tore at my heart.

"Sarah, believe me, your father isn't thinking about anything except how much he loves you and how badly he needed to find you."

"But after his relief lifts. . ." She grabbed my arm, wincing at the pain in her fingers. "How did he treat John? Did they have words? What—"

"Whoa. They were both too worried about you to be upset with each other. You might be surprised. Maybe this situation will bring them together."

The sound of angry, raised voices took the wind out of my hopeful declaration. "You stay in bed," I told Sarah, whose eyes had grown large with fear. "Let me see what's going on. I'll be right back."

I closed the door gently behind me and hurried down the stairs. I followed the sound of shouting to the kitchen. Sweetie was near the stove, holding a pot of coffee, her mouth hanging open. Sam stood between Gabe and John, one hand on each man's chest.

"If your relationship with my daughter is as innocent as you make it out to be," Gabe said loudly, his face red with anger, "why did you hide in the shadows? Why did you skulk around behind my back?"

"Because your daughter asked me to keep my feelings for her secret. She was afraid to tell you. Afraid of your reaction. You caused us to sneak around. I hated it. I told Sarah more than once that we should tell you the truth, but her fear of you—"

"Fear? What are you talking about? My daughter is not afraid of me!"

John opened his mouth to lob back what promised to be another accusation, but I shouted at them to shut up. They turned to look at me, their faces masks of resentment.

"What are you doing?" I said crossly. "Sarah can hear you yelling at each other, and she doesn't need that right now."

Gabe pointed a finger at John. "If he'd stayed away from her, she wouldn't be suffering now. She'd be safe at home where she belongs."

"What are you talking about?" John's fierce scowl signaled their argument was far from over. "It's the way you reacted when you found out about us that drove her to run away. This entire situation is your fault."

Gabe took a menacing step toward John, and Sam quickly pushed him back. "Stop it," he said sharply. "Grace is right. Sarah doesn't need to listen to you two go at each other. Sarah made the decision to jump in that buggy. She's an adult." He glared at Gabe. "That's something you don't seem to get." His voice softened slightly. "I know you've been hurt, Gabe. But Sarah isn't your ex-wife. And John isn't the man she took off with. These are two good people who fell in love. That's all."

Gabe's face blanched. "I know that. Sarah isn't anything like Greta. She loves God. Greta only loved what she thought the world could give her."

"Then why do you treat Sarah the way you do?" I asked. "Why don't you give her a chance to prove she is capable of making good decisions?"

Gabe stepped away from Sam and dropped into one of the chairs at the kitchen table. "I do trust her, but she can't have a relationship with someone outside our church. It would be an unequal yoking. I don't want her to make a choice that will only hurt her in the end. Sarah's faith is everything to her." He fastened his eyes on John. "If you really knew my daughter, you'd know that. If she betrays her faith, she will be miserable. It will haunt her the rest of her life."

"I would never ask her to give up her faith," John said forcefully. "Why would you think that? I realize it's part of who she is."

"Not part," Gabe replied. "Everything. If she married you, she would be turning her back on scripture. It is a commandment not to be unequally yoked."

John slid into a chair next to Gabe. "Look, I may not go to church, but I do believe in God. Anyway, I think I do. I'll go to church with her. Maybe her faith will rub off on me. But it has to be real. I can't pretend to believe the way she does. It would not only dishonor her; it would dishonor God."

I sat down across from the two of them. "You're both good and decent men," I said tentatively. "I hope you can at least see that about each other. And if Sarah and John should take their relationship further, I pray you can have peace with it, Gabe. Going back to the way things were—locking Sarah away—not allowing her to have a life. That's not the right way to do things."

"I know that now," he said. "Even if I wanted to, Sarah wouldn't allow it. She showed me that clearly today." He covered his face with his hands. "I'm so afraid for her," he said brokenly. "Making this decision will bring her so much pain, and I can't stop it."

"I think you can't stand the thought of losing her." John's comment seemed to hit home.

"You're right," Gabe said, taking his hands from his face. "I'm afraid to be alone, but I'd do it for Sarah, gladly, if I thought she would be happy. But believe me, marrying outside her faith won't do that. It will destroy her."

"Papa!" Sarah's voice was so faint we almost didn't hear her. She stood in the doorway, holding on to the frame for support. Her long black hair cascaded past her shoulders and fell across her chest. In my white nightgown, the contrast was startling. Even though she was still abnormally pale, she had never looked more beautiful. I heard John's sharp intake of breath.

"Daughter, what are you doing out of bed?" Gabe rose to his feet and started toward her, but Sarah held up her hand for him to stop. "Papa, I must say something. Then I will go back to bed."

She gazed at John, who seemed almost transfixed by her presence. There was no mistaking the naked emotion in her face. It was obvious she loved him. That's why her next words took me by surprise.

"I'm sorry, John, but my father is right. There's no future for us. It's best that we end things. Besides, our relationship was never that serious. You never even kissed me." With that, she turned and started to leave the kitchen. I noticed that she faltered, obviously still weak and unsteady.

I jumped up to assist her. "You all stay here," I ordered the three men. "I'll help Sarah back to bed."

I slid my arm around her tiny waist while she leaned against me. A few times as we climbed the stairs, I worried she would fall. Finally I got her back into bed. Although she tried valiantly to look calm and resolute, I could feel her body tremble as I pulled the covers over her. Before she turned her head away from me, I saw the stark pain on her face.

"You love him very much, don't you?"

No answer.

"Sarah, you can talk to me. Really. I won't repeat anything you tell me."

Her small body began to heave with sobs. I sat down on the bed next to her and opened my arms. She sat up and wrapped her slender arms around my neck. I could feel her tears falling on my skin.

"Oh, Gracie. I do. I love him more than I can bear."

"Then why? Why would you say what you did? Surely this can be worked out."

She shook her head. "No. No, it can't." She let go of my neck and put her head back on the pillow, tears running down the sides of her face. "You heard Papa. He is afraid to be alone." She reached for my hand, and I gave it to her. Her grip was surprisingly strong.

"My father raised me after Mother left. It was so hard for him, Gracie. I know he was devastated by her betrayal. He loved her so. But he kept going for me." Sarah stared at the ceiling, her expression resolute. "What if John and I wanted to marry? I would have to leave home. I will not do that to my father."

I started to protest, to tell her that she couldn't spend the rest of her life taking care of Gabe, but she put her fingers up to my mouth, softly touching my lips.

"Hush, dear friend. I know what you would say. I know the Bible talks about leaving our mothers and fathers and cleaving to our husbands. But I cannot leave him. Not yet. Not until I know he'll be okay. Right or wrong, I know it's what I must do." She smiled sadly. "Maybe the day will come when things change. I don't know. But I can't build happiness on my father's pain. It's impossible." Her eyes searched mine. "Do you understand—even a little?"

I had to bite my lip to keep the words I wanted to say inside. Sarah deserved a life. Her mother's abandonment had hurt her, too. Her father certainly wasn't the only victim. Yet as I gazed into her face, I knew she spoke the truth. Sarah didn't have it in her to hurt Gabe. With her gentle spirit and loving nature, to do so would rip her to shreds. "I understand, Sarah. I'll support you, whatever you decide." I squeezed her hand and saw her wince. "Are your hands still sore?"

She nodded. "And my feet. They are very painful. I didn't want to say anything."

I stood up. "I need to check with John. He should know."

A look of terror washed over her features. "Please, Gracie. Don't let him come here. Not now. I—"

"Nonsense." John's sharp retort startled me. I turned to find him standing in the doorway, frowning at us. "I'm still the doctor here. No matter what else, I intend to take care of your physical needs, Sarah." He came into the room, Gabe close on his heels. Before approaching the bed where Sarah lay, he stopped and looked at her, almost expressionless. "I've talked to your father. I want you to know that I agree with you. Whatever we thought we had is over. I see now that it was never meant to be. I was fooling myself to think that someone like you could love me. And it was wrong to put you in a position where you would have to choose between your religion or me. You can't give up your beliefs, and I can't manufacture beliefs I simply don't have. So I guess that makes our choice clear. Now I want to look at your hands and feet. As your doctor. Is that all right with you?"

Sarah was so still her nod was almost imperceptible. Her dark eyes looked huge in her delicate face, and I could only imagine her emotions as John approached her. He sat on the side of her bed and took her hands in his, turning them over and asking questions. Her response was either "Yes" or "No" to each inquiry. John moved to the end of the bed and uncovered her feet, asking her the same questions. Finally he stood up.

"Everything is fine. The tingling and pain are actually signs the skin is recovering. When you get her home, Gabe, just let her rest, and make sure she has plenty of fluids. She'll recover completely."

"Thank you, John. For everything." Gabe walked over to John and held out his hand. John took it and covered it with his other one.

"The one thing I ask of you," John said in a husky voice, "is that you don't pull back from your friends again. It isn't right. For you or for Sarah. Please don't let my selfishness cause you to cut yourself off from us again."

Gabe's eyes widened, and he placed his other hand over John's. "I promise. I don't want that for either one of us. I'm sorry for the way I acted. I was just so hurt. . .and afraid."

"I know exactly how that feels. But this town, and these people. . .well, they changed me. I want you and Sarah to be happy here, too."

"You have my word."

I couldn't stop the tears that filled my eyes. I glanced over at Sam, who stood in the doorway watching. He had to wipe his own eyes. But my joy at seeing these two men find reconciliation was marred by the pain I knew Sarah and John felt. Were they doing the right thing? I couldn't be sure, but one thing Gabe said made sense. Sarah did love God. How could she become involved with a man who didn't? I watched as Sarah smiled, seeing her father and John make peace, yet the sadness in her eyes caught at my heart.

Sweetie's shrill voice suddenly disrupted the quiet atmosphere. I looked over at Sam. "What's she yelling about?"

He shrugged. "Hold on. I'll check." He stuck his head out the door and called loudly to his aunt.

I heard her clomping up the stairs. "I said, there's someone outside. Looks like Dan and Dale Scheidler."

"I'm surprised they got through," Gabe said. He looked toward his daughter. "Will you be all right for a few minutes?"

"I'm fine, Papa. Go ahead." The men followed Sweetie down the stairs.

I picked up the teapot on the tray by Sarah's bed. "I'm going to get you more tea. This is lukewarm. I'll be right back."

"Thank you," Sarah said. "But to be honest, I'm tired. I think I'd like to sleep for a while if it's okay."

I wasn't certain whether she wanted to be alone because she was sleepy or if she just needed some time to cry, but either way, I understood. "Okay. I'll come back and check on you in an hour or so." I patted her shoulder. "You get some rest."

She nodded and turned away from me, her long dark hair in

stark contrast to the white bedspread covering her. Once again she reminded me of Snow White. I couldn't help but wonder if this beautiful princess would ever experience love's first kiss. I left the room and closed the door quietly behind me.

As I came down the stairs, I heard the sound of excited voices. Dale and Dan had just entered the foyer when I heard Dan exclaim, "We were trying to clear some of the roads when we found something."

As I joined the group gathered around the two brothers, Sam said, "You found something? What are you talking about?"

"We found a body, Sam," Dale said in a somber voice. "It's Rand McAllister. Dead as a doornail."

Chapter Nine

W hat do you mean dead?" Sweetie's nonsensical question only echoed the shock I felt at Dale's stunning announcement.

The brothers stared at her like she was demented. "Dead, Sweetie," Dale said. "Can't put it any other way. He's frozen stiff as a board." He fixed his gaze on John. "Glad to find you here, John. Heard you used to be a doctor. Can you take him off our hands?"

John's mouth dropped open. "Take him off your hands? And just what would you like me to do with him?"

Dale shrugged. "Have no idea, but he can't stay with us."

"We need to call the police," I said. "Or the sheriff. Or someone."

"Good idea," Sam said, "except the phones don't work, and I doubt they could get here anyway."

"The phones in town were okay earlier," Dan said. "When we get back, we'll call the sheriff. It may take a while though. It's mighty slow going. It could be a few hours before we can contact anyone."

"And we can't guarantee the phones will be working by the time we get there," Dale interjected. He looked at his brother.

"Doesn't Joe Loudermilk still have that old CB radio he plays with in his back room?"

Dan shrugged. "I have no idea, but if the phones are out, we could ask him about it."

"But Joe's probably at home," I said. "How will you get into his store?"

The brothers both frowned at me. "We just take the key off the hook by the door."

Living in Harmony took some getting used to. Obviously I hadn't completely retrained my thinking from the way things are done in the big city. "Sorry. Guess I hadn't thought it out."

The brothers nodded at me simultaneously. For a second, I was reminded of Tweedledum and Tweedledee from *Through the Looking Glass*. I shook my head. Second time today I'd compared someone who lived in Harmony with a fictional character. Somehow it just seemed appropriate.

"Well, if you men could help us get Rand off the roof of the tractor cab—"

"He's on the roof?" I asked, aghast. "Why is he on the roof?"

There was the look again. "Just where would you have put him?" Dale asked while Dan nodded briskly. "Guess we could have dragged him along behind us, but it didn't seem. . .well. . .respectful. Thank goodness we had some rope with us. We just strapped him up there and drove to the closest farm." The brothers looked at each other. "Seemed like the polite way of handling the situation."

"Polite? Tying someone on the roof of a tractor?" I was obviously out of my league, so I just gave up. "Now what?" My question was directed to Sam, but Sweetie answered.

"Just put him in the barn," she ordered. "On the big wood table in the middle. And for cryin' out loud, cover him up with a horse blanket or somethin'."

The brothers nodded together again. "Good idea," Dan said.

"He'll stay nice and cold out there until someone comes for him."

"What about his family?" I said. "Someone needs to let them know."

Once again the brothers shook their heads at the same time. "Too far from here. Rand's place is halfway to Sunrise. It may be some time before we can get word to them."

"We'll help you take care of Rand," Gabe said. "Let us grab our coats and meet you outside."

Sweetie trotted quickly toward the front door, probably wanting to see Rand McAllister hog-tied to the top of a tractor cab. I, on the other hand, didn't need that image in my mind. I turned the other way. Sam followed me to the kitchen.

"Guess I'll go with them." His expression made it clear he wasn't enthusiastic about the proposition. But there really wasn't much choice. Moving frozen dead bodies was definitely men's work. At that moment, I was thoroughly grateful to be female. He returned my smile with a sickly one of his own and left the room to help the men take care of their macabre business.

As I fixed myself a cup of hot tea, I wondered how Rand got caught outside in the middle of a storm. Sam had told me more than once that snowstorms could be brutal in this part of the country. Surely Rand knew that. Maybe his car broke down, and he tried to go somewhere for help, just like Sarah. I felt bad for him and for his family. He'd been a very unpleasant man, but anytime someone dies tragically, it's a sad event.

I sipped my tea while Sweetie spent her time checking her chicken and rolling out dough for biscuits. She didn't share what she'd seen when she rushed out to see Rand's body, and I didn't ask. Actually, we didn't talk much at all about anything. It had been an extremely stressful day. I was exhausted, mentally and physically. Sweetie must have felt it as well. For her to spend thirty minutes in silence was something that didn't happen very often.

Finally Sam, John, and Gabe came back into the house. Their expressions were grim.

I stood up when they entered the kitchen. "Is. . .is everything. . .um, taken care of?"

Sam and John sat down in the chairs at the kitchen table while Gabe leaned up against the wall near the door.

"Well, he's in the barn," Sam said. "It doesn't feel quite. . .proper. But I can't think of anything else we could possibly do. Hopefully Dale and Dan will be able to contact the sheriff." He shrugged. "I have no idea how long it'll be until he's picked up."

"John, did you, um, look at him? Did he die of exposure?"

John shook his head. "It's impossible to be certain without a thorough examination, but it's a very good possibility. One thing I can tell you for certain, though. He's been dead awhile." He gestured toward the window. "This storm didn't do it. My guess is he got drunk and lost his way. Wandered off and passed out. He probably never woke up."

"So he was already dead by the time this storm hit?" I asked.

"I'm just guessing, but I think it's the reason he didn't show up for his meeting with Eric Thursday night."

I frowned. "I know Rand hasn't lived in Harmony as long as the rest of you, but he's been here through several winters, right?"

The men nodded in unison.

"You're wondering how he could get caught out in a storm like this." Gabe said it matter-of-factly. "I think John's right. He must have been three sheets to the wind. That's the only way he'd be wandering around outside in the winter. He knew better."

"I hope you're right," Sam said. "I'd hate to think his wife and daughter got stranded somewhere, and he was out looking for them."

I couldn't hold back a gasp. "Oh, Sam. Surely not."

He rubbed his hand over his face. "Let's not worry about it yet.

My guess is that John and Gabe have it right. Man, I sure wish the phones were working so we could check on them, though."

Great. One more thing to think about. I'm a snow nut. Love it. But even I have my limits. This blizzard had exceeded them. First Sarah got stranded; now Rand was found dead. Jessica's sad face floated through my mind. I said a silent prayer for her protection as well as her mother's.

"Don't start worryin' about that girl," Sweetie said, breaking her silence. "Her mama's too smart to let her run around outside in nasty weather." She pointed her spatula at us. "Look, I know I get cranky and say things I shouldn't about people, and I know it's wrong to speak ill of the dead, but what no one is sayin' here is that Rand McAllister didn't have the sense God gave a duck. Makin' bad choices was par for the course with that man. Seems to me his last bad choice was. . ." Sweetie stared at us for a moment. "Well. . .his last bad choice. It's an awful tragedy, but now it's our job to help take care of his family. Isn't that what the Good Book says to do? What was that scripture about takin' care of widows and orphans?"

"James 1:27," Gabe said. " 'Pure religion and undefiled before God and the Father is this, To visit the fatherless and widows in their affliction, and to keep himself unspotted from the world.' "

"That's it," Sweetie announced triumphantly. "Boy, I used to think religion was just a bunch of rules and regulations. When I read that scripture, I saw God in a whole new way."

"Wait a minute," John said. "You people believe in more than just helping widows and orphans. I thought you loved your religion."

"We love God," I said gently. "Religion is a set of beliefs, but it isn't necessarily a relationship with God. Jesus had some pretty harsh things to say about the religious leaders of His day."

"God is love," Sam said. "Religion can actually push love out while it tries to enforce rules and restrictions on people." He looked down at Buddy, who was curled up at his feet. Snickle leaned up against his old friend. Both snoozed away, oblivious to life's trials. "It's kind of like having a pet. I can try to train him through rules and punishment. Or I can love him. Develop a relationship of trust. Buddy would do anything I asked him to do because he trusts me so much. It would never occur to him that I would lead him in a direction that would hurt him. It's kind of like that with God. He wants us to obey Him because we love Him and trust Him so much. Not because we're trying to follow a set of regulations." He sneaked a quick look at us, and his face flushed pink. "That's probably an overly simple explanation. . . ."

"It's a perfect explanation," Gabe said. "Take it from someone who's been doing it the wrong way." His gaze drifted toward the hallway stairs. "I've spent too much time trying to teach Sarah the rules. Not enough time showing her God's love." He smiled at John. "I still don't believe you and Sarah should be together, son. But I like you very much. I hope we can be good friends."

"That would make me very happy," John said. He shook his head. "You people are something else. I've spent a little time around religious people, and it made me want to run away. But there's something different about Harmony. About most of the people. I would hate to leave here."

"Why, there ain't no way you're gonna get outta here, John Keystone," Sweetie said. "You're a part of us now. Besides, we're still hopin' you'll take up doctorin' again. Sure could use you around here. Shoot. We can get all the meat we want in Sunrise."

He chuckled. "I don't know whether to be touched or offended, Sweetie. I think you just told me my business is inconsequential."

Everyone laughed. Watching John and Gabe together seemed to be a miracle happening right in front of me. I'd been afraid finding out about Sarah and John might send Gabe back to his former temperament. Thankfully it hadn't. If John hadn't backed off, perhaps things would be different. But at least for now, there was peace. And that was good enough for tonight.

While the rest of us got cleaned up for dinner, Gabe slipped away to tell Sarah about Rand McAllister. I hated that she would be faced with another unpleasant situation, but when Gabe came downstairs, he assured us that she had taken the news as well as could be expected.

Sweetie served us a delicious meal. Sam told us that Dan and Dale planned to come back in the morning. The men would be helping others dig us out from the almost two feet of snow that had been dumped on us. The snowfall totals were bad enough, but the winds had created monster snowdrifts that had trapped people in their homes and on their farms. Sam promised me Ida's would be the first place they'd check.

"I guess we'll know in the morning if the Scheidler brothers got through to the sheriff," I said.

He nodded while chewing a big bite of roasted potatoes and gravy. "Not sure how long it will be before he can get here after he gets the news. Council Grove got hit just as bad as we did."

I swallowed hard. "You—you mean we might have to keep Rand in the barn indefinitely?"

He raised his eyebrows. "I don't like it either. But we might as well get used to the idea. He's not going anywhere for a while."

"I wonder if this will change things in regard to that retirement community," John said. "With Rand dead, I guess Thelma could sell their farm to Eric and his investors."

I almost dropped my fork. "Wow. I'd almost completely forgotten about that with everything that's been happening." I sighed. "I sure don't look forward to watching everyone get all riled up again."

"Me neither," Sweetie said as she passed around her hot rolls for a second round. "Never seen people snipin' at each other like they were at that town meetin'. And I ain't interested in seein' it again. Wish that Eric Beck had never come to this town. Ain't brought nothin' but trouble."

"That's not fair," I retorted. "Eric wanted to do something to help Harmony. Rand is the one who caused all the trouble. Besides, you forget that working on that project was supposed to be my bread and butter. Without the work, I don't know if I can stay here."

"Don't say that," Sweetie snapped. "I told you we'd take care of you. You ain't got nothin' to worry about. I could feed this whole town, let alone a little, skinny girl."

"Sweetie, you're a doll," I said. "But you're forgetting things like utilities." Sam started to say something, but I quickly stopped him. "Before you tell me you'll cover my utilities, let me make it clear that I would never accept that. Besides, I also have student loans that have to be repaid. The truth is, unless I can get some fairly steady freelance work, I won't have a choice. I'll have to move back to Wichita."

Sweetie snorted. "It ain't gonna happen, and that's all I want to hear about that now. For land's sakes, been enough drama around here to last a lifetime. Let's not stir up any more worries tonight. How about a game of checkers after we eat?"

"You all go ahead," I said. "I'm going to take some dinner up to Sarah and see if she feels like coming downstairs."

"Don't be silly, Gracie," Gabe said. "I'll take care of my daughter."

I shook my head at him. "I think you'd better relax this evening and get to bed early. Sounds like you guys will be working pretty hard the next few days. Besides, Sarah's my closest female friend here. I like taking care of her."

"Come on, Gabe," John said good-naturedly. "Or maybe you're afraid I'll beat you at checkers."

Gabe laughed. "You know something funny? Games were frowned upon when I was a boy. Competition and all that. But a neighbor taught my brother and me how to play checkers. We made our own board and hid it in the barn. We made pieces out of our dad's metal washers. And we got pretty good." He looked over at me. "Tell Sarah I'll check on her later if she doesn't feel like joining us."

"I will." I got up from the table and took an extra plate from the cupboard. Then I filled it with servings of Sweetie's fine food.

Sam offered to help Sweetie clean up, but she shooed everyone out of the kitchen. "Won't take me more than a few minutes to straighten this mess up. Then I'll come in and play a round of checkers with whoever's ahead." She grinned at the assembled men. "Ain't no one alive able to best me at checkers. You all are on notice."

Sam grinned. "You might think she's kidding, but I assure you she's not."

"Well, let's do the best we can until she comes after us," John said.

The men kept teasing each other good-naturedly as Sam got the checkerboard and checkers out of the cupboard and set them up on a card table in the living room. I took Sarah's plate upstairs while Sweetie followed me with a fresh pot of tea and a tray. When we walked into the bedroom, Sarah sat up in bed. She looked much better. There was some color in her cheeks, and her eyes didn't look as tired as they had earlier.

"Oh my, you didn't have to bring dinner to me. I could have come to the kitchen," she said. Although her voice was a little stronger, it was clear she would need more time to recover completely.

"Pshaw," Sweetie sputtered. "You take it easy until you get all your strength back. Gracie and I don't mind waitin' on you some. Kinda reminds me of the time I tended to my pa. It ain't work when you're helpin' someone you care about."

Sweetie didn't talk much about the time she took care of her father after he was severely injured in a farming accident. It had to have been very difficult. I could see her swipe at her eyes with the back of her hand after she set the teapot down. She was an enigma. Just when I thought I had her figured out, she went a different direction. Maybe her determination to follow the Lord more closely was beginning to show. No matter what it was, my affection for her grew every day.

She carried the tray over to the bed, pulling out metal legs that fit over Sarah's lap. She motioned for me to put her plate down on the top. "I gotta get back downstairs and clean up the kitchen," she said to Sarah after she poured her a fresh cup of tea and grabbed the old pot. "I'll check on you later. If you're hungry enough, I'll bring you a piece of my peach pie."

Sarah smiled at her. "I don't know if I can eat everything you just brought, but if I can't eat pie now, I'd love a piece later." She shook her head. "I wish you'd teach me how to cook the way you do. I'm so awful at it."

If Sweetie liked Sarah before, her comment garnered her undying favor. There was nothing you could say to Sweetie that went straight to her heart faster than praising her culinary skills. Of course with Sweetie, that wasn't hard. She had a natural gift for cooking, thus the extra ten pounds I'd taken home to Wichita. Obviously I needed to practice restraint from here on out or there might be talk of little brothers and sisters to go with the imaginary baby I'd already given birth to.

"When you get to feelin' better, why don't you and Gracie come over once a week, and I'll teach you both to cook?"

"Hey, how did I get pulled into this?"

She pointed her finger at me. "I heard you tell Sam you can't cook. I ain't havin' my nephew saddled with some gal who can't keep him strong and fed right." She turned and walked out of the room mumbling something I couldn't hear. Sarah and I both giggled after she left.

"Looks like while you're teaching me how to do wood-block printing, Sweetie will be teaching us both how to cook."

Sarah took a bite of the roast chicken on her plate. "Oh my," she said after she put her fork down. "If I could learn to cook like this, maybe Papa wouldn't be so skinny."

I sat down next to her on the bed. "John's on the thin side, too, you know."

She didn't respond, just took another bite of food.

I reached over and took her hand. "Look, I know what you said earlier, and I won't keep bugging you. But don't shut that door completely, okay? God can do miraculous things."

She smiled sadly and stared at the food on her plate. "I know you're right, but unless John finds the Lord, there's no way we can ever be together. I never should have allowed these feelings to start. I knew better. I honestly can't explain how it happened. It took me by surprise. His warmth and. . .kindness. . .touched me." When she looked at me, her eyes were shiny with tears. "I know Papa loves me, but no one has ever listened to me like John does. It's as if everything I say is important. I really opened up to him and expressed feelings I didn't even know I had." Her eyebrows knit together in a frown. "Does this make any sense? Am I babbling?"

I squeezed her hand gently. "No, you're not babbling. I understand completely. I hadn't really thought about it before, but Sam makes me feel the same way."

"Well, as you said, I will put this in God's hands. But for now, I know we must keep our distance. It will be difficult. . . ."

"You know what? John knows this is what you want. He'll respect that and make it as easy as possible." I wanted to add that John's motive was his great love for the quiet Mennonite girl, but saying it wouldn't help anything. "Now let's see if we can get the rest of Sweetie's delicious dinner down. How do your hands and feet feel now?"

Sarah's eyes widened. "I hadn't thought about it, but they don't sting anymore. They feel perfectly normal."

"That's great. I predict you'll start getting back to your old self before long."

She nodded and took a bite of potatoes. "When will Papa and I be able to go home?"

I explained about the roads and the conditions. I also told her that the men would be leaving in the morning to help clear some of the snow away. "You might as well plan on staying here for a couple of days."

"Oh my. That means we'll have to spend the Sabbath here."

I chuckled. "Don't look so alarmed. We actually worship God on Sundays, too. I promise we won't do anything weird like build an altar and sacrifice one of Sam's animals."

Sarah's worried expression disappeared as she laughed. "I'm sorry. Of course you're right. It's just that Papa and I have wor shipped with other Old Order believers since I was a child. That is, until last spring when we began to go to Bethel." She sighed. "I love it there. It's not that I didn't care for our other brothers and sisters; it's just that there is so much fellowship and joy now in our services. I can hardly wait to get to church every Sunday. Those are my only two group worship experiences."

"Besides you, your father, and Ida, who else in Harmony belongs to the Old Order?"

"Of course you knew that your uncle Benjamin used to be part of us."

515

I nodded.

"There are three other families. There is a large farm on Faith Road about two miles north of you. The Voglers have three children. Then there are two bachelor brothers, the Beckenbauers, who live a mile out of town to the south of us." Her brow furrowed and a troubled look crossed her delicate features. "The only other person is Abigail Bradley, who lives not far from Papa and me."

"I know the large farm you mentioned on Faith Road. I've seen the children outside playing, but I've never met them. I don't believe I've ever met the other people you mentioned."

"You wouldn't. They don't come into town much. They're fairly self-sufficient. We used to take turns having services in the homes of the Beckenbauer brothers and the Voglers. We still meet during the week for Bible study, and they respect our decision to attend Bethel on Sundays. In fact, the Voglers talk about joining us someday. It's possible the brothers will come one day as well. They're rather quiet and keep to themselves."

"And this Abigail woman?"

A shadow fell across Sarah's face. "We don't see her anymore. She's a very strange person. I think she prefers to stay away from other people. One of the Beckenbauer brothers checks on her from time to time."

Sarah yawned and handed me her tray. "I'm sorry, Gracie. I'm still rather weary. Do you mind if we talk more tomorrow?"

I wondered at the way she cut off any further questions about Abigail Bradley. What was that about? But I knew Sarah was telling the truth about being tired. I could see it in her face.

"How about that peach pie?"

She gave me a tired smile. "Let's try that tomorrow, okay? I'm stuffed." She yawned again. "Please tell Sweetie how much I enjoyed everything, will you?"

I told her I'd take care of it and watched as she scooted down in the bed and pulled up her covers. "I'm sure your father will want to say good night. I'll send him up."

She nodded, but her eyes were already closing. I carried the tray out of the room and down the stairs. The men were intent on their game, and I could hear Sweetie rattling dishes in the kitchen.

"Gabe, Sarah's calling it a night. She's waiting for you to tuck her in."

He slapped down a checker and said, "Perfect timing. That's the game!"

Sam shook his head and tossed me a quick smile. "He's beat us every game so far. John and I don't stand a chance."

Gabe stood to his feet. "You two go ahead and play each other until I get back. At least that way one of you should win."

"Now just hold on there." Sweetie came into the room, wiping her hands on her overalls. "I think I can keep that from happenin'."

I winked at her. "You put these men in their places while I load Sarah's dishes in the dishwasher. Then we'll both show them how to really play checkers."

"You got a deal," she said. "Come on, boys, set 'em up again."

I carried the tray into the kitchen while Gabe went upstairs to check on Sarah. John followed me. "How's she feeling?"

"Much better. Her hands and feet have stopped tingling. She's still a little tired, though."

"Good." He looked relieved. "She'll be just fine. Thanks for taking such good care of her."

"No problem."

He left the room without saying anything else. Maybe he really would be able to keep his distance from Sarah. They both seemed committed to breaking the bonds of their relationship, but I had my doubts. When they looked at each other, their strong feelings were evident and the haunted expression in their eyes identical. While I rinsed Sarah's dishes and put them in the dishwasher, I prayed for them both.

The rest of the evening was spent playing games and having fun. It was as if the storm had never happened, outside or inside the hearts of those gathered together. And also as if there wasn't a dead body out in the barn.

We all headed to bed around ten o'clock, after a round of peach pie and ice cream had been served. Thankfully the big house had plenty of room for everyone. I slept in the bedroom next to Sarah's with the connecting door open enough so I could hear her if she cried out in the night. Either she slept very soundly or I did, because I woke up to sunlight streaming in the windows. I got dressed, checked on Sarah, who was still sleeping, and went downstairs. Sweetie was in the kitchen, sitting at the table. It was evident breakfast had already been served. The smell of bacon hung in the air.

"They're already gone," she told me before I could ask. "Don't know what time they'll get back tonight. Sam said to tell you he would make sure Ida was okay and would also find out if Thelma and Jessica heard yet about Rand."

I grabbed a cup from the cupboard and poured myself some coffee. The rich, hot liquid chased away the remnants of sleepiness that tried to hold on to me like an uncomfortable, heavy coat.

"Did Sam take his truck?"

"Nah. That old thing just ain't reliable enough with this much snow. Dan drove his tractor with the snowplow, and Dale brought their SUV. Guess they're roundin' up other farmers with tractors and plows. We have a tractor, but it's not heavy enough. With all of them workin' together, they should make some good headway today."

"I wonder if anyone's been able to reach Sheriff Taylor."

"Nope. According to the brothers, phones are out all over

town, and Joe's old CB is busted. But believe me, first chance that nasty old sheriff gets, he'll show up."

I thought about what waited for him out in the barn and shuddered.

"You cold, honey?" Sweetie sputtered. "You sit down, and I'll rustle you up some breakfast."

"I'm not cold. And I'm not very hungry. I'm still full of your peach pie."

She laughed. "Peach pie can do that, all right. How about some oatmeal?"

"Perfect. That would hit the spot."

Sweetie nodded and set about making round two of breakfast. I should have offered to help, but for some reason my energy was zapped. Not sure why. Maybe it was all the excitement from the day before.

"What's the latest on the cold snap the forecasters have been predicting?"

Sweetie whirled around, a large spoon in her hand. "Land sakes, I'm plumb worried about it. Last I heard it could be comin' today or tomorrow. Not sure how long it will last. If the temperatures hit below zero and stay that way too long, we could lose our trees."

"Sam said something about burn barrels?"

She nodded. "Yep, we got 'em all over the orchards, but with all this snow keepin' the ground even colder. . . I just don't know, Gracie girl. It ain't lookin' good. If the clouds come back in, things will warm up a bit. If not, there's no tellin' what will happen."

I told her about praying for God's protection and quoted the scripture in Psalm 91 that I'd mentioned to Sam.

"My, that's a good one," Sweetie said. "It brings peace to my soul." She stirred the pot a couple of times. Then she took it off the burner. "You know, my papa believed everything that happened in this world was God's will. That we just take whatever comes and thank Him for it." She shook her head. "Wished I knowed God then the way I know Him now. I woulda showed my papa that we gotta have faith in God's Word to chase the devil away. That we ain't supposed to be ignorant of his devices. Maybe my papa and I coulda fought that ole snaggletoothed liar, and Daddy woulda been here today." Her eyes met mine. "Can you imagine thinkin' the devil's dirty deeds are God's will?" She dabbed at her eyes with her apron. "My daddy jes' didn't know no better. I think about that quite a bit, you know. Wonderin' if I coulda made things turn out different."

I reached for her hand. "Sweetie, I'm sure God doesn't want you blaming yourself or your father for his death. I'm not a Bible scholar or anything, but I've figured out one thing. Even if the devil gets one over on us in this life, he still loses. Your father is living in God's glorious heaven, waiting for his beautiful daughter to join him. No regrets. Just joyous anticipation."

Sweetie threw her head back and laughed. "My goodness, girl. Your middle name Pollyanna or somethin'?"

"No, but isn't it cool that no matter what happens, when we know God, we always have hope?"

She ambled back to the stove to check on her oatmeal. "I guess it is. Like the Good Book says, nothin' is impossible with Him." She tended to the stove a minute then said something I didn't hear at first.

"What? Did you say something?" I asked.

"Yes," she said a little louder. "I sure was worried you and Sam weren't going to work things out, but God made a way." She turned around and stared at me as if she wanted to say something. I waited, but she didn't open her mouth. Just kept watching me.

"I believe He did. Don't you?"

She folded her arms across her chest and rocked back and

forth on her heels a few times. "I don't want to cause you no undo concern, Gracie girl. I hope everything is fine and dandy. It's just that I know my nephew pretty well. To be perfectly honest, I don't think he's settled in his mind about his mama yet." She rubbed her arms as if she felt cold. "I mean, think about it. The way he reacted to that story about the baby. Well, it showed he still had lotsa bad feelin's about the past. I mean, to treat you the way he did. Then suddenly everything's all right? Like nothin' ever happened?" She shook her head. "It just don't make sense to me. Through all these years, I've watched Sam stuff his real feelin's in a place down deep inside himself. In fact, he's spent a lot of his life doin' that." She stared at me, her expression guarded. "Just be careful, Gracie," she cautioned. "Make sure he's got all that sad stuff out and dealt with. If you don't, it could hurt you and him both." With that she turned her attention back to her oatmeal.

Her warning struck deep. The same thought had crossed my mind more than once. That Sam had changed too quickly after my emotional upheaval. Maybe Sweetie was right. Maybe it was a bad sign. My mother had the same kind of personality. She would always pick herself up after an emotional hurt and act like everything was okay. She'd done that after she was diagnosed with cancer, but one day her fear and anger boiled over, taking all of us by surprise. She began acting like a different person, yelling at my father and me, treating us as if everything we did irritated her. The change was so abrupt and so obvious that we knew immediately something was wrong. After some tears, venting, and counseling, she finally started to express her fear and frustration.

I learned a huge lesson from her. That to exercise our faith and walk in it, we must first deal honestly with our emotions. God can only help us when we admit we need it. Once my mom got hold of this important truth, she began to trust God for her complete healing. And she received it. She finished chemo with a positive attitude. I was thinking about her when a knock on the door almost made me spill my coffee.

"Now who in tarnation could that be?" Sweetie declared. "Shouldn't be nobody out 'cept our men, and they're gone." She frowned at me. "Can you get that? I gotta stir this oatmeal."

I hopped up from the table and hurried to the door. When I saw who waited on the porch, my mouth dropped open in surprise. Standing there as if there weren't six-foot snowdrifts surrounding us stood Sheriff Pat Taylor, his arms crossed, his feet spread apart, and his face screwed up into a fierce scowl.

"I hear you got another dead body to contend with, young lady. You wanna show me just where you stored this one?"

Chapter Ten

After changing my clothes and checking on Sarah, I led Sheriff Taylor to the barn, where Rand McAllister was laid out on a large wooden table used to hold feed for Ranger and Tonto, Sam's horses. The feed had been moved to accommodate the very deceased Mr. McAllister.

Thankfully he was covered with a blanket. I turned my head as the sheriff pulled up one edge to get a look at the dead man.

"Still pretty frozen," he grumbled. "Dang fool thing to do—wanderin' around outside in this weather." He paused a moment. "Any idea what he was doin' out there?"

I quickly looked his way and saw that he'd re-covered Rand's face. "I have no idea, Sheriff. I didn't really know him. Sam and a couple other men found him in the snow not far from here."

"Near here, huh? Figures."

"What does that mean?" I asked hotly. "Look, the last couple of days have been very stressful for everyone. Now a cold front is moving in, and I'm worried about Sam's trees. He could lose them. I don't feel like sparring with you about Rand McAllister."

The surprised sheriff rocked back on his heels, his eyes wide.

"Now just a minute, young lady. It might do you some good to speak a little more respectfully to me. After all, I am the sheriff in these parts."

"Yes, you are. And you certainly let everyone know it. You've been throwing your weight around ever since I got to Harmony. Even before that, now that I think about it. Why did you stop me on the highway the other day? There's nothing wrong with my taillight. Surely you have something better to do than detain innocent people and make up stories. Now we have this body. I mean, a man has died, and all you can do is attempt to blame me somehow."

I felt like a balloon that suddenly ran out of air. Deflated, dejected, and dumb. Of course, I'm pretty sure a balloon can't feel dumb—or anything else for that matter. I would have slapped my hand over my mouth if it wouldn't have looked too dramatic. We stood there and glared at each other for a while. To my chagrin, Taylor began to look somewhat amused. I, on the other hand, was not. Finally I decided to break our stalemate while trying to retain a shred of my shattered dignity. "I'm sorry. I've been under a lot of stress. I shouldn't have yelled at you."

He kept staring at me strangely. Then he reached for his handcuffs.

"Whoa! I don't think you can arrest someone for losing their temper," I sputtered. "This is America."

"I'm not arresting you, Miss Temple. I'm getting my handkerchief." With that he put his hand in his pocket, ignoring the nearby handcuffs hooked on his belt.

"I—I don't need a handkerchief. I. . ." With a start I realized that tears were dripping down my face. Oh brother. Another emotional meltdown. This was getting ridiculous. Taylor walked over and held out his handkerchief. I took it and wiped my face. The thought crossed my mind of blowing my nose and handing it back, but I'd already given the grouchy lawman more than enough reason to shoot me and call it self-defense. Putting a snotty hankie in his hand might be the last straw. With my face dry and my leaky eyes under control, I gave him back his only slightly used handkerchief. "Sorry," I said again.

He grunted.

I wasn't sure how to interpret that, not being fluent in grunts, so I just nodded. "So what now? Are you going to, uh. . ."

"Take Rand off your hands?"

I nodded again. At that moment nonverbal responses seemed safer. I couldn't risk going off again. Next he might actually pull out those handcuffs on purpose.

"So you're sure McAllister got caught out in the snow," he said. "No foul play or anything?"

I sighed with exasperation. "Look, Sheriff. Just because I used to have a dead body on my property, and just because I figured out who killed him. . . Well, that doesn't make me Jessica Fletcher. I assume Rand McAllister got caught out in the snowstorm and died of exposure. The same thing almost happened to my friend Sarah."

He frowned at me. "Who's Jessica Fletcher?"

I opened my mouth to respond but closed it before actual words came out. There wasn't anything I could say that wouldn't sound condescending and make the sheriff grab his handcuffs—or his gun.

He crossed his arms and examined me much the way a hawk might look at a field mouse running for its life. "Did you look at the body?"

I shook my head. "As much fun as that sounds, I'm not big on viewing corpses. But John Keystone helped bring him in here. I'm sure he checked him over."

The lawman's eyes widened. "So you think the butcher's

opinion of the deceased's condition oughta be good enough to determine COD?"

I flashed him a grin. "I do watch *CSI*, Sheriff. John Keystone used to be a doctor. I'm sure if he'd seen anything that made him suspicious in terms of *cause of death*, he would have said something."

"Good show. Wait a minute. The butcher used to be a doctor? Now that's just plumb funny."

"Not really. And how is it you've watched *CSI* but you have no idea what *Murder, She Wrote* is?"

His bemused expression switched to one of confusion. "Someone wrote you about a murder? Who was it?"

By this point my limbs were beginning to freeze, and I was becoming convinced the sheriff was playing mind games with me. Besides, I'd begun to feel rather outmatched. "Is there anything else I can do for you?" I asked, hoping the answer would be "no."

He shuffled back and forth on his feet. "Yep, little lady. You can tell your doctor/butcher friend to give me a call. And you can help me move Mr. McAllister to my truck."

Wow, this really wasn't *CSI*. Those guys would have crime scene technicians all over this place before the coroner moved the body. But I was standing in the middle of Harmony, Kansas. I guess here we just throw 'em in a truck and forget it.

"In case you're wondering," he said, as if reading my mind, "I can't get anyone out here. Not the coroner's office or an ambulance. I'd just leave him where he is until the roads clear up, but since the butcher thinks this death is natural, I might as well take him off your hands." He took a deep breath like he was getting ready to jump in a lake for a swim. "Now if you'll just grab his feet. . ."

I held up both hands. "Hold on there. I have no intention of starting my day by grabbing a dead body and flinging it around. Call me a wimp, but there are just some things that will now and forever stay out of my repertoire of life experiences."

"I could force you to help me at gunpoint."

"Funny. But I have another idea." I pointed to a wheelbarrow behind us. "Let's try that first."

"Hard to get a wheelbarrow through all the snow."

"Good point. But if you'll drive your truck up to the barn door, we won't have to worry about it."

He considered my idea for a moment. Thankfully the scenario seemed to work for him. "Bring the wheelbarrow. I'll slide him in and then get my truck. You think you can at least roll him up to the door?"

Although I couldn't think of anything else I would rather *not* do, I was smart enough to realize I was getting off easy. So I just nodded, since the words "I'd love to push a frozen dead body in a wheelbarrow like some kind of macabre game at a church picnic" didn't seem appropriate.

Taylor got the wheelbarrow and brought it over to the table. I turned my head as he put the body in it, but the thump I heard as the transfer was made would probably stay lodged in my memory for the rest of my life.

"Okay," he said in his deep, raspy voice. "I'll get the truck, and I'll honk when I'm ready."

"Fine."

There was a prolonged silence. Then I heard, "Miss Temple?"

"Yes?"

The sheriff cleared his throat. "Do you have some kind of plan to push the wheelbarrow without looking at it?"

"No."

"Okay. So. . ."

I reluctantly swung my head around. Great. Frozen bodies don't fit perfectly in a wheelbarrow. This was going to be a delicate balancing act. "Hey, maybe you could. . ." But I was talking to Taylor's backside. He left through the barn door without looking back. Obviously I was alone. Well, not completely alone. But alone enough.

I took a deep breath and grabbed the handles of the wheelbarrow, trying to completely avoid Rand's boots that stuck out from under the blanket. I noticed his blue socks showing through the holes in the bottom of his boots. Odd that he would wear lightweight boots like these outside—especially in the snow. It seemed to line up with John's assessment that Rand had gotten smashed and accidentally ended up outside. As I carefully navigated the barrow toward the barn door, trying desperately to keep the body balanced so it wouldn't slide off, the thought occurred to me that Rand might not be wearing socks after all. The idea made me a little nauseated. I could have checked out my theory, but let's just say that being right isn't always the most important thing.

We finally made it to the door. I waited while the sheriff backed his truck up next to us. I'd begun to notice that everyone and their brother owned trucks in Harmony. At first I wondered if it was just a country thing, but now I realized that trucks could make it through snow, high water, and the kind of rough terrain that cars like my Slug Bug couldn't. Although I had no intention of getting a truck, the idea of trading in my beloved Volkswagen for something more appropriate was noodling around in my head. What good is having a car you can't drive?

I turned my head once again as the sheriff loaded poor Rand up into the back of his truck. Kind of an undignified way to be transported to wherever he was going.

I heard the door on the truck bed slam shut. "Guess that's it," Taylor said. "You folks gonna be all right here?"

Did this tough character care about us or was he just being nosy? "Um, we'll be fine. Sure would like to get our phone service back, though."

The sheriff rubbed his stubbly chin. "Anyone I can call for you?" I thought about my parents, but they were used to big snows since they lived in Nebraska. Not hearing from me for a couple of days wouldn't worry them. "Sam and the other guys should be contacting everyone I'm concerned about. But thanks anyway."

"And who are these folks?"

"My friend Ida Turnbauer and of course Thelma and Jessica McAllister."

He nodded. "I ran into your boyfriend on my way here. He and his friends had already been to Mrs. Turnbauer's and were on their way to the McAllisters'. I guess you can quit worryin' about them."

"So that's how you found out about Rand."

He nodded.

"Then you were already on your way to Harmony? With the roads in such awful condition?" I shook my head. "Why? Surely you had enough going on in your own town."

He shrugged. "Had my reasons." He left me standing there as he got in his truck and slowly began driving back to the road. Even though his vehicle was heavy, it slipped on the ice several times.

I stood there and watched him go. Why would he come to Harmony if he didn't know about Rand? What was it here that interested him so much? I remembered Sam's stories about Taylor hanging around and asking questions not long after he took office. Between his bad attitude toward Harmony, his unusual interest in its citizens, his stopping me on the highway into town for no reason, and the fact that right after a major blizzard his first action was to head here—something wasn't right. A blast of bitter wind convinced me I needed to get indoors. Sweetie was waiting for me. She'd probably been keeping watch over the entire procedure.

"That old sheriff take Rand with him?" she asked as I came up the stairs.

"Yeah. He's gone."

She held the door open. I gladly left the cold behind and entered the house. It felt like walking into a warm hug.

"Goodness, honey. You go sit by the fire. I'll bring you a nice cup of hot cocoa."

At that moment a cup of hot chocolate sounded like the most fantastic thing in the world. I headed for the living room, ready to curl up in front of the fire and let the warmth seep into my chilled bones. When I got there, I was pleasantly surprised to find Sarah on the couch, a comforter tucked around her.

"Hey, you're downstairs. I take it you're feeling better?"

"Yes, I am, thanks to you and Sweetie. I know I'm supposed to take it easy, but I just couldn't stay upstairs anymore. I'm lonely."

"Boredom. A sure sign of recovery. I remember when I was sick as a child and had to stay home from school. As soon as I told my mother I was bored, she knew the worst was over."

Sarah giggled. "I guess that's exactly where I am. So I must be getting better."

"I'm glad."

She pulled her legs up and pointed to the other end of the couch. "Sit with me for a while, will you? I want to talk to you."

I scooted into the area left open and tucked my legs under me so I could face her. "Sure. Anything you want to talk about, I'm here for you."

"I know that, Gracie. The last time I had a close friend was before my mother left. Having you in my life means more than you could possibly know."

I reached over and patted her knee. "And you're the best friend I have in Harmony. I miss our teaching sessions. When you're better, let's start them again. I've been working on a couple of things I'd like you to look at."

She laughed lightly. "Oh, Gracie. You really don't need me to teach you any more about wood-block printing. The process is easy, and you've got a knack for it."

I shook my head. "Well, my 'knack' isn't anything close to your wonderful talent, Sarah. That's something I'll never learn, but I'd like to at least watch you work. I truly enjoy it."

She pushed her long dark hair back behind her ear. "I would love to spend more time with you, too. Surely by next week the roads will be clear, and we can all get back to normal."

"I hope so. Right now, though, I'm concerned about the weather forecast. They're calling for temperatures around zero. Sam's worried about his fruit trees."

Sarah frowned. "I hadn't heard that. But he has smudge pots, right? Hopefully that will help."

"He has them, along with the burn barrels already in the orchards. I have no idea how they work, but yes, he intends to use them if necessary."

"I will pray for him," she said earnestly. And I knew she meant it.

At that moment, Sweetie came into the room carrying a tray with two bowls of oatmeal and two cups of hot chocolate topped off with big dollops of whipped cream.

"You two need somethin' to warm you up. Oatmeal with cinnamon and sugar along with some good old hot chocolate oughta do it."

"Sounds perfect, Sweetie," I said. "But you didn't need to bring us breakfast. We could have gone into the kitchen."

"Nah," she retorted. "It's nice and warm in here. You two just relax in front of the fire."

"Oh my," Sarah said. "I love oatmeal, and you make the most

wonderful cocoa, Sweetie. I could almost swear it has medicine in it. Every time I drink it, I feel stronger."

Sweetie's weathered face broke into a huge grin. "I ain't never had no one compare my hot chocolate to medicine, but I guess if it makes you feel better, it's all right with me!"

I laughed. "As long as it doesn't *taste* like medicine, it's okay with me, too."

"Sweetie, why don't you sit with us for a while?" Sarah urged.

"Why, thank you, honey. How 'bout later? I got some cookin' to do. Them boys is gonna be hungry when they get back. I wanna be prepared."

"Can we help?" I asked.

She waved her hand at me. "You two sit and have some girl talk. I work better alone."

"Okay, but don't forget. You promised you'd teach us both to cook."

"I won't forget. If you ever intend to hook my nephew, you gotta learn to fix his favorite foods."

I giggled. "Hook him? You make him sound like a fish."

Sarah laughed and almost spilled her hot chocolate. A couple of drops splashed on her blanket.

"Well, men are kinda like fish sometimes. You gotta have the right bait on your hook."

For some reason, the picture of a fish with Sam's face wiggling at the end of a fishing line popped into my mind. I had to set my cup down so I wouldn't suffer the same fate as Sarah. I picked up the bowl of oatmeal Sweetie had put on the table in front of me and took a bite. It was the best I'd ever tasted.

Sweetie flushed. "Now it ain't funny at all. The way to a man's heart is through his gullet. And that's just the truth."

I wanted to ask her why, if she was such an expert on men, she was still single. But I knew some about Sweetie's difficult past and the reason she was still alone. "You're right," I said, straight-faced. "When can we start the lessons?"

"Let's get past the weekend, girls. Next week we'll start. I'll have you two cookin' like old pros in no time."

"Thank you," Sarah said with a big smile. "I can hardly wait. We'll have so much fun."

I wasn't so sure learning anything from Sweetie, who could be caustic and difficult to get along with even on a good day, was really going to be "fun," but I voiced my agreement anyway.

Sweetie left the room with a spring in her step, buoyed by the prospect of whipping Sarah and me into shape.

"Oh, Gracie. This is so exciting," Sarah said.

"Will your father approve?"

"Yes. Papa and John have made up. I don't believe Papa is upset anymore. Of course my silly stunt probably frightened him so much that he will spoil me for a while." She sighed. "I'm really sorry I scared him."

"We were all frightened. Especially your father. . .and John."

Sarah stared down into her cup, her expression so sad it touched my heart. "John really does love me, you know," she said softly. "And I love him, too."

"I know that. And I understand why you both made the decision to break off the relationship. You're worried about your father."

She nodded slowly. "Yes, my father. But not just my earthly father. I did it for my heavenly Father, too."

"Because of that scripture about not being unequally yoked?"

"Yes."

"What if John became a Christian after the two of you married?"

"There are no guarantees of that," she said. "What if he didn't? How could we have a good marriage if we don't share the most important thing there is? The most important aspect of my life?"

I knew that would be her response. I agreed with her stand, but I felt sorry for them—two really good people who truly loved each other. In my mind's eye, I could still see John lifting Sarah from the snow, although the expression on his face was something I never wanted to see again. Fear and intense love are powerful companions, but they certainly aren't friends. I thought about the scripture that says perfect love casts out fear. The only way to have perfect love is to have the perfect One in your life. And John didn't have Him.

"I know you're right," I said. "But I also know you're both hurting. You're trying to protect your father and obey God, and John is trying to protect you." I sighed. "I guess I'm just one of those people who believes in happy endings."

"But life is not a fairy tale, Gracie," Sarah replied. "Sometimes the endings aren't the ones we envisioned. However, if God is in them, we can find joy and blessing. He doesn't want us to be unhappy. He wants us to have joy. Leading us away from things that will hurt us is His way of directing us to the abundant life He has for us. He's the Good Shepherd, you know."

"You're a very wise woman, you know that?"

"Sometimes. When I'm not getting lost in a snowstorm."

At first I thought she was serious, but then I noticed her mouth quiver. We both laughed at the same time. It was great to see her on the road to recovery from her ordeal, but I sensed the pain over her broken relationship with John was still strong. Hopefully she would begin to heal, but right now I felt she needed to think about something else. I started to change the subject and bring up our scheduled cooking lessons when we heard a loud sound from outside, like the roar of an engine. Sweetie heard it, too. She came hurrying out of the kitchen, drying her hands on her apron.

"Are they back so soon? I figgered they'd be gone most of the day."

I got up and followed her to the front door. When Sweetie swung it open, I saw her expression instantly change. I peeked around her to see Eric standing on the porch.

"What in blue blazes do you want?" Sweetie said, her tone not the least bit welcoming.

Eric looked taken aback. "I—I came to see if everything was all right here. I went to Gracie's, but no one was there."

I stepped in front of Sweetie, who stood her ground, not giving me much room to maneuver. "I'm here, Eric." I shot Sweetie a sideways glance of disapproval. Reluctantly, she moved back. "Come on in." I pushed the door open and Eric came inside, although hesitantly. Sweetie's fixed glare obviously made him nervous.

"Seems that big fancy truck of yours can stay on the road when you want it to," Sweetie said sarcastically.

His eyes widened as he looked to me for help.

"Excuse me a minute, will you, Eric?" I grabbed Sweetie's arm and pulled her down the hall and into the kitchen. "What are you doing?" I whispered once we were out of Eric's line of vision.

"That man almost ruined things between you and Sam," she hissed. "He's a snake in the grass for sure."

"Sweetie, Eric didn't do anything wrong. At all. Sam misread the entire situation. You know that. Why are you acting like this? You're embarrassing me."

"I don't trust him as far as I can pick him up and toss him." She spoke a little too loudly for my comfort.

"You don't trust anyone. You barely trust me."

"Now that's just not true, Gracie. I trust you completely."

I grabbed her hand. "Then prove it. Eric is a very nice man. He risked coming here today through the snow just to make sure

535

we're all right. And you treat him like he's an escaped criminal."
The pitch in my voice had risen close to a tone only dogs could
hear. In fact, Buddy got up from his favorite spot under the table
to see what was going on. Snickle followed him. Seeing them
scrutinize me like I was some kind of interesting phenomenon
made me want to laugh. But I needed to make sure Sweetie
backed off of her unreasonable attitude, so I kept my cool.

She looked into my eyes for a moment; then she dropped her
head. "Okay, Gracie. You say he's a good guy, so I'll believe you.
I won't pick on him no more."

I would have asked her to apologize to Eric, but that would
have been pushing my luck. I left the kitchen and hurried back to
the front door.

"I'm sorry," I said to Eric. "Sweetie gets things in her head
sometimes. It's hard to reason with her, but I think everything
will be okay."

"Man, I was worried about Sam. I had no idea I'd be facing his
aunt's wrath as well."

I smiled at him. "Sam's not mad at you. In fact, no one is mad
at you. Come on in."

He followed me down the hall to the living room. Sarah was
gone. Her blanket had been folded and was draped over the arm
of the couch.

"I heard about Rand McAllister. I can hardly believe it," Eric
said, his eyes darting toward the kitchen.

"That was fast. Who told you?"

"Dale Scheidler. He was clearing off the intersection at Faith
and Main." He shook his head slowly. "At least I know now why
he wasn't returning my calls."

I motioned toward the couch. "Sit down. How about some
coffee?"

"I'd love it. Thank you."

"How do you take it?"

"With a little cream if you have some."

I grinned. "You're in Sweetie Goodrich's house. There isn't a food created she doesn't have. Anyway, I've never found it."

I heard him chuckle as I left the room. In the kitchen, I found Sweetie chopping vegetables with a little too much zeal. Even though she'd apologized, I could tell she was still bothered by Eric's presence in her house.

I got a cup from the cabinet and poured coffee into it. Then I got the cream from the refrigerator and mixed it into the cup. Sweetie didn't utter one word. It was almost worse than having her go off on a tangent. I set the cup on the counter and eyeballed her. "Sweetie, you have to trust God. If Sam and I are meant to be together, there is no man on the face of the planet who will be able to break us up. If you don't trust me, can you at least trust Him?"

When she turned around, I was shocked to see she'd been crying. Sweetie didn't cry very often. She usually yelled when she was upset.

"More than anything in this world, I want to see my boy happy," she said. "I'd give everything I own for that. And I know he will have that with you." She wiped a tear from her eye. "He's had so much pain in his life, and I've done all I can to make it better. But I know what he needs now can't come from me." She paused for a moment and cleared her throat. "It's time for me to become less important in his life. He needs—he needs someone to love. Someone to share his life." She focused her gaze on me. "He needs you, Gracie. And the idea that something could go wrong—that he might be hurt again. . . Well, I just can't bear to think about it."

I took her hand. "Like I said, if Sam and I are meant to be together, it will happen. You and I both need to believe that."

She shook her head. "But sometimes things don't seem to work out right. What about Gabe and his wife? I bet he thought they'd be together forever, and she walked out on her husband and daughter without so much as a fare-thee-well and spit in your face."

I was trying to figure out what a "fare-thee-well and spit in your face" was when I heard Sarah's voice coming from behind me. "Oh no."

I turned to find her dressed in her dark blue frock, her hair back up and covered by her matching prayer cap. Although she was beautiful no matter what she wore, I missed seeing her hair down.

"My mother wasn't dedicated to God, Sweetie," she said. "That's the difference between Gracie and Mama." She came into the kitchen and sat down at the table. There was still a shadow of weariness in her face. "She was raised in the Old Order ways, but she followed them because she had to. She married my father because he was the only boy close to her age that she liked at all." Sarah clasped her hands together and stared at them. "You see, she never really gave her heart to the Lord—or to our faith. So when she met the man she left with, all she could see was a new and different life. In her mind, a better life." She raised her head and smiled sweetly. "But Gracie has chosen her faith. She has chosen her God. And that is the difference. We cannot serve God because our parents do—or even because we think it is the right thing. Our commitment needs to come from our hearts—not just our minds." A frown creased her smooth forehead. "Am I saying this clearly? Do you understand?"

Sweetie nodded. "I think I do. I was readin' somethin' 'bout that the other day. Jesus asked Peter if he knew who He was, and Peter said Jesus was the Son of God. Then Jesus said somethin' that I had to read a few times before I got it. He spoke about flesh and blood not tellin' Peter who He was. But that his knowin' the truth about Jesus came straight from God." She frowned. "What Jesus said then was kinda amazin'. He said that the gates of hell couldn't come against that. I finally figgered out He was talkin' about the devil not bein' able to take away what we get straight from heaven." She looked at Sarah questioningly. "Is that what you mean?"

Sarah smiled at her. "That's exactly what I mean. Peter knew about Jesus because God revealed it to him. Not because someone else told him. I believe we all must have that moment when we choose to believe of our own free will." A sad countenance came over her. "My mother never made that choice. When she did finally choose, she chose the wrong thing."

"Sarah, in all these years have you or Gabe ever heard from your mom?"

"A few years ago a letter came. I will never forget my father's expression when he looked at the return address. He stared at it for the longest time. Then he threw it away without reading it or mentioning it again." She shrugged her thin shoulders. "He never said, but I think it might have been from my mother."

"You never asked him?" I said.

"No. I felt it would cause him pain. And to be honest, I feel more committed to caring about the parent who stayed with me—who raised me—than the one who walked away."

"I understand if Gabe just tossed out that letter," Sweetie said. "I kept things from my father the last year of his life because I didn't want him to worry. After his accident, he was so sick it was all I could do to keep him alive. Worryin' about things he couldn't fix. . .well, it just seemed wrong. Your papa didn't want your mama to cause you any more hurt. That's why he didn't open that letter."

Sarah nodded. "And I guess it isn't just the parents who protect their children. Sometimes the children protect the parents. And they may never know it."

Like Sarah was protecting Gabe from his fear of being alone. I had to wonder what Gabe would think if he knew the truth. "I'd better get this coffee to Eric before it gets cold," I said. "Sarah, would you like to meet him?"

"That would be nice."

I carried Eric's cup into the living room. He'd probably begun to wonder what was taking so long. "Eric Beck, this is Sarah Ketterling, Gabe Ketterling's daughter."

Eric stood to his feet. "Nice to meet you, Miss Ketterling. I visited with your father at your store in downtown Harmony. Unfortunately, he wasn't too enthusiastic about my project."

Sarah nodded at him and sat down in a chair across from the couch. Eric sat down as well.

"I hope he wasn't rude, Mr. Beck. My father is rather opinionated on most subjects."

Eric smiled. "No, he wasn't rude. He was just suspicious. And please, call me Eric."

"I would be happy to, but you must call me Sarah."

"Thank you." Eric finally had a chance to sip his coffee. I hoped it was still hot.

"Eric, can you tell me what will happen to your project now? Now that Rand McAllister is. . .deceased?"

"I honestly don't know. I'm actually in a rather difficult situation. Time is ticking away on this deal, but I can't run over and talk to Thelma right away. It wouldn't be respectful. I'm not sure just what I'll do."

"Perhaps Pastor Mueller could intercede for you," Sarah said. "I'm certain he will be spending time with Thelma and Jessica as they deal with their loss. Maybe you could speak to him, and he could broach the subject?"

Eric's face brightened. "That's a wonderful idea. Thank you, Sarah."

"I tend to wonder if Thelma will be ready to move for a while," I said to Eric. "I mean, her husband dies, and she's going to sell her home right away? I don't know. That might be a lot of upheaval for someone dealing with grief."

"I know," Eric said. "But the problem is that unless we move quickly, this deal will fold. The investors are looking at some property in northwest Kansas. Lakefront property. Of course, that would be the most desirable choice."

"Well, maybe they should just buy it and forget about Harmony," I said.

"They're thinking seriously about it. It's much more expensive than Rand's property, but a better site overall."

I frowned at him. "Why don't they just buy some of the property around Trouble Lake? The lake is large, and except for my place and Sam's, the area hasn't been developed."

Eric smiled and picked up his coffee cup. "We looked at that first, but your place and Sam's are the only privately owned land around the lake. The rest of it is owned by the county, and they're not selling." He took a sip of coffee and put the cup down. It had to be cold by now.

"Let me warm that up for you," I said, rising to my feet. "What about you, Sarah? Can I get you anything?"

She shook her head. "No, thank you. I'm fine."

As I walked away, I heard Sarah say, "But if you could buy affordable land on Trouble Lake, your investors would probably decide to build here?"

"Absolutely. This area is still their first choice."

When I got to the kitchen, Sweetie wasn't there, but the door to the basement was open. She kept an extensive pantry downstairs. I'd found most folks who live in the country have big pantries. When you don't have a grocery store nearby, you have to stock up for situations just like the blizzard we'd just gone through. Anytime a big storm was predicted for Wichita, the stores ran out of bread and milk almost immediately. I always found that funny. How much bread and milk can anyone use at one time? Well, in Harmony, most women made their own bread and there were enough milk cows around to make sure everyone had all they wanted. Those weren't the items folks around here stocked up on.

The coffeemaker was still on, so I poured Eric a fresh cup of coffee, added cream, and headed back to the living room. As I entered the room, Eric was telling Sarah about growing up in Mound City, Kansas.

"I've never been to Mound City," I said as I set Eric's cup down on the table in front of him, "but I had a friend in Wichita who grew up there. She had such fond memories of her childhood. Sounds like a nice place."

"It is. I miss it. My folks still live there." He flashed me a grin. "Go, Hawks!"

"You played sports?" Sarah asked.

"Baseball. Nothing like playing for a high school team in a small town. Everyone comes to the games."

"I grew up in a small town in Nebraska," I said as I sat down, "and you're right. The games were the most exciting thing going. People brought their grills and cooked hot dogs and hamburgers before the game. We certainly never went hungry."

Eric laughed. "I know exactly what you mean."

"It sounds wonderful," Sarah said.

I'd heard that a lot of Mennonite children weren't allowed to play sports as children. Gabe had mentioned as much. Not wanting to make the conversation uncomfortable for Sarah, I changed the subject back to something I'd heard before I went into the kitchen. "Eric, did I hear you say something about your investors having an interest in lakefront property?"

"Well, sure. Anytime you can build a property near a lake, it adds to the value. Especially if you can offer swimming, boating, and fishing."

"How much land do you need?"

"As much as we can get, with most of the property next to the water," he said. "I'd want to give a majority of the condos a view of the water with easy access to the shore."

"I was just thinking that since originally my land was used for farming and I'm not doing that, maybe I could sell off part of it to help the town."

"You're very generous. I wish it was the answer, but there's just not enough acreage. Rand's place is a little over forty acres, and yours is what. . .around thirty?"

I nodded.

"Excuse me," Sarah said softly. "I don't understand something. Even though Gracie's land is smaller, wouldn't your. . .investors. . .rather build a smaller community instead of giving up altogether?"

"The problem is that right now they're thinking about bailing out of the project completely since it seems our original plans won't work. And it isn't just the size of the land. Rand's place was just off a paved country road that connects to the highway. To reach Gracie's, you have to travel quite a distance on a dirt road. It's just not as attractive to older residents. My recent experiences in the snow show the importance of well-developed and well-maintained roads."

"So even if you could buy my place and Sam's, you still couldn't move the development here?" I asked.

"Well, I'd have to get the county to pave the road. I suppose if they were agreeable, we might be very interested." He smiled at me. "If the investors could be talked into looking at the possibility, there's a chance they'd be willing to offer you a great deal of money. Lakefront property is hard to come by. I'm sure they'd pay a lot more for your land than they would have for Rand's." He hesitated for a moment and then frowned at us. "But your property is much closer to downtown Harmony than Rand's. How would the residents feel about having the retirement community so close to town? The last thing I want to do is bring division to Harmony. This is a very special place." He shook his head. "On the other hand, having the development closer would definitely make shopping in Harmony more attractive to our residents."

The prospect of making Harmony stronger appealed to me. If Eric's project would really help the town, I'd actually be willing to move. But of course Sam and Sweetie would never sell their home or their orchards. This place was in their blood. And I couldn't stand to see the big red house destroyed. I pushed the idea out of my head. I'd just started to ask Sarah and Eric if they wanted more coffee when I heard the front door open.

I excused myself and hurried to see who it was. Sam stood in the hallway with the door still ajar. He was staring at Eric's Hummer parked in the driveway.

"What's he doing here?" he asked when he saw me.

"Well, hello to you, too."

"Sorry. Just wasn't expecting to find Eric here. I figured he'd hole up in Council Grove until the highways were in better shape."

I peered outside. Gabe and John had gotten out of the truck and were coming up the stairs.

"He came to help," I whispered. "You be nice. He was worried about all of us."

Sam glared at me but didn't pursue it.

"I thought you'd be gone all day. Why are you home so early?"

"We weren't the only ones out clearing the roads. Lots of men are working to make things passable. I decided the best place for me was back here. I have a lot of work to do before the freeze sets in."

"I guess you've been through this before?"

"Yeah, several times. And I've lost trees. I don't want to lose any more if I can help it."

With his mind on his orchards, at least he wasn't concentrated on Eric—or so I thought. When we walked into the living room, something in his expression must have alarmed Eric, who looked concerned when he spotted Sam. Sam still hadn't shared everything he'd said to Eric when he drove him to his truck the night of the storm—just that he'd threatened to kick him out if he tried to explain the awkward situation. If anything else had transpired, both Sam and Eric were keeping it to themselves. I had the distinct feeling it would be best to let it stay that way.

"Gracie says you drove through the snow to make sure everyone here was okay," Sam said. He hesitated a moment while I prayed he wouldn't say something I might regret. "Thanks." Although he more or less mumbled it, I was relieved. Eric appeared to feel the same way.

"You're welcome," he said. "I heard on the news that temperatures are supposed to keep dropping. They interviewed a farmer near Garden City who was worried about his orchards. It made me wonder if you needed some help."

Sam sat down on the couch and stretched his legs. I could tell he was tired. "That's exactly why we came home early. I've got to clean out my barrels and set out some smudge pots. John and Gabe plan to help. I could use you, too, if you're interested."

"That's why I'm here."

At that moment John and Gabe both came into the room. John noticed Sarah up and dressed. The weariness in his face disappeared, and he broke into a wide smile. He opened his mouth to say something but suddenly stopped. Sarah lit up when she saw him, too, but when she observed his hesitancy, she immediately broke her gaze from his and focused it on her father. Gabe didn't seem to notice.

"Why, Sarah," Gabe said, "you must be feeling better."

She offered her father a small smile, but the color that had flushed her cheeks moments before faded. "I am, Papa. Gracie and Sweetie have been such wonderful nurses."

He walked over to where his daughter sat and grabbed her hand. "Thank you, Gracie," he said to me. "I'll have to thank Sweetie, too."

"Well, you can do that in my kitchen." Sweetie stood in the doorway, her apron speckled with flour and other ingredients from this evening's dinner preparations. "You all need some good food inside you before you tackle the orchards. Alls I got right now is some sandwiches, but I'm cookin' up the best pot roast you ever ate for dinner later on. Now everyone get on in here, and let's have a little lunch before you go outside."

As if obeying orders, we all followed her to the kitchen. I went last and was able to see the exchange of glances between John and Sarah. I also caught a warning glare Sam sent to Eric. I shook my head. Two situations with different kinds of emotions bubbling below the surface. Before the weekend was over, I wondered if one or both of them would boil over.

Chapter Eleven

Sweetie's idea of "a little lunch" wouldn't meet that definition by anyone's standards. Thick slabs of turkey on homemade bread topped with pepper bacon and thick mayonnaise was accompanied by creamy red potato salad. And of course, pie. In Sweetie's kitchen, pie was served like a condiment. You have coffee, you have pie. You have lunch—pie. Dinner—pie. Before bed—pie. I was waiting to come down to breakfast to find a thick slice of peach pie and whipped cream instead of the usual bacon, eggs, and pancakes. I ate half a sandwich, a couple of bites of potato salad, and said no to pie.

During lunch I told Sam and the others that the sheriff had stopped by to pick up our unwelcome guest.

"Seems kind of odd," Sam said. "But I guess if the coroner can't get here, there isn't much choice."

I shrugged. "He died of exposure. Nothing nefarious about that."

"Nef-fairy. . .what?" Sweetie frowned at me.

"Nefarious. Shady."

"Well then, why don't you just say shady?" she retorted. "Ain't no reason to use fancy-schmancy words when plain old proper

English will work just as good."

I looked sideways at Sarah, who wouldn't meet my gaze. Her short bout of coughing was nothing more than an excuse to cover a case of the giggles. I fought to keep my composure. "You're right, Sweetie. Sorry."

John's raised eyebrow told me he also found Sweetie's admonition to use "plain old proper English" humorous. There wasn't a phrase Sweetie couldn't fracture, and she was incredibly fluent in colorful expressions.

"So just what are we doing this afternoon?" I asked Sam, trying to change the subject before Sarah embarrassed herself.

"*We* aren't doing anything. The men are going out to the orchards. *You* are staying here."

"Nonsense." I felt my temper flare. "I can work just as hard as you can."

"I know that, Gracie," Sam said patiently, "but Sarah is still recuperating. I think you should stay here with her."

"I'm fine, Sam," Sarah said with a smile. "Gracie doesn't need to watch me. Besides, Sweetie will be here."

"Only reason I won't be out there helpin' in my orchards is 'cause I need to keep an eye on what's in the oven," Sweetie snapped. "Don't you go tellin' any womenfolk where they belong, boy."

"I'm not trying to tell the 'womenfolk' anything," Sam said with a sigh. "I'm just pointing out that someone needs to stay with Sarah." He paused. "And watch the food, it seems. Sweetie, you and Gracie work it out between you. Whichever one of you wants to help, get bundled up. It's cold and getting colder. You're liable to be looking at frostbite before we're done."

"I—I didn't bring any gloves, and I'm afraid these pants aren't very thick," Eric said.

"No problem," Sam said. "I've got the proper clothes you can borrow—if you still want to help. If you don't, I totally under-stand." Maybe no one else noticed the touch of sarcasm in his tone, but I did. I scowled at him when Eric wasn't looking. I knew what he was up to. He was hoping Eric would give up and leave.

"Thanks, Sam," Eric said. "I'll take you up on that."

I smiled at Eric. Good for him. Sam wouldn't discourage him so easily. It was obvious Eric really wanted to help. Hopefully today would start to change things between Eric and Sam. I had no idea how long the young real estate developer would actually be hanging around Harmony. It depended on what happened with his quest for land. But however much longer it was, it would be helpful if the two men could bury the hatchet and find a way to get along.

After a brief argument with Sweetie about who would go and who would stay, I won. Or maybe I lost. The jury's still out on that. The winning point was struck when I pointed out that if I stayed to watch her food, I couldn't guarantee anything. Fear that her pot roast might not survive—and that any gravy from said pot roast might have more lumps than a prizefighter's head—sealed the deal. She would stay to watch Sarah and the food, and I would work in the orchards.

I changed into my heaviest jeans and the thickest sweater I'd brought with me. Double socks and my boots seemed to pass inspection with Sam, but he made me wear one of Sweetie's knit caps and a jacket that was so bulky I was reminded of the little boy in the movie *The Christmas Story* who complained that after his mother bundled him up against the cold, he lost the abil-ity to "put my arms down." Feeling like a big, stuffed snowman, I clomped down the stairs and joined the men. We drove both trucks over to the orchards.

The first order of business was to dump the snow out of the burn barrels that were situated at various locations throughout the trees. This was difficult since the snow had blown up next to them, almost cementing them to the ground. Sam worked with me while directing John, Gabe, and Eric to follow our lead. I marveled at how well John and Gabe worked together. It was as if there had never been any tension between them. They seemed to really like each other. Maybe in the end, that was enough of a victory. Still, I couldn't help but hope that one day Gabe, Sarah, and John would be a real family.

"Hey, pay attention," Sam barked at me. I realized I'd been staring into a barrel Sam was trying to loosen while I did nothing to help him.

"Sorry, just thinking about Sarah and John." We were far enough away from the others that they couldn't hear us, so I didn't try to keep my voice down.

"You're wasting your time worrying about it." Sam grunted as he tried to wiggle the barrel loose. "Sarah isn't going to leave her faith. And I sure don't see John throwing in with their Old Order beliefs."

"You know, the gap between people like Abel and Emily and Mennonites like Gabe and Sarah seems to be closing rapidly. Ida has a phone now. And almost every Conservative Mennonite in Harmony has electricity. I think the old ideas about some of the modern conveniences are changing. I read something the other day that said there really aren't many true Old Order sects left."

Sam finally freed the barrel. He and I turned it upside down to shake out the snow. "I've lived in Harmony almost my entire life," he said after we set it back down. "And one thing I've learned: Just like with all people everywhere, you can't put titles on the folks in this town." He stopped for a minute and stared toward Gabe and John. "They all live by what they think is best for them and their families. Most don't have television, but some do. Most have cars, but some don't. Most have electricity, but a very few, like

Ida and Gabe, don't. And everyone respects individual choices. You might be right. Someday soon, some unimportant differences might fade. But the faith of the people here will remain. Gabe doesn't care whether John has electricity. But he does care that John knows God, and that won't change. Ever."

He was right. Gabe and Sarah had made the decision to put God first. Sarah's feelings for John had been pushed to second place. . .well, third place actually. Behind her heavenly Father and her earthly father.

A surprised shout rang out from Eric. Sam and I turned to see him backing up from a barrel that was lying on its side. He'd started to set it right side up when he jumped back, tripped, and almost fell. Gabe's laughter brought us running. One look inside the barrel explained Eric's reaction. A mother raccoon looked up from a nest she'd made in the barrel. Several baby raccoons snuggled up next to her. The mother's bared teeth made it clear no one would be removing her and her family without a fight.

"Let's carefully move the barrel near the barn," Sam said with a grin. "They'll be warmer there. We've got plenty of other barrels."

Gabe, Eric, and I watched John and Sam pick up the barrel and carry it as gently as possible so as not to disturb the new family.

"I almost stuck my hand in there," Eric said, his voice quivering. I couldn't be sure if it was from fear or the cold.

"Good thing you didn't, son," Gabe said. "Raccoons are cute, but they can be vicious. Especially when they're protecting their young."

Eric's expression testified to the fact that Gabe's words brought no reassurance.

Gabe and I kept our eyes on Eric as he carefully approached the next barrel. He gingerly peeked over the edge before attempting to clean it out. Gabe grinned at me, but neither one of us said anything. I appreciated Eric's willingness to help out and had no desire to ridicule him—even though it was pretty funny.

The five of us worked for several hours. Sam and John pushed the snow out of the orchards the best they could so the barrels and pots could warm the ground as much as possible. Sam drove his tractor with the plow on the front while John shoveled snow by hand and dumped it in piles outside the tree line. Finally they began bringing out bunches of kindling wood, which we placed inside the large metal containers. As the weather forecasters had predicted, the temperature continued to plummet. My hands and feet were almost numb, but I didn't complain. None of the men mentioned the cold, so I didn't either. A couple of times I came close, but I felt protective of Sam's trees and determined to save them. After the barrels were ready, the men began dragging the smudge pots out of the barn. Black metal, with a long pipe that stuck out of the top, they were positioned in various spots around the orchard. Then the men put logs soaked in oil in the bottoms of the pots, added more fuel, and lit them. The flame shot out of the top flue and burned so hot it was almost invisible. After that they began lighting the kindling in the barrels.

"Go on back to the house," Sam shouted to me as I stood back to watch. "You've done all you can do. We'll finish up."

I wanted to argue, but I was really beginning to worry about my extremities. Besides, I could let Sweetie know they would be coming in soon, so she could have dinner ready. It was already dark, although I had no idea what time it actually was. I trudged back to the house, praying my feet would get some feeling back. Worry about Sam's trees filled my mind. What if the orchard was lost? What would Sam and Sweetie do?

As I neared the house, I caught myself. What was I doing? Even though I felt as if I would freeze to the spot if I didn't keep moving, I stopped.

"Father," I said out loud, "You said that without faith it is impossible to please You. You also said we're not to be anxious about anything, but with thanksgiving to send our requests to You. So I'm doing that now. I thank You for giving Sam this incredible home and these magnificent trees. I'm asking You to protect them, and I believe You will. Thank You for loving us so much and for caring about every part of our lives. Amen." I felt better and realized my feet had begun to tingle. I guess they weren't going to fall off after all.

When I reached the house, Sweetie stood by the door that led to the screened-in back porch. " 'Bout time someone came in. It's after seven o'clock. You people been out there for hours and hours." She held the door open and frowned at me. "Where's the rest of 'em?"

The fires from the barrels and pots lit up the encroaching darkness, so my answer seemed unnecessary, but I explained anyway. "The men are starting the fires. Sam told me to come in."

"Can you feel your feet?" she asked.

"Kind of."

"Come on over here and sit down. We'll get you warmed up while I get dinner on the table. Those men are gonna be ready to chow down when they get back."

I gladly entered the warm kitchen. Sarah sat at the table drinking something hot. I didn't even care what it was; I just pointed at it and plopped down in the nearest chair. She poured me a cup of what turned out to be coffee. I pulled off my gloves and wrapped my frozen fingers around the cup. It felt so good my whole body shivered.

Sweetie knelt down next to me and pulled off my shoes and socks. Then she went to the sink and poured some water in a tub. "Let your feet dangle in this for a while," she said, carrying it over and putting it down in front of me. "I'll go get you some nice warm socks."

Grateful for her help, I stuck my toes in the water. Immediately it felt as if thousands of little needles pierced my skin. I instinctively pulled my feet out.

"Put 'em back in," Sweetie said gruffly. "I know it stings, but that water is just room temperature. It won't hurt you."

Gingerly I lowered my tingling digits back into the tub. Slowly the rest of each foot followed. It didn't feel quite so bad this time.

"Are the men almost finished?" Sarah asked after Sweetie left the room.

"Yes. It was a lot of work. I hope it does the trick."

"It's usually pretty effective, I guess. The past few winters have been rather mild, so it's been awhile since I've seen it done."

"Between our work and our prayers, I'm expecting good results. I'd hate to think I almost sacrificed my toes for nothing."

She smiled. "I would, too."

I drank the last of the coffee in my cup. "This might be the best coffee I've ever tasted."

"That's because you're cold and tired." She reached for my cup and went to the coffeemaker to pour me another cup.

"Oh, thank you. I think I'm beginning to feel human again."

Sweetie came into the room carrying a thick pair of clean socks and a towel, which was thrown over her shoulder. She knelt down and removed my feet from the water. She dried them carefully and pulled a sock over each one. Her actions reminded me of Jesus washing the feet of His disciples. I almost pulled away, embarrassed to have someone do something so personal for me, but I felt a still, small voice tell me not to. As I stared down at Sweetie, who was focused on caring for me, I didn't realize I was weeping until a tear fell from my face and onto my lap. I wiped my face, but not before Sweetie noticed.

"Well, for cryin' out loud, girl. Whatcha bawlin' about? I ain't hurtin' you, am I?"

I shook my head and smiled through my tears. "No. You're not hurting me. I guess I'm just a little tired."

She grunted and gave me a worried look. "After I get you warmed up, I want you to take it easy. That's hard work out there. Shoulda left it for the men."

"Actually, I would have enjoyed it if we hadn't been out there for such a serious reason and it wasn't so cold. It feels good to work hard." I told the women about the barrel with the raccoons and Eric's reaction to it. They both laughed along with me.

"How many times have you and Sam had to do this, Sweetie?" Sarah asked.

After getting the new warm socks on my feet, Sweetie picked up the tub and towel and stood up. She paused a moment and squinted like she was trying to see something far away. "Let's see. Altogether I'd say we've been hit five or six times with temperatures below zero. Some was real serious." She smiled and bobbed her head up and down. "But every time the good Lord was faithful and answered our prayers. I know He'll do it this time, too."

Sarah sighed. "You have such faith. I wish I had more. I worry too much about things."

I wiggled my now-warm feet around, trying to make sure the circulation was back. "You worry about people, Sarah. Not things. There's a difference."

Sweetie dumped the water from the tub into the sink, splashing some of it on her apron. "Worry is worry, girls. Faith is faith." She turned around, leaned against the sink, and stared at us, her features wrinkled in thought. "I been wonderin' a lot about this faith stuff." She shook her head. "I started worryin' about it until I realized I was worryin' about not worryin'!" She let loose a raucous laugh. "Now don't that just take the cake?"

Then her expression turned somber. "You know, I'm right

grateful to God for all He done for me. Sendin' Sam into my life. Helpin' me to have this wonderful place to live and all. And most of all, lovin' a rough old broad like me. All He asks me to do is to trust Him and to cast my care on Him. I been figgerin' that since He's done so much for me, it's a pretty little thing He's askin' me back. I'm gonna try harder to do just that. I really am." With that she turned around and went back to rinsing out her tub and sink.

Sarah and I just looked at each other. Sweetie Goodrich surprised me almost every day with her homespun wisdom. She had a way of talking about herself and convicting me right down in the bottom of my heart without knowing she'd done it. Seemed like lately she'd been full of little sermonettes. The time she'd spent studying God's Word was starting to show.

"Sweetie, I think you're a pretty smart woman, you know that?" Sarah's tone was soft but sincere. "And I truly believe you're right. It *is* a pretty little thing to ask. I think we'll all quit worrying about the orchards and believe they'll be just fine. How about that?"

I could only nod at her. The concern over Sam's trees lifted, and I had a knowing down deep inside me that we would pass through this trial and come out victorious. A peace came into the room—and with it, a loud rumble from my stomach. "When is dinner ready, Sweetie?" I asked. "I'm starving!"

Just then the front door opened, and we heard the men clomping down the hall.

"It's ready right now," she said. "I've been keepin' things warm for you all."

I started to get up so I could help her, but she stopped me. "You stay right there, young lady. You're plumb tuckered out. I got this well in hand."

Sam stuck his head in the kitchen. "We're gonna clean up a bit; then we're ready to eat." He sniffed the air. "Wow, that smells amazing. I could eat my dinner and everyone else's."

Sweetie jabbed a big spoon at him. "You ain't eatin' anyone's food but your own. You ain't never starved for nothin' in my kitchen and you never will!"

Sam laughed and left the room. Within a matter of minutes, Sweetie had the table loaded with enough food to feel a small army. Even though I wasn't allowed to do anything, she did let Sarah help set the table and carry over some delicious-looking dishes. The aroma from Sweetie's roast beef along with huge browned potatoes, onions, and carrots made my mouth water. A broccoli and cheese casserole sat next to a big bowl of homemade applesauce. And big fluffy rolls came out of the oven, browned and slathered with butter. It didn't take long for the men to file in. Sam said grace and we began filling our plates. No one spoke for a while. I could tell the men were even more exhausted and hungry than I was. Sam shoved his food down faster than anyone. Then he stood up and looked at his watch.

"It's almost nine," he said. "I'm taking the first watch. John, you volunteered for the second. Eric, you have the third, and Gabe, you offered to take the fourth. Am I remembering that right?"

"What are you talking about?" I asked. "Aren't you through?"

Sam's smile only emphasized the weariness in his eyes. "Can't leave those fires burning without someone watching them. Along with the cold, we need to be concerned about the wind. If any of those pots blow over, it could start a fire and cause us some real damage. Also, we need to make sure the fires don't go out. Someone has to be on guard almost constantly." He shook his head. "I'd feel better if we had more than one person at a time, but we're all too tired to pull that off. As long as we're careful, we can take turns."

"I can take a shift," I said.

Sarah and Sweetie both jumped in at the same time to offer their services. I could tell Sam was starting to say no, but I stopped him before he could get any further. "Look, Sam. You've spent time clearing the streets and now this. Except for tonight, I've been sitting around doing nothing. I admit I was a little tired before we ate, but I'm fine now. For crying out loud, all I have to do is watch the barrels and the pots, right? If there's anything wrong, I'll come and get you." Again he started to say something, but I held my hand up. "Listen, if you guys get a couple hours of shut-eye, you'll have a better chance of staying awake out there. You sit around for long in the cab of a warm truck, as tired as you are now, you won't last more than fifteen minutes. Why don't you let me take the first watch? You all get some rest, and someone can relieve me in two hours. Okay?"

It was clear he wanted to argue with me, but it wasn't any use. My logic was too sound. Truthfully, I was still a little bit tired, but at least I wasn't sleepy. I knew I could stay awake. Sam and the other guys were fighting to keep their eyes open. After some hesitation, he shrugged.

"All right. I have to admit that your way makes more sense." He dug the keys to his truck out of his pocket and handed them to me. "Just drive up near the orchards. Park and watch for a while. About every fifteen minutes, drive all the way around. You're looking for fires that have gone out or pots that have blown over. If you see anything that concerns you, come and get me. Don't try to deal with it yourself."

I threw him a mock salute. "Yes, sir. I understand."

He smiled at me and then turned his attention to his aunt and Sarah. "Sweetie, I think you need to stay here. You're cooking for a houseful of people." She began to protest, but he interrupted her. "Let me finish. These are your orchards. Whatever you say goes. If you want to take a shift, that's up to you."

"Well, thank you for that. I was startin' to wonder if you thought I was just some weak-willed woman." She thought for a minute. "Why don't I take the shift after Gracie? While she's gone, I'll put some breakfast casseroles together. That way in the mornin' alls I gotta do is pop 'em in the oven. That'll give you guys four hours of sleep."

"That sounds wonderful. But if either of you run into trouble, you hightail it back here and wake me up. Better yet, where are our walkie-talkies?"

"They're right here." Sweetie got up and went over to a drawer next to her sink. She pulled it open and removed two black instruments.

"So that's how you guys keep in touch when you're working outside?" Eric asked. "I noticed my cell phone is worthless out here."

Sam nodded. "Cell phone service is spotty at best. These work great." He turned his attention back to me. "I'll keep one with me. If you need help, you call me." He looked around at everyone seated at the table. "When your shift is over, you give your walkie-talkie to the next person."

He handed the walkie-talkie to me, and I got up from the table. "I'd like to change my clothes first. I won't take long."

"You go get ready," Sweetie said. "I'll make you a thermos of coffee to take with you. Should help to keep you alert. In fact, I'll keep the pot on all night. If any of you want to take the thermos with you, just wash it out and fill it. Pass it to the next one."

Everyone around the table expressed their thanks, but Sarah looked troubled. "What about me? Can't I take a shift?"

"Daughter, we're still concerned about you," Gabe said. "You need to rest. Why don't you help Sweetie?" Seeing her crestfallen expression, he smiled. "Tell you what, if you want, you can come with me. That way I know I can stay awake. Besides, you haven't driven a truck like Sam's before."

She bristled at his comment. "I *have* driven a truck, Papa. I drove Uncle Matthew's truck when we went to visit. And I can drive our tractor."

Gabe tried to hide his quick grin. "Uncle Matthew's truck is an automatic. And you drive the tractor in one gear, Sarah. You can't do that with Sam's truck. I don't want you to get stranded outside in this weather—again."

Sarah still looked somewhat disappointed, so he added, "I'll tell you what, with Sam's permission, while we're keeping an eye on things, perhaps I could give you a driving lesson." He looked at Sam for agreement.

"I think that's a great idea," Sam said. "Please feel free."

Sarah's face lit up, and she clapped her hands together. I noticed that color had come back into her cheeks. I was relieved to see her looking more and more like her old self.

I excused myself and ran upstairs. I had to change my jeans. The bottoms were still damp from the snow. After getting myself ready as quickly as I could, I said good-bye to everyone and headed for the orchards, Sweetie's thermos beside me. A drive around the outer rim revealed everything was okay. I parked the truck and poured some steaming coffee into the cup on top of the thermos. I tried to sip it, but it was too hot, so I let it cool for a couple of minutes.

I was wishing I'd brought Buddy with me for company when I spotted something that looked odd. A smudge pot appeared to be missing. Although I couldn't memorize every position of every pot and barrel, I was certain I'd seen it at a particular location my first time around. But now there was only a dark space where the pot had been. Had it fallen over? Sam not only had warned all of us earlier about a fire starting from a tipped pot but also had mentioned that kerosene was deadly to the trees. The wind didn't seem that strong at the moment, though.

Where could it be? It seemed silly to call Sam until I knew

something was actually wrong, so I left the truck running and jogged into the orchard to get a closer look. When I reached the spot where the pot was supposed to be, I found nothing. I started to chalk it up to my own confusion, when I looked down and saw a bare spot where heat from the pot had melted the snow that still remained on the ground. So how could a large metal pot completely disappear? It didn't make sense. I'd just turned to go back to the truck and call Sam when a sharp pain exploded on the side of my head, and everything around me turned dark.

Chapter Twelve

I lay on my bed in the purple bedroom, but for some reason it was really, really cold. I noticed a fire blazing in the fireplace. I tried to get closer to it, but it grew too big, pushing past the fire screen as if it were trying to reach me. Instead of drawing nearer, I found myself pushing away. The heat was intense. Sam began to call my name.

"Gracie, are you all right? We need to get you out of here. Come on, let's get you up."

I started to tell him I was trying to get away from the fire, when I remembered where I really was. In the orchard, lying in the snow.

"Come on, young lady. Can you stand up?"

Now why was Sam calling me "young lady"? I stared up at the figure that stood over me. "Sam? Is that you?"

"No, it's not Sam. It's Sheriff Taylor."

As my vision cleared, I realized it really was the sheriff who stared at me, not Sam at all. "Wh—what happened?"

He grabbed my arms and pulled me to my feet. The orchard spun around me. "You got hit on the head," he said gruffly. I realized with a start that the orchard was on fire.

"The trees are burning," I gasped.

"Yes, I know. Can you drive back and get some help?"

I nodded. The action caused pain to shoot through my temples. The feeling was all too familiar. A good strong helmet might have to be added to my clothing list if this kept up. "Th–there's a walkie-talkie in the truck. I can call Sam."

"Do it, and then go back to the house. Alert everyone about the fire. I'm going to do what I can until they get here." He peered into my face. "Do you understand what I'm saying?"

I rubbed my head. "Yes, I understand what you're saying. My head hurts, but my brain is intact."

I staggered toward the truck while the sheriff went the other way. What was he doing here? As I reached the truck, I turned around to watch him. Could he have started the fire? And if so, would he try to do more damage after I left? In my fuzzy mind, the only thing to do was to get Sam and the other men out here as quickly as possible. I flung the door to Sam's truck open.

It wasn't running, even though I was certain I'd left it that way. A quick search revealed no walkie-talkie and no keys in the ignition. I slammed the door shut and had decided to run to the house, even though I felt unsteady on my feet, when I spotted the sheriff's truck parked a few yards away. I hurried over to it, opened the driver's door, and saw the keys in the ignition.

The sheriff had disappeared into the trees, so I jumped in, started the truck, and drove as quickly as I could toward the house. As I neared Sam's, I couldn't help but wonder if Pat Taylor was the one who attacked me. I looked around the truck cab, trying to see if there was anything he could have used as a weapon. Nothing fit the bill.

I steered with one hand and popped open the glove compartment with the other. I had to turn on the interior light to see what was inside. I pulled out registration papers and a manual for the truck, along with a small personal phone book and a receipt for new tires. As I tried to shove the papers back where they'd come from, something fell out and dropped to the floor. Shoot. I couldn't reach it and drive with any kind of safety, so I waited until I pulled up in front of the house, quickly picking up what had fallen out and holding it under the light. It was a picture of a woman and a small child. A boy.

Frankly, it startled me. It hadn't occurred to me that Pat Taylor had a family. I put the picture back in the glove compartment. Then I jumped out of the truck and ran inside the house, hollering at the top of my lungs. It didn't take long for everyone to come running. When I announced the fire in the orchards, the men began grabbing their coats, hats, and gloves from the closet, and their boots from the front hall where Sweetie had put them on a towel to dry. As they all rushed to get to the orchards, I quickly told Sam what had happened.

"Someone hit you?" he asked, stunned.

"Yes, I have no idea who did it. Sheriff Taylor found me."

"Sheriff Taylor?" Sam and Sweetie echoed his name at the same time.

"What in blue blazes is he doin' here?" Sweetie's tone had raised itself several notches.

Sam grabbed my shoulder. "Grace, could he have done it?"

I shook my head. Ouch. "Maybe. He acted like he was trying to help me. Honestly, I just don't know."

Sam looked troubled, but we didn't have enough time to talk about it any more. The men raced for the door. John stopped and looked at me before he followed them.

"Sit down. Take some aspirin. Don't exert yourself. I'll check you when I return." He sighed. "You know the drill since we've been through this before."

I smiled weakly. "Yeah. But I think this will do it for a while. I've been told I'm hardheaded, but I really need to stop testing that out."

"You've got that right," John said. And with that they were gone.

"Land sakes, Gracie. Get in there and sit down." Sweetie took my hand and led me into the living room. Sarah followed behind us. She wore my flannel nightgown and her hair was down. She looked like an angel. I sat down on the couch and pulled off my boots. Sweetie held her hand out for them.

"Better put them on the towel," I said, "or that snow will melt all over the place."

"I will, but I guess that system didn't work so well. Someone's boots left a trail of water and dirt all down the hallway. I'm gonna clean that mess up and get you some aspirin."

"Some hot tea would be nice, too," I said, shivering involuntarily.

"Gracie, you need to change clothes," Sarah said. "You're wet."

I'd forgotten I'd been lying in the snow. I jumped up from the couch before I made a mess of it.

"You stay there. I'll get you something. Do you have another nightgown like this one?"

"Yes, it's in the drawer in my. . .I mean, your room."

"Why don't you go strip off those clothes in the bathroom, and I'll bring it to you. Along with some fresh underwear and socks."

I agreed and walked slowly to the bathroom, still feeling a little dizzy. Man, I was running through socks—and heads—like nobody's business. Once in the bathroom, I stared at myself carefully in the mirror. I looked like I'd been "rode hard and hung up wet," another one of Sweetie's colorful colloquialisms. I had no idea what it meant, but if anyone ever fit the description, it was me. Maybe the first time I'd hit my head it had been my own fault. But not this time. Someone had deliberately attacked me and then set the orchard on fire.

The orchard! I'd been thinking about myself so much, I'd almost forgotten about it.

I stripped off my clothes, which were now soaked. Then I dried off with a towel that I wrapped around my body. My hair was a tangled mess and smelled of smoke. Thankfully there was a brush on the counter. I brushed my hair out the best I could and waited for Sarah. When she knocked on the door, I reached out and took the clothes she held out to me. The warm flannel night-gown felt good on my skin.

There's something about flannel nightgowns that makes me feel safe. They remind me of the gowns my grandmother used to make for me. Beautiful, soft colors with ribbons sewn into the neckline. Although it was impossible to buy a nightgown as nice as my grandmother's, I still loved them. I felt like a child when I wore them. And I was. A child of my heavenly Father. I prayed quietly for the men, asking God to help them. Then I prayed that Sam's trees would survive the fire. I hung my wet clothes over the shower curtain rod and opened the door.

"What's going on in the orchard?" I asked Sarah, who stood waiting on the other side.

"I don't know. Sweetie's on the back porch."

I grabbed her hand and we hurried to the porch. The windows of the enclosed room faced the orchards. Sweetie stood at the window near the outside door. Sarah and I joined her. Although I could see the fire from the barrels and the smudge pots, I could only see one tree ablaze. I sighed with relief.

"I was afraid the entire orchard would be lost," I said. "But it doesn't look so bad."

Sweetie shook her head. "No, it doesn't. Even if we lose a few trees, we'll be all right. As long as the cold snap doesn't do the rest of them in."

"Wow, growing fruit is a lot tougher than I realized."

Sweetie snorted. "It sure ain't for sissies, I can tell you that."

I reached over and took her hand. "You're certainly not a sissy, Sweetie Goodrich. In fact, you're one of the strongest people I've ever met. I hope I can be even half the woman you are."

She didn't respond, but I didn't care. I'd grown used to her inability to accept praise or personal gestures, so it surprised me when she suddenly put her arms around me and gave me a big hug.

"Thank you, Gracie. That means more to me than I could ever say." She released me and went back to staring outside.

I still felt a little shaky and was in need of that aspirin she'd promised me, but I knew she wanted to keep an eye on her trees. I excused myself and went into the kitchen. There on the table was the bottle of aspirin sitting next to a glass of water. She hadn't forgotten. Tea steeped on the stove. I took about four pills and poured myself a cup of hot raspberry tea. I took it into the living room and settled down on the couch, covering myself with the same quilt I'd used for Sarah. Although I didn't mean to, after sipping about half a cup of tea, I promptly fell asleep.

"Gracie? Are you all right?"

Sam's voice again. I woke with a start. Was I back in the orchard? No. This time it really was Sam, and I was still on the couch. His face was streaked with soot, but he looked happy.

"What happened? Are the trees okay?"

He sat down next to me. "Only a couple burned. The rest are fine." He shook his head. "You may not believe this, but the sheriff actually saved most of them. He shoveled snow around the bottoms of the trees. When the fire reached the snow, it burned out." He leaned closer to me. "That fire was deliberately set." He kept his voice low and his eyes darted around to see if anyone was within hearing range. "Someone poured kerosene around about ten of my trees and sprinkled more on the ground so the fire would spread. Thanks to the sheriff's quick actions, the plan didn't succeed."

"But who—"

"I have no idea," he said, interrupting me. "But I don't believe it was Sheriff Taylor." He sighed and shook his head. "For the life of me, I can't think of anyone who would want to burn down my orchards. Someone must really have it out for me."

"That doesn't make sense."

He shrugged. "Not to me either. There aren't any more buried bodies you haven't told me about, are there?"

"No, no buried bodies. No murderers trying to keep me from discovering their crime." I pulled myself up to a sitting position and frowned at him. "Are you sure someone actually set the fires, Sam? Is there any way the smudge pot could have blown over and rolled near the trees? Maybe the kerosene just escaped on the ground."

He shook his head. "I thought the same thing at first, and to be honest, if the trees had burned more, I would have come to that conclusion. I found the missing pot near the base of one of the trees. But the trail of kerosene was way beyond the path of a rolling smudge pot. Besides, two things make that theory even more unlikely."

"What do you mean?"

"Well, I'm not convinced it's windy enough to blow over those pots in the first place. And someone smacked you on the head. Someone who didn't want you to catch them. You're sure you didn't fall over your own clumsy feet this time, right?"

"Hey, my feet aren't clumsy. And no, I'm sure of it. I was standing perfectly still."

He nodded. "I checked all around the area where the sheriff found you, just in case a large branch had broken off and fallen on you. But there wasn't anything like that."

"Man, Harmony may be a small town, but it's always interesting."

Sam chuckled and ran his fingers down the side of my face. "I need you to stay here. John wants to check you out. Again. I think he also wants to tell you that frequent hits on the head can have a lasting effect. You really need to stop it. I can't have the woman I love forgetting my name."

"That will never happen, Seymour," I said with a smirk. "Now get out of here. You need to sleep. Who's taking the next watch?"

"If I tell you, you won't believe it."

"I have no idea."

"Sheriff Taylor. He said he's well rested and pointed out that he has a gun. I took that two ways. Number one is that he is fully capable of watching the orchards and protecting himself. And number two is. . ."

"Never argue with a man who has a gun?"

"You got it." He kissed me, and then he rose slowly to his feet. I could see how tired he was. "I'll get John. Then I'll see you in a few hours."

"Not if I see you first."

"Look, I don't want you out of Sweetie's sight while I'm gone. Do you understand me?"

I rubbed my head. "Why?"

"Because I'm not sure what's going on here, and I want you to be safe. Promise me."

I held up my hand. "I solemnly swear to stay near Sweetie at all times. Like she'd let me get away from her anyway."

He leaned down and kissed me again. "I happen to love you. Do you know that?"

"I believe I do."

He left, and I closed my eyes. I'd almost drifted off to sleep again when John came in.

"We've really got to stop meeting like this," he said with a smile. "I told you I was just a general practitioner. You seem to have confused me with a neurologist."

I grinned at him. "Actually, I'm just waiting for the day you quit practicing and become a real doctor."

He sat down next to me on the couch. "I can tell your sense of humor is still operational. Now let's see if anything else has held together." He felt my head and then looked into my eyes. "You have a bump. Surprisingly it's not too far from your previous bump." He sighed deeply. "The next time could you go for the other side of your head? This one is about used up."

"Sure. The next time a crazy arsonist approaches me, I will immediately offer the other side of my head to him. No problem."

"Are you having a lot of pain?"

"No. In fact, it hurts less this time."

"I think you're just getting used to it." He frowned at me. "Well, Gracie, everything looks okay. But now I really want you to drive to Sunrise when the roads clear and get yourself checked out. I mean it. Will you do it, or do I have to forcibly deliver you myself?"

I knew he was serious. And quite honestly, I was beginning to wonder how many times one person could get knocked in the noggin before it caused complications. "You have my word. I will get myself to Sunrise and ask them to check me out for drain bramage."

"Funny. I'm going to follow up and make sure you do. Now get some rest."

"Yes, sir."

He started to rise, but I grabbed his arm. "John, don't you think this whole thing is a little weird? Why would anyone want to burn Sam's orchards?" I lowered my voice so no one else could hear me. "And one other thing. If the sheriff hadn't come along, and if the fire had caught the way whoever started it had wanted it to, what would have happened to me? I was unconscious and pretty close to the kerosene."

John's face paled. "I hadn't thought of that. If you hadn't been found or if you'd been hit harder, you could have been seriously injured."

"Just what was this guy after? Sam's orchards—or me?"

"Well, if it's any consolation, I doubt anyone would have set the trees on fire if you were the target. Wouldn't they have just finished you off and left? Why start a fire?"

"I don't know. And the sheriff showing up when he did. Don't you find that strange?"

He shrugged. "He says he was in the area, trying to make sure everyone was okay, when he saw the flames. Makes sense to me. Doesn't it to you?"

"I guess so. Still, something feels odd about it."

"I don't know what to tell you, Gracie. I'm just glad you're okay."

"Thanks. I think I'll shove down some more aspirin and get some sleep."

"Sounds like a great idea. Good night."

After John left, I got up and went to the kitchen for a glass of water and some more aspirin. After swallowing them, I sat down at the kitchen table for a while. The house was dark and silent. I took the time to pray for wisdom. I couldn't help but remember something Ida had said. About having a bad feeling—a stirring in her spirit telling her that something was wrong. I had that same feeling now, and I had no idea why.

Chapter Thirteen

Though I speak with the tongues of men and of angels, and have not charity, I am become as sounding brass, or a tinkling cymbal. And though I have the gift of prophecy, and understand all mysteries, and all knowledge; and though I have all faith, so that I could remove mountains, and have not charity, I am nothing. And though I bestow all my goods to feed the poor, and though I give my body to be burned, and have not charity, it profiteth me nothing. Charity suffereth long, and is kind; charity envieth not; charity vaunteth not itself, is not puffed up, doth not behave itself unseemly, seeketh not her own, is not easily provoked, thinketh no evil; rejoiceth not in iniquity, but rejoiceth in the truth; beareth all things, believeth all things, hopeth all things, endureth all things. Charity never faileth.' "

With that, Gabe closed the Bible and put it on the kitchen table. Instead of sitting down in his chair, he remained standing, his eyes cast downward. After several seconds, he looked up at us. "I haven't always lived by these scriptures. I guess I don't really need to tell you people that. You've seen the worst side of me. Bitterness and anger ruled my life." He hesitated a moment and then cleared his throat. "I hope you will all forgive me. I've realized that Paul's admonition to forget the past and press on toward the future must also be my goal. And it starts with love." He smiled at us, but his mouth quivered slightly. This was clearly an emotional moment for him. "I know that none of us can completely trust human beings. We're fragile, and from time to time we all fail. But we can always trust God, and His way is the way of love. To leave behind anger, to trust, to hope, and to keep no record of wrongs. I'm afraid I had quite a lengthy ledger of the wrongs that I thought had been done to me. And to be honest, I've realized that when others do things that hurt you, they are the ones who should be pitied. I just want to tell all of you, my dear, dear friends, that I am letting go of the past today and intend to press on—with my friends and my God." He sat down.

John slowly stood to his feet. "First of all, thank you for allowing me to sit in this morning. I—I know I don't really belong in this group, not being a Christian and all, but would it be all right if I said something?"

"Of course," Gabe said. "This is just an informal gathering of friends."

I glanced around the table at the rest of our group. Sweetie, Eric, Sam, Gabe, Sarah, John, and me. An eclectic group to be sure, but everyone seemed to be enjoying our makeshift Sunday service.

"I came to Harmony on a quest to find my father," John continued, "and I certainly accomplished that. Unfortunately, as most of you know, my quest turned up harsh truths that were difficult for me to accept. Like Gabe, I held resentment and anger, not only toward my father, but toward the world in general. That anger was directed at some of you. So I'm also asking for forgiveness, and like Gabe, I'm determined to leave the past where it belongs. In the past." He ran his hand through his thick black hair. "I have to admit that I've been thinking about what happens next. My first reaction was to leave Harmony. I thought it would be best for me—and for Sarah and Gabe. But if it's okay with them, I'd like to stay. I feel at home here, and I've never felt that way before. In fact, I think it might be time to turn my meat shop into something different—like a doctor's office."

I heard Sweetie's sharp intake of breath. Having a doctor in Harmony was a dream come true for all of us.

"But here's the thing," he said, his dark eyes full of concern. "I can't make that decision alone. Those scriptures Gabe read made it clear. If my living here would be hard for you, Gabe, or for you, Sarah, I'll leave. No argument, no hard feelings. If staying causes either one of you pain, well, I just won't do it." He watched Gabe closely. "So what would you like me to do? It's all up to you."

He sat down slowly, and for quite a while Gabe didn't say anything. The rest of us kept quiet, waiting for his response. I could feel my heart pounding. Surely he wouldn't send John away.

"I appreciate how you feel," Gabe said finally. "And I appreciate your concern for Sarah and me. In many ways it would be easier if you left. But I won't ask you to do that. You see, I've spent years trying to protect Sarah—and myself—from pain. But all I did was make it worse." He reached over and took his daughter's hand. "Sending you away seems wrong." His eyes sought John's. "I believe you're an honorable man, John. I believe you when you say you won't pursue Sarah. Besides, I trust my daughter completely." He broke his gaze away and looked at Sarah. "If I tell you to leave, it will be out of fear. Not faith. And not love." He directed his attention to John again. "I don't want fear to rule me anymore. Do you understand?"

I thought John would look relieved, but he didn't. "I do understand. But since we're being completely honest, I have to say one more thing. And it may cause you to change your mind."

Gabe gave him a tight smile. "You mean that you're still in love with my daughter?"

John's mouth dropped open, but no words came out.

"I know that, son. I'm not stupid. And I know my Sarah loves you, too. If that wasn't true, this decision wouldn't be difficult at all. Your promise would be easy, and I know it isn't. I still want you to stay."

"Thank you," John said quietly. "Then I will do that. And I intend to make you glad I did."

There was silence at the table. I had no idea what to say, and everyone else seemed to be in the same boat I was.

Finally Sweetie broke the quiet. "Well, land sakes, Gabe. There for a while you had me nervous as a long-tailed cat in a room full of rocking chairs. If you'd sent this young man packin', I woulda been right disappointed in you." She flashed him a toothy grin. "You done the right thing here."

"Thank you, Sweetie. Coming from you that means a lot."

"I hate to hurry off," Sam said, "but I need to get outside. Please continue. Don't end early for my sake."

Gabe let out a long sigh that seemed to come from somewhere deep inside. "Frankly, I'm drained. How about a prayer, and we'll bring this to an end?"

Everyone agreed. We held hands and Gabe led us in prayer. Then before he left, Sam made sure Sweetie and I had Sheriff Taylor's number.

"He's still in the area," Sam said. "He told us to call him if we need anything or if we see someone hanging around who doesn't belong here."

"That would be a mite sight easier if the phones were working," Sweetie said.

"I know that. But until then, if you need something, all you have to do is come out to the orchards and get me."

"Wish we had them walkie-talkies. Did you ever find 'em?"

Sam sighed. "No. Haven't found them or the keys to the truck. Thankfully I have another set of keys. Maybe we'll run across them today since the sun's up. Couldn't see much of anything last night."

Sam left the kitchen to get his coat. Eric had offered a ride home to Gabe and Sarah, and they'd accepted. I hated to see them leave, but they wanted their own clothes and their own beds. Besides, Sarah was worried about Molasses. I prayed the horse had made it home safely. I knew Sarah would blame herself if she didn't.

I got another cup of coffee while everyone got ready to leave. Then I sat back down at the kitchen table to relax a little. When the phone rang, it startled me so much I almost spilled my coffee.

"Glory be, the phone's workin'!" Sweetie screeched. She grabbed it and hollered, "Hello?" so loud, I hoped the person on the other end hadn't lost some of their hearing. "Why, howdy, Pastor," she said. "Glad to hear from someone. Our phone's been out for a couple of days." After listening to his response, she handed the instrument to me. "Pastor wants a word with you, Gracie."

I took the phone from her.

"Gracie? You all doing okay over there?"

"We're fine, Abel. Had some trouble in the orchards last night, but everything is under control now. How about you?"

"Everyone's fine. We're all digging out."

"Same here."

"Listen, Gracie. I need to talk to you, but I don't really want to do it on the phone. Are you planning to come into town anytime soon?"

Uh-oh. What now? Another letter? "I'm not sure. Is something wrong?"

Abel's gentle laugh drifted through the receiver. "No. Nothing's wrong. The baby's mother came to see me this morning. I want to talk to you about it, but as I said, I'd rather do it in person."

I was thrilled to hear the news but unsure how soon we'd be able to make it to town. I told Abel I'd have to speak to Sam and get back to him.

I hung up the phone, thrilled the mother had been found, but disappointed that Abel wasn't willing to tell me more until I saw him. Just then, Sam came into the kitchen.

"Can I get a thermos of coffee, Sweetie?" he asked his aunt. "It's really cold out there."

She laughed. "I'm way ahead of you, son." She handed him the thermos, already prepared. "And here's an extra cup for John. This should last for a while."

"Thanks." He came over and put his hand on my shoulder. "We'll be out there most of the day, Gracie. You and Sweetie could really help out by watching the weather forecasts. According to the most recent report, this cold spell could break sooner than expected. If it does, I need to know right away."

I nodded. "No problem, but I have a question. When are we going into town again?"

"If the temperature goes up the way they're predicting, we could go tonight. I'd like to take you both to dinner. Sweetie needs a break. She's been cooking for a houseful of people. I'd like to have someone cook for her instead."

"Sounds great. Abel says he knows who the baby's mother is and wants to tell me about it."

"You let me know what the weatherman says. If we can get up another twenty degrees and they tell us we'll stay above zero for a while, we'll put out the fires and go to town, okay?"

"Sounds good."

"Sounds real good to me, too," Sweetie said. "I love cookin', the Lord knows I do, but I gotta admit that I'm tuckered out. I ain't as young as I used to be, you know."

"Well," Sam drawled, "none of us are, Sweetie."

"Are you sassin' me, boy?"

"No, ma'am." He turned his face and winked at me. "I would never sass you."

Sweetie took after him with a hand towel, ready to snap it on his backside, but he quickly kissed me on the cheek and side-stepped his aunt. Laughing, he bade us both good-bye and hurried out of the kitchen before his aunt regrouped.

Sweetie came over and sat down next to me. She was quiet until she heard the front door close. "Gracie girl, I'm worried."

"About what happened in the orchard?"

She nodded. "Sam hasn't said much to me because he doesn't want me to stew about it, but I know somethin's wrong. I got a gut feelin' there's more goin' on than meets the eye. I want you to tell me what really happened out there."

As I began telling her the events of the night before, her face wrinkled up in a frown. The longer I talked, the more worried she looked.

"And that sorry excuse for a sheriff just *happened* to show up when he did?" She snorted. "That's plumb ridiculous. There's somethin' wrong with that man. I been feelin' it ever since I first met him. There's deep, dark water runnin' under the surface of his pond."

"But Sweetie, he saved the trees, and he probably saved me. If the fire had spread and someone hadn't found me. . ."

"Don't you even go there," she said, shaking her head with vigor. "Ain't nothin' bad gonna happen to you. I pray much too hard for you, Gracie Temple."

I squeezed her arm. "Thank you. I seem to need all the prayer I can get."

"Has it occurred to you that the sheriff only pretended to save you so he could cover up his tracks? I mean, maybe he wasn't countin' on anyone findin' out what he was up to. Maybe when you showed up, he had no choice but to play the hero."

I could only stare at her. "But why not just run away? Why slug me?"

She shrugged. "Maybe he couldn't get away without you seein' his face."

"Maybe," I said slowly. "But what about my keys and the walkie-talkie?"

"I been ponderin' that," she said in a conspiratorial whisper. "Maybe he didn't actually want you to get back to the house for help. Maybe he thought if it took you longer, the trees could burn faster. You fooled him by takin' his truck. Then he had no choice but to put the trees out." She frowned. "If that's true, then he ain't done, 'cause he ain't accomplished what he set out to do."

I considered her words. They made a twisted kind of sense. "I don't know, Sweetie. All we can do is pray for God's protection and keep our eyes peeled. But I'm still not convinced about the sheriff. He acted really concerned about me—and about the orchards."

"Well, here's somethin' else, Gracie. Somethin' I forgot to tell you. It didn't seem all that important until now, but while you was gone, I saw Taylor at your place, snoopin' around. In fact, one night he was out there after dark with a flashlight."

My head snapped up. "A flashlight? You didn't tell Sam about it?"

She shook her head. "Nah. He gets aggravated at me sometimes when I complain about folks. I'd already been tellin' him that snoopy sheriff was hangin' around too much. I knew he'd think I was hallucinatin' or somethin'. I was gonna tell you, but with everything going on, it slipped plumb outta my head." She frowned at me. "Is it important?"

I told her about seeing someone in the woods behind my house the first night I came back.

"See what I mean? I'm tellin' you, Gracie. There's somethin' goin' on with that man. Somethin'. . .nefa-fairy-us."

Even though our conversation was serious, I couldn't hold back a smile. "I thought you said *nefarious* was a fancy-schmancy word."

She grunted. "Well, it certainly fits in this situation." She got up and went to the coffeemaker, grabbed the carafe, and carried it back to the table. "All I know is we need to do what Sam said. Keep our eyes open for anything suspicious." She filled our cups with fresh coffee. "I swear, I wish things would settle down for a while. The past few days have been real confusin'." She carried the carafe back and placed it on the warmer. "I can't shake this strange feelin' in my gut," she said when she came back to the table. "I think that old lion, the devil, is roamin' around, and we need to make sure we got our armor on good and tight."

Her declaration sent a shiver down my spine. I was just getting ready to respond when Sarah came into the kitchen.

"We're getting ready to leave," she said. "I wanted to thank you both so much for everything. There's no way I could ever repay you for your kindnesses to me or my father, but I would love it if you'd come by the shop next week after we open and pick out something you'd like."

Sweetie rose from her chair and gave Sarah a hug. "That's real nice of you, Sarah, but you don't owe us nothin'. We're all family, and lookin' out for each other is just what we do."

She smiled at us. "I know that, but I still would like to bless you in my small way."

"Thank you," I said. "I appreciate it. Hopefully all the businesses will be ready to open this week. We're going to try to go to town tonight if the temperatures keep rising."

"Papa said the forecaster predicted several days of below-zero weather. Has that changed?"

I nodded. "This morning they said the severe cold could break as early as today."

Sarah beamed. "God is answering our prayers, isn't He? This is wonderful news. I will continue to pray until the trees are safe."

"Please do," I said. "Where's your father? I wanted to say good-bye to him."

"I'm right here." Gabe's bass voice rang out loud and clear. "I'm sure Sarah has thanked all of you for your incredible help in finding her and nursing her to health, but I also want to express my gratitude. You've made both of us feel welcome. I won't ever forget it."

I went over and hugged Sarah. Then I held my hand out to Gabe. I wanted to hug him as well but wasn't sure if it would offend him. I shouldn't have worried. He disregarded my hand and wrapped me up in a big bear hug. I found my nose buried in the scratchy material of his thick wool coat. It felt wonderful.

"Well, I guess we need to get going," he said when he let me go.

Eric came up behind him. "Whenever you two are ready, we can head out. I've already been outside. The truck started." He grinned at me. "And I have no intention of turning off the engine until I get to my hotel."

"That's probably a good idea," I said, smiling. "When you go back to Wichita, you might look into trading that thing in for something more reliable."

"You've got that right," he said, shaking his head. "Believe me, I've learned my lesson." He smiled at Sweetie. "Thank you so much for your hospitality—and your magnificent food." He patted his stomach. "I'm going to avoid the scale for a few days. The hotel food should help me lose whatever I put on here. You're an incredible cook, Sweetie."

"Young man, I ain't usually wrong about people, but it seems I've been a mite unfair to you. I ain't sayin' I trust you completely. And I ain't sayin' I'm not still a little peeved with you, but you jumped in to help us when we needed it, and I'm mighty grateful. You're welcome back here anytime."

Sweetie's little speech took all of us by surprise, including Eric. "Well. . .well, thank you. I don't know what to say. That means a lot to me."

Sweetie nodded at him. "Now you all get out of here and get home." She pointed at Eric. "I'd be obliged if you'd give us a call when you get to your hotel. Let us know everyone made it back safe."

"I'll do that," Eric promised.

I followed them to the front door, grabbing Eric's arm before he could leave. I pulled him back a bit, letting Sarah and Gabe go ahead. "I wanted to thank you, too," I said. "And to apologize for the way you were treated. Sam and Sweetie were out of line. I'm glad everything's okay now."

"I wouldn't say it's okay," he said quietly. "Sweetie may have come around, but Sam still doesn't trust me."

"I'm sorry. I know he appreciates your help."

Eric's deep blue eyes peered into mine. "You know what Gabe said this morning about John still having feelings for Sarah?"

"Yes."

"Sam shouldn't trust me. If I thought I had a chance with you, I wouldn't hesitate to tell you how much I care about you. How deeply I'm attracted to you."

I shook my head at him and took a step back.

"Don't worry, Gracie. Like John, I'm a man of honor. I have no intention of acting on my feelings. I know how much you love

Sam. You're safe. I just thought you should know." With that he walked out the door.

I stood and stared at the closed door, my heart beating so hard I could feel it. At the beginning of this strange weekend, I'd forecast that hidden emotions would come to the surface. Well, they certainly had. But I'd been looking in the wrong direction, never dreaming my prediction would come back to haunt me.

Chapter Fourteen

Sweetie and I spent the afternoon cleaning up after our guests—doing all the dishes, washing sheets, towels, and blankets. The entire time we kept one ear open to the weather forecasts. The temperature climbed into the thirties by late afternoon, and the announcer finally declared that although at first they'd expected it to stay below zero for several days, things had changed. It would stay bitterly cold, but the temperatures were predicted to stay well above zero. Sweetie and I thanked the Lord together for answering our prayers. When Sam came in around three o'clock, we told him the good news.

"Hallelujah." He sighed with relief. "Except for the two trees that burned, they all seem okay. Of course, we can't be sure until spring, but all in all, I'm very optimistic."

"So what now?" I asked.

"Now we put out the fires, and I tell John to go home. I'll put the smudge pots away tomorrow."

Sweetie crooked her finger toward him. "Does this mean we get to go out tonight? I could use me one of Mary's great steaks." The eagerness in her face made Sam smile.

"I think that sounds like a great idea."

"How do you know Mary will be open?" I asked. "You two act like she lives there."

Sweetie laughed. "Maybe that's because she does. Mary's got an apartment over the restaurant. Cute little place. I saw it once when Sam and her was seein' each other."

"I guess that explains why she didn't seem worried about getting home the other night after our first round of snow. I never really thought about it."

"It's also one of the reasons she's always open," Sam said. "Besides the fact that she enjoys having people around her. I think she's pretty lonely when the restaurant is closed." He shook his head. "Twenty-nine years old, and her life revolves around that place."

I felt a wave of pity for Mary. She seemed so self-confident and comfortable with people. Goes to show we just don't know what's really hiding below the surface. "She asked if I could come by and have dinner with her tomorrow night. Do you think my Bug will be able to make it back and forth?"

Sam shrugged. "I guess we'll get a better idea of road conditions tonight. I expect some of the snow has melted, but it's likely to refreeze later. Let's leave early, okay? That way we can get back before it gets too slick."

"Hey, you're the one who has somethin' to do," Sweetie reminded him. "We're ready to go whenever you are."

"Why don't you see if John wants to come?" I said. "He deserves a night out. On you."

Sam grinned. "You're right about that. I'll ask him."

After he left to put out the fires, Sweetie and I finished up our work. About an hour later, Sam came stomping in the door, trying to shake the snow off his boots.

"Hey, there," he said when he saw me on my way upstairs with an armload of clean towels and sheets to put in the linen closet. "Give me about thirty minutes to wash up, and we'll take off."

"What about John?"

"What about me?" John had come in the door without my hearing him.

"What about going to dinner with us?"

He looked down at his clothes. "I appreciate the offer, but I'm a mess."

"I've got clothes you can borrow," Sam said. "We'd really like you to come."

John grinned at him. "I'm already wearing your clothes."

"The clothes you had on when you came here are clean," I interjected. "If that makes any difference."

"Well, it just might at that," he replied. "I would like to rinse off some, though."

"No problem," Sam said. "You can use the downstairs bathroom. I'll use the one upstairs."

Something suddenly struck me. "Wait a minute. I've been so excited about the trees being okay, I just realized we've forgotten something. We can't go to town. What about the orchards? Whoever started the fire last night might come back."

"I already thought of that," Sam said. "Sheriff Taylor came by while John and I were outside. He offered to keep an eye on things while we're gone."

"But what if he's the arsonist? We could be making a big mistake."

Sam frowned. "What? Sheriff Taylor had nothing to do with that. You've got him all wrong, Grace. He's trying to help us. He saved the trees—and you. Why are you so suspicious of him?"

I told him what Sweetie had said about Sheriff Taylor snooping around my house late at night.

He frowned at me. "So what? He's the sheriff. He could have

been investigating something. I'm sorry, but a sheriff outside with a flashlight sounds perfectly normal."

"Then why didn't he come and tell me why he was out there?"

"I have no idea. But I think you're being paranoid."

"Can I interrupt here?" John said. "I think Gracie has a point. We really don't know much about Sheriff Taylor. I mean, he might be a good guy and all, but why take chances? You guys go to town, and let me stay here. I'll keep an eye on things until you get back."

"No way," Sam said. "You've got to be exhausted. We'll just go another night."

"Don't be goofy," John said. "I saw some leftover meat loaf in Sweetie's fridge. I'd love nothing more than to sit in a quiet house, eat a meat loaf sandwich, and spend some time with Buddy and Snickle. To be perfectly honest, tonight I'd really like some time to myself. I love you guys, but I live alone. I'm not used to this many people around all the time. It kind of wears me out."

I started to object, but John stopped me. "Please. I'm with you, Gracie. Someone needs to watch this place until we know who started that fire. You all may be stuck at home for a while. Let this be my gift to you. Let me be your tree sitter for tonight. Besides, there will be lots of other times to go out to dinner. It's not like you don't know where to find me."

"It's up to you, Sam," I said. "These towels and bedsheets are heavier than they look. Why don't you two duke it out? I'll be back in a minute."

I continued up the stairs, put the towels and sheets away, and was headed back down when Sam came bounding up the stairs.

"So what's the verdict?" I asked.

"Get spruced up, good lookin'. We're going out."

"John talked you into it?"

"Yeah, I think he really wants to stay here. We need to get away, and he wants to be by himself for a while." He chuckled.

"Besides, I think he's serious about Sweetie's meat loaf. I know how he feels. It's great."

I had to agree. Sweetie had a way with meat loaf. I wasn't sure what she put in it, but it was better than my mother's. Even better than my grandmother's. "Okay. I'm going to call Abel and tell him we'll be at Mary's tonight. Maybe he can meet us there."

"That's the real reason you want to go to town. Admit it. You want to know the identity of the baby's mother." He reached over and tweaked my nose.

"Hey, don't do that!" I gave him a lighthearted slap on the hand. "It's not just because I'm nosy, although I have to admit I'm really curious." I sighed. "As much as I love this house, I would like to see some different walls for a few hours."

He grabbed my hand and kissed it. "And so you shall. The next walls you see will be a weird shade of blue and decorated with grease splatters." He offered me a goofy bow. "Only the best for you, my dear."

"Stand up straight, you big dork," I said, laughing. "You really do need a night out, don't you? And by the way, those walls are cerulean blue. And they're not the least bit weird."

He got to his feet. "It's a little bright for me. I guess I like my blues a little more subtle."

I kissed his cheek. "Because you have no imagination, my friend. Now get your shower. Trust me, you need it."

He grinned and put his hand over his heart. "You have wounded me to the depths of my soul. I shall take my stinky body to the showers, posthaste."

"Not posthaste enough. Now get out of here."

He bowed again and headed down the hall to the bathroom. My heart felt lighter than it had for a while. Even though we still had no idea who'd tried to destroy the orchards and given me a second bump on the head, Sam was obviously so relieved that his fruit trees were safe, his spirits were flying high.

I changed clothes and waited downstairs while Sam got ready. John made it to the kitchen first with his own clean clothes on. "Wow. Feels good to wear my own stuff. Not that I don't like Sam's wardrobe, but I'd started to feel like a homeless waif who had to rely on the kindness of others."

"And how do you know how a homeless waif feels?" I asked innocently.

"Okay. You got me. I'm just guessing about that. But now I'm about to beg for my dinner, so I'm right back where I started."

"You ain't gotta beg for nothin'," Sweetie said, walking into the room. John and I both did a double take. Sweetie's ever-present overalls had disappeared. Instead she wore a pair of nice black slacks and a cream-colored sweater with beadwork on the bodice. And her ratty tennis shoes were replaced with black pumps. Her dark gray hair was still in a bun, but it was neatly wrapped and accentuated with a decorative, beaded comb. Although Sweetie abhorred makeup, I could detect a slight bit of blush, mascara, and lipstick.

"Wow. You look great, Sweetie," I said.

John nodded his agreement.

"Well, for cryin' out loud," she barked. "You know I been goin' to Abel's church. Did you think I was wearin' my coveralls there every Sunday?"

"No. . .I guess not," I agreed. "I've never seen you right after church. I don't know what I thought."

"Goodness gracious, Gracie. I'm not some hick from the sticks, you know."

John and I exchanged quick glances. He turned away and stared out the window.

"Now about the food you thought you had to beg for," she said, opening up the refrigerator. "I heard you wanted a meat loaf sandwich, is that right?"

John had recovered enough to turn and face her. "Yes, ma'am," he said with a smile. "I've had your meat loaf sandwich on my mind all day."

"How 'bout some of my homemade potato salad and a big piece of peach pie to go with that?"

I could almost feel John's contentment rise and fill the room. "That sounds perfect."

"Everyone about ready?" Not only was Sam clean; he looked incredibly handsome in a black sweater and blue jeans. The sweater highlighted his blond hair and gray eyes. I almost gulped when I saw him, but forced it back. I'd have felt like a cartoon character. Next my tongue would be rolling out of my mouth and my eyes would pop way out of my head. None of those options seemed particularly attractive.

"Let me finish gettin' this young man somethin' to eat," Sweetie admonished. "Then we can get goin'."

"Hey, you look beautiful," Sam said to me, his eyes sweeping over me with appreciation.

"Funny, I was going to tell you the same thing."

He laughed easily. "And Sweetie, you look gorgeous, too. Maybe we're all too good-looking for Mary's Kitchen."

John snorted. "Guess it's a good thing I'm not going with you guys. I hate to lower the beauty bar."

"Thank you," I said sweetly. "We really appreciate that."

He stuck his tongue out at me but quit paying attention to the rest of us when Sweetie put his plate in front of him. Sweetie's meat loaf had taken over his brain, and further communication would fall on deaf ears.

"I'm going outside to warm up the truck," Sam said. "You two ladies join me when you're done here."

"Won't be more than a minute," Sweetie said while cutting

John a piece of pie big enough for two people.

"As soon as I eat, I'll take a tour of the orchards, Sam," John said with his mouth half full.

"That's great," Sam replied. "But remember what I said. Once every hour is plenty. You can see almost everything from the back porch. I don't expect any trouble tonight. Not with you here and the sheriff circling around."

The expression on John's face agreed with my feelings. Watching Sheriff Taylor might be the most important part of John's vigilance. But neither of us said anything.

Sam left to start the truck, while Sweetie made sure John was set up with enough food to feed a small army. While she fussed with him, the phone rang and I picked it up. It was Eric letting us know that everyone had made it home safely. I thanked him and hung up. I still felt uncomfortable with what he'd said to me as he was leaving. I hoped it wouldn't hurt our working relationship should he find a way to complete the project.

We got our coats and went outside. Fitting the three of us in the front seat was pretty snug, but the arrangement actually offered additional protection against the cold. Maybe the temperature was climbing, but you couldn't prove it by me. It was still chilly enough to make me wonder if staying home and having a meat loaf sandwich hadn't been the wiser choice.

The roads were in much better shape than I'd imagined, thanks to Sam and the other men who'd worked so hard to clear away the snow. As Sam had predicted, some of the snow had melted. As the temperature rose, the roads would get even better, although it would be a long time until the snow was gone.

As we drove past the spot where we'd found Sarah, I shuddered involuntarily. I couldn't help but wonder what would have happened if we hadn't found her when we did. Gabe and Sarah's buggy was gone, but I had no idea who had moved it or where it was. Hopefully it was back at their house. I forced myself to push the thoughts of Sarah from my mind. Tonight was supposed to be a fun break from the tension of the past few days. My mind needed a vacation just as much or more than my body.

Although we had to drive slowly, we made it to downtown Harmony just fine. These streets looked as if they'd received very careful attention. There were quite a few cars parked near Mary's. I recognized many of them. They belonged to members of Bethel who'd stopped in for dinner before church began at seven. We parked next to Abel's car.

"He's here," I said.

"I'm sure happy to know that poor little baby is back with its mama," Sweetie said. "I hope things go good for her. Wonder if there's somethin' I can do to help."

"I thought you said someone who left their baby wasn't much of a mother," I said. "Now you want to help her? That's a big change. What happened?"

Sweetie sighed and looked at Sam. "I figgered out that I was just mad at my sister for leavin' Sam. I don't know this baby's mama or why she thought she had to walk away." She looked at me and smiled. "I'm far from perfect, Gracie. But at least I'm aware of it. I asked God to help me change 'cause I know I can't change myself. And you know what? He's doin' it. I'll start to say somethin' that I wouldn't have thought about twice a few months ago, and suddenly the Holy Spirit reminds me that my words ain't right. That I'm gettin' ready to say somethin' I shouldn't. It might take me a bit longer than most to clean up my act 'cause I been so mean-minded for so long, but God don't give up on us—ever."

"Good for you, Sweetie," I said, hugging her. "I'm proud of you. Very proud of you." I looked over at Sam, but he seemed preoccupied.

"You both stay in the truck until I get you," he ordered.

"There's still some snow and ice near the steps, and I don't want you slipping and falling."

He climbed out and came around to the passenger door. First he escorted Sweetie up to the front door of the restaurant and then came back to get me.

"You need to say something encouraging to your aunt," I said quietly as he helped me out of the truck. "She's trying so hard to change."

"Humph," he grunted. "She's said stuff like this before. Let's see how long her newfound personality lasts. Just a couple of days ago she ripped some TV commentator to shreds because she didn't agree with his politics."

"Wow. That's a really negative attitude. How about cutting her a little slack, Mister Self-Righteous?"

He grunted. "Okay, I get the point. You're right." We walked up the steps to where Sweetie waited for us.

"Man, I can hardly wait to rip into one of Mary's rib-eye steaks. Hector does somethin' to 'em that makes 'em so juicy, you think you're drinkin' meat instead of eatin' it."

As we entered the restaurant, I tried to get the concept of liquid meat out of my mind. Mary spotted us when we came in.

"Hey, I've been wondering about all of you. How are you guys?"

Before Sam or I had a chance to open our mouths, Sweetie launched into a diatribe of our experiences over the last few days. By the time we sat down, Mary had been thoroughly briefed. The only things Sweetie didn't reveal were my bump on the head and our suspicion that the fire that started in the orchard was arson. I was pleased she hadn't spilled out all our business.

"I'm glad the trees are okay," she said, "but what about Sarah?"

"She's fine," I said, "but we sure were worried at first."

"She's such a sweet person," Mary said with a frown. "I hate the idea of her being out in that blizzard by herself."

"Thank God He led us right to her," Sweetie said. "It was a miracle if you ask me."

Mary nodded. "Sounds like it." She took her notepad out of her pocket. "What can I get for you all?"

We placed our drink orders, but I asked Mary to give us more time to decide what we wanted to eat. She left our table and I glanced around the room, looking for Abel. I spotted him across the room sitting with Emily and Hannah. I hadn't seen either one of them since I got back to town. I excused myself and headed for their table. Abel saw me coming and waved me over.

"Gracie," he said with a big smile, "I'm so glad to see you. I heard about the fire in Sam and Sweetie's orchard. Glad everything's okay."

"Who told you about that?" I asked, surprised.

Emily grabbed my hand and squeezed it. "It was Sheriff Taylor," she said. "We ran into him here at lunch. We don't usually eat out twice in one day like this, but the road to our house is still pretty bad. Abel decided we should hang around town today so we wouldn't run into any problems getting back for tonight's service."

Abel chuckled. "I was as surprised as anyone when he came up to our table to talk to us. I was giving Mary my order when he interrupted and told us about the fire. He seemed very concerned about all of you. Said he intends to keep a watchful eye on Sam's place."

"For a minute, I wondered if we were under arrest," Hannah said, giggling. "He doesn't like Mennonites, you know."

"Hannah!" Emily said. "Don't tell tales. As far as I know, he's never specifically said he doesn't like *us*."

"My wife's right. I don't think it's just Mennonites the man finds so repulsive. I think he feels the same about all faiths. He's an equal opportunity heathen." Abel eyes twinkled and he winked at me.

"Abel! My goodness. Calling a law enforcement official a heathen," Emily said with a sigh. "I'm glad we're going to church tonight so you can repent." Even though she sounded serious, I noticed the sides of her mouth curve up.

"When can we get together to paint?" Hannah asked. Even though I'd only been gone a couple of months, I could see the gorgeous blond-haired, blue-eyed girl maturing right before my eyes. Not only did she possess God-given talent; she'd been blessed with a delicate, almost angelic beauty.

"If the weather holds, we'll get together this week sometime. How's that?"

Her face lit up. "That would be wonderful. I've missed you, Gracie."

I leaned over and kissed her on the cheek. "I've missed you, too, Hannah."

"Add me to the list," Emily said with a smile. "Why don't you come to dinner one night during the week? You and Hannah could paint afterward."

"I'd love it. Can I call you tomorrow to set it up?"

She squeezed my arm. "That would be wonderful."

Abel stood to his feet. "If you both will excuse Gracie and me for a moment, I'd like to talk to her privately."

"You're always talking privately to people," Hannah said. Her bottom lip stuck out slightly.

Abel raised one eyebrow and stared at his daughter through narrowed eyes. "You're right, Hannah. It comes with the territory. I'm a pastor. Maybe you weren't aware of that."

She blushed. "I know, I know. But I'd like to have a secret once in a while."

"Tell you what," I said. "When we get together, I'll tell you a secret about me. As long as you promise to keep it to yourself."

"Oh, Gracie," she breathed. "I promise."

I winked at Emily, who smiled at me. I had no idea what secret I could share with the teenager, so I'd have to do some thinking first. I said good-bye to the women and followed Abel to an empty table.

"I'm almost glad Hannah mentioned secrets, because this will have to be a secret between us for now. The mother's identity won't stay quiet for long since people will see her with the baby, but it's up to her to decide how to tell people."

"I understand, but boy, Sweetie and Sam are really going to be disappointed."

He chuckled. "Emily respects my position, but she's tried once or twice to get me to reveal the truth."

"You mean Emily doesn't even know?"

"No. A pastor isn't any different than a priest or a psychiatrist when it comes to protecting the privacy of our parishioners. The only person I have permission to tell is you."

"I don't understand."

Abel leaned in closer to me. "I told her about the letter and how it had upset you. She felt you should know, and she asked me to apologize to you. Not only for being accused of something you didn't do, but also for running away from you the night she brought me the baby. She saw you fall down but was too afraid to go back and check on you. She feels bad about it."

"Please tell her I'm fine. There aren't any hard feelings. And the letter certainly wasn't her fault." I scooted my chair nearer to him. "I don't suppose the letter writer has also confessed?"

He shook his head. "Sorry. I still have no idea who wrote it. What about you?"

"Not a clue."

"I'm still hoping we'll find out one of these days. I keep talking about the seriousness of gossip and false accusations in my sermons, hoping the culprit will confess. But so far no one has said anything." He laughed softly. "I think my congregation is getting a little nervous. I was told that the ladies' Bible study had a real revival last week. They were crying and repenting and carrying on so loudly our outreach committee left their meeting to find out what was wrong."

I giggled at the picture that popped into my mind.

"Now to the reason I asked to see you."

His tone turned solemn, and I suddenly felt apprehensive. Was the mother someone I knew? Would I be shocked?

"Not only is the mother almost a child herself, only seventeen, but this past week has been a terrible time for this family. You see, her father just passed away."

I shook my head, puzzled by his comment. I had no way of knowing who had recently died in Abel's church. I started to tell him that when the realization exploded in my mind. "Oh my goodness. Do you mean. . . ?"

"Yes. The baby belongs to Jessica McAllister."

"Oh, Abel. That poor girl. She just lost her father. How awful."

"Yes, it is awful," he agreed. "But there's more to it than you know."

"What do you mean?"

"Well, let's just say that Jessica brought the baby to me for protection. Rand McAllister was a very abusive father. She feared for the child and for herself. When Rand found out about the baby, he was furious. Thelma and Jessica had kept her pregnancy a secret right up until a few weeks before the baby's birth. Rand threatened to kill his daughter and her child unless she figured out a way to get rid of it. He told them he had no intention of supporting Jessica's illegitimate child." Abel winced. "Of course, he didn't use the word *illegitimate*."

"Boy, he really was an awful man. So after he was found dead, Jessica came to claim the little girl?"

He nodded. "That's right. And the look on her face when she saw that baby." He dabbed at his eyes with a handkerchief he took from his pocket. "Well, let's just say that I'm not the least bit worried about the baby getting all the love she needs. And Thelma is just as crazy about her. They named her Trinity, by the way."

"Oh my. That's lovely."

"Yes, it is."

"I hesitate to say this, but from what you've told me, it almost sounds like Rand's death was a blessing in some ways."

He studied the surface of the table for a moment before replying. "The death of any man who doesn't know God is a tragedy beyond description," he said. His voice broke. "Believe me, I stay up some nights thinking about people like him. People I couldn't get through to. I wonder if I'd done something different—or better—maybe they would have found the Lord."

I started to say something, but he shook his head. "I know those thoughts are wrong. The Holy Spirit convicts every person, and in the end, it is their decision. But thoughts like these are part of the territory when you're a minister." He cleared his throat. "But back to your comment. As far as Thelma and Jessica, yes. Their lives will be much better now that Rand is gone."

"That's a sad commentary on anyone's life," I said.

"It certainly is."

"Will they be okay? Financially, that is?"

Abel smiled. "You know better than to ask that."

I returned the smile. "You're right. Sorry. The church will step in and take care of them."

"That's what we're called to do. And we love doing His work."

A thought popped into my mind. "Will they sell their property to Eric now?"

Abel frowned. "Strange about that."

"What do you mean?"

"Thelma has no idea what Rand was thinking in trying to sell his land to Mr. Beck. Rand had mortgaged the place to the hilt. Of course, he didn't spend the money on his family. He used it for drinking and gambling. I guess he was a regular at a casino near Topeka. All Thelma can surmise is that Rand figured he could pay off his first mortgage and get another loan on the house so he could throw that money away as well."

"And then he got greedy and decided he wanted to not only pay off his loan but make a little more from Eric and his investors."

Abel shrugged. "That's about the only thing that makes sense. I think he kept the fact that he didn't have a clear title from Mr. Beck."

"So if Thelma sells her place to Eric, will she make any money?"

"Not much after paying off the mortgage. But it doesn't really matter since she never wanted to leave her home in the first place. Thelma feels as strongly about Harmony as most of us do. She wants to stay here—in her own home."

"So what now?" I felt overwhelming compassion for Thelma and her daughter. Rand had certainly left them an unhappy legacy.

"That's an interesting question. Seems when Thelma started calling family this afternoon to tell them about Rand's death, she found out Rand has a life insurance policy. It was taken out on him when he worked for the family business back in Iowa. After Rand left to come to Harmony, Thelma's brother kept it going because he was concerned about Thelma and Jessica. With Rand's drinking, he figured there was a good chance he'd die early, and the brother wanted his sister and niece to be protected. It's enough money to pay off the mortgage and get the farm back on its feet."

"Oh, Abel. That's wonderful news. I can hardly believe it."

"God is already providing," he said with a wide smile. "And the church will make sure those fields are taken care of the way they should be. Thelma will have enough money to live comfortably on her land as long as she wants."

I didn't say anything for a moment, and Abel noticed the pensive look on my face.

"What's wrong?" he asked.

"Nothing. It's just that. . ."

"That Rand's death has actually benefited his family?"

I nodded.

Abel put his hand on my arm and patted it. "Rand chose to use the gift of life God gave him to be selfish and cruel to the people he should have cherished. His life could have been completely different. We can do a lot of things to help others, but we can't make their choices, Gracie. Even God Himself won't override our will."

I nodded my agreement. There wasn't much else to say. It was a sad ending for a sad man.

"I won't keep you any longer," Abel said. "I'm sure after the past few days, you're looking forward to enjoying some time relaxing with Sweetie and Sam." He patted his round stomach. "And eating Mary's food." He beamed. "I recommend the sauerbraten. It's delicious."

I laughed. "Is there anything Hector can't cook?"

"He is a marvel, isn't he? Please keep him and his family in your prayers. His wife, Carmen, is pregnant and has been having some problems. Her doctor has ordered bed rest for the last three months of her pregnancy. That means she has to leave her teaching job at the school in Sunrise. With three other children, things are already tight. Hector has no idea how they'll make it."

"I'm sure folks here will pitch in and help."

"Of course. Several of the town's women have volunteered to help Carmen around the house and with the children. But that's as much as Hector will allow us to do. He won't accept financial assistance. He believes supporting his family is his responsibility."

"I respect that, but all of us need help sometimes."

Abel sighed. "I agree. But I have to respect his wishes."

"I'll definitely keep him and his family in my prayers."

"I know you will." He rose to his feet. "I think I see Mary with my sauerbraten. Now I must enjoy my dinner—but without showing too much enthusiasm."

I stood up, too. "I don't understand."

He leaned over and whispered in my ear. "Because if my wife suspects I enjoy Hector's sauerbraten more than hers, I'll never hear the end of it." He stepped back with a big grin on his face. "You be sure and call us so we can set up a time for dinner. And bring Sam with you."

I kissed the big man on the cheek. "I can hardly wait. And thanks, Abel, for telling me about the baby. Please thank Jessica for me, too."

"I will. God bless you, Gracie."

I watched him go back to his table. Emily and Hannah waved at me. What a great family. And what wonderful friends they had become. I could hardly believe that when I first came to Harmony, I'd been so negative toward Abel and his religion. Just proves it's impossible to judge justly through preconceived opinions and prejudices.

When I got back to our table, Sam and Sweetie looked at me expectantly. "Well," Sweetie said, "who's the mother?"

I sat down. "I can't tell you."

"What?" Sweetie screeched loudly enough to be heard by dogs in the next county. Several patrons turned and looked our way. I noticed the Crandalls sitting in a booth across the room. They smiled at me, and I raised my hand in greeting.

"Hush," I scolded. "The mother has asked Abel to keep her identity secret—for now. You'll know the truth soon."

Sweetie wasn't happy about being kept out of the loop, but she grudgingly accepted my promise that she wouldn't have to wait long for the information she wanted. "Why did Abel tell you who the mama is?" she asked in a subdued voice.

"Because of that awful letter. The mother felt bad about it and asked Abel to apologize to me."

"Well, it wasn't her fault," Sam said. "But that's very thoughtful." He shook his head. "When the truth comes out, I hope the person who wrote that letter feels like the judgmental gossip they are."

"Most critical, judgmental people are too busy thinking about everyone else to look at themselves. I think that's why God commanded us not to judge people. We can't see into another person's heart, and we have no idea what we're talking about."

"Besides that, we got that huge two-by-four stuck in our eyeballs," Sweetie added.

I chuckled. "You've got it right, Sweetie."

Sam winked at me.

"Here you go," Mary said, stepping up to our table with a tray of drinks. She put a coffee pitcher and two cups down in front of me and Sweetie. Then she handed a huge glass of Mountain Dew to Sam. "I don't know how you can drink caffeine this late in the day. It would keep me up all night."

"Sweetie and I can drink coffee almost up to bedtime, and it doesn't bother us," I said.

She grinned. "I wasn't talking to you." She looked at Sam. "I never understood how you can drink that stuff any time of the day and never have a problem."

He smacked his lips and took a big gulp. "Best drink on the

face of the earth," he said with a sigh. "Hardly ever go through a day without it."

"That's the truth," Sweetie said. "I cart that stuff back from Sunrise by the caseload."

"You guys decide what you want?" Mary asked.

"Abel recommended the sauerbraten," I said. "Think I'll go with that."

"You won't be sorry. It's fabulous." Mary scribbled my order on her pad. "It comes with potato pancakes and sauerkraut—is that okay?"

"Sounds great."

"And what about you two?"

"Bring me the biggest, juiciest rib eye you got," Sweetie said. "I've got a real hankerin' for steak tonight."

Mary wrote down her order, not asking about side dishes because she already knew what Sweetie wanted. "Sam?"

"Put me down for the second biggest, juiciest rib-eye in the place," he said. "After all that work in the orchards, I've got the same hankerin'."

"You got it," Mary said. As with Sweetie, she didn't ask about sides. "Hey, Gracie, you still coming here tomorrow night? The roads should be pretty good by then."

"Sure. It sounds great. What time?"

"I'll close up around seven. It might take me another thirty minutes to get everyone out of here. Will that work for you?"

"Perfect. I'll be here. I look forward to it."

She left to take an order at a nearby table. I recognized Bill Eberly, the kind man who had moved his car for Ida and me the day of the meeting. I held my hand up and smiled at him. He waved back. I noticed he sat alone at his table. "Sam, do you know Bill Eberly?" I asked when Bill turned his attention to Mary.

"Sure. Nice man. He and your uncle got along really well. He and his wife moved here about ten years ago with their two kids. A boy and a girl. They're both in college now. One's in California and the other is somewhere back east. Edith passed away almost four years ago. Cancer, if I remember right."

"So he lives all alone?"

Sam nodded.

"He's about Joyce Bechtold's age, isn't he?"

"Yep, they're about the same age," Sweetie said. "But it won't do you no good to try to fix them two up. Bill ain't been interested in any woman since Edith passed. He's a one-woman man, I guess. And anyways, Joyce is gone."

"What do you mean she's gone?" Joyce had been in love with my uncle for many years before he died. Although I was certain he'd felt the same way about her, he'd never acknowledged it. Before I left town the last time, Joyce and I had spent several hours painting the last birdhouses, feeders, and rocking chairs my uncle had crafted before his death. Working together had been a joy, and we'd begun developing a real friendship.

"Her sister died, and Joyce moved to Dodge City to take care of her nieces and nephew," Sam said. "She left about a month ago."

"I wonder why she didn't tell me." I couldn't help feeling a little hurt. Maybe we weren't as close as I thought.

"To be honest," Sam said, "I'm not sure her brother-in-law needs her that much. I think Joyce just wanted to get away. Harmony reminded her of your uncle. She needs time to heal. Maybe she'll come back someday."

I sighed. "Well, I hope so. We still had some birdhouses left to paint."

"She finished 'em," Sweetie said. "I shoulda told you, but with everything goin' on I just forgot. They're all stacked up in the basement. She told me to tell you to do whatever you want with them."

"Don't take it personally," Sam said kindly. "Joyce didn't leave you; she left her painful memories. She thinks the world of you."

"Well, I'll miss her. Guess I'll have to come up with someone else for Bill."

Sweetie snorted. "You don't listen much, do you? I told you he ain't looking for nobody."

I smiled at her. "Everyone's looking for someone, Sweetie."

Sam laughed. "You're incorrigible, you know that?"

"Why, thank you so much," I replied. "I resemble that remark."

Sweetie and Sam started talking about what work needed to be done on the farm during the upcoming week. I'd certainly learned the hard way that farmwork continues even when the trees aren't blooming. My attention began to drift when Cora, Amos, and Drew Crandall approached our table.

"I'm so sorry to interrupt," Cora said in her sweet, high-pitched voice.

"Not at all," I said, happy for a reprieve from farm duties. "How are you guys?"

"We're doing very well," Amos said. "Thanks to Sam and the other men who cleared the roads near our house."

"We didn't get to every street," Sam said. "Wish we could have done more."

"Well, you made it possible for us to get home and to church tonight," Cora said. "We want to thank you."

"You're very welcome," Sam said with a smile.

"We're really looking forward to spending some time with Mr. Hampton tomorrow," Cora said.

"Grant?" I said. "I don't understand. I figured he was on his way back to Wichita."

"He called us yesterday and asked if he could talk to us about Drew. He has a special son like ours." Cora put her arm around Drew, who gave his mother a big smile. "I told him we are far from perfect, but we would be happy to help him in any way we can. He's staying a few more days so we can spend some time together."

I was touched that Grant had seen something helpful in this wonderful couple. "I know you'll be able to give him some needed advice," I said. "He really does need it."

"I hope we can be of assistance," Amos said. "We intend to do our best." He tipped his hat. "You folks have a nice dinner. It's time for us to head over to the church."

We said good-bye, and I watched them as they left. "What wonderful people. Isn't it odd that with all the organizations and social workers in Wichita, it took a Conservative Mennonite couple in Harmony, Kansas, to give Grant the support he's been looking for?"

"Maybe Grant needed to see someone like Drew," Sam said. "Probably gave him hope."

"You must be right."

Just then Mary arrived with our food. We spent the next hour talking, laughing, and stuffing ourselves. It was just the break I needed. On the way home, I told Sam that if the roads were clear enough, I felt I could drive home. "Besides, I really want to check on Ida."

"Remember what I said about the roads being slick tonight," he said. "Why don't you stay one more night and go home in the morning?"

The possibility of icy roads, along with my growing sleepiness, made me easy to convince, so I agreed.

Sam smiled. "Good. Besides, when you leave, Buddy will have to start sleeping with me again. And he seems to prefer you."

"He does like curling up next to me. Snickle used to do that, but he hasn't been sleeping on my bed since I got here. I'm not sure where he goes at night."

Sam's truck suddenly hit an icy patch, but he was able to

regain control. Just as he had predicted, the moisture on the roads was refreezing.

"I'm not so sure about you driving alone to Mary's tomorrow night," Sam said. "If it's like this. . ."

"Tell you what. If it seems bad, I'll call you. Or maybe Mary can put me up for the night. I'm not a hero when it comes to icy roads. Trust me."

He hesitated.

"Look, Sam. I really want to do this. Mary and I need to get the past behind us for good. I promise I won't put myself in a bad situation."

"For crying out loud, Sam," Sweetie said. "Gracie's not a dummy. She'll be fine."

He sighed. "Well, with two opinionated females against me, I guess I don't have much choice."

When we pulled onto Faith Road, we could see John's truck still in the driveway, but behind it was Sheriff Taylor's patrol car.

"What's he doin' here?" Sweetie grumbled.

"He said he'd be keeping an eye on things," Sam said with a frown. "I still don't see why you two have such a problem with him. We should be thanking him, not criticizing him."

Sweetie mumbled something under her breath that even I couldn't understand, and I sat right next to her. Since I was positioned between her and Sam, he probably didn't hear her either. Probably for the best.

When we pulled up to the house, Sheriff Taylor came walking around the side of the house with John.

"I hope nothing else has happened," I said.

Sam didn't respond, but he turned off the truck engine and jumped out, jogging over to where the two men stood. Sam almost always opened the truck door for me and Sweetie, so I knew he was concerned. We got out and joined the three men.

"Is something wrong?" I asked.

"Everything's fine," Sam said. "Sheriff Taylor drove by and didn't recognize John's truck. He wanted to make sure John wasn't trying to burn down our orchards."

John grinned. "I was getting a little concerned about coming up with bail money."

Sam laughed. "I wouldn't worry about it. As long as your crime isn't too costly, you can count on me."

"So how are the roads into town?" John asked. "I was thinking about going to the store before I head home."

Sam shook his head. "They were pretty good going in, but they're refreezing. I'd wait if I were you." He cocked his head toward me. "Of course, Miss Demolition Derby here is planning a late-night private dinner with Mary tomorrow night."

"Might be best if you don't do that," Sheriff Taylor said gruffly. "Sounds like you'd do better to stay where you are."

I wanted to thank him for his advice and inform him that I didn't need him to tell me where I could go or what I could do, but I just smiled and nodded. "I'm going inside," I said. "It's too cold out here for me."

"I'm with you," Sweetie said.

We left for the house, the three men still deep in conversation. Once inside, Sweetie pulled her coat off and almost threw it into the closet. "I still don't trust that man, Gracie." Her harsh tone echoed her suspicions toward the lawman. "I mean, why is he showin' up here all the time? What about the rest of the county? I'm tellin' you, somethin' is wrong here. Real, real wrong."

I had to agree with her. A county sheriff shouldn't be hanging around one of the smallest towns in the state with as much frequency as Taylor. It didn't make sense.

"I don't understand it either. I still think we need to keep an eye on him."

"Both eyes would be better," she grumbled. "Well, I'm gonna head to bed a little early. I'm plumb tuckered out. 'Sides, there's a show I don't want to miss. Hope I can stay awake through the whole thing."

Almost every night Sweetie turned on the small TV set in her room before she went to sleep. And almost every night she fell asleep with it on. She appeared to use it as a sleeping aid. Didn't speak much for whatever she watched, but it seemed to work for her. I said good night and went into the living room. The fire in the fireplace was getting low, so I added a few more logs. Knowing that this was my last night in the beautiful house made me a little sad. I hadn't been on the couch long before Sam came in the front door and called out my name.

"I'm in here," I said.

A few seconds later, he stuck his head around the corner. "There you are. I sent John home. Things seem to be quiet. I'll get up a couple times during the night to look around outside, though. Sheriff Taylor told me to call him if anything happens." He came over and plopped down next to me on the couch.

"Where will Sheriff Taylor be?"

"He's headed back to Council Grove, but he said he'd check in sometime tomorrow."

I wanted to say that the orchards might actually be safe with him gone, but I decided to keep my comment to myself since Sam seemed to trust the sheriff.

"Hey, I want to talk to you about something," Sam said, drawing his words out with hesitation.

"Sure. As long as this isn't the 'It's not you—it's me' speech."

He laughed nervously. "Well, in a way. . ."

My heart almost leapt from my throat. "What are you saying?"

He put his arm around me and pulled me up close to him. "Relax. This isn't *that*; it's something else."

I leaned against his chest. "Okay, hit me. What's going on?"

He took a deep breath and released it slowly. I could hear the air leave his chest, followed by the beating of his heart. "I've been doing a lot of thinking. About the way I reacted when you showed me that note. I realized that I've never really forgiven my mother for leaving me. I thought I had. I thought putting it out of my mind was forgiveness. But it wasn't. Now don't get me wrong. When we forgive someone, eventually we need to quit thinking about it. Dwelling on it. But if we just refuse to think about it, well, it just isn't forgiveness." He ran his hand over my hair. "And that's why I acted so badly with you. It brought back those painful memories. Waiting at that church for my mother. Wondering where she was. Finally realizing she wasn't coming back. The looks of pity on the faces of the people at the church when they realized I'd been abandoned." At this, he choked up.

I sat up and grabbed his hand. "What happened to you was awful, Sam. No child should ever go through something like that."

He quickly wiped his eyes. "No, you're right. But I know in my heart that my mother thought she was protecting me. Giving me a better life. Her drug habit cost us both plenty. Many times we didn't have food. Sometimes we had nowhere to live. We slept out on the street or crashed at some other druggie's house. A few months before she left me, things seemed to have turned around. She had a job, and we lived in a decent apartment. But right before she took me to that church, I could tell she was using again. It was the way she acted. Her mannerisms and our lack of money." He paused for a moment and gazed into the fire. When he started speaking again, his voice was so low it was hard to hear him. "I know that's why she decided to send me to live with Sweetie. She didn't want to put me through that again."

"But you didn't know that at the time?"

He shook his head. "No. I began to realize it as the years went by." He shrugged. "Even though I started to understand her decision, I held on tight to my anger. It took my reaction to the note to finally make it clear to me that I've got to forgive my mother if I have any hope of having a normal life." He squeezed my hand and looked deeply into my eyes. His own gray eyes were shiny with tears. "Or to have a good future with you." He smiled crookedly. "That's why I said that our problems weren't you. They were me." He leaned over and kissed me.

When he pulled back, he reached for my other hand. "I've decided to forgive my mother, Grace. Completely. And to let go of the past so we can have the kind of life together I know is within our grasp. And I also want to ask you to forgive me for treating you the way I did. I hope you understand why I acted so badly."

It was difficult to answer him with a catch in my throat and tears in my eyes, but I have to believe that the long kiss I gave him said what words couldn't begin to express.

Chapter Fifteen

After a breakfast of Sweetie's homemade waffles with bacon crumbled into the batter, I felt fortified enough to drive home. I was sad having to say good-bye, but I actually looked forward to some time at home. Snickle's low rumbling from inside his carrier made it abundantly clear that all the going back and forth between cities and houses was beginning to fray his kitty nerves. I tried to reassure him, but watching for slick spots didn't allow me to focus much of my attention on my irritated feline friend. Sam had been right about the roads freezing overnight. If the trip to my house hadn't been a short one, I might have turned back.

All in all, though, I didn't have much pity for Snickle. Last night, during a midnight trip to the bathroom, I heard Sweetie's TV still playing loud enough to make it difficult for me to go back to sleep. I sneaked quietly into her room, expecting her to be sound asleep—which she was. But what I didn't expect was to find Snickle contentedly curled up next to her. This solved the question of where he'd been at night. I turned off the TV, petted him, and whispered, "Fraud," to Sweetie even though she was out like a light.

By the time I got home, I'd decided to take Sam's advice about driving after dark. Even though he'd offered to come and get me, I didn't want him out on icy roads either. I called Mary to see if I could stay the night if the conditions were treacherous. She reassured me that her foldout couch was at my disposal. Feeling better about my plans, I set about doing some housework, unpacking, and washing my laundry. But instead of even trying to use the dryer, I hung everything up on the clothesline I'd put up in the basement. I could hardly wait for the day when the electrical setup in the house was more dependable. As I pinned my clothes on the line, I thought about Ida, who did this all the time. Maybe having certain conveniences spoils people when they have to go without them, but not having them in the first place keeps you from ever missing them. Perhaps it was that way for Ida, Sarah, and Gabe.

After I felt caught up, I drove slowly over to Ida's to check on her.

"Ach, Gracie," she said when she opened the door. "You and Sam are too worried about me. I am used to this kind of weather, you know. I grew up where winters were much harsher than they are in Kansas."

I entered the door she held open. "I know, but with the phones out, we wanted to make sure."

She clucked her tongue at me. "I did not even realize the phone was inoperable."

I went over and picked up the receiver, happy to hear a hum. "Well, it's working now. And you have my word. We'll quit bothering you so much."

"My dear, I love knowing you and Sam care so much for me. You may drop in anytime. You are always welcome."

I stayed for a little while to visit, telling her about Sarah, the fire in the orchard, and lastly about Rand McAllister.

"Ach, no," she said sadly. "Poor Thelma and Jessica. How will they get by?"

Although I didn't tell her that Jessica was the abandoned baby's mother, I did share the news about the insurance policy.

She clapped her hands together. "God is so good, ja? He goes before us and provides for situations we don't even know are coming."

I also left out my hit on the head because I knew she'd worry. But passing the fire off as an accident didn't get past her sharp mind.

"How could a fire start like that, Gracie?" she asked with a frown. "I know about burn barrels and smudge pots. Although the pots can blow over, it is rare. It did not seem windy enough that night to cause such a problem."

I shrugged and tried to look innocent. "I don't know much about this kind of thing, Ida."

She searched my face for a moment. The thought crossed my mind that I wouldn't want to play poker with the astute Mennonite woman. I'd lose. But there was little chance she'd be caught dead playing poker anyway. A mental picture of Ida with a cigar hanging out of her mouth, saying, "I'll call your five and raise you ten," flashed in my mind, and I smiled. For some reason the gesture seemed to reassure her, and she changed the subject.

"So how does Rand's death affect the sale of his land to Mr. Beck?"

"It doesn't. Thelma wants to stay in Harmony. She never wanted to sell the land in the first place."

Ida breathed a deep sigh. "Good. So maybe the development will go somewhere else?"

"Unless he finds other property." I had no intention of telling her I'd asked Eric if he was interested in part of my land. Being so close to her place, I was certain she'd be horrified.

Suddenly she grabbed my arm. "Listen to me, child. There is

still something that disturbs my peace. Even this news does not calm it. You must promise that you will be very careful the next few days. I feel. . .I don't know. . .as if you might be in some kind of danger."

I could see the sincerity in her face. "Okay, Ida. I will. I promise." Although I still believed Ida's overdeveloped sense of protection toward Harmony was the cause of her disquiet, her warning made me even more committed to staying off the roads after dark tonight. My assurance seemed to bring her a little comfort, and we visited for another hour. Then I left, promising to come back soon. The temperature had risen some, and the drive home was better than the drive there. Snow, melting some from the large piles pushed up against the sides of the road, had turned into wet, sloppy mud. Not a good sign since it was definitely supposed to drop down below freezing tonight.

I puttered around the house until six thirty then took off for Mary's, bringing a change of clothes and some pajamas. When I got to the restaurant, Mary was shooing out the last of her customers, including the ever-present Harold.

"Thanks for coming, guys," she said to one family who'd just paid for their meals. "Sorry to rush you out, but I've got plans tonight."

" 'Bout time you had something to do besides boss me around," Harold interjected as he waited next in line.

Mary laughed. "Someone's gotta do it, Harold. And it's my pleasure. Now you get out of here. Why don't you go visit Esther Crenshaw? I saw her making goo-goo eyes at you in church last week."

Harold's florid face lost some of its color. "Esther Crenshaw? That woman's a menace. All she does is gossip. And those wigs of hers." He shook his head. "No thank you." A smile lit up his face. "But I might stop by that pretty Kay Curless's place."

Mary's mouth dropped open. "Why, you old rascal. Have you been seeing Kay?"

Harold blushed. "We got together to play cards last week. I asked her to come to dinner with me Thursday night. We'll be here around six."

Mary came around the counter and gave him a hug. "I'll have the best seat in the house waiting for you two. I'm so happy to hear this news. Kay is a lovely woman."

With that, Harold said good night, stopping first to ask me how Sam was doing. I assured him that the fruit trees were fine without going into details. After the door closed behind him, Mary rushed over and locked it. She'd already turned the OPEN sign to CLOSED. But now she pulled down all the shades.

"That should do it," she said with satisfaction. "I rarely close early, but almost every time I do, people keep coming—trying the door and hollering for me. For some reason when I pull down the blinds, they take it more seriously."

"Out of sight, out of mind?"

She chuckled. "Maybe so." She waved toward a table in the back that had been specially set. "Have a seat. I have our dinner warming in the oven."

"Is Hector gone?" If he was still here, I wanted to say hello. I'd grown to like the friendly man who'd taken me so graciously under his wing after the first storm though he'd been under so much pressure.

"Yep. I told him to take off after he cooked the last order. Nice chance for him to spend a night with his family."

I sat down at the table, which had been covered with a beautiful white linen tablecloth and set with flowered china. "Pretty fancy for just us gals," I quipped.

"We deserve the best, don't we?" Mary disappeared into the kitchen while I waited. I'd been a little nervous about this dinner, but her easy manner and extra effort put me at ease. I had high hopes we could be good friends. Not an easy thing to do with a background like ours. The silence in the restaurant felt strange. Usually this place bustled with chatter and laughter. Drifting through the overwhelming quiet, I was certain I heard low voices. A conversation. But Mary said no one else was here. Who could it be? I got up to check out the kitchen when Mary suddenly pushed the door open and came toward me with two large plates of food.

"I thought I heard you talking to someone," I said. "Is there anyone else here?"

She laughed. "Just me talking to myself. I do that from time to time. Sorry."

"Wow. Thought I heard two different voices. Must be the strain of the last few days."

Mary placed the plates on the table and pulled out my chair. "Sit back down. Hopefully dinner will help to take some of that stress away."

I sat down and checked out my plate. "This looks incredible. What is it?"

"Chicken paprikash with spaetzle. It's a family recipe. My mom was famous all around M—Marion for this dish. The secret is the paprika. It can't be just any old paprika. I get mine shipped from a special store that orders their spices from Europe."

"Marion? Is that where you're from? My friend Allison grew up in Marion. Did you know the Cunninghams?"

Mary cleared her throat and stared blankly at me. "No. . .no, I don't think so. But we moved away when I was eleven. I don't remember many people." She picked up the glasses on the table. "I made raspberry tea, but if you'd rather have coffee, I've got a pot on."

"I adore raspberry tea. Maybe I'll have a cup of coffee after dinner if it's okay."

"Sure. I'll get the tea and rolls and be right back."

"Mary, you shouldn't have gone to all this trouble. This wonderful food and the raspberry tea. How did you pull it off after working all day?"

"I've been looking forward to this for quite some time, Gracie. It was a pleasure to cook this dinner for you." She smiled and headed back toward the kitchen.

For a moment she'd seemed uncomfortable. Was it my question about Marion? And I couldn't believe she hadn't known the Cunninghams. Mr. Cunningham was the principal of the elementary school. Had been for thirty years. But maybe she'd just forgotten. Still, it seemed odd. Just then she came back into the room.

"Here we go. Fresh iced tea and rolls hot from the oven. Hope you enjoy everything. Although I can cook pretty good main dishes, desserts are not my specialty. I bought a cake from Menlo's. They make a carrot cake to die for."

"Yummy. I can hardly wait."

Mary sat down across from me and picked up her fork. Then she set it down. "Oh. I guess we should say grace. Why don't you do it?"

I bowed my head and thanked God for the food. Then I prayed blessings over Mary and her restaurant, also asking God to bless our friendship and help it to grow into something that honored Him. When I raised my head, I found Mary frowning at me, the same funny look on her face she'd had earlier. I wanted to ask her if something was bothering her, but I didn't want to come off as nosy or paranoid. Again I blamed it on the strain of the last several days.

I'd started to take a bite of my paprikash when Mary stopped me.

"Here," she said. "Put some extra paprika on it. It really brings out the flavor."

Simple Deceit

As I took the bottle from her, I noticed a ring she always wore. I'd never looked at it up close. At first I didn't recognize it, but suddenly I remembered where I'd seen the exact same ring before.

"That ring," I said slowly. "It's a high school ring. From Mound City." I raised my eyes to meet hers, which had grown wide. For several moments there was silence between us. Finally I said, "Mary, what's going on? You don't know Mr. Cunningham who was the principal of the school when you lived in Marion. And you act like you don't know Eric Beck, who went to school in Mound City at the same time you did. The school was too small for you two not to have known each other."

My mind began acting like a minicomputer, processing comments and different incidents, bringing them together. One dot connected to another until the picture that was left seemed extraordinarily ugly and unthinkable. Unfortunately, the conclusions couldn't be denied. Why hadn't I seen it? The truth had been right in front of me the whole time. "But you do know Eric, don't you? You. . .you and Eric. . . What have you been up to?" I set my fork down. "I don't understand, Mary. Obviously you two are working together to accomplish something. But what?"

Mary's face was blank, devoid of emotion, but there was something in her eyes. Was it fear?

I took the linen napkin off my lap and put it on the table and stood. "I don't think this dinner is a good idea. Unless you want to tell me why you and Eric have kept your relationship secret, I don't think we have anything to talk about. Some really strange things have been happening in Harmony, and they started not long after Eric arrived. I don't think it will take a lot of effort to trace most of them, maybe all of them, back to one or both of you. Maybe Sheriff Taylor would be interested in putting the pieces together."

Mary opened her mouth to say something, but no words came

out. Her eyes darted quickly to a spot behind me.

"Sit down, Gracie. Unfortunately, you won't be going anywhere."

I turned around to find Eric Beck standing at the kitchen door, a gun in his hand. And it was pointed directly at me.

Chapter Sixteen

I told you to take off that stupid ring."

Eric's scolding seemed to vanquish whatever spark of willpower remained in Mary's body. Her shoulders slumped and her eyes became lifeless. "I—I couldn't get it off. I've put on weight since high school, and I didn't want to ruin it." Tears filled her almost expressionless face. "Please, Eric. You don't have to hurt Gracie."

Eric pulled up a chair from a nearby table and sat next to me, his gun still leveled at my chest. "Actually, I really do have to hurt her." Gone was the kindness I'd thought I'd seen in him. It had been replaced by a cold hardness that sent chills throughout my body. He glared at Mary. "Thanks to your incompetence, it's our only way out."

Although I had no desire to anger him, for some odd reason I felt the urge to keep him talking. "If you're going to shoot me anyway, why don't you explain what's going on?" I said. "I get that you and Mary have been trying to acquire land in Harmony, but why go through all this? Did you ever really want Rand McAllister's property?"

Eric, seemingly pleased to have a chance to spout off about his plan, some of which I'd already figured out, sat back in his chair and relaxed his grip on the gun. "No, I never wanted Rand's property. Waste of time, piece of dirt. I paid him to pretend I wanted his land, then to back out after everyone in town was pumped about having a new development to help the town.

I shook my head. "But why did you feel you had to go through all this? A quiet retirement community would be a blessing here. Unless that's not what you intended at all."

Eric grinned. I couldn't understand what I'd ever seen in him. There was no warmth or compassion in this man—absolutely nothing appealing.

"Smart girl," he said. "No, there's no retirement community. My investors are looking for a resort that will be close to the new casino being built near the highway."

"Casino? I haven't heard anything about a casino in this area. I doubt the citizens of this county would vote one in."

Eric's laugh was full of contempt. "The hicks who live around here won't have a say. Not when several of their county officials are in the pocket of the group I work for. There are ways to push things through without asking permission, you know."

"A casino near Harmony would ruin the town," I said, stating something I was sure Eric already knew.

He shrugged. "Maybe. Maybe not. It will still bring in revenue."

"And a lot of other influences we don't need here. Harmony is. . .special. Your plan would destroy the very qualities that make this place unique."

He sighed. "Not my problem."

Again something whispered inside me to stall. "So if you didn't really want Rand's property, what did you want?"

Even before he opened his mouth, I knew the answer. I looked at Mary. "You said something once about grandkids fishing and swimming at the retirement community. At the time I thought it was odd, since there's no place like that around here. I should have paid more attention. I thought it was just a slip of the tongue." I swung my gaze back to Eric. "You want my land, don't you?"

He grunted. "Not just yours. Your boyfriend's, too. My investors want lakefront condos for their high rollers." He jabbed his finger at Mary, who'd sat silently since he'd come out of the kitchen. "I told you your stupid slipups would cost us. Good thing she didn't figure it out until now. When it's too late."

Mary's head drooped lower, and she wouldn't look at me.

"So when did you two put this thing together?"

"It's been in the works ever since Mary and I ran into each other at a bar in Topeka. I hadn't seen her since high school. When I told her I needed lakefront property for a new resort near a future casino, she mentioned Harmony—and you and your boyfriend's property. But she told me you wouldn't sell outright. That I'd have to trick one or both of you out of your land. We've been working on this ever since." He slapped the table with the hand that didn't hold the gun. "Your sites are the only spots in the right area that will work. They're perfect."

I shook my head. "But why, Eric? Is this deal really so important you'd risk everything to put it through?"

"He owes money to the men behind the casino." Mary's first words since Eric sat down were matter-of-fact. "If he doesn't pay them, they'll hurt him. Maybe even kill him." She lifted her head a little higher. "If he doesn't get your land, his life isn't worth a plug nickel."

Anger flashed in Eric's eyes. "Shut up."

Instead of heeding his warning, Mary turned toward me. "The plan was to split you and Sam up. If you left Harmony, Eric would buy your place and the building would begin. He figured that would force Sam to sell his property, too. Trust me, Sam and

Sweetie wouldn't be happy living next door to the kind of people the resort would bring in."

"You two started the rumors about the baby, didn't you? And you told Esther the baby was mine. Did you write the note, too?"

"Mary wrote it. I delivered it," Eric said. "I thought it was a great opportunity dropped right into our laps. Too bad it didn't work."

I frowned at Mary. "You knew about Sam's past, didn't you? You figured making him think I'd done the same thing as his mother would destroy our relationship."

She shrugged. "Sam told me once about his mother dropping him off at a church. I could tell it still bothered him."

"But why, Mary? Do you still hate me that much?"

"I did. I don't know; I guess I do." She shrugged. "Eric promised me money—and a new life. I planned to leave Harmony and start over with him." She sighed. "I know you love this town, but I want out. I'm tired of seeing the same people day after day. Having the same conversations over and over. Not everyone wants what you do, Gracie."

"I thought you were happy here. I thought this place meant something to you."

"It does. But just not what it means to you."

I frowned at Eric as a mental picture flashed in my mind. "It was you in the orchard, wasn't it? Sweetie said one pair of boots was still wet after she put them on the rug to dry. They were yours, weren't they?"

His grin made my stomach turn. He was pleased with the evil he'd done. He was proud of the web of deceit he'd woven throughout Harmony.

"I snuck out after everyone went to bed. Sam said something about the wind knocking over the smudge pots. It was a spur-of-the-moment decision. I had no idea what would happen. I planned to set quite a few trees on fire. In retrospect, my actions were ill conceived. The fire probably wouldn't have caused the kind of damage I'd hoped for."

"And hitting me on the head? What was that for?"

He laughed harshly. "I thought you were on the other side of the orchard, but you surprised me by showing up when I wasn't expecting you. I couldn't allow you to find me out there. After you passed out, I took your car keys and your walkie-talkie. I had to stall you long enough for me to get back into the house and act surprised when the fire was discovered." He shrugged. "I wanted to give Sam a reason to sell his property. If his trees were destroyed, that would have done it."

"She could have been killed out there," Mary said. "You said no one would get hurt." Although she still seemed somewhat disconnected, I could see something smoldering in her eyes. Maybe Eric was losing his partner in crime.

Keep stalling. The words were so loud in my mind I almost looked around to see who else was in the room.

Eric waved the gun around wildly. "I told you I didn't *plan* to hurt anyone." He glared at Mary and swung the gun her way. "I guess things change, don't they? If the fire had done its job, I'd be sitting pretty right now. With Gracie dead, everything would have fallen into place. I could buy her place and poor, distraught Sam would gladly hand over his property." He turned his attention back to me, his lips drawn up in a snarl. "I should have finished you off, but I didn't have enough time to come up with a plan to make it look like an accident. If that nosy sheriff hadn't shown up when he did, I could have figured out a way to do it without having to count on that stupid fire." He banged his hand on the table. "Don't look at me like that," he yelled at Mary, who stared at him like she'd never seen him before. "I've only done what I was forced to do. None of this is my fault."

"What really happened to Rand?" I asked, trying to keep my voice calm and steady. Eric was losing it. If he suddenly went completely off the deep end, the results could be tragic. "I knew something was wrong with the story that he'd accidentally wandered outside."

"What is she talking about?" The timbre of Mary's voice climbed a couple of notches. "You said Rand's death was an accident."

"But it wasn't, was it?" I asked Eric. "Did he renege on your deal?"

"Little creep figured out something big was up," Eric sneered. "He thought he could get more money out of me. Threatened to go to the sheriff with what he knew." He let out a long, slow breath. "He tried to extort more money out of me. What happened to him was his own fault."

Mary rose partially to her feet. "You. . .you killed him? You murdered Rand McAllister?"

He laughed harshly. "You're really stupid, you know it? I killed him on Thursday night after I took Gracie home. Then I brought him back here and stuffed him in one of your empty freezers until I got the chance to pick him up and toss him in the snow. You never even knew it." He laughed again and looked at me. "Now you know what I was really doing before I ditched my truck and walked back to your house that night."

Mary's face turned ashen and she looked ill. Her eyes sought mine. "I didn't know, Gracie. I swear I didn't know."

"Shut up, Mary," Eric shouted. "Just shut up." His fierce gaze swung back to me. "I gave you every chance to get out of this alive. If you and your boyfriend had parted ways, I could have bought you out lock, stock, and barrel."

"But I offered you my property once," I said.

"No. You offered me part of it. I need all of it." He chuckled.

"My plan was to get you to willingly hand it over. After disposing of Rand, I arranged that supposed breakdown so your boyfriend would find us in a compromising position and break up with you. I figured you'd leave town after that. Like I said, if I got your place, I knew I could drive Sam and his old-maid aunt out." He put his head back and giggled crazily. "I even turned on the charm, hoping you'd decide to leave your hick boyfriend behind and go for me. Then I planned to nicely talk you out of your place."

"Well, it seems that none of your brilliant plans worked. So now what?"

He grinned wildly, his eyes frightening orbs of madness. "Now you have an accident, just like Rand. You know, the roads are slippery. After you leave Mary's, your little car runs off the road and you're fatally injured. Or at least that's what it will look like."

At that moment several things happened at once. Mary shouted, "No!" and stood to her feet. Eric pointed his gun at her, and I heard a gunshot. But instead of seeing Mary take a bullet, I watched a slow stain of blood spread across Eric's chest as he fell to the ground.

Chapter Seventeen

Sam reached for another hot muffin. "I feel like a fool," he said. "I should have realized Eric was up to no good." He put the hot muffin on his plate next to the sausage and cheese omelet Jessica had just delivered to the table. "I thought the only thing he had his eye on was you."

I shook my head. "I guess I'm not as irresistible as you thought. Turns out my land was my best asset in Eric's eyes."

"This whole thing is my fault," Grant said. "I should have realized something was wrong with that guy. When Eric first came to me, he said I'd been recommended to him, but he didn't seem to know any of our clients. I should have pressed him, but I didn't. I realize now he only looked me up so he could get to you."

"Mary told him about you, Grant. You had no way of knowing what Eric was up to. And you have nothing to feel bad about. Eric fooled everyone. He and Mary are the only people at fault. They're the ones who chose a path of deceit."

"Well, Eric will have a long time to think about his choices in prison." Sheriff Taylor stuck a mouthful of Hector's banana pancakes in his mouth.

"I sure was wrong about you," Sweetie said to the sheriff. "Here I thought you were a meddlin' busybody, and it turns out you was keepin' an eye on those two rattlesnakes all the time." She cut off a piece of sausage and held it up to her mouth. "But how'd you know they was up to no good?"

Pat swallowed his food and wiped his mouth. "I heard rumors about Eric Beck from several sources—that he was working with a group of very questionable people and that he had his sights set on this area. I didn't know Harmony was the target at first, but after following him around some, his motives became pretty clear. I did some research on him and found his high school records. I saw that Mary Whittenbauer had gone to the same school. I started hanging around here, keeping an eye on both of them. When I heard her act like she'd never met him before, I knew they were in on it together."

"That's why you was near the orchards the night of the fire. You was watchin' Eric," Sweetie said. "You mighta saved Gracie's life."

He shrugged. "I wasn't sure what he was going to do at the time. I figured he wouldn't risk another murder. I was sure wrong about that." He scooped up a big forkful of scrambled eggs. "I did try to protect Sam and Gracie by telling that Mennonite pastor I was watching Sam's place after the fire so Mary would hear me and carry the information back to her partner. I just didn't count on Eric confronting Gracie here. Good thing Sam told me you were having dinner with Mary Monday night," he said to me. "I followed you and snuck into the back." He shook his head. "No one locks their doors in this town. Strangest thing I've ever seen. Glad the back door was open that night, though. I almost waited too long."

"Yeah. Thanks for delaying until the very last second to waltz in and shoot Eric," I said. "Made everything much more exciting."

The sheriff grunted and stuck the eggs in his mouth.

"And by the way, just what were you doing behind my house with a flashlight?" I asked.

He chased the eggs down with a mouthful of coffee. "Just following Eric. He'd been out there earlier in the day. I think he was just sizing up your property, trying to figure out how many trees they'd need to clear out for their resort."

"That explains why he knew just where my driveway was even though it was covered with snow. And he was aware that I own thirty acres. I'd never told him that. Wish I would have put two and two together a little sooner."

"None of those comments caught your attention because you never suspected Eric was up to anything," Sam said. "I was suspicious of him, but not for the right reasons. I was too busy being jealous to realize what was really going on."

"I guess you're right," I said. "But now I can see all the clues I missed. Mary's mention of fishing and swimming and Eric's comment about Rand making money 'free and clear' from the sale of his property. Eric would have known there was a mortgage on that land if he was really going to buy it." I shook my head. "And that stupid story about his supposed ex-girlfriend. He concocted that to make me unsure of our relationship. To make me doubt you." I reached over and took Sam's hand. "I'll never allow anyone to come between us like that again." I laughed lightly. "Of course, the biggest clue I missed wasn't anything natural. It was spiritual."

"What do you mean?" Grant asked.

"When an old Mennonite woman told me she had 'a stirring inside my spirit that tells me something is wrong,' I should have listened. Ida was right all along. Next time something stirs inside her, I will be the first person in line to pay attention."

"Pat, when did you suspect Eric had killed Rand?" Sam asked.

"Right away. I wish I'd seen that comin'. I'd like to have prevented it. In the end, all I could do was get the body to the coroner as quickly as possible so he could back up my suspicions. After he got a chance to look closely at him, he discovered that Rand had been asphyxiated before he was dumped in the snow. I knew Eric was responsible, but I still had no direct evidence." He shook his head. "I'm just sorry things got so serious before I was able to prove his guilt."

I grunted. "No one's as sorry as I am. I think I lost about ten years of my life that night in the restaurant. Thank God you came in when you did. I thought Eric was going to shoot Mary—or me."

"Unfortunately, he almost did."

"So he'll recover completely?" Sam asked.

Pat chuckled. "Yes, but I doubt he'll be able to use that right arm to hold a gun for a long, long time."

"And what about Mary?" Sweetie asked. "Is she goin' to jail?"

"I think she'll get a deal from the prosecutor for turning state's evidence. Whether or not she gets jail time or probation. . . I just don't know. But I don't think she'll be back here anytime soon—if ever. Turning the restaurant over to Hector seems pretty final."

I agreed with him that we'd probably seen the last of Mary, but in an odd way, I felt some pity for her. She'd been stupid and careless, but she almost died in an attempt to save my life. The notion that all this time she'd hated me because of Sam made me sad. Shows what unforgiveness and deception can do. Mary's life would never be the same. Learning a lesson from the tragic results of the last few days forced me to forgive her—and Eric— as quickly as I could. I didn't want the same kind of poison festering inside my soul.

"More coffee?" Jessica's smile was evidence that her life was improving. Her daughter, Trinity, was at home with her grandmother. She'd taken a job working at the restaurant after deciding she didn't want to go back to school. I wasn't certain it was the best decision, but Jessica didn't want to face the boy who had taken advantage of her insecurity and then pushed her away when she became pregnant. At least for now, she had a place to work and a loving environment at home.

Sweetie held up her cup. "I'll take some more. Hector makes a good cup of coffee. Not as good as mine, but it comes pretty close."

"I'm glad you like it," she said. She filled Sweetie's cup and warmed up everyone else's.

"Thank you, Jessica," I said with a smile.

"Actually, it's Jessie," she responded. "I—I decided I want to be called Jessie from now on."

"I like it," I said. "Jessie it is."

She twirled around and headed toward another table. A new name for a new person. It was a good sign.

I gazed around the room. The restaurant was full. Mary's Kitchen would continue but with Hector at the helm. Running the restaurant was the answer to his prayers. Several of the town's women were helping Carmen stay in bed by doing her housework and caring for her children, and now the Ramirezes wouldn't have to worry about paying the bills.

"I'm still worried about that casino," Sweetie said, her mouth full of scrambled eggs. "What's gonna happen with that?"

Pat chuckled. "Let's just say that our county government is going through a thorough housecleaning. Everyone involved with Eric's shady group is being shoved out of office. Several will be prosecuted for taking bribes. I don't think anyone will be talking about a casino in this area for a long, long time."

"Well then, everything turned out all right, didn't it?" She stabbed another sausage and happily stuffed it in her mouth.

"I guess it did," he replied.

The sheriff finished his breakfast and stood to his feet. "Thanks for askin' me to eat with you folks. I enjoyed it. But it's time for me to head back to the office. I've neglected it way too long chasin' after this case."

Sam stood up and held out his hand. "Thanks for everything, Sheriff. I don't know what we would have done without you."

"Happy to help. Y'all take care now."

I grabbed my coat. "Wait a minute, Sheriff. I'll walk out with you."

Sam gave me an odd look, but I smiled and motioned for him to sit down. I had something to talk to Pat about that couldn't wait. He held the door open for me, and I stepped out into a cold but sunny day. The roads had improved greatly, although snow still covered everything else. When we got to his car, the sheriff turned to me.

"Did you walk me out here because you think I'm too old to make it alone, or did you have another agenda? You've thanked me enough for a while."

I leaned against his truck and stared at him. "Well, I have a question, Sheriff. Just when do you intend to tell Sam the truth?"

He eyed me suspiciously. "Tell him the truth about what?"

I wrapped my arms around myself to stave off the cold. "The night I drove your truck from the orchard to the house, I went through your glove compartment. I was looking for evidence because I suspected you were the person who'd knocked me out." I waited for his reaction, but his expression didn't change. "I saw the picture. At first I didn't recognize the people, but the boy seemed so familiar. It kept bothering me. And then a couple of days ago I remembered something you said to me when you pulled my car over on the way to Harmony. You mentioned blood ties. Finally everything clicked."

He stared past me. "And what was it that clicked, Gracie?"

"You're Sam's father."

He didn't say anything, just kept looking at something over my shoulder.

"That's why you started hanging around, asking questions right after you took office. It's also why you kept such a close eye on us throughout this whole ordeal. You were protecting your son. Actually, I should have figured it out sooner. When you pulled me over on the way to Harmony, probably so you could check me out to see if I was someone you wanted in Sam's life, you made that strange comment about blood ties. You were talking about yours and Sam's."

Finally he met my gaze. I detected a shadow of apprehension in his eyes. "I didn't know about him until two years ago. Bernie found me in Colorado. It wasn't hard. I was the sheriff of a much larger area than this. She was sick. Real sick. She told me about Sam and gave me that picture. Then she told me where he was. Not long after that, I found out Morris County needed a sheriff because theirs had quit. I offered to fill in until a new sheriff was elected. Luckily, I won the election."

"I can't keep this from Sam for long, you know. If he finds out I knew and didn't tell him. . . Well, I can't take that chance. One thing I've learned since coming to Harmony is that secrets don't keep here. Eventually the truth comes out. It would be best if you told him yourself, though. And soon."

He nodded. "I know. But give me a little time, please. I want him to trust me before I tell him who I am."

I patted his arm. "You saved my life, you know. I don't think there's much more you can do to get on his good side."

He grunted. "I'll tell you what. If you'll keep my secret for a while, I'll tell you one. And trust me, you really want to know this."

"Okay. As long as you realize I won't wait too long."

He stuck his hand out. "Agreed."

I shook it. "Okay, so what's the secret?"

"I ran into Sam yesterday in Council Grove. He was coming out of Meyer's Fine Jewelry." He grinned at me. "He had a little black box in his hand and a great big smile on his face."

He tipped his hat and started toward his car. But before he opened the door, he turned around and looked at me. "By the way, you're right," he said. "I was checking you out that day on the road to Harmony. Just so you know, you passed." With that, he got in his car and took off.

I stood there and watched him drive away. I'd meant what I said about secrets. I'd had to tell Sam that Eric had kissed me, and that I'd told him about Sam's mother. It wasn't easy to confess, but I knew if we had a future together, he needed to know. He not only understood; he blamed himself for putting me in a situation where I felt I had no one to talk to. I think I fell in love with him even more at that moment—if it's even possible. I'd keep Pat's secret for a while. I owed them a chance to work it out. I prayed Sam's decision to let go of the pain from his past would allow him to open his heart to his father.

Cora Crandall called out my name, and I waved to the three of them as they went into the restaurant to meet with Grant. I looked across the street to see Molasses hitched to Gabe and Sarah's buggy, waiting to take her owners home. All in all, Harmony was back to normal.

Hopefully things would stay quiet for a while. I'd learned something important over the last few days. Just because a storm comes, it doesn't necessarily mean you've stepped out of God's will. It just means you have to find the rock God sends to hold you up. I had no doubt I was exactly where I was supposed to be. For a while I'd looked at the storm. From now on, I intended to keep my eyes on the Rock.

I looked up as the sun poked its head from behind the clouds that had covered Harmony for quite some time. Today promised to be a beautiful day. Sam had asked me to dinner at a very nice restaurant in Topeka. He said he had something important to ask me.

I headed into Mary's with a smile on my face. Yes, today certainly promised to be an exceptionally beautiful day.

DISCUSSION QUESTIONS

1. Gracie moved to Harmony because she loved Sam and she loved the town. She believed her life would be peaceful and happy there. But can a place or a person actually give us happiness or peace? Were her expectations unrealistic? Where does true peace come from?

2. Was Abel's decision to keep the abandoned baby until he could find the mother the right choice, or should he have called the authorities immediately? What would you have done in his place?

3. When Sam read the note claiming the baby belonged to Gracie, why did he react the way he did? Is there anything in your past that might cause you to react unreasonably in a similar situation?

4. What did Sam finally do to break free from his past? Do you need to do this in any area of your life?

5. Why did Gracie have feelings for Eric? Was there something lacking in her relationship with Sam? Or was the problem inside Gracie herself?

6. Should Gracie have been more understanding about Sam's insecurities, or were her feelings understandable?

7. What was it that Eric and his investors offered the citizens of Harmony? Were the residents right to get excited, or should they have been more protective of what they already had?

8. There is nothing wrong with wanting good things for your family, but when it looked as if there might be a problem with the development project, people began to turn on each other. What should they have done? What would you have done?

9. Were you surprised to find out who the baby's mother was? Did you have compassion for her, or did you feel angry with her decision?

10. Deceit can cause all kinds of evil. Is deceit always an outright lie? What about choosing not to tell the complete truth? What about lies that protect someone? Was Sweetie right to tell Sam to lie? Was Sam wrong for not telling Gracie the truth sooner? Is it ever right to deceive someone?

Simple Choices

ACKNOWLEDGMENTS

For this last visit to Harmony, I want to thank the people who made this journey so special.

As always, to Judith Unruh, Alexanderwohl Church Historian in Goessel, Kansas: You kept me on track throughout the series. I can't thank you enough.

To Sarah Beck, owner of Beck's Farm in Wichita: Thanks for all your help. The Harmony Series was made better because of you.

To Deputy Sheriff Pat Taylor—the real one: Thank you for always being available to help me with research, and thank you for allowing me to use your name. I hope I didn't besmirch it too much. LOL!

My thanks to Doctor Andy (Andrea McCarty) for being the world's best doctor and for helping me with all my medical questions! You're the greatest!

Thank you to Marjorie Vawter, my wonderful editor. Your hard work is always appreciated.

Thank you to Alene Ward, owner of DesignsbyAlene.com, who is one of those "divine connections" God puts in our lives. Thank you for creating "Sweetie's Christmas Quilt." One for our contest and another one for me! I will treasure it for the rest of my life. I look forward to the future and more adventures together!

To Penny and Gus Dorado: Thank you for always being ready to help in any way you could. You're both very precious to me.

To my agent, Janet Benrey: Thanks for your help along the way. You will always have a special place in my heart.

As always, my thanks to the folks at Barbour: Becky, Mary, Shalyn, Ashley, and Laura. You gave me a chance, and I will always appreciate that.

To the Mennonite people and their rich heritage: I hope you feel I've represented you well.

Special thanks to my wonderful husband, Norman. I'm so thrilled that we're working together now. There's no one else I'd rather share my journey with. I love you.

To my son, Danny, who has always encouraged me: I am still amazed that God has allowed me to be your mother. You are one of the most incredible people I've ever known. I'm so blessed.

And finally, to the One who has set my feet in a broad place: Without You, I have nothing. With You, I have everything. Without You, I am nothing. With You, I can soar like an eagle, move mountains, and become more than I ever dreamed I could be. I love You so much. My most fervent prayer is that when people read my books, they will see You.

DEDICATION

To Fred Mehl, my wonderful father-in-law, who battled the great darkness that is Alzheimer's. You were never diminished in the eyes of those who loved you. We always saw the real man you were—a man of strength, love, character, and incredible creativity. I've tried to represent your struggle through the character of Papa Joe. I pray I've succeeded. We all still miss you.

Chapter One

"Y ou will get packed right now because. . .because. . .I said so!" Yikes! I almost turned my head to see if my mother had crept up behind me. *Because I said so?* Isn't that what parents say when they can't think of anything else?

"You are *not* my mother, you know," Hannah said defiantly.

Like I wasn't very well aware of that. I shook my head, trying to come up with something that sounded wise. I could use some of Sweetie's good old homespun smarts right now. She'd know what to do. Several of her past pearls of wisdom flitted through my head, but none of them seemed to fit this situation. There was something about pigs flying, but that didn't seem appropriate either. Feeling defeated, I slumped down into a nearby chair. "Listen Hannah, you know how hard it was to talk your parents into letting you come to Wichita for six weeks and take art classes. I fought for you. I promised to take care of you and not let you get into trouble. But. . .but just look at you!"

The beautiful young woman who stood in front of me certainly didn't resemble the chaste, quiet Mennonite teenager I'd brought to

Wichita six weeks earlier. Her simple clothing had been replaced with jeans and a sleeveless T-shirt that stated TODAY WILL BE THE BEST DAY EVER! I had the distinct feeling this would not prove true.

"Robin gave me these clothes so I wouldn't feel like such a freak, and I like them," she responded. Her bottom lip stuck out in a definite pout.

A twinkle of silver caught my eye. "She gave you that bracelet, too?"

Hannah raised her wrist. "It's a friendship bracelet."

The bracelet was made with silver and colored beads, and a silver heart dangled from it.

"It says 'Love, Friend, and Forever.'" She pointed to engraved inserts evenly spaced between the beads. "It means Robin and I are forever friends. But you want to send me back to Harmony where I don't have any real friends at all!"

I sighed so forcefully, it was a wonder the girl stayed on her feet. "That's ridiculous. You have all kinds of friends in Harmony. I actually thought I was one of them."

No response. Just more pouting.

"Listen," I said forcefully, "I want you to put on the clothes your parents sent with you. I'm responsible to them, and I can't take you back to Harmony looking like this." I stared closely at her. "Is—is that mascara? And are you wearing lipstick?"

"Everyone wears it." Her bottom lip stayed in the pout position.

I pulled myself up from my chair, fighting the urge to say *If everyone jumped off a cliff, would you jump off, too?* Boy, I really *was* turning into my mother. "We're leaving this afternoon, and that's all there is to it. Allison is returning from her vacation in the morning, and she wants her apartment back. We are going home to Harmony!" The note of hysteria in my voice seemed to startle Hannah, and she took a step back. Had I scored a point? Maybe becoming slightly unhinged would get the results I so desperately needed. I was trying to come up with something really over the edge when Hannah's bottom lip began to quiver and tears filled her eyes.

"I—I love it here," she said, her voice breaking. "And Mr. Monahan said I could live with him and his family and attend a high school that has special art classes. He practically guaranteed me an art scholarship to college."

My anger began to melt. Hannah wasn't really fighting against me—she was fighting for her dream. Unfortunately, I couldn't help her. "Look, Hannah, I understand. I really do. But this is not the way to go about it. We need to go home and talk to your parents. I'll explain the opportunity Jim's offered you. If it's meant to be, then it will happen." I frowned as my eyes traveled up and down her body. "But you need to get rid of those clothes and clean off your face. If you go back looking like that, they'll never agree to let you leave Harmony. Or even your room for that matter."

She stared down at her sandals. "They won't let me live here," she said, her voice so soft I could barely hear her. "We both know that."

I didn't respond, but I was fairly certain she was right. However, sharing that thought at this moment might trigger another bout of resistance that I didn't have time to deal with. "Your parents love your paintings," I said, trying to sound reassuring. "They know you have real talent. You can't be completely sure they'll say no. But even if they do, you're only a year away from graduating and turning eighteen. Remember that Jim said if you couldn't go to high school here, he'd still try to get you into a good art school or college. Your grades are excellent, and you have a good shot at being accepted." I walked over and put my hands on her shoulders. "Hannah, you have to go home. Your parents love you, and you love them. You can't stay here without their permission. If you put up a fight now, you'll lose Jim's support as well as mine—and you'll hurt your mother and father. I know you don't really want to do that." I put my hand under the teenager's chin and pulled her face up so she had to look at me. "You know I'm right."

Tears spilled from her china-blue eyes. "I—I know. It's just..."

"You're afraid if you leave, you'll never find a way to come back?"

She nodded, and her face crumbled. "It's so wonderful here, Gracie," she blubbered. "Wichita is exciting and full of so many opportunities. If I get stuck in Harmony, I'll never be anything!"

I raised one eyebrow at her, wondering if she'd forgotten that I'd chosen Harmony over Wichita. I'd found the love of my life, and my freelance work as a graphic artist was going very well. "If your parents won't let you come back and finish high school in Wichita, in a year you'll be free to determine your own future." I let go of her chin and shook my finger at her. "But if you want me to talk to them about Jim's offer, you'll clean your face, change your clothes, and get packed. If you don't, I won't raise a finger to help you when we get home. And I mean that."

The young girl's eyes grew wide as she weighed her options, but both of us knew she had no real choice. She turned slowly and headed toward the guest bedroom. While she packed, I set about writing Allison a quick note, thanking her for the use of her apartment. As I wrote, I couldn't help but compare myself to Hannah. Here she was fighting hard to stay away from Harmony while I was fighting just as hard to get back. Odd how two people can see the same thing in totally different ways. I loved the small Mennonite town with its friendly residents and old-fashioned flavor. Yet Hannah regarded Harmony as her prison.

I folded the note and put it under the glass candy dish on Allison's fireplace mantel, aware that she'd see it since she never actually put candy in the dish. She only used it to hold her car keys. I stared at my reflection in the mirror over the mantel. Although I still looked the same—reddish-brown hair and green eyes—the apprehension in my face was obvious. Quickly looking away, I sat back down in the chair next to my already-packed suitcases.

I felt like a traitor. I'd never suspected our visit to Wichita would turn out like this. If I had, I never would have pushed Emily and Abel Mueller to let Hannah come. They'd resisted my old art teacher's offer to enroll their talented daughter in his six-week summer art course. Their concern for Hannah had made them reluctant to let her go. But I'd finally convinced them to trust me, and now their worst fears had been realized. Hannah's view of the world outside Harmony had changed her. How would I be able to explain it? I chewed my lip and worried for a while. Finally, I picked up the phone and called Sam, hoping he could make me feel better. No answer. Great. He and Sweetie were probably out in the orchard picking apples and peaches.

Sam and his aunt worked hard on their fruit farm. Correction. Soon to be *our* fruit farm. My wedding to Sam was now only two weeks away. Thankfully, my absence hadn't caused any major problems since we'd planned a small ceremony, and Sweetie had taken over all the preparations. It was Saturday and my parents would be arriving on Monday—along with my grandfather.

I'd been surprised when my mother called to tell me Papa Joe was coming. My grandfather's Alzheimer's was originally considered to be advanced, but recently he'd seemed to rally. Doctors said his lack of speech and other symptoms may have had more to do with depression than the disease. When new medication began to help lift the hopelessness he felt after losing my grandmother and moving into the nursing home, he began to talk again. Although Alzheimer's still continued its evil and devastating march against him, according to my parents, there were times when he almost seemed like the man he used to be.

Now Joe wanted to see Harmony once more before he died, and my parents felt he should have the chance before he slipped into the darkness of the disease for good. I looked forward to seeing him even though the last time we'd been together, the man I'd known had seemed so far away. I had some fear that this visit wouldn't be any different. Seeing him as just a shell of the robust man he'd once been broke my heart.

With the conflict between Hannah and me finally behind us, I felt more relaxed than I had in days. I'd almost drifted off to sleep when Hannah called my name. I opened my eyes to see the girl I'd brought to Wichita. Her pastel pink dress and plain brown shoes replaced the contemporary clothing her friend Robin had given her, and her long blond hair had been pulled into a bun and tucked under her white prayer covering. I rose from my chair and looked closely at her face. No sign of makeup.

"Thank you, Hannah. I know this is hard for you, but. . ." I reached out to touch her, but she jerked away from me.

"Don't tell me you know how I feel, because you don't. Maybe you like hiding out in Harmony, but I don't intend to spend the rest of my life buried there."

I felt a rush of indignation. Somehow I'd turned into Hannah's enemy even though I'd gone out of my way to give her this opportunity. It didn't seem fair. I grabbed my bags. "Let's get going," I said sharply. "We're already leaving later than I'd planned."

Without a word, Hannah picked up the soft cloth valise her mother had sent with her, and we walked out of the apartment. On the way to the car, all I could do was wonder what would happen when we reached Harmony. An uneasy sense of dread filled me—and it stayed with me all the way home.

Chapter Two

Iwas kinda afraid somethin' like this would happen," Sweetie said, handing me a tall, cold glass of her home-brewed iced tea. "That girl ain't never seen nothin' outside Harmony and a few small towns around here."

She joined Sam and me as we sat in white rocking chairs on the huge wraparound porch of their beautiful red Victorian house. Even though it was July, a cool breeze helped to push the hot, humid air away. It felt good to be home, but I couldn't get the situation with Hannah out of my mind. "Abel told me that sometimes they drive to Topeka to eat dinner," I said. "I assumed since she'd seen a larger city, she wouldn't be overwhelmed by Wichita."

"Pshaw," Sweetie spat out. "That Chinese restaurant they go to is right on the edge of town. Hannah ain't never been all the way inside Topeka."

"Man, good thing I didn't take her to Kansas City or St. Louis. She would have really gone off the deep end."

Sam reached over and took my hand. "It's not your fault,

Grace. You were trying to help her. You couldn't possibly have anticipated her reaction. Quit beating yourself up."

I threaded my fingers through his and squeezed lightly. "I'm glad you feel that way, but I have to wonder how Emily and Abel are going to react."

"They're not stupid people," Sweetie said. "And they love you. Besides, they're not gonna give Hannah permission to live in Wichita with some guy they don't even know. It ain't never gonna happen. After that child figgers it out, she'll settle down."

"I hope you're right."

"Truth is, the Muellers oughta be thankin' their lucky stars. Those girls that went missin' in Topeka still ain't been found—alive or dead. At least Abel and Emily know where their daughter is."

Sweetie was referring to the disappearance of two young women who'd vanished about a month apart before I left for Wichita. At first, it was assumed they'd taken off on their own. But investigators now suspected they'd been abducted.

"I don't think anyone in Harmony really took much notice," I said. "You know Harmony. No one believes something like that could happen here."

"Seems strange after two murders that occurred right on their own turf," Sam said.

I shrugged. "One took place over thirty years ago, and the other was committed by an outsider. I'm not saying folks in Harmony aren't wary of strangers, but most of them truly believe God has blessed this place with special protection."

"And so He has," Sweetie said. She sat up in her chair and stared at me. Her ever-present bun had fallen to the side of her head, making me think of Princess Leia in *Star Wars*. Of course, Sweetie would need another bun on the other side, hair coloring to cover her gray, and a lot of plastic surgery to come close to looking like Carrie Fisher. She yanked at the T-shirt under her cutoff overalls, trying to adjust it so it wouldn't tug so tightly at her neck. "Anyways," she croaked loudly, "we need to stop talkin' 'bout all this bad stuff and start thinkin' 'bout your weddin'. I got almost everything ready, but I need to go over it with you. There's a few decisions left that you gotta make."

I sighed, let go of Sam's hand, and settled back comfortably in my rocking chair. "Let's talk about it later, okay? I'm really tired, and I need to go home and unpack. Besides, I'm sure Snickle is ready to get home, too."

As if on cue, a plaintive *meow* came from around the corner. Snickle, my cat, and Buddy, Sam's dog, trotted up to us. Snickle greeted me by rubbing up against my leg while Buddy jumped up in my lap, almost spilling my tea. Snickle and Buddy had become great friends, and I had to wonder if Snickle really would be happier at our house. Staying with Sweetie and Sam while I was in Wichita may have changed his perspective as to what home really looked like. I wasn't too concerned though. After the wedding, we'd be living here anyway, so I guess in the long run, being with me for two weeks wouldn't ruin him. As if reading my mind, Sweetie piped up.

"Are you gonna drag that poor cat back to your place again? Why don't you just leave him be? He loves it here, and you're over every day anyway. Wouldn't that be easier on you both?"

Sweetie, who had sworn up and down that she hated cats, was crazy about Snickle. And he was nuts about her, too. Frankly, he spent more time hanging around her than he did me. Persnickety feline.

"You're probably right," I said, stroking Buddy. "If you don't mind, I think I will leave him here. With my parents and my grandfather coming, it might be best."

Snickle ran over to Sweetie and nuzzled her leg as if thanking her for allowing him to stay with his good doggy pal. Sweetie chuckled and bent down to stroke the calico cat that had become her friend. "You know, we tried keepin' him inside since he ain't got no claws to defend himself with, but he kept slippin' out. Funny thing is, Buddy keeps him in line. If Snickle starts to wander too far, Buddy barks and barks. Then he starts rounding this silly cat up and pushin' him home. I ain't never seen nothin' like it before." Snickle jumped up in Sweetie's lap, turned around once, and lay down. He didn't even look my way.

"Guess I know where I stand," I said with a smile.

"If it makes any difference, *I* like you," Sam said laughing.

"That's good, 'cause in a couple of weeks, you won't be able to get rid of me."

"You decided what to do with your house yet?" Sweetie asked.

"No. I can't sell it; it's been in the family too long." My father and his brother had been raised in that house. And Benjamin, my uncle, had left it to me when he passed away. I'd thought about renting it out, but that didn't feel right either. "Guess I'll let it sit until God gives me some direction."

"Good idea," Sweetie said. "Ain't smart to get ahead of the Lord. You'll know what to do when the time comes."

We sat quietly sipping tea until the sun began to set behind us. Rosy fingers of light reached out and touched the wispy clouds that floated over our heads. There was something about the skies over Harmony at sunrise and sunset. Stroked with God's paintbrush, they were a sight to behold. As I sat there with Sam and Sweetie, for the first time since driving Hannah home, serenity began to overtake my concern for her.

Our trip hadn't been pleasant. The silence between us was nothing like the relaxed atmosphere I enjoyed now. Although I'd counseled her to wait a few days to tell her parents about Jim's offer, I had no idea if she'd followed my advice. For all I knew, the Mueller household was in an uproar now, and I could be at the center of it. Abel, Emily, and I had been through a lot together. I prayed we could weather this storm as well.

Reluctantly, I lifted Buddy, kissed him on the head, and put him down. Then I stood to my feet. "Guess I'd better get home. I dumped my luggage inside the door before I came over. If I don't unpack and wash my dirty laundry, I may have to pull my winter clothes out of storage. And it's way too hot to wear anything heavy."

"Good thing I finally got your electrical problems solved while you were gone," Sam said. "Now you can actually turn on your lights and run your washer at the same time."

I grinned. "Much more convenient than washing my clothes in the dark. Thank you."

He stood up and took me in his arms. "I'm tired of saying good-bye to you," he whispered. "I can hardly wait for the day when all I have to say is good night."

I sighed and leaned into him. "Me, too." We stayed that way until we heard Sweetie clear her throat.

"I ain't in the way on my own front porch, I hope," she said with a throaty chuckle.

"Actually, you are," Sam said, finally letting me go. "But what can we do? We're used to you."

Sweetie's gruff laughter carried through the deepening shadows, almost drowning out the song of the cicadas as they serenaded the encroachment of night.

Moving into Sweetie's house after the wedding might seem strange to people who didn't know us, but it was as natural to me as breathing. Sweetie was family, and living with my husband and his aunt felt completely right. I couldn't help but think back to the first time I met Sweetie. Rough, nosy, and caustic, she seemed unpleasant—someone to avoid. Now she was almost a second mother to me. I'd learned an important lesson from Sam's aunt. Judging anyone too quickly is a big mistake. People have many layers, and if you want to really know someone, you've got to invest some time and patience. Beneath Sweetie's harsh exterior, I discovered a strong, brave, and humble woman who'd turned out to be a role model for me. Her difficult life had toughened her, but it hadn't broken her spirit or her ability to love. My respect for her only grew as I got to know her better.

"I'll walk you to your car," Sam said, grabbing my hand.

I waved good-bye to Sweetie and ran my hand over Snickle's back. Buddy followed us down the steps.

"Pick me up for church in the morning?" I said, as I leaned against my car.

"Sure," Sam said. "How 'bout lunch at Mary's afterward?"

Even though Harmony's only restaurant retained Mary Whittenbauer's name, Mary had departed our small town months ago. Her secret dealings with a shady real estate agent who'd wanted to build a resort and casino near Harmony had been exposed, along with her involvement in a grisly murder. After testifying against the agent and being granted immunity, Mary left the state. No one knew where she was now. Her former cook, Hector Ramirez, currently ran the restaurant, along with his wife, Carmen.

"Sounds good," I said, "but after we eat I need to go home and get things prepared for my family's visit."

"Need help?"

I grinned. "I'm not blind, you know. Even though I wasn't home long, it was obvious little elves had been cleaning the house and stocking my fridge."

Sam held his hands up. "I am guilty only by association.

Sweetie knew you wouldn't have much time to shop and dragged me to the store in Council Grove. And you know I don't clean, but I do follow my aunt's orders. She even forced me to move furniture so she could sweep under it. I really doubt you'll find much to do tomorrow."

I leaned over and kissed him. "Good thing I don't have privacy issues, huh?"

He chuckled. "You've got that right. It will only get worse when you move in here."

I laid my head on his chest. "I love this place—and you. And believe it or not, I'm just crazy about Sweetie. You know, if you ever want me to cook for you, I need to get back to those lessons Sarah and I started with Sweetie before I left."

"I think Sarah's passed you by. She never missed a lesson while you were gone. In fact, she's already graduated to frying chicken and baking apple cobbler." He rubbed his stomach. "I got to be the guinea pig. Tough job."

"Poor baby. I feel for you."

He sighed dramatically. "I know. It's a burden I must bear with bravery."

I laughed at the silly look on his face. "Can you forget food for a moment? Let's get back to Sarah. How's she doing?"

"I don't know." He shrugged. "I'm a guy. We're not very good at figuring out how women feel."

I reached up and brushed a lock of sandy-blond hair from his eyes. "You're one of the most sensitive, insightful people I've ever known. Even if you are male."

"Thanks, I think." His expression turned serious. "To be honest with you, I think Sarah's in a lot of pain. She and John have kept their word and stayed away from each other. But there's this deep sadness in their eyes." He stared at me for several seconds before continuing. "You know, if I ever lost you, I believe I'd look exactly the same way."

I kissed him softly. "You won't ever lose me, you know. In a few days, I'll be yours forever."

He wrapped his tanned, muscled arms around me. "I thought you already were mine forever."

We kissed again, and then I pushed him gently away. "If you keep that up, I'll never get home."

"Fine by me."

"Now I know it's time to go." I got into my bright-yellow Volkswagen Bug and started the engine. Sam motioned to me to roll down my window.

"I thought you were going to sell this car while you were in Wichita," he said frowning.

"I tried, but I couldn't find anything else I wanted to buy."

"In all of Wichita there wasn't one other car you liked? I find that hard to swallow."

"Well, you can believe what you want. If I have to get rid of my slug bug, I want a car with personality."

Sam pointed to his ancient truck, held together more by rust than metal. "You mean like that?"

"Definitely not the kind of personality I'm going for. No decent hillbilly would be caught dead driving that poor thing. Thanks anyway."

"Are you calling me an indecent hillbilly?"

I shrugged. "If the truck fits. . ."

"You just don't appreciate the kind of character brought about by use and age," he sniffed, trying to look offended.

I nodded. "You must be right 'cause I think that sorry excuse for transportation should be put out of its misery."

"Women just don't understand a man and his truck."

"Thank God for that."

He gave me his most pitiful look, which made me giggle. "And here I broke down and bought something new just to make you happy. You haven't said one word about it."

I gazed at the big, beautiful red truck parked in the circular driveway. His decaying, beaten-up model had been pulled up next to the barn as if it had been relegated to second place. "I apologize. I truly applaud you, but why keep the old one?"

"Because contrary to the theory that male members of society have no real feelings, I'm emotionally attached to it."

I gave him a big smile. "Well, you're emotionally attached to me, too. But if you ever test-drive a newer model, you'll end up in worse condition than that aged rattletrap."

He stuck his head into my window and kissed me soundly. "You have nothing to worry about. I'd rather stick with my old, comfortable model. The new versions with all the bells and whistles scare me."

I slapped his arm. "I'm not sure what that means, but I'm pretty sure I don't like it."

He stood up and pointed toward the road. "Go home. I'll see you in the morning."

"If you're lucky." I put the car into gear and started down the driveway.

"I love you, Grace," Sam hollered as I headed toward Faith Road.

"I love you, too!" I yelled back.

Getting to my house from Sam's didn't take long. We live a little less than a mile from each other. As I drove, my mind drifted back to our conversation about Sarah Ketterling and John Keystone. They were certainly star-crossed lovers, separated by differences in their faiths. Although I understood the reasons they chose to deny their feelings, my heart ached for them.

I pulled into the driveway of my cute yellow house. When I'd left, my grandmother's purple irises were in full bloom. But now, in the heat of summer, only green stalks remained. Knowing that I'd missed so much of their flowering beauty made me sad. Mama's irises were a special love we'd shared. "Irises represent faith, hope, and wisdom, Gracie," she'd tell me as she worked in the garden at her home in Nebraska. "They remind me of God's faithfulness. Through faith and hope we inherit His promises, and through His Word and His wonderful Holy Spirit, He gives us wisdom we could never gain from human knowledge. These purple irises also signify royalty. Someday our heavenly Father will put crowns on our heads because we are children of the King."

I could still hear her as she talked about her beloved flowers and the God she loved more than anything else. Even though she'd been happy in Fairbury, I knew she missed her irises in Harmony. How I wished she could have come back before she died to see them still growing. They were a reminder to me of her faith in God and her love for me. I felt blessed to tend them for her all these years later.

Thankfully, under the illumination of the yard light, I could see that the marigolds Sam had planted by the front porch were thriving. At least I would be able to enjoy them for a while. I was grateful for the light so I could find my way to my front porch. In the country, where there are no streetlights, on cloudy nights it can get so dark it's actually impossible to see your hand in front of your face.

I got out of the car and hurried inside. My suitcases still sat inside the door where I'd dropped them. I dragged the biggest one toward the kitchen, opened it up, and removed a plastic bag full of dirty clothes. A visit to the basement and a few minutes later, the washer was churning away. I'd put the wet clothes in the dryer tomorrow morning. Right now I needed a good night's sleep. I couldn't help but smile at the wringer washer Mama Essie had used to wash her clothes, sitting in the corner of the basement. When I first arrived in Harmony, it was all I had. Thankfully, when I was a child, Mama had taught me how to use the old-style washer. Even after leaving Harmony and her Old Order ways, she'd preferred the wringer washer to the "newfangled" machines.

As I trudged up the stairs, I was surprised to hear someone knocking on my door. I glanced at my watch as I hurried to find out who would visit this late. A little after nine o'clock. Normal in Wichita but really unusual in Harmony where the sidewalks are rolled up around seven.

I pulled the door open and found Pastor Abel Mueller standing on my porch, his face beet red. Before I could say anything, he blurted out, "Gracie Temple, why in heaven's name are you trying to destroy my family?"

Chapter Three

Abel was halfway through his second cup of cold cider before his color began to return to normal. I grasped my hands to keep them from shaking. I'd never seen the gentle Mennonite minister so upset. And he'd certainly never been this angry with me before. It hurt me deeply to think I was the cause of his distress.

"So you do understand," I said for the third time. "I had no idea until the lessons were almost over that Hannah felt like this. By then it was too late."

Abel set his cup down on the table next to the couch. "I'm trying, Gracie," he said. He shook his shaggy head, and his beard quivered. "But Emily is devastated. She and Hannah have always been so close. Now it's like we don't even know our own daughter."

I stared down at the floor. "I'm so sorry, Abel. I wish now I'd never taken her to Wichita. I was just trying to help."

"Somewhere inside I know that, Gracie. But right now my father's heart is breaking. Hannah has never been this rebellious toward us. Before I left to come over here, I had to send her to her room for yelling at her mother. She insists we let her live with that art teacher and go to school in Wichita. But we can't do that. It's our job to raise our daughter—not anyone else's. Besides, if this is how she acts after being in the big city for six weeks, what would happen to her if she lived there during an entire school year?"

"I don't know," I said, raising my head to meet his eyes. "To be honest, I planned to encourage you to let her go."

Abel started to sputter, but I held my hand up to stop him. "Let me finish. Jim really could do wonderful things for her. I'm confident she could get into a good art school or college—probably with a full scholarship. But with the way she's responded to being away from home, I can't recommend it now."

"Well, thank goodness," Abel said. "Maybe knowing that you've changed your mind will help to convince Hannah it's the wrong move. As far as college, she will have to make her own decision after she graduates high school. Most folks in our church believe a young woman should get married and settle down after school is over. And that's liberal compared to the old beliefs that eighth grade was far enough for any young person—especially the girls."

He took a deep breath and let it out slowly. "But things change, and I have come to believe that I must allow her to choose her own way in life even if it isn't the one I want for her. God isn't asking us to follow His path because we have to. He desires His children to pursue His will because we want to." His eyes sought mine. "But in this situation, I must wonder if I should have been stricter. Two of our elders came to me before Hannah left. They both felt I was making a mistake, and I dismissed their concerns. But now. . ."

He rubbed the back of his neck as if trying to relieve stress or pain. "When you first came to Harmony, you challenged me about our beliefs. Perhaps now you see why we live a separated life. Hannah leaves our church and our town for a few weeks, and she brings back the rebellion and disrespect rampant in the world outside our borders."

"I understand what you're saying, Abel. But there are many, many good Christian people living in big cities who still keep Christ as the center of their lives. I love Harmony, too, but this place isn't a panacea against evil. The people who live here have chosen to live a certain kind of life, and that's fine. But Hannah made a choice, too—one that none of us saw coming. The problem isn't Wichita. . ." I hesitated to complete my sentence, so Abel finished it for me.

"It's Hannah," he said, his words slow and methodical. He clasped his hands together. "But still, if she hadn't left our protection. . ."

"The problem would still be in her heart. There is something she longs for, Abel. Something she hasn't found here."

His face flushed and his jaw tightened. "Her art. One of the elders also cautioned me about this—this talent of hers. He said Hannah's interests could lead to vanity and self-involvement. I didn't pay any attention to him. It seemed silly and old-fashioned. Maybe I've been foolish. . ."

"But Abel, if that were true, why would God give her such a wonderful gift? That doesn't make any sense."

"But why would He give her something she can't handle? Something that would lead her away from Him and her family?"

I reached over and covered his hand with mine. "That hasn't happened. Hannah is acting out a bit, that's all. I think you're blowing this out of proportion."

"I don't know," he said hesitantly. "Maybe. I know some children rebel during their teenage years. I've certainly counseled many families in crisis. I just never thought Hannah would—"

"Be a teenager?" I smiled at him. "I think the best thing we can do is to let her work this out in her own mind. It could all blow over in a week or two. Hannah loves you and Emily. And Harmony is the only home she's ever known."

He nodded and patted my hand before pulling his away. "I believe it's wise to put the subject of her future on hold for now. We've told Hannah we expect her to adjust her behavior. As you say, perhaps she will settle down now that she's home. If God has a different plan for her life from what Emily and I would choose, we won't stand in His way. But right now, it's Hannah's heart that concerns me most."

Although I firmly believe God has a plan for everyone's life, I'm also aware that He doesn't force our steps. We all have the right and ability to pick a different direction—the one that isn't God's will for us. I prayed that wouldn't happen to Hannah.

I'd thought about mentioning Hannah's wardrobe malfunction in Wichita, but I just couldn't bring myself to do it. What would it help? The knowledge that she'd rejected her simple clothing for jeans and a T-shirt wouldn't give Abel and Emily additional peace of mind. They had enough to deal with now.

"What about our painting lessons?" I asked.

Abel stood up, his wide-brimmed straw hat in his hand. "Let's wait on that for now, Gracie. But please understand that Emily and I still love you. Just because we hit a bump in the road doesn't mean our buggy has completely turned over."

"I understand, and I promise to watch out for any future bumps. This one just snuck up on me."

He ambled toward my front door. "I know. When Hannah settles down, we'll consider restarting her lessons. I'm sure she'll be eager to continue."

"All right." When Abel closed the door behind him, I covered my face with my hands, trying to compose the emotions that raged through me. I prayed this situation would turn around, but frankly, not seeing Hannah for a while might be good for both of us. I'd said everything I could to encourage her to be patient. I was out of advice and although I would never admit it to Abel or Emily, I understood her desires. I'd felt the same way once. The big city had drawn me—as had the yearning for what I thought success entailed. But coming to Harmony had changed me. I'd found real peace and contentment here, something I'd never experienced in Wichita.

"Help Hannah find her way, God," I prayed quietly. "Show her the path You have for her, even if it isn't the same one someone else might choose for her."

I headed to the kitchen and made a cup of hot chocolate. The July heat hadn't chased away this nightly habit. Fixing cocoa from scratch takes longer than pouring a premade package of mix into a cup of hot water, but I really enjoy the taste of real cocoa powder, sugar, and milk, heated and topped off with whipped cream. I carried my cup upstairs to the bedroom and changed clothes. Then I turned on the small window air conditioner and the old, thirteen-inch television that sits on my dresser, wiggling the rabbit ears around until I got a halfway decent picture.

Television in my house is not without its complications. Sam and Sweetie have satellite TV, so when I want to watch something special, I go over there. Here, I just take whatever I can pick up through the tower Sam erected outside my house. At least I'm able to make out the news and a few programs I like. The many hours I used to spend in front of my set in Wichita has been reduced to only a few shows here and there. TV lost a lot of its pull on me after moving to Harmony. I chuckled to myself. Must be the Mennonite influence. The ten o'clock news was just coming on, so I set my cup of cocoa on the table next to my bed, got in, and wiggled under the covers.

"Police are investigating the disappearance of a young college student in Emporia," the grim-faced announcer said. "Melissa Dunham went missing after a night out with friends. Miss Dunham never returned to her apartment last night, according to her roommate. Police are treating the situation as suspicious. If you know anything about the whereabouts of Melissa Dunham, please notify the authorities." A picture of a young, fresh-faced woman with long blond hair and blue eyes filled my fuzzy TV screen. The girl looked remarkably like Hannah. "Police are still searching for two other young women who are still missing from Topeka. A local spokesperson declined to comment as to whether these cases might be linked to this most recent disappearance." Two more pictures popped up on the screen. Both girls had long blond hair, and at least one had blue eyes. I couldn't tell the color of the other girl's eyes from the photo. They both reminded me of Hannah as well. A strange sense of disquiet filled me, and it took much longer than usual to fall asleep. When I finally did, I kept seeing the missing girls' faces in my dreams, superimposed over the face of the young Mennonite girl I'd grown to love.

Chapter Four

It was a little after twelve thirty when church let out the next morning. It felt wonderful to be back among my friends at Harmony Church. Ruth Wickham hugged me so tightly I almost couldn't breathe, and Wynonna Jensen, the pastor's wife, squealed when she saw me. Pastor Jensen's sermon brought such peace to my troubled soul. He talked about how important it is to forgive ourselves as well as others. That it actually helps to show our faith in God's forgiveness. Many people, he said, say they believe God has forgiven them for their mistakes, but they continue to condemn themselves.

"If you truly believe in God's promise to be faithful in forgiving your sin," he said, "you would never throw that act of love and grace back in God's face by continuing to punish yourself. Do you think your faults are stronger than Jesus' sacrifice for you? True humility is believing God's Word and not trying to create a false sense of righteousness based on your own behavior."

His words led me to remind myself that taking Hannah to Wichita, and being away from Sam, Sweetie, and my friends, was a sacrifice done out of kindness. I hadn't purposely set out to cause a problem in Hannah's family. And besides, in the end, her reaction was her responsibility, not mine. I asked God to forgive me for beating myself up about it and submitted myself to His unending grace. I felt lighter and less troubled when we stepped out into the sunshine after church was dismissed.

"Let's get to Mary's before they're out of chicken," Sam said, gently pulling me away from the entrance.

Hector serves fried chicken family-style on Sundays, and the town turns out in droves to get their fair share. Thankfully, Abel usually preaches longer than Pastor Jensen so the members of Harmony Church get to their chicken dinners before the members of Bethel Mennonite. Harmony residents love to tease Abel about it. He always laughs and says, "I believe the good Lord cares more about your soul than your stomach." But the truth was, most of the Bethel folks went home to eat after church anyway, so it didn't really matter that much.

Sam left the truck parked in front of the church, and we walked hand in hand down the wooden sidewalk to the restaurant. Younger Harmony residents know many of the older folks like to eat out on Sunday, so they purposely park farther away, leaving plenty of spaces close to Mary's front door. We walked past the small stores that lined Main Street. Cora's Simple Clothing Shoppe, Harmony Hardware, Ruth's Crafts and Creations, and Menlo's Bakery were just a few of the small, homespun businesses along the way. All closed on Sunday, thank you very much. Sunday is the Lord's Day in Harmony, and no one would think of being open—except for the restaurant. Somehow hungry residents didn't seem to notice the inconsistency. But since Hector and his family always attended Mass during the week at the Catholic church in Sunrise, no one questioned the contradiction too closely. Harmony residents love to gather together at Mary's. It's akin to family dinner at Grandma's even though Hector certainly didn't look like anyone's grandmother.

I couldn't help but feel sad when I saw the large sign that says MARY'S KITCHEN still hanging on the two-story brick building that houses the popular eatery. I secretly hoped one day Hector would rename the establishment and remove the name of the previous owner. I had nothing against Mary, but seeing her name every time we came to town brought back painful memories.

We entered the bustling eatery with its old-fashioned diner feel. Blue walls filled with old photographs, wooden floors that squeak when you walk on them, booths with checkered tablecloths, and tables with yellow laminate tops. Every tabletop held red and yellow plastic containers for ketchup and mustard. The place was filling up quickly, but we managed to find a table. We had to wait awhile for service. Two women I didn't know were taking orders. A couple of Hannah's friends, Leah and Jessie, worked during the week, but being Conservative Mennonites, they never work on Sundays. Leah had been brought up in a stable, godly family. Unfortunately, Jessie's life had been a hard one so far. Her father, Rand McAllister, was abusive to her and her mother. His death last year was a tragedy—of sorts.

As awful as it sounds, since his funeral, his family seemed to blossom. Jessie actually smiled once in a while now. A rather unattractive girl when I'd first met her, she'd changed once her father's tyrannical rule ceased. A glow of happiness that brought life to her features replaced her usual sullen expression. The sallow-faced young woman now had color in her cheeks and a sparkle in her eyes. And she'd lost quite a bit of weight. Of course, working at the restaurant probably helped.

I have real respect for people who serve food to the public. I'm not sure I'd be able to last through an entire day on my feet, running orders back and forth. In Harmony, though, if one of

Hector's waitresses runs behind, it's not the least bit unusual to see a patron jump up, go back to the kitchen, and fetch their own food or get their own drink. In fact, most of the time, they'll even check with other customers to see if they need anything. Life in Harmony is a lot different from what I was used to in Wichita. Frankly, after being gone for a while, it takes a few days to adjust to the way things work here.

One of the women taking orders shuffled up to the table. "What would you folks like to drink?" She didn't bother to ask about food since chicken was the only thing on the menu today. Sam and I both ordered coffee with cream.

After she walked away, Sam crooked his head slightly to the right. "Something you don't know. Not long after you left, Bill Eberly started dating."

I looked toward the area Sam indicated. Bill Eberly sat alone in a booth against the wall. I caught his eye and waved to him. He smiled and returned the gesture. Bill Eberly is one of my favorite people—a kind man whose wife died several years ago. Sam's statement surprised me though, because I'd been told Bill was a one-woman man who would probably never marry again.

"Who?" I asked, turning my attention back to Sam.

His right eyebrow arched in amusement. "Guess. Go ahead, you won't believe it."

"I'm not going to guess. Either tell me or don't. Doesn't matter to me."

"Okay, never mind."

I reached across the table and lightly slapped his arm. "Okay, okay. Um, he's dating Ida. Is that it?"

"Well, if you're not going to be serious. . ."

My friend Ida Turnbauer is over eighty years old and an Old Order Mennonite. Sam was right. I wasn't being serious. "Would you just tell me? You know I hate guessing games."

"All right, but you sure take the fun out of stuff."

I guess the look on my face caused him some concern because he finally blurted out, "Thelma McAllister. He's dating Thelma, and it looks pretty serious."

"Thelma McAllister?" I gasped. "Jessie's mother? Rand's wife?"

"Well, she's not actually his wife now, you know. She would be his widow. But yes, *that* Thelma McAllister—like there are two of them living in Harmony."

At first, I could barely believe it, but as I considered the idea, it began to make sense. Thelma was a good woman who'd been beaten down by years of abuse by Rand. Just as Jessie had changed after Rand's death, Thelma had also come out of her shell. Well, maybe *shell* wasn't the right word. Perhaps cocoon described it better. When Rand was alive, she always carried herself like someone who'd given up on life—and on herself. Before I left for Wichita, though, I'd caught a glimpse of her one day in the restaurant, and I hadn't recognized her at first. She had a totally different countenance. Even her personality had transformed. She'd begun to open up and talk to people. In fact, she seemed to enjoy social interaction. And she was funny. I could see someone like Bill being drawn to her.

"Wait a minute," I said. "Thelma and Jessie aren't supposed to date anyone outside of their faith. Bill isn't Mennonite."

Sam paused while the waitress brought our coffee. When she walked away, he smiled triumphantly. "That's changed, too." Seeing my frown, he chuckled. "Do you think you have to be born into a Mennonite home to join the church? Well, you don't. Bill's been taking some instruction from Abel. When he's finished, he'll officially become a member. He and Thelma are already going to church together."

"Wow. Sounds like they're pretty serious."

Sam nodded. "I think they are. You should see them together. I've never seen Thelma so happy, and Bill reminds me of the man he used to be when Edith was alive."

I poured cream into my cup and stirred it. "How's Jessie taking their relationship?"

He shrugged. "I don't know. She doesn't act thrilled about it. I think she needs some time to get close to Bill, though. After the way Rand treated her, she will probably be a little hesitant about accepting him right off the bat."

I started to respond, but our waitress came over with a large tray full of food and began to fill our table. I thanked her, and she asked if we wanted anything else. I looked at the huge plate of fried chicken, the bowl of mashed potatoes and gravy, green beans, a basket of homemade rolls, and chuckled. "I can't think of one more thing we could possibly need."

She smiled and walked away. "Who is that woman?" I asked Sam.

"She's Carmen's sister, Connie. And the other woman is Connie's daughter."

"They don't live here, do they?"

"No. They both live in Council Grove. They just started coming to the restaurant on Sundays to help out. Carmen was running herself ragged without Leah and Jessie."

"That's nice of them."

Sam nodded in agreement. "Let's pray. I'm starved."

I felt certain Sweetie had cooked her usual Sunday morning pancakes and sausage and that Sam had partaken liberally, but I didn't tease him. He worked hard, and his lean, muscled body was a testament to the fact that he needed fuel to get all the necessary chores done on his large fruit farm. He prayed, thanking God for the day and for the food on the table. Then we dug in. I glanced around the restaurant and noticed several other people praying over their food. I hadn't witnessed much public praying in Wichita, but it was par for the course in Harmony.

As always, the chicken was crisp and buttery tasting, the whipped potatoes and gravy thick and creamy, and the green beans with bacon and onions were delicious. I took several bites while I built up the courage to ask Sam the question I'd wanted to ask ever since I got home.

"So did you spend any time with Pat while I was gone?" I said finally. Immediately I felt an emotional door slam shut.

The smile slipped from Sam's face. "You know we're very busy in the orchards right now."

"You're not so busy you couldn't have found a couple of hours to spend with your father."

Sam took a sip of coffee then put his cup down with a thud. "Look, Grace. You just got back. We'll talk about it at some point but not today, okay?"

"You said that before I left. There never seems to be a right time to discuss Pat."

"He abandoned me and my mother."

"For crying out loud, Sam. He didn't even know your mother was pregnant. How is that abandoning her?"

He brushed away a lock of hair that had fallen over one eye. "Well, he certainly didn't check to find out, did he? He took advantage of her, and then he was gone."

We'd been over this more than once. Sam seemed to judge his father by his own standards. "I get it, but as I've said before, neither one of them were living for God." I knew this was difficult for him and tried to keep my tone as gentle as possible. Truth was, his attitude frustrated me. "Even so, I don't believe your father would have left had he known your mom was expecting." I reached across the table and took Sam's hand. "It was your mother's responsibility to tell him, but she didn't. And remember, when she contacted him a couple of years ago, he immediately set out to find you. He even gave up an important job he loved to become sheriff of a rural county where most of the time the biggest crime he faces is chicken stealing."

Sam pulled his hand back, and a frown creased his handsome face. "Right. Except he waited for over a year to tell me who he was. And actually, he didn't even tell me. You figured it out."

Sam scooped another big helping of mashed potatoes onto his plate, a signal that our conversation had ended.

I couldn't help but sigh with frustration. Sheriff Pat Taylor became my friend last year during a particularly trying time. In fact, he'd saved my life. Through a series of incidents, I'd discovered he was Sam's real father. Since then, Pat had done everything possible to forge a relationship with his son. But Sam's resistance had stalled their connection and when they were together, the tension was palpable. Before I picked up my fork, I let out another deep sigh.

Sam stopped eating and scowled at me. "For goodness' sake, Grace. If you keep that up, you'll hyperventilate. We'll sit down sometime this week and have a long discussion about Pat if it will keep you conscious. Okay?"

I waved my fork at him. "Very clever. You know my folks will be here, and you're counting on my being too busy to talk to you." I jabbed my fork at him like a pointer. "It won't work. I'll definitely find the time. You've got to figure this out before the wedding. Your father should be sitting on your side of the church. He's family, you know."

For the first time since we'd begun this uncomfortable

conversation, Sam grinned. "Oh sure. And I suppose you're planning to sit him down right next to Sweetie?"

Touché. If Sam's acceptance of his father was minimal, Sweetie's was almost nonexistent. Although Sam's aunt had come a long way in her spiritual walk since I'd known her, the subject of Pat Taylor was "sorer than a boil on a pig's behind," as she would say. I'd even dragged both of them to a meeting with our pastor, Marcus Jensen. He'd done a great job of explaining forgiveness and how we had no right to withhold it from anyone after God had sacrificed so much to forgive us. For a while, I thought he had them. But when we walked out of his office, the Goodriches were right back where they started. It confused me some since they were both such kind, forgiving people in every other area. This was simply one stronghold they protected with ferocity. Meanwhile, Pat just kept trying. If he ever decided to give up and move on, I wouldn't blame him. But instead he'd dug his heels in, determined to ride it out. In truth, he was as stubborn as his son, although in my eyes, he was in the right while Sam stood with both cowboy boots planted squarely in the wrong.

Out of the corner of my eye, I saw someone walk up to our table. I turned to find Bill Eberly smiling at me. "Glad to see you back, Gracie."

"Thanks, Bill," I said, returning his smile. "It's good to be back."

Bill is a nice-looking man with an easygoing manner. His brown hair is sprinkled with gray, and his dark-green eyes almost always twinkle with humor. His road hadn't been an easy one since the death of his wife, Edith. Not long after her passing, his two grown children moved away, leaving him alone and grieving.

"So how did Hannah enjoy her art classes?" he asked.

"She did very well. The instructor thinks she's quite talented."

I congratulated myself on sidestepping the Hannah-fought-tooth-and-nail-not-to-return-to-Harmony issue. But my mouthy fiancé wasn't quite as clever.

"Yeah, she didn't want to come back," he offered. "Grace had to practically drag her home."

I shot Sam a look that made his eyes widen. Men. They have no clue when it comes to discretion.

"Wow," Bill said. "This certainly isn't a good time for young women to be where they shouldn't be. Have you two heard that another girl is missing? This one from Emporia?"

"I caught something about it on the news last night," I said.

Bill looked around and then stepped closer, lowering his voice. "I have a nephew who works for a newspaper in Topeka. He says the police think all three girls might have been kidnapped by the same man. They're trying to keep that away from the media, though, so they don't spook the guy. You know, in case the women are still alive. If the kidnapper thinks the authorities are closing in on him, the police are afraid he might harm them." He shook his head. "We need to pray for those poor girls and their families."

"But why do they think the cases are connected?" I asked. "I mean, maybe these girls took off on their own."

Bill shrugged. "My nephew has a friend on the police department." He lowered his voice again. I had to strain to hear him. "Please don't repeat this. My nephew's friend told him it was off the record, but in one of the situations in Topeka, someone saw the girl being picked up in a red truck. And in Emporia, there were truck tracks on the dirt road where that young woman disappeared."

"What about the other girl in Topeka?" Sam said.

"She was out walking and never came home," Bill said. "No one reported seeing her get into a truck, but all the girls look so similar."

"That's not much to go on," Sam said, frowning. "Lots of people in rural areas have trucks. Someone sees one red truck, and there are tracks from a truck at a second location?" He shook his head. "Doesn't make sense. Why would the police think these situations are connected based on flimsy evidence like that?"

"I'm not sure. Maybe they have something else that links the missing girls together." He grunted. "My nephew isn't the best source of sound information. He could be blowing his friend's comments out of proportion."

I frowned at Sam. "All the girls have long blond hair and blue eyes. Like Hannah." I could hear the alarm in my voice, and Sam noticed it, too.

"Hannah's not out running around by herself," he said reassuringly. "And she'd never get into a stranger's vehicle. Never. Besides, I'll bet none of the girls dressed like Hannah, did they, Bill?"

He shook his head and smiled at me. "No, these were modern girls, Gracie. Not Mennonite." He patted my shoulder. "I'm sorry. I didn't mean to alarm you. I shouldn't have said anything. I'm sorry."

"It's not your fault," I said. "Hannah's been on my mind, and some of her recent actions have me concerned. You're both right. This has nothing to do with her."

Sam grunted. "A red truck, huh? I have a red truck. You do, too, don't you, Bill?"

He nodded. "Yep, and so do a lot of other folks around here. Oh, I just remembered. The truck had an odd bumper sticker. The witness didn't get a real good look at it, but I guess she told the police something about it that they found helpful." He shrugged. "My nephew didn't go into any other details."

Sam pointed toward the front window of the restaurant. "I see four red trucks parked out there right now, and I can guarantee you that at least three of them have bumper stickers. The police are going to need a lot more than that to find this guy—if there really is someone out there abducting young women."

Bill nodded. "You're right about that." He straightened up and grinned at us. "Well, I better get going. I'm having dinner at Thelma's tonight before church. I need to take a nap and sleep off Hector's fried chicken before I tackle Thelma's yummy pot roast." He chuckled. "It's a hard life, but I'm doing the best I can."

Sam and I laughed, even though our previous discussion left me feeling decidedly uneasy. After Bill walked away, I finished my meal while Sam talked, but I couldn't concentrate on the discussion. Ida had taught me to listen when something disrupts my inner sense of peace. And I felt as if my peace was busy jumping up and down, frantically waving its arms.

Chapter Five

After lunch, Sam took me home. I spent the rest of the day trying to get ready for the arrival of my parents and Papa Joe. The situation with Hannah made it difficult for me to concentrate. I couldn't help but wonder what was going on at the Muellers'. I stopped and prayed once again that God would bring peace to them. Somehow I managed to get everything done I'd planned to do. The room my dad grew up in sat ready for my mother and father, and I'd cleaned out my room for Papa Joe since it had been his bedroom when he and Mama Essie lived in the house. I'd temporarily moved into Uncle Benjamin's room. When I surveyed the space I'd prepared for my family, I felt certain everyone would be comfortable. The rooms were clean, the furniture polished, and each bed was covered with one of the beautiful quilts I'd retrieved from trunks in the basement. Most of the furniture pieces had belonged to the room's original owner. Temple furniture was certainly made to last. I loved knowing that my family would be able to enjoy many of the furnishings they grew up with.

I finished much earlier than I'd anticipated thanks to Sam and Sweetie's efforts before I got home. There was plenty of food in the house and the main rooms had been cleaned so perfectly there was almost nothing left to do. I decided to run over and see Ida. Since she only lives half a mile from me, I chose to walk. I hadn't gone very far when I realized I'd made a mistake. The July sun beat down relentlessly on my uncovered head, and I remembered that Ida doesn't have air-conditioning. Even though I considered turning around more than once, in the end I kept going. If someone Ida's age could handle the heat, surely I could.

As I entered her yard, the front door swung open. "Ach, my Gracie! I have been hoping you would come to see me."

I hurried up the steps and flung my arms around her. "I missed you so much."

"Not as much as I missed you, my dear child," the old woman said, her voice breaking. "Please come inside. I can hardly wait to hear all about your trip." Her blue eyes, faded with age, shone with tears.

When I stepped inside Ida's simple home, I was pleasantly surprised. Although the interior of the house was warm, it wasn't as bad as I'd expected. The shades were drawn, keeping the room cooler, and a slight breeze from outside flowed through the space with vigor. Ida noticed my interest.

"My house was designed to circulate the air," she said with a smile. "The windows and doors in the front and back are situated in a way that brings the wind from outside through my main rooms." She chuckled. "However, it is still very warm."

"I've visited you when it was hot outside, but I never noticed that your house was designed differently from anyone else's."

"I believe you were not aware of the heat because you were comfortable here. But today you are thinking about the heat, so for the first time you see the difference. Is this not the answer?"

I nodded. "I think you're exactly right."

"Your house is designed in the same way," she said. "If you will open the windows in your living room and the windows near your back door, you will find that the air will move through your home just like mine."

"Maybe I'll try that in the fall, but on days like this, I'm afraid any cool air in my house will have to come from my air-conditioning. I guess I'm a wimp."

Ida laughed. "You are certainly not a wimp in my book. Now you sit here while I get something cold to relieve you."

Ida's refrigerator runs on propane. It seems odd that while propane gas burns under the appliance, the inside stays cool. I watched the elderly woman toddle off toward her kitchen. In deference to the hot summer temperatures, she'd shed her usual apron. The sleeves on her dress had been shortened, and the large collar she usually wore had been removed. But her dress was dark blue, not a good color in the heat, and her ever-present black prayer covering sat atop her head, covering her steel-gray hair, which had been pulled into a tight bun. I'd learned from my friend Sarah that in Harmony, married or widowed women wore black prayer coverings while single women, like her, wore white. Good way to let the gentlemen folk know you're available, I guess.

I wiped the sweat trickling down my face and rubbed my hands on my jeans. Shorts would have been more comfortable, but not wanting to offend Ida, I'd opted for jeans and a T-shirt. It's true that Ida's house was cooler than it could have been, but I was still second-guessing my clothing choice when Ida came back into the room carrying a large glass of lemonade. As I took it from her, I realized she wasn't sweating. It was obvious I was more sensitive to the high temperatures than she was. Maybe some people adjust to this kind of heat when they're not used to air-conditioning. Obviously, I would never be one of them. All I could think about was going home and sitting in front of the air conditioner until my face froze.

"Now, Gracie," she said, as she sat down again, "before we talk about anything else, you must tell me about Hannah. How did she do in Wichita? Was your art teacher able to help her?"

I took a big gulp of lemonade before answering her. "It—it didn't go well, Ida," I said. "Hannah loved Wichita. In fact, she wanted to stay there. My teacher offered to let her live with him and go to a local magnet school that specializes in art classes." I put the lemonade down and sighed. "The truth is, I had to force her to come home."

Ida was quiet for a moment. With anyone else, I would have expected a stern "I told you so," but that wasn't Ida's style. "My, my," she said softly. "And how do her parents feel about this?"

"What do you think? They're very disappointed. And not just in Hannah. They're upset with me, too. Obviously, taking her to Wichita was a mistake. A big mistake."

"*Ach, liebling.* I am not sure you are right about this."

I raised my eyebrows at her. "How can you say that? Hannah's angry and taking out her frustration on her parents. She's being a—a pill!"

Ida smiled. "Please understand that I am not saying Hannah's actions are correct. God says in His Holy Word that children should respect and obey their parents. She is clearly in the wrong. But is it not better that the Muellers find out how Hannah feels now when they can still have an influence over her? Would it have been better for Hannah to have moved away from those who love her and then had this reaction?" Ida shook her head. "No. I am a firm believer in God's promise that all things work together for our good for those of us who love Him and are called according to His purpose. Hannah loves God, Gracie. She will find the right way, and God will use this experience to teach her something very valuable."

"I hope you're right, Ida. I really do."

"I am certain God's Word is truer than the circumstances that surround us." She peered into my face. "And I am also sure that it is time for you to forgive yourself. You have done nothing wrong. Hannah is responsible for her own choices. What you did for Hannah you did because you care for her. That was the intent of your heart. You must remember this. You gave up six weeks of your own life to help someone else."

"Pastor Jensen preached about forgiveness this morning, and I know my heart was in the right place. I just wish I'd listened to you and the Muellers. You both warned me taking Hannah to Wichita might turn out badly."

The elderly woman laughed lightly. "And do I look like God to you? My dear sweet Gracie, people have opinions about things. Sometimes they believe they know what is right, but God is the only One who really knows the truth. You must not always take my advice to heart. You had to make a decision, and you chose the path you thought was right. We all make choices we wish we could take back. But I think our Father does not like it when we feel condemnation for our mistakes. He paid the ultimate price so there would be no separation between Him and the ones He loves. Why do we want to turn our back on His gift of forgiveness and righteousness?" She smiled. "Long ago I became convinced that true humility is believing what God says instead of following what we feel or think. So when God tells me that there is now no condemnation for those who are in Christ Jesus, I humbly choose to believe Him—even if I don't feel worthy of His acceptance." She shrugged her thin shoulders. "Only one of these things is true. Either there is no condemnation—or there is. I must choose. And I choose His truth over mine."

"That's exactly what Pastor Jensen said. God must be trying to tell me something." I reached over and hugged her. "Thanks, Ida."

"Just remember that God loves you, child. Every minute of every day, and that will never, ever change." She sighed. "And when you try to do something right, but it looks as if you were wrong, some people will misunderstand. I have certainly experienced this myself. That is why we must not seek to please people—but to please God. Trying to keep people happy with us is impossible and will always cause us unnecessary pain and confusion."

"I love Abel and Emily so much; it hurts that they blame me."

"Ach, no," Ida said with a wave of her hand. "I am certain they do not really blame you. These are godly people who know it is not your fault. They are just worried about their little girl. You must not take their words seriously right now."

"I'll try not to," I said, praying she was right. Abel and Emily were like family, and the idea of losing their friendship troubled me deeply.

"We must pray right now," Ida said, grasping both my hands. "We must pray for Hannah."

We closed our eyes and Ida began to pray. She thanked God for loving Hannah and giving her wisdom. She also prayed for peace in the Muellers' home. As she spoke, faith rose up inside me, and by the time she'd finished, I knew God had heard her prayer. I felt a wave of calm assurance wash through me.

When Ida let go of my hands, I picked up the glass of lemonade she'd brought me. I was suddenly so thirsty I could barely stand it. "This is delicious," I said after taking a long drink.

"Ja, my mother taught me to make lemonade," Ida said. "I will tell you the secret." She leaned over as if someone were listening, ready to steal her recipe, and sell it the masses. "It is honey." She straightened up, a look of pride on her face. "My mother used honey and I use honey."

I took another drink. It really was delicious. "It's wonderful. Where do you get the honey?"

"I used to buy it from Abigail Bradley. Unfortunately, I am on my very last jar. She sold her hives several months ago due to her poor health. She could no longer keep her honey business going." Ida frowned. "I do not believe you have met Abigail. She is a very private person. She does not leave her house anymore and has not done so for quite some time. Her neighbor gets her groceries when they buy their own, and they check on her when they can. However, in other areas she will not allow people to assist her. The house she lives in needs repair, but all offers to help her have been rejected. I assume it is her pride that compels her."

Abigail Bradley. I'd heard the name before but where? Suddenly I remembered. "Sarah mentioned her once. She seemed uncomfortable talking about her though. I believe Sarah actually called her 'strange.'"

Ida sighed and shook her head. "I understand how Sarah feels. Abigail is. . .unusual. But she has had a very hard and confusing life. Abigail is the only child of very strict parents. As a young woman, she spent many years in rebellion against them and their beliefs. Then she married a man named Bradley. During her marriage she chased after some very different kinds of religions. I believe her husband also had some odd beliefs. Now what was it. . ." Ida strained to recapture a fading memory. Finally she shrugged. "Oh my. I am not sure, but it was something unusual. If I remember right, spaceships were involved somehow." She gave me a small smile. "It was the seventies. A very strange time in the world. There were many curious beliefs circulating back then." Ida giggled at the look on my face. "You think I am so separated from the world, I do not know about the seventies?"

I grinned. "Nothing you know surprises me anymore, Ida. But I have to ask. Without TV or newspapers, where did you get your information?"

She chuckled. "Well, I like to visit with my friends at the restaurant, and they talk about many things." She held a hand up to her cheek. "In fact, I have heard conversations in that place that would have turned my hair gray if it had not already happened!"

Her expression made me laugh. "Why Ida. You're blushing."

"You see," she said, shaking her finger at me. "I am not quite as sheltered as you believed."

I'd lived in Harmony long enough to know that whatever Ida had overheard would be considered incredibly tame by most standards. But to her it was probably scandalous. "So tell me more about Abigail," I said, draining the last of my drink.

The old woman stood to her feet. "I will do so but first, more lemonade."

After she disappeared into her kitchen, I gazed around the sparse but comfortable living room. I knew Ida missed her husband, but she had adapted without complaining and feeling sorry for herself. In fact, I couldn't remember her ever voicing one word of self-pity. She was a remarkable woman, and when I compared myself to her, I definitely came up short.

"Here we go," she said, as she came back with two glasses in her hands. "I had a lemonade earlier, but I have decided to splurge and help myself to a second one." She shook her head. "Sometimes I think the honey stimulates me too much, but today I will not be concerned about that." She handed me my glass and sat down again. After taking a sip, she placed her drink on the table next to her. "Now where was I? Oh yes. Abigail. After her husband 'went off the deep end,' as she put it, she left him and traveled, trying to *find herself*, whatever that means." Ida's forehead wrinkled in confusion. "I have no idea why a person would need to find herself. We are with ourselves all the time, ja?"

I grinned. "Ja."

"Anyway, after running around the country for many years and becoming ill, she was taken in by a Mennonite couple who cared for her. Although they were not Old Order, their mother was. Abigail latched on to her like a puppy following its mama, I guess, although I am certain Abigail would express it differently. She told me the mother was her *mentor*. So, she adopted the Old Order ways." She held her hands up in a gesture of surrender. "That is the whole story. To be honest with you, I feel she became Mennonite not because she believed in our ways but because our lifestyle reminded her of the parents she left behind. And perhaps she was also looking for a place to hide." Ida frowned. "I do not want to escape from the world. I choose to keep my life free from distractions that may separate me from my precious Savior. However, I fear Abigail has a completely different reason for her choices."

"But how did she end up in Harmony?" I suddenly realized I was no longer feeling hot. Hopefully it was because of Ida's interesting story and not the first stage of heatstroke.

"Actually, the family she lived with brought her here during a visit to a relative who owned the house where Abigail now resides. When the family member died, Abigail bought the house and moved to Harmony with her son. Until then, the boy had been living with his father, but he died, leaving the child without a home. So Abigail brought him here, and he lived with her until he left for college. He moved away not long after your parents left Harmony. Abigail has stayed alone in that house ever since."

She rubbed her hands together like she was cold. "In truth, I was glad to see her son leave. He was such an unhappy boy. Abigail brought him up very harshly, with many rules and restrictions. Several people tried to help, to tell her she was hurting him. He became extremely withdrawn and would act out sometimes in town with the other boys. Unfortunately, after Abigail became frustrated with his behavior, she eventually kept him home almost all the time." She rubbed her chin. "I remember that he had a girlfriend once. He was very much in love with her. A beautiful girl as I remember with hair the color of wheat and startling blue eyes. What was her name?" Ida stared into space for a moment. "Melanie, I think. Melanie Pemberton. But Abigail's interference broke them up. The girl's family moved away not long after that, and I never saw C.J. smile again. It was so sad. I was glad to hear he was going to college." She sighed. "Higher education was discouraged back then in our group, but I believed C.J. needed to get away before Abigail broke his spirit."

"Did Abigail know my uncle Benjamin?"

Ida nodded. "Oh yes. In fact, I believe Abigail had some interest in him as a husband. Benjamin did not return her feelings, but he was close to the boy until he left Harmony." She smoothed out her skirt with her age-spotted hands. "Your grandfather did not like the boy, though. When they were young, he forbade your father and your uncle from spending time with him outside of school. I have no idea why, but Joe felt C.J. was a bad influence. I disagreed with him at the time because I felt C.J. needed good examples in his young life. Joe would have none of it." She sighed. "Joe could have been such a help to the boy. To this day I do not understand why he could not extend a hand of friendship. Joe wouldn't talk about it. So you see why I was happy when C.J. went away. I hope he has turned out right. He has been in my prayers for quite some time."

"When was the last time you saw Abigail?"

"It has been awhile," Ida acknowledged. "Our small group used to take turns meeting in each other's homes, but then she refused to leave her house. We started gathering together at her place, but now our numbers have dwindled, and there are no more home churches. Most of us have chosen to attend Bethel, including the Ketterlings and the Voglers. That just leaves the Beckenbauer brothers and Abigail. The brothers have both been too ill to attend church, so Abigail has been alone. I have invited her several times to Bethel, but she has declined my invitations. She believes the church is too liberal." She smiled sadly. "I have tried to talk to her about this, but it has been to no avail. I am not certain her standards are the only reason for her refusal. I think she is now too afraid to leave her home. The last time I saw her was in May when I hitched up Zebediah and rode over to see her."

"Are you worried about her?"

"Well, as I said, her neighbors were checking on her and buying her groceries, but with the wheat harvest going on, I am sure they do not have the time to keep a close watch on her. I must admit that I am concerned." She jabbed at her right leg with her finger. "This leg of mine has been so stiff and sore the last few months, and the trip to Abigail's takes quite awhile. But that is no excuse. I will ride over to see her after I visit with your parents and grandfather tomorrow." She clapped her hands together. "I am so excited. Do you know what time they will arrive?"

"Sweetie is hosting a big dinner tomorrow night to welcome them. One reason I came over was to invite you. Either Sam or I will pick you up around six if that's okay."

"Oh ja. I would love to go. But you do not need to worry yourself about me. I will hitch up Zeb and carry myself."

"I thought perhaps Zeb would rather stay in his shed since it's so hot. Wouldn't that be better for him?" The horse was as old and decrepit as its owner. I dreaded the day something happened to him. Ida treated him like a dear, beloved friend.

"Well, you may be right," she acknowledged. "If it would not be too much trouble. . ."

I stood up, leaned over, and kissed her cheek. "It would most definitely not be too much trouble. Now I must get home. I need to get to bed early so I'll be bright and cheerful when my family arrives."

Ida also stood to her feet. "Ach, I hope I will be able to sleep tonight due to my exhilaration. Do you believe your grandfather will remember me?"

Ida knew my grandfather was battling Alzheimer's. "I'm not sure, but it's his short-term memory that seems to be the most affected. I think it's very possible he will know exactly who you are."

"I hope so," she said, a tinge of sadness in her voice. "How awful for him to be trapped in a mind that does not work the way it should. It is so heartbreaking, ja?"

"Yes it is." I gave her a quick hug. "I'll see you tomorrow."

"See you tomorrow, *liebling*. And remember, we have prayed for Hannah and God has listened. I expect everything to turn out right. You must do so, too, ja?"

I nodded. "Thanks, Ida. I always feel better after speaking to you."

"That means more to me than you know, my dearest Gracie," she said softly.

I'd already opened the front door when a thought struck me. "Ida, what if I go by and check on Abigail sometime in the next few days. Would that help?"

"Oh Gracie, I do not know. She does not know you, although

I did tell her about you." She considered my question for several seconds. Finally she said, "Perhaps if you tell her who you are and that I sent you, she will receive you." She looked at me hopefully. "It would be wonderful if you could make certain she is well. And it would save Zeb and me from that long ride."

"Even if she refuses to see me, at least we'll know she's okay," I said. "Let me get my folks settled in, and then I'll drive over there. Don't worry about her, okay?"

"Ja, ja. Thank you, Gracie. You are such a blessing to me." Her face crinkled up in an angelic smile.

"And you are a blessing to me." I waved good-bye and closed the screen door behind me.

After I got home, I spent the rest of the evening adding a few last touches to the house. On the way back from Ida's, I'd picked some of the wildflowers that grew near the large lake behind my property. I placed the flowers in vases and scattered them throughout the house, making certain the upstairs bedrooms had the loveliest arrangements.

Although I climbed into bed early, I had trouble falling asleep. I kept thinking about seeing my family again. It had been awhile since I'd been to Nebraska, and it was the first time they'd been to Harmony in thirty years. Their departure had been under negative circumstances, and I couldn't help but wonder if they'd see the differences now. The tyrannical bishop who once ruled the town with an iron fist had been gone a long time. Abel Mueller's compassionate leadership helped to change Harmony's complexion—along with the commitment of its citizens to keep the peace they worked so hard to protect. I felt sure my parents would be pleased to find their hometown's current condition.

Finally, a little after eleven o'clock I fell asleep. It seemed like only minutes later when I awoke to the sound of pounding coming from downstairs. I struggled to sit up and focus my eyes so I could see the numbers on the clock that sat on the dresser across the room. Five thirty? The insistent knocking continued. Dressed only in a pair of boxers and a T-shirt, I grabbed a robe out of the closet and hurried down the stairs, trying to pat my hair into place. I flipped on the front porch light and swung the door open to find Abel and Emily standing there. The looks on their faces sucked the breath out of my lungs.

"She's gone, Gracie," Emily said, tears running down her face. "Hannah's missing!"

Chapter Six

By seven thirty, my little kitchen was full to overflowing with people. Sweetie and Sam drove over after my frantic phone call. I'd called Pat Taylor, and as he tried to sort out the situation with Abel and Emily, Sweetie glared at him while Sam stayed busy trying to ignore him.

"So you checked on Hannah around five o'clock this morning?" Pat said. "Isn't that a little early?"

Emily shook her head. Her large brown eyes reflected her fear. Her prayer covering sat crookedly on her head, and stray brown hairs touched with silver peeked out from underneath it due to a hastily pulled-together bun. "I wake up early every morning. It's my quiet time with the Lord." She stared at the bleary-eyed law enforcement officer who clearly hadn't expected to be rushed out of bed at sunrise. Her eyes spilled over with tears. "I—I just felt as if something wasn't right. When I opened the door to her room, I could see that her bed was empty."

Pat frowned. "Was the bed messy? Had it been slept in?"

Emily hesitated for a moment. "No. As a matter of fact, it was made up. I hadn't thought about it. What does that mean?"

He didn't answer. Instead his eyes darted around the room, studying each of us carefully. I felt like a bug under a microscope. Everyone but Sweetie met his gaze. "Anything unusual happen lately? Any reason this young woman has to be upset or angry?"

I quickly filled him in on Hannah's desire to stay in Wichita. "But that couldn't possibly have anything to do with this," I said. "For one thing, Hannah adores her parents and would never just leave without a word. She knows how much it would hurt them. And anyway, she has nowhere to go. Jim Monahan, the art teacher in Wichita, would never allow her to stay with him without her parents' permission."

"I'm gonna need his contact information," Pat growled. He put his notepad on the table and scowled at us. "Any other place she might go?"

"Not that I can think of. Well, maybe my friend Allison's since that's where we stayed. But she doesn't even know Allison. There's really no reason she'd head there."

"Give me the number anyway," he said, sighing. "You people really don't think a girl who didn't want to come home would run off if she's forced back? Have any of you actually thought this out?"

"Of course they have," Sam retorted. "Abel and Emily know their daughter, and they're frightened. Maybe you should pay attention to what they're trying to tell you."

Pat locked eyes with his son. "I'm paying attention," he said, his tone a little softer, "but Hannah hasn't been abducted. She's run away." He turned his gaze to Abel and Emily. "You said there was no sign of forced entry. Her bed was made. Did you happen to check to see if any of her clothes are missing?"

"Of course not," Abel snapped. "Our minds were a little occupied. Checking out her wardrobe wasn't our first concern."

"Look Pat," I interjected. "Even if she ran away of her own accord, you still need to find her. She could get into trouble."

"I agree, and I have every intention of looking for her," he said. "A girl who's lived the kind of sheltered life she has shouldn't be out there on her own." He stopped and studied Abel and Emily for a moment. "She would be on her own, right? Is there a boyfriend in the picture?"

"Hannah hasn't run off with a boy," I said.

"There's no boyfriend," Abel agreed.

"Well, actually. . ." Emily said, looking at her husband.

Abel's eyebrows knit together as he stared back at his wife. "What are you saying? There's a boy in her life? Why don't I know anything about this?"

Emily lifted the skirt of the apron she wore over her dress and wiped her eyes. "The boy isn't actually in her life, but Hannah told me last week she has a crush on Jonathan Vogler. I doubt he even knows it."

Pat picked up his notebook again and scribbled in it. "Won't hurt to check it out."

"What do you intend to do, Sheriff?" Abel asked, skepticism written clearly on his face.

"I intend to look for your daughter. I'd like to come by your place and inspect her bedroom, if you don't mind. Any clues I can find as to her frame of mind might help me to locate her."

Abel stood to his feet and held his wife's arm as she rose from her chair. "That would be fine. We'll meet you there."

"Don't straighten up," Pat said, his tone serious. "In fact, don't touch anything. Just wait for me."

"Yes, we understand. You have our address?"

"I do. You go on. I'll be right behind you."

"Abel—Emily," I said. "If you need anything. . ."

"I think you've done quite enough," Emily said angrily. "I'd appreciate it if you'd just stay away from us for a while." She turned and fled out my front door.

Abel waited until he heard the door slam. "I'm sorry, Gracie," he said gently. "Emily's nerves are on edge." He gave me a smile that didn't reach his eyes. "Please be patient with us." He quickly followed his wife out of my house.

I put my head in my hands. Emily's words played over and over in my mind. I could feel tears on my fingers, but I didn't care. The loudest voice in my head at that moment was the one that criticized me. Was this really my fault? Sweetie's voice cut through my thoughts.

"That's just ridiculous," she sputtered. "Gracie, don't you pay her no nevermind. You ain't done nothin' wrong. You was tryin' to help that girl. Don't you let them bad words get into your head, you hear me?"

I nodded but didn't say anything. Sweetie's sentiments echoed Ida's and Pastor Jensen's, but I still felt responsible.

After a long silence, Pat said, "Guess I better get going."

"Wait a minute," I choked out. I picked up a napkin on the table and wiped my eyes. "I didn't want to say anything in front of Abel and Emily, but what about those other girls who have gone missing? Hannah looks just like them."

Pat looked at me like my brain had just jumped out of my head and run out of the room.

"An unhappy girl running away has nothing to do with that," he said. "Besides, no one's sure those cases are even related."

Without telling him who said it, I recounted Bill's information. As I talked, Pat's eyebrows kept rising higher and higher. When I finished he glared at me. "And just who told you all this?"

"I—I can't tell you. It was said to us in confidence."

Sam let out a long breath. "Which actually means you're not supposed to share it with anyone."

I waved my hand dismissively at him. "This is important, Sam. Hannah's life could be at stake. I'm not going to risk her safety just to keep a secret."

"Except that it may not be correct. Word-of-mouth information isn't very reliable."

"I don't care," I said sharply. I ignored Sam and focused my attention on Pat. "Look, I have a bad feeling about this. I realize it looks like Hannah's run away. But things are different in Mennonite families. There's a bond that is too strong to be broken. Hannah would never just leave. She wouldn't. . ." Suddenly, something Hannah said before we left Wichita flashed through my mind. *"Maybe you like hiding out in Harmony, but I don't intend to spend the rest of my life buried there."* I gulped and stared at Pat with wide eyes.

"What?" he asked.

"N–nothing. It's just. . ."

"You might as well tell us, Grace," Sam said matter-of-factly. "Honesty is always the best policy."

I rolled my eyes at him. "And a stitch in time saves nine, but overused clichés aren't helpful right now."

"Quit stalling," he said. "You just remembered something. Did Hannah threaten to run away?"

"No. I mean. . .maybe." I stared back at the three pairs of eyes fastened on me. "Look," I said with a sigh, "she said something in the heat of the moment about not wanting to live in Harmony. But she wasn't referring to *now*. I'm sure she meant after she graduates."

Sweetie grunted. "I don't think you know what she meant." She shook her head. "Time was Mennie kids wasn't allowed to go past the eighth grade. Now they're finishin' high school and goin' off to college. Seems to me this girl is pushin' the line. She should be grateful she's got folks who support her as much as they do."

I felt my face flush. "I hardly think you're an expert on child rearing. In fact, none of you have a clue about what a real family should be. You can't even solve your own problems. I doubt seriously you can figure out anyone else's."

As soon as the words left my mouth I knew they were wrong. Sam's face flushed, and Sweetie's expression turned almost toxic.

Pat cleared his throat and stood up. "Look Gracie, I'm going to look for Hannah, and I'll post a missing person's report. But that's all I can do unless I find some compelling evidence that makes me believe something else is going on here besides a simple case of a girl who's left home because she didn't get her way." He picked his hat up from the table. "If you find anything that might send me in a different direction, you let me know. I'm going over to the Muellers' to look around. I'll keep you updated. Good-bye."

His last word was directed at everyone in the room, not just me. But I was the only one who responded. Sam and Sweetie's attitude toward Pat wasn't going to help us find Hannah. I waited until I heard the front door close. "I am so tired of this," I said pointedly to them both. "Can't you two forget your anger for a while? Hannah should come first now." I stood up and faced them, my hands on my hips. "You both sit in church every Sunday and hear about the goodness and forgiveness of God. But when it comes to practicing it, you're pretty pitiful."

Sweetie rose to her feet. "I'm headin' home. I got work to do." She pointed her finger at me. "I know the Word says I gotta forgive that man, and I'm tryin'. But it's not gonna happen overnight. When I do it, it's gotta be from my heart. And my heart just ain't in it yet." She frowned at me. "Besides, maybe you need to quit bein' Holy Ghost junior. Sam and I will deal with things in our own way—and in our own time." She dropped her hand to her side and stomped out of my kitchen.

I stood there with my mouth open. "I—I do not think I'm Holy Ghost junior," I stammered. "Why in the world. . ."

Sam came over and put his arms around me, covering my mouth with his before I could get another word out. Finally he took his lips from mine. "Listen," he said gently, "you're very passionate about the people you love, and I adore that in you. But sometimes you need to leave things alone and let people work situations out on their own. You've told me and Sweetie your opinion about Pat more times than I can count. Now hush and let us deal with it in our own way. Your comment about none of us having a clue about what family means was not only unkind, it was untrue. Sweetie and I understand family better than most people. That might be why we're so careful to protect it. Until Pat proves himself, we have no intention of opening ourselves up to a relationship that might end up being destructive."

I gently pushed him away. "I just want you to be happy. He's your father. . ."

"Grace," he retorted, "I know who he is. So does Sweetie. You don't need to constantly remind us."

I slumped back down in my chair. Sam went to the coffeemaker, picked up the pot, and carried it over to the table. After taking care of refills, he sat down, too. "I love you," he said with a smile. "And I respect you. But that's a two-way street."

His comment stirred up my indignation all over again. "I do respect you, Sam. How can you say something like that?"

"I can say it because sometimes you treat me like a child, and I'm not your child. I'm going to be your husband. It's okay to try to help me, but it's not okay to try to straighten me out all the time. Since I found out who Pat really is, you've tried to get your point across by shaming me, encouraging me, tricking me. . ."

"Hey, wait a minute! I've never tried to trick you."

Sam gave me a lopsided grin. "Oh really. What about that goofy story you read to me the other day from the Topeka paper? About the man who had a fight with his brother?"

"You mean the one where he finally decides to visit his brother and finds out that he's been dead inside his house for a year?"

Sam nodded.

"I wasn't sharing that story because of you and Pat. I read it to you because it was just. . .creepy."

His right eyebrow disappeared under his bangs, but he didn't say anything. He didn't have to.

"Okay, okay," I said heatedly. "I get it. I really do. No more comments about Pat. But I really do think. . ."

"Grace," Sam warned.

"I said *okay*." I took a sip of coffee. "Let's change the subject. I'm really worried about Hannah, Sam. Something's just not right. I really don't think she'd run away without a word."

He stared at the table for a few moments. "You know what? I tend to agree with you. Pat doesn't know Harmony the way we do. I realize Hannah saw something in Wichita that excited her, but to throw away everything she's believed in her entire life and leave this place and her parents behind? It's very hard to accept."

I sighed with relief. "Thank God someone believes me. But what can we do?"

"I don't know. Let's wait until Pat goes over to the Muellers' house. Maybe he'll find something helpful that will point him in the right direction. In the meantime, what was the name of that boy Hannah likes?"

"Jonathan Vogler."

"Aren't they that Old Order family that lives right outside of town?"

I nodded. "Ida said they just recently started going to Bethel. I've seen them, but I don't know them at all."

"I think I'll check up on him," Sam said. "See if he knows anything."

"Great. Can I come with you?"

"Well, I don't mean right this minute, Grace. But I will try to find out what I can as soon as possible. Besides, don't you need to hang around here and wait for your parents?"

I put my hand on the side of my face. "Yikes! My parents. I almost forgot." As realization dawned, a feeling of dread filled me. "Oh Sam, I promised my mom and dad that Harmony had changed. They think they're coming to a wonderful, peaceful town. Instead they're coming to a place full of anger—and most of it's directed at me."

"Grace, Harmony is *not* full of anger. For crying out loud, just because Emily's blaming you for the way Hannah's acting, it doesn't mean five hundred people are in some kind of uncontrolled frenzy."

His frustration made me realize I'd blown the situation out of proportion. "You're right. I'm just so anxious for this homecoming to go well. You know my parents wanted us to have the wedding in Fairbury. They were both reluctant to come back to Harmony. They only agreed because of me. If they get here and everything is messed up. . . Well, it just can't happen, that's all." I blinked back tears that threatened to spill down my cheeks again.

Sam reached over and put his hand under my chin. "We need to pray for Hannah, and we need to pray over your parents' trip. Then you need to trust God and stop worrying, okay?"

I nodded. Sam removed his hand from my face and took my

hands in his. We prayed for several minutes. When we finished, I felt better.

"Why do I keep forgetting that God doesn't want me to worry or fret about anything?" I smiled at Sam. "I'm so thankful I have you to get on my case when I start trying to do God's job for Him."

Sam stood to his feet and pulled me up with him. "Keeping you straightened out is my cross to bear, I guess."

I laughed. "Poor boy. Do you think you can handle it?"

He put his arms around me. "I'm a pretty determined fellow, willing to spend the rest of our lives finding out."

His warm breath on the back of my neck made me shiver, and I playfully pushed him away. "I need to clean up the kitchen and get ready for my folks. My dad said he'd call me before they left, and I haven't heard a word. I'm guessing he forgot. I have no idea when they'll show up."

"I've got some apple picking to do. I could come back when I'm done and wait with you."

"Oh that would be wonderful. That way I can introduce you to my folks when they arrive. And I wouldn't have to sit here by myself."

"Sounds good." Sam started to walk out of the kitchen, but at the doorway he stopped. Then he turned and frowned at me. "Do I have your word that you won't spend your time worrying about Hannah?"

I held my right hand up as if swearing an oath. "I promise."

I followed him out to the front porch and waved good-bye as he drove away. The rising sun spread its colors across the awakening sky with blues, pinks, and oranges. I stared out across the green farmland and lush trees that made up Harmony. But my mind was filled with thoughts other than the beauty of the countryside. Where could Hannah be? Was she safe? I tried to keep my promise and cast my care on the Lord, but uneasiness filled my heart. Of one thing I was certain: no matter what Pat Taylor said, I would do everything in my power to find the young Mennonite girl and bring her home.

Chapter Seven

Sam made it back to my place by two. A little after three o'clock I heard a car door slam outside and rushed to the front door. I flung it open in time to see my father get out of his car. When he saw me, he smiled widely and said, "Hi Snicklefritz!"

I ran down the steps and flung myself into his open arms. Even the use of a nickname I hated couldn't take away my joy at seeing him. There's something about fathers and their daughters. I can't explain it, but every time I see my dad I instantly feel safe.

"Don't lean on him," my mother exclaimed loudly. "His leg is still giving him problems."

I let go of him. "I thought your leg would be completely healed by now."

"It's getting stronger every day," he said. He scowled at my mother. "You hush, Bev. You're making me sound like an old man. I'm fine."

"Phooey," she retorted. She reached into the car and pulled out a black cane. "He still has pain. The break hasn't healed just right, and the doctor told him to take it easy."

703

She came around the car and handed the cane to my dad who took it reluctantly. "Well, bum leg or not, I'm still glad to see you."

"Me, too, Dad."

As I hugged my mother, I could smell her perfume. Chantilly. The only scent she ever wore. "I've missed you so much," I whispered to her.

"Not as much as I've missed you."

I looked toward Sam who had come down the stairs and stood watching us. I ran over and grabbed his arm, pulling him toward my parents. "Dad and Mom, this is Sam."

My father stepped forward and stuck out his hand. "Sam, I'm happy to finally meet you. I'm sorry it took us so long to get together. First I couldn't travel, and then Gracie spent all those weeks in Wichita. I regret that. I don't like meeting my son-in-law-to-be only two weeks before he marries my daughter."

I looked closely at Dad. There was an edge to his voice I recognized. He's a very civilized man, but I can always tell when he's upset. Sam obviously noticed, too, because his smile tightened.

"I'm sorry about that, too, sir," he said. "I would have come to Nebraska to meet you, but it seemed like every time I could find the time to leave the farm, Grace was in Wichita. I hope we'll have some quality time together before the wedding."

"I hope so, too." My father's serious tone matched his expression. An uncomfortable silence was interrupted by my mother's cheery voice.

"Well, I'm certainly grateful we're getting together now." She shot my father a quick look of disapproval. "We would have come to visit before now, but Daniel's leg and his attitude toward Harmony prevented it."

My father started to protest, but my mother hushed him. "Now Daniel, why don't we let Sam help us with our bags? You need to stretch that leg out, and it wouldn't hurt you and Papa to take a nap before dinner."

In the excitement I'd almost forgotten about Papa Joe. My father opened the car door to the backseat and held out his arm.

" 'Bout time," my grandfather said as he climbed out of the car. "Thought you were gonna leave me in there all day."

"Papa Joe," I cried. "I'm so glad to see you!"

Although he was frailer and his hair was much thinner, his smile reminded me of the grandfather I remembered. I was thrilled to see the old familiar twinkle in his eyes. I rushed over to hug him. He felt thin beneath his Windbreaker.

"I'm glad to see you, too," he said.

"It's Gracie, Dad," my father said loudly.

I let him go and looked into his face. Didn't he know me?

"I'm aware that it's Gracie, Daniel," he responded brusquely. "I haven't completely lost my mind."

My father shot me a quick look. He was obviously concerned, and I felt the same way. The last time I'd seen Papa Joe, I couldn't get him to talk to me at all. He'd just stared at me as if he'd never seen me before. I'm no expert on Alzheimer's, but I'd read that people can suddenly seem to snap out of it, and then without warning, retreat behind that black curtain again. Could that be what worried my father?

"Let's get you inside," I said, taking his hand. "I'll bet you'd like to rest a bit before dinner."

He took his hand from mine and wrapped it around my arm for more support. "I am a little tired," he confessed. "It was a long drive." He suddenly stopped and stared at the house. "Oh my," he whispered. I looked into his face and saw tears well up in his eyes.

"What is it, Papa?"

"I wondered if I'd ever get to see this place again." His eyes scanned the house and the yard. He pointed to the flower bed surrounded by bricks in the middle of the front yard. "Essie's irises," he said, choking up. He swung his gaze back to me. "Thank you for keeping this place, my darling Gracie. Thank you for letting me come home."

I hugged him, too emotional to speak. But in my heart I thanked God for guiding me to my decision to stay in Harmony so I could be a part of this moment. What if I'd sold the house the way I'd originally planned?

I saw my father wiping his eyes. My mother grabbed his arm and helped him up the steps and into the house. Papa, Sam, and I followed behind them. Thankfully, except for a few changes, I'd kept the inside as close to the way I'd found it as possible. Papa Joe stopped at the large cherry secretary and ran his hands over it.

"This is where I work, Papa." I opened the rolled top to show him my keyboard that pulled out on a sliding shelf. I also opened the cabinet doors so he could see my flat-panel monitor. Sam had removed one of the shelves so it would fit inside. He'd also added the sliding shelf. I loved the old secretary and was happy I could use it as a work space without compromising the integrity of the design. I'd purchased a padded antique chair that matched the secretary as if it had been made for it. My CPU was tucked away between the side of the secretary and the wall so it wasn't noticeable.

"It's beautiful, Gracie," Papa said, his voice so soft I could barely hear him. Then he made his way over to the rocking chair my uncle had crafted. He stared at it a few moments before lowering himself into it. "Benjamin made this, didn't he?"

"Yes, Papa. In fact, Harmony is full of his rocking chairs, birdhouses, and bird feeders."

He smiled. "I taught him how to build those things. We used

to work on them together. I'm glad he kept at it. He was very clever with his hands."

"Papa, why don't you stay there while Sam and I carry our luggage upstairs?" my dad said.

"I've got some cider in the refrigerator," I said. "I'll get everyone a glass while you're doing that."

"Sounds great." My father looked at Sam. "Maybe you'll help me get the bags from the car? Then we can get them into the appropriate rooms."

"Daniel Temple, you are not carrying suitcases up the stairs," my mother said sharply. "The doctor told you to rest that leg. Sam looks quite capable of getting our luggage by himself."

"Of course. I'd be happy to," Sam said with a smile.

My father grunted. "I guess working on a farm means he should be capable of manual labor." He glared at my mother. "I'll go out and show him what to bring in if that's acceptable to you."

"Of course it is. And maybe you can work on your attitude while you're out there."

My dad didn't say another word, just headed toward the front door. My rather confused fiancé followed behind him, casting a worried glance my way. All I could do was shrug.

In several phone conversations about my upcoming marriage, I hadn't caught a hint of animosity. His rude comment about Sam was out of character for my usually well-mannered father. I waited until the door closed behind them.

"What gives?" I asked my mother who stood near the kitchen door with her arms crossed. "Is Dad upset about the wedding for some reason?"

She shook her head. "I have no idea what's going on. He was fine until we started getting close to Harmony. Then suddenly he began complaining about not having time to get to know Sam before you get married." She sighed. "I think it's coming back here again. Bad memories. Then there's the pressure of watching Papa deal with this awful disease. Give your father a little slack. He's under a lot of pressure. I'm sure he'll snap out of it."

"I hope so. All I need is one more person who's upset with me."

My mother's eyebrows shot up. "Who's upset? Is something wrong?"

I put my hands up in a gesture of surrender. "Let's talk about it later, okay? I'm really happy you're here, and I'd rather spend the day catching up. I'll fill you in on all the Harmony drama tomorrow."

She hesitated. "Well. . .all right. But you know I don't like secrets."

I chuckled. "Yes, I'm very aware of that, but this has nothing to do with secrets."

I'd started toward the kitchen when Papa Joe spoke up. "Hey, Gracie. What do you get from a pampered cow?"

I grinned at him. "I don't know, Papa. What do you get from a pampered cow?"

A big smile creased his face. "Spoiled milk."

I laughed, although to be honest, I felt like crying. I never thought I'd hear my grandfather tell another one of his awful jokes again. It filled my heart with joy. Unfortunately, that feeling was short-lived, for his next comment reminded me of the cruelty of Alzheimer's.

His face lost its jovial look, and he stared at me through narrowed eyes. "Now Gracie, whatever you do, don't forget your grandmother's wedding present. She'll be upset if you do."

I opened my mouth, but no words came out. Papa looked quizzically at me, as if my reaction confused him. Suddenly my mother spoke up.

"Gracie won't forget, Papa. Thanks for reminding us."

A look of peace settled over his face, and he leaned back in the rocking chair as if her words had allayed his concerns.

"Let's get that cider, Gracie," Mom said quietly. "I'm sure Papa would love some."

A few minutes later, we all sat in the living room sipping the fresh cider Sweetie had left in my refrigerator. Sam had carried all the suitcases up the stairs under my father's direction. Dad seemed more relaxed when they came downstairs.

"This is delicious," Dad said. He smiled at me. "Thanks for putting Mom and me in my old room. I can't believe how good it looks." He shook his head. "It's almost as if I just walked out the door of this house yesterday. Almost everything is the same."

"Except for the lights and air-conditioning," my mother said laughing. "That's one thing about Harmony I don't miss. Surely everyone has electricity by now, don't they, Gracie?"

"Just about. There are a few holdouts. Ida Turnbauer doesn't, but she has a phone. And there are a few families outside of town that still live without the modern conveniences."

"I can hardly wait to see Ida," Dad said. "She was so good to me and Benjamin growing up. A truly kind lady. Your grandmother was very close to her."

I nodded. "She's become a very good friend."

"She's a good friend to everyone in town," Sam added. "I would say she's probably the most loved and respected woman in Harmony."

My dad smiled. "I'm glad to hear that. It means a lot to me to know that she's happy." He looked at Sam. "I can hardly believe your aunt is Myrtle Goodrich. She was the most beautiful woman in Harmony when I was a boy. And as stubborn and hardworking as they come. When her father had his accident, everyone pitched in to help her." He chuckled. "And believe me, it wasn't an easy task. She had her own way of doing things and was bound and determined not to be seen as needy. We almost had to convince her she was doing us a favor by letting us help with her farm. I'm glad she was able to sell it and buy her new place. I got a glimpse of it on the way here. Incredible. Doesn't look anything like it did when we left Harmony. I can't wait to get a closer look."

"You'll get your chance at dinner tonight," I said, relieved that his mood had finally lightened.

"I look forward to it." He put his glass down and stood up. "I think I'd like to lie down for a bit before supper. And I think you wanted a quick nap, didn't you, Papa?"

Everyone looked at my grandfather who just stared into the distance, as if no one else were in the room.

"Papa?" I said. "Are you ready for a nap?"

"Never mind, Gracie," my father said. "We'll all go upstairs together." He grabbed his cane and leaning on it, walked over to where my grandfather sat. He helped him to his feet. "Come on, Papa. I'll take you upstairs."

"Daniel, let me do that," Mom said. "Your leg. . ."

"I can take care of it, Bev," my father snapped. "I'm not completely useless."

My mother frowned at him, but she didn't say anything.

Papa Joe looked at his son as if he'd never seen him before, but my father ignored the lost expression on his face and led him to the stairs like an adult would lead a little child, speaking to him in soft tones and encouraging him to keep going. No one in the room said a word until we heard the door to Papa's room close.

"You told me he was a lot better," I said to my mother.

She sighed. "He is. A few weeks ago he suddenly began to have moments of clarity. Then he started talking again. As we told you on the phone, he's on a new medication. Papa was severely depressed after Mama died. When the doctor started treating him for his depression, Papa got better. His emotional condition could have caused a lot of the symptoms we saw." She smiled sadly. "I can't explain why he suddenly has the ability to relate to his surroundings, but it's important to remember that he still has Alzheimer's. That hasn't changed. Several people from our Alzheimer's support group told us their loved one went through a period of improvement toward the end. I have no idea if the change we're seeing is the medicine. . .or something else." She hesitated. "This may sound silly to you two, but I almost wonder if it isn't a gift from God—a brief reprieve before he dies." She smiled sadly at me. "Besides the Alzheimer's, he has serious heart problems. This may sound awful, but I hope he dies from his heart condition before the Alzheimer's robs the last vestiges of his personality."

"I understand," I said. "But I still pray for healing. I believe with all my heart that it isn't God's will for Papa Joe to suffer."

Mom smiled. "I believe that, too, Gracie. But to be honest, I don't think Papa wants to be healed. He misses Mama a great deal. I think more than anything else in this world he wants to be with her." Her brow wrinkled in thought. "Strange though, how he rallied because of this trip. It was so important to him. He said it's because he wants to see Harmony again, but I get the feeling there's another reason as well. Something he doesn't seem willing to share with us."

"Maybe he wanted to see me," I said.

Mom patted my hand. "I'm sure that's true." She smiled. "Here I am trying to figure out what someone with Alzheimer's is thinking. I don't really have a clue why this trip meant so much to him, but he was absolutely determined to come. And you know

711

Papa when he makes up his mind about something."

I laughed. "Yes, he's like a mad dog with a bone. You might as well just give in and forget it. I hope he gets whatever he wants from this visit. I'm certainly thrilled to see him." I sighed. "Boy, I hate Alzheimer's."

"No more than your father and I do," my mother assured me. "And please understand that we still pray for healing, too. We know nothing is impossible with God." She choked up. "When his mind seems to clear, every time I hope it's a sign. . ."

I got up and went over to her, wrapping my arms around her neck. "Papa is so fortunate to have you in his life. You've always loved him like he was your own father."

"Your other grandparents live so far away, and we don't see them very often. Papa and Mama were always near us after they left Harmony. They really have been like my very own parents all these years."

"I know."

I sat back down and drank my cider while Sam and my mother talked about the fruit farm. My mother is a great conversationalist. I think it's because she's really interested in people. Sam had just started sharing about the new pumpkin patch he and Sweetie just planted when my dad came back into the room.

"Papa's lying down now," he said. "He'll be confused sometimes. The best way to handle it is to just go along with him."

"We learned in our support group that some people try to straighten out loved ones who have the disease when they get confused," Mom said. "But it only frightens them." She leaned her cheek on her hand. "One day I pretended to be Essie an entire afternoon. It made him very happy."

"That makes sense," I said, but truthfully, none of this made sense at all. I couldn't comprehend why a man like Papa Joe, who had lived his life as a good, decent Christian man, should have to face something this awful at the end of his life. Where was the justice in it?

My mother rose to her feet. "Well, I don't know about anyone else, but I think I'll join Daniel for that nap. This has been a tiring day."

"I'd better get going," Sam said. He stood up and smiled at my parents. "I'm looking forward to this evening. I know Sweetie and Ida can hardly wait."

"We're looking forward to it, too, Sam," Mom said. "I believe Gracie said we should be there at six, is that right?"

"We'll eat at six, but you can come early if you'd like, and I can show you the orchards."

"We'll have plenty of time to see your farm while we're here," my father said. "Six is soon enough. Bev and I need to get some rest this afternoon."

There was that tone again. I shot him a look, but he ignored me.

"Sure, that's fine," Sam said. "Whatever's best for you."

He turned to leave, and I followed him. "Let me walk you out," I said. Once we were on the front porch, I closed the door behind us. "I'm sorry, Sam. My dad is usually so easy to get along with. It's just stress. Coming back to Harmony, worrying about Papa Joe. And of course his leg. . ."

Sam grabbed my hand and pulled me down the stairs. Then he wrapped his arms around me. "I understand, Grace. Really. Don't worry about it. Tonight he'll get to see some old friends, eat some good food, and have the chance to relax a little. We'll be fine. Stop worrying."

I leaned against him. "I wish we were already married. Maybe we should have eloped."

He put his hand under my chin, raised my face to his, and

gazed into my eyes. His own eyes always reminded me of the gray clouds that paint Kansas skies before a storm. "I disagree. You see, I'm waiting for that moment."

"What moment?"

He smiled. "That moment when you walk down the aisle. When everyone sees the incredibly beautiful woman who has decided to become my wife. I want to promise before God that I will love you for as long as I live. And I want to put my ring on your finger so the whole world knows you're mine." He shook his head. "No eloping for us. I intend to experience every moment of our wedding and keep it in my heart for the rest of my life."

"Okay," I whispered. "Let's do this right." I ran my hand down his cheek. "I love you so much, Sam. I can hardly wait to be your wife. Every day seems like an eternity."

"But it's not," he said, kissing the top of my head. "Eternity starts the moment we each say 'I do.'" I felt his body stiffen. He let me go and took a step back, his gaze locked on something over my shoulder.

I turned to see what he was looking at. My father stared out the window at us.

"Oh great," Sam said softly. "Now he thinks I'm pawing his daughter."

"Don't be silly. He isn't thinking any such thing." I grabbed his hand and walked with him to his truck. "I'll see you at six."

He opened the truck door and climbed into the cab. "I love you, Grace," he said as he started the engine.

"I know."

While I watched him back out of my driveway and turn onto Faith Road, I thought about how blessed I was to have found someone like Sam Goodrich. Then I turned to go into the house. Once inside I found that my father had abandoned his spot by the window, and everyone had already gone upstairs.

After pouring myself another glass of Sweetie's delicious cider, I went back out on the porch and sat down in my uncle's rocking chair. I certainly shared Sam's feelings about our wedding, but Hannah's disappearance left me wondering if the ceremony would really happen on time. How could we celebrate our new life unless Hannah was home? And if she'd actually been abducted, what would the outcome be? If it was terrible, Harmony would be in mourning, and a wedding would be inappropriate. I hadn't shared my concerns with Sam because there were no decisions to be made yet. The guilt I'd been fighting against returned to haunt me as I considered the harsh truth that kept invading my thoughts. If I'd listened to Abel and Emily in the first place, Hannah would never have gone to Wichita. And she might not be missing now. If something awful happened to her, I would never be able to forgive myself. And Harmony, as loving as it was, would not forgive me either.

I finished my cider, put the glass on the floor next to me, and prayed.

Chapter Eight

We got to Sam's a little late. My parents and Papa Joe got out of the car at Ida's and spent several minutes in the old woman's house hugging and reminiscing. I was a little worried since Sweetie doesn't do well when people arrive late for dinner. But surprisingly, when we pulled up to the house, she came out on the porch with a huge smile on her face. Her overalls were gone, replaced by her Sunday church clothes. She looked very nice. I was touched to know that seeing my family was so important to her. Sam came out on the porch behind her.

"Oh my goodness," Sweetie said as we got out of the car. "Daniel and Beverly. I'm so glad to see you again. It's been such a long time." She hurried down the stairs and grabbed my mother's hand. "Why Bevie, you're just as pretty as you was the last time I seen you. I woulda knowed you anywhere."

"Oh Myrtle," my mother said, "I think you're stretching the truth a bit, but please keep it up." They both laughed and hugged each other.

Then Sweetie turned her attention to my father. "If it ain't

Daniel Temple," she said, her voice breaking slightly. "Still as handsome as the day you left." She looked over at me and smiled. "Your father is one of the best people it was ever my pleasure to know. Even as a boy, every last soul in Harmony knowed they could rely on Daniel and Benjamin Temple. They was young men to look up to." Then she spotted Papa Joe who waited a few feet behind my father. She blinked back tears. "And here's the reason why. Joe. I can hardly believe it."

"Why if it isn't little Myrtle Goodrich," Papa Joe said with a smile. "Still as beautiful as I remember."

I figured it wouldn't be appropriate to point out that Papa's memory wasn't what it used to be. I'd seen pictures of Sweetie as a young woman, and if I hadn't known better, I would never have made the connection. Years of working outside in the sun had damaged her once-flawless skin and aged her beyond her years. But Sweetie beamed like someone who had just been given a million dollars. Sam came over and put his arm around me. He looked pleased to see our families together.

"Why Joe, you always was the kindest man I ever met." Sweetie walked over and gave Papa a hug. "I remember you used to love green bean soup with ham. Essie cooked up some for my father, and she gave me the recipe. I made it for dinner hopin' you'd enjoy it."

Papa chuckled. "Schaubel Zup! Oh my goodness, Myrtle. I haven't had Schaubel Zup since I lost Essie. I can hardly wait to taste it again."

"And I got friendship bread warmin' in the oven. I hope it's as good as Essie's, but I wouldn't bet my farm on it."

Papa smiled at me. "Your grandmother made the best friendship bread in Harmony."

"I thought Mama didn't make bread." The story I'd been told

717

was that because her parents had put such an emphasis on bread making when she was young, Mama refused to do it after she got married.

"You're right about that," Papa said. "But friendship bread isn't like regular bread. It's more like dessert." He laughed. "Just you wait. You're in for a real treat."

"Well let's get outta this hot sun and cool off inside," Sweetie said, taking Papa's arm. "The food's ready and the company's here. Can't ask for nothin' better than that."

I noticed my dad watching Papa and Sweetie climb the stairs together.

"Papa seems like his old self today," I said to him in a low voice. "You'd never know there was anything wrong."

Dad nodded. "He's been swinging back and forth like this for the past month or so. He seems confused and upset, and then suddenly he's Papa again." My father put his arm around my shoulders. "Don't get too excited, Gracie. We've been through this before. In an instant everything can change."

"I know, but this is nice. I really never thought I'd get more time with him. Whatever's going on, I'm grateful."

He was silent as we went into the house. I saw my mom take his hand. I couldn't imagine what my dad was feeling. Watching his father suffer through this insidious disease had to be incredibly hard on him. Hopefully Papa would be alert for the rest of the day.

"Come on in and sit down," Sweetie called out as we came down the hall. "We're eating in the dining room tonight."

Usually when I come over for supper we eat in the kitchen. Sweetie's beautiful dining room is reserved for special occasions. The walls are a lovely shade of deep red with white wainscoting almost halfway up. Crown molding accents the ceiling, which supports a large, intricate brass chandelier with small bulbs that flicker like candles. The long windows along one wall let in the light, and cream-colored valances with red flowers sit atop each one. Over the large white-marble fireplace, a gorgeous painting portraying the outside of the house gives the room a unique feeling of history. The dark mahogany furniture could easily overpower the room with its size and design, but instead it fits perfectly. It's certainly hard to believe that the rough-edged and sometimes unkempt Sweetie Goodrich lives in this house. But anyone who judges her by her physical appearance or her misuse of the English language will miss seeing her for who she really is. There is depth, intelligence, and beauty in the heart of this rugged woman. The dining room table was covered with her fine linen tablecloth and matching napkins. And her good china, an incredible blue-and-red-designed pattern called Bird of Paradise, sat waiting for dinner. I had no idea how much it was worth, but I knew it was expensive and very collectible.

"Your home is beautiful," my mother said. "I have to admit I was a little nervous about seeing this house again. When we left Harmony, Bishop Angstadt lived here, and my visits were never pleasant." She gazed around the room. "But there's not a trace of him left, Myrtle. You even painted the outside red. It changes the entire look of the place."

Sweetie grunted. "That was surely my intention. Ain't no hint of that man here no more."

"Beverly is right," Ida said, adjusting her long black skirt under her as she sat down. "This is the most attractive home I have ever seen."

"Why, you've been here before, Ida," Sweetie said. "Many times."

The old woman smiled. "Yes, and every time I come, I think the same thing."

I knew Ida meant every word she said. Even though she lived a much simpler life than Sweetie, there was no judgment, no condemnation toward others who didn't choose her lifestyle. Ida had taught me many things, but one of the most important was the grace God has toward His children. That even though some of us may choose different paths in our lives, our roads all still lead home—to Him.

Sweetie excused herself and left the room. When she returned a few minutes later, she carried a large china soup tureen in her hands. Sam jumped up and helped her place it in the center of the table. She took off the lid and the wonderful aroma I'd caught when we'd come in, filled the room. "Schaubel Zup," she proclaimed with a smile. "Sam, why don't you help me bring in the rest of the food?"

He followed his aunt to the kitchen. They returned with homemade rolls, Sweetie's wonderful, creamy coleslaw, and peach marmalade made from the peaches they grow on the farm.

"Joe, I wonder if you'd ask the blessing," Sweetie said when she sat down.

I cast a quick glance at my father, wondering if Papa Joe was capable of handling the task Sweetie had just given him. When he was younger, he could "pray the devil back to hell" as Sweetie would say. But could he do it now?

"I'd be happy to, Myrtle." Papa reached out and took my hand and my father's hand. I reached for Sam. Feeling his strong fingers cover mine gave me a sense of security.

"Dear Lord," Papa prayed, "we thank You for family and dear friends. We thank You for this wonderful food and ask that You bless the hands that prepared it. May God, who supplies seed to the sower and bread for food, supply and multiply our seed for sowing and increase the harvest of our righteousness. Amen."

Simple Choices

Everyone around the table echoed Papa's "Amen." I opened my eyes to see my father's mouth quiver with emotion. He probably hadn't heard Papa pray for a very long time. I picked up the pitcher of iced tea sitting next to me, filled my glass, and gave the pitcher to Sam who got up to make sure everyone who wanted iced tea was served.

"If you'll pass me your bowls," Sweetie said, "I'll fill 'em up with soup." While we did as she'd requested, my mother started asking Ida about the changes in Harmony since they'd left.

"Oh my, Beverly," Ida said, shaking her head. "So much has changed. Since Bishop Angstadt died, we have become a new town." She put her hand on her chest. "Please understand that I am not his judge. What I say is only what I have seen since his passing. Perhaps we were not as understanding of Bishop Angstadt as we should have been. I do not know, and I do not presume to know his heart. There is one Judge who will decide at the end of time what our deeds deserve. I am content to let Him determine those things. But I can certainly tell you that when the bishop was gone, it was as if our little town emerged from the shadows." She paused as Sweetie spooned soup into her bowl, thanking her when she finished. "Many of the women, including me, gathered together and prayed for Harmony—that it would deserve the name it had been given from that moment on. We asked God to bless our town with peace. And He has." She picked up her soup spoon and paused. "I hope you will see us with new eyes. Surely there are also good memories from your life here."

My mother laughed lightly. "I have wonderful memories of Harmony, Ida. You certainly are one of them." She leaned her head against my father's shoulder. "And, of course, I found true love in this town. It gave me my husband and my child, as well as the best mother- and father-in-law any woman could have.

And now Gracie is here, and she loves it. She has found her soul mate here just as I did." She nodded. "Yes, there are many good memories—and more to be made, I'm sure. Besides, it was never Harmony that was the problem. It was the bishop."

"There were others in the church who should have stood up to him and didn't," Dad said, frowning.

"I wonder if you mean me," Ida said. Her eyes searched my father's face.

"Oh my goodness no, Ida," he said quickly. "You were always so supportive of us. I can never thank you enough for your constant love and encouragement. And Herman." Dad shook his head. "What a good man he was. I miss him." Herman Turnbauer had been Papa's best friend. They worked in the fields together and lived like brothers. My father smiled. "Herman always had a story for Benjamin and me. Stories from the Bible. He really made the Bible come alive. I still remember learning about Joseph. A man who wouldn't turn his back on God or feel sorry for himself, no matter what happened to him."

Papa Joe chuckled. "When times were hard, Herman would call me by my given name, Joseph, just to remind me that we couldn't give up, and that circumstances never change God's plan." He smiled at Ida. "I still hear him sometimes. 'Joseph, don't give up. Stand up straight. God has deliverance in His mighty hand!'"

Ida gave a soft cry and put her napkin to her face. When she lowered it, there were tears in her eyes. "Oh Joe. Sometimes I swear I hear him whisper to me in the dark before I go to sleep. I miss him so."

"I know, Ida, I know. There are moments when I'm sure Essie is sitting right beside me. Or she comes up behind me and puts her hand on my shoulder." Papa stared down at the table the smile gone from his face.

"Goodness gracious," Sweetie said, loudly. "You all are gonna turn this celebration into a sobfest if you don't stop it." She sniffed and dabbed at her eyes with the bottom of her apron. "Now, let's get to eatin' this good food before it gets cold."

"Sounds good, Myrtle," Papa Joe said, pasting a smile on his face with effort. "I'm so hungry I could eat a horse." He winked at me. "Gracie, do you know what made the pony cough?"

"No, Papa. What made the pony cough?"

Papa looked around the table as if he was getting ready to tell the funniest joke ever written. "Because he was a little horse," he said chuckling.

Everyone laughed. "Oh Joe," Ida said, her eyes twinkling with laughter. "I must admit that I have missed your jokes. Essie and I used to giggle together every time you told a new one."

Papa pointed a finger at her. "You told me you laughed because they were so bad. I remember that."

I snorted. "Well, don't worry. They're just as bad as they used to be."

Papa's smiled widely. "I take that as a compliment."

"You should," Sweetie said with a smile. " 'Cause that's about the only one you're gonna get for a joke like that."

After another round of laughter, we began eating Sweetie's soup. I had no idea if she'd ever made this dish before, but I'd certainly never had it in all the times I'd eaten dinner at her house. Big chunks of ham, fresh green beans, carrots, and potatoes floated in a creamy broth. I filled my spoon and brought it to my mouth. An explosion of flavor greeted me. The ham was tender and the vegetables perfect. And the broth combined creaminess and spice at the same time. It was absolutely delicious.

Papa Joe took his first taste. "Goodness," he said dreamily. "It's wonderful." He smiled at Sweetie. "You've outdone yourself,

Essie. You really have."

His words caused my stomach to clench. My father's face fell, and an uncomfortable silence filled the room. But Sweetie didn't miss a beat.

"Why thank you, Joe," she said, her tone upbeat. "I'm so happy you like it."

"I do," he said, holding up another spoonful. "Now Daniel, you and Beverly eat your soup. We won't wait for Benjamin. He knows better than to show up late for supper." He shook his head. "I can't count the number of times I've told that boy to be home before your mama puts food on the table. He may find himself missing his meal tonight. I just might send him to his room hungry." He turned toward Ida. "And where's Herman tonight, Ida? I know he doesn't like to miss Essie's cooking."

Ida nodded. "You are right about that, Joe. He would have loved to be here, but unfortunately he could not get away."

Papa patted her arm. "He's such a hardworking man. Why don't we send some soup home with you? You can heat it up for him later."

"Thank you, Joe. I would appreciate that."

Papa looked over at me. "Now who is this young lady again? I'm sorry. I just don't seem to remember your name."

"That's okay, Papa," my mother said. "I may have forgotten to introduce you. This is Gracie. She's a friend of mine."

I opened my mouth to respond, but I just couldn't. Sadness overwhelmed me, and I sat there, trying desperately to hold back a flood of tears. How could he go from the Papa I knew so well to this confused man? Mumbling out a lame excuse about needing to check on something, I fled the room. A few moments later, my dad opened the door to the screened-in back porch where'd I'd escaped to cry.

"I—I'm sorry, Daddy," I said tearfully when he sat down next to me on the white wicker love seat. "I tried, I really did. I just couldn't. . .couldn't. . ."

"Pretend?" My father stroked my hair. "It's okay, Snicklefritz. I know exactly how you feel. I've had to walk away many times myself."

"How could God let this happen?" I asked, wiping my face on my arm. My father reached into his pants pocket and pulled out a handkerchief. Outside of Harmony, he's one of the few men I know who still carries one.

"Oh Gracie. God doesn't *let* it happen. Disease and illness were never His plan, but sin and destruction came into the world. Again, not His plan and certainly not His will." He smiled at me. "Believe me, God hates what's happening to Papa even more than we do. I think we always need to remember that there is no sickness or destruction in heaven. That knowledge should help us to know who God really is, and what He really wants for His children." He shrugged. "And remember people get healed all the time. I've seen people wonderfully delivered from disease. Of course I've also known some who weren't."

"Why doesn't everyone get healed, Dad?"

He sighed. "I don't know, honey. It could be for a variety of reasons. We aren't going to understand everything in this life, but I do know one thing."

"What's that?" I sniffed, blowing my nose into his hankie.

"That whether we're delivered from our circumstances or we have to walk them out, God is with us every step of the way. His love never changes, and it never fails. He'll always find a way to bring us through every trial of life if we trust Him."

"Seeing Papa Joe like this makes me feel so sad." I leaned against my father's shoulder.

"It makes me sad, too." He put his arm around me. "But you know what? Most of the time, Papa's very happy. When he's with us and when he's not. The times he drifts away he almost always goes to happy places where my mother is still alive and where his life was good."

"What about the other times?"

"Well, when he quit talking we thought he'd left us forever. When we'd go to visit he'd just stare at us—as if he had no idea who we were. He's verbal now, and we're grateful. But there have been a few times when he's gotten terribly upset. It's as if he's trapped between reality and the disease. I'm sure it's horribly confusing to him, and he lashes out."

"He's not violent, is he?"

My father was quiet for a moment, and then he hugged me tight. "A couple of times he's been rather physical."

"That's not Papa at all."

He kissed the top of my head. "No, it's not. I think the darkness begins to come over him, and he simply tries to fight his way out. It has nothing to do with anyone around him. The first time it happened, I took it personally. But I've learned to let him get it out of his system. When he calms down he's fine."

"So what will happen to Papa now?"

"I don't know. When he stopped talking we assumed the end was near. But now that he's communicating again, we're not sure what to expect next. My guess is that at some point he'll fall silent once more."

"W–will Papa die here?"

My dad sat up straight and gazed directly into my eyes. "No, Gracie. If he gets too bad before we leave for home, Mom and I will get him transferred to a hospital or nursing home nearby. After the wedding, we'll take him back to Nebraska."

"Okay." I wiped my face once again and handed the handkerchief to my dad.

He smiled. "You keep it."

I couldn't help but laugh. "Okay. I'll wash it and then give it back to you."

"I would appreciate that very much. Now let's get back in there before Papa sends me to my room. I didn't like it when I was a kid, and I doubt I'd like it any better now."

I giggled. "I think I'd enjoy seeing that. Payback for all the times you did it to me."

He grunted. "Yes, I'm sure you would. Hopefully I can spare myself the humiliation." He grabbed my hand and pulled me up. "Now get going, young lady. And no more tears in front of Papa, okay?"

"I'll try."

My dad and I went back to the dining room together. Mom grabbed my hand as I walked past. "You okay?" she whispered.

I nodded. Papa Joe was busy eating his soup, smacking his lips with delight. I sat down next to Sam who reached over and gave me a quick hug. It seemed that my grandfather hadn't noticed my unexplained exit. I breathed a sigh of relief.

"Sweetie was telling us about the girl who's missing, Gracie," my mother said. "Isn't Hannah the one you took to Wichita?"

I nodded. "Yes. We're not sure if she just ran away or if something else happened."

"Oh honey. I'm sorry. You must be very worried. I know you care a great deal about her."

"She's very special to me. Everyone's concerned." I launched into the story of Hannah's reaction to Wichita and how she seemed to change.

"I hope you're not blaming yourself," my dad said. "It's certainly not your fault. Take it from two people who know what it's like to want a different kind of life."

I glanced over at Ida who smiled at me. "I did at first. But a dear friend straightened me out." I pointed my soup spoon at my father. "This situation isn't the same as yours, Dad. You and Mom wanted to get married, and Bishop Angstadt wouldn't allow it—ever. But Hannah knows she can go to art school in a year. I can't believe she'd leave her parents and her home just because she's impatient."

"You could be right," he said. "But when Mom and I lived here, there were other people our age who left for the same reasons you said Hannah gave. It happens."

"Well maybe." I turned his comment over in my mind. Was I wrong? Had Hannah really run away because she saw a future beyond Harmony? As hard as I tried, I just couldn't believe it. I started to say that when the doorbell rang.

"Now who in tarnation can that be?" Sweetie murmured. "Botherin' people when they're tryin' to eat." She got up and went to the door, mumbling all the way. Most people in Harmony knew better than to bother Sweetie at suppertime. I felt sorry for whoever was waiting on the other side of her front door. We heard voices and then footsteps in the hallway. Pat Taylor came in, his hat in his hands.

"Pat needs to talk to you, Gracie," Sweetie said. Her sour expression made it clear she wasn't happy about her impromptu visitor.

I started to stand up, but Sam grabbed me and pulled me back into my seat. "Is this about Hannah?" he asked.

Pat nodded, and I gasped.

"Why don't you tell all of us, Pat," Sam said. "If something has happened. . ."

"It's not bad news," he said quickly. "We still haven't found

728

her." He gazed around the table. "I don't want to interrupt your dinner."

"A little late for that," Sweetie grumbled.

Pat nervously rotated his hat with his fingers. "Maybe I should come back some other time."

"Nonsense," my dad said. He stood up and pointed to an empty chair at the end of the table. "We've all heard about Hannah's disappearance. Why don't you have a seat and tell us what's going on? I know we're all very interested."

"Yes, Pat. Please sit down," I said. "Are you hungry?"

He looked at Sam who didn't offer any kind of encouragement, but he slid into the chair next to my dad anyway. "Uh, no. That's okay. I just wanted to bring you up to date. I should have called first, but I was in the area. I tried your place first, but when I found out you weren't home, I thought I'd check to see if you were over here."

"I'm glad you did, Pat," I said.

My father stuck out his hand. "I'm Daniel Temple, Sheriff. I'm Gracie's father. And this is my wife, Beverly, and my father, Joe."

"I'm happy to meet you," Mom said.

My grandfather didn't say anything, but he nodded at Pat.

"Daniel Temple," Pat said. "Your brother was Benjamin?"

"Yes, that's right," Dad said. "Did you know him?"

Pat shook his head. "No, not really. I only met him a couple of times. I hadn't been sheriff for that long before he died. He seemed like a very nice man."

I glanced over at Papa. A few minutes ago he'd thought Benjamin was still alive. How would he react to Pat's statement? Thankfully, he didn't appear to have heard it. Instead he seemed to be focused on buttering his roll.

"Thank you," my father said. "So what is this news you've brought about Hannah?"

Pat scooted up closer to the table. "The girl who disappeared from Emporia has been found. She ran off with her boyfriend. And although neither one of the girls from Topeka have been located yet, the police are pretty sure they know who abducted one of them. An ex-boyfriend threatened her the day before she went missing, and he hasn't shown up for work since the day she disappeared. The police are confident he's got her. They just don't know if they'll find her alive."

"How awful," my mother said. "I can't imagine what her parents are going through."

"About the same thing Abel and Emily are, I imagine," I said. "So only one girl is left who could have been abducted by a stranger?"

"Yes. The girl who got into the red truck is the only remaining mystery." He shrugged. We'll probably find out it's another case of someone running off with a boy her family doesn't approve of." He looked at me. "I wanted you to know about this so you'd quit worrying about Hannah being abducted."

"I appreciate that, but I still have a hard time believing she took off because she's mad at her parents," I said.

Pat grunted. "Maybe this will change your mind. Some snooping around uncovered a little more going on between this Vogler boy and the Mueller girl."

"What do you mean?" I asked.

"Seems that before Hannah left for Wichita, they'd been meeting pretty regularly behind their parents' backs."

"That doesn't sound like Hannah," Sam said. Hannah was special to him. He'd encouraged her in her art and even made frames for her pictures.

"Well, Jonathan Vogler came clean when I questioned him. They think they're in love but didn't want their parents to know.

Afraid they wouldn't approve. One more reason for her to be unhappy at home."

"Hannah couldn't have loved him very much if she wanted to stay in Wichita," I said.

Pat shrugged. "I have no idea. Maybe he planned to meet her there."

"So you're absolutely convinced she ran away?" I was starting to wonder if he was right.

He nodded slowly, but an odd look flickered across his face.

"What?" I asked. "Is there something else?"

"It's probably nothing, but. . ."

"Tell me," I said, pressing him.

"The Muellers can't figure out what Hannah was wearing when she left. All of her dresses seem to be in her closet. At first I doubted they could remember every article of clothing their daughter owns, but I guess Mrs. Mueller makes all her daughter's clothes so. . ." His eyebrows knit together with concern. "Gracie, are you okay?"

I'd felt the blood drain from my face so it wasn't hard to imagine how shocked I looked. "I—I—I mean. . ."

"Grace, what's wrong?" Sam peered into my eyes.

I gulped and took a big breath. "Hannah's clothes. She—she got some jeans and a T-shirt from a girl she met in Wichita. I don't know why I didn't realize. . . I mean, she must have taken them with her when we left town."

"You mean she could have been wearing these new clothes when she left her house?" Pat sighed and pulled a notebook out of his pocket. "You should have told me this from the beginning. I put out an all-points bulletin based on my assumption she was wearing something more. . ."

"Mennonite?" my dad said.

Pat nodded at him. "Exactly. I figured she wouldn't be hard to find dressed like that. But if she blends in. . ."

"She could have slipped right past anyone who was looking for her," I said. "I'm so sorry, Pat. I just didn't realize how important it would be. I thought about telling her parents about the clothes, but they're already so upset with me. . ."

"Upset with you?" my dad said. "Why would they be upset with you? You're not responsible for their daughter's actions."

I recognized the irritation in my father's tone. Papa tiger defending his cub. Mix in a tendency to mistrust anyone with spiritual authority in Harmony. "Dad, the Muellers didn't want Hannah to go with me to Wichita. I talked them into it. Everything they worried about happened. Hannah changed in Wichita."

"I don't care," he said sharply. "It's their job to raise their daughter the right way. If she goes off the deep end the first time she gets away from them, they only have themselves to blame."

Oh dear. This wasn't going well. I grabbed Sam's hand under the table as a signal for help.

"They're just worried about Hannah, sir," he said, taking the hint. "They love Grace. I'm sure it's just the pressure they're under."

Sam's reassurance seemed to mollify my dad somewhat. "Well, I suppose that makes sense. I just don't want anyone trying to make my little girl feel guilty about something that's not her fault."

"Thanks, Daddy. I'm fine." Ida's words of encouragement had really helped me, even though I still wished I'd listened to Abel and Emily when they'd originally expressed their concerns. At the time, I'd been more focused on Hannah's art than on her heart. If only I could have that moment to do over. A quick look at Ida made me realize I was going in the wrong direction. . .again. I smiled at her and tried to push regret out of my thoughts. I needed to concentrate on Hannah—not myself.

"Describe these clothes," Pat said. "I'll correct the APB and get this information out as soon as possible."

I gave him a detailed description of Hannah's outfit. Good thing I'd looked at it so closely. "Oh, she probably had her hair down, and she might have been wearing makeup. Not a lot, but some."

He wrote everything down and then closed his notebook. "Unfortunately, if she was hitchhiking, she would have blended in with anyone else out there on the highway."

"Do children still hitchhike?" my mother asked. "I don't see many girls asking for rides anymore. Too dangerous."

Pat nodded. "You're right, they don't. But is Hannah aware of that? She's lived such a sheltered life I have no idea if she knows how to protect herself from danger."

"But that just proves my point," I insisted. "That she could be in real trouble."

"I understand that, Gracie," Pat said. "But it doesn't change the fact that she's listed as a runaway, and as far as we know right now, that's exactly what happened. Finding out that she put these clothes on of her own volition before leaving home makes it even clearer that she had a plan. And it wasn't to stay in Harmony. I figure she's on her way to Wichita. I've talked to your art teacher and your friend Allison. Neither one of them have seen her. Is there anyone else she might contact?"

I thought for a moment. "Her friend, Robin. The one who gave her the clothes. And you might check with Jim again. It's possible she made friends with someone else in her class that I'm not aware of."

He flipped his notebook open again. "Do you have Robin's contact information?"

I shook my head. "But Jim would."

"Okay, I'll call this Monahan guy again." He stopped writing and looked up at me. "Have you talked to him since you got back?"

"No, I tried to call them before we came over tonight but they were both out. I left messages to contact me if they hear from Hannah."

This time after he closed his notebook he put it back in his pocket. "I guess that's all I need now." He stood up. "Again, sorry to interrupt your family dinner. I'll be on my way."

"Are you sure you won't eat with us?" my dad asked. "There's plenty, and this soup is out of this world."

Pat's eyes darted toward Sam. "No, but thanks anyway. . ."

Sam stood to his feet. "Of course you'll stay. Sit down. I'll get you a bowl from the kitchen."

"Sam!" Sweetie hissed.

He ignored her while Pat gazed at him with his eyebrows arched in surprise. "I should have introduced Sheriff Taylor when he first got here," Sam said. "This is my father."

"Your father?" my dad said. "Why, I had no idea. . . Gracie, I thought you told me Sam's father wasn't around."

"Daniel, hush," my mother said in a loud whisper. "I'm happy to meet you again, Pat," she said smiling. "Now you *must* sit down and share dinner with us."

"Yes, sit down, Pat," Sam said. "Please."

Pat lowered himself slowly back into his chair. "Thank you. This looks really good."

"Oh for cryin' out loud," Sweetie said. "Sit down, Sam. I'll get the bowl." She stood up and stalked out of the room.

"Sam and Pat just recently reunited," I explained to my mother and father, hoping my brief explanation would satisfy them for a while. I could see the questions in their expressions. I prayed they'd hold them until I could get them alone and fill in the details.

"Well that's wonderful," Dad said jovially. "I'm so glad this happened before the wedding. Now we can all celebrate together."

Grateful Sweetie was in the kitchen during this little announcement, I picked up my spoon and went back to work on my soup. It was a little cold, but I could almost swear it tasted even better now.

"Pat, we're planning to go into town tomorrow," Dad continued. "My wife and I haven't seen Harmony for a long time. Maybe you could join us for lunch?" He looked over at me. "What time did you plan for us to eat?"

I broke open a roll and reached for the butter. "I don't really care. Whatever works for everyone else. I intend to drive over to Abigail Bradley's place in the morning, but that shouldn't take long. I'll be home in plenty of time for lunch."

"Then how about meeting us at eleven thirty at the restaurant in town?" Dad said, smiling at Pat.

"I'll do my best," Pat said, "but I'll have to check in to the office first. Why don't you folks go ahead, and I'll try to meet you there."

As Sweetie came into the room with another soup bowl in her hands, my father said, "So I guess you were very involved with uncovering the body of Jacob Glick on our property last year, Pat?"

Before Pat had a chance to respond, Papa Joe jumped to his feet, flinging his arms around wildly, his eyes wide with alarm. His hand hit Sweetie who was nearby, and the china soup bowl in her hands flew across the room and shattered against the fireplace.

"You've got to stay away from him, Beverly," he shouted, staring at me. "I've seen the devil in his eyes! Please! You've got to stay away!"

Chapter Nine

The air conditioner in my car had a hard time working against temperatures that promised to hit one hundred degrees by the afternoon. Even though it was only ten in the morning, the air outside was already stifling. As I drove down dirt roads to Abigail's house, the terrible scene from last night's dinner played over and over in my mind. It had taken quite some time to calm Papa Joe down.

No one had suspected that Jacob Glick's name would evoke such powerful emotion. Obviously Papa's long-term memory was still working. He remembered Glick and had been aware of his proclivities toward young women and girls. Last night he'd been reminded of his concern for my mother when she was young and had thought she was still in danger. After my grandfather calmed down, my dad took him back to my house to rest. Papa stayed confused until my parents finally got him to bed. He'd kept shouting something about evil and that he had to protect us.

"This may have been a mistake," my father had said when he came downstairs. "I expected some confusion, even extreme

736

disorientation from time to time. But I had no idea Papa would come unglued like this. Gracie, I'm sorry if Papa embarrassed you in front of your fiancé and his family. Maybe Mom and I should take him back to the nursing home. We could be back within the week and still have plenty of time to help you get ready for the wedding."

"I don't want him to go, Dad. This might be the last chance I have to spend time with him. We'll all just be more careful and try not to say anything that will upset him."

After some cajoling, my father finally agreed to give it more time. In the light of a new day, I wasn't certain I'd made the right decision, but I knew having Papa here on the day I married Sam was extremely important to me.

At breakfast, Papa seemed to have no memory of his outburst the night before. In fact, he was relaxed and happy. The only glitch came when he tried to ask for pancake syrup but couldn't remember what it was called.

I spotted the road Abigail lived on and turned down it. A couple of miles later, I saw a large white house looming ahead. As I got closer, I could see it was badly in need of paint and upkeep. A screen door on the side of the house hung by its bottom hinges, and an old, rusted tractor sat in the yard. Various items littered the yard including pieces of farm equipment and discarded furniture. Sitting back from the house was an ancient barn and off to its side was a large shed that looked deserted.

I turned into the dirt driveway, being careful to avoid several rusted tools and pieces of lumber lying on the ground. The house appeared to be abandoned. Could Ida's friend have moved without telling anyone? I stopped my car, got out, and made my way to the rickety front porch, passing a large tree that looked as dead as everything else on the property. The boards on the decrepit porch squeaked and groaned with each step I took. I found myself watching my feet and praying the rotting wood wouldn't splinter under me. When I finally reached the entrance, I knocked on a screen door that was so loose it jiggled each time I rapped my knuckles against it. After trying several times to roust someone, I decided to make my escape before the entire structure buckled and crashed down around me.

"Can I help you?"

I was already spooked enough by the ghostly look of the disintegrating property, but hearing a man's voice from behind me caused me to emit a high-pitched shriek that should have toppled the house without any further assistance. I swung around to find a shirtless man about my father's age standing at the foot of the steps. His reddish-blond hair almost glowed in the sunlight. He was well built and muscular, but his fair skin was turning red from exposure to the elements.

"I'm sorry. I was looking for Abigail Bradley. A friend of hers sent me to check on her. . .to make sure she's okay."

He came up to the steps and held out his hand. "I think you'd better get off that porch before you go right through the boards. I haven't had a chance to fix it yet."

I took his arm and held on while carefully making my way back to solid ground. When I got to the bottom, he let go of me but stuck his hand out again. "I'm C.J., Abigail's son."

When I shook his hand, I noticed his firm grip. "Oh, I had no idea you were here. Ida Turnbauer told me about you. I understand you live out of state somewhere?"

He let go of my hand and smiled. "Yes, I live in California, but Mom had an accident and broke her leg. One of her neighbors called, so I took some time off work to care for her while she recovers." He motioned toward the house. "I had no idea this place was in such bad shape. I'm trying to fix it up before I leave."

"How long has it been since you've been back to Harmony?"

He sighed. "Too long, obviously. Mom is very independent and always told me she was fine in her letters." He shook his head. "I should have checked on her sooner. I feel bad about it."

"Well, it's great you're here now." I gazed at the house. "Looks like you've got your work cut out for you."

C.J. chuckled. "That's the truth. Two different families who live nearby have already offered to help." He pointed to a pile of lumber lying next to the house. "One of them brought this by, along with a case of nails, and the other has offered me some white paint when I'm ready for it."

I laughed. "That's Harmony. Don't be surprised if a truckload of people show up to help with the work. No one is an island here." I put my hand up to shield my eyes from the sun and stared at the house again. "In fact, I'm surprised people haven't been by before now to help your mother get the house in shape."

"Oh, they tried, but Mom shooed them off. Like I said, she's pretty independent."

The dilapidated screen door suddenly opened. An old woman dressed in black and in a wheelchair appeared in the doorway. She wore a black prayer covering over her gray hair. "C.J., who is that you're talking to?" she asked in a thin, reedy voice.

"Hello, Mrs. Bradley," I called out. "I'm Gracie Temple, Daniel Temple's daughter. Ida Turnbauer asked me to check on you."

"Daniel Temple," she hollered, her tone rising. "Benjamin's brother?"

"Yes ma'am."

C.J. put his foot on the bottom step. "Mama," he said sternly, "don't come out on the porch. It won't support you and that wheelchair."

"But I want to talk to this girl," she whined.

"I told you it's not safe."

Abigail moved her wheelchair back and angrily slammed the door shut. C.J. looked embarrassed. "If you have time to visit, you can use the back door. Until I support the porch and replace the rotten boards, she can't come out here."

"I totally understand." I looked at my watch. "I don't have much time right now, but maybe I could come back some other time for a visit?"

He smiled. "Mom would love that. Give me a few days to make some improvements, then come by anytime. I'd tell you to call, but my cell phone doesn't seem to work very well out here, and Mom doesn't have a phone." He sighed. "Or air-conditioning. I'm not used to this heat."

"You should come into town. The restaurant has great food, and it's nice and cool."

"Sounds wonderful. I'll do it." He stuck his hand out once again. "I'm glad to meet you, Gracie, and I hope to see you again soon."

I shook his hand and smiled at him. "Same here."

As I headed to my car, I looked back to see Abigail sitting at the front window, watching me. I waved to her, but she just closed the curtain. Ida's description of Abigail Bradley was right on the button. She was definitely strange, but at least Ida could stop worrying about her now.

The temperature had continued to climb, and the interior of my car felt like an oven. I rolled down the windows, but all I managed to do was let in more hot air. As I headed back onto the dirt road that led to Abigail's house, I had no choice but to roll the windows up again. Driving on unpaved roads meant dust—and lots of it. The air conditioner blew hot air at first, but after driving a few minutes, a little cool air started to eke out of the vents.

I couldn't help but think about C.J. and his attempts to fix his mother's house. Noble sentiments, but in this heat, not such a good idea. When I got home, I'd tell Sam about it, and see if he could find some people to help. Unfortunately, Sam and Sweetie were picking fruit right now and had very little extra time. What few hours Sam could find were being spent with me and my family.

I'd just started to turn onto Faith Road and head for home when something shiny in the road caught the rays of the sun. The light hit my windshield, and the reflection was so bright it made it hard to see for a moment. I pulled over and got out, wondering what it could possibly be. It took me a minute to find it, but when I did, the discovery took my breath away. Lying in the dirt by the side of the road was a silver bracelet with colored beads. A silver heart hung from a chain, and the three inserts were engraved with *Love*, *Friend*, and *Forever*.

Hannah's bracelet.

Chapter Ten

Sam put the phone down and shook his head. "Pat's been called out on another case, Gracie. It will be awhile before he can get here. He can't make it to lunch today and asked that we explain the situation to your parents. He also said to remind you that he's got the whole county to take care of and can't keep running to Harmony for every little thing."

"Every little thing!" I snapped. "Finding Hannah's bracelet proves something's wrong, Sam. We've got to find her. She's in real trouble!"

We sat at the table in his kitchen. Sweetie was out in the orchard working alone. My frantic cries had brought Sam inside to find out what was going on.

He ran his hand through his sun-bleached hair and sighed with frustration. "Explain to me why you're so convinced this means something. So Hannah dropped her bracelet. In my book, it proves she really did take off on her own. She changed into her new outfit, walked out to the road, and probably found a ride. Her bracelet fell off by accident."

I started to say something, but he held up his hand and shushed me.

"Before you go off on a tangent, I totally understand that she shouldn't be out there by herself. There are dangerous people who would be more than willing to pick her up for all the wrong reasons. But at least we know she wasn't abducted like the girl in Topeka. Hannah left under her own power."

"You're missing the entire point!" I held up the bracelet for him to see. "Don't you notice anything odd?"

Sam stared at the silver jewelry in my hand. Finally he shook his head. "No, Grace. It looks like a bracelet. Nothing more."

I flung it down on the table. "Would you like to explain to me just how it fell off when the clasp is still fastened?"

"Obviously it slid off her wrist."

I picked the bracelet up and held it out to him. "Hannah's tiny, I grant you. But this bracelet is too small to slide off anyone's wrist—even hers." I unclasped the catch, put the bracelet on my own wrist, and snapped it shut again. I grasped it with my other hand, showing him there wasn't any wiggle room at all. "I'm not big either, and even though my wrists may be a little wider than Hannah's, there's not that much difference. Look at this. Can you see that there's no earthly way this bracelet could have fallen off accidentally?"

He stared at my wrist with a dubious expression. He even reached over and pulled at the bracelet to see just how tight it fit. After a brief silence, he let out a deep breath. "Okay. I see your point. So how did it come off?"

I snapped the clasp open and took the bracelet off, putting it on the table in front of us. "Hannah purposely removed it and dropped it on the ground." My voice quivered with emotion. "She left it behind so we'd know she needed help, Sam. It's the only thing that makes sense."

I watched his expression as he turned this information over in his mind. "What if she just didn't want to wear it for some reason? Maybe it was uncomfortable. Or maybe she decided she didn't like it."

"No," I said emphatically. "She loved that bracelet because Robin gave it to her. And I saw it on her wrist. It fit perfectly."

"Maybe she had it in her pocket, and it fell out accidentally."

I shook my head. "Those jeans are tight, and the pockets are more for looks than for function. If she could have gotten the bracelet inside one of them, there's no way it could have just fallen out."

His frown only deepened as he considered the possibilities. "Are you certain this is Hannah's bracelet? Maybe it belongs to someone else in Harmony."

"Oh sure," I said with a snort. "Lots of conservative Mennonite girls wear bracelets like this. The odds are astronomical that anyone else in Harmony would have a bracelet sold at an upscale shop in Wichita. Give me a break."

"Okay," he said finally, "I see what you mean. It's probably Hannah's bracelet. She wouldn't have just tossed it away because she didn't want it anymore; it couldn't have fallen off her wrist or out of her pocket. She probably took it off on purpose. But why close the clasp again? Why not just drop the open bracelet on the ground?"

"Because then it would look like it actually had slipped off," I said, trying to keep the impatience I felt out of my voice. "She was trying to leave a clue behind that would let us know she needs help."

"You think she'd have the presence of mind to think that through?"

"Yes, I do," I responded quickly. "Hannah is extremely intelligent.

With the time she had available, this was the only thing she could come up with."

"But who would know about this bracelet?" he asked. "You're the only one. How could she know you'd find it?"

"This is Harmony. People don't steal from each other here. Whoever found it would take it to town and show it around, hoping to find the owner. Of course it would eventually get around to me."

He raised an eyebrow. "And you think Hannah thought all that out in what was probably a matter of seconds?"

I shook my head. "No. I think she only had a short amount of time, and the bracelet was the only thing at her disposal. Hannah played a Hail Mary—and it worked. That's all that matters."

"I guess. . ."

"Look, Sam. You have to admit this bears looking into."

His gray eyes peered into mine. "Okay. Yeah, I guess so. But if you start insisting that Hannah really has been abducted, and she shows up at her boyfriend's, you're going to have a lot of explaining to do. This is a very serious conclusion to reach—that Hannah really was taken against her will."

I scowled at him. "You think? I've been trying to get someone to listen to me since she first went missing."

"Yeah, but that's because you thought some guy had been abducting young women from around here. Now we know that at least two of those women weren't kidnapped."

I rubbed my temples to try to relieve the beginnings of a tension headache. "Oh, do we? We actually only know that one wasn't abducted. The police *think* the other girl in Topeka was taken by her ex-boyfriend. But until they find her with him, they don't actually know for sure, do they?"

"I guess that's true." He was quiet for a moment while he

pondered my argument. "Oh by the way," he said finally, "I decided not to bug Jonathan Vogler or his family. Sounds like Pat's already checked out his story. I don't want to scare the Voglers or make them feel responsible for what's happened."

I shrugged. "That's fine. I doubt there's much more he can tell us at this point. I'd rather have you help me convince Pat that he needs to take finding Hannah's bracelet seriously."

He grunted. "We'd better leave that to you. When it comes to getting Pat to do something, you seem to have more influence than I do." His gaze swung to the clock on the kitchen wall. "We're supposed to meet at Mary's at eleven thirty, right?"

I nodded and looked at my watch. "Shoot. It's already a few minutes after eleven. I've got to get home and round everyone up. I also need to call Ida and tell her Abigail's okay." I started toward the kitchen doorway but stopped and turned back. "I know you think I have some kind of magic influence over Pat, but it's not true. He listens to you. Will you please call him one more time? Explain to him that the bracelet is important new evidence."

Once again Sam's eyebrows disappeared under his long bangs. "New evidence? Can I put it another way? You know how he hates it when you act all Nancy Drew."

"Put it however you want. Please, just convince him to talk to me, okay?"

Sam smirked and gave me a snappy salute. "Yes, Miss Marple. I am ever your loyal Mr. Stringer."

"I shouldn't have introduced you to those Miss Marple movies," I retorted. "You've been throwing Miss Marple in my face ever since."

"You do remind me of her in many ways," he said with a grin. "But I am grateful you don't actually look like Margaret Rutherford."

"That would make two of us." I waved good-bye, hurried out of his house, and headed back to my own. When I got there I called Ida to let her know Abigail had broken her leg but that her son was staying with her. She was upset to find out about her friend's accident. Probably feeling guilty that she hadn't checked on her sooner. Although last night I'd asked her to go with us, today she'd turned me down because of all the walking we planned to do. I checked with her once more.

"Ach, thank you, Gracie, but this leg of mine would only slow you down. I believe I will stay in today and rest. All the excitement from last night wore me out. But thank you for wanting me."

After the phone call, I cleaned up a bit. Then we all piled into my dad's Crown Vic since my Bug would have been a tight fit, and we drove into town. We ran a little late because my parents had an argument about Dad's cane. At first he refused to take it even though my mother insisted. Probably a pride thing. Eventually he gave in and tossed it in the car under protest.

On the way to town I told my parents about finding Hannah's bracelet. They agreed with me that the discovery was troubling. "We'll keep Hannah in our prayers," my mother said. "God is an expert at leading the lost home."

When we pulled up in front of the restaurant, Sam's truck was already there. As we got out of the car, I noticed my mother's tears.

"Mom, are you okay? Is something wrong?"

She closed the car door and reached into her purse, pulling out a tissue. "Oh Gracie," she said, dabbing at her eyes, "it's been thirty years since I've been in this town. In all that time, I never allowed myself to miss Harmony. But now that I'm here..." She stood next to the car and gazed around at the shops and the people, a good number of them wearing the simple clothing worn by many of the

Mennonite townspeople. Next to us sat a buggy and a horse, tied up to a post. "I can hardly believe it, but it looks almost the same. I mean, the names of some of the shops are different, and there wasn't any restaurant back then, but the buildings all look just like they used to. And the wooden sidewalks. . ." She blew her nose into her tissue. "And the people. I'd almost forgotten the beauty of long skirts and prayer coverings. It's been so long. . ."

"Oh for crying out loud, Beverly," my father grumbled. "It's just a town." But I noticed that as he helped Papa Joe from the car, his eyes swept the scene around him. Although he refused to meet my gaze, the emotion on his face was obvious.

We finally made it inside the restaurant, although it took some time due to my dad's leg and Papa's slow gait. Sweetie and Sam already had a table and waved us over. As we sat down and greeted each other, Sweetie watched Papa Joe carefully, probably concerned after the scene last night. Thankfully, Papa seemed to be fine this morning, although he was rather quiet.

I spotted Jessie heading our way. She smiled when she saw me. "Hey, I heard you were back," she said as she came up to the table. I introduced her to everyone. She put her hand on my shoulder. "Everyone's heard about Hannah. Anything new?"

"Not that I know of. Sheriff Taylor put out an APB, but so far she hasn't been found."

"Well, kids run away. It happens all the time." She shook her head. "I did it once myself, but when I found out there was no place to go, I came home. Hannah will show up before long. I'm sure she's okay."

Knowing about Jessie's abusive father, I would have been surprised if she hadn't tried to leave home. "I hope you're right," I said. "We're praying for a good outcome."

"Everyone is, Gracie," she said seriously. "I've seen this town pray together before. Incredible things happen." She turned her attention to the other people at the table. "If you folks will tell me what you want to drink, I'll get it while you look over the menu."

Everyone gave her their drink order, and she shared Hector's daily specials, which were fried catfish nuggets and chicken and noodles. I watched as she walked away, still amazed by the difference in her since her father died. Jessie would be all right, as would her daughter, Trinity. I was sure of it.

"So what's good here?" my dad asked.

"Everything is top-notch," Sweetie said. "I consider myself pretty good in the kitchen, but Hector gives me a run for my money." She glanced at the menu, although it wasn't necessary. Everyone in Harmony had already memorized the available dishes. When you only have one restaurant, it's not hard. "I like the steaks. Hector uses a steak rub that makes 'em tender and delicious. And his fried chicken is somethin' to write home about."

"And Dad, he makes really good fried liver and onions," I said.

Although my mom hates liver, my dad and I love it. Really good liver, fried, with crispy edges and tender in the middle, can't be beat when surrounded by a pile of onions browned in the same grease. My mother just sighed, and Sam looked at me with a puzzled expression.

"I didn't know you like liver. I don't remember you ever ordering it."

"I've got news for you, big boy. There *are* a few things I do without you sometimes. Eating liver and onions is one of them."

"Well, it's a fine time to learn that your fiancée likes liver a week and a half before the wedding. Seems the husband-to-be is always the last to know."

"Very funny."

"Okay you two," Dad said, laughing. "Let's knock it off about the liver. I want to concentrate on the menu."

"And I want to concentrate on the wedding," Mom said. "Sweetie, now that I'm here, I'm ready to help you."

"That's great, Bevie. Why don't you come to the house for a while after we're done in town, and we'll go over everything. I could surely use the help."

Now that was a surprise. Sweetie actually allowing someone else to be a part of her plans. Sweetie was a lone wolf who usually didn't like anyone near her projects. Of course, planning a wedding takes more work than cooking a meal or decorating a room—both endeavors I'd been shooed away from in the past. But Mom was the bride's mother, and she had every right to be involved in the wedding plans. Apparently even Sweetie recognized this.

We chatted until Jessie came back with our drinks. I kept an eye on the entrance, hoping Pat would show up. A few minutes later, we ordered. Dad and I went for the liver. Mom ordered the catfish nuggets and Sweetie asked for fried chicken. Sam's order was no surprise. He ordered a rib-eye steak. Sam's nuts about steak. It's his very favorite food. Papa Joe settled on the chicken and noodles. Mama used to make great chicken and noodles. I hoped Hector's recipe would hold up next to Mama's.

Sweetie and my father started a conversation about people and events from years ago—before I was born. As they talked, my attention was divided between watching for Pat and listening to Dad talk about his childhood in Harmony. I figured he could tell I wasn't giving him my full attention, but he seemed to have his own distraction to deal with. I caught him frowning at Sam more than once. His reaction to Sam when they first met troubled me. Something wasn't right, but I had no idea what it was. Certainly, it would have been better if they'd met before now, but the reasons were pretty clear. I couldn't believe Dad would hold something against Sam that wasn't his fault. My father had always been a fair man. In dealing with him, it was always best to confront the situation head-on. Next chance I got, I'd ask him directly to explain his odd response toward Sam. With Hannah's situation, Papa Joe, and the wedding looming, I didn't need one more weird situation to deal with.

In a small town where everyone knows each other, my parents and Papa Joe drew attention. Several people came up and spoke to them. Ruth was taking a break from her store, and I was happy to introduce her and tell my parents that she donated flowers every month to put on Benjamin's grave. Joe Loudermilk from the hardware store stopped by the table. Although Joe moved to Harmony after my grandparents left, his dad had known Papa. I couldn't tell if Papa really remembered Joe's father, but he acted like he did, and they had a nice but short visit. The Scheidler brothers from the local farm implements store came over, too, and I introduced them.

By the time our food arrived, my parents had met almost every single person in the restaurant. Even Hector came out to greet them and Papa. Before he left, he told them their lunch was on him—a kind of welcome back to Harmony gift. Once our plates had been delivered, we were left alone to eat. Harmony folk were nothing if not well mannered. Dad said a quick prayer over our food, and we all dug in.

"Oh Daniel," my mother said softly, "this catfish is wonderful. I've forgotten what fresh catfish tastes like."

My dad laughed. "We've had fresh catfish since we left Harmony, Bev."

She shrugged. "Well, maybe so, but it didn't taste like this."

"How's your liver, Dad?" I asked.

He grinned. "It's the best I've had in years. You know your

mother never makes it. I always have to sneak some when she's not around."

"Sneak it?" Mom said, raising her quiet voice a bit. "Are you sneaking it now, Daniel? My goodness. You make me sound like an old nag who doesn't want her husband to enjoy his favorite foods."

My dad winked at me. "I'm sorry, dear. I didn't mean to make you sound that way. When we get home, you can make lots and lots of liver and onions for me. I look forward to it."

My mother's look of disgust made me giggle. She pointed her fork at my dad. "You're making me look silly," she said, trying hard not to laugh.

He blew her a kiss. "Again, I apologize. It's just so easy."

Sweetie chuckled. "You two act just the same as you used to. I remember you teasing each other when you was kids. Some things never change."

"I agree," Papa said smiling. "Beverly is just as sweet and beautiful as she was back then. I've never seen any woman keep her looks the way you have, Bev. Except Essie. She was the most beautiful woman I ever saw—right up to the day she died."

"Yes, she was, Papa," my mother said, tears filling her eyes. "She certainly was."

"Sam," my father said, "we didn't get a chance to look around your farm yesterday. When we get back, I'd love to have a tour."

Sam, who had just stuck a big piece of steak into his mouth, nodded, chewed quickly, and swallowed. "I'd be happy to take you around, sir. You, too, Mrs. Temple."

My mother smiled. "I think you can start calling us Daniel and Beverly, Sam. We're going to be family."

"Thank you, Beverly," he said. "I'd like that."

I just started to say something about joining them on the

tour, when I noticed everyone's attention drawn toward the front door of the restaurant. I looked over to see a woman dressed in a black two-piece suit come into the room. Wearing black in July, unless you were Old Order Mennonite, was unusual in this heat. Actually, anyone wearing business apparel in this town stuck out like a sore thumb.

Jessie was at a table near the door, talking to the Scheidler brothers. I saw her walk over to where the woman stood, looking around the restaurant. They spoke briefly, and then the woman left. I wondered what she'd wanted, but I had to wait until Jessie came back to check on our drinks before I could ask her.

"She was looking for Abel," Jessie said. "She's already been to their house. I suggested she go over to church. I think I saw his car there when I came in."

"Did she say why she wanted to talk to him?" I asked.

Jessie shook her head. "No, but she seemed pretty serious. I hope it's nothing bad about Hannah."

My stomach turned over as I looked toward the front window of the restaurant. I could see the woman standing next to her car, writing something down on a pad of paper. "Excuse me," I said to everyone at the table. "I'll be right back." I hurried out the door and down the steps, reaching the woman's car just as she was getting in.

"I'm sorry to bother you," I said. "But I was told you're looking for Abel Mueller. Does this have anything to do with his daughter, Hannah? I don't mean to be nosy, but I'm a friend of the family, and I've been so concerned. . ."

The woman squinted at me, her eyebrows knit together in a frown. "I'm sorry, but I'm not able to share anything about the Muellers with you. You'll have to ask them for information. Right now, I'm just trying to locate them."

I glanced over at the church. Sure enough, Abel's dark-blue car was parked next to the side entrance. "Well that's his car." I pointed toward it. "You should try the side door because he may not hear you if you knock on the front door."

She put her hand up to shield her eyes and stared toward the church. "What in the world is wrong with that automobile?" she asked. "It looks like someone has painted the bumpers black."

"That's right. It's a Mennonite thing. Some people believe keeping their car as plain as possible will help to curb envy." I shrugged. "Abel only did it because he didn't want to offend people in his congregation who hold with the practice."

"That's the silliest thing I ever heard," she snapped, each word said with emphasis. "What is wrong with these people?" She turned to look at me with suspicion. "Do you paint your bumpers, too?"

"No, I'm not Mennonite. But Abel. . ."

"How well do you know the Muellers?" she said, interrupting me. "What can you tell me about them?"

Her rude attitude was beginning to bug me. "Actually, you'll have to talk to them yourself," I said sharply. "I don't know you, and I have no idea why you're here. If you'll excuse me." I'd turned on my heel to leave when she called out to me.

"What's your name?"

I whirled around. "I'm Gracie Temple. And you are?" I knew my tone now matched hers, but I didn't care.

"You can call me Mrs. Murphy."

"Then you can call me Miss Temple." With that, I stomped off toward the restaurant, irritated and angry. When I got to the table, Sam grabbed my arm.

"Who is that?" he asked.

"I have no idea. She wouldn't tell me. But I don't think she's up to any good, and she's headed to the church. Should I call Abel and warn him?"

"You don't even know what she wants. Why do you assume she's out to hurt Abel?" he said.

"Them business-suited types is always up to no good," Sweetie interjected, waving a piece of chicken around to highlight her pronouncement. "I'd call if I was you."

My dad shook his head. "What do you intend to say? Watch out, Abel, a woman in a business suit is coming your way? Doesn't that sound a little silly?"

"I—I guess so," I said slowly. I still felt alarm bells going off inside me, but rather than jump in the middle of Abel's business, I elected to keep my nose where it belonged—for now.

Halfway through lunch, Pastor Jensen came into the restaurant, and I introduced him to my family. Since he was performing the wedding ceremony, they were especially glad to meet him. He sat with us for a few minutes while he and my parents went over details for the rehearsal. Jessie came back to refill our drinks and overheard them talking.

"Who's making the food for the reception?" she asked.

"I plan to," Sweetie said. "The Menlos are making the wedding cake."

Jessie frowned. "How many people are you expecting?"

"It's a small wedding," I said. "Only about twenty people."

Jessie laughed and winked at Sweetie. "So you're planning to start a war in Harmony, are you?"

"What do you mean?" I asked, alarmed.

"Well, I kinda tried to tell you. . ." Sweetie said.

"This is Harmony, Gracie," Sam said, grinning. "The whole town will just assume they're invited. You're going to have some hurt feelings if you try to keep them out."

"But you never said anything..."

Sam shook his head. "I started to, and so did Sweetie. But then you left for Wichita, and we never got another chance."

"I've lived here all my life," Jessie said. "They're telling you the truth. I'd expect at least a hundred people. Maybe more."

"A lot of folks feel they know you, Gracie," Pastor Jensen said. "With finding Jacob Glick's body on your property and catching his killer, you're already famous in Harmony. A real celebrity. And Sam knows lots of people through his fruit farm." He smiled reassuringly. "It's your wedding—yours and Sam's. If you only want twenty guests, we'll find a way to do it. But I can't promise you that people won't be offended."

I glanced at Papa. The last time someone brought up Jacob Glick's name, his reaction was severe. But he seemed to be staring at some of the old pictures on the wall and didn't appear to be listening to us. I'm sure he recognized many of the people and places. Thankfully, the one picture with Glick in it had been removed.

Relieved that we weren't going to experience another outburst, I shrugged at Sam. "What do you think?"

"I think we should let everyone who wants to attend do so. Besides, we'll get more gifts that way, won't we?"

I slapped him lightly on the arm. "It's not about the gifts."

"I'm more than willing to do whatever I need to do," Sweetie said. "But I'm not sure I'm up to cookin' for over a hundred people."

"That's why I brought it up," Jessie said. "Hector would love to prepare the food for your reception. If Sweetie would allow him to help, together they could do a great job."

"What do you think, Sweetie?" I asked, preparing myself for an explosion. Again, she surprised me.

"I think that would be great," she said with enthusiasm. "Tell

Hector I'll come back by this afternoon when it's slow and go over the details with him." She swung her attention to my mother. "You can come with me, Bev, if that's okay. We can work on it together."

Mom happily agreed to her proposal, and I was left to wonder what had happened to the real Sweetie. It was like watching *Invasion of the Body Snatchers* played out right in front of me. She had definitely changed since our first meeting. God was busy moving out the negative personality traits and keeping the good ones. Thankfully Sweetie was still Sweetie, and there wasn't anyone else like her.

With my reception plans on the way to completion, and the size of my wedding blown up at least five times, everyone seemed happy. Jessie went back to the kitchen to inform Hector, and Sweetie and Mom put their heads together to decide what kind of food should be served. I kept waiting for them to ask my opinion, but I seemed to be a side note at this point. Fine with me. I couldn't care less what people ate as long as they were happy.

I glanced over at Papa to see how he was holding up. He'd started off pretty good, but now he seemed distant again. As if he were somewhere else. His silence concerned me. Dad tried to engage him several times, but Papa just nodded, seemingly focused on his food. I'd begun to wonder if we needed to take Papa home when the front door of the restaurant swung open and C.J. Bradley walked in. I was glad to see him, but I'd hoped it was Pat. I waved him over.

"I see you took my advice," I said when he reached our table.

"You were right," he said, taking off his cap. "It feels great in here." His sunburned face made it clear the cap was a new addition. One he should have added quite some time ago. "I needed a break and your suggestion was too good to pass up."

I introduced C.J. to everyone at the table. "I remember you both," he said to my parents. "But just barely. You left town not long after I arrived."

My father shook his head. "I'm sorry. It's been a long time, and my memory's not what it used to be."

"Well, I remember you," my mother said. "You were friends with Melanie Pemberton when I knew you."

C.J. nodded. "Yes, that's right. Melanie and I planned to be married, but she moved away."

"I don't suppose you've kept track of her down through the years."

C.J. grinned. "As a matter of fact, we recently connected again. Believe it or not, after I finish getting Mom back on track, we intend to take up where we left off all those years ago."

My mother clapped her hands together. "Oh how wonderful. I'm so thrilled to hear that, C.J. Please tell Melanie I said hello."

"I certainly will do that."

My father frowned as he looked at C.J. "I sure apologize for not recalling you. It seems I should."

I remembered Ida telling me that Papa wouldn't allow my father and Benjamin to play with C.J. when they were boys. Obviously this was why Dad couldn't clearly place him. This was one situation where Papa's memory lapse was a blessing. It would be embarrassing if he said something rude to C.J. I glanced at Papa, but there was no recognition on his face when he looked at C.J.

"It's all right," C.J. said. "I'm sure Beverly only remembers me because she was friends with Melanie. After your parents moved away, I got to know your brother, Benjamin. He was very kind to me." He smiled. "He showed me how to make birdhouses and we put several rocking chairs together before I went to college. I was

758

so sorry to hear he passed away. I wish I'd gotten the chance to see him again." He turned his attention to Papa Joe. "It's certainly good to see you again, Mr. Temple. It's been a long time. How are you, sir?"

He stuck out his hand, and Papa took it, but his expression was blank.

"I'm fine, thank you," he said. "Nice to meet you."

C.J. looked a little surprised as he released Papa's hand. Next time we were alone, I'd have to explain Papa's condition.

"So you haven't been back to Harmony since you left for college, C.J.?" my mother asked. "That's a long time, isn't it?"

"Oh no. I've been back to see Mama several times. I just hardly ever make it into town. My mother prefers to stay on her own property." He ran his hand through his short reddish hair. "Honestly, I think she may be slightly agoraphobic. Of course she swears she's fine and just wants to be left alone."

"How long are you staying?" my father asked.

"I'm not sure. I don't see how I can go until Mama's back on her feet and the house is in better shape."

"This is a busy time for our wheat farmers," Sam said. "They're working hard to bring in their harvests, but I'm sure I can round up a few men to come out and help you."

C.J. smiled. "Thanks, I really appreciate it, but to be honest, right now I'm just assessing the problems and taking care of the emergency fixes. Let's wait until I have a better idea of how to proceed." He sighed. "Besides, my mother doesn't take to visitors very well. I'd have to get her permission, and I'm not sure she'll give it."

"Well why don't you let me know after you get a better idea of what needs to be done. And if she'll agree to it, we can help you get your repairs done a little faster."

"I appreciate that more than I can say," C.J. said. "I may have been gone from Harmony for quite some time, but I certainly remember the way neighbors helped neighbors here. You don't find that in California."

"Harmony is different, that's for sure," Sweetie said. "I've been here a long time myself. Sure don't remember seein' you and your mama together. Sorry. I guess we just didn't run in the same circles."

"Oh Miss Goodrich. I'm sure you don't remember me, but I couldn't possibly forget you. All the boys in Harmony knew who the prettiest gal in town was."

Sweetie blushed. "That was a long time ago."

"I guess so, but I recognized you right away."

I fought a grin. C.J. was nothing if not diplomatic. He certainly didn't tell Sweetie she hadn't changed, yet his words made her happy. Good for him.

"I bet you was one of them rowdy boys who used to watch me whenever I came to town," Sweetie said. She narrowed her eyes and stared at him a minute. "In fact, I think you was the boy who used to whistle at me sometimes, ain't you?" Her face lit up with recognition. "Tarnation, your hair was bright red back then, weren't it?"

C.J. broke out laughing. "Oh no, my sins have come back to haunt me. You're right. That certainly was me."

Everyone at the table joined in the laughter except Papa Joe. He smiled and looked around the table, but I could tell he was lost. It was like we'd all gotten in our car to take a trip and left him standing on the curb watching us go.

"Them was some happy times back then," Sweetie said, chuckling. "You boys was always gettin' in trouble, though, as I remember."

C.J. nodded. "The pastor of the church wasn't too happy with us most of the time. But there was another man. . .what was his name?" His face wrinkled as he tried to pull up the memory. "Ugly man. I think he was the church custodian. Anyway, I swear that man hated us with a passion. I always got the feeling he was sweet on you, Miss Goodrich."

"Call me Sweetie," she said. "My friends do. And you're talking about Jacob Glick."

C.J. snapped his fingers. "That's it. Jacob Glick." He shook his head. "Hope he's not hanging around here somewhere. That's one man I'd rather not ever run into again."

"I guess your mama didn't tell you," Sweetie said. "Glick died about thirty years ago now, so you don't have to worry about him no more."

I waited for Sweetie to say something more about Glick, but thankfully she didn't. Good. I didn't want to see Papa upset again, and besides, I was tired of thinking about Glick. Better to let sleeping dogs lie. I cringed inwardly. Another Sweetie-ism. Yikes. I certainly didn't mind emulating her in many ways, but there were some aspects of Sweetie's personality that should remain with her alone.

Just then Jessie returned to our table. "How about some dessert, folks? Hector just took some peach cobbler out of the oven."

I'd been convinced I didn't want dessert, but Hector's peach cobbler was something no one could resist. Sam, Sweetie, and I nodded in unison.

"Think I'll pass," Mom said. "I'm full."

"Bring her a small piece, Jessie," I said. I held up my hand when my mother started to protest. "Trust me, Mom. If you don't want it, I'll take it home. You really don't want to pass up Hector's hot peach cobbler."

"That's good enough for me," my father said, smiling. "Bring Papa and me some, too." He looked up at C.J. "Why don't you join us? The cobbler's on me."

"Oh thank you," he said. "But I've bothered you folks long enough." He patted his pocket. "I brought my trusty notepad with me, and I plan to do some scribbling in it until I have some kind of workable repair schedule. But thank you for asking. Maybe some other time?"

My dad nodded. "Definitely. We'll be here for another week and a half. Let's get together soon."

"Thank you, Daniel." He put his cap back on his head. "So nice to talk to all of you. Hope you have a wonderful afternoon."

We all echoed his sentiments. C.J. found a table near the door and sat down. Sure enough, he brought out his pad and pen and began to write.

"Nice fellow," Dad said. "Good to run into people who lived here when we did."

Sweetie snorted. "He does seem like a nice fella now, but he was a little terror when he was a kid."

"Now Sweetie," Sam said. "Most boys are a handful when they're young."

"Well, you weren't," she said, one eyebrow raised higher than the other. "And Daniel and Benjamin weren't neither."

"But I'm exceptional," Sam said grinning. "I was raised by the most beautiful and wonderful woman who ever walked the streets of Harmony."

"Now wait a minute," Dad said. "I think I married the most beautiful and wonderful woman who ever walked the streets of Harmony."

"You two are both incorrigible," my mother said. "Hush up."

My father's expression turned from amused to alarmed. I

followed his gaze and realized that Papa Joe was drawing a steak knife across his palm. A line of blood began to form.

"Papa!" Dad exclaimed. "Stop that." He reached out and grabbed the knife from his other hand. "What do you think you're doing?"

"Evil, evil, evil, evil. . ." Papa stared at his hand while repeating the word over and over.

Chapter Eleven

My mother jumped up and wrapped her napkin around Papa's hand, her face lined with worry. "Gracie, didn't you say Harmony has a doctor now? The cut isn't very deep, but I think we need to have someone look at it."

Jessie set a large tray filled with bowls of cobbler and ice cream on our table. "Here you go, folks," she said as she began to pass them out.

I stood up. "Jessie, will you take the ice cream off mine and Papa's and keep our cobbler warm? We've got to go across the street for a few minutes."

Dad started to protest, but I stopped him. "You guys eat your cobbler. The doctor's office is just across the street. I'll take Papa over there and have John take a look at him. When we're done I'll bring him right back."

"But Gracie. . ." Mom said.

"No *but Gracie*s," I retorted. "Dad needs to rest his leg. Besides, Papa's my grandfather, and I can take care of this. We'll be back as soon as John's done." I took Papa's arm. "Come on, Papa. We're going across the street, okay?"

"Sure, Gracie," he said with a smile. "That sounds fine."

Dad started to object again, but my mom put her hand on his arm. "Let her do it, Daniel. She's very capable, and Papa is safe with her."

My father sighed. "All right. Thanks, Gracie. But if you need us. . ."

"I know just where you are. Besides, now you can grill Sam without me around. I'm sure you'll enjoy that."

Sam's face fell. "Maybe I should come with you. . ."

"Nothin' doin'," Sweetie said. "You stay here and take your medicine." She winked at me. "If it gets too intense, I'll come runnin' for you, Gracie."

"It's a deal." I led Papa to the door of the restaurant and we stepped outside to the sidewalk. I held tight to him as we went down the stairs. When we got to the bottom, he grabbed my arm with his other hand.

"Gracie, you've got to protect yourself. He's evil. He's so evil."

"Papa, who are you talking about? Jacob Glick?"

That veil of confusion dropped over his face again. "Yes. . . yes. . .Jacob Glick. He's evil. Don't let him hurt you. You've got to protect yourself."

I squeezed his arm. "Papa, Jacob Glick is dead. He's been dead almost thirty years. He can't hurt me—or anyone."

He shook his head vigorously. "He's evil. Evil, evil, evil. I caught him. I caught him."

"Caught him doing what?"

Papa stared at me like he didn't know me.

"Papa, you caught him doing what?"

My grandfather shook his head and patted my hand. "We need to get home, Essie," he said. "The boys will be wanting dinner. Hope the buggy's nearby."

"Oh Papa." I couldn't keep the sadness out of my voice.

"It's okay, Essie. We'll make it in plenty of time."

Ken and Alene Ward, a young farm couple who lived about a mile down the road from Ida, had come out of the restaurant and were standing behind us. I wasn't sure just how much of our conversation they'd overheard, but as I began to pull Papa away, I felt a hand on my shoulder.

"We're going through the same thing with my father," Alene said softly. "We'll be praying for you."

"Th–thank you," I said, trying to keep myself from bawling. I finally convinced Papa to come with me, and we made our way across the street to what used to be Keystone Meats. Now the sign read, JOHN KEYSTONE, M.D. Our small town had gained a doctor, but thankfully we hadn't lost our meat store. Rufus Ludwig, a newcomer to Harmony, opened up a new shop in a nearby abandoned building. Rufus was a genial man whose past was rather mysterious. He would only say that he'd moved to Harmony from Illinois and was someone who needed to start over. Most folks in Harmony respected his privacy, although there were a few busybodies like Esther Crenshaw who had decided he was an ex-con. Regardless, Esther bought her meat from Rufus along with everyone else. Ludwig's Meat was a blessing for the restaurant as well as our residents. Although it's not the only source of beef available since we have two local townspeople who raise cattle and sell fresh meat from their farms, it's a lot easier to run to Ludwig's when you need something for dinner.

Papa and I walked into John's office and found four members of the Breyer family waiting. The Breyers are a very large family who live on the edge of town. Cecil Breyer works at a grain elevator near Emporia. His job is considered the most dangerous in Kansas. Every year, people die from accidents at grain elevators. But Cecil's love for his eight children keeps him going back since the pay and benefits are so good. For some reason, at least one of Cecil's kids seems to always be sick. Good health insurance was vital to the family.

"Why hello there, Gracie," Abbie Breyer said when she saw me. "Doc's with Moses now. Shouldn't take more than a couple more minutes."

Before I could respond, the door to the back room swung open and John came out with little Moses. John smiled when he saw me.

"Abbie," he said, patting the small boy on the top of his head, "Moses has the flu. I gave him a shot. All you can do now is make sure he rests and give him lots of liquids." John pointed at Moses. "And by liquids I mean water or juice. Not pop."

"Ah Doc," Moses moaned. He pushed the bangs of his long brown hair out of his face. "Pop makes me feel better."

John chuckled. "Well, it doesn't make your body feel better." He smiled at Abbie. "Water and juice, Abbie, okay?"

She nodded. "What should he eat, Doc? I tried to get some soup down him, but he wouldn't have none of it."

"I hate soup," Moses said glumly. "It tastes like throw up."

"Moses!" Abbie said, her face reddening while the other two children with her giggled with childish delight. "I'm sorry, Doc. Sometimes the things he says. . ."

John laughed and shook his head. Then he knelt down in front of the small boy. "Okay, Moses. Just what kind of food doesn't taste like throw up?"

Moses' face brightened immediately. "Ice cream," he said with a dreamy smile. "Ice cream doesn't taste like throw up."

John stood up. "Abbie, you still make your own ice cream, don't you?"

She nodded. "Don't like all the chemicals in the store-bought stuff. I've been making these children ice cream their whole lives."

"Then I prescribe ice cream," John said, trying to look serious. "Feed him ice cream three times a day until he's hungry for something else."

Moses' eyes got big as he stared up at John who towered over him. "You are the very best doctor in the whole world," he said, his voice full of awe.

"Well thank you, Moses. That's not what you said when I gave you the shot, though."

Moses thought this over. "Well," he said slowly, "people change."

Abbie turned her face away so Moses wouldn't see her laugh. She covered her mouth and tried to make it sound as if she had to cough. A few moments later, after composing herself, she turned back toward her son. "Okay, Moses. Tell Doctor Keystone good-bye, and let's get going. Gracie needs to see him now."

John frowned at me. "Are you okay, Gracie?" Then he saw the white linen napkin wrapped around Papa's hand. "Oh, looks like you cut yourself," he said to Papa.

"John, this is my grandfather, Joe Temple."

"How do you do, Mr. Temple?"

Papa didn't respond, he just stared at John as if he was trying to place him. But since Papa had never met John before, it was an exercise in futility.

John smiled at Papa anyway and pointed toward the back room. "Go on in, and we'll take a look."

John said his good-byes to Moses, his mother, and his brother and sister. Then he followed Papa and me into his exam room. I gazed around, impressed by the change. It had gone from a place that stored meat to an exam room that was clean and nicely stocked with medical equipment.

"Almost looks like you know what you're doing," I quipped.

"Almost," John said with a grin. He led Papa over to a chair. "Let's take a look at that hand."

Papa's gaze was locked on John's face, his eyes wide, his hand clenched tightly around the cloth napkin. I started to explain where we were and why we were here but suddenly I remembered that John looked quite a bit like his father, Jacob Glick. Except Glick's face was twisted in a way that displayed the evil in his soul, while the same features in his son turned out quite differently. John's aquiline nose accented his good looks. Glick's nose had just added to his long, horsey face. John's dark hair and eyes echoed his father's, but where Glick's overgrown black eyebrows had made him seem to be permanently scowling, John's eyebrows fit his features. And the dimple in John's chin was manly and attractive whereas his father's had given his face a misshapen appearance. But did Papa see the difference, or did he think he was looking into the eyes of Jacob Glick? Would he have another episode? The possibility frightened me.

I touched John's shoulder. "Can I talk to you just a moment? It's really important."

I explained to Papa that I had to speak to the doctor for just a few minutes and asked him to stay where he was. He nodded, but his eyes were still glued to John.

John looked at me strangely but agreed to come with me. We stepped into a supply room next to the exam area. I quickly explained Papa's condition and his reaction to John's father's name.

"So you're afraid he'll think I'm my father?" he asked.

"Maybe. You don't look like him really, but your coloring is the same. And the shape of your face. I just wanted to warn you. . ."

"Okay, I understand. I'll do my best to treat him, but we should probably get back in there. I don't think we should leave a confused man alone for very long."

"One other thing," I said slowly. "He—he cut himself on purpose. We were eating lunch at Mary's, and when I looked over at him, he was slicing his palm with his knife."

"I hate to say this, but you need to keep a close eye on your grandfather. Keep him away from objects that could injure him. Don't let him near a hot stove or even hot water without watching him. I've seen some really awful accidents."

"Have you treated many people with Alzheimer's?"

"A few, although I'm certainly not an expert. My best advice is to try to keep him as calm and relaxed as possible. If he's confused, don't try to 'snap him out of it.' Too many people do that in my opinion, and it only makes it worse."

"That's the same thing my parents said."

He smiled. "Good, then they're on the right track. Now let's get back in there. I'd hate for your grandfather to get any more disoriented. . .or bleed to death in my exam room. It would be such a bad way to start out my new practice."

I chuckled. "The cut's not *that* deep, but we thought it would be good if you'd take a look anyway." I reached out and grabbed his arm before he had a chance to leave. Then I peeked around the corner and checked on Papa. He sat docilely in his chair, staring off into space. "Before you go," I said quietly, "how are things going between. . . Well, you know, with you and. . ."

"Sarah?"

"Yes, Sarah. I've been gone six weeks, you know. Has anything changed?"

He shook his head. "I realize you've been gone six weeks because it's been that long since anyone stuck their nose in my business."

I felt my face flush. "Well, it's not like I don't know about you two."

John reached out and put his hand on my shoulder. "Yes, I know. You've been right in the middle of it, haven't you?" He sighed, removed his hand, and ran it through his thick black hair. "We've kept our promises, if that's what you mean. But it hasn't been easy. Seeing her walk past me—not talking to her. It takes something out of me each time it happens."

"And Sarah?"

He shrugged. "She doesn't seem to see me at all. If we're in the same room, she acts like I'm not there. Her father came in last week, and she waited outside."

"I'm sorry, John. I'd hoped things would be easier by now."

His dark eyes peered into mine. "I don't think they'll ever be easier, Gracie. My love for her hasn't diminished one bit. If anything, it's stronger now than it was before." He stuck his hands in his pockets. "But there's nothing that can be done. She won't walk away from what she believes, and I can't believe in God just because she does. If I tried to pretend, she'd know. And I'd know. We'd be living a lie, and I can't allow that to happen."

"I understand." I admired John for his ethics, realizing that some people might not be quite so honest.

"Well, let's see what we've got." He pushed the door open and we went back into the exam room. Papa still sat in his chair. He was quiet but smiled when we came in.

"Mr. Temple, I'm Doctor Keystone. I understand you cut your hand?"

Papa held out the hand covered with the napkin. "I believe I did, Doctor," he said. "I have no idea how it happened. Just clumsy, I guess."

John pulled up a stool and positioned himself right in front of Papa. He gently removed the cloth and inspected the cut, which had stopped bleeding. "It's not too bad. I think we can just clean and bandage it. Stitches aren't necessary."

"That's good, Doctor," Papa said. "Thank you."

Papa appeared to have moved past his initial response to John. I breathed a sigh of relief. While John rounded up the antiseptic and bandages, I glanced at the certificates on his wall. "So the medical profession allowed you back, huh? How many hoops did you have to jump through?"

"Not too many. I had to get licensed in Kansas, and because I'd been out of the loop for three years, I had to take some brush-up courses. But all in all, it wasn't too painful."

"Well, the town is certainly thrilled. How do the more conservative Mennonite residents respond to you?"

John sat down again and began to clean Papa's palm with disinfectant and a large cotton ball. "Great. They have no problem with me at all. I think a long time ago some Old Order Mennonites may have gotten their medical services through their local area oversight committee. But as far as I know, that doesn't really happen anymore."

"So everything's smooth sailing?"

He turned around and grinned at me. "I didn't say that. I'm still not used to having my bill paid in food."

I laughed. "What kind of food?"

He turned his attention back to Papa who smiled up at me. "Anything you can think of. Baked goods, meat, corn. . . Last week, one woman tried to give me a beautiful quilt her mother made. I turned her down. I couldn't take something that meant so much to her."

"Gracie," Papa said, frowning, "have you found your grand-mother's wedding present yet? She'll be very upset if I don't make sure you get it."

I shot John a quick look. "No, Papa. I haven't found it. But let's not worry about it right now, okay? We need to get your hand taken care of. Then we'll find Mama's gift. Okay?"

Papa nodded slowly. "Okay, Gracie. But I can't have Essie upset with me."

I patted his shoulder. "I know. I know. We'll look for it when we get home."

"Okay. Well, am I gonna keep my hand, Doc?"

"I think you will, Mr. Temple." John finished wrapping gauze around Papa's hand and secured it with tape. "Gracie, I'm sending some bandages home with you. Just keep the cut covered and clean. Change the bandages once a day. In a few days it should be fine."

"We will," I said. "Are you ready, Papa?"

"Yes, I believe I am." He frowned and rubbed his stomach. "Are we late for dinner? I'm getting hungry."

I smiled at him. "We had to leave lunch because you cut your hand. Let's get back to the restaurant, okay?"

"Why yes. That sounds good." He held out his other hand to John. "Thank you very much, Doctor. What do I owe you?"

John shook Papa's hand. "Nothing, Mr. Temple. All I did was clean out your cut and put a bandage on it. I have no intention of charging you for something so trivial."

Papa studied John for a moment. "Well, it isn't trivial to me, son. And I think you can call me Joe now."

John smiled. "Thanks, Joe. I appreciate it."

Papa continued to stare at John for a while. His forehead was wrinkled in thought, and I was almost certain it was because of John's resemblance to his father. I took his arm, attempting to get him out of the office before he made the connection. "Come on, Papa. Let's let Doctor Keystone go back to work. We need to get to the restaurant before someone decides to toss out your peach cobbler."

Papa's eyes widened. "Can't let that happen. Let's get moving, Gracie girl."

I laughed and waved good-bye to John. When we stepped out onto the sidewalk, the heat was invasive. As folks in Kansas say, "It's not the heat, it's the humidity." Today it was both. I led Papa across the street and into Mary's. My father got up when he saw us and then came over to take Papa's arm and help him to the table.

"I hope Jessie kept Papa's cobbler warm," I said. "He's still hungry."

"It's waiting for him in the kitchen," Dad said. "Along with yours."

Papa smiled at his son. "Good for you, Daniel. Waste not, want not."

Dad smiled. "I know, Papa. You taught us that very well."

I was just about to sit down when I heard someone call out my name. Pat had just walked in the front door, and he waved me over. I excused myself and hurried over to meet him.

"It's about time," I said. "Where have you been?"

"I've been a little busy. Didn't you get my message?"

"Yes, but I really need to talk to you. It's important."

He glanced quickly around the room. "I need to speak to you, too. Can we go outside for a moment?"

His grim expression caused a shiver to run down my spine. I gazed back at the table where Jessie had just put my cobbler on the table again. After catching my father's eye, I held up my finger as a way to let him know I was going outside and would be back soon. "Okay, let's go," I said to Pat.

I followed him out the door and down the steps. He finally stopped next to one of the wooden rails where residents who rode horses or drove buggies into town tied them up. He leaned against it and stared at me, his arms crossed. "Look, I know how you're going to react to this, but I want you to try to keep your cool."

A prickling sensation spread across my scalp. "Is—is it Hannah?" I croaked out.

"No, we still haven't found Hannah, but the police have found the girl who went missing from Topeka. The one they believed was abducted by her boyfriend. She wasn't with him at all. Thankfully, she's fine. Just took off on her own for a while."

"That's wonderful news."

"We also found the other girl. The one who got into that red truck."

I breathed a sigh of relief. Maybe there wasn't some kind of crazed serial killer running around Kansas after all. "Okay, and what's her story?"

"She was in the middle of a cornfield about ten miles from here." He hesitated a moment, his eyes locked on mine. "She's dead, Gracie. She was murdered."

Chapter Twelve

I guessed I swayed a little because Pat reached out and grabbed me by the shoulders. "Come over here and sit down," he ordered. I lowered myself to the edge of the wooden sidewalk behind us. Truth was, I did feel a little dizzy.

"You say she was murdered? How—how do you know that? Could she have died accidentally?"

He sat down next to me. "No, Gracie. She'd been strangled, and there was evidence she'd been bound for several days before she was killed."

"Do they have any idea who did it?"

Pat took off his hat and ran his hand over his closely cropped hair. "There are some things about this killing that match several others across the country over the last several years. The FBI thinks it might be the same man. He's never been in Kansas before, but he may be here now."

My eyes filled with tears that trickled down my face. My previous relief over the absence of a serial killer in the area evaporated. "But—but that means Hannah. . ."

"That means absolutely nothing as far as Hannah is concerned," he said gruffly. "I still think Hannah ran away. It's just a coincidence that it occurred at the same time. Believe me, I've seen this happen before. There can be a couple of similar circumstances in cases that cause concern during a situation like this. But it doesn't mean they're connected."

I started to ask him how he could possibly know this seeing he was just a sheriff over a small county in Kansas, but then I remembered that he used to work in an area that probably gave him a lot of experience dealing with awful crimes. "But Pat, this is a serial killer!" I cried. "Hannah looks just like the girl in Topeka. How can you possibly tell yourself that these disappearances aren't related? The truth is that Hannah may have been abducted by the same man!"

He stared at the hat he held in his hands. "If the girl in Topeka *was* killed by this guy, and that hasn't been confirmed yet, he doesn't stick to blonds. Remember that the other two girls are okay. It's just a coincidence they all had blond hair like Hannah. There's no real link between the murdered girl and Hannah."

"But I have proof she was taken against her will."

He frowned at me. "And what would that be?" The impatience in his voice made it clear he was beginning to get frustrated.

"I found her bracelet on the road out of town."

He shook his head and sighed. "And how does this tell me she was taken against her will?"

I slowly explained the entire thing—about how the bracelet couldn't have slipped off her wrist. And how it had to be a message from Hannah that she was in trouble. Throughout my entire diatribe, his stoic expression didn't change. Surely I was getting through to him, but I couldn't tell. Finally I stopped talking and waited for his reaction.

"Look, I've already turned over the information about Hannah to the Kansas Bureau of Investigation so they can determine whether or not Hannah's case could be related to the others. Finding a bracelet that may or may not have been owned by Hannah isn't going to change anything."

"But it's proof. . ."

"No, it isn't proof," Pat said, his tone sharp. "It's just a bracelet. The KBI isn't going to find this *evidence* compelling."

"Well, maybe they would if they ever hear about it." I wiped my face with the back of my hand.

Pat took out his handkerchief and started to hand it to me.

"No thanks. I think I'm through. For now anyway."

He stuck the piece of cloth back into his pocket. "Look Gracie, I'm not going to lie to you. The KBI has no interest in Hannah's disappearance. There are certain signs they look for. Hannah's case doesn't have any of them."

"Like what?" I demanded.

He sighed. "I'm not going to tell you what they are. Why don't you just let the people who are experienced in this sort of thing do their job? You need to concentrate on your wedding."

"I know about the red truck—and the weird bumper sticker."

His eyes widened. "And how did you hear about that?"

"I can't tell you."

He glared at me like I'd just committed a felony. "Okay. Did anyone see Hannah picked up by someone in a red pickup with a 'weird' bumper sticker?"

"Well no, but. . ."

"But nothing," he said. "There is no evidence whatsoever that ties Hannah to the guy they're looking for."

I could feel my temper rise. "What kind of evidence, Pat? What do you need to believe she's been kidnapped?"

"Something a lot more solid than your feelings and a lost bracelet."

I shook my head. "It's all I have." I looked into his eyes. "How about going the extra mile because we're family? Does that mean anything to you?"

"That's not fair."

"I don't care. Nothing will make me give up on Hannah. Nothing."

Pat sighed. "Gracie, I'm not giving up on Hannah. That's ridiculous. But my years of work in law enforcement tell me this girl ran away. I can't just ignore that."

"I'm not asking you to," I said emphatically. "All I want you to do is open up your mind to the possibility that something else *could* have happened to her. Share what you know with me. Let me in, Pat."

He scowled at me. "You'd make a great interrogator, you know that? I swear, if you breathe a word of this to anyone else. . ."

I held up my hands in mock surrender. "I won't. I promise."

Pat scanned the area around us, looking to see if anyone else was in earshot. When he seemed satisfied, he leaned in closer. "It would be nice to find the truck. No one is completely sure what the bumper sticker says, but there's a bear on it."

"A bear? So the killer is a hunter?"

"Or he loves the zoo," Pat said sarcastically. "I have no idea why there's a bear on his bumper sticker."

"Okay, but at least that helps. Is there anything else?"

Pat blew his breath out slowly. "Well, there's the way that he kills his victims, but you don't need to hear about that."

I didn't argue. He was right. I didn't want those kinds of images in my head.

Pat put his hat back on his head and stuck his finger in my face.

"If you tell anyone else what I just told you, I'll find something to charge you with and lock you up until the day of your wedding." He shook his finger several times for emphasis. "And I mean that."

I pushed his hand down. "So is that it? A bear on a bumper sticker? You put me through all that for something so insignificant? How are we going to find Hannah with nothing more to go on than that?"

Pat shrugged. "Believe it or not, I've had cases with even less. At least it's a start."

"So the FBI is investigating every man with a red truck?"

"No, of course not. But they are tracking the ones with violent criminal records who have attacked women." He sighed and shook his head. "The problem is that his truck's been mentioned in the media. Chances are he'll dump it."

"That means authorities wouldn't have anything to tie him to the murders."

"That's not true. They have solid DNA evidence."

"Oh great," I said, unable to keep the sarcasm out of my tone. "Don't they actually have to find a suspect before they can test for DNA?"

Pat rubbed his eyes, and I realized for the first time how tired he looked. "I know. It's not much, but right now it's all we've got." He pointed at me again. "You stay out of this, understand? If you think you have any more *evidence*, you come to me and me only. All the KBI needs is some little red-haired girl sticking her nose where it doesn't belong."

"Seems to me they need all the help they can get," I retorted. "We have no idea how much time Hannah has left."

"I've told you from the beginning that Hannah isn't part of this," Pat said in a low voice.

"But the bracelet. It just doesn't make sense."

"Look, could you trust me just a little? Hannah ran away. She'll find out she can't make it on her own and come home. Just concentrate on your upcoming nuptials. Really."

"But what about this murder? Abel and Emily will panic when they find out about it."

"I'm going over to talk to the Muellers right now. I think they need to hear about it from me before anyone else. Please keep it to yourself for now."

I shook my head. "This will terrify them."

He grunted. "I'll assure them that we still believe Hannah's situation isn't related." He frowned. "Besides, I thought you Christian types weren't supposed to be afraid of anything because you believe God takes care of you."

"That's true. But sometimes it takes time on our knees and our willingness to fight the good fight of faith to get us through the stormy parts of life. Christians aren't perfect, you know."

"Yeah, I know," he said wryly. "You're just forgiven. I've heard it all before." He stood to his feet and helped me to mine. "You okay now?"

"Yes. But why did you come to me about the murder before the Muellers?"

"I tried to talk to them first, but they're meeting with someone from Child Protective Services."

My mouth dropped open. "Mrs. Murphy? Is that who she is?"

"You know her?"

I explained my encounter with the woman outside the restaurant.

Pat nodded. "Yep, that sounds like her. I've had run-ins with her before. She's good at her job, but she certainly isn't the easiest woman to deal with."

"But why would she be bothering Abel and Emily?"

Pat put his hat back on his head and pulled the brim down to shield his eyes from the sun. "Someone phoned in a complaint. Said the Muellers' lifestyle forced the girl to flee from her home."

"What?" I sputtered. "That's ridiculous. The Muellers are wonderful parents."

"Well, someone in Harmony doesn't seem to agree with you." He held his hand up to stop any further protests. "Look Gracie, give Mrs. Murphy a chance. She's actually pretty fair-minded."

"She could use some better people skills," I muttered. I turned and stared over at the church. Abel and Emily's car was still there along with another car that most probably belonged to the infamous Mrs. Murphy. "I'll bet it was that nasty-minded Esther Crenshaw who called in. She's got her nose in everyone's business, and she's always ranting on and on about how wrong the Mennonites are about everything."

Pat grunted. "I thought Christians weren't supposed to judge others."

I snorted. "Unfortunately, some of us don't seem to have gotten the message." I looked at him carefully. "That's the second time you've made a snide remark about Christians. Christianity isn't based on what Christians do, you know. Every time I hear that old excuse I recognize it for what it is. A cop-out. It's not hard to figure out that we're called to follow Christ, not each other."

Pat's eyes narrowed. "What do you mean it's a cop-out? A lot of people out there aren't interested in your religion because you people say one thing and do another."

"Hey, it's not called Gracieanity, you know. Christ alone is our example. We're trying to become as much like Him as we can, but it's a process. None of us will reach perfection in this life." I stuck my finger into his chest. "And you're smart enough to know that. That's why I said your excuse is a cop-out." I grinned at him. "The good news is that Jesus will even take someone as ornery as you."

Pat tried to glare at me, but his mouth quivered and he ended up laughing. "You're something else, Gracie Temple. If anyone could get me to darken the door of a church, it would be you." His voice softened. "But don't count on it, okay?"

I shrugged. "I'll keep praying for you anyway."

"You do that."

I gave him a quick smile before changing the subject. "Pat, I'd like to check on Abel and Emily after that woman is finished. I need to make sure they're all right."

"Not until I'm done," Pat said sternly. "You wait until I'm gone to pounce on them."

I started to protest his use of the word *pounce* when we both turned our heads at the sound of a car door slamming. The dark sedan parked next to Abel's car took off slowly from the church. It pulled into the street and started coming our way. I saw Mrs. Murphy behind the wheel. She stared at me as she drove past.

"That's my cue," Pat said. "You get back inside with your family. And remember what I said. Keep your mouth shut until after I leave the church." He glared at me. "Do you understand me? Not a word."

"Trust me, I don't intend to mention anything about the murder to my family. It's gruesome and depressing, and I don't like being the bearer of bad news."

"Good." He patted me on the shoulder and took off toward his cruiser. I watched as he drove away and whispered a prayer for the Muellers and Hannah. After Pat got out of the car and went into the church, I hurried back into the restaurant. Of course, by the time I got back to the table, everyone was getting ready to leave. A small foam box sat where my plate had once been. My cobbler. At least I could take it home and eat it later. Dad went up front to pay for our meal, but Carmen, Hector's wife, shook her head when he tried to hand her the payment. Obviously Hector had informed her that our lunch was to be a gift. My father put his money back in his billfold, and he and Carmen talked for a few minutes. I waited until they were finished for a chance to say hello to Carmen. She hugged me and told me how happy she was that my family had come to visit. Since she and Hector had taken over the restaurant, Carmen had become one of my favorite people. After thanking her profusely for their generosity, I started to walk out of the restaurant. Before I reached the front door, I heard Jessie call my name. I turned to see her coming my way.

"Gracie, can I ask you a quick question?" she said, her voice low.

"Sure. What is it?"

She took my arm and led me a few feet away. I motioned to my parents to go on. My father nodded and started herding everyone out the door.

"I'm really sorry to bother you while you're with your family," she said.

"It's okay," I assured her. "Is something wrong?"

She crooked her head just a little. "That man over there. What's his name?"

I let my eyes follow the direction of her slight gesture. "Oh, that's C.J. Bradley, Abigail Bradley's son." I noticed the troubled look on her face. "Why?"

"Well, it's odd. When I first waited on him, everything seemed fine. In fact, we were having a nice conversation. And then I mentioned Trinity."

"I don't understand."

She shrugged. "Me either. When I brought up her name, he asked about my husband. When I told him I wasn't married, he got real quiet. Now he's. . .I don't know. Cold. Like I've offended him. Any idea why?"

I remembered what Ida had told me about C.J.'s mother. "I think he might have been brought up under rather strict religious rules, Jessie. He may have been a little shocked that Trinity was born. . .you know. . ."

"Out of wedlock?" she finished for me. She sighed. "This town has been so supportive of me and my daughter I guess I'm not used to getting that judgmental attitude. I know God has forgiven me, and that's what matters most."

"C.J. seems like a nice man. Just forget it and move on. I'm sure he'll come around. Sometimes we have automatic reactions to situations before we think them through. I'll bet that's what happened."

"I hope you're right. Having to wait on someone who dislikes me isn't much fun, but I'll do it if I have to."

"Do you want me to talk to him?"

She shook her head. "No, but thanks. I'm sure you're right. He'll probably get over it." She gave me a quick hug. "Thanks for letting me talk about it."

"Anytime, Jessie. You know that."

I watched as she walked away, and then I looked over at C.J. He was busy writing in his notebook and didn't notice me. He didn't seem like the kind of person who would be put off by Jessie's situation, but I didn't really know him. Besides, it could be Jessie's imagination. Maybe if it happened again, I'd speak to C.J., but right now, I had other things to deal with.

I jogged out the door to catch up with my family. Today wasn't going to be very enjoyable with a murder filling my thoughts. My concern for Hannah had grown every second since she'd gone missing. Finding her bracelet had convinced me she was in trouble but knowing the girl from Topeka had been murdered made me feel even more strongly that she was in danger. After we finished our tour of Harmony, I intended to pull Sam aside and persuade him it was time we took Hannah's disappearance and recovery into our own hands. I didn't want to upset Pat, but I was beginning to wonder if someone should contact the media about the missing Mennonite girl. People should be looking for her. And if she really *had* run away, which I doubted, maybe she would see the report and contact her parents. The more I thought about it, the more sense it made.

While everyone else waited, I ran into Ruth's and picked out some flowers. Then we all drove to the cemetery where my Uncle Benjamin was buried. I worried about Papa's reaction. Would he remember about Benjamin? As we got out of the car, I pulled my father aside.

"Dad, I'm concerned about Papa. Maybe I should stay with him in the car. What if he doesn't remember that Benjamin is dead?"

My father gazed out across the cemetery. "Papa deserves to see his son's grave. I won't take that away from him. If he seems too disoriented, I'll distract him, lead him away. But I have to give him this chance."

I wasn't convinced it was the best decision for Papa, but it wasn't my business to argue with my dad. Benjamin was his brother and Papa his father. It was his call. We walked past the monuments until we found Benjamin's grave. Although I hadn't been there since before I left for Wichita, a bunch of wildflowers had been placed in the cement vase at the base of the engraved stone. Who had put them there?

"Sweetie and Ida tended to the grave while you were gone," Sam whispered in my ear, answering my question.

I nodded, unable to speak. What precious friends I had, and how grateful I felt for them at that moment.

" '"Tis Grace that brought me safe thus far and Grace will lead me home,'" my mother read on the headstone. She turned tear-filled eyes to me. "And Grace did bring him the peace he couldn't find on this earth," she said. "I'm so proud of you."

I shook my head. "I only proved what I already knew in my heart: that Dad couldn't possibly take another person's life. I only wish Uncle Benjamin had found the truth before he died." I reached out and took my father's hand. "His love for you and his desire to protect you kept him from having the kind of relationship two brothers should have had."

My father wiped tears from his cheeks. "You know what, Gracie? The older I get, the less it matters what happens in this life. I know my brother and I will have eternity together. And that's what I cling to." He looked around at our assembled group. "And that goes for all of you. Even if we have to say good-bye for a while in this life, we are assured that it won't be for long." He squeezed my hand. "I'm so grateful to God for His wonderful promise."

Papa knelt down on Benjamin's grave. "I'm grateful, too, son," he said brokenly. "I can hardly wait to give Benjamin a hug. I know Essie is with him now and that they're waiting for the rest of us." He looked up at us. "You know, I'm fully aware that I have one foot in heaven and one foot on the earth. Soon I'll set both of my feet on that side, and Essie, Benjamin, and I will be there to greet you when you arrive. That will be a great day, won't it?"

My father bent down and helped Papa up. Then he wrapped his arms around him. "Yes, Papa," he whispered. "That will truly be a great day."

We stayed at Benjamin's grave for a little while, and then we walked through the rest of the cemetery. Mom and Dad pointed out the graves of people they'd known. Several times they linked their arms together and wept at the names of people they'd loved. Sweetie knew most of the names and was able to bring my parents up to date on past history—marriages, children, and how people had died. She had some great stories about Harmony residents that I'd never heard before. By the time we finished, I felt even more tied to Harmony. As if I'd been raised here, just like my parents.

One grave was missing though. John had allowed Abel to perform a small memorial service for his father, more for John's comfort than to memorialize Jacob Glick. Then Jacob's ashes had been scattered somewhere private. John had never shared the location and as far as I knew, no one ever asked. Although he wouldn't have faced opposition had he wanted to bury Jacob in the Harmony cemetery, John refused. His concerns weren't for himself but for those his father had harmed.

We drove back into town to visit the shops. Mom and Dad knew several people including the Menlos who owned Menlo's Bakery. Papa's memory seemed clear as a bell while they talked about old times. They all reminisced for quite a while, and Mr. Menlo insisted they try some of his baklava. By the time we left, we had an apple spice cake, a bag full of Mrs. Menlo's fudgy brownies, and a box of the best baklava I've ever tasted. We stopped back by Ruth's Crafts and Creations, and my father was able to see some of Benjamin's beautiful birdhouses and feeders. Most of them had been purchased by townspeople, but there were three houses and two feeders left. Dad ran his hand over them slowly. He'd seen the ones I had at the house, but these were brand new, not faded by time and weather like mine.

Ruth came from behind the counter and stood next to my

father. "When you get ready to leave town, you come on by here," she said softly. "I'll have these packed up for you."

He nodded. "Thank you. If you'll just make up a bill, I'll pay you when my wife decides what else she wants." He winked at Ruth. "I'm glad my car has a big trunk. Looks like she's buying out your inventory."

Ruth shook her head. "You don't understand, Daniel. I'm giving them to you."

My dad started to argue with her, but she grabbed his arm. "Now hush. This is what Benjamin would have wanted, I'm sure of it. I don't want to hear another word about it."

My father, who prides himself on his self-control, paused only a second before wrapping his arms around the stout shop owner. I turned away and concentrated on some hand-painted plates mounted to the wall. I'd cried so many times lately, I was afraid of drying out my insides. We spent quite awhile in Ruth's and by the time we left, my father's words had proven true. My mother's stack of new acquisitions was impressive. I'd shown them some of Hannah's paintings, and they'd agreed that she was incredibly talented. As I stood in front of the colorful pictures, I couldn't help but wonder if she'd ever paint again.

Papa spent most of his time gazing at a display of beautiful quilts, mumbling to himself. When I went to fetch him so we could leave, he grabbed my hand.

"Now Gracie, have you found Essie's wedding present yet? She's gonna scold us both if you don't find it. It's really, really important."

"I'll find it, Papa. We've still got plenty of time."

This seemed to satisfy him, and he followed me out of the shop, first stopping to receive a hug from Ruth. She'd been a young woman when Papa knew her and her parents, and she clearly remembered him, even bringing up times they'd spent together. Even though he pretended to recall the events she mentioned, it was obvious he had no idea who she was. Ruth's sad expression as she watched Papa leave made my heart ache.

We spent some time in Cora's Simple Clothing Shoppe talking to Amos and Cora Crandall. Although they hadn't lived in Harmony when my parents and Papa were here, it turned out Amos's parents had. They shared several stories passed down to them and we discovered that Amos's father and Papa used to go fishing together. Their conversation sparked some animation in Papa's face. Thankfully he remembered Norman Crandall and could even tell us a couple of big "fish stories" that made everyone laugh.

My mother grew nostalgic over some of the garments sold at the store and ended up buying two lovely pastel dresses. I had little faith that she would actually ever wear them, but since I had several similar dresses in my own closet, I certainly wasn't the person to protest her choice.

We made the rounds of quite a few other places in town, including Joe Loudermilk's hardware store and the Scheidler brothers' farm implements store. My mother loved Nature's Bounty, a shop that sells dairy products, fresh fruits, and vegetables. The store used to be owned by Joyce Bechtold, a woman who had been in love with my uncle. Even though I believe he loved her, too, he'd never reached out to Joyce. Instead, he'd remained trapped, trying to protect a family secret that didn't need protecting. After he died, Joyce left town, brokenhearted. Now the shop was run by Florence Avery, wife of a dairy farmer who supplied most of the milk, eggs, and cream. Flo was a very nice woman, and my parents purchased assorted fruits and vegetables that Sam and I toted back to the car. Their stash was growing. Hopefully we'd be able to get the trunk closed after loading everything that waited at Ruth's.

The last visit on our route was to Ketterling's Candles and Notions. I could hardly wait to see Sarah and her father, Gabe. My mother pulled me aside before we reached the front door.

"This is Sarah? The girl you told me about?" she asked quietly.

I nodded. "Yes, she's the one who's in love with Dr. Keystone."

I'd told my mother all about Gabe and Sarah and how that although we were now dear friends, my first introduction to Gabe was pretty bumpy. A man hurt by the devastation of losing his beloved wife to an outsider, he'd withdrawn into a world he thought he could control. Unfortunately he'd dragged Sarah into it, too. Thanks to the efforts of a loving community, Gabe had finally come out of his shell and joined the human race— to an extent. His complete commitment to his faith kept certain boundaries strong, including not allowing his daughter to become involved with an unbeliever like John Keystone.

"Their story is so similar to ours. I feel such compassion for them," Mom said.

"Except that you and Dad were both believers. John isn't. I can't fault Gabe for not wanting his Christian daughter to marry someone who doesn't know God."

"Does Sarah feel the same way?"

Dad, Sam, and Papa were busy looking over farm equipment through the Scheidler brothers' window so we sat down on one of the many benches along the boardwalk.

"Yes, she believes that she shouldn't be unequally yoked," I said. "But she's also very protective of her father. I told you that his wife, Sarah's mother, ran off with another man. Gabe's carried that hurt for a long, long time." I wiped the sweat off my forehead with the back of my hand. It seemed much hotter now than when we'd started our tour. "Sarah believes if she left her father, it could destroy him. She loves him too much to risk it."

My mother sighed and stared off into the distance. "But that's not her job, Gracie. We need to find our fulfillment from our relationship with God, not from other people. Her father needs to let her go so she can experience the life God has called her to live."

"I know, Mom. I tried to tell her, but she doesn't want to hear it. If I say anything else about it, I could ruin our friendship."

The men had finished their survey of farm machinery, so Mom and I got up and followed them to the candle shop. As we entered, Gabe looked up from something he was working on behind the counter.

"Gracie!" he said, his face breaking out into a big smile. "I heard you were back."

He held out his arms and embraced me in a big hug, something he never used to do. I was still adjusting to the changes, although I loved seeing the difference in his personality. Then he approached my father. "You must be Daniel," he said, holding out his hand. "I knew your brother. In fact, we were friends. I'm so happy to meet you."

Dad seemed somewhat taken aback by Gabe's Old Order attire and customary beard. I was sure it brought back memories from his youth. Gabe and Sarah were one of the few Old Order families left in Harmony. But ever the trouper, Dad quickly regained his composure and took Gabe's hand.

"Good to meet you, too, Gabe. I've certainly heard a lot about you—and your daughter."

I quickly made the rest of the introductions. When I got to Papa, Gabe nodded. "My family and I moved here shortly before you and your wife left Harmony," he said to Papa. "I'm sure you don't recall me, but I certainly remember you. You were very highly thought of in this community. I'm honored to see you again."

Papa took his hand and smiled, but the blank look was back. He stared at Gabe's clothing and beard and frowned. I wondered if he was also remembering the past. But whatever his thoughts, he kept them to himself.

"I still remember coming here when Levi Hoffman ran this store," Dad said. "We bought candles and lanterns for our home. Levi was a good friend of our family."

Gabe nodded. "He was a good friend to many people here. What happened to him was sad. I hope someday he'll return to Harmony. People in this town still pray for that day."

"Yes," Dad said. "We pray for that, too."

Just then the curtain that separates the main shop from the rooms in the back parted and Sarah entered the room.

"Gracie!" she said, laughing. "I've been waiting for you."

I ran over to the beautiful young woman in the dark dress and apron, her raven-colored hair tucked under her prayer covering, and hugged her tightly. I was startled to feel her bony frame under my grasp. She looked even thinner than she had before I left.

"I've missed you so much," I said, feeling somewhat emotional. Sarah was my very best friend in Harmony. An Old Order Mennonite and a very modern girl from the big city. Strange combination, but somehow it worked.

She finally let me go and stepped back to smile at me. "I've been keeping up my cooking lessons with Sweetie. I think I've passed you by, you know. Will you be ready to begin again soon?"

"I think we can work in one more lesson before the wedding. Can I call and let you know when? I really need the rest of this week to go over wedding plans and spend some time with my family."

Sarah looked at her father. "That would be wonderful as long as Papa will let me take off some time from the shop."

Gabe's eyes crinkled with amusement. "Saying no would only hurt me in the long run. I'm the one benefiting from your lessons." He patted his stomach, which was flat as a board. "I may have to go on a diet if this keeps up, but it's worth it. Sarah is becoming quite the cook." His face lost its jovial look for a moment. "Can't figure out why I keep gaining weight and she seems to be losing it though. Doesn't make sense."

"You do look thinner, Sarah," I said. "Are you feeling all right?"

She blushed slightly and looked down toward the floor. "I think I've been working too hard and forgetting to eat. But I promised Papa I'd do better, and I will." She swung her gaze up to me. "Now, no more talk of how much I weigh. I want to hear all about Wichita."

Gabe leaned back against the counter behind him. "Of course, we've heard about Hannah. The whole town is abuzz. What's really going on, Gracie? Did she run away?"

I hesitated before answering, torn between keeping folks in Harmony from becoming frightened by the idea of a killer who might target their daughters and an overwhelming desire to warn these people I loved so much. Not certain if Pat was finished talking to the Muellers, I decided not to share everything quite yet. "We honestly don't know, Gabe. Sheriff Taylor thinks she's a runaway. A few other people aren't so certain." I sighed. "I just wish she'd show up. I can't help but blame myself some for this situation. If I hadn't taken her to Wichita. . ."

"Don't be silly, Gracie," Gabe said. "Even though Sarah and I believe in a separated life, we don't believe that alone will keep us unspotted from the world. People have free will. They have the right to make decisions. Good ones or bad ones. Hannah Mueller has godly parents who taught her right from wrong. Her reaction to what she saw in Wichita was her own." He shook his head. "It's unlikely she would have lived all her life here anyway." He motioned toward my father. "In the old days, young people were expected to stay in their hometowns. Schooling past the eighth grade was not only discouraged, but in many families it was forbidden. Do you remember?"

Dad nodded. "My brother and I were allowed to finish high school and my parents knew we intended to go to college. But my mother and father were rebels in their day." He smiled at Papa who returned his smile. "But yes, that's the way it was."

"Today, children are allowed to go to college even in the more conservative communities," Gabe said. "I believe the Muellers would have allowed Hannah to leave if she had that desire, so she would have seen life outside our little town eventually. It was something inside her, Gracie, that sparked a fire. It wasn't you." He shook his head and his eyebrows drew together in a frown. "Sometimes I wonder, though, if the old ways aren't better. I worry about the world and its effect on young people." He smiled at my father. "Of course I've changed my mind about many things since your daughter came into my life. I'm sure I'm not through learning, but I thank God all the time for her friendship. I know I'm better for it."

I felt my face get hot. "Th–thanks Gabe," I stuttered, surprised by his kind comments.

"I know Hannah will come back, Gracie," Sarah said reassuringly. "And then she might not want to leave Harmony again. Some people do, and some don't. Papa and I have seen folks take off, thinking they can't find happiness here. But after being out in the world for a while, they realize how special this town is and they come home."

I nodded. "Funny how different we all are. Here I left the big city for Harmony, and Hannah wants to leave Harmony for the big city. I love this place and can't imagine my life anywhere else."

Out of the corner of my eye I saw my parents exchange looks. I knew they felt differently. They couldn't get out of Harmony fast enough, but I was learning that we all have a path to follow. One that God has prepared for us. Reasoning has nothing to do with finding the place you belong. He is the only One who knows the way—and my way was in this town. And with this man. I grabbed Sam's hand.

"Well, we'd love to look around your shop," my dad said, changing the subject. "Gracie has been going on and on about some stationery you make, Sarah. And we must have some Honeysuckle Grace candles. Gabe, I understand you created these candles as a tribute to my daughter?"

Gabe smiled. "Yes, I did. They're over here."

Dad followed Gabe to a large shelf full of candles while Sarah led my mother over to a display table with sets of stationery she'd designed through a procedure called woodblock printing, a craft not practiced much anymore. Blocks of wood are carved with special knives, creating grooves in the wood. One design can actually be made up of several different blocks using various colors. Once the design is carved into the block, paint is rolled over it. The paint fills the grooves and then the paper is placed on top of the wood. A rubber roller is moved back and forth lightly until the pattern emerges. It takes real skill. Too much paint can cause unsightly blobs and an uneven design. Also, rolling unevenly can ruin a pattern. I'd destroyed many sheets of expensive paper before finally gaining some skill. Even still, not everything I did turned out right. Complex designs and colors mean that more blocks are carved, loaded with paint, and the paper that has already been rolled is rolled again. If done right, the second, third, and sometimes fourth blocks will deepen the design and add interesting details. Making a mistake with the last block was frustrating to say the least. The entire procedure would have to be started again. With Sarah's help I'd created a few patterns of my own, but I wasn't anywhere close to her level of expertise.

I took Papa's hand and led him over to a small bench in the corner of the room. We sat next to each other and watched as Mom and Dad looked over all the wonderful items for sale in the shop. Papa took a deep breath, enjoying all the incredible aromas in the room. There's nothing like a candle shop to excite the senses.

Papa pulled on my arm. "Gracie, who is that man?" he whispered. "I don't know him."

"No, I'm sure you don't, Papa," I said. I quickly explained that Gabe had moved to Harmony not long before he and Mama left. "You probably didn't get the chance to meet him and his daughter."

Papa shook his head. "I understand that, but something is wrong," he said slowly. "I know this place. But not this man."

"Oh Papa, I'm sorry. I should have explained. You're thinking of Levi Hoffman who used to run this shop. But he—he moved away." No sense in telling him that Levi was in prison. Papa didn't need to know that.

His expression brightened some. "Yes. Yes, that's it. I used to come here when Levi ran this store." He patted my knee. "Thank you, Gracie. I was confused for a moment."

"That's okay, Papa. I understand."

We sat there quietly, but Papa seemed much more relaxed. As she had in several other shops, my mother bought everything she could get her hands on. Funny thing, usually my mother was a very frugal person. I'd never seen her spend money like this.

Finally we left the candle shop, picked up Mom's purchases

from Ruth, and headed home. My dad, who'd wanted to tour Sam's farm this afternoon, asked for a rain check. I could tell his leg was bothering him. Besides, both my parents looked really tired. Sweetie offered to meet with Hector by herself and get some different ideas for the reception. My mother gratefully accepted. Being outside in the heat all afternoon had drained everyone's energy. I was grateful we'd have an afternoon to rest. Running around in Sam's orchards didn't sound very appealing to me either. When we got to the house, Dad took Sam aside for a few minutes while Mom and Papa went inside the house. I waited until they finished talking, then I walked Sam to his truck to say good-bye. I'd asked him and Sweetie over to my place that night for dinner, but they'd declined.

"You need some time with just your parents," Sam had said. "We'll get together tomorrow."

Instead of getting into his truck, he paused with his hand on the door handle. "Your father just told me he wants some time to visit with me tomorrow while Sweetie and your mom talk about the wedding. I guess we'll walk around the farm for a while." His handsome features twisted with concern. "I'm not sure he approves of me, Gracie."

"Don't be silly. He just wants to get to know you better. I'm sure he likes you."

"Well, I hope so. But sometimes I catch him looking at me...I don't know. Strangely."

I laughed. "I look at you strangely all the time, and I like you."

"Very funny." He ran his hand through his long blond hair. "Well, I guess I'll find out tomorrow how he really feels."

I leaned into his chest. "Don't worry. If he forbids me to marry you, we'll change our names, run off to a foreign country, and start a new life."

I felt him heave with laughter. "And what will our new names be?"

I stared up at him. "Hmmm. Let's see. How about Grace Marple and Sam Stringer? No one will ever suspect it's us."

"Okay. But which one will you be?"

I pushed myself away from him. "I can be Sam and you can be Grace. That should really confuse people."

"That would confuse me, too. Maybe we should just stay here and work it out."

I raised my hands in a gesture of surrender. "Okay, but I'm offering you a life of excitement and intrigue."

He leaned down and kissed my nose. "Trust me. Being with you gives me all the excitement and intrigue I can handle."

"Good. That's my goal."

I kissed him good-bye and sent him on his way. When I got inside, Papa had gone upstairs for a nap, and my mother was busy unloading all her purchases. I glanced over at my dad who watched her with a worried expression. He'd obviously found her uncharacteristic buying spree troublesome. After unwrapping everything, she suddenly announced she was tired.

"I'll put all this stuff away later," she said, yawning. "But for now, a nice nap would help get my energy levels back up to normal. The heat really takes it out of me."

"You go on, honey," Dad said. "I intend to rest my leg a bit. Think I'll stay down here and find a way to prop it up for a while."

"How's it feeling, Dad?" I asked. "I noticed you left your cane in the car when we had lunch, but you took it when we walked around town."

He nodded. "It's a bother, but thankfully, my leg's feeling stronger every day." He raised his hand before my mother had a chance to say anything. "I know, Bev. I'm supposed to use my cane all the time. At least I used it most of the day. That should certainly make you happy, so no nagging, okay?"

Mom pointed her finger at him. "This has nothing to do with making *me* happy. We'll all be happy if you'll just be responsible and take care of yourself. And any nagging you get will be well deserved."

"I know, I know. Now get to bed, young lady. We need to be on high alert tonight. Gracie's cooking."

She smiled at me. "I know whatever you make will be wonderful, Gracie. I have utmost confidence in you."

My father gave a dramatic shudder. "I can't forget the last meal she cooked for us. It almost turned out to be our actual last meal. I swelled up like a fat balloon."

"Oh Dad," I retorted, "you know that wasn't my fault. The recipe in the paper was a misprint."

My parents both laughed.

"Most cooks would realize that a cup of salt for eight servings of beef stew is too much," my mother said.

"Well I know that *now*. But you can't fault a gal for trying."

"Maybe we should look over the recipe for tonight," Dad said. "You know, for our own protection."

"I'll have you know that Sweetie taught me how to prepare tonight's main course. I've made it twice already, and no one has died."

"That's just the kind of recommendation I like before I eat," my father mumbled. "Here, try this. No one has died."

My mother shook her head and waved a hand at us. "I've had enough of you two comics. I'm going to bed. See you later."

She climbed the stairs, leaving my father and me alone. "How about something to drink?" I asked him.

"Sounds crazy since it's so hot outside, but I'd love a cup of coffee with cream. How about you?"

My father and I shared a love of coffee. One thing I missed in Harmony—Starbucks. An iced caramel macchiato would taste great right about now. But coffee with plain cream was growing on me. "Sure, I'll put a pot on."

Dad followed me into the kitchen and sat down at the table. "This place brings back so many memories," he said quietly. "Mama fixing breakfast in this kitchen. All of us crowded around the table. Papa praying. Then we'd talk about what was going on in our lives." He stared out the kitchen window. "I think families are missing out on something important nowadays. Gathering together around the supper table. Really listening to each other. We're becoming a generation that tunes each other out, I'm afraid."

I filled my metal coffeepot with coffee and water and set it on the stove to percolate. Dad frowned at me. "You have electricity now. Why don't you have a coffeemaker?"

I turned on the gas burner under the pot. "Oh, I have one, but I like the taste of coffee in a regular pot, and I don't have a lot of counter space in here. Do you mind?"

He shook his head. "Not at all. I like coffee made the old-fashioned way. Has a deeper, richer taste."

I came over and sat down at the table. "Sam tells me you want to talk to him tomorrow. Mind if I ask what that's about?"

He just shrugged but didn't answer me.

"Look Dad. Anyone who spends time around Sam can see what a wonderful man he is. But I've noticed. . .I don't know. You've spoken to him rather harshly a few times. And I've caught you looking at him in a weird way. I mean, you *do* like him, don't you?"

My father let out his breath slowly. "Yes, I like him, Gracie. It's just that in all the time you two have known each other, it's hard to believe you couldn't find a few days to come to Nebraska and introduce Sam to your mother and me. After all, we are your parents." He leaned back in his chair and crossed his arms. "It's not like I don't know what it's like to be young and in love. But I truly don't believe I'd have left Harmony with your mother unless Mama and Papa knew my bride-to-be and approved of her. I've never been given the chance to approve or disapprove of Sam. What if Mom and I didn't like him? Would it make any difference?"

I thought about his question for a moment. "Well, I'm certain beyond a shadow of a doubt that Sam and I are meant to be together. What you're actually asking me is if you and Mom wanted me to disobey God's will for my life, would I do it? I guess the answer to that question is no."

He was quiet for a little while, and his gaze drifted back toward the window. Finally, he sighed. "I understand, Gracie, and it sounds right. Maybe some of those old ways are still inside me, but I would have felt better about this marriage if you and Sam had made more of an effort to visit us before becoming engaged. And I really would have liked it if Sam had asked us for your hand."

I snorted. "Asked you for my hand?" I searched my father's face but couldn't see any sign that he wasn't serious. "Wow, Dad. Does anyone do that anymore?"

He frowned at me. "Yes, Grace Marie, they do. Milton Olshaker's son-in-law went to him first before he asked their daughter, Debbie, to marry him."

I raised an eyebrow. "Who in the world is Milton Olshaker?"

"You know the Olshakers? From church?"

"Oh wait a minute. I *do* remember them." I grinned at him. "Debbie Olshaker? I imagine Milton and his wife were thankful *anyone* wanted to marry Debbie."

"Grace Marie," my father gasped. "That's unkind. Besides, Debbie looks better now. She got her braces off and has started plucking her eyebrows..." Although he tried to fight it, he burst out laughing. I joined in. "Okay, okay. Bad example," he said, wiping his eyes. "But the point is..."

"The point is, my dear old dad," I said softly, "you feel left out. I'm sorry. I really do understand. What can Sam and I do to make it up to you?"

He reached over and grabbed my hand. "Nothing," he said. "You're right. I guess I feel like I'm losing my little girl." He let go of my hand and pointed his finger in my face. "And please don't tell me I'm gaining a son. I'm not quite ready for that yet."

"But you will be, Dad," I said gently. "When you get to know Sam the way I do you'll be proud to call him your son. Besides, Sam could really use a father figure in his life."

"But he has a father, although I must admit they don't seem very close."

I told my father the story of Sam and Pat, getting up in the middle of my story to turn down the burner and pour our coffee. I got the cream out of the refrigerator and put it on the table. Then I finished explaining the confusing relationship the best I could.

"Oh my," Dad said when I was done. "I had no idea." He shook his head. "I feel sorry for them both, but Sam needs to forgive his father and find a way to build a relationship."

"That's what I keep telling him, but he's still trying to work through some issues."

Dad nodded. "People have to deal with their feelings. They just fester inside if you don't." He smiled. "If Sam is the man you say he is, he'll find a way."

"I'm counting on it. I was so encouraged last night when he

insisted that Pat join us for dinner. That was a real step in the right direction."

"I'm not so sure his aunt felt the same way."

"Sweetie's having a hard time. She blames Pat for leaving her sister."

"So what really happened to Sam's mother? You said she contacted Pat and told him where Sam was."

"That was a few years ago. After she wrote to Pat she moved from the town where she'd been living. Left no forwarding address. Pat's looked everywhere for her, and he has lots of ways to track people. More than a regular person would have at their disposal. But he hasn't been successful in finding her. She said in her letter that she was really sick and wanted to tell Pat the truth before she died. Pat's even checked through death records, but he hasn't found anything."

"Has Sam talked to Pat about his mother?"

I shook my head. "No, and he doesn't like to talk about her with anyone. I've learned not to bring up the subject."

"Sounds like he's carrying some unresolved problems into your marriage."

I shrugged. "Maybe. But look at the mother- and father-in-law I'm giving him. I figure we're even."

Dad wrinkled his nose at me. "Ha, ha." He sipped his coffee. "Mmmm. Very good. Why is it everything tastes better in the country?"

"I have no idea, but I know exactly what you mean."

My dad stared into his cup for a moment. "One other question about Sam, then I'll leave it alone."

I raised my eyebrows at him. "And that would be?"

"Why does he always call you Grace? I've never heard him call you Gracie. Not once."

"Sam believes God's grace brought me into his life. Calling me Grace is meaningful to him. A way of letting God know he's grateful for His gift."

My father sighed dramatically. "Well, if that isn't the corniest thing I've ever heard."

"Dad!"

We both burst out laughing, and my father almost spilled his coffee.

"Oh my," he said when we settled down a bit. "I couldn't pass that up. You set me up so perfectly."

"Glad I could assist your attempt at humor," I said grinning.

"Actually, I really appreciate that he sees you that way. Your mother and I named you Grace for a reason. After doctors said we might never have children, we prayed that God would do what medical science couldn't. And a couple of months later, you were conceived. That's why we named you Grace. Sam's got it right."

"Oh Dad."

"I love you, Grace Marie," he said, his voice full of emotion. "I want you to be confident of that every moment of your life."

"I am, Dad. I really am."

My father picked up his cup. "I noticed you talked to Pat for quite awhile outside the restaurant today. Is everything all right?"

"No. No, it's not." I told him about the police finding the body of the girl in Topeka.

"That's terrible. Does Pat think the cases are related?"

"No, he doesn't. He still thinks Hannah ran away."

My thoughts turned back to my conversation with Pat, and my attention drifted away until Dad said, "Gracie, you're twirling your hair again."

I let go of the strand of hair wrapped around my finger. "Sorry. I just don't know what to think. I mean, according to Pat, Hannah's situation doesn't match the profile of the other cases."

"Other *cases*. What do you mean?"

"I guess there are some similarities between this murder and several others. The police think the killing in Topeka is the work of a serial killer."

My father frowned. "I just can't believe something like that could touch Harmony."

"Why? There have been two murders in Harmony. Living simply doesn't keep evil away, Dad. It takes more than that."

"I know, I know. It's just. . ."

I smiled. "Evil doesn't belong here?"

He chuckled. "Yes, I guess that's what I mean. There's something different about Harmony. Something. . ."

"Yes, I know. Something special. That's why I moved here. You seemed so upset when I made that decision, I figured you'd never understand."

My father ran a finger around the rim of his cup. "Oh, I understand, Gracie. You know, when your mom and I left Harmony, it was one of the hardest things I've ever done. I've been so angry. . ."

"Because of the way you were treated?"

He stopped and stared past me, out the window again. I couldn't blame him, it's a beautiful sight. Deep-green grasses sprinkled with colorful wildflowers and lush trees that line a crystal-clear lake. After pausing for several seconds, he shook his head. "You know, I thought that's why I had such negative feelings toward this place. But now I don't know. I'm starting to wonder if I was more upset about what was happening to Harmony than how your mother and I were being treated. Funny I didn't see that until we came ho. . .back."

"You started to say 'home.' Wow, Dad. After all these years

and all the negative things you've said about this place, you still see it as home?"

He was quiet as he stared at his coffee cup for a while. "Isn't it silly? Yes, I guess I do. My bitterness toward some of the people here made me forget all the wonderful things about this place." He rubbed his hand across his face. "Funny how we do that to ourselves. A couple of unpleasant memories can drive out all the good ones if we let them."

I started to agree with him when a shout from the living room stopped our conversation cold. We both jumped up and hurried out of the kitchen just in time to see Papa standing at the top of the stairs, his eyes wild and his hair messed up.

"I can't find it!" he yelled. "I can't find it anywhere! Essie will be so upset..."

Before either one of us could rush to his side, Papa stepped out as if he were standing on a solid floor. We watched in horror as he tumbled down the stairs.

Chapter Thirteen

"Thanks again for coming over here," I said to John. "I know it's an inconvenience."

He put his stethoscope back into his medical bag. "Like I said, it's no problem. My only other patient was Franklin Marshall. Lancing the boil on his foot can wait a bit."

"The life of a doctor is really glamorous," I said, grinning.

John smiled. "No kidding."

"So my father will be all right?" Dad asked.

"He's fine," John said. "He'll probably be a little sore. Just make him rest for a couple of days. If he complains of any unusual pain, let me know, but I can't find any broken bones."

"What a stupid thing to do," Papa said, adjusting the quilt I'd tucked around him as he lay on the couch. "I can't imagine what I was thinking."

Papa had no memory of even getting out of bed, and he had no explanation what it was he'd been attempting so hard to find. Ever since he'd arrived, he'd been trying to find something—a wedding present from Mama. My father believed it was something lodged in his memory from long ago and triggered by all the talk of my upcoming wedding.

"Don't worry about it, Papa," I said, putting my hand on his shoulder. "Must have been a bad dream. I'm just glad you're okay."

Papa mumbled something unintelligible, and his eyes closed.

"I gave him something for the pain," John said. "He'll be a little sleepy." He held out a bottle to me. "You might give him one of these every four to six hours for a day or two. Then just if he complains of pain."

"Will they make him more confused?" my mother asked.

"Maybe a little, but he'll be comfortable and relaxed. Alzheimer's patients can get agitated quickly. You shouldn't have any more outbursts for a while."

"I shouldn't have brought him to Harmony," Dad said slowly.

John shook his head. "Look Daniel, it's not my job to tell you what you should or shouldn't do. But do you think your father would be happier in a nursing home or here with his family? Yes, there will be some confusion. Some problems. But he really wants to be in Harmony. I guarantee you he's more at peace here than he would be back in Nebraska." He slapped my dad lightly on the back. "You can do this. Someday when he's gone, you'll be glad you made the effort. Regrets are poisonous. Trust me. I had to learn that the hard way. Living with them is tougher than enduring the problems you're having now. As long as you keep him safe—make sure he doesn't hurt himself or wander off— he'll be fine."

"Someone will have to stay down here with him if he can't be upstairs," Mom said. "What if he gets up in the middle of the night and tries to go outside or something?"

I chuckled. "Mom, this is Harmony. Even if that happened, he'd have to walk twenty miles to the highway. There's nothing out here that can harm him."

"Still. . ." she said, her face twisted with worry.

"I'll put my sleeping bag in the living room and camp out on the floor. It's no problem."

"You don't need to do that, Snicklefritz," my father said. "I'll do it."

I snorted. "Oh sure. You lying on the floor with your bum leg. Mom and I will end up with two patients."

My father started to respond, but I held up my hand. "Just give it up. I don't mind a bit. In fact, it will give me more time with Papa before you all go home. I'd really like that."

My mother grabbed my father's arm. "Quit fighting your daughter, Daniel," she scolded. "You don't have to be the one to do everything. Let us help sometimes."

"Very good advice," John said. "Gracie, call me if you need anything. I think I'd better head back to the office. A boil awaits."

I laughed and walked with him to the door. Before he left, he gave me a hug. "You'll be fine," he whispered in my ear. "You're the strongest person I know."

I stood staring at the front door after he closed it. John Keystone was so different from the cold, angry man I'd first met. I suspected his love for Sarah was the main reason. Love can certainly change people.

"Nice man," my father said. He came up and put his arm around me. "You certainly have made a home for yourself here. I wish. . ." His voice trailed off. I started to ask him what he was going to say when my mother interrupted.

"My goodness, it's almost five o'clock. Do you need help with dinner?" she asked.

"No. You two relax awhile. I'll get busy."

"And just what are we supposed to do?" my father grumbled.

"No TV, except for that sad little set in your room."

I put my hands on my hips. "Well, for crying out loud. What did you do for entertainment when you lived in Harmony?"

My father got a mischievous look on his face. "I used to sneak out into the woods with your mother and neck."

"Daniel Christopher Temple!" my mother exclaimed. "I was a proper Mennonite girl. I never, ever necked!"

I burst out laughing. "Why, Mom. I'm shocked. Here you made me think you never even kissed Dad until you were married."

"Oh you two," she said, her face red, "I never said anything like that."

I started to fire back a smart-alecky answer when someone knocked on the door. "John must have forgotten something." I quickly swung the door open and was surprised to find the infamous Mrs. Murphy standing on my front porch. I was so shocked I couldn't think of anything to say.

"I'm sorry to bother you," she said frowning. "I'd like to talk to you for a few minutes if you don't mind."

Mrs. Murphy's dark hair, pulled back in a tight bun, gave her an almost oriental look. The severe hairstyle seemed to match her uptight personality.

"I—I don't know," I said hesitantly. "If you're trying to find dirt on Abel and Emily Mueller, you've come to the wrong place."

She sighed and her stern features softened a little. "Well, that's just it. I've talked to the Muellers, and I've spoken to several other people in town. I'm not getting any information that makes me think Hannah Mueller ran away because she was being abused. I still don't understand the rigid rules these people live by, but I don't find any reason Hannah should be removed from her home once she's found."

"Well that's a relief. But what is it you want from me?"

She glanced at her watch. "I wonder if I could buy you dinner in town? I'd like to talk to you a bit so I can wrap this case up."

I just stared at her, not knowing what to say. I needed to fix supper for my family, yet I was willing to do anything I could to send this woman packing. Maybe getting her to ease up on Abel and Emily would help to make up for the trouble I'd caused them.

"You go ahead, Gracie," my mother said from behind me. I turned to find her standing a few feet away, listening to our conversation. "I can cook for us tonight. You fix supper another night."

"Okay," I said slowly. I looked at Mrs. Murphy. "Can I meet you at Mary's in about twenty minutes?"

"That would be fine." She turned, went down the stairs, and headed out to her car without saying good-bye. Her brusque manner was certainly intact even if her suspicions about Abel and Emily had abated some.

I closed the door and turned to look at Mom. "I don't trust her. What if this is some kind of trap? What if she tries to make me say something awful about the Muellers and then uses it against them?"

"Do you actually know anything awful about them?" my father asked as he watched the exchange between my mother and me from the rocking chair.

"Well...no."

"Then I think you're safe."

My mother grabbed my hand. "Now show me what you were going to make for supper. I may not fix it quite the way you planned to, but I'll try not to poison anyone."

"You're a great cook," I said with a smile. "I think the chances of doing bodily harm to this family is much more likely with me standing over the stove."

Simple Choices

"Wow," Dad said. "I think I'm grateful to Mrs. Murphy for showing up when she did."

My mother giggled. "Come on." We walked hand in hand to the kitchen where I showed her the ingredients I'd put together for Sweetie's famous meat loaf recipe.

"No problem," she said. "And I'll make sure there's something left in case you and your grandfather decide you want to make a meat loaf sandwich in the middle of the night."

I'd actually forgotten about our late-night forages into the refrigerator when I was young. Mama and Papa would come to visit, and Papa would wake me up after everyone had gone to bed. He'd make us meat loaf sandwiches, and we'd watch TV together until we were both too sleepy to stay up any longer. Papa and meat loaf sandwiches. The best sleeping pill in the world.

I went to the bathroom and freshened up a bit. Then I decided to change my blouse since I'd sweated much more than was ladylike that afternoon. It only took a few minutes to run upstairs, pick out a clean blouse, throw the sweaty one in the laundry hamper, and hurry back down to the living room. I checked on Papa who was still fast asleep, then said good-bye to my parents.

When I got to the restaurant, I discovered that Mrs. Murphy had already gotten us a booth in the corner. I assumed she wanted as much privacy as possible. I tried to quell the nervousness I felt. This was my chance to help the Muellers. I prayed God would give me the right words and keep me from saying anything stupid.

"I hope this booth is okay," Mrs. Murphy said as I approached.

"It's fine." I scooted in across from her. "I'm still not sure what you want from me, though. The Muellers are wonderful parents. If you think I'm going to disagree with the other positive things you've heard about them, you're mistaken."

She shook her head and started to say something when Leah, another one of Hannah's friends, came up to the table. A beautiful, delicate girl with deep-chestnut hair, she'd caught the attention of most of Harmony's young men. But Leah was very devout and not easily impressed by anything except a heart committed to God. I admired her. She's definitely the kind of young woman a mother would like to see her son marry.

"Can I get you something to drink?" she asked.

Mrs. Murphy and I both ordered iced tea.

"Do you need a few minutes to decide what you want?"

"Well, I think it might be nice if I had a chance to look at the menu before I give you my order," the social worker snapped.

To her credit, Leah didn't respond. She walked over to where the menus were kept and grabbed a couple, handing them to us. "I'll be back in a few minutes," she said softly. I could see the hurt in her eyes.

"People here aren't rude to each other," I said when Leah walked away. "Most of us have memorized the menu and don't need to see it."

Mrs. Murphy shook her head. "I'm sorry. Guess I'm used to things working a little differently. I can be impatient." She gazed around the room. There were a couple of Conservative Mennonite families eating supper together, dressed in plain clothing, the women and girls with prayer coverings over their buns or braids. Other patrons wore overalls or jeans and T-shirts, having just come in from harvesting. The room was filled with the aroma of sweat and grain dust mixed with the great smells emanating from Hector's kitchen. "I just don't get this place. This is the first time I've ever been in a town that was so...so..."

"Peaceful?" I interjected helpfully.

She glared at me. "I was going to say *backward*."

"I'm sorry, maybe I misunderstood you. I thought you said you were forming a positive opinion about this town—and the Muellers. Am I mistaken?"

She sucked in a deep breath and let it out slowly. "You're right. Sorry again. I spend so much time interviewing the world's worst parents, when I find good ones, I'm still suspicious."

I raised my eyebrows with interest. "So you're admitting Abel and Emily are good parents?"

Leah came up to the table with our drinks. She put them down and then hesitated.

"Sorry, Leah," I said. "Give us a couple more minutes. I don't think Mrs. Murphy has looked at her menu yet."

She nodded and started to walk away.

"Wait a minute," the social worker said. "I–I'm sorry I was rude. It's been a bad day, but I shouldn't have taken it out on you. Forgive me."

Leah gave her a beatific smile. "I already did that, ma'am. Please don't worry about it. I'll be back in a bit." She left to tend to another table.

"Now see? That's just what I mean," Mrs. Murphy said, exasperation showing in her expression. "What's up with that? The people here aren't. . .aren't *human!*"

I couldn't stop my mouth from dropping open. "Surely you've met Christians before. It's not like we live on another planet."

She grunted, picked up her tea, and took a long drink. Then she set it down with a thump. "Oh yes, I've met *Christians* before." She said the word in the same way someone might say *cockroaches* or *poisonous snakes*.

"I take it you weren't impressed."

She unfolded the napkin wrapped around her silverware and

put it neatly on her lap. "Look, let's not get into some kind of religious debate. I didn't ask you here for that."

"Fine. You said you wanted to talk about the Muellers. Just what do you want to know, Mrs. Murphy?"

"First of all, you can call me Susan if you wish."

There was a little voice inside me that wanted to tell her she could continue to call me Miss Temple, but I quashed it. "I'm Gracie. So what is it you want to know. . .Susan?"

She took another sip of her iced tea, and I noticed her hand trembled slightly. What was that about? I spotted Leah watching us from across the room. "Why don't we decide what we want to eat before we talk? That way Leah won't have to wait for us."

Susan reached up to pat her hair. As if a stray hair had a chance of escaping that tight bun. Her hair almost looked sprayed on. "It's hardly our job to make our waitress comfortable. She can wait until we're ready to order."

I could almost feel my blood start to boil. Her earlier show of humility hadn't lasted long. "Look here, Susan. . ." I drew out her name with emphasis. "Maybe you treat people that way in Topeka. . .or wherever you're from. But we don't do that in Harmony. Either you decide right now what you want for supper, or I'm out of here."

She actually bit her lip to keep from saying whatever was on her mind. Then she flung open her menu and perused it quickly. I waited a few moments then waved at Leah to come over. She walked up, flipped open her notepad, and waited.

"I'd like a fruit salad and a slice of banana bread," I said with a smile.

Leah wrote down my order. "And for you, ma'am?" she asked Susan.

Susan's look of disgust as she stared at the menu couldn't have been any more obvious. "I don't know. I suppose I'll try the fried chicken dinner."

Leah explained the sides, and Susan picked mashed potatoes, green beans, and salad. As Leah walked away, Susan leaned over and said in a loud whisper that Leah could hear, "Surely even a cook in a greasy spoon like this can figure out how to fry chicken."

Leah didn't turn around, but I knew she'd caught the mean comment. I'd had enough. As Sweetie would say, "This ole dog ain't gonna hunt no more."

"Listen, *Mrs. Murphy*," I said harshly. "I gave up dinner with my family to come here because I care about the Muellers. But I don't intend to spend another minute with you. You think this is a hick town? There isn't anyone living here who doesn't have more class in their little finger than you do in your whole body. At least in Harmony we have manners. We know how to act. You obviously don't." I slid out of the booth and stood up. "I'll wait in the kitchen and take my dinner with me. You can sit here by yourself. That way you'll get to spend time with your very favorite person in the whole world. My guess is it won't be a new experience for you."

I started to storm out, but Susan stood up and grabbed my arm. "Please," she said, desperation in her voice. "Please don't go. I'm sorry. If you'll just let me explain. . ."

I had no intention of falling for that again, but as I tried to wrestle my arm out of her strong grip, I heard a voice that seemed to come from inside me. It was so loud, I looked around to see if someone nearby had actually said it. I clearly heard, *"Don't go."* That was it. Two words. *Don't go.* I took my other hand and pried her fingers off my arm. Then I sat back down.

"Okay," I said in a low voice. "But this is it, lady. I mean it. Knock it off."

I was shocked to see tears streaming down her face, and I started to feel like a heel. *Wait just a minute*, I told myself sternly. *She's the one who was nasty and hateful. Why am I chastising myself?*

"I—I just found out today that my husband is seeing another woman," Susan said between sobs. "Someone from our church. Can you believe that? Someone I thought was my friend."

Rats. Now I was going to feel sorry for her. Not fair. Not fair at all. "I'm sorry, Susan. I really am." That not only explained her attitude, I now understood the comment about Christians. I reached out and put my hand over hers. "Look, I'm not an expert about this kind of thing, but I do know God will help you through it."

She pulled her hand away. "Well He sure didn't take very good care of my husband. If this is the best He can do, I'll take care of myself, thank you."

The words were said quickly, but they were heavy with pain. My previous dislike for the woman turned to compassion. "People make choices," I said gently. "Sometimes they're not God's will at all. He's not a giant puppet master pulling our strings, you know."

She used her napkin to wipe her face. "I thought God controlled everything," she sniffed. "Everything that happens is His will."

I smiled. "Now that really doesn't make sense, does it? If that were true no one would ever go to hell. No one would suffer. Didn't Jesus pray that God's will would be done on the earth as it is in heaven?"

She stared at me for a moment. "I—I guess so."

"You've read what heaven is like, right?"

Looking more composed, she put her napkin back in her lap and glanced around to see if anyone had noticed her outburst. Even if they had, Harmony residents were too kind to let her know it. No one appeared to be paying any attention. "To be quite honest, Gracie, I don't know much about the Bible. Our minister says it's just a nice guide, but it doesn't mean much today."

Wow. One of those. I prayed quickly and quietly for help. "I don't believe that, Susan. The Bible is God's Word to us. His love letter, if you will. His Word is spirit and life. Not just words on a page."

"So you believe in heaven?"

"Yes, with all my heart. And just like it says in the Bible, it's a wonderful place without pain, sadness, death, or sickness."

She sighed so deeply, she sounded like a big balloon losing all its air. "So you're saying that this world isn't like heaven because people make poor decisions?"

I nodded. "That started a long time ago when a man and woman named Adam and Eve made some really bad choices. God gave them the right to do it though, because He wants us to be His children, not His robots."

She stared down at the table for a moment while she made circles with her finger on the surface. "So it's really not God's fault that my husband made the choice he did."

"No, Susan. It's your husband's fault. God loves you so much. He'll comfort and support you through this if you'll let Him. And if your marriage can be saved, He'll help you with that, too."

"You—you seem to really know God," she said, another tear rolling down her cheek. She picked up her napkin once again and dabbed at it.

"Well, not as much as I want to, but I'm working on it. What about you?"

Her grief-filled eyes locked onto mine. "The way He's presented in my church, He feels so far away. Like someone I know *about* but not someone I really *know*. Does that make any sense?"

I nodded. Here I thought I came to meet with this woman so

we could talk about Hannah and her parents, and now it looked like I was going to lead her to the Lord. Life is weird. I couldn't help but wonder what would have happened if I hadn't listened to that voice telling me to keep my rear end stuck in this booth. I took a deep breath and began to tell her about the great exchange. The life that Jesus died to give us—one free of sin and full of forgiveness. I explained that knowing who Jesus is isn't enough. We must know why He came and what He did for us. Then we must accept the exchange of our sinful life for His righteous one. I also told her that God has a plan for each of us. A wonderful plan that He formed before we were born. Not only can we find forgiveness and acceptance but we can also discover His personally crafted path made just for us.

"I want that new life, Gracie," Susan said, her voice breaking. "I need forgiveness, and I want to find out what kind of life God has for me. I'm tired and unhappy. My way isn't working at all. I want His way."

Right then and there we bowed our heads and prayed together. Susan asked Jesus to forgive her and promised to live every day of her life for Him if He would come into her life. By the time we finished, we were both crying. And Leah, who waited until we were finished, had tears in her eyes as well when she returned to our table. She put our plates in front of us and then leaned over and gave Susan a big hug. I tried to hold my breath, afraid of making this odd hiccup noise that happens when I get too emotional. Unfortunately, although I tried my hardest not to let it out, it showed up anyway. This of course, sent Susan and Leah into gales of uncontrolled giggles. I could feel my face get hot, and I looked around the now-crowded restaurant to find the other customers staring at us. But instead of looking at us like we'd lost our minds, they were smiling.

I guess most of them realized what had just happened. All I could do was shake my head. Being a Christian is certainly not boring.

"What was that noise?" Susan finally asked when she could breathe again and Leah had left the table.

"I'm not really sure. I've had it ever since I was a kid. Unfortunately."

She chuckled. "It's so funny."

"Yeah, thanks."

"Oh Gracie, if I can get saved in a diner, in front of all these people, you can certainly get over making a weird noise."

She had a point. "Okay, I guess that's fair." After praying over our food, I dug into my fruit salad. It was delicious. Flavorful chunks of apples, oranges, blueberries, and bananas mixed with strawberry slices and walnuts. And to go with it, the best banana bread I'd ever tasted. It was still warm from the oven. Hector was an artist in the kitchen, and Harmony was blessed to have him. Although I was certain seeing Susan ushered into the family of God had helped to make everything, including my salad, seem much sweeter.

Susan took a bite of her chicken. Her eyes widened with surprise. "Oh my goodness," she said after swallowing. "This is the best fried chicken I've ever had. Even better than my grandmother's."

"Not bad for a greasy spoon, huh?" I said with a wink.

She smiled. "Sorry about that. I've been so upset all day. When I got to Harmony, I was looking for someone to unload on. Then I saw the way the people dressed, and for some reason it made me even angrier. I don't know why." She stared past me for a few moments. "I—I guess I was mad at God, and seeing these people. . .well, I decided to take it out on them."

"But then you met Abel and Emily."

"But then I met Abel and Emily," she repeated softly. "The love of God just flowed out of them, and I knew I didn't feel what they felt. My relationship with God wasn't like theirs. It confused me." She studied me closely. "I really do want to talk to you about this situation with Hannah, but to be honest, I think I searched you out because I knew I needed help. I couldn't talk to the Muellers since I'm investigating them. But they said so many wonderful things about you, as did several other people I spoke to, I just knew somehow you were the person I could reach out to."

I put my fork down. "Well, I'm not sure why anyone would be saying nice things about me. I'm the one who took Hannah to Wichita. That trip seemed to set this whole thing off."

She shook her head. "I don't think so. I spoke with the Vogler boy. . .Jonathan? He said Hannah was on her way to see him when she disappeared."

My mouth dropped open. "Wait a minute. Do you mean she was only going to meet with Jonathan? She wasn't running away?"

Susan shook her head. "No. According to Jonathan, she wanted to show him her new outfit, and they were going to try to figure out what she should do next. But she never said anything to him about leaving home before school was over."

My heart dropped to my feet. "Sheriff Taylor talked to Jonathan, but the boy didn't tell him that Hannah was going to meet him that night."

"I know. Jonathan said he was afraid of the sheriff so he kept that to himself. But when I talked to him myself, he came clean because he's so worried about her."

"Oh Susan. I've been trying to tell Pat that she didn't run away, but he wouldn't believe me. You know about the woman in Topeka who was found dead?"

Susan nodded and took a bite of her mashed potatoes. "Wow,

delicious." She pointed her fork at me. "Yes, the story's all over the news. Why? Do you think Hannah's disappearance is related?"

"I don't know, but I think it's possible."

Susan seemed to mull over this information. "It sounds like Hannah's case should be carefully investigated."

I agreed with her, even more convinced that Hannah could be in serious trouble. We ate quietly for a while until I broke the silence.

"Susan, I'd like to ask you a question."

She nodded.

"It's about the reason you came to Harmony."

"Well, we almost always follow up complaints filed by someone in the community."

"Can you tell me who called you about Hannah?"

She shook her head. "Sorry, that's confidential. I will tell you that it's someone who claims to know the family."

I frowned at her. "I'll bet anything it was Esther Crenshaw. Just so you know, Esther's a busybody who's always causing trouble."

She didn't confirm my suspicions, but a quick look of recognition at Esther's name told me everything I needed to know.

"Don't worry about it," she said. "I intend to report that there's no evidence of any kind of abuse. Right now, I'm more concerned about this serial killer thing."

"Me, too. Is there anything you can do to get someone to take Hannah's disappearance more seriously?"

She chewed and swallowed another bite of chicken. "I think so. We work with the KBI frequently. Let me see if I can get someone to look into it."

I reached across the table and squeezed her arm. "Oh thank you, Susan. I'm so grateful."

She shrugged. "You save my soul, I ask someone to take a

closer look into a missing child case. Seems fair."

"*I* didn't actually save your soul, but at this point, I'll take any help I can get."

We both laughed. I focused on my food, and Susan did the same. Between bites, she told me how she'd gotten involved with helping children. Her own childhood had been anything but ideal. Even as a little girl, she'd dreamed of helping other children escape the pain she'd endured. I knew that many abused children have a hard time trusting a God who calls Himself a Father if their earthly father was cruel. Susan's road wasn't going to be easy, but I truly believed she would be okay. Now that she and God were walking together, He could bring real healing and restoration into her life. Beauty for ashes. I purposed in my heart to keep her in my daily prayers. Sometimes healing can be painful. Facing our fears isn't always easy.

After scooping up my last juicy bite of apple, I asked, "So what will you do about your husband and your friend?"

She rested her chin on her hand and stared at me. "I have no idea, but I think I'll take some time off work and get away by myself for a while. God and I need to spend some quality time together. If I immerse myself in His presence, and in His Word, maybe I'll know what to do next."

"Do you mind if I ask you how you found out your husband was cheating?"

"No, I don't mind." She looked down at her plate. I got the feeling she was trying to screw up her courage. "My supposed friend came to me and told me about it. She insisted I give Brad up. She tried to convince me that it was God's will. That they're supposed to be together, and that our marriage is a mistake they're trying to correct."

"Susan, God doesn't work that way. He doesn't condone

adultery, and He hates divorce."

She frowned at me. "So if I decide to leave my husband, God will hate me?"

Her question hurt me down deep inside. "Absolutely not. God will never, ever hate you. Never. It's not possible. He loves you, and He'll love you every single day of your life. No matter what you do."

"But does He want me to stay with Brad?"

"I can't answer that. I'm sure God will heal your marriage if that's what you both want. But God doesn't expect you to stay in an adulterous relationship. If you want to stay, I guess it's going to be up to Brad."

Susan was quiet, and I felt I should also be silent and allow her to think things through. As Sam had pointed out, I'm not Holy Spirit junior.

Leah came to pick up our plates. "How about dessert?"

Susan started to say no, but I told her about Hector's cobbler. We sent Leah to the kitchen to bring us back some cobbler, along with a pot of coffee.

"I'll have to diet for a week to make up for this dinner," Susan said as we waited.

"Keeping my weight under control is a constant battle in Harmony. My only hope is working out in the orchards with my fiancé. It's a better workout than what I used to get in the gym."

Susan asked some questions about my life, so I told her about my upcoming wedding and shared a little about the kinds of freelance jobs I was doing. My description of trying to send work over a dial-up Internet line made her laugh. She had a few questions about the conservative Mennonites who live in Harmony, and I explained their way of life to her the best I could. She seemed to understand. I noticed that she carefully steered our conversation away from her personal life during the rest of our time together. That was okay with me. She'd already shared a lot with someone who was really a stranger. We finished up our visit pleasantly, and when we parted company outside the restaurant, she vowed to see what she could do on her end to get more KBI interest in the search for Hannah. She also gave me her card and made me promise to keep in touch with her.

I stood outside by my car as she drove away, heading back to Topeka. Thankfully, a nice breeze made the heat almost bearable. I'd just started to open the door when I noticed a red truck parked on the other side of the street. A sticker was attached to the back bumper. I closed the door and ran across the street to get a closer look. Even though it was getting dark, a nearby street lamp made the image clear. I stepped back into the shadows as someone came out of one of the stores and got into the truck. Rufus Ludwig started the engine and drove away. I stared at his bumper sticker as he passed by me.

I could clearly see the image on the sticker as I watched him disappear down Main Street. A big, black bear.

Chapter Fourteen

I woke up Wednesday morning after a night full of bad dreams. My worst nightmare was easy to interpret. Hannah in the back of a red truck, calling for help. A bear chasing after her and gaining ground. I woke up from the first round of dreams, my body drenched in sweat.

Sleeping on the floor in the living room certainly wasn't as comfortable as my bed. I pretended it was just fine, though, because I knew my father would feel badly if he thought I hadn't rested well.

I'd called Sam when I got home and told him about Rufus's truck. He sounded interested but not alarmed. Then I called Pat and gave him the lowdown on Rufus and repeated what Susan told me about Jonathan. Pat was more than a little angry that the boy hadn't been honest with him about meeting Hannah, but my hope that this information might convince him that Hannah had been abducted was dashed.

"This still doesn't prove she didn't take off on her own, Gracie," he said gruffly.

I sighed with frustration. "But you have to admit that she obviously wasn't planning to run away when she left home. She didn't tell Jonathan about it. And what about the fact that none of her clothes were missing?"

"I considered the clothing. But if she was leaving her Mennonite roots behind, I figure she wouldn't take any of those long dresses anyway."

"Look, Pat. There's no reason to believe she was planning to leave Harmony that night. Please, just keep an open mind, okay?"

"I believe I am. I think I proved that when I talked to the KBI about Hannah. You need to give them time to do their jobs."

"Okay, okay. What about Rufus's truck?"

"I'll look into it. I doubt seriously that Rufus is the man we're looking for, but the last thing I need you to do right now is to make him suspicious. Stay away from him," he warned. "Do you understand me, Gracie?"

After giving him my promise more than once to mind my own business, I hung up the phone. I tried to focus instead on my plans for the day, but it wasn't easy. I prayed Rufus wouldn't get apprehensive and try to run. I also prayed that Pat would move quickly. We couldn't take a chance on losing the only suspect we had.

After a hearty breakfast, we all planned to go to Sam's. Dad and Sam intended to tour the orchards and get to know each other better, a proposal Sam found slightly terrifying, while Mom and I went over wedding plans with Sweetie. I'd told Pat where I'd be so he could keep me posted on Rufus. Hannah had been gone two days now, although it seemed much longer.

I cooked a big breakfast of scrambled eggs, bacon, and toast, and then Mom and I cleaned up the kitchen.

"Dad and Papa took baths last night," Mom said as she put

the last of the clean dishes away. "Do I have time to take a quick bath myself?"

"We're not due at Sweetie's until two," I said. "There's plenty of time." I looked up at the clock on the kitchen wall. "I think I'll drive over to Abel and Emily's and see how they're doing. Do you think Dad can keep an eye on Papa?"

My mother laughed. "Asking your father to watch over any member of his family is like asking a mother hen to guard her eggs. It's part of his nature. Just let him know you're going."

I hung up the dish towel on the rack and went off to find Dad. He and Papa were on the front porch. Papa rocked in the rocking chair while my father sat on the top step drinking his coffee. I knew he felt nostalgic here, remembering his boyhood. For a moment it struck me as rather odd that thirty years after leaving Harmony, he and Mom were finally back. But now his daughter lived in the house he'd grown up in, and he was a man, taking care of the father who'd once taken care of him. I stood in the doorway and watched them for a while before I said anything, touched by an odd feeling of enchantment I couldn't explain. I just knew I didn't want it to pass me by too quickly.

"Think I'll run into town," I finally said, keeping my voice soft so as not to frighten Papa.

Dad cranked his head around and smiled at me. "Sounds good. Have you asked Ida if she'd like to come with us today?"

Man, I'd been thinking so much about Hannah and her situation, I'd almost forgotten about Ida. "You know, I haven't. I'll go call her right now. She'd probably enjoy being part of the wedding plans."

Papa grunted. "Weddings were simple affairs in our day. The bride wore a blue dress. The groom wore a black suit. Then after the ceremony there was a banquet with singing and storytelling.

The first night, the couple stayed with the bride's parents. And after that, they visited the homes of other relatives and friends who attended the wedding. There were no wedding rings and few if any flowers."

I pushed the screen door open and came out on the porch. "You weren't at Mom and Dad's wedding, were you?"

Papa took my hand, and I sat down on the porch rail next to him. "No," he said shaking his head. "We wanted them to get out of town and away from Harmony. You know, we should have followed them. It's one of the greatest regrets of my life—and of Essie's, too. But we were conflicted back then. Even though we believed Daniel and Beverly belonged together and we encouraged them to leave, we also felt we couldn't just up and go with them. We thought being submissive to our bishop was being submissive to God. We were wrong. Our bishop was the one who wasn't submissive to God. It took several years for us to see it."

"But you encouraged us to go, Papa," Dad said. "And gave us enough money to get started. You have nothing to feel badly about. You and Mama were wonderful parents. Always."

Papa didn't say anything, just kept rocking in the warm July morning air, holding my hand.

"So what did Mom wear when you got married?" I asked my father. "She told me once it was just a plain dress because it was all she had."

"She wore my mother's dress," Dad said with a smile. "Dark-blue linen that brought out the color in her eyes." He sighed. "She was the most beautiful thing I'd ever seen. We were married in the home of a Mennonite pastor and his wife, friends of my parents who left Harmony before we did. We stayed the night with them, and they treated us like their own children."

"Owen and Darlene Papke," Papa said. "Two of the finest

people I ever knew."

"They live in Florida now," Dad said. "We still exchange Christmas cards and call each other at least twice a year. They mean the world to your mother and me."

"What dress will you wear at your wedding?" Papa asked.

"I bought one while I was in Wichita. It's lovely. White, with embroidered flowers around the neckline."

"Look, Gracie," my father said slowly, "maybe I should warn you. Your mother actually brought the blue dress with her—just in case you wanted to wear it. But she fully understands that you may have something totally different in mind. So be prepared when she brings it up, but don't feel pressured. You know your mother. She's the most sentimental person I've ever known, but she also loves you more than her own life. The blue dress is only here in case you want it. You're under no obligation whatsoever to wear it."

I was a little stunned. An old blue linen dress? For my wedding? "Thanks for the heads up, Dad. I'll just tell her I already have a dress. I'm sure she'll understand."

"Of course she will, Snicklefritz. Don't worry about it."

I let go of Papa's hand, got up, and kissed him on the cheek. "I'll get you both some more coffee. Then I'm going to call Ida and head over to the Muellers for a visit. I'll be back in plenty of time to go to Sam's."

I took their cups and got them both fresh, hot coffee, and then I called Ida. She was thrilled to be included in the wedding plans. I thought about calling Abel and Emily, but I was afraid they wouldn't let me come, and I was determined to see them, even if Emily was still angry with me. To get to their house, I had to drive through the middle of town, right past Ludwig's Meats. I realized why I hadn't noticed the bumper sticker on Rufus's truck sooner.

831

He always backed his truck up to the store so he could unload new purchases of meat from local ranchers. Unless I walked down the sidewalk in front of his business, I couldn't possibly see the back of his truck.

I drove past the church, but Abel and Emily's car wasn't there. During the week, Abel could usually be found in his church office, but since Hannah left, he and Emily spent most of their time at home in case she showed up. Sure enough, I found their car sitting in its usual place at their house. Gathering up my courage, I parked behind it and walked to the front door. I waited awhile before knocking, butterflies beating their wings furiously inside my stomach. A few moments later the door opened. Abel smiled when he saw me.

"Oh Gracie," he said. "How nice of you to come by." He hesitated and glanced away from the door. After a moment he turned back to me. "Please, come in."

"I don't want to upset Emily," I said quietly. "Is—is it okay?"

He put his big, meaty hand on my shoulder. "Of course. She'll be glad to see you."

I wasn't so sure about that, but I walked into the house anyway. "Have you heard anything, Abel?"

The big pastor shut the door behind me. "Nothing. Not a word." He pointed toward the interior of the house. "Emily and Jonathan Vogler are on the back porch.

"Jonathan? I hear Hannah was on her way to meet him when she disappeared."

Abel nodded. "Yes, we just found that out recently. Jonathan's parents sent him here to explain what happened. We've just started talking to him. Why don't you join us? Maybe you can add some insight to our conversation."

I followed him, but I wasn't certain I'd be able to help much.

When we entered the lovely enclosed back porch, Emily's favorite room, I was shocked by her gaunt appearance. Her haunted eyes locked on mine. I winced at the pain I saw there and waited for her to rebuke me for coming. But she didn't. Instead she rose and put her arms out.

"I'm so sorry I blamed you for causing Hannah to leave us," she said. "You've been a wonderful friend. I've just been so frightened." She raised her face from my shoulder. "I—I can't sleep at night. I don't know where she is or what's happening to her, Gracie." A shudder racked her frail body. "I don't know how much more of this I can take."

I wanted to comfort her. I wanted to tell her everything would be all right—that all we could do is trust God to take care of Hannah. It was the truth, but for some reason I felt she would take it as a rebuke. I didn't want to sound judgmental or sanctimonious. As I held her I sought heaven. What could I do to help? Again, just like at the restaurant, a voice spoke to me sweetly and softly. When Emily released me, I led her back to the chair where she'd been sitting.

"Abel," I said, "I wonder if you'd read the ninety-first Psalm to us? It's so comforting, and I think it would help now."

"That's a wonderful idea, Gracie," he said in his deep, re-assuring voice. I knew his emotions were as raw as Emily's, but as the man of the house, he was working hard to maintain a calm exterior for his distraught wife.

Abel took his Bible from the table next to him, flipped it open, and began to read the comforting scriptures to us. I glanced at Jonathan. His eyes were wide with fear. Perhaps his concern was for Hannah, or perhaps it was for his role in her disappearance. But whatever he was feeling, I watched as he visibly relaxed. Emily's face changed as hope began to ignite a spark inside of her. The wonderful words became life in that room. They encouraged us to trust God, to make Him our refuge. Emily took a deep breath as Abel read that God has given His angels charge over us—to keep us in all our ways. And as Abel finished the psalm, the promise that God will be with us in trouble and deliver us when we call on Him, filled the atmosphere around us as if God Himself had just made us a personal promise. I could tell I wasn't the only one who felt it.

Abel closed the Bible and gazed lovingly at his wife. "Emily, I know that Hannah will return to us. I believe it with all my heart. God has spoken to us today."

For the first time since I'd come into the room, Emily smiled. She wiped her wet eyes with the tissue in her hand. "I feel it, too," she said in her quiet voice. "No, it's more than just a feeling. I believe it in my heart." She looked at me. "Thank you, Gracie. God has used you to bring us comfort. Hannah will be all right."

I believed it, too, but I also felt an urgency in my spirit. Time was of the essence. I silently asked God to show me whatever I needed to know. Whatever I needed to see in my efforts to help bring Hannah home.

"We were just talking to Jonathan about the night Hannah went missing," Abel said. He turned his attention to the young boy. "Would you please start over, Jonathan? I'd like Gracie to hear everything."

Jonathan was dressed in jeans and a plain, blue shirt. I noticed that his shirt had no buttons but instead was closed with hooks and eyes. This was an Old Order style that not many Mennonites wore anymore. His long chestnut hair hung longer than most boys his age, and his large dark eyes were fastened on Abel. He was a handsome boy, and I could see why Hannah was attracted to him.

He cleared his throat, obviously nervous. "L–like I said, sir, she told me during the day, after church, that she wanted to see me that night." He hung his head. "We'd met a few times at night before she left town. We shouldn't have done it. I know it was wrong. I—I'm so sorry. Maybe if I'd said no. . ."

"Never mind, son," Abel said gently. "I'm tired of hearing how everyone blames themselves for what happened. The truth is that Hannah chose to sneak out of our house. Her decision put her in danger. I know you would never have done anything to hurt my daughter."

The boy's eyes filled with tears. "It's true, sir. Hannah means a great deal to me. If I can do anything to help. . ."

"You should have told the sheriff about this when he questioned you," I said, not bothering to keep the edge of anger I felt out of my voice.

"I—I know. I was just so scared when he showed up. I'm trying to make up for that."

"Just finish your story," I said. "And this time, please don't keep anything back. Maybe you'll tell us something that will help us to find her."

He nodded and swiped at his eyes. "Hannah told me to meet her at our special place." He looked at me shamefacedly. "We used to meet in a clearing behind your house. You know, where they found that body."

My mouth dropped open. "Why would you want to get together there?" I remembered that my mother and father used to meet at the same spot when they were young. What was so special about that clearing?

"It's so beautiful," the boy said. "There's a place where you can sit and see the lake, but no one can see you. The trees hide you. And besides, it's halfway between our houses. It only takes us about twenty minutes to walk to it."

I looked over at Emily who had gone pale. This was the same spot where she used to sit and gaze out at the lake before she was raped by the man who was later buried there. The memory of that pain must be assailing her now, at a time she didn't need to be thinking about it. She met my eyes, smiled bravely, and visibly gathered herself together.

"Go on, Jonathan," she said. "How often did you meet there?"

He shrugged. "Several times before she left for Wichita. Maybe five or six times. We would just sit and talk." He hung his head. "I could talk to Hannah about anything. She understands how I feel about...well, everything."

"So that night, the night she disappeared, you went to this same spot?" I asked.

At my question, his eyes grew large. "No. That's just it. My father and I worked hard in the fields that day. It was so hot, and I was so tired, I couldn't stay awake. I didn't wake up until the next morning." He stared at Abel. "If only I'd gone, I could have saved her."

I thought about the place I'd found the bracelet. It was about a mile away from my house, but it was on the road to Jonathan's.

"Would Hannah have tried to walk to your house if you didn't show up?" I asked the upset young man.

He thought about it for a moment. "I—I don't know. I don't think so. We'd told each other that if something should happen, if our parents weren't sound asleep when we were supposed to leave, we should just forget it. If one of us didn't show up, the other one was supposed to go home."

This information sure didn't explain how Hannah's bracelet got to where I'd found it. "Did she say what she wanted to talk to you about?"

He nodded. "She said she had something to show me. Some new clothes she got in Wichita."

"Anything else?"

"Yes. She had a gift for me. Something someone gave to her that she wanted me to have."

I picked up my purse and dug around in it until I found what I wanted. "Is this what she planned to give you?" I held up the bracelet I'd found on the road.

He shrugged. "I don't know. She didn't tell me. She did say it was something I couldn't wear in public. That I'd have to keep it a secret."

"It has to be this bracelet," I said to Abel. "She didn't bring anything else back that I know of." I showed him the spacers that declared *Love*, *Friend*, and *Forever*. "I think she meant this as a way to tell Jonathan how she felt about him."

Abel took the bracelet from my hand. "But how did you get it?"

I took a deep breath and told him about finding it on the road and how I was certain it was a message from Hannah to let us know she was taken against her will. I knew the knowledge wouldn't comfort her parents, but I believed they needed to know the truth. About everything. When I finished telling them about the bracelet, I made a quick decision to spill my guts about the rest of it.

When I finished, Abel was silent. "The sheriff told us about the girl who was murdered, but he assured us that it had nothing at all to do with Hannah."

"He might be right, but I think we need to consider it. The most important thing is that we realize she's in trouble. Finding the bracelet where I did, and the fact that it was closed, is an indication that Hannah was trying to send us a message."

"Someone told me that the girl in Topeka was kept alive for several days before she was killed," Abel said, his voice trembling. "So if this is true, and if Hannah was abducted by this man, she might still be alive?"

"Yes. That's why it's so necessary for us to find her as quickly as possible."

"But why did Sheriff Taylor tell us Hannah wasn't abducted?" Emily said, her hands clasped together so tightly her knuckles were white. "He keeps assuring us that she's just run away and that he'll find her."

"Because he really believes that," I said. "I tried to tell him that he might be wrong, but he hasn't listened to me. The good news is that he's finally contacted the KBI about Hannah. And Susan Murphy is also going to get in touch with them."

"Mrs. Murphy? The social worker?" Abel looked puzzled. "Why would she help us? She seems committed to taking Hannah away from us when she comes home."

"She's not going to do anything like that," I reassured them. "She and I had a long talk, and she thinks you're great parents. She's trying to help us find Hannah, too."

The Muellers were silent. I knew I wasn't supposed to tell them about the serial killer theory, but I couldn't help it. I felt time was of the essence.

"I don't like being kept in the dark about my daughter's disappearance," Abel said. "Sheriff Taylor should be giving us this information, not you, Gracie. I think we need to ask him to come over here and speak to us. If there's anything else. . ."

"There is," I said. I felt like someone had opened the floodgates. A part of me tried to hold back, but I couldn't seem to control myself. I told them about the red truck and the bumper sticker. Then I told them about Rufus.

Abel jumped to his feet. "You're telling me that this man may have my little girl?" His face was red with anger. "Why hasn't the sheriff looked into this? You told him this last night?"

"Yes, and he's probably checking it out now," I said, flustered by his reaction. "It's important that we let him do his job. If we tip Rufus off too soon, we might not find Hannah."

I stood up and tried to grab Abel's arm. He shook me off. "Nonsense," he growled. "I'm going over there now and get my daughter." He pointed at Emily. "You stay here. I'll call you as soon as I can." With that, he stormed out of the house.

I jumped up and ran to the phone in the hallway, fear squeezing my chest. I called the sheriff's department in Council Grove. Pat wasn't in the office, but they patched me through to the radio in his car.

Thankfully, he picked up right away. I quickly explained the situation. After bawling me out profusely, he hung up. He'd just left Harmony but promised to turn around and hightail it to Rufus's shop. After a quick word to Emily and Jonathan, I ran out to my car and took off after Abel. His car wasn't even in sight. By the time I got to downtown Harmony and parked in front of Ludwig's Meats, Abel was already inside the shop. I jumped out of my car and pushed open the front door. As I did, I saw Pat's patrol car speeding up the street. He almost ran into a horse and buggy that had pulled out from the curb. He squealed his brakes and swerved to avoid a collision. Then he slid up next to my car, jumping out and pointing at me. I figured he was trying to tell me to stay out of the store, but I couldn't let something bad happen because I'd shot my mouth off before I should have. I pushed the front door open and ran into the main shop area. Abel was there all right, and he had Rufus in a headlock. The frightened man was trying to say something, but no words came out of his mouth. Probably because Abel was cutting off his air supply.

The door swung open behind me and Pat rushed past. "Abel, let him go!" he yelled.

"He has Hannah," Abel cried. "He has my little girl!!"

Pat grabbed Abel's arms and pulled. "No, he doesn't," he shouted. "Abel, Rufus had nothing to do with Hannah's disappearance. He wasn't even in town the night she went missing."

Abel didn't seem to hear Pat. He just held on to Rufus who was beginning to gasp frantically for air.

"Abel! Listen to me," Pat said loudly, putting himself only inches from the enraged father's face. "Rufus doesn't have Hannah. He doesn't. You've got the wrong man."

Finally, Abel's grip seemed to loosen a bit. I heard Rufus take a deep breath. Then he began to struggle, trying to get out of Abel's arms.

Pat pulled hard and finally forced Abel to loosen his grip. The meat store owner dropped to the floor and then half-crawled and half-scurried to the other side of the room. Pat held on to Abel for dear life. Then he pushed him up against the counter, pinning his arms behind him.

"Abel, I checked Rufus out right after Gracie told me about the truck. He told me he spent the night with his sister in Topeka and then picked up a new freezer Monday morning before driving back to Harmony. I checked out his story first thing this morning. It's all true. He wasn't even in town the night Hannah disappeared. He didn't get back until the next morning." He turned and glared at me. "And it might interest you to know that the other murders associated with the serial killer you're so interested in couldn't have been committed by Rufus because he was in the army—and in Iraq during the last two. Before that, he lived all the way across the country from where the other killings occurred. And his bumper sticker is about the Chicago Bears, the football team? Rufus is from Illinois. Gracie, I asked you to keep quiet about this. Do you see what your interference has caused? What if Abel had seriously hurt this man?"

My lips couldn't form a response. He was right. It was my fault. I'd jumped the gun and had almost caused a tragedy. I turned around and fled the building. Then I drove home as quickly as I could, determined to keep my nose out of anything further having to do with Hannah Mueller. I almost ran off the road several times because I couldn't see through the tears that flooded my eyes.

Chapter Fifteen

Although I didn't want to explain to my family what I'd done, it was obvious I was upset when I came in the door. Mom and Dad took me into the kitchen and sat me down at the table so Papa couldn't hear us. After I spilled out the whole story, my mother scooted her chair over next to mine and held out her arms. I fell into them.

"Honey," she said in a soothing voice, "you were trying to help. Your zeal to find Hannah overcame your sense of discretion. It happens. Especially to someone like you who cares so much. Pat will understand, and so will Abel. You need to forgive yourself." She held my tear-stained face in her hands and looked deeply into my eyes. "Your concern for others is one of the qualities that makes you so special. You meant no harm, you just wanted to rescue Hannah if there was any way possible."

I nodded but couldn't stop crying. "I really did. But Mom, you should have seen Abel. I didn't know he could get so angry. I thought Mennonites were supposed to be peaceful."

My father chuckled. "Snicklefritz, I don't care who Abel is,

842

he's a father. He saw the chance to save his daughter, and he went for it." Dad reached over and stroked my arm. "He did the same thing you did. He reacted out of his emotion. Trust me, he's just as sorry as you are. Maybe even more so. He's not blaming you right now. He's blaming himself."

"Re—really?" Somehow knowing that Abel had messed up, too, made me feel a little better.

As my parents tried to comfort me, the phone rang. My dad left the kitchen and went into the living room to answer it. A few minutes later, he returned. By then, my mother had fixed me a meat loaf sandwich and a tall glass of milk. Comfort food, but it helped. Somehow I couldn't be too upset munching on a meat loaf sandwich. The ketchup on top combined in a weird way with the mayo my mother had slathered on the thick pieces of white bread. It was delicious.

"That was Pat," Dad said when he came back into the kitchen. "He said to tell you everything is all right. Abel apologized to Rufus who took it pretty well considering. Pat's on his way here."

"No!" I exclaimed, spitting out a good chunk of meat loaf onto the kitchen table. "I don't want to talk to him." Listening to him yell at me was the last thing I wanted to endure right now.

"Gracie, he just wants to make sure you're okay. He's not mad. In fact, he said to tell you he understands."

That sure didn't sound like something Pat would say. But I couldn't see my father joining forces with Pat against me. Maybe it was his job to hold me down while Pat took out his revolver and ended my trail of terror. "Whatever," I said finally. "But I've had all the conflict I can take for one day."

"Speaking of today, what time are we leaving for Sam's?" Dad asked.

"We're supposed to be there by two." Then something struck

me. "What about Papa? Will he be able to come?"

"He's still pretty sore," Mom said. "I'm staying here with him. You and Sweetie go over the wedding plans by yourselves. You can tell me all about it when you get home, and then we'll all get together again in a few days. This will give us time to talk about everything and see if you want any changes."

"Wait a minute," I said, shaking my head. "You're the mother. Your part in the planning is crucial. Maybe I could. . ."

"Stay here?" she said with a smile. "Sorry. I think the bride needs to be present." She came over and hugged me. "It's okay, sweetie. Really. Dad wants to get to know Sam a little better, and you need to hear what Sweetie's come up with so far. I'm really not necessary this time around. Besides, I love spending time with Papa. Once you make the big decisions, I'll help with the details."

I chewed and swallowed the last bite of my sandwich, not certain my mother was really happy to be stuck at home. But I had little choice. Since my father was determined to talk to Sam today, she seemed to be the only person available to watch Papa.

"Okay, I guess," I said slowly. "But I still think you should be going."

"Why don't you see if Sweetie can come over here Friday for lunch?" Mom said. "I'll fix us all something and that way no one will have to stay home alone with Papa. And I'm sure he'd love to see Sweetie again."

"That sounds good." A loud knock on the door made me jump. Pat. I was extremely embarrassed by my actions and had no idea how I could face him. If Rufus really had been involved in Hannah's situation, I could have scared him away. I'd spoken out of turn and did so after Pat had trusted me with information I should have kept confidential. From now on, I was pretty sure he'd never tell me anything he didn't want the whole world to know. And how was I ever going to face Rufus? I might never be able to set foot in downtown Harmony again.

My father started to get up.

"You stay off that leg, Dad. I'll get it." Reluctantly I went to open the front door, but before I had the chance, Pat pushed it open and came in. I didn't say anything, just stood there, waiting for the inevitable.

"That was quite a scene," Pat said, his expression solemn. "I guess I don't really need to say anything about what happened, do I?"

"No. I'm sorry. I just got so...so..."

"Enthusiastic?" he finished for me.

"I was going to say manic, but enthusiastic sounds better."

"Pat, have a seat," my dad said pointing to the rocking chair. Papa was on the couch, sound asleep, so I stood next to my father who sat in a chair across from Pat.

"Just wanted you to know that the situation is under control," Pat said. "Rufus survived, and Abel has calmed down. He's thoroughly appalled by his actions."

"Mennonites are taught to live at peace with everyone," my father said. "He must be extremely upset about the way he treated Rufus."

Pat shrugged. "Most of the cases I'm called out on have to do with families who can't get along. For all his religion, seems Pastor Mueller didn't do much better than anyone else."

I looked over at my dad who frowned at Pat. Were we going to get into a debate on religion? I'd been praying for Pat for months, but I wanted the Holy Spirit to prepare the ground of his heart before I tried to sow seed. Right now, his heart seemed too hard to receive the love of God. My father must have sensed the same thing because he stayed quiet. Not the way my volatile father usually did things. I was very well aware of where my "enthusiasm" came from.

"So now what?" I asked. "Maybe Rufus isn't the killer. But someone has Hannah. We've got to find her before it's too late."

Pat raised one eyebrow and stared at me. "Well, with your friend Susan Murphy bugging the KBI, we may end up with too much attention focused on Hannah. I'd rather have avoided that."

"What are you talking about?" I asked with fervor. "We need all the attention we can get. Time is running out!"

Pat shook his head. "If Hannah has been taken by a stranger, and I'm emphasizing the word *if*, the more activity you stir up, the more likely he is to take off or kill her. But I don't suppose you thought of that, did you, Miss Marple?"

I stared at him with my mouth open. "Why did you call me that? Sam is the only one..." I pointed at him. "You got that from Sam, didn't you?"

"I plead the fifth." He stood to his feet. "Now you listen to me, Gracie Temple," he said, his eyebrows knit together so tightly they looked like a unibrow. "Under no circumstances whatsoever are you to put your pretty little nose into this investigation again. And I'm as serious as I can be about this. Believe it or not, I actually know what I'm doing. I realize you don't believe it, but it's true nonetheless." Pat looked at my father. "Can I enlist your help to keep her concentration focused on her upcoming wedding instead of my case?"

"Your case?" I sputtered. "You said there wasn't any case. You said Hannah ran away. You said..."

"What I *said* was that I'd take care of it," Pat said sternly. "I've been listening to you. If you can remember just a couple of hours ago, during the ruckus you caused at the meat store, I told you I'd followed up on your information about Rufus, remember?"

I thought about it for a moment. "I—I guess you did."

"Yes, I guess I did. And if you have any more great ideas, I want you to share them with me. But I want you to let *me* take care of checking them out. Am I making myself clear?"

I nodded. "Got it. I'm not looking to cause any more violent confrontations for a while." I studied his face for a few seconds. "Wait a minute, just *when* did Sam tell you about the Miss Marple thing? He certainly didn't do it while I was around."

Pat headed toward the door. He put his hand on the knob and smiled at me. "Well, maybe he told me this morning when we had breakfast."

"You and Sam had breakfast? Are you serious? Does this mean..."

"It means that we may be making some progress." He glared at me. "And I think it will continue unless I have to lock up his fiancée for impeding the course of an investigation."

"I am *not* impeding anything! I've been trying to..." The look on his face brought a quick halt to the rest of my protest.

"Grace Marie..." my father warned.

"Okay, okay," I snapped. "If I have any more bright ideas, I'll contact you first before I do anything about them."

"You promise?" Pat said.

I held my right hand up. "I swear. But please, please, Pat. Do everything you can to find Hannah. I believe she's alive, but we need to locate her soon."

Pat took his hand off the doorknob and his eyes sought mine. "And why are you so sure she's still alive?"

"Because God told us she is."

"God told who, Gracie?" he asked slowly.

"The Muellers and me."

Pat didn't respond, but the look on his face spoke volumes.

"Look, you don't believe in God, but we do. And I'm telling you that God told us she's alive and that she's coming home."

"Then why do you need me?"

I shrugged. "Maybe God wants to show you that He really does exist and that He has a plan for you. Maybe saving Hannah is part of that plan."

Pat shook his head and stared at me like I'd just escaped from a loony bin. I could take his anger, but I really hated to be on the other end of his pity. "Gotta go," he said finally. "Work on your wedding. Stay away from anyone else you think looks like a good suspect."

"I said I would." I could hear the petulance in my voice, but I was tired and disgusted. Mostly with myself.

Pat was halfway out the door when he stopped again. Now what?

"Hey, one other thing. Something that's been bothering me. I need you to tell me who told you about the color of the truck and the odd bumper sticker."

I hadn't wanted to reveal the source of the information, but I no longer cared about protecting secrets. I just wanted Hannah to come home. I told Pat about Bill, carefully going over the conversation I'd had with him at the restaurant. "Why did you want to know?" I asked when I'd finished. "Is it important?"

"No, not really. It's just odd, that's all," Pat said. "No one was supposed to know about it."

"Bill's nephew works for the paper, and he has a friend on the police department." I watched his expression change. Doubt was clearly written on his face. "Do you have some reason to think Bill wasn't telling the truth?"

"Not really. I guess that makes sense, but the police swear no one leaked that information. Just seems weird, that's all." He said good-bye to my dad and told me once more to mind my own business—for good measure, I guess. Then he left.

I started to ask my father if he'd thought Pat's manner was a little odd, when Papa suddenly moaned from the couch. Dad got up and went over to him.

"You okay, Papa?" Dad asked.

"Yes, fine," he answered. "But I need to take a trip to the bathroom, and I'm a little unsteady on my feet. Would you give me a hand, son?"

My father helped Papa up and guided him toward the bathroom. I checked the clock. A little after one. Less than an hour until we were due at Sam's. I sat down at my kitchen table and thought about Pat's interest in the source of my information. Surely he couldn't suspect Bill of anything. He was one of the nicest men in Harmony. Then I remembered Bill's red truck. What if he didn't really have a nephew on the Topeka paper?

My conversation with Pat echoed over and over in my mind. Suddenly I realized how ridiculous my suspicion sounded. Bill Eberly wouldn't hurt a fly. And why in the world was I so focused on men in Harmony anyway? It didn't really make much sense. Pat said the murderer had committed crimes in other states. As far as I knew, Bill had lived here all his life. Jumbled thoughts collided with each other inside me, and I could almost feel my blood pressure rise. Pat was right, I was out of control. Bill Eberly was not and never could be a murderer.

I thought back to the strong sensation back at the Muellers' when Abel read the ninety-first Psalm. I was certain God had reassured us that everything would turn out okay, but I still felt this nervous fear rolling around inside me. A sermon I heard in church popped into my head. It was about God's wisdom being peaceful. Well, I sure didn't feel peaceful. Either I would have to have faith that God was watching over Hannah, or I'd have to follow fear. I chose faith. It took an effort to push the voice of panic away from me, but I made the decision to do it.

"You okay, Snicklefritz?"

My dad's voice startled me. He was helping Papa back onto the couch. "I'm fine, Dad, thanks. How are you feeling, Papa?"

"With my fingers, Gracie," Papa said. He lowered himself gingerly to the couch and my father covered him up with the quilt.

"Can I get you anything?"

"A cup of hot chocolate would be very nice." Papa smiled. "Essie used to make me hot chocolate when I was sick, and it always made me feel better."

"She did the same thing for me," I said. "Right now a cup of cocoa sounds like the perfect prescription for both of us."

My mother came into the room from the basement where she'd been washing clothes. "What's the perfect prescription?" she asked.

"Hot chocolate."

She laughed. "It's almost one hundred degrees outside, and you people want hot chocolate?"

"Hey, sounds good to me," my father said. "It's great anytime and in any weather."

"Well, Gracie Marie," Mom said with a smile, "I think the womenfolk should retire to the kitchen and whip up some cups of hot chocolate. What do you think?"

"I completely agree."

We started toward the kitchen, but I stopped when Papa called out my name. "Hey, Gracie," he said with a grin. "What do you call a cow with no legs?"

My parents joined in and we all said together, "I don't know,

Papa. What do you call a cow with no legs?"

We laughed when he exclaimed, "Ground beef!"

My mother and I worked together to prepare the hot cocoa. Then my family and I spent the next thirty minutes talking and enjoying each other until it was time to pick up Ida and go to Sam's. For just a little while, the world felt normal, and everything seemed to be the way it should be. But there was someone missing. Until Hannah was home, nothing would really be the way it was supposed to be again.

Chapter Sixteen

When we got to Sam's, he was waiting on the front porch. He'd changed his regular work clothes for clean jeans and a light-blue shirt that brought out his blue-gray eyes. I could tell he was nervous, but I had no doubt Sam would win my father over completely. Sam was everything a father could ever want in a son-in-law. He was certainly everything I'd ever dreamed of in a husband. Sam and my dad took off toward the orchard while Ida and I followed Sweetie into the kitchen.

"Been workin' on these plans for a long time," she said when we sat down.

She poured us both a glass of iced tea and put a plate of cookies on the table. Sweetie's coconut pecan cookies. They were out of this world, but I only took two. My wedding dress was tight enough. If I ate too many, I'd never get into it.

"Sorry to dump so much of this on you," I said. "I really appreciate everything you're doing to help me."

"Oh, pshaw," she retorted. "Ain't much work at all. I did expand things a bit, though, since you decided everyone who wanted to come was welcome."

"Expand things, how?" I asked, not sure I wanted to hear the answer.

"Well, I asked Pastor Jensen if we could move the ceremony from the small chapel to the main sanctuary. He said that weren't no problem. 'Course this means we'll need more decorations, but the women's Bible study has taken over all that. They're gonna put big white-ribbon bows on the ends of the pews with purple silk irises in the middle. And you'll carry a bouquet with red carnations, yellow dandelions, and purple irises."

Ida's eyebrows shot up. "What an unusual bouquet, Gracie. Why those flowers?"

I smiled at her. "The red carnations are a symbol of love, the dandelions remind me of the wildflowers that grow in Harmony, and purple irises are my favorite flower. They were my grandmother's also."

Ida reached over and put her hand on mine. "What a beautiful sentiment. This will be an extraordinary bouquet."

"I hope so. I saw one like it on an online wedding site a while back, and I fell in love with it."

"There will be a large bunch of the same flowers in a vase on the stage where you say your vows and another bouquet on the table at the reception," Sweetie continued. "Ruth has a long red floor runner we'll use for you to walk on up to the front of the church." She squinted at me. "How's all this sound so far? Is this what you wanted?"

"It's perfect," I said. "What's going on with the food?"

Sweetie shuffled through her notes and pulled out a handwritten piece of paper. "Hector has suggested three different menus. He said you should look them over and see what sounds good to you." She chuckled. "And he said to tell you if you don't like these ideas, toss 'em out and tell him what you want. Whatever it is, he'll find a way to do it."

Ida glanced at the list Sweetie put on the table. "Ach, this is so much fancier than what I had at my wedding."

"What food was served at your reception?" I asked.

"It was very simple. Much too simple for young people today, I imagine." Ida wrinkled her nose as she sought to remember. "We had the most delicious roast chicken with stuffing, along with mashed potatoes and gravy. I believe my mother made creamed celery and coleslaw. Of course, there was homemade applesauce." She covered her mouth with her fingers and giggled. "It was very good, but it was not as good as yours, Sweetie. My mother would not be pleased to hear me say this." She lowered her hand and screwed up her face again. "I remember delicious cherry pie and tapioca pudding with bread. There were warm biscuits fresh from the oven served with butter and jelly." She closed her eyes and sighed. "It was quite a feast."

"My father said Mom wore a blue dress for her wedding," I said. "What did you wear?"

Ida nodded. "Ach, yes. A blue dress. Plain without additional adornment. And a black prayer covering to show I was now a married woman." She smiled at me. "I know this sounds unattractive to you, liebling, but Herman whispered into my ear that I was the most beautiful bride he ever laid eyes on." She sighed. "And I believed him. Herman always made me feel he was blessed to be my husband. No woman could ask for more, ja?"

I nodded my agreement.

"I guess all this wedding folderol seems foolish to you," Sweetie said to Ida.

"Not at all," she responded. "A wedding is about the bride and groom and their commitment to God. I know Gracie and

Sam will put Him first in their lives. I have no doubt of their love or their ability to pursue the life God has for them." She reached over and patted my shoulder. "The traditions we follow at a wedding shouldn't be our main focus, child. It is what is in our hearts that matters, and how we live after our vows."

"Wise advice," Sweetie said.

I sighed. "Yes, it is, but all these details sure seem important right now." I frowned at Ida. "My mother brought her blue dress for me to wear."

"Tradition used to be that the wedding dress was only worn once and then kept as a remembrance because it is so meaningful," Ida said. "It is very touching that she has offered it to you."

"I'm sure it is," I said, shaking my head. "But I bought a beautiful white wedding dress in Wichita, and I planned to wear it."

"Then wear it," she said emphatically.

"I don't know. I've been thinking. . ."

"Wait a minute, Gracie girl," Sweetie said. "This is your wedding. You wear what you want. I know your mama feels the same way. Just 'cause she brought that dress with her, it don't mean she expects you to wear it."

"Sweetie is right," Ida chimed in. "I know your mother wants your wedding to be everything you desire. Why are you thinking about this?"

I let out a deep breath. "I don't know. It's just been on my mind. She never got the wedding she wanted. If it would make her happy. . ."

"It is *your* day," Ida said. "One day when we are allowed to be a little selfish. You let your heart lead you, liebling."

"Okay." I smiled at the two women who were so important to me. "It was just a thought. Let's move on." But it was more than just a thought. The idea had been rolling around in my mind ever since my father told me about the dress. The idea of being married in Harmony—in the same dress my mother had worn at her wedding tugged at my heart. It gave me a sense of being a part of something really special. A connection to the past. "Ida, tell me more about your own wedding," I said, pushing the menu from Hector out of the way.

Ida described a day that began at four o'clock in the morning. All the chores were done first, and then the wedding helpers arrived around seven. Weddings were usually held in the bride's home unless it wasn't large enough. First the ushers, dressed in black suits with bow ties, took their places near the front door. Their wives stood with them. When the guests arrived, they were seated on long wooden benches that had been brought in just for the ceremony. The wedding actually started at eight thirty in the morning and lasted about three hours.

"Three hours," Sweetie exclaimed. "My goodness, after gettin' up so early folks would be plumb tuckered out by the time the couple finally says 'I do.'"

Ida laughed. "Believe it or not, no one seemed the least bit tired. It was such a wonderful day, I suppose the excitement kept us going."

"Did you go on a honeymoon?" I asked.

"Well, it was not the kind of honeymoon that brides and grooms go on today. We spent our first night in my parents' home, and then the rest of the winter we visited many of the other relatives and friends who attended the wedding and stayed at least one night with them."

"Yikes," I said. "That's not my idea of a honeymoon."

Sweetie snorted. "And just where are you and Sam going after the wedding?"

"Well, with the harvest and everything. . ."

Sweetie winked at Ida. "They ain't goin' nowhere. They're stayin' here to finish pickin' fruit."

"Yes, but that's because there's nowhere else we want to be," I said quietly. "Being in Harmony as Sam's wife, and living in this beautiful house... Well, there's no honeymoon spot on this planet that appeals to me more."

"Ach, liebling," Ida said. "This is why Sam is the most blessed man in the world, and you are the most blessed woman. You have found God's will for your lives. In His will is more joy and peace than any place or possession the world could ever offer."

We spent the rest of the afternoon going over other details of the wedding. As we double-checked the guest list, I thought of C. J. Bradley.

"I wonder if C.J. would like to come to the ceremony," I said. "I don't know him very well, but since the whole town is turning out anyway, it might be a good chance for him to connect with some of the town's people. Might help us round up some additional help for him, too."

"I think he'd like that," Sweetie said. "But why don't you just ask him? I don't think we need to send out another invitation, do you?"

"No problem. I'll run by there and invite him."

"I am so glad C.J. is home and caring for Abigail," Ida said. "It puts my mind to rest."

"Me, too," I said. "Oh, and remember the story you told me about C.J. and the girl he loved when he was young?"

She nodded.

"Well, they're together again after all these years. Isn't that wonderful?"

Ida looked surprised. "I am glad to hear that. Maybelline Parker told me she thought Melanie had passed away. I am so pleased to know that she is alive and well." She frowned. "I wonder if Abigail knows about Melanie. She would not be happy."

Sweetie made a clucking noise with her tongue. "That woman is just plain cantankerous. I'm glad to see her plan to break those two kids up didn't succeed after all. It mighta taken awhile, but the good Lord put back together what Abigail tried to destroy. Good for Him."

"Yes," Ida agreed. "I will pray that this time C.J. finds happiness with the woman he loves."

"I'll pray for him, too," I said.

Ida laughed softly. "Ach, I just remembered what his initials stand for."

I raised my eyebrows. "Must be good. What is it?"

"He was born during Abigail's involvement in some kind of odd religion. His mother named him Cosmic Journey."

Sweetie burst out laughing. "Are you kiddin' me? That poor man."

"Oh my." I covered my mouth with my hand. "I'd rather be called Snicklefritz than something like that."

Ida nodded. "A name left over from the sixties, I believe. Maybe C.J. has had it changed. Anyway, I hope so."

"And I thought being saddled with Myrtle was bad," Sweetie said, giggling.

I didn't mention that most people wouldn't want to be called *Sweetie*, but she loved her nickname. Ida cast a quick glance my way, and I grinned at her. She was probably thinking the same thing I was.

We moved on to looking over Hector's choices for the reception dinner. I finally decided on a menu, and we set a time for the wedding rehearsal.

"The rehearsal dinner will be here," Sweetie said. "I may not be cookin' for the reception, but I sure as tootin' can handle dinner for the families and Pastor Jensen."

We'd just started talking about that menu when the front door opened and my father's voice boomed out. "Anyone here?"

"We're in the kitchen," I hollered.

Sam was a few seconds behind my dad, and as soon as I saw his face I knew something was wrong.

"You about ready to go, Snicklefritz?" Dad said. He ignored Ida and Sweetie, which wasn't like him.

"I—I guess so." I looked at Sweetie. "Why don't you finish the menu for the rehearsal dinner on your own? I trust your instincts."

She nodded but didn't say anything. I could tell she'd picked up on the tension in the air. Part of me wanted to throw my hands up in the air and say, "What now?" Surely there was enough drama going on around me without my father and my fiancé having problems.

"Dad, why don't you and Ida go on out to the car? I want to talk to Sam a minute."

My father hesitated for a second or two, but finally he helped Ida up and silently guided her down the hall and out the door.

"Okay, what in the world is going on?" I asked Sam after we heard the front door close.

He slumped down in a nearby chair. "Wow. I really don't know what happened." He shook his head. "Everything was going just fine, and then all of a sudden your dad went off on me."

"What do you mean he went *off on you*?" I couldn't keep the exasperation I was feeling out of my voice.

Sam rubbed the side of his face. "We were talking about the farm. You know, why Sweetie and I chose peaches and apples. Then he started asking about our berry crop. Suddenly, he started going on and on about weather and crop failure. What would happen if we had a couple of bad seasons? I tried to explain how we operate, that we have savings in reserve in case we have a poor crop, but he wouldn't listen to me. Your father seems to think I can't take care of you properly."

"I have a job, too," I said. "It's not like we're completely dependent on the farm to—"

Sam slapped the table with his hand. "I don't need your money. I can take care of us just fine."

Stunned, I couldn't form a response fast enough. "I—I . . ."

He stood up, his face flushed and angry. "I don't need you or anyone to support me, thank you. If you don't believe I can provide for you. . ."

"All right, that's enough, you two," Sweetie bellowed. "I won't have you goin' at each other like this." She jabbed a finger into Sam's chest. "Sit down, young man. And I mean now!"

Sam slid back into his chair like a whipped puppy.

"And you. . ." she said, narrowing her eyes at me. "You watch the way you talk to this man. He don't want no woman supportin' him. It ain't respectful to talk to a husband like that."

I wanted to ask just what she knew about husbands seeing that she'd never been married, but I wisely kept my mouth shut. Sweetie was on a rampage, and it was best to stay out of the way when she let loose.

"Now the way I see it, you're both wrong. . .and you're both right." She pointed at Sam again, but this time kept her finger out of his midsection. "Gracie has a talent, boy. And she not only wants to use it to help support the family you're gettin' ready to make, she has a responsibility to use the talents the good Lord gave her. You don't need to sound like some old-school, he-man type who's gonna take care of his little woman. This here marriage is gonna be a partnership, buddy. And you better get used to it." She swung her gaze over to me, her irritation making her look like she'd been "suckin' on a pail full of lemons." Another one of Sweetie's favorite expressions. "You gotta understand that Sam is gonna be the head of your house, young lady. You gotta treat him like you respect him, even when you don't." She shook her head. "I may not be married, but I done watched some folks down through the years. It's the marriages where both people treat each other with respect that make it through the storms of life. I seen some women pick, pick, pick at their husbands until they turn into almost nothin'. Man's gotta feel like his wife looks up to him." She moved her face a little bit closer to mine. "And if you want your husband to change, you go talk to God about it. Don't nag him yourself. Only God can change the inside of a human bein'. I seen folks turn into different people when their spouse quits harpin' at 'em, and they put the situation at the Lord's feet." She glanced at Sam. "This is for both of you. You both gotta love the good stuff and turn the other over to God. It's the only way it'll work. I'm as sure of that as I'm sure Gracie's daddy is gonna come around."

"And how could you possibly know that?" I asked.

Sweetie nodded and looked off into the distance. It was obvious she was thinking about her answer. After a moment she said, "That man is dealin' with the past. He ain't mad at you, son. He's mad at himself. You two gotta give him time to work it out. He'll be okay. I guarantee it."

My father, who was supposedly "gonna come around" honked his car horn as a sign he was getting impatient.

"Sweetie, I hope you're right," I said. I got up, went over to Sam, and wrapped my arms around his neck. "I'm sorry. I'm sure everything will be okay. Give me time to find out why my dad's upset." I smiled over at Sweetie. "Correction. Give me time to pray for my dad. Sweetie's right, we've got to give God a chance to work this out."

"And if He doesn't?" Sam asked glumly.

Nancy Mehl

I slapped him playfully on the head. "How about we just believe, and leave the rest of it up to Him? My mother told me once that faith doesn't have a Plan B. There's no option for failure. I say we stick to Plan A."

Sam was quiet for a few seconds before he chuckled softly. "I have no chance against two women of faith, do I?" He reached up and grabbed my arms, pulling me down to him. Then he kissed me. "Okay, okay. Plan A all the way."

My father's car horn blared again, longer this time. I kissed Sam once more, ran over and threw my arms around Sweetie, hugged her, and then hurried out the front door. I opened the car door and slid into the backseat. Ida sat silently in the front passenger seat. The air was thick with tension, and I got the feeling that Ida and my father had been talking before I came out of the house. Must not have gone well. Dad drove Ida home and started to get out of the car so he could assist her to her door, but I jumped out quickly and announced that I would help her instead. I had Ida's door open before my dad could protest. Holding on to my arm, she got out of the car and we walked slowly toward her porch.

"Your father is dealing with some painful feelings," she said quietly as we stepped up on her stairs. "You must be patient, liebling. God is speaking to his heart." She smiled up at me. "Everything will work out the way it is supposed to. I believe it in my heart of hearts."

When we reached the top of the stairs I hugged her. "Sweetie said the same thing. I think you're both right, although I can't figure out what he's so upset about. I know he's felt bad about Uncle Benjamin, but I thought he was just about over that."

Ida glanced back at the car where my father sat waiting. "Sometimes we make choices, Gracie. At the time, they may seem right in our minds, but in our hearts they may not set as well.

We might ignore the voice of the heart; we may even cover it up with other things. But one day we will face it again, and then we must decide. Was the choice wrong or right? And if it was wrong, what can we do about it now?" She shook her head. "We make a mistake if we torment ourselves about the past since it does not really exist anymore. It is nothing more than a memory without weight or substance. The key is to leave the ghosts of yesterday behind and move forward with new choices. It is never too late with God." She reached over and kissed me on the cheek. "Now your father faces a past choice—and a new one. I am afraid Sam only represents the choice he made long ago—one he may now regret. When Daniel realizes that today he can choose again, and that's it's not too late to get back what he lost, he will drop his misplaced anger toward Sam. I promise this." She stroked my cheek. "You trust God, liebling, ja?"

I wrapped my arms around her. "Ja," I whispered. "Ja." I waited until Ida's front door closed behind her before I went back to the car. I glanced at my father when I got into the front seat, but his expression didn't invite conversation. We pulled out onto Faith Road and had almost reached my house when I noticed something strange on the road ahead. A black buggy was stopped on the side of the road, not moving. No one seemed to be near it.

"Dad, I want to check out that buggy. It looks like Gabe and Sarah's."

He drove past the house and parked on the side of the road. I got out and walked up to the side of the black buggy. Sarah Ketterling lay slumped over in her seat. I jumped up next to her and called out her name. Then I tried to rouse her, but she didn't appear to be breathing.

Chapter Seventeen

My father helped me lift Sarah out of the buggy and onto the ground. He winced more than once from supporting her weight on his leg, even though she felt light as a feather to me. After checking her breathing, he yelled at me to go home and call John while he did CPR. I got in his car and quickly drove the short distance back to my house. I pulled the car up near the house, jumped out, and ran inside to the phone. Thankfully, John answered right away. My breath came in fast spurts as I told him about Sarah.

"I'm on my way, Gracie," he said. "Try to get her cool and continue CPR until I get there."

I hung up the phone and ran to the kitchen to get a pail of cool water and a towel while trying to explain what was going on to my mother. She promised to pray for Sarah as I hurried to the car.

When I got back to my father, I told him what John had said.

"She's breathing," he said, "but it's shallow." He frowned. "Help me get her out of these clothes."

"Oh Dad. I don't think. . ."

He stared into my face, his jaw tight. "Gracie, do you care more about this girl's modesty or her life?"

I reached down and unfastened Sarah's cap. Then with Dad's help I rolled her onto her side and untied her apron.

"Foolish to wear all these clothes in hot July weather," Dad said, his face flushed with frustration. "She probably has heatstroke."

"Maybe that's why John wanted us to cool her down." I unpinned the back of her dress and pulled it down. From a situation last winter when Sarah had been found in the snow, I knew she wore a kind of sleeveless undergarment with an attached slip under her dress. She was still covered but now would feel much cooler. I moved the heavy clothes to the side and put her head on my lap. Then I began to wipe her face with cool water. My father bent over to check her breathing.

"We need to watch her carefully in case we need to start CPR again." He tried to find a comfortable position kneeling next to the unconscious girl, but the pain on his face was evident.

"Dad, I know CPR. If she needs it, I can do it."

"We may both need to assist her."

"No. I can take care of it myself." I gently pushed him away. "You get off that leg. I don't need to take care of both of you."

He started to argue with me, but his face suddenly went white from pain. He struggled to stand up. I left Sarah and helped him to his feet, guiding him over to the buggy where he sat down on the back axle. Once I knew he was comfortable, I returned to Sarah and continued to keep her face, chest, and arms damp. Finally, I heard a small noise, and her eyes fluttered open.

"Sarah, can you hear me?"

She seemed confused at first, but then she stared up at me. "Oh my," she whispered. "What happened?"

"You fainted."

She started to sit up, but I gently pushed her back down. "We don't know why you passed out, Sarah. I need you to stay still until John gets here. You're probably just overheated, but we need to make sure."

Although I'd been concentrating on making sure she was breathing, I was stunned by how thin she was. Her breastbone and ribs were visible beneath her damp undershirt.

"John?" she said, her voice thin and high pitched. "John's coming here?"

I wiped her face with the wet rag. "Yes, of course. He's a doctor."

Sarah's hands flew to her chest and she felt the thin material of her undershirt. "Oh Gracie! I can't have him see me like this. Please. . .please. . ."

"Young lady," my father said in a gruff tone, "wearing all that heavy clothing on a day like today is ridiculous. No wonder you fainted."

Sarah's dark eyes were huge in her pale face. "Gracie. . ."

The plaintive plea in her voice moved me to action. I pulled up the top part of her dress, covering her chest. "I will not put the rest of it on, Sarah," I said, trying to sound as firm as possible. "I just won't do it."

Her thin fingers encircled my wrist. "Thank you, thank you. This is enough." Once again, she struggled to sit up, and once again I resisted her efforts. It didn't take much. She was so weak.

"Stay still," I scolded. "You're not moving until John takes a look at you." The hot sun beat down on us. I could see how easy it would be to get heat exhaustion on a day like today. However, Sarah's condition seemed to be more than simple heatstroke. Her obvious weight loss and the blue tinge to her lips worried me.

The sound of a car's engine caused me to look up. John

screeched to a halt a few yards from us. He jumped out of his SUV and ran toward us, a leather bag in his hand.

"She's breathing now and awake," I told him as I gently put Sarah's head on her folded cape and stepped back so he could get close to her. While he looked her over, I checked on my father. He still seemed to be in pain and sweat ran down his face. "Let's get you back in the car where there's air-conditioning." Surprisingly, he didn't argue.

"I'll just wait for you," he said, leaning on my shoulder and hobbling toward the car. My father's not the kind of person who likes to sit on the sidelines during an emergency. By the time I got him situated, my concern for him had grown.

"Gracie!" John was calling my name, so I made sure Dad was okay, and then I ran back to where John knelt in the road next to Sarah.

The look on his face alarmed me. He handed me a card. "This is the number of Emergency Services in Sunrise. I need you to call them right away and ask them to send an ambulance as soon as possible."

"What's wrong, John?"

He spoke softly to Sarah and got to his feet, leading me a few feet from the silent young woman who lay prostrate in the road. "This isn't heatstroke. She's been having chest pains, and she's very weak." He glanced back at Sarah, his expression one of desperation. "I think it's her heart. It's serious, Gracie. Very serious."

I grabbed his arm. "John, she's going to be okay, isn't she?"

With fear-filled eyes he shook his head. "I don't know, Gracie. I really don't."

"I'll call this number and be right back." I raced toward the car without saying another word. When I got in my father could see I was frightened.

"What's going on?"

"Sarah's in trouble, Dad. I've got to call an ambulance." I pulled into my driveway and opened my door. "You stay here. Mom can get you inside while I call for help." I ran up the steps and into the house, yelling for my mother who hurried in from the kitchen. After a brief explanation, she went out to get my father. I dialed the number on John's card and gave our location to the dispatcher who answered the phone. He promised to have someone there within the next fifteen minutes. I hung up and jogged out to the porch, ignoring Papa who sat on the couch, watching all the turmoil.

"Let us know what happens, Gracie," my mother said as I raced past her and my father. Dad was going up the steps slowly, but at least he was home where Mom could look after him. One patient out of the way.

I backed out of my driveway, almost knocking over my mailbox. Then I gunned the motor and sped back to where Sarah and John waited. After assuring John I'd placed the call, I knelt next to Sarah whose frightened eyes sought mine.

"John says something might be wrong, Gracie." Her voice was so soft I could barely hear her. "I haven't felt good for a while, but I thought it would pass. We've been working so hard in the shop. . ."

"That's not it," John interrupted, his tone harsh. "You didn't do anything about it because you were afraid to come to my office. You've risked your health because of me."

Sarah's already pale face turned even whiter. "No, that's not true. Please. . .please don't say that. . ."

Without any warning, her eyes rolled back in her head and she fainted. John called her name several times, but she didn't respond. I cried out involuntarily because she looked dead. John pulled her dress down and began doing chest compressions, his face grim.

"Watch for the ambulance, Gracie," he said in a tone that shook me to my very core. "Make sure they don't miss us."

I ran out on the road so I could see any approaching vehicle. Within a few minutes, I spotted the ambulance barreling down the road, creating a storm of dust behind it. I waved my hands like a crazy person, making sure they saw us. They pulled up next to the buggy and two emergency workers jumped out, carrying equipment. John shouted instructions to them. One of the emergency workers inserted a needle in Sarah's arm, attached to a plastic bag of clear liquid. The other moved into the spot where John had been working and put his head on Sarah's chest. He took out something that looked like large scissors and cut down the length of the rest of her dress, throwing it aside. Then he opened the metal box he had with him and grabbed a couple of paddles. After adjusting some knobs on the instrument, he put the paddles on her chest and jolted Sarah. Her body jumped. He checked her, shook his head, and then repeated the procedure. Once again, he shook his head. In the meantime, the other worker gave her a shot and told the man with the paddles to try again. This time, he seemed satisfied with the results and ran over to his vehicle to get a gurney out of the back. All three men loaded Sarah up into the back of the ambulance. I heard the emergency technicians talking to John, but I couldn't distinguish what they were saying. It was like my heart was pounding in my ears, and all I could hear was the sound of it beating. I began to pray with all my might, not caring who heard me or if I sounded deranged. One of the men jumped up into the back of the vehicle with Sarah while the other ran to the front, jumped in, and sped off. John jogged back to me.

"They wouldn't let me go with them so I've got to follow in my car."

"John, please tell me she's going to be okay." My voice shook, and I felt tears course down my cheeks.

"I—I don't know, Gracie," John said. "I really don't." He grabbed my hands. "You say this God of yours is good—that He loves us. If that's true, He'll save Sarah." The anguish in his voice was palpable. "You've got to pray. . .please. Please pray that she lives."

I lowered my head and prayed with every ounce of faith in my heart. "Dear God, thank You for providing everything we need for life. We draw on Your goodness and Your mercy for our friend Sarah. We declare that she will live and not die, and that she will completely recover. Thank You for hearing our prayer." I started to say "amen," but surprisingly, John began to speak out loud.

"God, I know You don't know me, but I believe You're there. I've seen You in the lives and hearts of these people in Harmony. In the life and heart of Sarah Ketterling. Please God, I love her. Save her. Heal her. If You do, I'll serve You the rest of my life. I promise."

I waited a moment and then said, "Amen."

John hugged me and hurried toward his car.

"Call me!" I yelled after him. "Call me after you check on her!"

I had no idea if he heard me or not. He drove away so quickly that when the dust cleared, I couldn't see his SUV any longer. I got in my dad's car and drove home. After parking in my driveway, I put my head down and prayed again. This time, I prayed for two lives. One for continued life in this world, and the other for a life in eternity.

Chapter Eighteen

Friday morning dawned with cloudy skies and rain. It was most welcome. We desperately needed it to help cool down temperatures and aid thirsty crops. There was more good news. Sarah had been moved to a hospital in Topeka and had improved so much it looked as if she could come home by Monday. She'd been diagnosed with cardiomyopathy, a disease that attacks the heart muscle. Caught early, it can be treated successfully with medicine. Sarah had ignored her symptoms for a while, causing her to feel weak and finally lose consciousness. According to John, if her condition had been left untreated, she could have easily died. He called me several times from Topeka, but I hadn't actually seen him since Sarah's collapse. Except for running back and forth to Harmony for a few patients who couldn't wait, he stayed by her side constantly.

I'd promised Ida I'd drive her to Topeka to see Sarah that afternoon. The drive would take us around an hour and a half each way. I was happy to have some time to spend with Ida, and frankly, I needed a break from Papa. He seemed to be having more and more confused episodes. His insistence about finding a wedding present from Mama had grown stronger. It was all we could do to talk him out of it. My father finally told him we'd found it, and everything was all right. I didn't like lying to Papa, but Dad said it was the kindest thing to do. At first it seemed to calm him down, but last night, he woke up about three in the morning, worried once again about this imaginary gift. Although his delusion bothered me and losing sleep didn't thrill me, I was touched that he longed to give me something for my wedding. And though he was doing better physically after his fall, the decision was made to keep him downstairs so we wouldn't have a repeat of his previous accident. Besides the 3:00 a.m. episode, my concern for Hannah and Sarah kept me tossing and turning at night. Hannah had been gone five days now. After a visit with Jessie yesterday when I went to lunch with Sam, my concerns about Bill had returned. When I'd asked her about her mother's new relationship, her response reignited my suspicions.

"Mom seems happy," she'd said, "but I don't know. Bill makes me uncomfortable. I get the feeling he's hiding something."

That was enough to send me over the edge and hound Pat until he did some checking up on Bill. Although he did have a child who lived in the area where a couple of young women had been abducted and killed, he hadn't been there during the time it happened, and had never been to Arizona or New Mexico in his life. Ever. Turned out Jessie's "uncomfortable" feelings were nothing more than that, probably a leftover reaction to the abuse she suffered at the hand of her father. Pat reminded me after spending time following up another useless lead that Rufus still wasn't speaking to me—and might not for quite some time.

"For crying out loud, Gracie," he'd said in a tone that didn't invite further discussion, "just because this guy *might* have struck in Topeka, and we're still not sure of that, it doesn't mean he lives around here. You're imagining things, and it's causing me a lot of trouble."

"I never said he lived here," I'd answered hotly. "But Hannah is gone and whoever picked her up was in this area. It's entirely possible that he's been here before."

His answer, mumbled under his breath, wasn't something his mother would be proud of. I'd pointed that out to him, but it didn't do any good. He'd just hung up on me.

After everything that had been happening in Harmony, going to Topeka sounded like a vacation. And although it was almost impossible since there was an APB out on Hannah and no one had spotted her, in the back of my mind, the thought that I might find her on the road between here and Topeka was overwhelming, even if it was unlikely.

Every day that Hannah was gone gave Abel and Emily more opportunity for stress. But the supernatural assurance they'd received when we'd read the ninety-first Psalm seemed to hold them up. I could see the battle to believe in their faces, but I also observed the peace of God sustaining them. They were determined to trust God with their daughter's safety, and my respect for them grew immensely. Faith is easy when the stakes are small, but to see them walk in assurance when the life of their beloved child was on the line showed their true devotion to their God.

A little before three o'clock I said good-bye to my parents and left to pick Ida up. She wanted to stop by and see Abigail before we left town, and I'd gladly agreed to take her. I'd been planning to ask C.J. to the wedding, and I looked forward to seeing the progress he'd made on his mother's house.

Ida was ready when I pulled up to her place. She sat on her porch with a basket in her lap. I got as close as I could so she wouldn't get too wet. Then I jumped out of the car to assist her.

"What have you got in the basket?" I asked when I reached her.

"I made us a nice supper," she said with a smile. "I thought perhaps we could stop along the road and eat."

"I'd planned to take you out to a restaurant. There are some great places to eat in Topeka."

"Oh my, Gracie," she said, getting to her feet while holding the basket in her hands. "That is not necessary even though I appreciate it very much. I have two roast beef sandwiches, and two tuna salad sandwiches, homemade pickles, apples from Sam's trees, and some of Mr. Menlo's baklava. We will not need to buy anything when we have such good food with us."

I reached out for the basket. "Sounds delicious, Ida. We'll put it in the backseat so it will stay cool. We might want to eat before the hospital so nothing will spoil."

Ida took my other arm, and I helped her down the steps. "I think that is a good idea. I am so excited about our trip. I can hardly wait to see Sarah. I have been praying for her." She leaned her head against my shoulder for just a moment. "Thank you so much for taking me today. It blesses me so."

We stepped carefully through the puddles on the ground while the rain fell steadily. "I'm looking forward to it, too," I said. "Sweetie is coming to my house today to talk wedding plans with my mother, and frankly, I need a break. I know it's my wedding, but I just want to walk down the aisle and say, 'I do.' I want to be Mrs. Sam Goodrich, and I wish I could do it without all the fuss."

Ida waited until I opened the car door. She carefully folded her long skirt beneath her and positioned herself into the passenger seat. I closed the door and went around to the other side of the car, placing the basket in the backseat before I got behind the wheel.

"I know it feels that way now, Gracie," she said when I got inside the car, "but someday you will cherish the memories of your wedding. Even though my ceremony was very simple by today's standards, it was very special to me, and I think of it often." Her voice grew soft, and she looked away from me and out the window. "Especially when I lost Herman. Then the memories came rushing back like a flood. Herman looking so young and handsome in his black suit. The look on his face when we were declared man and wife. The joy we shared with our friends and families. It was one of the best days of my life." She turned to look at me. "It will be this way for you, too. Please do not take it lightly, ja?"

I nodded. "I won't, Ida. Thank you. I think everything else that's going on is stressing me out. My mind is on Hannah and Sarah. And Papa has gotten worse the last few days. It's hard to concentrate on anything else."

Ida was silent for a moment. When she spoke, there was hesitancy in her voice. "Perhaps this will bring you some comfort, liebling. I had a dream last night about Hannah." She smoothed the thick material of her dress with her aged-spotted hands. "She was in a dark place, but there was an angel standing beside her, and the light from the angel began to drive away the blackness that surrounded her. And there was peace, Gracie. Great peace. The angel looked at me as if I stood in that place with them, and he said, 'Fear not. God is watching over Hannah and she will come home soon.'" The old woman looked at me with tears in her eyes. "Many people believe that God no longer speaks through dreams and visions, but this is not so. 'And it shall come to pass in the last days, saith God, I will pour out my Spirit upon all flesh: and your sons and your daughters shall prophesy, and your young men shall see visions, and your old men shall dream dreams.'" She touched my arm. "I believe this dream is inspired, Gracie. I believe our Hannah will come home."

Something rose up inside of me after hearing Ida's words and strengthened my faith. Her dream confirmed what the Muellers and I believed God had already told us. I'd learned to trust this elderly Mennonite woman who knew God in a way many people didn't. "Oh, Ida," I said. "I also believe God still speaks today, and I'm so glad you shared this with me. This is the second time He's sent reassurance of Hannah's return."

"Ja, ja," she said, "but this is not all."

"There's more? What is it?"

"The angel said one more thing. He said, 'Tell Grace she must have eyes to see and ears to hear.' And then I awoke."

I was so surprised, I swerved the car before gaining control and slowing down. Thankfully there was no other traffic on Faith Road. "Th—the angel mentioned me by name? What does that mean?"

"I believe it means God will use you to bring this precious girl back to us," she said simply. "You must remember what he said and make sure your eyes see and your ears hear."

"I have no idea what that means, Ida."

"Ach, Gracie. You must just pay attention. God will show you what He wants you to know. You must stay open to Him." She made a clucking sound with her tongue. "And do not let your mind fill up with worry and fear. I find it is harder to hear what God has to say when these two emotions crowd out my peace."

Ida and her *peace*. Her peace guided her constantly, and I'd begun to understand that her peace was the voice of the Holy Spirit living inside her. She'd taught me to look for *my* peace and follow it. And something inside told me her dream and the words she'd shared with me were very important. I turned them over in my mind until we pulled up into Abigail's driveway. The difference in the house in just the short time C.J. had been working on it was impressive. The yard was cleaned up, and the porch had been rebuilt. Other repairs had been made, and the house was being painted.

"Oh my," Ida said when she saw it. "This is so wonderful. So many people have tried to help Abigail, but her pride turned them away. I guess it took her son to accomplish what an entire town could not do. And just look at the wonderful results."

"Yes, he's done a marvelous job, hasn't he?"

She nodded. "I know we cannot stay long," Ida said, "but perhaps Abigail will at least see us for a few minutes."

As if on cue, the rain began to come down in torrents. "Wait here," I told her. "I have an umbrella in my trunk. I'll get it." I popped the trunk latch, got out of the car, and hurried to the back. Thankfully, the umbrella was still there. I'd been worried I'd taken it in the house when I'd cleaned out my car. I slopped around to Ida's door, opened it, and helped her out. We both tried to stay under the large umbrella Allison had given me on my last birthday. Clear plastic with colorful dots, I felt a little ludicrous holding it over Ida's bonneted head. I'd always thought the umbrella was cute, but now it just seemed silly. Although it was slow going, we finally made it to the porch. With the rotting wood replaced, the floor felt sturdy and safe. I knocked on the new door that had been installed, and a few moments later, it swung open.

"Gracie!" C.J. said with a smile. "I'm so glad you stopped by. Come in, please."

I helped Ida inside first. There was a rug near the door and we both carefully wiped our wet feet. C.J. looked at Ida oddly and hesitated. Then recognition showed in his face. "Mrs. Turnbauer?" he said. "Is that you?"

Ida smiled. "C.J., it is so good to see you again. It has been a long time, ja?"

"Yes, yes it has." He held out his arm. "May I take your cape?"

"Ja, ja. It is very wet though. I do not want to make a mess."

"That's no problem. I'll hang it up on the coatrack. There's a rug underneath to catch the water."

"Thank you, young man," she said gratefully.

I quickly scanned the room. The furniture was old and worn, but the room itself was neat. A metal fan whirred from a corner. Since I knew Abigail had no electricity, I was surprised. C.J. noticed.

"It runs on batteries," he said. "It's been so hot working here without air-conditioning, I went to Council Grove and bought a couple of them. The other one is in my bedroom."

The rain outside had lowered the temperature quite a bit, and with the fan running, the inside of Abigail's house was quite pleasant.

"Where is your mama?" Ida asked. "I don't want to bother her, I would just like to say hello. We are on our way to Topeka to visit a friend in the hospital, so I thought we would stop by for a minute or two."

"I'm glad you did," he said. "Mama is lying down, but if you'll wait, I'll be glad to tell her you're here."

"I do not wish to wake her," Ida said hesitantly. "Perhaps we should come back another time."

"No, she's not sleeping. Sometimes she gets uncomfortable in her wheelchair and likes to stretch out for a while. I'm sure she'll be thrilled to see you."

"C.J.," I said, "before you get your mother, I—I wanted to explain something. Why Papa Joe didn't recognize you. He–he's ill. It's Alzheimer's."

His face fell. "I'm so sorry, Gracie. I guess that explains it. I mean, it's not as if we were close when I was young, but I really thought he'd remember me. Joe wasn't too crazy about me back then, and I certainly don't blame him. I was rather rebellious, I'm ashamed to say."

"Well, I just wanted you to know. I didn't want you to be offended."

He shook his head. "I'm not offended, but I'm certainly sad to hear about his condition. Joe Temple is one of the finest men I've ever known."

"Thanks," I said sincerely.

He nodded. "I'll get Mama." He pointed toward an old couch that had seen better days. "Please have a seat. She'll be out in a minute."

Ida and I sat down gingerly on the faded piece of furniture. I brushed something that looked like cookie crumbs from one area, and we had to avoid a spring that had pushed its way through the material.

"I know you and Abigail believe in a simpler life," I whispered to Ida, "but does that mean you can't have decent furniture?"

She shook her head. "We try not to make material things too important, but perhaps Abigail needs furniture that will not cause injury to her or those who visit her." She leaned in closer to me. "Help has been extended to her, but she refuses it." She put her hand on mine. "Real humility isn't found in living a life of poverty, Gracie. Outside expressions do not reveal the heart. True humility comes from believing and obeying God above our own thoughts and feelings. I am afraid Abigail thinks that if she looks poor it is proof she is humble. I believe it is actually misplaced pride. She is too proud to let others bless her. I do not think this is pleasing to a God who wants to provide for His children through the love of His people. How can we fulfill His mandate to give when people like Abigail will not receive?"

She put her hand back on her lap, and I thought about what she'd said. There was a man in our little church back home in Fairbury who made a big show of being poor. Because he had so little in worldly goods, to him it signified that he was more spiritual than the other people in the church. One day when his car broke down and couldn't be repaired, my mother and father, who'd just purchased a new car, decided to give the man their old one, which was still in very good shape. My father took it to a mechanic and had him go over everything, spending almost three hundred dollars in repairs. When my parents gave the man their car, he seemed to accept it gratefully. But the next Sunday, when he pulled into the church parking lot, the once-beautiful vehicle was a complete mess. The windshield was cracked and the body was covered with dents and dings. My father was horrified, thinking the man had been in an accident. He rushed over to see what had happened, my mother and I following behind him.

"Were you in collision?" Dad asked. "Are you okay?"

"Oh no," the man said, his chest swelling with a sense of importance. "I took a sledgehammer to it so I wouldn't become proud of driving something that looked so nice." The man's wife and child stood behind him. The wife stared at the ground while the man's ten-year-old son just looked embarrassed.

My father was so angry he couldn't speak. He turned around, grabbed my mother's arm, and ushered us into the church building. That was the last time my parents ever tried to help him. Eventually his wife left him and took their son with her. I'd wondered for years what had happened to them, but ever since I continued to pray that they would discover who God really is and wouldn't be permanently scarred by this man's strange behavior.

Eventually, the pastor confronted him about his confused ideas, but this so-called humble man didn't take kindly to the correction. He left the church after standing up in a service and railing against the "pride and arrogance" of the pastor and the other members. Then he left to find another church where he could play his game of false humility.

"You are very quiet, child," Ida said. "Have I offended you?"

"Not at all," I answered. "In fact, you've just explained a situation that I hadn't thought about for a long time." I quickly told her the story.

"Ja, ja," she said, nodding her head. "This is a very good example of what I mean. This poor man tried to build his own righteousness through his works, and we cannot do that. Our righteousness is of God only." She took a deep breath. "This is what I have tried to tell Abigail down through the years, but I am afraid I have been unsuccessful. As I have told you before, living the life I live is a choice. Not a judgment on others, and not a source of spiritual pride. But Abigail. . . Well, I do not think she believes the same way."

A noise from the other room stopped our conversation. C.J. pushed a wheelchair into the living room. I was somewhat surprised to see Abigail up close. She wasn't as old as I'd thought she'd be. She looked to be in her late fifties or early sixties although I knew she had to be almost seventy. Her hair was pulled back from her face, probably in a tight bun, and her head was covered with a black bonnet similar to Ida's. She was dressed in black from head to toe, except for the white plaster cast that peeked out from under her heavy skirt. Once again, I wondered how anyone could wear so many clothes in the summer.

"Oh Abigail," Ida said, getting up from the couch. I held her elbow as she struggled to her feet. "I am so sorry to find out about your leg. I should have checked on you sooner."

Abigail arched one eyebrow and stared at Ida without smiling. "Well, I hear you have been busy attending that liberal church in town. Perhaps they don't teach taking care of your neighbors there?"

Ida toddled up next to Abigail and kissed her on each cheek. "Now Abigail, the church is not liberal. They also live a simple life. You should visit. I believe you would enjoy it. The pastor is a man of great love and deep understanding."

"Humph," she uttered. "We had a wonderful church until you broke it up. I believe you've also convinced the Vogler family to abandon true doctrine."

Ida laughed gently. "No, Abigail. I do not convince anyone to do anything. God alone is able to lead His sheep. And you know that our number began to dwindle because our dear brother Benjamin died. And then Gabriel and Sarah decided to attend Bethel, as I did. The Voglers made their decision later without any help from me. And the Beckenbauer brothers are too ill to attend church at all. It might interest you to know that Abel and Emily Mueller visit them regularly and help to care for them. They have become very good friends."

"Oh, pshaw," the woman spat out. "The brothers are taking help because they have no other choice. I would help them if I could." Her voice took on a whiny tone. "But as you can see, I can't do much for anyone." She leaned over and rubbed her cast. "I've been in this chair for a month now. It doesn't get any better." She reached up and grabbed C.J.'s hand. "Thank God my son is here to take care of me."

C.J., who still stood in back of his mother's wheelchair, winked at us. "Now Mama, you know the doctor said your bones were healing nicely and that you should be able to start getting around with crutches before long."

Abigail quickly pulled her hand from her son's. "You just say that because you want to abandon me again." She put her hands up over her face. "I am so alone. There isn't anyone who cares about me."

"How did you break your leg, Abigail?" Ida asked, ignoring her friend's attempt to gain sympathy.

"I tripped on the stairs carrying my laundry to the basement," she said. "I lay on the floor for days because no one cared enough to check on me."

"But I believe Kenneth and Alene Ward bring you groceries almost every week, isn't that true?" Ida said.

Abigail turned her face away and wouldn't answer.

"That's who found her," C.J. said. "And it was only a couple of hours after she fell. Not days. They called an ambulance and stayed with her at the hospital. They also called me. Nice people."

"You have no idea how long I was on that hard cement floor!" Abigail cried angrily. "You were nowhere around and haven't been for years. You don't care anything about me."

"Now Abigail Bradley," Ida said emphatically, "you stop this right now. Your son left his job to come here and help you. This is not the right way to treat people. Especially your own flesh and blood."

Abigail's expression turned even more irate, but she clamped her thin lips shut.

C.J. sighed. "I'm sorry for my mother's behavior." He patted her on the shoulder. "She has been in quite a bit of pain. I'm sure it's not easy to stay cheerful when you hurt so much." He smiled at us. "May I get you ladies something to drink?"

Ida leaned over and hugged her friend, and then she walked back over to where I sat. "No thank you, C.J.," she said. "As we told you, we are on our way to see a friend in the hospital. I just wanted to check on Abigail. We should be on our way."

"Just like you to rush off," Abigail barked, abandoning her momentary attempt at silence. "You leave me alone for months, and then when you do come by, you only stay a few minutes. I guess you can check me off your list of things to do now."

"Mama!" C.J. said. "That's enough. I think it's time for you to go back to bed. Maybe a little sleep will help calm you down. And perhaps another pill?"

"No! You give me those pills to keep me quiet." She looked at us, her eyes wide. "He tries to keep me asleep so I won't complain."

I couldn't help thinking that if I were C.J., keeping his mother knocked out on medication would be a temptation I wasn't sure I could resist. However, it was obvious he was going out of his way to care for her.

"We must be going, Abigail," Ida said. I stood up and held out my arm so she could hold on to me. "I will check back with you soon. And C.J., please let me know if there is anything I can do to help you. Gracie, can you give him my telephone number? I can't ever remember it." She turned and smiled at him. "I know there is no phone here, but if you need to reach me, you can do so in town, from the restaurant."

I opened my purse and pulled out a small notepad. I wrote down Ida's number and then my own and handed the paper to C.J.

"Thank you, ladies. I truly appreciate it. So far we're doing fine, but if I do need something I'll certainly call you."

"I'd like to invite you to my wedding, C.J." I gave him the details while his mother glared at me. "I understand if you're too busy, but I'd love it if you could come."

"I'll certainly try. I appreciate the invitation." He took Ida's cape from the coatrack and helped her into it.

We made our way to the front door to the sounds of Abigail grumbling about being deserted by people who called themselves her friends. I couldn't wait to get out of there and away from that unpleasant woman. We said good-bye to C.J. and he closed the door behind us. The rain was still coming down so I popped open the umbrella and held it over us until we were inside the car.

"Man, that woman is something else," I said when we were both safe inside. "How can you be so kind? I just wanted to punch her."

Ida's nose wrinkled up as she giggled. "Oh, Gracie. I do not think you would ever strike a woman in a wheelchair. No matter how obnoxious she was."

"I wouldn't place a bet on that," I said under my breath. I started the car and began backing out of the dirt driveway we'd come in on. My concentration was on my rearview mirror, and I forgot about the big mud hole I'd driven around when we'd arrived. My back tires suddenly sank down into it, and it was clear after several attempts that I would need assistance to get free.

"We're stuck, Ida," I said. "I've got to go back to the house and get some help."

The old lady nodded. "I'm sure C.J. will give us the assistance we need."

I started to open my door, thinking what a mess I was going to be after wading through the mud hole in the rain, when my door flew open. C.J. stood there in a gray plastic rain covering, a hood over his head.

"Stay in the car," he said. "I'll get my truck and pull you out."

"Oh thank you so much," I responded with relief. "I'm sorry. I should have gone around it."

He smiled, water dripping from the edge of his hood and past his face. "No, I should have filled it before this happened. It's my fault." He pointed to the front of my car. "I'm going to put a chain around your bumper and attach it to the back of my truck. I don't think you're stuck too badly, so I don't believe it will cause any damage to your car."

I grinned at him. "That's fine. I'd rather mess up my bumper a little bit than sit in this hole until it dries up."

He laughed and shut the door. Ida and I waited a few minutes until C.J.'s truck came around the back of the house. Of course it was red, just like every other Tom, Dick, and Harry in the county. I almost laughed. I had no intention of falling for this again or leveling any further accusations toward anyone in Harmony.

C.J. pulled around in front of us and wrapped a couple of thick chains around my bumper. I'd turned off my wipers so it was hard to see him. He came back to my window. I rolled it open.

"Turn off your engine and put your car in neutral," he instructed.

"Okay." I rolled my window back up and turned off the engine. Then I shifted into neutral. It was almost impossible to see anything with the rain pouring down and hitting the windshield, but I heard C.J.'s motor rev up. Then slowly we began to move. Within a couple of minutes, we were out of the hole. C.J. got out of his truck, removed the chains, and waved us on. I lowered my window once again and yelled "Thank you!" to the now thoroughly drenched man. I started the car and turned on my windshield wipers. For the first time I got a good look at C.J.'s red truck.

And his bumper sticker with a big black bear emblazoned on it.

Chapter Nineteen

I drove the rest of the way to Topeka without saying anything to Ida about C.J.'s truck. For crying out loud. Did everyone with a red truck have a compulsion to stick an image of a bear on his bumper? I'd made Pat investigate two men because they had red trucks. Only one had a bear bumper sticker. Besides, what if the witness who saw the truck in Topeka was wrong? What if the animal on the bumper sticker wasn't a bear at all but some other animal? Rufus's Chicago Bears bumper sticker wasn't the least bit odd seeing as how he'd moved here from Chicago. Maybe the image on C.J.'s sticker was something else entirely. With all the rain, I hadn't seen it clearly. I'd feel pretty stupid if the sticker was actually a shout-out for the *I Love Koalas Club*. I decided to stop back by Abigail's and get another look at that truck before I did anything stupid. I tried to put it out of my mind, but I couldn't help thinking if Hannah showed up in a day or two, sorry that she'd run away and thinking that she could just waltz back into town after causing all this trouble, the next person Pat might have to physically restrain would be his future daughter-in-law.

We were almost to Topeka when I spotted a park by the side of the road with covered shelters. The rain had slowed down to a light sprinkle. I pulled off the road and into the park. "Maybe we should eat here," I said to Ida. "What do you think?"

"Ach, it is just lovely, Gracie," she said with a smile. "Yes, let's stop here."

I parked as close as I could to the shelter, and we both got out. I carried the picnic basket to one of the covered tables. Surprisingly, it was clean and didn't need to be wiped down, a condition not always true when it came to eating outside. I surveyed the area. Very nice. Lots of trees and pleasant landscaping. I compared it to the park in Harmony, which was one of my favorite spots in town. One reason I loved it so was because it reminded me of a special place in Wichita where I'd spent many happy days.

O. J. Watson Park is the epitome of what a park should be. It contains a beautiful lake full of ducks, geese, and even a crane or two, with tall trees full of lush leaves and wildflowers that grow along the paths. And Watson Park has something else unique to Kansas—an actual yellow brick road that winds through it. It's still my favorite walking trail. I used to go there on the weekends just to walk the road, enjoy nature, and watch children laugh as they rode ponies, pushed paddleboats across the sparkling water, or caught a ride on a special train that chugs around most of the perimeter of the park. Over the years, the friendly park staff had grown to know me, and every time I went there, it was like visiting dear friends. My love for Watson Park had helped me to realize that this city girl longed for the beauty and silence of the country long before I was able to recognize it.

"Are you here with me, Gracie?" Ida said, chuckling. "You look so far away."

I laughed. "I guess I was. I was remembering a special place I used to visit in Wichita. This park made me think of it."

Ida breathed deeply. "Ja, this is lovely. I would rather eat outside any day than sit in my house or in a restaurant. Many days I take my lunch out on the front porch and eat it there."

I'd just started to open the picnic basket when I remembered we had nothing to drink. I mentioned my concern to Ida.

"Ach," she said with a smile, "I remembered. Open the basket."

I looked inside. There were two Mason jars with iced tea nestled between a thick towel so they wouldn't hit against each other and break. I removed the jars and the food, and we spent the next forty minutes enjoying our supper. The sandwiches were delicious, the pickles crisp and tart, and the baklava sweet and flaky. By the time we finished, I couldn't eat another bite.

We packed up, got back in the car, and drove to the hospital. I was using directions copied from the Internet, but I missed our turnoff the first time. The second time around I found the hospital without any problem. I parked, and Ida and I went inside. I had Sarah's room number, but I wasn't sure how to get there. A kind receptionist gave us directions. It was amusing to see all the odd looks aimed Ida's way. In Harmony, conservative Mennonite clothing went unnoticed. Ida's was somewhat more severe than most, but no one ever paid any attention to her. Here, she stuck out like a sore thumb. I was certain she wasn't used to the stares since she hardly ever left Harmony, but she carried herself as if she had no idea she was garnering attention. Finally we found Sarah's room. The door was open, and as we entered we immediately saw Sarah sitting up in her bed. She looked so much better than she had when she collapsed, I was filled with joy.

"Gracie! Ida!" she called out when she saw us. Her face lit up in a smile. She wore a hospital gown, and her long black hair hung down past her shoulders. "I am so glad to see you both!"

I hurried over to her side and put my arms around her. "I'm thankful to see you looking so well, and I'm grateful to God for taking such good care of you."

She patted my back with her small hand. "God is good, isn't He? He brought just the right people to me when I needed help." She tightened her arms around me. "Thank you, Gracie. Thank you for all you did for me. And thank your father for me, too, won't you?" She let me go and lay back on her pillow. "The doctors say I can go home soon. Then I'll be able to offer my thanks to your father in person."

"He'll be happy to see you."

Ida, who'd gone around to the other side of the bed gave Sarah another big hug. "I prayed for you, dear, sweet Sarah," she said, her voice cracking with emotion. "I knew the God who heals would keep you safe."

"He has done exceedingly above and beyond, Ida," Sarah said solemnly. "The most recent tests are good. The doctors say I am responding very well to the medicine they've prescribed. I'm already feeling much better than I have in a very long time."

"That's wonderful," I said.

"Well, well. Look who's here." Gabe's deep voice rang out from behind us. I turned around to find him smiling at us. "Gracie and Ida. Two of my very favorite people. I'm so glad to see you."

He held out his arms, and I embraced him. Goodness, he really was turning into a great big teddy bear in Mennonite clothing. He also greeted Ida, and then helped her into a nearby chair.

Sarah asked about Hannah.

"Nothing new," I answered. "It's been five days now. I'm ready for her to come home."

"I feel badly for Abel and Emily," Gabe said. He walked over to Sarah's bed and took her small hand in his. "I know how it feels to wonder if you might lose the most important person in your life." His voice broke.

I reached over and put my hand on his shoulder. "I know you do. We're all so grateful nothing really awful happened."

Sarah gave me a beatific smile. "And that's not all God has done, Gracie. You'll never guess."

I frowned at her. "I give up. What else has He done?"

"Great and mighty things." I immediately recognized the voice that boomed from behind me. John came up next to the bed. I almost gasped at the change in his expression and the different look in his eyes. There was a light that hadn't been there before.

"Oh John," I said, overcome with emotion.

"Now, now, Gracie," he said, grabbing my hand. "No tears. I've spent the last two days being weepier than any man should be."

"Ach, my dearest John. You have met my friend Jesus, ja?"

He smiled. "Yes, Ida. I've met your friend. And it didn't happen just because He saved Sarah's life, although that started it. After we got to the hospital, while the doctors were working with her, I went to the chapel, got down on my knees, and asked God to reveal Himself to me. I'd heard the story of salvation many times and rejected it because I couldn't be sure it was true. I needed to *know* God. To know in my heart He was real. I couldn't believe just because people told me I should—or even because the message of the cross was so appealing. I needed to experience the presence of God for myself." He tried to blink away the tears in his eyes. "And I did. I can't really explain it. All I can tell you is that God visited that room. He visited this man, and I will never, ever be the same."

If we hadn't been standing in a hospital, I think I would have jumped up and down and shouted at the top of my lungs. Even the sedate and dignified Ida looked as if she had some Holy Ghost fire in her belly.

I threw my arms around John and hugged him as hard as I could. "I'm so happy, John. So very happy."

"Now you're more than my friend," he whispered into my ear. "You're my sister."

"And proud to be," I replied softly. I let go of him and smiled at everyone in the room. "Now if Hannah would just come home, everything would be perfect."

Sarah nodded. "We will all keep praying."

"I know the whole town of Harmony is praying as well," Gabe said.

His reminder about Harmony made me think about Sam. I rifled through my purse, only to realize I'd left my cell phone at home. Cell phones are so useless in Harmony, I tend to forget I have it. "Is it okay if I use your phone, Sarah? I'd like to call Sam and tell him we got here safely."

With Gabe's encouragement, I called Sam's house collect. He answered after the second ring. I waited while the operator confirmed that he would accept the charges.

"So you made it," he said after the operator left the line.

"Yes, we're here. I'm in Sarah's room, and she looks incredible."

"Did you have any problems with the rain? It poured buckets and buckets here."

I briefly told him about getting stuck at Abigail's, but I left out the part about the truck. I was determined to look at C.J.'s bumper once more before I said anything to anyone else, even Sam. And especially Pat.

"I'm just glad you're okay," Sam said. "I told you to get rid of that car. It's too small and lightweight for the country."

"Could we deal with this some other time?" I asked impatiently. "Is Sweetie over at my house?"

"Yep. She's been there for a couple of hours. Took some

strawberry pie with her."

"Sweetie and her pie. For goodness' sake. And why didn't you go with her? I mean, this is your wedding, too. Maybe you should get more involved."

There was silence on the other end. Finally he said, "Look, Gracie. I'm putting on a monkey suit. That should be the only thing the man has to do. The rest of it belongs to the woman."

"You did not just say that," I retorted. "When I get back there..."

He burst out laughing. "I'm kidding."

"Laugh all you want, monkey suit boy. You're still in trouble."

"Hey, that Murphy lady called. She needs to talk to you. I told her you were going to Topeka. She wants you to call her. She says she has something important to tell you."

I thanked him, told him what time I thought we'd be home, and then hung up. Gabe, John, Ida, and Sarah were visiting and didn't seem to be paying any attention to me, but I didn't want to take the chance they might overhear my conversation with Susan. I stepped out into the hall and asked a nearby nurse if there was another phone I could use. She directed me to an empty room. I dug through my purse and found the business card Susan had given me. I dialed the number and after several rings, she answered.

"Susan, it's Gracie. Sam said you'd called?"

"Yes, Gracie." She lowered her voice a couple of notches. "I told you I'd check with the KBI about Hannah Mueller? Well, I did. As you suspected, until recently they were treating her disappearance as that of a runaway. Pat Taylor has already asked them to see if Hannah's situation could be tied to the murder in Topeka. I voiced my own concerns as well, and they promised to step up their efforts." She sighed. "I hope it helps. I pushed about as much as I dared."

"Thank you so much," I said, deciding not to mention that Pat had already told me about her involvement. "I'm glad Pat actually followed through, but I'm sure your input will push the investigation forward even more. I'm so relieved to know that the KBI is finally taking Hannah's case seriously." I cleared my throat and hesitated.

"Is there something else?"

I carefully explained my concerns about C.J. Bradley. "I don't want to overreact, Susan. It just seems odd. C.J. showing up now and his truck matching the description of a vehicle that might belong to a serial killer."

"You should probably contact Sheriff Taylor first," she said.

"I would, but so far, he's been less than enthusiastic about my suggestions."

She grunted. "I understand completely. He's got a hard head." She paused, and I could hear papers shuffling in the background. "Give me a few more details about this C.J. person."

I quickly told her everything I knew. "Let me see what I can do," she said. "Hopefully, they'll follow up on this lead now that they're headed in the right direction."

"Can you please keep my name out of it? There's already one former suspect who won't talk to me. I don't want to make another enemy."

"I'll try. If I find out anything helpful on this end, I'll contact you. And keep me updated, okay? I'm still praying Hannah will just show up. She may be a little worse for wear, but she may also be much more thankful for her good home and her loving parents."

"I sure hope you're right." I thanked her again and hung up. I felt bad going over Pat's head again, but after the bawling out I got about Rufus, I had no intention of mentioning C.J. to Pat.

Even if I did, I felt pretty sure he wouldn't take it seriously.

I headed back to Sarah's room, ready to apologize for interrupting our visit to talk on the phone. But when I entered her room, I saw something that made the words stick in my throat. John stood by Sarah's bedside, holding her hand. And Gabe, who was only a few feet away, was smiling. He must have noticed the dumbfounded look on my face because he laughed.

"Now don't get emotional," he said, "but the three of us are working things out." He slapped John on the back. "If things keep going well, there may be more than one wedding in Harmony this summer."

I felt so overwhelmed I grabbed a nearby chair and sat down. "I can hardly believe it," I said rather breathlessly. "Can this be true?"

Sarah giggled. "Why, Gracie Temple. You're the one who told me God could do anything—that I shouldn't give up hope. Now look at you."

"You're right. It's just that. . .well, Gabe. . ."

"I told you that Sarah couldn't be unequally yoked," Gabe said. "Now Sarah and John are one in the Spirit. John has made it clear that he respects Abel Mueller and our church and has no problem attending there."

"And I also told him that I'd wear sackcloth and ashes if it made him happy," John interjected. "What I wear is meaningless to me. What I feel on the inside means everything."

Gabe cleared his throat. "Which also helped me to realize that it isn't our traditions that make us who we are. It's our hearts. And John has one of the most honest, sincere hearts I've ever come across. I love him like a brother now. Loving him as a father won't be hard at all."

"And guess what else?" Sarah said. "Papa says I can wear

prettier colors from now on. Like the other ladies in church."

Gabe nodded. "Abel has convinced me that dressing modestly doesn't mean we must look as if we're on our way to a funeral."

"I pointed out that if God painted all the flowers with color, why wouldn't He want His people to be clothed the same way?" Sarah's eyes twinkled, but I knew it wasn't because of the new dresses she would be wearing. It was because God had saved John and given them both the deepest desire of their hearts.

I sighed with happiness. So many wonderful things were happening in Harmony. Maybe it was a sign that Hannah's situation would soon be resolved as well.

We visited for about another twenty minutes, but it was clear Sarah was getting tired, so Ida and I excused ourselves and headed home. We were both so happy that we chatted nonstop all the way. I wondered if Ida would agree with Gabe's acceptance of John before he actually joined the church, but I needn't have worried. She was ecstatic, but not just because it looked as if Sarah and John would finally be together. The elderly Mennonite woman rejoiced more that John had finally found his way to God.

As we headed down the road to Harmony, I told her I needed to make one quick stop. "There's something at Abigail's house I need to check," I told her. "If you don't mind, I'd rather not explain. Would it bother you to sit in the car for a few minutes and wait for me?"

She frowned. "No, liebling. If it is something you must do, I will be glad to wait. But is there something that troubles you? Is there anything I can do to help?"

I assured her there wasn't and asked her to trust me. Then I turned down the road that led to Abigail's house, grateful that the rain had stopped so I wouldn't end up soaked by the time I finished my mission. Thankfully, there was a line of trees that hid a section of the road from the house. I left Ida in the car while I trudged down the road with a small flashlight I kept in my glove compartment. I left it off since there was still enough light left to see the way. However, it wouldn't last long. Any daylight peeking through the still cloudy skies overhead would soon disappear. The flashlight would help me to see C.J.'s bumper and would also guide me back to my car. The flashlight was my dad's idea. He had a strict list for my glove box. Registration, title, and flashlight. Check. I sent up a prayer of thanksgiving for my father as I approached the house. I felt fairly safe. Unless someone specifically looked out the windows on the west side of the house to see if some crazy girl was wandering through the field, I wouldn't be noticed. Even so, as I got closer, I tried to be as quiet as possible. Unfortunately, the rain had created a lot of mud. My sneakers weren't as sneaky as they should have been. A weird sucking sound occurred every time I took a step. It was noticeable to me, but I consoled myself with the knowledge that it wasn't something anyone inside the house could hear.

I made my way around to the back of the house and was surprised to find nothing. No truck. Had C.J. gone into town? Was ruining my best sneakers all for nothing? A quick glance through the yard revealed the large outbuilding I'd noticed during my first visit. The door on the front was unusually large. More like a garage door. Maybe the truck was inside. I crept up to the building. Although the structure appeared to be decrepit, it was actually much sturdier than I'd originally thought. I found a regular door in the back and pulled on the latch. The loud creak made my heart race. I peeked around the corner toward the house to see if anyone else had heard it, but no one stirred. I could see that the windows were open and the curtains were drawn back, probably to get some air circulating. The shimmering lights from inside came from oil lamps. Even though they usually have a glass hurricane cover to protect the flame, air can still get inside from the top and make the flames flicker. It gave the house an eerie look, creating shadows that appeared to be caught in some kind of macabre dance. A shiver ran down my spine, but I reminded myself that no one knew I was there.

I slipped inside the dark building. Sure enough, the truck was parked inside. Feeling my way around the side with my hand, I made my way to the back. Turning on the flashlight, I aimed it on the right bumper. There was a bear on the sticker all right, standing on top of a hill. I moved the beam of light along the bottom border. It read CALIFORNIA REPUBLIC, and over the bear, on the top left side, was a star. "It's a California flag," I whispered into the dark. Well, that didn't seem very ominous. How many people from California had them? I sat on the bumper for a moment, trying to decide what to do. Should I let this go? Or should I call Pat? The war in my mind waged against the feeling in my gut. Where was my peace? I knew that's what Ida would ask. At that moment, I had no idea. Ida. I needed to get back to her before she began to worry. I stood up and started toward the door when I heard a loud thumping noise. It frightened me so much a small scream escaped my lips. Was C.J. out there? Had I been discovered? I waited several seconds, but there was only silence. I crept closer to the door. There it was again! Two thumps this time. Was someone knocking on the wall outside the makeshift garage? I had two choices. I could step outside slowly and confront whoever was out there, or I could take off running like the devil was chasing me. After looking carefully around the corner and seeing no one, I chose the latter. Of course, with all the mud, the devil probably could have simply strolled next to me and not broken a sweat. But I moved as fast as I could, keeping the light from the flashlight in front of me. At this point, I didn't care who was watching. It was so dark outside, no one would be able to clearly see me.

"Look, Mama," C.J. might say. "There's a strange light bouncing through the field."

That was a lot better than, "Look, Mama, Gracie Temple is running around outside like an insane person. Wonder what she's up to?"

I finally made it back to the car, but my sneakers were so caked with mud I could barely lift my feet. I opened the car door, sat sideways, and pulled them off. A weird slurping sound accompanied my task. Now what? I felt a hand on my shoulder.

"Hand them to me, Gracie," Ida said. I swiveled around and saw that she'd removed a towel from the basket and had it on her lap. "I was certain you would need help with your shoes when you returned. Let me clean them for you while we. . .make our getaway? Is that the correct phrase?"

I started to protest, to tell her that my schlepping through a muddy field in the middle of the night had nothing to do with anything underhanded, but she wouldn't have believed me. And she would have been right. So I just handed her the shoes, closed the car door, backed up a bit, turned the car around, and headed back to the main road. I waited to flip on my headlights until I was certain my car couldn't be seen from the Bradley house. I kept looking in the rearview mirror to see if a red truck was on our tail, but no one followed us. When we turned onto Faith Road, I breathed a sigh of relief. Ida carefully wiped my shoes off the best she could, leaving globs of wet mud inside the towel, which she held on her lap. The entire time she didn't utter a word.

"Aren't you going to ask me what I was doing?" I said finally.

"No, liebling." Her voice was soft in the dark interior of the car. "You do not have to explain everything to me. If it is my business, you will tell me."

Odd how the fact that she *didn't* ask for an explanation made me want to give her one, but I decided not to. Lobbing false accusations against your neighbors was a big no-no in the Bible. However, in my mind *thinking* about it wasn't quite as bad. I needed some time to sort things out before adding C.J. to my list of bogus suspects.

"Thanks, Ida. I appreciate it. I'll tell you one of these days why I did this. But for now, if you don't mind, I'd rather not."

"I trust you, Gracie. In fact, I knew you were someone I could trust from the first moment I met you. Nothing has changed. Nothing ever will."

And that was it. I glanced over at the elderly Mennonite woman, dressed in her Old Order clothes, and was surprised to realize that Ida Turnbauer was one of the best friends I'd ever had. As much as I loved Sarah, I wasn't as close to her as I was to Ida. I started to get a little emotional, so I tried to turn my thoughts back to C.J. Bradley before I burst out into a chorus of "Wind Beneath My Wings." A song Ida had probably never heard in her entire life.

The fear of offending C.J. and the real possibility that my actions could cause Pat to consider using his gun to stop me from causing any more trouble played against my overwhelming desire to find Hannah. By the time we reached Ida's, I'd made my decision.

I helped Ida up the stairs with her basket. "If you'll give me that muddy towel, I'll wash it and return it," I said when we reached the porch.

"No, liebling," she said. "I am happy to wash the towel. It is no trouble at all."

I knew arguing with her would be useless so I didn't. "Thank you, Ida. I had a wonderful day. Spending time with you is a joy."

"Why, my precious girl," she said, patting my cheek with her hand. "That means more to me than you could possibly know. You are such a dear friend."

"As are you." I kissed her cheek and waited while she opened her front door. Then I set the wicker basket inside. "I'd be happy to carry this to the kitchen."

"Thank you, Gracie. But that is not necessary. It will be fine here until I am ready to clean it out."

I said good-bye and left, still basking in the glow of treasured friendship. On the way home, I looked at the clock on my dashboard. Nine o'clock. I had one last thing to do before bed. I had no plan to tell Pat I'd asked Susan to follow up on C.J. It would make more sense to hang myself now and get it over with. But if I voiced my suspicions about C.J. and he contacted the KBI himself, there was a chance he would never know about Susan's involvement. It was a chance I was willing to take. So when I got home I called Pat.

One more time.

Chapter Twenty

Let's just say that the phone call didn't go well. At all. The first time, he just hung up on me. After letting the phone ring and ring the second time around, he finally picked up. I launched into a lengthy explanation as to *why* I felt he needed to follow this lead. Then I promised profusely that this would absolutely be the last time I bothered him with a possible suspect. That seemed to finally get his attention, although I had to listen to several minutes of ranting and raving, including the use of some words I'd actually have to look up to understand. I had the distinct feeling these pearls of "wordom" would not be found in my handy Funk and Wagnalls. When he finally calmed down a little, I tried again.

"Look," I said firmly, "we can't leave any stone unturned. If it makes you feel any better, I think this is the last red truck in Harmony you'll need to worry about. I've probably checked out all the rest. I just didn't see this particular truck until today."

"Well thank goodness for that," Pat replied, although it sounded more like, "Well. Thank. Goodness. For. That." I had no idea why his words were spoken with so much emphasis and definition. Perhaps getting them out coherently took extra effort.

"C.J. isn't from around here," I explained. "He's from California, and he probably lived there when some of those murders took place. And you said there were others in Arizona and New Mexico, right? Obviously, your killer lived somewhere in that part of the country. C.J. fits the bill."

The silence from the other end of the phone line wasn't very reassuring. Finally a long, drawn-out sigh came through the receiver. I wondered if he had any air left. "All right, Gracie. One last time. But I mean it. This is the end. My deputies are beginning to think I've lost my mind. Spending all this time on a runaway."

I bit my lip and didn't utter what had become my mantra the past few days. *Hannah is not a runaway.* I didn't have the nerve to say it again or to tell him that thanks to Susan, the KBI might get more involved in his case even without his help. I wasn't sorry I'd contacted Susan. I couldn't take the chance that Pat would drop the ball or refuse to follow up on C.J. At least now I had two people pushing for an investigation of C. J. Bradley. Hopefully, this plan wouldn't blow up in my face. After all, Pat was about to become my father-in-law. Holiday dinners could be tense.

"Changing the subject for a moment," he said. "Sam called and invited me to the wedding rehearsal. And the dinner."

"Oh Pat. That's great news." And I meant it.

"I'm assuming that means I'm also invited to the wedding?"

"You haven't gotten an invitation?"

"Not yet."

Mom told me the invitations were mailed out several days ago. Pat obviously hadn't gotten one because he wasn't on Sweetie's list. She'd handled most of the local invitations while my mother worked mainly on the relatives that lived out of state. I was determined Pat would get an invitation if I had to mail it myself.

"I'll follow up on that," I said. "But you're definitely invited."

"Good. I think Sam and I are starting to make progress. For the first time I'm beginning to feel like a real father."

"Just remember that you're also a real father-in-law. No matter how much I irritate you."

He snorted. "I keep trying to remind myself of that. Frankly, it's getting harder and harder."

"Thanks." I heard Mom and Dad getting ready to head upstairs for bed. "Hey, gotta go. Will you let me know what you find out?"

"Yes, Gracie. *If* I find out anything."

I said good-bye and hung up the phone feeling a little better. Suddenly Ida's dream popped back into my mind. *Eyes to see and ears to hear.* Maybe noticing C.J.'s bumper was what I was supposed to *see.* Perhaps we were finally getting close to finding Hannah. After hearing about Ida's dream, I felt even more certain that Hannah wasn't dead. My hope was high, and I had no intention of backing off the search for her.

"We're going upstairs," Mom said. "Will you be okay down here?"

"I'm fine. Might raid the fridge though. I'm a little hungry."

"We gave Papa a pill about an hour ago," my father said. "I think he'll be quiet for a while. If he wakes up during the night again, don't hesitate to give him another one."

"Okay," I said. "By the way, how's your knee?"

"Dr. Keystone stopped by this morning on his way to Topeka," Mom said. "He looked at your father's leg and told him what I've been saying for months. He hasn't been allowing his injury to heal properly. John wrapped it up and handed Daniel his cane with a warning that if he doesn't start using it all the time, he'll put your father back in a cast."

"I just saw John in Topeka earlier today. When was he here?"

"About thirty minutes after you left," Mom said. "He had a couple of emergencies earlier today. Then he stopped by to see Daniel. He told us he was on his way back to Topeka. He must have passed you."

"He sure is putting miles on that SUV of his," I said. "With what people around here pay him, I hope he doesn't go broke."

"I think his mind is on love," Mom said smiling. "Not money."

I laughed. "I'm sure you're right about that."

After they went upstairs, I checked on Papa. Sure enough, he was sound asleep and snoring. Smelling something good coming from the kitchen, I investigated and found that my mother had made peanut butter cookies. I grabbed several, made some hot chocolate, and went into the living room. It seemed silly to try to be quiet when talking to my parents hadn't roused Papa, but I tiptoed to the rocking chair, put my food on a nearby table, picked up the phone, and called Sam. I kept my voice as low as I could but loud enough so Sam could hear me while I gave him a rundown of my day. As I'd expected, he scolded me for going back to Abigail's.

"You might as well save your breath," I said. "I'm glad I did it. We have to know if C.J. *is* involved. There's no way I can simply ignore the situation. He's probably innocent, but if that's true, he has nothing to worry about."

"Well, here's something you might not have thought of, Grace," Sam said, his tone a couple of notches higher than normal. "What if C.J. *is* the serial killer, and he saw you sneaking onto his property and spying on him? What do you think he would do?"

His words brought me up short. "I—I hadn't thought of that." And I hadn't. I'd been so focused on Hannah that the whole idea of my own safety never occurred to me.

Sam exhaled loudly. First Pat and now Sam. I seemed to be

making the men in my life breathless. "Did he see you?"

I shook my head before realizing Sam couldn't actually pick that up through the phone. "No, I'm sure he didn't. I was careful, and no one followed me when I left."

"Did you leave anything behind that might tell him you were snooping around?"

"No. Nothing." *Except big, muddy footprints all around the area where his truck was parked.* While Sam continued to reproach me, I tuned him out and thought about those footprints. But with relief I realized the ground had been really wet. It wouldn't take long for mud to ooze back into my tracks. There shouldn't be any sign of my visit by morning. I started to relax a bit.

"Did you hear me?" Sam said.

"Certainly. I agree completely." It was the only thing I could come up with. Hopefully it fit.

"Thank goodness. I thought I'd have to fight with you about it."

Uh-oh. "Um, could you just repeat that one more time for clarification?"

Silence. After a long pause, he said, "You weren't listening, were you?"

"I'm sorry, Sam. My mind drifted. It's been a long day. Tell me again?"

"Forget it. It wasn't important." His tone softened. "I know it's been rough. We'll talk more tomorrow. Any family plans?"

"Not yet. Problem is, Papa can't go anywhere right now. Unless you guys come over here, there's no way we can all get away together."

"Maybe it's better that way. I don't think your father wants much to do with me."

"I *am* going to talk to him, Sam. I just haven't had much time. Trust me, everything will be all right."

"And just how do you know that?"

"I know that because God put us together, and I'm fully confident He'll take care of this situation. Besides, my father is a just man. Something's bothering him, and it has nothing to do with you. Dad's pretty introspective so I know he's trying to figure out why he's so upset. As soon as he deals with whatever's on his mind, he'll make things right with you. I guarantee it."

"I hope you're right. We need to get this straightened out before the wedding."

I heard a noise behind me. Papa Joe was sitting up on the couch, staring at me. "Hey, Papa's awake. I gotta go. Don't worry, I mean it."

"I love you, Grace."

"I love you, too, Sam. Good night."

I put the phone down, quickly downed the last of my chocolate, and went over to check on Papa.

"Why, Gracie girl," he said when he saw me. "Has everyone else gone to bed?"

"Yes, Papa. It's after ten."

He swung his legs around and sat facing me. "All this sleeping during the day has made it hard to get any shut-eye at night. I've got to get on a better schedule."

His shifts from normalcy to confusion were emotionally draining. How long would he be with me before retreating into that other world again? Although the good times made me happy at first, I'd actually begun to hate them. It was like being teased. First you soar and then you crash.

"I think I missed dinner, Gracie. How about a meat loaf sandwich?" he said with a smile.

"Sounds great, Papa." I got up to go into the kitchen. Papa rose shakily to his feet, obviously intending to follow me.

"You wait here," I said. "I'll bring it to you."

"I've been rotting on this couch all day. If you don't mind, I'd love to sit in the kitchen with you for a while."

I offered him my arm, and we made our way slowly to the kitchen.

"Are you still sore?" I asked.

"Just a smidgen. But those goofy pills they give me take away most of the pain. I feel pretty good right now."

"I'm glad, Papa." I helped him into a chair, and he watched me while I got the meat loaf out of the refrigerator.

"Gracie, when was tennis mentioned in the Bible?"

I turned to stare at him, wondering if he was drifting away again. But his quick smile and the twinkle in his eye told me he was still there.

"I don't know, Papa. When was tennis mentioned in the Bible?"

He winked at me. "When Moses served in Pharaoh's court."

I laughed. "Oh Papa. That's awful."

"I know." He fell silent while I got out the mayonnaise and bread from the bread box.

"Gracie, it's time for us to get your wedding present."

The jar of mayonnaise almost slipped from my hand. "Oh Papa." I set it down on the counter. I couldn't stop my tears even though I knew I wasn't supposed to let Papa see my pain.

He got up slowly and came over to me. Taking my hand, he led me to a chair. "Gracie," he said, sitting across from me, "I know there's something wrong with me, but this isn't part of that. You need to trust me."

I couldn't speak, so I just looked at him.

"Your grandmother made a wedding present for you right after you were born. She loved you so much, and she wanted to create something special for the day you became a bride. When we left Harmony, it was left behind. It's my fault, I took the wrong trunk. Your uncle Benjamin was given the task of protecting it. He knew it was to be yours, and he swore to get it to you someday. Of course he died before he could honor his word. Your grandmother never forgot that gift, and before she died, she made me promise I would get it to you. That's the main reason I wanted to come with Daniel and Beverly. Of course, I wanted to see Harmony again, and more than anything else, my beloved granddaughter. But I also knew I had to fulfill that promise to Essie." He shook his head slowly. "Sometimes I forget exactly where it is or how to find it. But tonight, my mind is clear." He reached out and grabbed my hands. "We must retrieve it now, Gracie. I can't trust my mind past my next thought. Do you understand?"

I nodded, picked up a napkin from the table, and wiped my face. "Where is this gift, Papa?"

"Unless someone has moved it, it's in the basement." He waved his hand toward the meat loaf sitting on the counter. "Let's have our sandwiches after we find it. There is no time to waste."

"But you're not supposed to go down the stairs."

"I understand. But I can tell you where to look, and you can find it yourself."

Oh please, God. Don't let this be his imagination. "All right, Papa. Where is it?" I knew every inch of that basement. There couldn't be anything hidden down there that I hadn't seen. Fear made my chest tighten, and I tried to shake it off.

"Is there still an old trunk in the basement made out of wood with a metal latch on the top? Do you know the one I mean?"

I nodded. "Papa, I've been through that trunk. There were some pieces of silver, some old papers, and a couple of quilts that I put on the beds upstairs."

"Yes, that would be the right one."

I frowned. "One of those items is my wedding present?"

He shook his head. "Remove them from the trunk. You'll find a leather tab on one side of the piece of wood at the bottom of the trunk. It's a false bottom, Gracie. Pull the tab up. The gift is under there. Essie put it in the trunk to keep it safe from air and from moths."

"Okay, but you have to stay here, okay? Don't leave this chair."

"I promise, but please hurry." He looked at me strangely. "Sometimes the lonely place comes for me, and I can't fight it off."

I nodded, not trusting my voice at that moment. I got up and opened the door that leads to the basement, being careful to shut it behind me. Fear that Papa would try to follow me made me hurry so quickly I caught my foot on one of the steps and almost tumbled the rest of the way down. Thankfully, I was able to grab the banister just in time. When I reached the bottom of the stairs, my heart pounded so hard it felt as if it might jump from my chest.

The basement was dark, so I switched on the light. The trunk Papa referred to was in the far corner, covered with drop cloths and supplies used when Sam and I painted the house. I quickly moved everything out of the way, praying that this wasn't some kind of wild goose chase. Papa had been talking about a "gift" from Mama ever since he'd arrived in Harmony. Had he been right all along? Had this been more than a result of the disease that ravaged his brain?

I unlocked the trunk, opened the lid, and carefully removed the items inside. Two old quilts in worn condition that I'd taken from upstairs; some pieces of family silver, simple in design but treasured by my grandparents; a pair of Mama's shoes wrapped in plastic, too precious for me to throw away; and an old album full of school papers belonging to my father and Uncle Benjamin. Once these had been removed, there was nothing left. No "tab" evident to my eyes, and the bottom of the trunk felt solid. I was just about to give up when I had an idea.

I jumped up and ran to a large closet full of old tools that had once been used by my grandfather. Inside one of the tool chests I found a thin piece of metal shaped almost like a fingernail file. I hurried back to the chest and tried to insert it between the bottom of the trunk and the side, figuring this was probably an exercise in futility because there wasn't any space below the wood bottom. But surprisingly, the tool slid in several inches. I stopped and examined the outside. Sure enough, the bottom appeared to be higher than the edge of the trunk that sat on the floor. I tried to wiggle the tool out, but it was stuck. After several attempts, it finally released. The piece of metal slid out, but something was attached to it. I pulled it a little more and discovered a piece of leather. Could this be the tab Papa talked about?

I yanked on it. Nothing. I pulled again, and the bottom of the chest moved a bit. I kept tugging until the piece of wood was loose enough I could grab it with my fingers and remove it. After putting it on the floor next to me, I stared down at the trunk. There was definitely something there, covered with material. With trembling fingers, I peeled back the layers. Underneath, I found a quilt. I lifted it out, put it on the floor, and began to unfold it.

As the design started to emerge, I began to sob. It was the most beautiful quilt I'd ever laid eyes on. The middle was splashed with various hues of breathtaking purple irises. The gorgeous flowers were just as vibrant as the day Mama stitched them together with love. They were surrounded by reddish blocks, just like the bricks that encircle Mama's garden. The quilt's background was the color of a Harmony sky, and additional irises and colorful pinwheels added to the overall depth and beauty. A deep-purple border framed the entire quilt like a picture frame. I looked closer,

Nancy Mehl

and although it was difficult for me to see through my tears, I found the words *Faith*, *Hope*, *Wisdom*, and *Royalty* stitched into the corners of the incredible design. I could see the tiny pieces of thread around the purple border, and in my mind's eye, I could envision Mama sewing each small stitch. How could Mama Essie have known almost twenty-five years ago that irises would be my very favorite flower just as they were hers? I'd chosen purple irises as my wedding flower, and now, as if she'd known it long ago, she'd sent this gorgeous quilt just in time for my marriage to Sam. I felt her gentle strength and overwhelming love in that room with me. This truly was a wedding present from my grandmother. And my grandfather had delivered it, just as he'd promised. I wept for a while, wiping my eyes on the hem of my shirt. Then I remembered Papa. I folded the quilt and carried it upstairs. He still sat in the chair where I'd left him.

"I found it, Papa," I said, my voice shaky. "It was right where you said it would be."

He let out a deep breath. "I kept my promise," he said softly. "I kept my promise."

I sank down on the floor in front of him, holding the quilt next to me. "Yes Papa, you kept your promise. It's the most beautiful wedding present anyone could give me. Thank you."

I laid my head against his legs, and he reached down and stroked my hair. After a few minutes he said, "Gracie, why don't cannibals eat clowns?"

"I don't know, Papa. Why don't cannibals eat clowns?"

He didn't say anything for a moment. Then softly he said, "Because they taste funny."

"Oh Papa," I said laughing through my tears. "Now that joke is the best one yet."

"Always end with your best material," he said. "I'm tired,

912

Gracie girl. I really need to lie down."

"What about your meat loaf sandwich?"

"Not tonight. Maybe tomorrow."

"That sounds good, Papa." I got up, carefully put the folded quilt over a nearby chair, and helped Papa to his feet. He leaned into me as we walked back toward the living room. When we reached the couch, I quickly straightened his pillow and pulled back the covers. He sat down slowly.

"Thank you, Snicklefritz," he said. "This was one of the best evenings of my life." He sighed deeply and sank down on the couch. I pulled his covers up. "Sorry I didn't get to tell Daniel and Beverly good night." He reached out and grabbed my fingers. "If I'm asleep in the morning when they get up, will you tell them I love them?"

I patted his hand. "Of course Papa. But you can tell them yourself."

He nodded. "That's right."

Suddenly he blinked several times. "Gracie, one other thing. You must stay away from. . .from. . ." He shook his head. "He's evil. You know who I mean, right?"

"Yes, Papa. I know who you mean. I promise to stay away from him." Papa's revulsion of Jacob Glick had survived the years in fine shape. I thought about reminding him once again that Glick had been dead for thirty years, but I knew it didn't really matter. Papa would only forget. Hearing him drift away once again made my heart ache, but I was grateful for the time we'd been given tonight. It meant more to me than I could say.

"That's fine, Gracie. Think I'll nod off for a while." He brought my hand to his lips and lightly kissed my fingers. "I love you, you know." Suddenly he sat up. "Why Essie, there you are. It's about time." He smiled at an empty corner of the room. "Gracie knows you love her, Essie." He looked at me. "Isn't that right, Snicklefritz? You know your grandmother loves you?"

"I know, Papa. I know."

I got up and fetched the quilt from the kitchen. Then I pulled my rocking chair near the couch and watched Papa as he fell asleep, Mama Essie's beautiful quilt on my lap. I woke up a couple of hours later when someone kissed me on the head. Startled, I turned around to see if Mom had come downstairs, but no one was there. I was alone.

I sat there for a while, running my hands over the beautiful quilt, remembering how Mama Essie used to wake me when I'd fallen asleep as a child—with a kiss on the head. I thought about the times we'd spent as a family—Papa telling his silly jokes and singing "I've Been Working on the Railroad" while he swung me around with his strong arms. The way he used to tease Mama, and the funny way she wrinkled up her nose when she laughed, making her look like a little girl even when her hair was gray and the spring had left her step. Mama and Papa had built a strong family through faith in God, the love they had for each other, and the determination to always believe that with God, anything was possible. Like Papa fighting against the shadows that tried to overtake him because he'd made a promise to the woman he loved.

And like Mama Essie kissing me on the head to let me know everything was all right.

After a few more minutes, I gathered my courage and got up to check on Papa Joe, confirming what I already knew in my heart.

Papa and Mama were finally together again, and the darkness that had tried to defeat my grandfather had been conquered once and for all.

Chapter Twenty-One

I think we should postpone the wedding."

Dad shook his head. "Papa would be horrified by that idea, and you know it. He wouldn't want to be the cause of disrupting your special day."

"But it feels too soon. How can we celebrate my wedding so quickly after Papa's funeral?"

My mother was making sandwiches while Dad and I sat at the table in my kitchen. We'd arranged for a funeral home in Sunrise to make the arrangements for Papa's service. Papa had always made it clear that he only wanted a graveside service. "I don't want people sitting around telling long-winded stories about me," he'd say. "Just plant my body in the ground. As long as the good Lord knows where it is, that's all I care about."

"You're sure about burying Papa here?" I asked. "I thought he'd want to be next to Mama."

My father cleared his throat and stared at the tabletop for a moment before answering. "Actually, we're probably going to have Mama moved here, too."

915

His statement took me by surprise. "Wow. I—I don't understand. Didn't Papa and Mama buy a double plot in Nebraska? Isn't that where they wanted to be buried?"

Mom stopped her lunch preparations and gazed at my father, a strange expression on her face. "I think you need to tell her, Daniel."

I looked back and forth between them. "Tell me? Tell me what?"

"Your mother and I had a long talk on the way up and back from the funeral home," Dad said. "It was clear we needed to face some feelings we've both been having. Papa's death brought everything out into the open."

I was tired and although the sadness I felt over losing Papa was overshadowed with the knowledge that he and Mama were finally together, I wasn't in the mood for riddles. "I guess you need to explain what you mean. I'm not getting it."

My father cleared his voice again. "Haven't you noticed that your mother and I have been behaving a little. . .oddly since we've been in Harmony?"

I smiled for the first time since Papa died. "As opposed to?"

My father's eyes narrowed. "Okay. Let's say our behavior is a little stranger than normal, will that do?"

I nodded. "I can accept that."

"Gee, thanks." He shook his head, but I saw the corners of his mouth turn up.

Mom came up behind me, carrying our plates. She'd made us sandwiches with potato salad. "Your father has been concerned about my impromptu buying spree. Of course there's nothing wrong with buying whatever I want, but you know me, Gracie. I'm usually. . ."

"Cheap?" my father interjected.

She frowned at him. "I was going to say *thrifty*, thank you."

"I have to admit I was curious about all the purchases you made in town," I said. "You could almost open your own store. So what was that all about?"

She got three glasses down from the cabinet. "Well, the explanation happens to be the same reason your father took a dislike to Sam."

"Okay, now I'm confused. What do those two things have to do with each other?"

My father sighed. "Well your mother was trying her best to buy Harmony, and I've been jealous of Sam even before I met him. And it's because. . ."

"You miss Harmony." The light had finally come on, and I was surprised by the revelation. "I thought you two were thrilled to get away from here. What gives?"

My mother got a pitcher of tea out of the refrigerator. "We weren't thrilled to go, Gracie. We hated leaving. We loved Harmony. But Bishop Angstadt's hold over our church stood in the way of God's will in our lives. In the end, we had no choice."

As she filled our glasses, Dad picked up where she left off. "When we moved away, I think we tried to put Harmony out of our minds. It got easier when Papa and Mama followed us to Nebraska. And when Benjamin cut himself off from the rest of the family, the only thing that made sense was to turn our back on Harmony for good." He shook his head. "But the truth is, we never really forgot this place. It's always been home." He reached over and took my hand. "When I met Sam, I disliked him because he had what I'd lost—a home in Harmony. It sounds so selfish, but in my defense, I didn't realize why I reacted so strongly to him. . .until Papa died."

"But what does Papa's death have to do with anything?"

Mom brought us our drinks and sat down beside me. "Because when we thought about sending Papa's body back to Nebraska, we both felt the same way. That we didn't want his grave that far away from us."

I frowned at her. "But he wouldn't be far away from you. He'd be. . ." I stopped and stared at them, my mouth hanging open. "You're moving back to Harmony, aren't you?"

My mother leaned over and put her arm around me. "Only if it's okay with you, Gracie. We realize you've made a life here, and we don't want to butt in—"

"Are you serious?" I exclaimed, cutting off the rest of her sentence. "I would *love* to have you here!"

Dad grinned. "Then it's settled. We'll start looking for a house right away."

"You don't need to do that. You can live here."

Mom squeezed my shoulder. "But this is your house, Gracie. We don't want to. . ."

"Now how many houses do you think I can live in at one time, Mother? It's perfect. After the wedding, I'll move into Sam's, and this house will be yours."

"We'll buy it from you, Gracie," Dad said.

"Don't be ridiculous. I don't want to sell it to you. This house should have been yours in the first place. If Uncle Benjamin hadn't been so confused about things, it would have gone to you anyway. I know he'd want you to have it, Dad. And you know it, too."

My parents stared at each other for a moment. Then my mother broke out in a smile. "Okay Gracie, if you're sure. After the wedding, we'll go home and put the house in Nebraska up for sale. Then we'll come back here for good."

"And we'll bring Mama back, too," Dad said. "Our family still owns several plots in the Harmony cemetery. Mama and Papa will be right next to each other. The way they should be."

I picked up my glass of iced tea and took a big gulp. Then I put it down and smiled at my parents. "Papa's last gift wasn't the quilt from Mama. It was bringing his family back together."

My father grabbed my mother's hand. His voice broke as he said, "I believe that's exactly right, Gracie. He brought us all home. And with the quilt, even Mama is here with us."

For some reason, I didn't tell him about Mama's kiss. My pragmatic father might not believe me, and for now, it was between Mama, Papa, and me. And I wanted to keep it that way.

We spent the rest of the day together. It felt right, sharing memories of Papa while planning his funeral. Sweetie brought over enough food to feed us for a week; Ida hitched up Zeb and drove over to comfort us. She added her own tales of Papa and Mama, and it helped all of us to be reminded of how many lives they'd touched. Abel came by to see if he could help us. He looked tired, and when he offered to do the graveside service, at first my father refused, not wanting him to think about us until Hannah was found. But when Abel convinced him that he needed to concentrate on something besides his missing daughter, my parents gratefully accepted. Pastor Jensen stopped by while Abel was there, and they both went outside on the front porch for a while. I think it was just what Abel needed. Pastors minister so much to others, sometimes they don't get much ministry themselves. They were out there a long time. When I checked on them after an hour or so, they were praying together.

By the time supper rolled around, we were all exhausted from answering the phone and receiving people who stopped by to drop off food or offer their condolences. Finally, around seven o'clock, the only people left were Sam and Sweetie.

"You folks sit still," Sweetie told my parents. "I'll heat up some of this food for you, and then Sam and me will get outta your way."

"I wish you'd stay," Dad said. "And Sam, I'd like to talk to you for a few minutes, if you don't mind."

I hadn't had a chance to tell Sam about my dad's recent revelation. I smiled reassuringly at him, but the look on his face made it clear he was apprehensive about what my father planned to say. Dad led him out on the porch, and they took up the same spots Marcus and Abel had shared earlier in the day. While Sweetie fixed dinner, Mom and I shared the good news that they were moving back. Sweetie was so happy, she got weepy. Something she doesn't do often.

"It's been me and Sam for so long," she said, sniffling. "Then our darling Gracie came along, and now you two. It's startin' to feel like a real family. I ain't had one since I was a small girl. I'm feelin' really happy about it right now."

I laughed. "I'm feelin' real happy about it, too."

Right before dinner was served, Sam and Dad came back into the house. Sam looked relieved, and Dad looked more relaxed than I'd seen him since he'd come to Harmony. I knew he missed Papa but even though no one said it, we all felt that Papa's burden had been lifted. Watching him disintegrate from Alzheimer's was much worse than knowing he was rejoicing with Jesus and dancing on streets of gold with Mama. Alzheimer's is a thief, and what it had tried to rob from Papa had been restored by God. I'd prayed for a healing on earth, but Papa had been healed in heaven instead.

After dinner I showed Sam and Sweetie the quilt Mama had made for me.

"Why, land's sake if that ain't one of the most beautiful things I ever seen," Sweetie said. She ran her fingers lightly over the top. "But it looks almost brand new." She scrunched up her face. "You say it had some kinda material around it?"

"Yes. It was in a wooden compartment below the main part of the trunk."

"Mind if I take a look?"

I told her to go ahead, and she went down in the basement for a while. When she came back up, she had a smile on her face. "You're real blessed that the quilt lasted the way it did. Your grandma was one smart lady. The wood was varnished and she wrapped the quilt in unbleached muslin. Best way in the world to keep a quilt in good shape. She knowed just what she was doin'."

Sam loved the quilt and didn't even complain about the flowers. We agreed it would be hung on the wall somewhere in the house. Sweetie had already informed us that the beautiful purple room would belong to us. I had a feeling the quilt would end up there.

After Sam and Sweetie left, my parents headed to bed. We were all wiped out from the day's events. We'd decided to have the funeral on Tuesday, and keep the wedding on Saturday. Since the invitations had already been sent, it seemed the easiest solution. For just a moment, I felt badly that Papa wouldn't be able to see me get married, but I had a witness in my heart that he and Mama would be watching.

Sam drove Sweetie home and then came back. We sat on the front porch, holding hands, and rocking next to each other until way after the sun went down.

"One more week, and we'll never have to say good-bye at the end of the day again," Sam said as stars began to light up the heavens.

"I know, I know," I whispered. "Just good night."

The next day we all went to church and after the service had lunch at Mary's. People kept stopping by the table to offer their condolences. Carmen, Hector's wife, informed us that they had finally decided to change the name of the restaurant from Mary's Kitchen to The Harmony House.

"Hector thought about changing it to Hector's House, but he felt it would be better to honor the town instead of drawing attention to one person."

Connie overheard her sister and came up to the table. "He also think about calling this place Ramirez Restaurant," she said with a heavier accent than her sister, "but he afraid everyone believe we only serve Mexican food." She laughed and took off to greet Harold Price and Kay Curless. Harold, a widower who had made the restaurant his second home, beamed. And Kay, a beautiful woman who had also been a widow for many years, looked as happy as she could possibly be. It was apparent that these two wonderful people would no longer be alone.

We were getting ready to leave when Pat walked in the front door looking upset. "Good afternoon, folks," he said when he reached our table. "Sorry to disturb you, but I wonder if I could talk to Gracie for a moment."

Sam shook his head. "Why is it that every time you say that, I get a bad feeling?"

Pat grunted. "Probably past experience."

Sam nodded. "You've got that right."

I put my napkin down and excused myself. "Please don't let anyone take my plate. I'm not finished."

"Well, that's what happens when you get hauled off by the police before you finish eating," Dad said.

"I'm not being hauled off by the police," I protested. Unfortunately I spoke a little too loudly. People at several nearby tables looked at us with interest. I followed Pat over to a table across the room where we wouldn't be overheard.

"What now?" I asked once we were seated. "Is there any news about Hannah?"

He shook his head. "Nothing about Hannah. But your friends at the KBI have certainly been busy."

I offered him my most innocent look. "What are you talking about?"

He glowered at me. "I think you know exactly what I mean." My continued silence seemed to exasperate him. "It might interest you to know that pulling your social worker friend into things may have backfired on you. Big-time."

"What are you talking about?"

"The KBI looked into Hannah's disappearance all right. And the first thing they did was stop by and question C. J. Bradley."

"Oh no." I felt the blood drain from my face. "They weren't supposed to. . ."

"I thought so," Pat said with a note of triumph.

I just stared at him. "Does C.J. know?"

"Does he know what? That you're the one who contacted the KBI about him?"

I swallowed hard. "Yes."

"I'm not sure. I wasn't there so I have no idea what was said to him. I just know they had quite a long visit."

I thought for a moment. "If he's the person they're looking for, they've just tipped him off. What if he runs?"

Pat folded his arms across his chest and leaned back in his chair. "I don't think he'll be doing anything like that."

"How in the world can you know that?" When several customers turned to stare at us again, I realized I needed to calm down. I lowered my voice. "There's no way to tell what he might do next."

"I'm pretty sure he's not going to take off because he's not the serial killer we've been looking for. If he leaves, it will probably be because someone called the KBI on him."

I sighed with exasperation. "You're not making sense. What are you trying to tell me?"

"I'm trying to tell you that authorities in Kansas City caught the guy."

I was stunned. "What do you mean they 'caught the guy'?"

"How much clearer do I have to make it? A couple of hours after the boys in black interrogated your friend C.J., the police cornered the killer they've been looking for in an apartment in Kansas City. C.J. had nothing to do with the murder in Topeka." He held up his hand. "And before you ask me if they're sure they've got the right man, the answer is yes. Without a doubt. The DNA matches, and to top it off, he confessed. Seems he's pretty proud of himself and wants everyone to know what he's done. A real nut job."

The reality of what Pat told me hit me like a ton of bricks. "But that means. . ."

"That Hannah is a runaway, just like I said. This guy was singing like a noisy canary. He was asked about Hannah, along with a couple of other runaways. He didn't know anything about them. He killed the girl in Topeka all right, but he had nothing whatsoever to do with Hannah's disappearance."

"Then where is she, Pat? What's happened to her?"

"I can't answer that question, Gracie. I'm still in touch with your friends from Wichita. No one's seen her." Connie came up to the table to see if Pat wanted anything, but he waved her away. "I know you're worried, but I just don't believe she was taken against her will. As far as that bracelet, she just lost it, and that's all there is to it." He leaned forward, his forearms on the table. "Look, I'm going to keep searching for her. You need to concentrate on burying your grandfather and getting married. Let me take this on for you, okay? Let it go. . .just for a while."

His attempt at kindness touched me. "I won't let it go until Hannah is home, but I'll try to ease off a bit. If you promise to do everything you can to find her."

"I really have been doing my best, but I'll go over it all again. If there's any way to bring her back, I'll do it. You have my word."

"What about C.J.? Does he know the killer's been caught?"

Pat nodded. "I went over there myself and told him. Apologized for bothering him. He was very gracious about it, but he wasn't thrilled about being suspected of serial murders. He talked about going back to California."

Guilt washed over me. "But his mother needs him." I put my head in my hands. "This is all my fault."

Pat reached over and pulled my face up. "You were trying to save your friend, Gracie. Sorry I came on so strong. Don't beat yourself up because of me. There's no harm done. The KBI halted their investigation of C.J., and he won't be contacted again."

"They were actually investigating him? How far did they go?"

"Well, they started a background check. And of course they questioned him and were checking out his whereabouts around the time of the murders."

"Would C.J. have any way to know about the background check?"

"No, I don't think so."

I took a deep breath. "Well at least that's something."

"So now what are you going to do?" Pat asked.

"About what?" I was pretty sure what he meant, but I hoped I was wrong. I wasn't.

"About C.J. Don't you think you should talk to him? Explain? Apologize? Something? You might be able to talk him into staying if you tell him why you suspected him of taking Hannah."

I stared at Pat, trying to come up with a reason that I *shouldn't* confess to C.J. and beg his forgiveness. Problem was, no sensible reason sprang to mind. "All right," I said finally. "I'll do it. Even if he hates me forever, maybe he'll stay and finish the work he started on his mom's house."

"Good girl." Pat stood up. "I'll see if I can dig up any new leads on Hannah, and you spend time with your family. Is that a deal?"

"Hey, one last question?"

Pat raised an eyebrow. "What?"

"This serial killer. Did he have a red truck and a bumper sticker with a bear on it?"

He grinned. "He was driving a purple truck, and the only bumper sticker he had said GIVE A SQUIRREL A HOME. PLANT A TREE."

"No bear?"

He shook his head. "Nope. Just a squirrel."

"So he doesn't mind killing human beings, but he's worried about squirrels?"

Pat shrugged. "Gracie, the guy's insane. I don't think I'd take his bumper sticker too literally."

"I guess," I said glumly. "Boy, this has been a rough couple of days."

He smiled at me and held out his hand. I took it, and he pulled me to my feet. "Everything's going to be fine. I promise."

I nodded but didn't respond. Nothing would be "fine" until Hannah was safely home.

I went back to the table. Thankfully my food was still there, and Connie had refilled our bowls of mashed potatoes, creamed corn, gravy, and coleslaw. A new platter of fried chicken had also appeared. Before I had a chance to finish what I'd started to eat before my discussion with Pat, Connie whisked my old plate away and put a new one in its place.

"Cold food no good for you," she said. "You eat nice hot food now, sí?"

"Thank you, Connie," I said, grateful for her kindness. "Hot food is always better."

She bobbed her head in agreement and left the table with a big smile on her face.

I ate Hector's delicious dishes until I felt like the buttons on my lightweight summer dress might pop off and cause injury to some of the other diners.

After we left the restaurant, we drove to the Harmony cemetery where my father pointed out the other gravesites that belonged to our family. As I stood there, seeing where Papa and Mama would be laid to rest, the thought crossed my mind that someday, Sam and I might also be buried here. The idea gave me the shivers. Good thing the real me would be in heaven, not caring one little bit about the shell that had contained me on this earth. The cemetery was actually situated in a gorgeous location. It sat about a mile out of town and was surrounded by tall trees that shaded almost the entire area. Large monuments of carved angels or other figures decorated the grounds, and carefully tended flowers offered color and graceful beauty. After the initial creepy feeling that came from possibly standing on my own grave, I had to admit that this was the most beautiful cemetery I'd ever seen.

We went home and everyone took a nap, including me. Not something I usually do, but with all the stress of losing Papa, I was physically and mentally exhausted. At first I tossed and turned on my bed, but when I did finally fall asleep, I dreamed that Hannah was calling my name, pleading with me to save her. She kept saying the same thing over and over. "Help me, Gracie. Use your eyes and ears. Please use your eyes and ears."

After a couple of hours, I woke up, drenched with sweat. By the time I got up, took a quick shower, and changed clothes, it was almost dinnertime.

"Can you guys heat some of this food up?" I asked my parents after my shower. "I have a quick errand to run."

"We're still stuffed from lunch," my mother said. "If your father gets hungry, I'll make him something. I'm not the least bit interested in eating."

"Thanks. I shouldn't be too long."

"Where are you going?" Dad asked. "Or are you too old to account for your whereabouts?"

I grinned at him. "I get the distinct impression I'll never be old enough for that in your eyes."

"You've got that right," he said, peering over the top of his reading glasses. My father reads the paper religiously every Sunday. He doesn't care about the newspaper during the week, but Sunday never passes without him sticking his nose into newsprint and only coming up for air when absolutely necessary. My dad's copy of the Topeka paper could only have come from the restaurant. Since the paper isn't delivered to Harmony, Hector faithfully drives to Sunrise every Sunday morning and buys twenty or thirty copies for residents who want to read it. Dad must have gotten to the restaurant very early to snag one of the prized copies.

I grabbed my purse and my keys. "If you must know, I'm going to apologize to someone. Since I don't do it very often, I might be a little while."

My mother smiled at me. "If you're apologizing to Sam, take your time. It's not good to have tension between you two right before the wedding."

I started to tell her my mea culpa had nothing to do with

Sam, but trying to explain the whole story of my transgression against C.J. Bradley seemed like too much effort. Besides, I was still extremely embarrassed about it. I nodded, said good-bye, and left.

My drive to the Bradley place seemed to take longer than normal. Probably because I wasn't anxious to get there. As I pulled into the driveway, I didn't see C.J. anywhere. I thought about knocking on the door, but if he'd followed through on his threat to leave town, I was pretty certain his mother wasn't going to be glad to see me. I got out of my car and checked the back of the house, hoping I'd find him working. Nothing. Then I looked in the garage to see if his truck was still there. I swung the door open. No truck.

I stepped inside the large, empty building, allowing the door to close behind me. I needed to think. Maybe he'd just gone to town. It didn't make sense for him to take off so quickly. I noticed tools lying around on the ground, as if someone had left in the middle of a project. Surely he would have taken the time to put them away if he was leaving Harmony for good. I was headed toward the door when my foot caught on something, and I almost fell.

"What the heck?" I said out loud. As I leaned down to see what it was, a strange thumping noise startled me. It was the same sound I'd heard when I was there the last time. This time, instead of running out, I decided to find out what it was. There it was again. It sounded as if it was coming from beneath the floor. I reached down to see what I'd stumbled over. There was a large metal ring lying on the ground. When I tried to pick it up, I realized it was attached to the floor. Another *thump*.

I could have sworn I heard someone whisper, *"Tell Grace she must have eyes to see and ears to hear,"* and I felt a presence in that garage. It was almost overpowering. Sweat broke out on my forehead that had nothing to do with how hot it was. I got down on my knees and pushed the dirt away from the ring. I tugged on it as hard as I could, but it didn't budge. I realized there was a latch secured with a lock several inches from the ring that kept the trapdoor from opening. Spotting a pair of metal cutters mounted on the wall along with several other tools, I got up, removed them, and went back to the latch. It took me a couple of minutes to finally cut the lock open. Sweat poured down my face. Even before I pushed the trapdoor open, I knew exactly what I would see below the floor of the Bradley's garage.

And I was right.

Hannah Mueller stared up at me.

Chapter Twenty-Two

"Gracie, is it really you?" Hannah's voice was weak, and she blinked as if the light hurt her eyes.

"Yes, it's me," I said softly. "We've got to get you out of there, Hannah. I don't know where C.J. is."

"There aren't any steps down here. Can you find a ladder?" She began to sob. "Hurry, Gracie. He's crazy. He'll be back soon."

I spotted a stepladder against the wall and ran to get it. I'd just started to lower it to Hannah when I heard a noise. I whirled around and found C. J. Bradley standing near the garage door.

"What do you think you're doing?" he demanded. "You're trespassing on private property."

"Trespassing? Are you serious?" My fear of C.J. began to turn into rage. "Have you had Hannah here this entire time? Do you know how worried her parents have been?" Other questions exploded in my mind that I was afraid to ask. But right at that moment I was only thinking about the fact that Hannah was alive. He took a step closer, and I bent down and grabbed the pitchfork that lay at my feet.

"I don't know what you're talking about. There's no one named Hannah here. Just Melanie. I came back to Harmony, and there she was, just walking along the road. She waited for me all these years." His tone took on a kind of singsong quality, and he looked at me the way someone might look at a child. He shook his head and gave me an odd smile. As the setting sun peeked in through a window beside me and lit up his features, I realized I was looking into the face of madness. Hannah was right. C.J. Bradley was definitely crazy.

I attempted to control my anger and think clearly. I had to save Hannah. "C.J., Melanie isn't happy down there." I tried to push the emotion out of my voice and sound as soothing as possible. Keeping him calm might help us get out of the spot we were in. "I know you love her and don't want to see her unhappy. Why don't you let her go? Then you can really be together."

He cocked his head to the side as if listening to a voice I couldn't hear. Then he shook his head slowly. "No, I can't do that. Melanie tried to run away from me. I can't let that happen." He shrugged. "Wedding jitters, I guess. It will pass."

I could feel my heart pound as if it would burst through my chest. "But don't you think she'd relax more if she could walk around some? She doesn't look comfortable."

He looked at me like a chicken might study a bug before pouncing upon it. "Yes, you're right. It's time for her to come out. She won't run away again. Melanie loves me. She told me she does. I'm taking her back to California. We'll get married there. Maybe on the beach." He stared at me. "You're not going to interfere, you know. I won't have it. My mother ruined my life once. I won't let it happen again." He took a large hunting knife from his pocket and pointed it at me. "Get back so I can help her up the ladder. Then we're leaving. You can stay down there until someone finds you.

I'm—I'm not a killer, Gracie, but this is my last chance to get it right. No one will stop me this time. Not even your grandfather."

"What are you talking about?"

He snorted. "He caught me once when I was a kid. You know, with a girl. I let her go. No one got hurt. But he told me to stay away from all the girls in the town. And he told my mother what I did. She talked to Melanie's parents. They said I couldn't see her anymore. Then they left town and took Melanie away from me." His voice got soft. "Mama tried to beat the devil out of me. She promised Joe Temple I would never do that again so he wouldn't tell anyone else." He shook his head. "But the devil came back. He always comes back, you know."

My poor grandfather had recognized C.J., but hadn't been able to communicate the truth about him to us. Instead, he'd just exploded, warning us about evil. I'd thought he was talking about Jacob Glick. If only I'd realized. . .

C.J. brandished his knife and took another step toward me. "Now get out of the way, Gracie. Right now."

"There's no way I'm letting you take Hannah from here. No way in this world." I stepped between him and the hole in the ground where Hannah cowered, holding the pitchfork up between us.

"Then whatever happens is your fault," he said, raising the knife up over his head. But before he could get any closer, the door to the shed opened slowly and Pat Taylor came inside, his gun drawn.

"Put the knife down right now, C.J.," he growled, "or I'll blow a hole so big in you I'll be able to walk right though you instead of goin' around you. You got it?"

C.J. hesitated for a moment, and then after what seemed like an hour, let go of the knife. Pat immediately moved in, kicked it away, pushed C.J. to the ground, and handcuffed him. While he called for backup, I lowered the ladder down to Hannah and she climbed up. She was dirty and disheveled, but I'd never seen anything so beautiful in my entire life. She collapsed to the ground, and I got down beside her, holding her as she wept.

"I'm gonna lock this piece of pond scum in the back of my car so you all don't have to look at him anymore," Pat said, pulling C.J. to his feet. He looked completely disoriented—almost as if he didn't know where he was. "Are you both okay?"

"We're going to be fine," I said. "This is the second time you've saved my life, you know."

"Yes, I realize that. And it's gettin' old. Let's put a stop to it."

I stroked Hannah's matted hair. "And just why are you here, Pat? I didn't tell anyone where I was going."

"I'm aware of that. From here on out I'd like your daily itinerary if you don't mind. It will make rescuing you much easier." He pushed C.J. toward the door. "That background check the KBI started on this guy turned up some interesting information. He's a sex offender registered in California, and they suspect him of two attempted kidnappings in the past six months. Both of them girls about Hannah's age and description. I put two and two together—and then I figured you could only be right where you shouldn't be. And surprise. Here you are."

I smiled. "Thanks. Again."

He nodded and pushed C.J. out of the garage.

I put my hand under Hannah's chin and asked the question I didn't want to. "Hannah, did he. . .hurt you?"

She shook her head. "No, Gracie. I'm fine. He—he acted like we knew each other. Like we'd been engaged for a long time or something. He kept calling me Melanie. At first I tried to tell him I didn't know him. And I begged him to let me go." A sob tore from deep inside her. "But it made him mad. Really mad. I was afraid he was going to kill me. So I started acting like I really was this Melanie person, hoping he'd let me out. But he didn't. It's so dirty down there, and sometimes he forgot to feed me. I haven't eaten for a couple of days."

I smiled at her. "We can certainly take care of that. This is Harmony. Everyone and their cousin will be bringing you food."

She laughed through her tears. Then she grabbed my hand. "Thank you, Gracie. Somehow I knew it would be you who would find me. I prayed so hard that you would."

"Well God heard you. And so did Ida Turnbauer."

"What do you mean?"

"I'll tell you about it later. I expect there are a couple of people who would love to see you as soon as possible." I put my arm around her. "Can you walk?"

She nodded. "Let's get out of here."

I pulled her up, and she leaned against me. "Yes, let's." We walked over to the door, I swung it open, and Hannah and I stepped out into the light.

Chapter Twenty-Three

Sweetie's dining room was full for the rehearsal dinner. Not only had she put all the leaves in her dining room table, but she'd had to put up two other card tables to accommodate everyone. In her usual capable way, the room looked beautiful and the meal delicious. Prime rib, new potatoes with fresh green beans, Waldorf salad, homemade rolls with apple jam, and a chocolate mousse cheesecake that was so good it rivaled any dessert I'd ever tasted.

The atmosphere was light and happy, but there were questions about the strange events over the past two weeks.

"So no one knew how disturbed C.J. Bradley really was?" Pastor Jensen asked as we enjoyed cheesecake and coffee.

"Papa Joe knew," I replied. "And I should have. The clues were all there. Papa's reaction every time he saw C.J. His story about getting back together with Melanie. Although I'd forgotten, Ida told me Melanie had blond hair and blue eyes like Hannah. C.J. had a twisted view of life—and particularly of women. I saw that when he reacted badly to Jessie, but I dismissed it. His mother brought him up in her own deformed brand of religion. The world she created was void of love but full of judgment. And her anger toward men after her husband left caused her to pass some perverted ideas about relationships to her son. C.J. began acting out with local girls when he was a boy. When my grandfather caught him and informed his mother, she only made it worse by trying to 'beat the devil out of him,' as C.J. said. Then he lost Melanie because of his destructive behavior. I think he built Melanie up in his mind as the only way to save himself. If Melanie could forgive him and love him, he'd be free of the demons that had haunted him for so long. Add that to Abigail's religious views that stripped real love out of the equation, and C.J.'s life became a breeding ground for mental illness. If Abigail hadn't distanced herself and her son from almost everyone in Harmony, someone might have recognized how much trouble the boy was in. Perhaps he would have gotten the help he so desperately needed."

"But then he left to go to college," Mom said. "You'd think he'd be able to figure it out for himself once he got around normal people."

"It was too late for him by then," Susan said. Although she wasn't actually part of the wedding party, I'd invited her to dinner. Abel and Emily were so grateful for her help in getting the KBI to dig up the information that led to C.J.'s arrest, they'd wanted to thank her personally. Their profuse expressions of appreciation obviously embarrassed the social worker, but I could tell she was pleased to have helped bring their daughter home.

"What about them other women he assaulted?" Sweetie asked. "I mean, thank God he didn't hurt Hannah. . .physically anyway. But sounds like he treated her differently from the rest."

Susan shrugged. "I don't have any details about the other cases, but my guess is he's been trying to replace the love he lost for a long time. He sees Melanie as the perfect woman. Something about the women he hurt made him angry. He probably discovered they were flawed, and he couldn't accept it. Hannah never did anything to ruin that perception." She shook her head. "This may sound crazy, but it's possible that hiding Hannah in that cellar saved her life. If he'd spent more time around her and discovered she was just as human as everyone else, he might have harmed her."

"Not long ago, he found out Melanie had passed away," Pat said. "Is that what pushed him over the edge?"

Susan nodded. "I'm certain he couldn't accept knowing that he'd lost her forever. Lost his opportunity for some kind of redemption. So he decided he had to get her back. The night he saw Hannah walking down that dirt road, his warped mind turned her into Melanie. Hannah was his last chance for happiness."

"And he kept her hidden because he didn't want his mother to see her?" Dad asked.

Susan nodded. "Or anyone else. Maybe old Abigail was the world's worst mother, but her son's fear of her helped to protect Hannah. Also, people kept showing up at the house to help with repairs even though he tried to keep them away. Obviously he didn't want anyone to uncover his secret. It's possible that all the attention kept him from leaving town sooner with Hannah. If he had, she might not have been found in time." She smiled. "Please understand that as far as C.J.'s mental condition, I'm just guessing. I'm not a trained psychologist, but I've seen a lot of abuse."

"Well, it rings true to me," Pat said. "That man definitely has a screw loose somewhere."

Sam nodded his agreement. He and Pat were on their way to building the kind of relationship I'd been praying for. Pat had saved my life twice, and Sam's appreciation was helping to bridge the gap between them. Even Sweetie seemed to be accepting Pat. She certainly hadn't thrown her arms around him and welcomed him to the family, but she wasn't shooting him dirty looks anymore either. So progress had been made.

"How is Hannah?" my mom asked the Muellers.

"Much better," Emily said. "She wanted to come tonight, but I think she needs some time alone to sort out her feelings."

"Did she explain why in the world she got into C.J.'s truck in the first place?" Pastor Jensen asked.

"Yes, she did," Abel said. "She was walking over to Jonathan's house when C.J. pulled up next to her. He introduced himself as Abigail's son and told her Emily and I were looking for her. Hannah believed him. But after she got into the truck, she realized he wasn't taking her home. That's when she knew something was wrong. The only thing she could think to do was to toss her bracelet out the window when he wasn't looking."

"Thank God she did," I said. "If I hadn't found that bracelet, I might have accepted the idea that she'd run away."

Hannah's views of Harmony and her Mennonite lifestyle had changed—for now. Her "modern" clothes had been taken by detectives for evidence, but she wasn't the least bit sorry to see them go. She'd run back to her simple dresses and her prayer covering almost as if they were a special kind of protection against evil in the world. Sadly, I knew that wasn't true, but her desire to stay home and out of trouble was the best thing she could do for the time being. I had no idea if she would one day leave Harmony and go to Wichita—or some other large city—but at least she was safe and would have plenty of time to heal from the scars C. J. Bradley had caused through his own brokenness.

"Will C.J. go to jail?" Ida asked.

"Hard to say," Pat answered. "For now he's locked away. He's being evaluated to see if he's competent to stand trial. I suspect he's not."

Ida smiled at me. "I am so grateful you had 'eyes to see and ears to hear,' liebling. God used you to bring our Hannah back to us."

I sighed. "But I was way off. I thought Hannah had gotten mixed up with a serial killer, and here she was in Harmony all the time, right under our noses. I can't help but wonder whether we would have found her sooner if we hadn't gotten distracted by the man who killed that woman in Topeka."

Pat grunted. "I didn't get distracted by the girl in Topeka, and I missed it completely. You kept telling me Hannah had been abducted, but I wouldn't listen. If anyone's at fault for not finding her sooner, it's me. Not you. Thanks to you and your snoopiness, Hannah Mueller is home safe. No one could have done better than you did."

"You're giving me way too much credit, Pat. You're forgetting that I accidentally stumbled on her. You're the one who followed the leads and saved us both."

"That's true," Abel said, smiling. "But only after you wouldn't let it go, Gracie. Pat got those leads because you kept pushing."

Pat grunted. "Yeah, and I have a feeling I'm in for a lotta years of being pushed around."

I grinned at him. "You can count on that."

"Well, all I know is that my daughter is home, safe and sound," Emily said, her bottom lip quivering. "And I'm grateful to everyone who had anything to do with it. Thank you from the depths of our hearts."

"Amen," Abel said.

"Well," my father said, standing to his feet, "why don't we move on to the reason we've gathered together tonight? To celebrate an upcoming wedding." He frowned. "Now just who is it that's getting married? I can't quite remember."

"Very funny," I said, laughing.

"Oh yes. I remember now. I think my beautiful daughter Gracie and her handsome fiancé Sam plan to say their vows two days from now." He smiled at me. "Gracie Marie Temple, you have been our treasure from God from the day you were born. We are thankful every day that He chose us to be your parents." His voice caught, and he paused a moment before continuing. "You know, it's not easy to give away something that's precious to you. When I first arrived in Harmony, I wasn't sure about this strapping, blond farm boy you'd fallen in love with. That is until I realized there wasn't anything wrong with him at all. In fact, Sam Goodrich is everything I ever wanted to be—but wasn't. Stupidly, I took it out on him. I'm grateful to God that He helped me to realize what I was doing before I caused damage I couldn't fix." He rested his gaze on Sam. "I know you've forgiven me, son, but I want to say publicly that I'm sorry for ever making you feel uncomfortable." He reached over and took my mother's hand, pulling her to her feet. "Beverly and I want to welcome you to our family with open arms. We both want you to know that if we'd been asked to create the perfect man for our Gracie, we couldn't have designed anyone better than you."

"Now Daniel and I want to share something with you and Gracie," my mother said, smiling. "I hope it's advice that will guide you throughout your years together the way it has helped us. Our marriage has lasted for thirty years because we've tried our best to walk in the love of God, and fulfill His calling for us. So many Christians spend their lives searching for 'their ministry,' yet they miss the most important ministry God will ever give them. Gracie, if you will wake up every morning knowing that your first ministry is to Sam, and Sam, if you will wake up every morning knowing your most important ministry is toward Gracie, you will both see miracles in your lives. When God can trust you in this important calling, He'll lead you into other exciting areas because He knows your priorities are right. If you will remember to put each other first in every situation, you will forge a relationship that adversity can't destroy and the devil can't steal. Please understand that there will be storms. I wish I could say they won't come, but they will. But please trust us when we tell you that if you will build your house on the Rock, you will stand." She leaned against my father and gazed into his eyes. "Daniel and I have had our share of trouble, but thanks to God, we have had victory through each and every situation." She reached over and picked up her glass of iced tea. "Sam, I want you to know that in our eyes we don't see you as our son-in-law. The law of love is even stronger than the law of man. You are our son from this day forward. We will support you no matter what happens. We will always believe the best about you. Our words, our actions, and our hearts will always express the confidence and love we have for you."

My dad picked up his glass. "Gracie, you will always have an important place in our hearts—one that no one else will ever fill. But your mother and I want you to know that we are stepping back to take second place in your life. Behind your husband. We are here to love you both, to support you both, and to help you in any way we can. But we won't get in your way. Your mother and I release you to your husband. And now," my father said, "will you all stand and raise your glasses to Sam and Gracie."

Everyone at the table stood to their feet.

"May their lives be full of God's grace, and may their home always be overflowing with His love." Dad smiled at me, tears glinting in his eyes. I felt Sam grab my hand. "To Sam and Gracie."

"To Sam and Gracie," everyone repeated.

I couldn't speak, and Sam blinked back tears. "Thank you,"

he said to my parents. "I feel so blessed to be part of this family. And blessed to finally have my father in my life." He paused in an attempt to rein in his emotions. "But if no one minds, I'd like to take this opportunity to thank the one person who's always been there for me." He turned toward his aunt. "Sweetie, you stepped into my life when there wasn't anyone else. You gave me a home and all the love anyone could possibly need. I will be eternally grateful to you. I love you more than I can say and so does Gracie. If it wasn't for you, I wouldn't be standing here now, and I wouldn't have the wonderful life you've made possible." He held up his glass of iced tea. "I know tonight is supposed to be for Gracie and me, but I'd like to ask everyone to raise their glasses to Sweetie, who took a chance on a skinny, frightened, messed-up boy, and in doing so, brought us all together."

Sweetie's face crumbled as everyone in the room toasted to her. She tried to say something but couldn't get the words out. The love in the room was palpable, and I was overwhelmed by it. In this special moment, I felt an odd sense that my whole life had been rushing toward this place and these extraordinary people. Even more, to the heart of this incredible man who would soon be my husband.

"If you don't mind," Abel said smiling, "I'd also like to offer a toast to Harmony, a special place that God has blessed with protection and love. We've had our challenges, but He has been faithful. Emily and I have seen His hand many times down through the years. And now, in bringing our Hannah home to us." He looked at Ida who stood next to him. "And I want to honor Ida Turnbauer and the other women of Harmony who prayed over this place so long ago. God has answered that prayer in a mighty way. We've been faced with evil, but the Spirit of God has always prevailed." He held out his glass and said, "To the praying women of Harmony."

Every person in the room echoed his words.

"Is there anyone else we should toast?" my father said jokingly.

Pat cleared his throat. "If it's okay," he said softly. "I didn't plan to say anything, and I don't want to take attention away from Gracie and Sam."

"Of course it's all right," Dad said. "I think this is a night for saying what's in our hearts."

Pat nodded and turned toward Sam. "If I'd known about you sooner, son, I would have been there for you. It's important to me that you know that. I also want to tell you how much I regret my casual actions toward your mother. All I can say is that I was young and irresponsible. But I will never, ever regret the result of our relationship. You've turned out to be the kind of son any father would be proud of. And you're marrying one of the best women I've ever met." He paused for a moment, his jaw working. When he continued, his voice shook. "I'm not a churchgoing man, but I can't dispute the feeling that there is a divine hand in all of this. I look around this room, and I have to believe that there is a loving God who has a plan for all of us. Even though it's hard to believe that I could be a part of His grand design, tonight I feel it so strongly I can barely express my gratitude." He took a deep breath and held it a moment before letting it out. "Sam, thank you for allowing me into your family. And my thanks to all of you for opening your arms to me. I intend to spend the rest of my life making you glad you did." He held out his glass. "To family."

Once again, everyone repeated the toast. I looked at Sam who had tears streaming down his face. This was a night neither one of us would ever forget. A look around the table didn't reveal anyone else who felt the need to speak—or who wasn't so moved they couldn't even if they'd wanted to. When we sat down, almost everyone was in tears. After a few moments of silence, conversation began to break out once again. I gazed around the table and felt such deep gratitude to God for my good fortune. In Harmony, I'd found more than just a simple town full of loving people. I'd found my life, and I'd grown to know my heavenly Father more intimately.

Earlier in the day I'd experienced a tinge of melancholy knowing that Mama and Papa wouldn't be sitting in the church on Saturday when I walked down the aisle. But I had a strong sense that somehow they were with me and it helped. Somehow I knew they would be watching when I said my vows to the man of my dreams.

It was another hour before guests began heading home. Sam and I stood at the front door to say good-bye and thank them for coming. The Muellers and Ida were the last to leave except for Pat and my parents.

"Oh Gracie, thank you from the bottom of my heart for everything you've done for us," Emily said as she came up to me. She put her arms around me and hugged me tightly. "God brought you to this town—and to me. I love you, and I will always be your friend."

Emily's sweet comments touched my heart. "And you'll always be mine," I whispered back. "Tell Hannah everyone is praying for her, will you?"

She let me go but kept her hand on my arm. "She knows that, and she wanted me to tell you that she will be at the wedding." She looked at her husband. "Abel, will you go out to the car and get Hannah's wedding present to Gracie?"

Abel nodded and went out the front door.

"I know wedding gifts are usually given after the ceremony, but Hannah asked that we give this to you tonight," Emily said.

Ida, who had been waiting next to Emily, stepped up to me

and opened her arms. "Oh, liebling," she said softly, "I am so happy. The joy of the Lord wells up like rivers of living water in my spirit."

I wrapped my arms around her and she stroked my hair. "God has used you in great ways in my life," I told her. "I wish I had the words to tell you what you mean to me."

Ida released me and chuckled softly. "Ach, Gracie. We do not need words. I understand because I feel the same way about you."

She gazed up into Sam's face and took his hands. "I know you will take good care of my Gracie, and she will take good care of you. I pray that you will know the kind of love my Herman and I shared. The same kind of love that Gracie's grandparents had for each other. And the kind of devotion her parents feel for each other. If you will put God first and follow the words they spoke to you tonight, you will live with joy unspeakable and full of glory. Putting others first is the love of God, is it not? He gave everything for us. Now we follow His example and give our lives to each other."

"Thank you, Ida," Sam said, leaning down and kissing the old woman's cheek. "And if I ever forget, even for a minute, I expect you to remind me."

She laughed. "Ach, you can count on it, liebling." She reached out and took Emily's arm. "And now I must go back to my little house and rest. I must confess that the excitement of the last few days has made me very weary."

Just then Abel came back into the house with a large wrapped gift in his hand.

"I'm going to help Ida to the car while you deliver Hannah's present," Emily told her husband.

He held the door open for the two women who made their way outside to the porch and down the stairs. I turned my attention back to Abel who handed me the large square-shaped package.

I grinned at him. "I know what this is. Why don't we go into the living room where I have more room to open it?"

Sam and Abel followed me down the hall. Pat, Mom, and Sweetie were busy clearing dishes from the dining room. I put the package down on the living room table and started tearing off the paper, handing it to Sam. As I suspected, a large wood frame and canvas were revealed. After unwrapping it completely, I turned it over to reveal a beautiful painting.

"Oh my," I said, tears once again filling my eyes. I'd need massive amounts of water to replace all I'd lost that night. I even felt a little dehydrated. "Sam, look."

In the painting, a man and woman stood in the middle of an orchard. Although you couldn't see their faces, it was clear the couple was Sam and me. We were surrounded by beautiful trees, full of ripened fruit. A golden light from above bathed us in a soft radiance. My head was on Sam's shoulder, and his strong arm circled my waist. Even the ground beneath us glowed. It reminded me of Adam and Eve in the Garden of Eden. Written at the bottom of the canvas were these words: *And God Almighty bless thee, and make thee fruitful.*

"It's—it's incredible," I said, my voice catching from the emotion that overtook me. "Abel, tell her this picture will be have an honored place in our home forever."

"I will." The big pastor smiled. "I thought you'd like it. We gave Hannah permission to paint again, and this is what she chose to do. Her mother and I have agreed that she has been given a gift from God that must be used for His kingdom. When you're ready, we'd like you to start Hannah's lessons again."

Sam stuck his hand out to Abel who grabbed it. "It's an awesome gift," he said after clearing his throat. "Please tell

Hannah how precious she is to us."

Abel shook Sam's hand with vigor. "Why, Sam. She already knows that." He smiled at both of us and left the room. Sam and I remained, staring at the painting. The style made me think of Thomas Kinkade. The scene absolutely glowed with almost unearthly light. It took everything I had to tear my gaze away.

"We've got to find a wonderful place for this," I said to Sam. He started to answer me when Sweetie's voice interrupted.

"Gracie? Sam? Where are you two?"

Sam put the painting on the coffee table. "We're in the living room, Sweetie," he called loudly.

"Well, get into the kitchen. Pat has something to talk to us about."

Sam and I looked at each other. "Wonder what this is about?" he said.

"One way to find out." I grabbed his hand and pulled him toward the hallway.

When we reached the kitchen, we found everyone gathered around the table except for Sweetie who was rinsing dishes at the sink.

"Please, sit down," Pat said in a solemn tone. The expression on his face was one I'd seen before, and every time it had preceded bad news. But that couldn't happen tonight. Hannah was home, C.J. was locked up. What could he possibly say that could make a dent in this perfect evening?

"Sweetie, I need you to sit down, too."

Sweetie started to argue with him, but she was trying hard to turn over a new leaf with Pat, so she put her dish towel down and came over to the table. She plopped down next to my mother. Sweetie was quiet, but her frown expressed her irritation. She couldn't abide a dirty kitchen.

All eyes were fixed on Pat, who cleared his throat and rubbed his hands together before finally speaking. "Right before dinner, I got a call from a detective friend in Colorado." He hesitated again.

"Well for cryin' out loud, Pat, spit it out!" Sweetie declared. "Ain't nothin' you can't say. We're family now, remember?"

He nodded. "Yes, I know. And this is family business. That's why I waited until everyone else left."

"What is it, Pat?" I asked. "Is something wrong?"

He shook his head. "No. I mean, I don't believe anyone will feel that way. Anyway, I hope not."

Sweetie glared at him. If he didn't get to the point soon, that family feeling she had could be in serious jeopardy.

"Terry called to tell me that he's located Bernie."

A small bomb exploding in the middle of Sweetie's kitchen table couldn't have produced more shocked expressions.

"Bernie who?" Dad asked.

"Bernice Goodrich," I said quickly. "Sam's mother."

"Oh my," Mom said breathlessly.

I grabbed Sam's arm. His face had gone white.

"Where is she?" Sweetie asked.

"She's in a hospital in Wyoming. She's been there over a month," Pat said.

"Is—is she all right?" Sam choked out.

Pat shook his head. "No, not really. She's pretty sick. Hepatitis." He gazed into his son's eyes. "But she's clean. I wish I could tell you more about her condition, unfortunately I just don't know. I called the hospital, but they wouldn't tell me anything since I'm not family."

"Well, I'm sure as shootin' family," Sweetie barked, standing to her feet. "You give me the number of this place, Pat. I'll call them right now."

He reached for his wallet, pulled it out of his pocket, and opened it. Then he removed a folded piece of paper and handed it to Sweetie. "That's it. Sure would appreciate it if you'd let me know how she is."

Sweetie took the paper from his hand and stared at it for a moment. Then she came around the table to where Pat sat. She put her hand on his shoulder. "I'll make sure you know all about how Bernie's doin', Pat. Thank you for bringin' her back to me. I'll never forget it. Never." She patted his shoulder then left the room. Sam sat silently. He looked stunned.

"How do you feel about this, Sam?" my father asked.

"I—I don't know," he said softly. "To be honest, I never thought I'd hear from my mother again."

Pat stood up. "I should have given you this before," he said to Sam. "Just wasn't sure you'd want it. But now I think you should have it." He reached into his shirt pocket and pulled something out. "It's Bernie's letter. The one she sent me when she told me about you." He held it out toward Sam who only stared at it. "She writes about you, son. About how much she loves you and how she only left you because she was afraid of ruining your life. Maybe she made the wrong choice, but she made it out of love. I think if you'll read this, you might understand her a little better."

Sam's gaze seemed locked on the letter, but he still didn't reach for it. I was about to grab it for him, when he suddenly took the folded paper from Pat's hand. "I can't promise I'll read it right away, but I will when I'm ready." His own eyes sought his father's. "Guess I'm learning that forgiveness and understanding brings peace. Holding a grudge only causes pain." Sam and Pat stared at each other for several seconds. Then Sam said, "Thanks. . .Dad."

Pat hung his head, nodded quickly, and mumbled something about having to get home. For just a second I thought about following him, but then I realized the tough lawman needed to be alone. Sam and I heard the front door close.

"Good for you," I said.

"You know what?" Sam said, sliding the letter into the pocket of his slacks. "It *is* good for me. I've wanted to call someone 'dad' my whole life. It feels absolutely fantastic." His smile lit up his face.

"I think Pat feels just about as good as you do."

"I hope so." Sam yawned and stretched his arms behind his head. "I could use some coffee. How about you?"

"Sounds good."

Mom and Dad begged off, deciding to go home. Dad's leg was bothering him and they were both tired. I kissed them good-bye and promised to let them know about Bernie. It was hard to watch them leave without me. Frankly, I was exhausted and wanted nothing more than to go home and fall into bed. But even more than I wanted sleep, I needed to know what Sweetie found out about her sister. We'd just poured our coffee when Sweetie came into the kitchen.

"I called the hospital and told 'em who I was. They're gonna check with Bernie before they'll tell me anything."

"Will she let them speak to you?" I asked.

Sweetie sighed deeply. "Land sakes, I hope so. Wish I could predict what Bernie will do, but I just can't. All we can do is sit and wait."

Sam got up and poured Sweetie a cup of coffee. We all sat at the table until the phone finally rang. Sweetie jumped up and answered it. She was silent for quite some time, listening to whoever was on the other end. Finally she said, "Tell her I said not to worry. I'll take care of it. I'll call her back tomorrow. You tell her that, hear me?" Seemingly satisfied with the answer, she said good-bye and hung up. Sam and I stared at her expectantly as she came back to the table and sat down.

"Well, she's sick, but there's hope. She's gonna need a liver transplant. She's on a list, and her chances look okay. Nothing for certain, but if she can last long enough for a liver to become available, she might actually pull through."

Sam let out a deep breath. "Can we talk to her?"

His aunt stared at him for a moment, her expression unreadable. Then she smiled at both of us. "She'll certainly be talkin' to me, son. I'm goin' up there to be with her until she's well."

Sam's mouth dropped open. "What do you mean? You can't leave."

Sweetie reached over and took his hand. Then she grasped mine. "You two have each other now. Bernie has no one." Her eyes filled with tears. "Lord knows I love you both so much it hurts, but you don't need me no more."

Sam started to say something, but she hushed him.

"When you was a little boy, you needed me real bad," Sweetie said gently. "And I loved bringing you up. I loved every single moment of it. But now you got Gracie." She moved our hands together and took hers away. "You gotta be able to see this as clearly as I do. My sister is all alone, and you both could use some time together without someone else hangin' around. It's the perfect solution." She chuckled. "Don't be thinkin' you're gettin' rid of me though, Sam Goodrich. You have my word. If Bernie gets better, I'll bring us both back here." She rubbed her eyes. "And if she don't, well I'll come back alone. But either way, I'll come home one of these days."

"I can't imagine living here without you," Sam said in a choked voice.

"I know," his aunt said softly. "But this is my choice, son. And

I need you to support me."

Sam didn't speak, but he nodded slowly. At Sweetie's suggestion, we all went outside and sat on the porch, rocking quietly until the sun went down and the air cooled. No one said it, but we all realized it would be the last time the three of us would be alone together for a long, long time.

Chapter Twenty-Four

Saturday was the most wonderful day of my life, but it rushed past me like a mighty wind that sweeps in and out so quickly you're not sure it was ever really there. A few memories will always stay burned into my memory, though. Sam, standing at the front of the church in his black suit. As I walked down the aisle, I was certain he was the most handsome man I'd ever seen in my entire life. My mother told me once that in her eyes, my father outshone every man she'd ever met. As the years went by, she never changed her opinion. At the time, I couldn't understand why she didn't seem to notice his wrinkles, the extra skin under his chin, or the way his stomach got a little larger every year. But on Saturday, I understood it completely. I knew that the rest of my life, I would see Sam standing there, his sun-bleached hair combed neatly into place, his incredible gray eyes looking at me beneath dark lashes, his expression one I will always remember. He told me after the ceremony that he was so overcome by my beauty he could barely breathe.

And I will always recall my mother's face when she saw me

wearing her blue dress, a white-lace shawl around my shoulders, and a bouquet of red carnations, yellow dandelions, and purple irises in my arms. My white dress was packed away in a trunk, waiting for the day my daughter would decide between it. . .or a plain blue dress that carried more meaning than beauty.

A sea of faces passed before us that day. My mother and father, Pat, Ida, Gabe, Sarah and John, Sweetie, Emily and Abel. Each face precious to me. Every person part of a large, extended family. And of course, Hannah. Although we didn't get much time to speak, she hugged me tightly and whispered "Thank you," into my ear.

There was great food, courtesy of Hector and Carmen, and wonderful gifts given by all the people who love us. Our reception overflowed with laughter and the joy of the Lord. But little by little, people drifted away. Bill Eberly drove Sweetie to the airport after the reception. It was hard to see her go, but Sam and I both knew she had made the right choice.

As quickly as the whirlwind of excitement that weddings bring reached its peak, it was over. My mother and father went home to the house that had sheltered the Temple family for over fifty years. Sam and I drove home to the big red house, our truck stuffed full of gifts we'd find places for later. Although everything we'd been given blessed us, my grandmother's quilt and Hannah's painting would stay at the top of the list.

We changed clothes and went out to sit on the porch. We were finally alone. Buddy curled up at my feet, and Snickle lay down on Sam's lap. The third rocking chair sat empty, and Sweetie's absence was deeply felt. We pulled our rocking chairs together and held hands until the sun went down.

Finally Sam said, "I think it's time to go inside, Mrs. Goodrich."

"I agree." I turned to look into the stormy gray eyes of the man I would spend the rest of my life with. "Hey Sam, why don't cannibals eat clowns?"

He chuckled softly. "I have no idea. Why don't cannibals eat clowns?"

"Because they taste funny."

Sam's warm laughter drifted into the night air. "Is this what I can look forward to for the next fifty years?"

I squeezed his hand. "You got it, bub."

He leaned over and kissed me gently, and then he stood up. "I can hardly wait."

I let go of his hand. "Hey, give me just a minute alone, okay?"

He smiled. "Just don't take too long."

"I won't."

He called Buddy and Snickle, ushering them both into the house. When the door shut behind him, I looked up into a sky full of glittering stars. A verse from the eighth Psalm popped into my mind. *When I consider your heavens, the work of your fingers, the moon and the stars, which you have set in place, what is mankind that you are mindful of them, human beings that you care for them?* Tearfully, I whispered a prayer of thanks to the One who had led me to Harmony, Kansas, so He could reveal His plan for me—a plan far beyond anything I could have ever dreamed. I rocked for a while in the soft, summer air, wrapped in His love. Then I got up and opened the front door of the house I'd loved from the first moment I'd seen it, and went inside, ready to begin a brand-new, wonderful adventure.

Discussion Questions

1. Did Gracie make a mistake when she took Hannah to Wichita? Explain your answer.

2. Should Abel and Emily have allowed her to go? Do you think they should feel any responsibility for Hannah's reaction? Why?

3. Why do you think Hannah felt so drawn to Wichita? What was she really looking for?

4. Papa Joe's family decides that the best way to deal with the confusion caused by Alzheimer's disease is to go along with his delusions rather than to correct him. Do you agree with this? Why or why not?

5. Have you ever known anyone stricken with Alzheimer's? Was the portrayal of Papa Joe similar to your experience? How was it similar? How was it different?

6. Sam and Sweetie have a hard time accepting Pat into their family. Do you think their concerns about Pat are fair? Do you understand their resistance at first? Why or why not?

7. What did you think about the social worker who came to Harmony? Do you think her reaction to the Mennonite citizens of Harmony was justified? At first, do you think she was actually concerned

about Hannah's welfare or was she operating out of prejudice?

8. Sarah Ketterling and John Keystone tried to stay away from each other because of the differences in their beliefs. Was this the right thing to do? Why or why not? How did you feel about the way the relationship ended?

9. Why did Abigail Bradley adopt the Conservative Mennonite lifestyle? Were her motives right? Why or why not?

10. If she had made different choices, do you think her life would have turned out differently? If yes, how?

11. What was the most important message you took away from *Simple Choices*?

ABOUT THE AUTHOR

NANCY MEHL lives in Wichita, Kansas, with her husband, Norman, and her rambunctious puggle, Watson. She's authored eleven books and is currently at work on her newest series. All of Nancy's novels have an added touch—something for your spirit as well as your soul. You can find out more about Nancy by visiting her website at: www.nancymehl.com.

OTHER BOOKS BY NANCY MEHL

HOMETOWN MYSTERIES

Missing Mabel
Blown Away